NOBLE HOUSE

Volume 2

James Clavell

NOBLE HOUSE

A Novel of Contemporary Hong Kong

Volume 2

DELACORTE PRESS/NEW YORK

41

Claudia picked up a mass of notes and letters and replies from Dunross's *out* tray and began to leaf through them. Rain and low clouds obscured the view but the temperature was down and very comfortable after the heavy humidity of the last weeks. The antique clock set into a silver gimbal on the mantel chimed 8:30.

One of the phones jangled. She watched it but made no attempt to answer it. It rang on and on then ceased. Sandra Yi, Dunross's secretary, came in with a new batch of documents and mail and refilled the *in* tray. "The draft of the Par-Con contract's on the top, Elder Sister. Here's his appointments list for today, at least, the ones I know about. Superintendent Kwok called ten minutes ago." She blushed under Claudia's gaze, her *chong-sam* slit high and tight, her neck collar fashionably high. "He called for the tai-pan, not me, Elder Sister. Would the tai-pan please return his call."

"But I hope you talked to Honorable Young Stallion at length, Younger Sister, and swooned and sighed marvelously?" Claudia replied in Cantonese, then switched to English without noticing it, still leafing through all the notes as she talked, stacking them into two different piles. "After all, he really should be gobbled up and safely in the family before some Mealy Mouth from another clan catches him."

"Oh yes. I've also lit five candles in five different temples."

"I hope on your time and not company's time."

"Oh very yes." They laughed. "But we do have a date—tomorrow for dinner."

"Excellent! Be demure, dress conservatively, but go without a bra—like Orlanda."

"Oh, then it was true! Oh oh do you think I should?" Sandra Yi was shocked.

"For young Brian, yes." Claudia chuckled. "He has a nose that one!"

"My fortune-teller said this was going to be a wonderful year for me. Terrible about the fire wasn't it?"

"Yes." Claudia checked the appointment list. Linbar in a few minutes, Sir Luis Basilio at 8:45. "When Sir Luis arrives p—"

"Sir Luis's waiting in my office now. He knows he's early—I've given him coffee and the morning papers." Sandra Yi's face became apprehensive. "What's going to happen at ten?"

"The stock market opens," Claudia told her crisply and handed her the larger stack. "You deal with this lot, Sandra. Oh and here, he's canceled a couple of board meetings and lunch but I'll deal with those." Both looked up as Dunross came in.

"Morning," he said. His face was graver than before, the bruises enhancing his ruggedness.

Sandra Yi said prettily, "Everyone's so happy you weren't hurt, tai-pan."

"Thank you."

She left. He noticed her walk, then Claudia's look. Some of his gravity left him. "Nothing like a pretty bird. Is there?"

Claudia laughed. "While you were out your private phone rang twice." This was his unlisted phone that, by rule, he alone picked up, the number given only to family and a handful of special people.

"Oh, thank you. Cancel everything between now and noon except Linbar, old Sir Luis Basilio and the bank. Make sure everything's VIP for Penn and Miss Kathy. Gavallan's taking her to the airport. First get Tightfist Tung on the phone. Also Lando Mata—ask if I can see him today, preferably at 10:20 at the Coffee Place. You saw my note about Zep?"

"Yes, terrible. I'll take care of everything. The governor's aide called: will you be at the noon meeting?"

"Yes." Dunross picked up a phone and dialed as Claudia left, closing the door behind her.

"Penn? You wanted me?"

"Oh Ian, yes, but I didn't phone, is that what you mean?"

"I thought it was you on the private line."

"No, but oh I'm ever so pleased you called. I heard about the fire on the early news and I . . . I wasn't sure if I'd dreamed it or not that you'd come back last night. I . . . I was quite worried, sorry. Ah Tat said you'd left early but I don't trust that old hag—she wanders sometimes. Sorry. Was it awful?"

"No. Not bad actually." He told her about it briefly. Now that he knew everything was all right with her he wanted to get off the phone. "I'll give you a blow-by-blow when I pick you up for the airport. I checked on the flight and it'll leave on time . . ." His intercom buzzed. "Hang on a moment, Penn . . . Yes, Claudia?"

"Superintendent Kwok on line two. He says it's important."

"All right. Sorry, Penn, got to go, I'll pick you up in good time for your flight. 'Bye, darling. . . . Anything else, Claudia?"

"Bill Foster's plane from Sydney's delayed another hour. Mr. Havergill and Johnjohn will see you at 9:30. I called to confirm. I hear they've been at the bank since six this morning."

Dunross's uneasiness grew. He had been trying to talk to Havergill since 3:00 P.M. yesterday but the deputy chairman had not been available and last night was not the time. "That's not good. There was a crowd already outside the bank when I came in at 7:30."

"The Vic won't fail, will it?"

He heard the anxiety in her voice. "If they do we're all up the spout." He stabbed line two. "Hi, Brian, what's up?" Brian Kwok told him about John Chen.

"Jesus Christ, poor John! After giving them the ransom money last night I thought . . . what bastards! He's been dead some days?"

"Yes. At least three."

"The bastards! Have you told Phillip or Dianne?"

"No, not yet. I wanted to tell you first."

"You want me to call them? Phillip's at home now. After the payoff last night I told him to miss the eight o'clock morning meeting. I'll call him now."

"No, Ian, that's my job. Sorry to bring bad news but I thought you should know about John."

"Yes . . . yes, old chum, thanks. Listen, I've a do at the governor's around seven but that'll be through by 10:30. Would you like a drink or a late snack?"

"Yes. Good idea. How about the Quance Bar at the Mandarin?"

"10:45?"

"Good. By the way, I've left word for your *tai-tai* to go straight through Immigration. Sorry to bring bad news. 'Bye."

Dunross put down the phone, got up and stared out of the window. The intercom buzzed but he did not hear it. "Poor bugger!" he muttered. "What a bloody waste!"

There was a discreet knock, then the door opened a fraction. Claudia said, "Excuse me, tai-pan, Lando Mata on line two."

Dunross sat on the edge of his desk. "Hello Lando, can we meet at 10:20?"

"Yes, yes of course. I heard about Zeppelin. Awful! I just got out with my own life! Damned fire! Still, we got out, eh? Joss!"

"Have you been in touch with Tightfist yet?"

"Yes. He's arriving on the next ferry."

"Good. Lando, I may need you to back me today."

"But Ian, we went through that last night. I thought I ma—"

"Yes. But I want your backing today." Dunross's voice had hardened. There was a long pause. "I'll . . . I'll talk to Tightfist."

"I'll talk to Tightfist too. Meanwhile I'd like to know I have your backing now."

"You've reconsidered our offer?"

"Do I have your backing, Lando? Or not."

Another pause. Mata's voice was more nervous. "I'll . . . I'll tell you when I see you at 10:20. Sorry, Ian, but I really must talk to Tightfist first. See you for coffee. 'Bye!"

The phone clicked off. Dunross replaced his receiver gently and muttered sweetly, "*Dew neh loh moh*, Lando old friend."

He thought a moment then dialed. "Mr. Bartlett please."

"No answer his phone. You want message?" the operator said.

"Please transfer me to Miss K. C. Tcholok."

"Wat?"

"Casey . . . Miss Casey!"

The call tone rang and Casey answered sleepily, "Hello?"

"Oh sorry, I'll call you back later. . . ."

"Oh, Ian? No . . . no, that's all right, I should . . . should have been up hours ago . . ." He heard her stifle a yawn. ". . . Jesus, I'm tired. I didn't dream that fire did I?"

"No. Ciranoush, I just wanted to make sure you were both all right. How're you feeling?"

"Not so hot. I think I must have stretched a few muscles . . . don't know if it was the laughing or throwing up. You all right?"

"Yes. So far. You haven't a temperature or anything? That's what Doc Tooley said to watch out for."

"Don't think so. I haven't seen Linc yet. Did you talk to him?"

"No—there's no reply. Listen, I wanted to ask you two to cocktails, at six."

"That's lovely with me." Another yawn. "I'm glad you're okay."

"I'll call you back later to . . ."

Again the intercom. "The governor's on line two, tai-pan. I told him you'd be at the morning meeting."

"All right. Listen, Ciranoush, cocktails at six, if not cocktails maybe late supper. I'll call later to confirm."

"Sure, Ian. And Ian, thanks for calling."

"Nothing. 'Bye." Dunross stabbed line two. "Morning, sir."

"Sorry to disturb you, Ian, but I need to talk to you about that awful fire," Sir Geoffrey said. "It's a miracle that more weren't lost, the minister's hopping mad about poor Sir Charles Pennyworth's death and quite furious that our security procedures allowed that to happen. The Cabinet have been informed so we can expect high-level repercussions."

Dunross told him his idea about the kitchens for Aberdeen, pretending it was Shi-teh T'Chung's.

"Excellent. Shitee's clever! That's a start. Meanwhile Robin Grey and Julian Broadhurst and the other MPs have already phoned for a meeting to protest our incompetent fire regulations. My aide said Grey was quite incensed." Sir Geoffrey sighed. "Rightly so, perhaps. In any event that gentleman's going to stir things up nastily, if he can. I hear he's scheduled a press conference for tomorrow with Broadhurst. Now that poor Sir Charles's dead Broadhurst becomes the senior member and God only knows what'll happen if those two get on their high horse about China."

"Ask the minister to muzzle them, sir."

"I did and he said, 'Good God, Geoffrey, muzzle an MP? That'd be worse than trying to set fire to Parliament itself.' It's all really very trying. My thought was that you might be able to cool Mr. Grey down. I'll seat him next to you tonight."

"I don't think that's a good idea at all, sir. The man's a lunatic."

"I quite agree, Ian, but I really would appreciate it if you tried. You're the only one I'd trust. Quillan would hit him. Quillan's already phoned in a formal refusal purely because of Grey. Perhaps you could invite the fellow to the races on Saturday also?"

Dunross remembered Peter Marlowe. "Why not invite Grey and the others to your box and I'll take him over part of the time." Thank God Penn won't be here, he thought.

"Very well. Next: Roger asked me to meet you at the bank at six o'clock tomorrow."

Dunross let the silence hang.

"Ian?"

"Yes sir?"

"At six. Sinders should be there by then."

"Do you know him, sir? Personally?"

"Yes. Why?"

"I just wanted to be sure." Dunross heard the governor's silence. His tension increased.

"Good. At six. Next: Did you hear about poor John Chen?"

"Yes sir, just a few minutes ago. Rotten luck."

"I agree. Poor fellow! This Werewolf mess couldn't've come at a worse time. It will surely become a *cause célèbre* for all opponents of Hong Kong. Damned nuisance, apart from the tragedy so far. Dear me, well, at least we live in interesting times with nothing but problems."

"Yes sir. Is the Victoria in trouble?" Dunross asked the question casually but he was listening intently and he heard the slightest hesitation before Sir Geoffrey said lightly, "Good Lord no! My dear fellow, what an astonishing idea! Well, thank you, Ian, everything else can wait till our meeting at noon."

"Yes sir." Dunross put the phone down and mopped his brow. That hesitation was bloody ominous, he told himself. If anyone'd know how bad things are it'd be Sir Geoffrey.

A rain squall battered the windows. So much to do. His eyes went to the clock. Linbar due now, then Sir Luis. He already decided what he wanted from the head of the stock exchange, what he must have from him. He had not mentioned it at the meeting of the Inner Court this morning. The others had soured him. All of them—Jacques, Gavallan, Linbar—were convinced the Victoria would support Struan's to the limit. "And if they don't?" he had asked.

"We've the Par-Con deal. It's inconceivable the Victoria won't help!"

"If they don't?"

"Perhaps after last night Gornt won't continue to sell."

"He'll sell. What do we do?"

"Unless we can stop him or put off the Toda and Orlin payments we're in very great trouble."

We can't put off the payments, he thought again. Without the bank or Mata or Tightfist—even the Par-Con deal won't stop Quillan. Quillan knows he's got all day today and all Friday to sell and sell and sell and I can't buy ev—

"Master Linbar, tai-pan."

"Show him in, please." He glanced at the clock. The younger man came in and closed the door. "You're almost two minutes late."

"Oh? Sorry."

"I don't seem to be able to get through to you about punctuality. It's impossible to run sixty-three companies without executive punctuality. If it happens one more time you lose your yearly bonus."

Linbar flushed. "Sorry."

"I want you to take over our Sydney operation from Bill Foster."

Linbar Struan brightened. "Yes certainly. I'd like that. I've wanted an operation of my own for some time."

"Good. I'd like you to be on the Qantas flight tomorrow an—"

"Tomorrow? Impossible!" Linbar burst out, his happiness evaporating. "It'll take me a couple of weeks to get ev—"

Dunross's voice became so gentle but so slashing that Linbar Struan blanched. "I realize that, Linbar. But I want you to go there tomorrow. Stay two weeks and then come back and report to me. Understand?"

"Yes, I understand. But . . . but what about Saturday? What about the races? I want to watch Noble Star run."

Dunross just looked at him. "I want you in Australia. Tomorrow. Foster's failed to get possession of Woolara Properties. Without Woolara we've no charterer for our ships. Without the charterer our present banking arrangements are null and void. You've two weeks to correct that fiasco and report back."

"And if I don't?" Linbar said, enraged.

"For chrissake don't waste time! You know the answer to that. If you fail you'll no longer be in the Inner Court. And if you're not on that plane tomorrow you're out of Struan's as long as I'm tai-pan."

Linbar Struan started to say something but changed his mind.

"Good," Dunross said. "If you succeed with Woolara your salary's doubled."

Linbar Struan just stared back at him. "Anything else? Sir?"

"No. Good morning, Linbar."

Linbar nodded and strode out. When the door was closed Dunross allowed himself the shadow of a smile. "Cocky young bastard," he muttered and got up and went to the window again, feeling closed in, wanting to be out in a speedboat or, better, in his car, racing the corners just too fast, pushing the car and himself just a little harder each lap to cleanse his head. Absently he straightened a picture and watched the raindrops, deep in thought, saddened by John Chen.

A globulet fell a wet obstacle course and vanished to be replaced by another and another. There was still no view and the rain pelted down.

His private phone jangled into life.

"Yes, Penn?" he said.

A strange voice said, "Mr. Dunross?"

"Yes. Who's this?" he asked, startled, unable to place the man's voice or his accent.

"My name is Kirk, Jamie Kirk, Mr. Dunross. I'm, er, I'm a friend of Mr. Grant, Mr. Alan Medford Grant. . . ." Dunross almost dropped the phone. ". . . Hello? Mr. Dunross?"

"Yes, please go on." Dunross was over his shock now. AMG was one of the few who had been given this number and he had known it was to be used only in emergencies and never passed on except for a very special reason. "What can I do for you?"

"I'm, er, from London; Scotland actually. Alan told me to call you as soon as I got to Hong Kong. He, er, gave me your number. I hope I'm not disturbing you?"

"No, not at all, Mr. Kirk."

"Alan gave me a package for you, and he also wanted me to talk to you. My, er, my wife and I are in Hong Kong for three days so I, er, I wondered if we could meet."

"Of course. Where are you staying?" he asked calmly, though his heart was racing.

"At the Nine Dragons in Kowloon, room 455."

"When did you last see Alan, Mr. Kirk?"

"When we left London. That was, er, two weeks ago now. Yes, two weeks to the day. We've, er, we've been to Singapore and Indonesia. Why?"

"Would after lunch be convenient? Sorry but I'm jammed till 3:20. I could see you then if that would be satisfactory."

"3:20 will be fine."

"I'll send a car for you an—"

"Oh there's, er, there's no need for that. We can find our way to your office."

"It's no trouble. A car will call for you at 2:30."

Dunross replaced the phone, lost in thought.

The clock chimed 8:45. A knock. Claudia opened the door. "Sir Luis Basilio, tai-pan."

Johnjohn at the Victoria Bank was shouting into the phone. ". . . I don't give a sod what you bastards in London think, I'm telling you we've got the beginnings of a run here and it looks very smelly indeed. I . . . What? Speak up, man! We've got a rotten connection. . . . What? . . . I couldn't care less that it's 1:30 in the morning—where the hell were you anyway—I've been trying to get you for four hours! . . . What? . . . Whose birthday? Christ almighty . . ." His sandy eyebrows soared and he held onto his temper. "Listen, just get down to the City and the Mint very first bloody thing and tell them . . . Hello? . . . Yes, tell them this whole bloody island may run out of money and . . . Hello? . . . Hello? . . . Oh for chrissake!" He started jiggling the plunger up and down. "*Hello!*" Then he slammed the receiver onto its cradle, cursed for a moment, then prodded the intercom button. "Miss Mills, I was cut off, please get him back quickly as you can."

"Certainly," the cool, very English voice said. "Mr. Dunross's here."

Johnjohn glanced at his watch and whitened. It was 9:33. "Oh Christ! Hold . . . yes, hold the call. I'll . . ." Hurriedly he put the phone down, rushed to the door, composed himself and opened it with forced nonchalance. "My dear Ian, so sorry to keep you waiting. How're things?"

"Fine. And with you?"

"Marvelous!"

"Marvelous? That's interesting. There must be six or seven hundred impatient customers queuing up outside already and you're half an hour to opening time. There're even a few outside Blacs."

"More than a few . . ." Johnjohn just caught himself in time. "Nothing to worry about, Ian. Would you like coffee or shall we go straight up to Paul's office."

"Paul's office."

"Good." Johnjohn led the way along the thickly carpeted corridor. "No, there's no problem at all, just a few superstitious Chinese—you know how they are, rumors and all that. Rotten about the fire. I hear Casey stripped and dived to the rescue. Were you at the track this morning? This rain's grand, isn't it?"

Dunross's unease increased. "Yes. I hear there're queues outside almost every bank in the Colony. Except the Bank of China."

Johnjohn's laugh sounded hollow. "Our Communist friends wouldn't take kindly to a run on them at all. They'd send in the troops!"

"So the run's on?"

"On the Ho-Pak, yes. On us? No. In any event we're nowhere near as extended as Richard Kwang. I understand he really has made some very dangerous loans. I'm afraid the Ching Prosperity's not in good shape either. Still, Smiler Ching deserves to take a drubbing after all his fiddling over the years in such dubious enterprises."

"Drugs?"

"I really couldn't say, Ian. Not officially. But the rumor's strong."

"But you say the run won't spread to you?"

"Not really. If it does . . . well I'm sure everything will be quite all right." Johnjohn went on down the wide paneled corridor, everything rich, solid and safe. He nodded at the elderly English secretary, went past her and opened the door marked PAUL HAVERGILL, DEPUTY CHAIRMAN. The office was large, oak paneled, the desk huge and clear of papers. The windows faced the square.

"Ian, my dear fellow." Havergill got up and extended his hand. "So sorry I couldn't see you yesterday, and the party last night was hardly the place for business, eh? How're you feeling?"

"All right. I think. So far. You?"

"I've got the trots slightly but Constance's fine, thank God. Soon as we got home I gave us both a good dollop of good old Dr. Colicos's Remedy." It was an elixir invented during the Crimean War by Dr. Colicos to cure stomach disorders when tens of thousands of British soldiers were dying of typhoid and cholera and dysentery. The formula was still a guarded secret.

"Terrific stuff! Dr. Tooley gave us some too."

"Damnable about the others, what? Toxe's wife, eh?"

Johnjohn said gravely, "I heard they found her body under some pilings this morning. If I hadn't had a pink ticket Mary and I'd've been there too." A pink ticket meant that you had your wife's permission to be out in the evening without her, out playing cards with friends, or at the Club, or on the town with visiting guests or wherever—but with her benevolent permission.

"Oh?" Havergill smiled. "Who was the lucky lady?"

"I was playing bridge with McBride at the Club."

Havergill laughed. "Well, discretion's the better part of valor and we have the reputation of the bank to think of."

Dunross felt the tension in the room between the two men. He smiled politely, waiting.

"What can I do for you Ian?" Havergill asked.

"I want an extra 100 million credit for thirty days."

There was a dead silence. Both men stared at him. Dunross thought he saw the flicker of a smile rush behind Havergill's eyes. "Impossible!" he heard him say.

"Gornt's mounting an attack on us, that's clear to anyone. You both know we're solid, safe and in good shape. I need your open, massive backing, then he won't dare proceed and I won't actually need the money. But I do need the commitment. Now."

Another silence. Johnjohn waited and watched. Havergill lit a cigarette. "What's the situation with the Par-Con deal, Ian?"

Dunross told them. "Tuesday we sign."

"Can you trust the American?"

"We've made a deal."

Another silence. Uneasily, Johnjohn broke it. "It's a very good deal, Ian."

"Yes. With your open backing, Gornt and Blacs will withdraw their attack."

"But 100 million?" Havergill said. "That's beyond possibility."

"I said I won't need the full amount."

"That's surmise, my dear fellow. We could become involved in a very big power play against our wish. I've heard rumors Quillan has outside financing, German backing. We couldn't risk getting into a fight with a consortium of German banks. You are already over the limit of your revolving credit. And there's the 500,000 shares you bought today which have to be paid for on Monday. Sorry no."

"Put it to the board." Dunross knew that he had enough votes to carry it over Havergill's opposition.

Another silence. "Very well. I'll certainly do that—at the next board meeting."

"No. That's not for three weeks. Please call an emergency meeting."

"Sorry no."

"Why?"

"I don't have to explain my reasons to you, Ian," Havergill said crisply. "Struan's doesn't own or control this institution, though you do have a large interest in us, as we have in you, and you are our valued customer. I'll be glad to put it up at the next board meeting. Calling emergency meetings is within my control. Solely."

"I agree. So is the granting of the credit. You don't need a meeting. You could do that now."

"I will be glad to put the request to the board at the next meeting. Was there anything else?"

Dunross controlled his urge to wipe the barely concealed smugness off his enemy's face. "I need the credit to support my stock. Now."

"Of course, and Bruce and I really do understand that the Par-Con down payment will give you the financing to complete your ship transactions and make a partial Orlin payment." Havergill puffed his cigarette. "By the way, I understand Orlin won't renew—you'll have to pay them off totally within thirty days as per the contract."

Dunross flushed. "Where did you hear that?"

"From the chairman, of course. I called him last night to ask if the—"

"You what?"

"Of course. My dear chap," Havergill said, now openly enjoying Dunross's and Johnjohn's shock. "We have every right to inquire. After all, we're Struan's bankers and we need to know. Our equity's also at risk if you are to fail, isn't it?"

"And you'll help that happen?"

Havergill stubbed out his cigarette with vast enjoyment. "It's not to our interest for any big business to fail in the Colony, let alone the Noble House. Oh dear no! You needn't worry. At the right time we'll step in and buy your shares. We'll never allow the Noble House to fail."

"When's the right time?"

"When the shares are at a value we consider correct."

"What's that?"

"I'd have to look into it, Ian."

Dunross knew he was beaten but he showed none of it. "You'll allow the stock to go down until they're at giveaway prices and then you'll buy control."

"Struan's is a public company now, however the various companies interlock," Havergill said. "Perhaps it would have been wise to follow Alastair's advice, and mine—we did point out the risks you'd take as a public company. And perhaps you should have consulted us before buying that massive quantity of shares. Clearly Quillan thinks he has you and you really are stretched a bit, old boy. Well, never fear, Ian, we will not allow the Noble House to fail."

Dunross laughed. He got up. "The Colony will be a much better place with you out of it."

"Oh?" Havergill snapped. "My term of office lasts until November 23. You may be out of the Colony before me!"

"Don't you think . . ." Johnjohn began, aghast at Havergill's fury, but stopped as the deputy chairman turned on him.

"Your term of office begins November 24. Providing the annual general meeting confirms the appointment. Until that time I run the Victoria."

Dunross laughed again. "Don't be too sure of that." He walked out.

Angrily Johnjohn broke the silence. "You could easily call an emergency meeting. You could eas—"

"The matter is closed! Do you understand? Closed!" Furiously Havergill lit another cigarette. "We've got problems of our own that have to be solved first. But if that bastard squeezes out of the vise this time I shall be very surprised. He's in a dangerous position, very dangerous. We know nothing about this damned American and his girl friend. We do know Ian's recalcitrant, arrogant and out of his depth. He's the wrong man for the job."

"That's not t—"

"We're a profit-making institution, not a charity, and the Dunrosses and Struans have had too much say in our affairs for too many years. If we can get control we become the Noble House of Asia—we do! We get his block of our stock back. We fire all the directors and put in new management at once, we double our money and I'd leave a lasting legacy to the bank forever. That's what we're here for—to make money for *our* bank and for *our* shareholders! I've always considered your friend Dunross a very high risk and now he's going to the wall. And if I can help hang him I will!"

The doctor was counting Fleur Marlowe's pulse beats against his old-fashioned, gold fob watch. One hundred and three. Too many, he thought sadly. Her wrist was delicate. He laid it back on the bedcovers, his sensitive fingers aware of the fever. Peter Marlowe came out of the small bathroom of their apartment.

"Not good, eh?" Tooley said gruffly.

Peter Marlowe's smile was weary. "Rather tedious actually. Just cramps and not much coming out, just a little liquid." His eyes rested on his wife who lay wanly in the small double bed. "How're you, pet?"

"Fine," she said. "Fine thank you, Peter."

The doctor reached for his old-fashioned bag and put his stethoscope away. "Was, er, was there any blood, Mr. Marlowe?"

Peter Marlowe shook his head and sat tiredly. Neither he nor his wife had slept much. Their cramps had begun about 4:00 A.M. and had continued since then with ever-increasing strain. "No, at least not yet," he said. "It feels rather like an ordinary bout of dysentery—cramps, a lot of palaver and very little to show for it."

"Ordinary? You've had dysentery? When? What kind of dysentery?"

"I think it was enteric. I, I was a POW in Changi in '45—actually between '42 and '45, partially in Java but mostly in Changi."

"Oh. Oh I see. Sorry about that." Dr. Tooley remembered all the horror stories that came out of Asia after the war about the treatment of British and American troops by the Japanese Army. "I always felt betrayed in a curious way," the doctor said sadly. "The Japanese'd always been our ally . . . they're an island nation, so're we. Good fighters. I was a doctor with the Chindits. Went in with Wingate twice." Wingate was an eccentric British general who had devised a completely unorthodox battle plan to send highly mobile columns of marauding British soldiers, code name Chindits, from India into the jungles of Burma deep behind Japanese lines, supplying them by airdrop. "I was lucky—the whole Chindit operation was rather dicey," he said. As he talked he was watching Fleur, weighing clues, sending his experience into her, trying to detect the disease now, trying to isolate the enemy among a myriad of possibilities before it harmed the fetus. "Bloody planes kept missing our drops."

"I met a couple of your fellows at Changi." The younger man searched his memory. "In '43 or '44, I can't remember when exactly. Or any names. They'd been sent down to Changi after they were captured."

"That'd be '43." The doctor was somber. "One whole column got caught and ambushed early on. Those jungles are unbelievable if you've never been in one. We didn't know what the devil we were doing most of the time. Afraid not many of the lads survived to get to Changi." Dr. Tooley was a fine old man with a big nose and sparse hair and warm hands, and he smiled down at Fleur. "So, young lady," he said with his kind, gruff voice. "You've a slight fev—"

"Oh . . . sorry, Doctor," she said quickly, interrupting him, suddenly white, "I, I think . . ." She got out of bed and hurried awkwardly for the bathroom. The door closed behind her. There was a fleck of blood on the back of her nightdress.

"Is she all right?" Marlowe asked, his face stark.

"Temperature's a hundred and three, heartbeat's up. It could just be gastroenteritis. . . ." The doctor looked at him.

"Could it be hepatitis?"

"No. Not this quickly. The incubation period's six weeks to two months. I'm afraid that specter's hanging over everyone's head. Sorry." A rain squall battered the windows. He glanced at them and frowned, remembering that he had not told Dunross and the Americans about the danger of hepatitis. Perhaps it'll be better just to wait and see and be patient. Joss, he thought. "Two months, to be safe. You've both had all your shots so there shouldn't be any problem about typhoid."

"And the baby?"

"If the cramps get worse she may miscarry, Mr. Marlowe," the doctor said softly. "Sorry, but it's best to know. Either way it won't be easy for her—God only knows what viruses and bacteria're at Aberdeen. The place's a public sewer and has been for a century. Shocking, but nothing we can do about it." He rummaged in his pocket for his prescription pad. "You can't change the Chinese or habits of centuries. Sorry."

"Joss," Peter Marlowe said, feeling rotten. "Will everyone get sick? There must have been forty or fifty of us thrashing around in the water—impossible not to drink some of that muck."

The doctor hesitated. "Of fifty, perhaps five'll be very sick, five'll be untouched and the rest'll be in between. Hong Kong *yan*—that's Hong Kongites—they should be less affected than visitors. But, as you say, a lot of it's joss." He found his pad. "I'll give you a prescription for a rather newfangled intestinal antibiotic but continue with good old Dr. Colicos's Remedy—that will settle your tummies. Watch her very carefully. Do you have a thermometer?"

"Oh yes. With . . ." A spasm went through Peter Marlowe, shook him and went away. "Traveling with young kids you have to have a survival kit." Both men were trying not to watch the bathroom door. They could half-hear her as her pain waxed and waned.

"How old are your children?" Dr. Tooley asked absently, keeping the concern from his voice as he wrote. When he had come in he had noticed the happy chaos of the tiny second bedroom off the small drab living room —barely big enough for its two-tiered bunk, the toys scattered. "Mine are grown up now. I've three daughters."

"What? Oh, ours are four and eight. They're . . . they're both girls."

"Do you have an *amah?*"

"Oh yes. Yes. With all the rain this morning she took the kids to school. They go across the harbor and pick up a *bo-pi.*" A *bo-pi* was an unlicensed taxi that was quite illegal but most everyone used them from time to time. "The school's off Garden Road. Most days they insist on toddling off themselves. They're perfectly safe."

"Oh yes. Yes of course."

Their ears were fine-tuned now to her torment. Each muted strain went through both men.

"Well, don't worry," the doctor said hesitantly. "I'll have the drugs sent up—there's a pharmacy in the hotel. I'll have it put on your bill. I'll come back this evening at six, as near to six as I can. If there's any problem . . ." He offered a prescription blank gently. "My phone number's on this. Don't hesitate to call, eh?"

"Thanks. Now about your bill . . ."

"No need to worry about that, Mr. Marlowe. The first order of business is to get you well." Dr. Tooley was concentrating on the door. He was afraid to leave. "Were you army?"

"No. Air force."

"Ah! My brother was one of the Few. He pranged in . . ." He stopped. Fleur Marlowe was calling out hesitantly through the door, "Doctor . . . cou . . . could you . . . please . . ."

Tooley went to the door. "Yes, Mrs. Marlowe? Are you all right?"

"Cou . . . could you please . . ."

He opened the door and closed it after him.

The sour sweet stench in the tiny bathroom was heavy but he paid it no attention.

"I . . . it . . ." Another spasm twisted her.

"Now don't worry," he said, calming her, and put one hand on her back and the other on her stomach, helping to support her tormented abdominal muscles. His hands massaged gently and with great knowledge. "There, there! Just let yourself go, I won't let you fall." He felt the knotting under his fingers and willed his warmth and strength into her. "You're just about my daughter's age, my youngest. I've three and the eldest has two children. . . . There, just let yourself relax, just think the pains away, soon you'll feel nice and warm. . . ." In time the cramps passed.

"I . . . God, sorr . . . sorry." The young woman groped for the toilet roll but another cramp took her and another. It was awkward for him in the small room but he tended her and kept his strong hands supporting her as best he could. An ache leapt into his back.

"I'm . . . I'm all right now," she said. "Thank you."

He knew she was not. The sweat had soaked her. He sponged off her face and dried it for her. Then he helped her stand, taking her weight, gentling her all the time. He cleaned her. The paper showed traces of blood and the bowl traces of blood mucus among the discolored water but she was not hemorrhaging yet and he sighed with relief. "You're going to be fine," he said. "Here, hold on a second. Don't be afraid!" He guided her hands to the sink. Quickly he folded a dry towel lengthwise and wrapped it tightly around her stomach, tucking the ends in to hold it. "This's the best for gippy tummy, the very best. It supports your tum and keeps it warm. My grandfather was a doctor too, in the Indian Army, and he swore this was the best." He looked at her keenly. "You're a fine brave young lady. You're going to be fine. Ready?"

"Yes. Sorr—sorry about . . ."

He opened the door. Peter Marlowe rushed to help. They put her to bed.

She lay there exhausted, a thread of damp hair on her forehead. Dr. Tooley brushed it away and stared down at her thoughtfully. "I think, young lady, that we'll put you into a nursing home for a day or two."

"Oh but . . . but . . ."

"Nothing to worry about. But we'd better give the baby-to-be every chance, eh? And with two small children here to fret over. Two days of rest will be enough." His gruff voice touched both of them, calming them. "I'll make the arrangements and be back in a quarter of an hour." He looked at Peter Marlowe under his great bushy eyebrows. "The nursing home's in Kowloon so it'll save any long journey to the Island. A lot of us use it and it's good, clean and equipped for any emergency. Perhaps you'd pack a small bag for her?" He wrote the address and phone number. "So, young lady, I'll be back in a few minutes. It'll be best, then you won't have to worry about the children. I know what a trial that can be if you're sick." He smiled at both of them. "Don't worry about a thing, Mr. Marlowe, eh? I'll talk to your houseboy and ask him to help make things shipshape here. And don't worry about the money." The deep lines around his eyes deepened even more. "We're very philanthropic here in Hong Kong with our young guests."

He went out. Peter Marlowe sat on the bed. Disconsolate.

"I hope the kids got to school all right," she said.

"Oh yes. Ah Sop's fine."

"How will you manage?"

"Easy. I'll be like Old Mother Hubbard. It'll only be a day or two."

She moved wearily, leaning on a hand and watching the rain, and beyond it, the flat gray of the hotel across the narrow street that she hated so much because it cut off the sky. "I . . . I hope it's not going . . . going to cost too much," she said, her voice weightless.

"Don't worry about it, Fleur. We'll be all right. The Writers Guild'll pay."

"Will they? I bet they won't, Peter, not in time. Blast! We . . . we're so tight on our budget already."

"I can always borrow against next year's drop dead check. Don—"

"Oh no! No we won't do that, Peter. We mustn't. We agreed. Other . . . otherwise you're trapped ag . . . again."

"Something'll turn up," he said confidently. "Next month we've got a Friday the thirteenth and that's always been lucky for us." His novel was published on a thirteenth and went on to the best-seller list on a thirteenth. When he and his wife were at bottom, three years ago, on another thirteenth he had made a fine screenwriting deal that had carried them again. His first directing assignment had been confirmed on a thirteenth. And last April, Friday the thirteenth, one of the studios in Hollywood had bought the film rights to his novel for $157,000. The agent had taken 10 percent and then Peter Marlowe had spread the remainder over five years —in advance. Five years of family drop dead money. 25,000 per year every January. Enough, with care, for school and medical expenses and mortgage and car and other payments—five glorious years of freedom from all the usual worries. And freedom to turn down a directing-screenwriting job to come to Hong Kong for a year, unpaid, but free to look for the second book. Oh Christ, Peter Marlowe thought, suddenly petrified. What the hell am I looking for anyway? What the hell am I doing here? "Christ," he said miserably, "if I hadn't insisted on us going to that party this would never have happened."

"Joss." She smiled faintly. "Joss, Peter. Remember what you're . . . you're always saying to me. Joss. It's joss, just joss, Peter. Oh Christ I feel awful."

42

Orlanda Ramos opened the door of her apartment and put her sodden umbrella into a stand. "Come in, Linc," she said radiantly. *"Minha casa é vossa casa.* My house is yours."

Linc smiled. "You're sure?"

She laughed and said lightly, "Ah! That remains to be seen. It's just an old Portuguese custom . . . to offer one's house." She was taking off her shiny, very fashionable raincoat. In the corridor he was doing the same to a soaked, well-used raincoat.

"Here, let me hang it up," she said. "Oh, don't mind about the wet, my *amah* will mop it up. Come on in."

He noticed how neat and tidy the living room was, feminine, in very good taste and welcoming. She shut the door behind him and hung his coat on a peg. He went over to the French windows that let out onto a small balcony. Her apartment was on the eighth floor of Rose Court in Kotewall Road.

"Is the rain always this heavy?" he asked.

"In a real typhoon it's much worse. Perhaps twelve to eighteen inches in a day. Then there are mud slides and the resettlement areas get washed away."

He was looking down through the overcast. Most of the view was blocked by high rises, ribbon-built on the winding roads that were cut into the mountainside. From time to time he could see glimpses of Central and the shoreline far below. "It's like being in an airplane, Orlanda. On a balmy night it must be terrific."

"Yes. Yes it is. I love it. You can see all of Kowloon. Before Sinclair Towers was built—that's the block straight ahead—we had the best view in Hong Kong. Did you know Struan's own Sinclair Towers? I think Ian Dunross helped have it built to spite Quillan. Quillan has the penthouse apartment here . . . at least he did."

"It spoiled his view?"

"Ruined it."

"That's an expensive attack."

"No. Both blocks are immensely profitable. Quillan told me everything in Hong Kong's amortized over three years. Everything. Property's the thing to own. You could make . . ." She laughed. "You could improve your fortune if you wanted to."

"If I stay, where should I live?"

"Here in Mid Levels. Farther up the Peak you're always very damp, the walls sweat and everything mildews." She took off her headscarf and shook her hair free, then sat on the arm of a chair, looking at his back, waiting patiently.

"How long have you been here?" he asked.

"Five, almost six years. Since the block was built."

He turned and leaned against the window. "It's great," he said. "And so are you."

"Thank you, kind sir. Would you like coffee?"

"Please." Linc Bartlett ran his fingers through his hair, peering at an oil painting. "This a Quance?"

"Yes. Yes it is. Quillan gave it to me. Espresso?"

"Yes. Black, please. Wish I knew more about paintings . . ." He was going to add, Casey does, but he stopped himself and watched her open one of the doors. The kitchen was large, modern and very well equipped. "That's like something out of *House and Garden!*"

"This was all Quillan's idea. He loves food and loves cooking. This's all his design, the rest . . . the rest is mine though he taught me good from kitsch."

"You sorry you broke up with him?"

"Yes and no. It's joss, karma. He . . . that was joss. The time had come." Her quietness touched him. "It could never have lasted. Never. Not here." He saw a sadness go over her momentarily but she brushed it aside and busied herself with the sparkling espresso maker. All the shelves were spotless. "Quillan was a stickler for tidiness, thank God it rubbed off on me. My *amah*, Ah Fat, she drives me insane."

"Does she live here?"

"Oh yes, yes of course, but she's shopping now—her room's at the end of the corridor. Look around if you like. I won't be a minute."

Filled with curiosity he wandered off. A good dining room with a round table to seat eight. Her bedroom was white and pink, light and airy with soft pink drapes hung from the ceiling that fell around the huge bed making it into a vast four-poster. There were flowers in a delicate arrangement. A modern bathroom, tiled and perfect, with matching towels. A second bedroom with books and phone and hi-fi and smaller bed, again everything neat and tasteful.

Casey's outclassed, he told himself, remembering the easy, careless untidiness of her little house in the Los Angeles canyon, red brick, piles of books everywhere, barbecue, phones, duplicators and electric typewriters. Troubled at his thought and the way he automatically seemed to be comparing them, he strolled back to the kitchen, bypassing the *amah*'s room, his walk soundless. Orlanda was concentrating on the coffee maker, unaware that now he was watching her. He enjoyed watching her.

This morning he had phoned her early, very concerned, waking her, wanting to remind her to see a doctor, just in case. In the melee last night, by the time he and Casey and Dunross had got ashore she had already gone home.

"Oh, thank you, Linc, how thoughtful of you to phone! No, I'm fine," she had said in a happy rush. "At least I am now. Are you all right? Is Casey all right? Oh I can't thank you enough, I was petrified . . . You saved my life, you and Casey . . ."

They had chatted happily on the phone and she had promised to see her doctor anyway, and then he had asked if she'd like breakfast. At once she had said yes and he had gone Hong Kong side, enjoying the downpour, the temperature nice. Breakfast atop the Mandarin, eggs Benedict and toast and coffee, feeling grand, Orlanda sparkling and so appreciative of him and of Casey.

"I thought I was dead. I knew I'd drown, Linc, but I was too frightened to scream. If you hadn't done it all so quickly I'd never . . . The moment I was under, dear Casey was there and I was alive again and safe before I knew it. . . ."

It was the best breakfast he had ever had. She had ministered to him, small things, passing him toast and pouring coffee without having to ask for it, picking up his serviette when it fell, entertaining and being entertained, assured and feminine, making him feel masculine and strong. And she reached out once and put her hand on his arm, long fingers and exquisite nails, and the feel of that touch still lingered. Then he had escorted her home and inveigled an invitation up to her apartment and now he was here, watching her concentrate in the kitchen, silk skirt and Russian-style rain boots, loose blouse that was tight to her tiny waist, letting his eyes flow over her.

Jesus, he thought, I'd better be careful.

"Oh, I didn't see you, Linc. You walk quietly for a man of your height!"

"Sorry."

"Don't be sorry, Linc!" The steam hissed to a crescendo. Jet droplets began to fill the cups. "A twist of lemon?"

"Thanks. You?"

"No. I prefer cappuccino." She heated the milk, the sound fine and the smell of the coffee grand, then carried the tray to the breakfast area. Silver spoons and good porcelain, both of them aware of the currents in the room but pretending there were none.

Bartlett sipped his coffee. "It's wonderful, Orlanda! The best I've ever had. But it's different."

"It's the dash of chocolate."

"You like cooking?"

"Oh yes! Very much. Quillan said I was a good pupil. I love keeping house and organizing parties, and Quillan always . . ." A small frown was on her face now. She looked at him directly. "I seem to be always mentioning him. Sorry but it's still . . . it's still automatic. He was the first man in my life—the only man—so he's a part of me that's indelible."

"You don't have to explain, Orlanda, I und—"

"I know, but I'd like to. I've no real friends, I've never talked about him to anyone, never wanted to, but somehow . . . somehow well, I like being with you and . . ." A sudden, vast smile went across her. "Of course! I'd forgotten! Now I'm your responsibility!" She laughed and clapped her tiny hands.

"What do you mean?"

"According to Chinese custom you've interfered with joss or fate. Oh yes. You interfered with the gods. *You* saved my live because without you I'd surely have died—probably would have died—but that would have been up to the gods. But because you interfered you took over *their* responsibility, so now you have to look after me forever! That's good wise Chinese custom!" Her eyes were dancing and he had never seen whites as white or dark brown pupils so limpid, or a face so pleasing. "Forever!"

"You're on!" He laughed with her, the strength of her joy surrounding him.

"Oh good!" she said, then became a little serious and touched him on the arm. "I was only joking, Linc. You're so gallant—I'm not used to such gallantry. I formally release you—my Chinese half releases you."

"Perhaps I don't want to be released." At once he saw her eyes widen. His chest was feeling tight, his heart quickening. Her perfume tantalized him. Abruptly the force between them surged. His hand reached out and touched her hair, so silky and fine and sensuous. First touch. Caressing her. A little shiver and then they were kissing. He felt her lips soft and, in a moment, welcoming, just a little moist, without lipstick, the taste so clean and good.

Their passion grew. His hand moved to her breast and the heat came through the silk. Again she shivered and weakly tried to back off but he held her firmly, his heart racing, fondling her, then her hands went to his chest and stayed awhile, touching him, then pressed against him and she broke the kiss but stayed close, gathering her breath, her heart racing, as intoxicated as he was.

"Linc . . . you . . ."

"You feel so good," he said softly, holding her close. He bent to kiss her again but she avoided his kiss.

"Wait, Linc. First . . ."

He kissed her neck and tried again, sensing her want.

"Linc, wait . . . first . . ."

"First kiss, then wait!"

She laughed. The tension broke. He cursed himself for making the mistake, his desire strong, whipped by hers. Now the moment had passed and they were fencing again. His anger began to flood but before it possessed him she reached up and kissed him perfectly. At once his anger vanished. Only warmth remained.

"You're too strong for me, Linc," she said, her voice throaty, arms around his neck but cautiously. "Too strong and too attractive and too nice and truly, truly I do owe you a life." Her hand caressed his neck and he felt it in his loins as she looked up at him, all her defenses settled, strong yet inviolate. Perhaps, he thought.

"First talk," she said, moving away, "then perhaps we will kiss again."

"Good." At once he went to her but, both of them in good humor now, she put her finger on his lips, preventing him.

"Mr. Bartlett! Are all Americans like you?"

"No," he said immediately but she would not take the bait.

"Yes, I know." Her voice was serious. "I know. That's what I wanted to talk to you about. Coffee?"

"Sure," he said, waiting, wondering how to proceed, gauging her, wanting her, not sure of this jungle, fascinated by it and by her.

Carefully she poured the coffee. It tasted as good as the first. He was in control though the ache remained.

"Let's go into the living room," she said. "I'll bring your cup."

He got up and kept a hand around her waist. She did not object and he felt that she liked his touch too. He sat in one of the deep armchairs. "Sit here," he said, patting the arm. "Please."

"Later. First I want to talk." She smiled a little shyly and sat on the sofa opposite. It was dark blue velvet and matched the Chinese rug on shiny parquet floors. "Linc, I've only known you a few days and I . . . I'm not a good-time girl." Orlanda reddened as she said it and carried on a rush over what he was going to say. "Sorry but I'm not. Quillan was the first and only one and I don't want an affair. I don't want a frantic or friendly tumble and a shy or aching good-bye. I've learned to live without love, I just cannot go through that all again. I did love Quillan, I don't now. I was seventeen when we . . . when we began and now I'm twenty-five. We've been apart for almost three years. Everything's been finished for three years and I don't love him anymore. I don't love anyone and I'm sorry, I'm sorry but I'm not a good-time girl."

"I never thought you were," he said and knew in his heart it was a lie and cursed his luck. "Hell, what do you think I am?"

"I think you're a fine man," she said at once, sincerely, "but in Asia a girl, any girl, finds out very quickly that men want to pillow and that's really all they want. Sorry, Linc, casual pillowing's not my thing. Perhaps it will be one day but not now. Yes I'm Eurasian but I'm not . . . you know what I'm saying?"

"Sure," he said and added before he could stop himself, "you're saying you're off limits."

Her smile vanished and she stared at him. His heart twisted at her sadness. "Yes," she said, slowly getting up, near tears. "Yes, I suppose I am."

"Jesus, Orlanda." He went over to her and held her. "I didn't mean it that way. I didn't mean it rotten."

"Linc, I'm not trying to tease or play games or be diffic—"

"I understand. Hell, I'm not a child and I'm not pushing or . . . I'm not either."

"Oh, oh I'm so glad. For a moment . . ." She looked up and her innocence melted him. "You're not mad at me, Linc? I mean I . . . I didn't ask you up, you really insisted on coming."

"I know," he said, holding her in his arms, and he was thinking, It's the truth, and also the truth that I want you now and I don't know what you are, who you are but I want you. But what do I want from you? What do I really want? Do I want magic? Or just a lay? Are you the magic I've been seeking forever or just another broad? How do you stack against Casey? Do I measure loyalty against the silk of your skin? Remember how Casey said once, "Love consists of many things, Linc, only one part of love's sex. Only one. Think of all the other parts. Judge a woman by her love, yes, but understand what a woman is." But her warmth was going through him, her face against his chest and once more he felt himself stirring. He kissed her neck, not wanting to withhold his passion.

"What are you, Orlanda?"

"I'm . . . I can only tell you what I'm not," she said in her tiny voice. "I'm not a tease. I don't want you to think that I'm trying to tease you. I like you, like you very much but I'm not a . . . I'm not a one-night stand."

"I know. Jesus, what put that into your head?" He saw her eyes were glistening. "No need for tears. None. Okay?"

"Yes." She moved away and opened her purse and took out a tissue and used it. "*Ayeeyah*, I'm acting like a teen-ager or a vestal virgin. Sorry, but it was rather sudden and I wasn't prepared for . . . I felt myself going." She took a deep breath. "Abject apologies."

He laughed. "Refused."

"Thank God!" She watched him. "Actually, Linc, I can usually handle the strong, the meek, and the cunning—even the very cunning—without too much trouble. I guess I've known every kind of pass it's possible for a girl to have and I've always figured I've an automatic game plan to counter them almost before they begin. But with you . . ." She hesitated, then added, "Sorry, but almost every man I meet, well, it's always the same."

"That's wrong?"

"No, but it's trying to walk into a room or a restaurant and feel those leering eyes. I wonder how men would handle it. You're young and handsome. What would you do if women did it to you everywhere you went. Say when you walked through the lobby of the V and A this morning you saw every woman of every age, from false-toothed old grannies, bewigged harpies, the fat, the ugly, the coarse, all of them, all openly leering at you, undressing you mentally, openly trying to get close, trying to stroke your behind, openly ogling your chest or crotch, most of them with bad breath, most of them sweating and foul-smelling, and you know they're imagining you in their bed, enthusiastically and happily doing the most intimate things to them."

"I wouldn't like it at all. Casey said the same thing in different words when she first joined me. I know what you mean, Orlanda. At least I can imagine it. But that's the way the world's made."

"Yes, and sometimes it's awful. Oh I don't want to be a man, Linc, I'm very happy to be a woman, but it's really quite awful sometimes. To know you're thought of as just a receptacle that can be bought, and that after it all you're to say thank you very much to the corpulent old lecher with the bad breath and accept your twenty-dollar bill and sneak off like a thief in the night."

He frowned. "How did we get on this kick?"

She laughed. "You kissed me."

He grinned, glad they were happy together. "That's right. So maybe I deserved the lecture. I'm guilty as charged. Now, about that kiss you promised me. . . ." But he did not move. He was feeling his way, probing. Everything's changed now, he thought. Sure I wanted to—what did she call it? To pillow. Sure. Still do, more than before. But now we're changed. Now we're in a different game. I don't know if I want in. The rules've changed. Before it was simple. Now maybe it's more simple. "You're pretty. Did I mention you were pretty?" he said, avoiding the issue that she wanted out in the open.

"I was going to talk about that kiss. You see, Linc, the truth is I just wasn't prepared for the way, to be honest, the way I, I was swamped, I guess that's the word."

He let the word linger. "Is that good or bad?"

"Both." Her eyes crinkled with her smile. "Yes, swamped with my own desire. You're something else, Mr. Bartlett, and that's also very bad, or very good. I, I enjoyed your kiss."

"So did I." Again he grinned at her. "You can call me Linc."

After a pause she said, "I've never felt so wanting and swamped, and because of that very frightened."

"No need to be frightened," he said. But he was wondering what to do. His instincts said leave. His instincts said stay. Wisdom told him to say nothing and wait. He could hear his heart beating and the rain hammering the windows. Better to go, he thought. "Orlanda, guess it's ab—"

"Do you have time to talk? Just a little?" she asked, sensing his indecision.

"Sure. Sure, of course."

Her fingers brushed her hair from her face. "I wanted to tell you about me. Quillan was my father's boss in Shanghai and I seem to have known him all my life. He helped pay for my education, particularly in the States and he was always very kind to me and my family—I've four sisters and a brother and I'm the oldest and they're all in Portugal now. When I came back to Shanghai from San Francisco after I'd graduated, I was seventeen, almost eighteen and . . . Well he's an attractive man, to me he is, though very cruel sometimes. Very."

"How?"

"He believes in personal vengeance, that vengeance is a man's right, if he's a man. Quillan's very much a man. He was always good to me, still is." She studied him. "Quillan still gives me an allowance, still pays for this apartment."

"You don't have to tell me anything."

"I know. But I'd like to—if you want to listen. Then you can decide." He studied her. "All right."

"You see, part of it's because I'm Eurasian. Most Europeans despise us, openly or secretly, particularly the British here—Linc, just hear me out. Most Europeans despise Eurasians. All Chinese do. So we're always on the defensive, almost always suspect, almost always presumed to be illegitimate, and certainly an easy lay. God how I loathe that Americanism! How rotten and vulgar and cheap it really is. And revealing about the American male—though, strangely, it was in the States that I gained my self-respect and got over my Eurasian guilt. Quillan taught me lots and formed me in lots of ways. I'm beholden to him. But I don't love him. That's what I wanted to say. Would you like more coffee?"

"Sure, thanks."

"I'll make some fresh." She got up, her walk unconsciously sensuous and again he cursed his luck.

"Why'd you bust up with him?"

Gravely she told him about Macao. "I allowed myself to be persuaded into the fellow's bed and I slept there though nothing happened, nothing —the poor man was drunk and useless. The next day I pretended that he'd been fine." Her voice was outwardly calm and matter-of-fact but he could feel the anguish. "Nothing happened but someone told Quillan. Rightly, he was furious. I have no defense. It was . . . Quillan had been away. I know that's no excuse but I'd learned to enjoy pillowing and . . ." A shadow went over her. She shrugged. "Joss. Karma." In the same small voice she told him about Quillan's revenge. "That's his way, Linc. But he was right to be furious with me, I was wrong." The steam hissed and the coffee began to drip. Her hands were finding clean cups and fresh home-baked cookies and new starched linen as she talked but their minds were concentrating on the man-woman triangle.

"I still see him once in a while. Just to talk. We're just friends now and he's good to me and I do what I want, see who I want." She turned the steam off and looked up at him. "We . . . we had a child four years ago. I wanted it, he didn't. He said I could have the child but I should have it in England. She's in Portugal now with my parents—my father's retired and she lives with them." A tear rolled down her cheek.

"Was that his idea, to keep the child there?"

"Yes. But he is right. Once a year I go there. My parents . . . my mother wanted the child, begged to have it. Quillan's generous to them too." The tears were rolling down her face now but there was no sound to her crying. "So now you know it all, Linc. I've never told anyone but you and now you know I'm, I wasn't a faithful mistress and I'm, I'm not a good mother and and . . ."

He went to her and held her very close and he felt her melt against him, trying to hold back the sobs, holding on, taking his warmth and his strength. He gentled her, holding her, the length of her against him, warm, tender, everything fitting.

When she was whole again she reached up on tiptoe and kissed him lightly but with great tenderness and looked at him.

He returned the kiss equally.

They looked at each other searchingly, then kissed again. Their passion grew and it seemed forever but it was not and both heard the key in the lock at the same time. They broke away, trying to catch their breath, listening to their hearts and hearing the coarse voice of the *amah* from the hall. "*Weyyyyy?*"

Weakly Orlanda brushed her hair straighter, half-shrugged to him in apology. "I'm in the kitchen," she called out in Shanghainese. "Please go to your room until I call you."

"Oh? Oh the foreign devil's still here is he? What about my shopping? I did some shopping!"

"Leave it by the door!"

"Oh, oh very well, Young Mistress," the *amah* called back and went off grumbling. The door banged loudly behind her.

"They always slam doors?" Linc asked, his heart still thumping.

"Yes, yes it seems so." Her hand went back to his shoulder, the nails caressing his neck. "Sorry."

"Nothing to be sorry about. How about dinner?"

She hesitated. "If you bring Casey."

"No. Just you."

"Linc, I think it's best no," she told him. "We're not in danger now. Let's just say good-bye now."

"Dinner. Eight. I'll call for you. You pick the restaurant. Shanghai food."

She shook her head. "No. It's too heady already. Sorry."

"I'll call for you at eight." Bartlett kissed her lightly, then went to the door. She took down his raincoat and held it out for him. "Thanks," he said gently. "No danger, Orlanda. Everything's going to come up roses. See you at eight. Okay?"

"It's best not."

"Maybe." He smiled down at her strangely. "That'd be joss—karma. We must remember the gods, huh?" She did not answer. "I'll be here at eight."

She closed the door behind him, went slowly to the chair and sat, deep in thought, wondering if she had scared him off, petrified that she had. Wondering if he really would be back at eight and if he did, how to keep him off, how to puppet him until he was mad with desire, mad enough to marry her.

Her stomach twisted uneasily. I have to be fast, she thought. Casey holds him in thrall, she's wrapped her coils around him and my only way is good cooking and home and loving, loving loving loving and everything that Casey is not. But no pillow. That's the way Casey's trapped him. I have to do the same.

Then he'll be mine.

Orlanda felt weak. Everything had gone perfectly, she decided. Then again she remembered what Gornt had said. "It's the law of the ages that every man has to be trapped into marriage, trapped by his own lust or possessiveness or avarice or money or fear or laziness or whatever but trapped. And no man ever willingly marries his mistress."

Yes. Quillan's right again, she thought. But he's wrong about me. I'm not going to settle for half the prize. I'm going to try for all of it. I'm going to have not only the Jag and this apartment and all it contains but a house in California and, most of all, American wealth, away from Asia, where I'll no longer be Eurasian but a woman like any other, beautiful, carefree and loving.

Oh I'll make him the best wife a man could ever have. I'll minister to his every need, whatever he wants I'll do for him. I felt his strength and I'll be good for him, wonderful for him.

"He's gone?" Ah Fat wandered noiselessly into the room, automatically tidying as she talked the Shanghai dialect. "Good, very good. Shall I make some tea? You must be tired. Some tea, *heya*?"

"No. Yes, yes make some, Ah Fat."

"Make some tea! Work work work!" The old woman shuffled to the kitchen. She wore black baggy pants and white smock and her hair was in a single long braid that hung down her back. She had looked after Orlanda ever since she was born. "I took a good look at him downstairs, when you and he arrived. For an uncivilized person he's quite presentable," she said speculatively.

"Oh? I didn't see you. Where were you?"

NOBLE HOUSE   597

"Down by the stairs," Ah Fat cackled. "Eeeee, I took good care to hide but I wanted to look at him. Huh! You send your poor old slave out into the wet with my poor old bones when what does it matter if I'm here or not? Who's going to get you sweetmeats and tea or drinks in bed when you've finished your labors, *heya?*"

"Oh shut up! Shut up!"

"Don't shut up your poor old Mother! She knows how to look after you! Ah yes, Little Empress, but it was quite clear on both of you the yang and the yin were ready to join battle. You two looked as happy as cats in a barrel of fish! But there was no need for me to leave!"

"Foreign devils are different, Ah Fat. I wanted him here alone. Foreign devils are shy. Now make the tea and keep quiet or I'll send you out again!"

"Is he going to be the new Master?" Ah Fat called out hopefully. "It's about time you had a Master, not good for a person not to have a Steaming Stalk at the Jade Gate. Your Gate'll shrivel up and become as dry as dust from the little use it gets! Oh, I forgot to tell you two pieces of news. The Werewolves are supposed to be Macao foreigners; they'll strike again before the new moon. That's what the rumor is. Everyone swears it's the truth. And the other's that, well, Old Cougher Tok at the fish stall says this foreign devil from the Golden Mountain's got more gold than Eunuch Tung!" Tung was a legendary eunuch at the Imperial Court in the Forbidden City of Peking whose lust for gold was so immense that all China could not satisfy it; he was hated so much that the next emperor heaped his ill-gotten gains on him until the weight of the gold crushed him to death. "You're not getting younger, Little Mother! We should be serious. Is he going to be the one?"

"I hope so," Orlanda said slowly.

Oh yes, she thought fervently, faint with anxiety, knowing that Linc Bartlett was the single most important opportunity of her life. Abruptly she was petrified again that she had overplayed her game and that he would not come back. She burst into tears.

Eight floors below, Bartlett crossed the small foyer and went outside to join the half a dozen people waiting impatiently for a taxi. The torrent was steady now and it gushed off the concrete overhang to join the flood that swirled in a small river down Kotewall Road, overflowing the gutters, the storm drains long since choked, carrying with it stones and mud and vegetation that came off the high banks and slopes above. Cars and trucks grinding cautiously up or down the steep road splashed through the whirlpools and eddies, windshield wipers clicking, windows fogged.

Across the road the land rose steeply and Bartlett saw the multitude of rivulets cascading down the high concrete embankments that held the earth in. Weeds grew out of cracks. Part of a sodden clump fell away to join more debris and stones and mud. One side of the embankment was a walled garage and, up the slope, a half-hidden ornate Chinese mansion with a green tiled roof and dragons on its gables. Beside it was scaffolding of a building site and excavations for a high rise. Beside that was another apartment block that vanished into the overcast.

So much building, Bartlett told himself critically. Maybe we should get into construction here. Too many people chasing too little land means profit, huge profit. And amortized over three years—Jesus!

A taxi swirled up, careless of the puddles. Passengers got out and others, grumbling, got in. A Chinese couple came out of the entrance, shoved past him and the others to the head of the line—a loud chattering matron with a huge umbrella, an expensive raincoat over her *chong-sam*, her husband meek and mild alongside her. Screw you, baby, Bartlett thought, you're not going to take my turn. He moved into a better position. His watch read 10:35.

What next, he asked himself. Don't let Orlanda distract you!

Struan's or Gornt?

Today's skirmish day, tomorrow—Friday—tomorrow's the ballbreaker, the weekend's for regrouping, Monday's the final assault and by 3:00 P.M. we should have a victor.

Whom do I want to win? Dunross or Gornt?

That Gornt's a lucky man—was a lucky man, he thought, bemused. Jesus, Orlanda's something else. Would I have quit her if I'd been him? Sure. Sure I would. Well maybe not—nothing happened. But I'd've married her the moment I could and not sent *our* child packing to Portugal—that Gornt's a no-good son of a bitch. Or goddamn clever. Which?

She laid it out nice and clean—just like Casey did but different though the result's the same. Now everything's complicated, or simple. Which?

Do I want to marry her? No.

Do I want to let her drop? No.

Do I want to bed her? Sure. So mount a campaign, maneuver her into bed without commitments. Don't play the game of life according to female rules, all's fair in war and war. What's love anyway? It's like Casey said, sex's only a part of it.

Casey. What about her? Not long to wait for Casey now. And then, is it bed or marriage bells or good-bye or what? Goddamned if I want to get married again. The one time turned out lousy. That's strange, I haven't thought about *her* in a long time.

When Bartlett had returned from the Pacific in '45 he had met her in San Diego and married within a week, full of love and ambition and had hurled himself into beginning a construction business in southern California. The time was ripe in California, all forms of building booming. The first child had arrived within ten months and the second a year later and a third ten months after that, and all the while working Saturdays and Sundays, enjoying the work and being young and strong and succeeding hugely, but drifting apart. Then the quarreling began and the whining and the "you never spend any time with us anymore and screw the business I don't care about the business I want to go to France and Rome and why don't you come home early have you a girl friend I know you have a girl friend. . . ."

But there was no girl friend, just work. Then one day the attorney's letter. Just through the mail.

Shit, Bartlett thought angrily, it still hurting. But then I'm only one of millions and it's happened before and it'll happen again. Even so *your* letter or *your* phone call hurts. It hurts and it costs you. It costs you plenty and the attorneys get most, get a good part and they cleverly fan the fire between you for their own goddamn gain. Sure. You're their meal ticket, we all are! From the cradle to the goddamn grave, attorneys kite trouble and feed off your blood. Shit. Attorneys're the real plague of the good old U.S. of A. I've only met four good ones in all my life, but the rest? They parasite all of us. Not one of us's safe!

Yes. That bastard Stone! He made a killing out of me, turned her into a goddamn fiend, put her and the kids against me forever and nearly broke me and the business. I hope the bastard rots for all eternity!

With an effort Bartlett took his mind off that gaping sore and looked at the rain and remembered that it was only money and that he was free, free and that made him feel marvelous.

Jesus! I'm free and there's Casey and Orlanda.

Orlanda.

Jesus, he thought, the ache still in his loins, I was really going back there. So was Orlanda. Goddamn, it's bad enough with Casey but now I've two of them.

He had not been with a girl for a couple of months. The last time was in London, a casual meeting and casual dinner then into bed. She was staying at the same hotel, divorced and no trouble. What was it Orlanda said? A friendly tumble and a shy good-bye? Yes. That's it. But that one wasn't shy.

He stood in line happily, feeling greatly alive and watching the torrents, the smell of the rain on the earth grand, the road messed with stones and mud, the flood swirling over a long wide crack in the tarmac to dance into the air like rapids of a stream.

The rain's going to bring lots of trouble, he thought. And Orlanda's lots of trouble, old buddy. Sure. Even so, there must be a way to bed her. What is it about her that blows your mind? Part's her face, part's her figure, part's the look in her eye, part's . . . Jesus, face it, she's all woman and all trouble. Better forget Orlanda. Be wise, be wise, old buddy. As Casey said, that broad's dynamite!

43

10:50 A.M.:

It had been raining now for almost twelve hours and the surface of the Colony was soaked though the empty reservoirs were barely touched. The parched earth welcomed the wet. Most of the rain ran off the baked surface to flood the lower levels, turning dirt roads into morasses, and building sites into lakes. Some of the water went deep. In the resettlement areas that dotted the mountainsides the downpour was a disaster.

Shantytowns of rickety hovels built of any scraps, cardboard, planks, corrugated iron, fencing, canvas, sidings, three-ply walls and roofs for the well-to-do, all leaning against one another, attached to one another, on top of one another, layer on layer, up and down the mountains—all with dirt floors and dark alleys that were now awash and mucked and puddled and potholed and dangerous. Rain pouring through roofs soaking bedding, clothes and the other remnants of a lifetime, people packed on people surrounded by people who stoically shrugged and waited for the rain to stop. Tin alleys wandered higgledy-piggledy with no plan except to squeeze another space for another family of refugees and illegal aliens but not really aliens for this was China and, once past the border, any Chinese became legal settlers to stay as long as they wanted by ancient Hong Kong Government approval.

The strength of the Colony had always been its cheap, abundant and strife-free labor force. The Colony provided a permanent sanctuary and asked only peaceful labor in return at whatever the going rate of the day was. Hong Kong never sought immigrants but the people of China always came. They came by day and by night, by ship, by foot, by stretcher. They came across the border whenever famine or a convulsion racked China, families of men, women and children came to stay, to be absorbed, in time to go back home because China was always home, even after ten generations.

But refugees were not always welcomed. Last year the Colony was almost swamped by a human flood. For some still unknown reason and without warning, the PRC border guards relaxed the tight control of their side and within a week thousands were pouring across daily. Mostly they came by night, over and through the token, single six-strand fence that separated the New Territories from the Kwantung, the neighboring province. The police were powerless to stem the tide. The army had to be called out. In one night in May almost six thousand of the illegal horde were arrested, fed and the next day sent back over the border—but more thousands had escaped the border net to become legal. The catastrophe went on night after night, day after day. Tens of thousands of newcomers. Soon mobs of angry sympathetic Chinese were at the border trying to disrupt the deportations. The deportations were necessary because the Colony was becoming buried in illegals and it was impossible to feed, house and absorb such a sudden, vast increase in new population. Already there were the four-plus million to worry about, all but a tiny percent illegals at one time.

Then, as suddenly as it had begun, the human gusher ceased and the border closed. Again for no apparent reason.

In the six-week period almost 70,000 had been arrested and returned. Between 100,000 and 200,000 escaped the net to stay, no one knew for certain how many. Spectacles Wu's grandparents and four uncles and their families were some of these, seventeen souls in all, and since they had arrived they had been living in a resettlement area high above Aberdeen. Spectacles Wu had arranged everything for them. This was more of the land that the Noble House Chen family had owned since the beginning that, until recently, had been without value. Now it had value. The Chens rented it, foot by foot, to any who wished to pay. Spectacles Wu had gratefully rented twenty feet by twelve feet at 1.00 HK per foot per month and, over the months, had helped the family scavenge the makings for two dwellings that, until this rain, were dry. There was one water tap per hundred families, no sewers, no electric light, but the city of these squatters thrived and was mostly well ordered. Already one uncle had a small plastic flower factory in a hovel he had rented at 1.50 HK per foot per month lower down the slopes, another had rented a stall in the market area selling tangy rice cakes and rice gruel in their Ning-tok village style. All seventeen were working—now eighteen mouths to feed with a newborn babe, born last week. Even the two-year-olds were given simple tasks, sorting plastic petals for the plastic flowers the young and old made that gave many of the hill dwellers money to buy food and money to gamble with.

Yes, Spectacles Wu thought fervently, all gods help me to get some of the reward money for the capture of the Werewolves in time for Saturday's races to put on Pilot Fish, the black stallion who, according to all the portents, is definitely going to win.

He stifled a yawn as he plodded on barefoot down one of the narrow twisting alleys in the resettlement area, his six-year-old niece beside him.

She was barefoot too. The rain kept misting his thick glasses. Both picked
their way cautiously, not wanting to step on any broken glass or rusting
debris that was ever present. Sometimes the mud was ankle-deep. Both
wore their trousers well rolled up and she had a vast straw coolie hat that
dwarfed her. His hat was ordinary and secondhand like his clothes and
not police regulation. These were the only clothes he possessed except for
the shoes he carried in a plastic bag under his raincoat to protect them.
Stepping over a foul pothole he almost lost his footing. "Fornicate all haz-
ards," he cursed, glad that he did not live here and that the rented room
he shared with his mother near the East Aberdeen police station was dry
and not subject to quirks of the weather gods like those here. And thank
all gods I don't have to make this journey every day. My clothes would be
ruined and then my whole future would be in jeopardy because Special
Intelligence admires neatness and punctuality. Oh gods let this be my
great day!

Tiredness wafted over him. His head was hunched down and he felt
the rain trickling down his neck. He had been on duty all night. When
he was leaving the station early this morning he had been told that there
was to be a raid on the old *amah*, Ah Tam, the one connected with the
Werewolves, whom he had found and tracked to her lair. So he had said
that he would hurry with his visit to his grandfather who had been taken
ill and was near death and hurry back in good time.

He glanced at his watch. There was still time enough to walk the mile
to the station. Reassured, he went on again, eased past a pile of garbage
into a bigger alley that skirted the storm drain. The storm drain was five
feet deep and served normally for sewer, laundry or sink, depending on
the amount of water therein. Now it was overflowing, the swirling runoff
adding to the misery of those below.

"Be careful, Fifth Niece," he said.

"Yes. Oh yes, Sixth Uncle. Can I come all the way?" the little girl
asked happily.

"Only to the candy stall. Now be careful! Look, there's another piece of
glass!"

"Is Honorable Grandfather going to die?"

"That's up to the gods. The time of dying is up to the gods, not to us,
so why should we worry, *heya?*"

"Yes," she agreed importantly. "Yes, gods are gods."

All gods cherish Honorable Grandfather and make the rest of his life
sweet, he prayed, then added carefully, for safety, "Hail Mary Mother
and Joseph, bless old Grandfather." Who knows whether the Christian
God or even the real gods exist? he thought. Better to try to placate them
all, if you can. It costs nothing. Perhaps they'll help. Perhaps they're sleeping or out to lunch but never mind. Life is life, gods are gods, money is
money, laws must be obeyed and today I must be very sharp.

Last night he had been out with Divisional Sergeant Mok and the

Snake. This was the first time he had been taken with them on one of their special raids. They had raided three gambling joints but had, curiously, left five much more prosperous ones untouched even though they were on the same floor of the same tenement and he could hear the click of mah-jong tiles and the cries of the fan-tan croupiers.

Dew neh loh moh I wish I could get part of the squeeze, he told himself then added, Get thee behind me, Satan! I want much more to be in Special Intelligence because then I will have a safe, important job for life, I will know all manner of secrets, the secrets will protect me, and then, when I retire, the secrets will make me rich.

They turned a corner and reached the candy stall. He bartered with the old toothless woman for a minute or two, then paid her two copper cash and she gave the little girl a sweet rice cake and a good pinch of the bits of oh so chewy and tangy bittersweet sun-dried orange peel in a twist of newspaper.

"Thank you, Sixth Uncle," the little girl said, beaming up at him from under her hat.

"I hope you enjoy them, Fifth Niece," he replied, loving her, glad that she was pretty. If the gods favor us she will grow up to be very pretty, he thought contentedly, then we can sell her maidenhead for a vast amount of money, and her later services profitably for the good of the family.

Spectacles Wu was very proud that he had been able to do so much for this part of his family in their hour of need. Everyone safe and fed and now my percentage of Ninth Uncle's plastic flower factory, negotiated so patiently, will, with joss, pay my rent in a year or two, and I can eat good Ning-tok rice gruel three times a week free which helps eke out my money so that I needn't take the squeeze that is so easy to obtain but would ruin my future.

No. All gods bear witness! I will not take the squeeze while there's a chance for SI but it's not sensible to pay us so little. Me, 320 HK a month, after two years of service. *Ayeeyah,* barbarians are impossible to understand!

"You run along now and I'll be back tomorrow," he said. "Be careful as you go."

"Oh yes!"

He bent down and she hugged him. He hugged her back and left. She headed up the hill, part of the rice cake already in her mouth, the cloying tacky sweetness oh so delicious.

The rain was monotonous and heavy. Flooding from the storm drain carried debris against the shacks in its path but she climbed the path carefully, skirting it, fascinated by the rushing water. The overflow was deep in parts and here where the way was steeper, almost like rapids. Without warning a jagged five-gallon can came swirling down the drain and hurled itself at her, narrowly missing her, to smash through a cardboard wall.

She stood stock-still, frightened.

"Get on, there's nothing to steal here!" a furious householder called out at her. "Go home! You shouldn't be here. Go home!"

"Yes . . . yes," she said and began to hurry, the climb more difficult now. At that moment the earth just below her gave way and the slide began. Hundreds of tons of sludge and rock and earth surged downward burying everything in its path. It went on for fifty yards or more in seconds, tearing the flimsy structures apart, scattering men, women and children, burying some, maiming others, cutting an oozing swath where once was village.

Then it stopped. As suddenly as it began.

On all the mountainside there was a great silence broken only by the sound of rain. Abruptly the silence ceased. Shouts and cries for help began. Men and women and children rushed out of untouched hovels, blessing the gods for their own safety, adding to the pandemonium and wails for help. Friends helped friends, neighbors helped neighbors, mothers searched for children, children for parents, but the great majority nearby just stood there in the rain and blessed their joss that this slide had passed them by.

The little girl was still teetering on the brink of the chasm where the earth had fallen away. She stared down into it with disbelief. Eleven feet below her now were fangs of rocks and sludge and death where seconds ago was solid ground. The lip was crumbling and small avalanches of mud and stones cascaded into the abyss, aided by the flooding from the storm drain. She felt her feet slipping so she took a tentative step backward but more of the earth gave way so she stopped, petrified, the remains of the rice cake still firmly in her hands. Her toes dug into the soft earth to try to keep her balance.

"Don't move," an old man called out.

"Get away from the edge," another shouted and the rest watched and waited and held their breath to see what the gods would decide.

Then a ten-foot slice of the lip collapsed and toppled into the maw carrying the little girl with it. She was buried just a little. Up to her knees. She made sure her rice cake was safe then burst into tears.

44

Superintendent Armstrong's police car eased its way through the milling angry crowds that had spilled over into the road outside the Ho-Pak Bank, heading for the East Aberdeen police station. Mobs were also clogging the streets outside all the other banks in the area, big and small—even the Victoria which was across the street from the Ho-Pak—everyone impatiently waiting to get in to get their money out.

Everywhere the mood was volatile and dangerous, the downpour adding to the tension. Barricades erected to channel people into and out of the banks were manned in strength by equally anxious and irritable police—twenty per thousand, unarmed but for truncheons.

"Thank God for the rain," Armstrong muttered.

"Sir?" the driver asked, the irritating screech of ill-adjusted windshield wipers drowning his voice.

Armstrong repeated it louder and added, "If it was hot and humid, this whole bloody place'd be up in arms. The rain's a godsend."

"Yes sir. Yes it is."

In time the police car stopped outside the station. He hurried in. Chief Inspector Donald C.C. Smyth was waiting for him. His left arm was in a sling.

"Sorry to be so long," Armstrong said. "Bloody traffic's jammed for bloody miles."

"Never mind. Sorry but I'm a bit shorthanded, old chap. West Aberdeen's cooperating and so is Central, but they've problems too. Bloody banks! We'll have to do with one copper in the back—he's already in position in case we flush one of the villains—and us up front with Spectacles Wu." Smyth told Armstrong his plan.

"Good."

"Shall we go now? I don't want to be away too long."

"Of course. It looks pretty dicey outside."

"I hope the bloody rain lasts until the bloody banks close their doors or pay out the last penny. Did you go liquid yourself?"

"You must be joking! My pittance makes no difference!" Armstrong stretched, his back aching. "Ah Tam in the flat?"

"As far as we know. The family she works for is called Ch'ung. He's a dustman. One of the villains might be there too so we'll have to get in quickly. I've the commissioner's authority to carry a revolver. Do you want one too?"

"No. No thanks. Let's go, shall we?"

Smyth was shorter than Armstrong but well built and his uniform suited him. Awkwardly, because of his arm, he picked up his raincoat and began to lead the way, then stopped. "Bugger, I forgot! Sorry, SI, Brian Kwok called, would you call him? Want to use my office?"

"Thanks. Is there any coffee? I could use a cuppa."

"Coming up."

The office was neat, efficient and drab, though Armstrong noticed the expensive chairs and desk and radio and accoutrements. "Gifts from grateful customers," Smyth said airily. "I'll leave you for a couple of minutes."

Armstrong nodded and dialed. "Yes, Brian?"

"Oh hello, Robert! How's it going? The Old Man says you should bring her to HQ and not investigate her at East Aberdeen."

"All right. We're just about to leave. HQ eh? What's the reason?"

"He didn't tell me, but he's in a good mood today. It seems we've a 16/2 tonight."

Armstrong's interest peaked. A 16/2 in SI terms meant they had broken an enemy cover and were going to take the spy or spies into custody. "Anything to do with our problem?" he asked cautiously, meaning Sevrin.

"Perhaps." There was a pause. "Remember what I was saying about our mole? I'm more convinced than ever I'm right." Brian Kwok switched to Cantonese, using oblique phrases and innuendoes in case he was overheard. Armstrong listened with growing concern as his best friend told him what had happened at the track, the long private meeting between Crosse and Suslev.

"But that means nothing. Crosse knows the bugger. Even I've drunk with him once or twice, feeling him out."

"Perhaps. But if Crosse's our mole it'd be just like him to do an exchange in public. *Heya?*"

Armstrong felt sick with apprehension. "Now's not the time, old chum," he said. "Soon as I get to HQ we should have a chat. Maybe lunch and talk."

Another pause. "The Old Man wants you to report to him as soon as you bring the *amah* in."

"All right. See you soon."

Armstrong put down the phone. Smyth came back in. Thoughtfully he handed him a coffee. "Bad news?"

"Nothing but bloody trouble," Armstrong said sourly. "Always bloody trouble." He sipped his coffee. The cup was excellent porcelain and the coffee fresh, expensive and delicious. "This's good coffee! Very good. Crosse wants me to bring her to HQ directly, not here."

Smyth's eyebrows soared. "Christ, what's so important about an old hag *amah?*" he asked sharply. "She's in my jurisdic—"

"Christ I don't know! I don't give the f—" The bigger man stopped his explosion. "Sorry, I haven't been getting much sleep the last few days. I don't give the orders. Crosse said to bring her to HQ. No explanation. He can override anyone. SI overrides everyone, you know how it is!"

"Arrogant bastard!" Smyth finished his coffee. "Thank God I'm not in SI. I'd hate to deal with that bugger every day."

"I'm not in SI and he still gives me trouble."

"Was it about our mole?"

Armstrong glanced up at him. "What mole?"

Smyth laughed. "Come on for chrissake! There's a rumor among the Dragons that our fearless leaders have been advised to find the bugger very quickly. It seems that the minister's even roasting the governor! London's so pissed off they're sending out the head of MI-6—presume you know Sinders arrives tomorrow on the BOAC flight."

Armstrong sighed. "Where the hell do they get all their information?"

"Telephone operators, *amahs*, street cleaners—who cares. But you can bet, old lad, at least one of them knows everything. You know Sinders?"

"No, never met him." Armstrong sipped his coffee, enjoying the excellence, the rich, nutty flavor that was giving him new strength. "If they know everything, who's the mole?"

After a pause, Smyth said, "That sort of info'd be expensive. Shall I ask the price?"

"Yes. Please." The big man put his cup down. "The mole doesn't bother you, does he?"

"No, not at all. I'm doing my job thank you very much and it's not my job to worry about moles or to try to catch them. The moment you catch and snatch the bugger there'll be another bugger subverted or put into place and we'll do the same to them, whoever the *them* are. Meanwhile if it wasn't for this bloody Ho-Pak mess this station'd still be the best run and my East Aberdeen area the quietest in the Colony and that's all I'm concerned about." Smyth offered a cigarette from an expensive gold case. "Smoke?"

"No thanks, I quit."

"Good for you. No, so long as I'm left alone until I retire in four years all's well in the world." He lit the cigarette with a gold lighter and Armstrong hated him a little more. "By the way, I think you're foolish not to take the envelope that's left in your desk monthly."

"Do you now?" Armstrong's face hardened.

"Yes. You don't have to do anything for it. Nothing at all. Guaranteed."

"But once you've taken one you're up the creek without a paddle."

"No. This's China and not the same." Smyth's blue eyes hardened too. "But then you know that better than I."

"One of your 'friends' asked you to give me the message?"

Smyth shrugged. "I heard another rumor. Your share of the Dragons reward for finding John Chen comes to 40,000 HK an—"

"I didn't find him!" Armstrong's voice grated.

"Even so, that'll be in an envelope in your desk this evening. So I hear, old chap. Just a rumor, of course."

Armstrong's mind was sifting this information. 40,000 HK covered exactly and beautifully his most pressing, long overdue debt that he had to clear by Monday, losses on the stock market that, "Well really, old boy, you should pay up. It has been over a year and we do have rules. Though I'm not pressing I really must have the matter settled. . . ."

Smyth's right again, he thought without bitterness, the bastards know everything and it'd be so easy to find out what debts I have. So am I going to take it or not?

"Only forty?" he asked with a twisted smile.

"I imagine that's enough to cover your most pressing problem," Smyth said with the same hard eyes. "Isn't it?"

Armstrong was not angry that the Snake knew so much about his private life. I know just as much about his, though not how much he has or where it's stacked away. But it'd be easy to find out, easy to break him if I wanted to. Very easy. "Thanks for the coffee. Best I've had in years. Shall we go?"

Awkwardly, Smyth put on his regulation raincoat over his well-cut uniform, adjusted the sling for his arm and put his cap to the usual jaunty angle and led the way. As they went, Armstrong made Wu repeat what had happened and what had been said by the youth who claimed to be one of the Werewolves and later by the old *amah*. "Very good, Wu," Armstrong said when the young man had finished. "An excellent piece of surveillance and investigation. Excellent. Chief Inspector Smyth tells me you want to get into SI?"

"Yes sir."

"Why?"

"It's important, an important branch of SB, sir. I've always been interested in security and how to keep our enemies out and the Colony safe and I feel it would be very interesting and important. I'd like to help if I could, sir."

Momentarily their ears focused on the distant wail of fire engines that came from the hillside above.

"Some stupid bastard's kicked over another stove," Smyth said sourly. "Christ, thank God for the rain!"

"Yes," Armstrong said, then added to Wu, "If this turns out as you've reported, I'll put in a word with SB or SI."

Spectacles Wu could not stop the beam. "Yes sir, thank you, sir. Ah Tam is really from my village. Yes sir."

They turned into the alley. Crowds of shoppers and stall keepers and shopkeepers under umbrellas or under the canvas overhangs watched them sullenly and suspiciously, Smyth the most well known and feared *quai loh* in Aberdeen.

"That's the one, sir," Wu whispered. By prearrangement Smyth casually stopped at a stall, this side of the doorway, ostensibly to look at some vegetables, the owner at once in shock. Armstrong and Wu walked past the entrance then turned abruptly and the three of them converged. They went up the stairs quickly as two uniformed policemen who had been trailing from a safe distance materialized to bottle up the front. Once the narrow passageway was secure one of them hurried up an even smaller alley and around the back to make sure the plainclothes detective was still in position guarding the single exit there, then he rushed back to reinforce the undermanned barricades in front of the Victoria.

The inside of the tenement was as dingy and filthy as the outside with mess and debris on every landing. Smyth was leading and he stopped on the third landing, unbuttoned his revolver holster and stepped aside. Without hesitation Armstrong leaned against the flimsy door, burst the lock and went in quickly. Smyth followed at once, Spectacles Wu nervously staying to guard the entrance. The room was drab with old sofas and old chairs and old grimy curtains, the sweet-rank smell of opium and cooking oil on the air. A heavyset, middle-aged matron gaped at them and dropped her newspaper. Both men went for the inner doors. Smyth pulled one open to find a scruffy bedroom, the next revealed a messy toilet and bathroom, a third another bedroom crammed with unmade bunks for four. Armstrong had the last door open. It let into a cluttered, filthy, tiny kitchen, where Ah Tam bent over a pile of wash in the grimy sink. She stared at him blankly. Behind her was another door. At once he shoved past and jerked it open. It was empty too, more of a closet than a room, windowless with a vent cut in the wall and just enough space to fit the small string mattressless bunk and a broken-down chest of drawers.

He came back into the living room, Ah Tam shuffling after him, his breathing good and his heart settling down. It had taken them only seconds and Smyth took out the papers and said sweetly, "Sorry to interrupt, madam, but we've a search warrant."

"Wat?"

"Translate for us, Wu," Smyth ordered and at once the young constable repeated what had been said and, as previously arranged, began to act as though he was the interpreter for two dullard *quai loh* policemen who did not speak Cantonese.

The woman's mouth dropped open. "Search!" she shrieked. "Search

what? We obey the law here! My husband works for the government and
has important friends and if you're looking for the gambling school it's
nothing to do with us but it's on the fourth floor at the back and we know
nothing about the smelly whores in 16 who set up shop and work till all
hours making the rest of us civ—"

"Enough," Wu said sharply, "we are police on important matters!
These Lords of the police are important! You're the wife of Ch'ung the
dustman?"

"Yes," she replied sullenly. "What do you want with us? We've done
noth—"

"Enough!" Armstrong interrupted in English with deliberate arrogance.
"Is that Ah Tam?"

"You! You're Ah Tam?"

"Eh, me? *Wat?*" The old *amah* tugged at her apron nervously, not recognizing Wu.

"So you're Ah Tam! You're under arrest."

Ah Tam went white and the middle-aged woman cursed and said in a
rush, "Ah! So it's you they're after! Huh, we know nothing about her except we picked her off the street a few months ago and gave her a home
and sal—"

"Wu, tell her to shut up!"

He told her impolitely. She obeyed even more sullenly. "These Lords
want to know is there anyone else here?"

"Of course there isn't. Are they blind? Haven't they raped my house
like assassins and seen for themselves?" the shrew said truculently. "I
know nothing about nothing."

"Ah Tam! These Lords want to know where your room is."

The *amah* found her voice and began to bluster, "What do you want
with me, Honorable Policeman? I've done nothing, I'm not an illegal, I've
papers since last year. I've done nothing, I'm a law-abiding civilized person
who's worked all her li—"

"Where's your room?"

The younger woman pointed. "There," she said in her screeching, irritating voice, "where else would her room be? Of course it's there off the
kitchen! Are these foreign devils senseless? Where else do maids live?
And you, you old maggot! Getting honest people into trouble! What's she
done? If it's stolen vegetables it's nothing to do with me!"

"Quiet or we shall take you to our headquarters and surely the judge
will want you kept in custody! Quiet!"

The woman started to curse but bit it back.

Armstrong said, "Now, what . . ." Then he noticed that several curious
Chinese were peering into the room from the landing. He stared back,
took a sudden pace toward them. They vanished. He closed the door, hiding his amusement. "Now, ask both of them what they know about the
Werewolves."

The woman gaped at Wu. Ah Tam went a little grayer. "Eh, me? Werewolves? Nothing! Why should I know about those foul kidnappers. What have they to do with me? Nothing nothing at all!"

"What about you, Ah Tam?"

"Me? Nothing at all," she said querulously, "I'm a respectable *amah* who does her work and nothing else!"

Wu translated their answers. Both men noticed that his translation was accurate, fast and easy. Both were patient and they continued to play the game they had played so many times before. "Tell her she'd better tell the truth quickly." Armstrong glowered down at her. He bore her no ill feeling, neither did Smyth. They just wanted the truth. The truth might lead to the identity of the Werewolves and the sooner those villains were hung for murder the easier it would be to control Hong Kong and the sooner law-abiding citizens, including themselves, could go about their own business or hobbies—making money or racing or whoring. Yes, Armstrong thought, sorry for the old woman. Twenty dollars to a broken hatpin the shrew knows nothing but Ah Tam knows more than she'll ever tell us.

"I want the truth. Tell her!" he said.

"Truth? What truth, Honorable Lord? How could this poor old body be anyth—"

Armstrong put up his hand dramatically. "Enough!" This was another prearranged signal. At once Spectacles Wu switched to Ning-tok dialect which he knew neither of them understood. "Elder Sister, I suggest you talk quickly and openly. We know everything already!"

Ah Tam gaped at him. She had only two twisted teeth in a lower gum. "Eh, Younger Brother?" she replied in the same dialect, caught off guard. "What do you want with me?"

"The truth! I know all about you!"

She peered at him without recognition. "What truth? I've never seen you before in my life!"

"Don't you remember me? In the poultry market? You helped me buy a chicken and then we had tea. Yesterday. Don't you remember? You told me about the Werewolves, how they were going to give you a huge reward . . ."

All three saw the momentary flash behind her eyes. "Werewolves?" she began querulously. "Impossible! It was someone else! You accuse me falsely. Tell the Noble Lords I've never seen y—"

"Quiet you old baggage!" Wu said sharply and cursed her roundly. "You worked for Wu Ting-top and your mistress's name was Fan-ling and she died three years ago and they owned the pharmacy at the crossroads! I know the place well myself!"

"Lies . . . lies . . ."

"She says it's all lies, sir."

"Good. Tell her we'll take her to the station. She'll talk there."

Ah Tam began shaking. "Torture? You'll torture an old woman? Oh oh oh . . ."

"When does this Werewolf come back? This afternoon?"

"Oh oh oh . . . I don't know . . . he said he would see me but the thief never came back. I lent him five dollars to get home an—"

"Where was his home?"

"Eh? Who? Oh him, he . . . he said he was a relation of a relation and . . . I don't remember. I think he said North Point . . . I don't remember anything . . ."

Armstrong and Smyth waited and probed and soon it was apparent that the old woman knew little though she ducked and twisted the probing, her lies becoming ever more flowery.

"We'll take her in anyway," Armstrong said.

Smyth nodded. "Can you handle it till I can send a couple of men? I really think I ought to be getting back."

"Certainly. Thanks."

He left. Armstrong told Wu to order the two women to sit down and be silent while he searched. They obeyed, frightened. He went into the kitchen and closed the door. At once Ah Tam pulled at her long ratty queue. "Young Brother," she whispered slyly, knowing her mistress did not understand Ning-tok, "I'm guilty of nothing. I just met that young devil like I met you. I did nothing. People of the same village should stick together, *heya*? A handsome man like you needs money—for girls or his wife. Are you married, Honorable Younger Brother?"

"No, Elder Sister," Wu said politely, leading her on as he had been told to do.

Armstrong was standing in the doorway of Ah Tam's tiny bedroom and he wondered for the millionth time why it was that Chinese treated their servants so badly, why servants would work in such miserable and foul conditions, why they would sleep and live and give loyal service for a lifetime in return for a pittance, little respect and no love.

He remembered asking his teacher. The old policeman had said, "I don't know, laddie, but I think it's because they become *family*. Usually it's a job for life. Usually their own family becomes part also. The servant *belongs*, and the *how chew*, the *good points* of the job are many. It goes without saying all servants cream off a proportion of all housekeeping money, all foods, all drinks, all cleaning materials, all everything, however rich or poor, of course with the employers' full knowledge and approval providing it's kept to the customary level—how else can he pay them so little if they can't make extra on the side?"

Maybe that's the answer, Armstrong thought. It's true that before a Chinese takes a job, any job, he or she will have considered the *how chew* of the job very carefully indeed, the value of the *how chew* always being the deciding factor.

The room stank and he tried to close his nose to the smell. Sprays of rainwater were coming through the vent, the sound of the rain still pelting down, the whole wall mildewed and water-stained from a thousand storms. He searched methodically and carefully, all his senses tuned. There was little space to hide anything. The bed and bedding were relatively clean though there were many bedbugs in the corners of the bunk. Nothing under the bed but a chipped and stinking chamber pot and an empty suitcase. A few old bags and a tote bag produced nothing. The chest of drawers contained a few clothes, some cheap jewelry, a poor quality jade bracelet. Hidden under some clothes was an embroidered handbag of much better quality. In it were some old letters. A news cutting. And two photographs.

His heart seemed to stop.

After a moment he went into the better light of the kitchen and peered at the photographs again but he had not been mistaken. He read the news cutting, his mind reeling. There was a date on the cutting and a date on one of the photographs.

In the honeycombed basement of Police Headquarters, Ah Tam sat on a hard, backless chair in the center of a large soundproofed room that was brightly lit and painted white, white walls and white ceiling and white floors and a single, flush white door that was almost part of the wall. Even the chair was white. She was alone, petrified, and she was talking freely now.

"Now what do you know about the barbarian in the background of the photograph?" Wu's flat, metallic Ning-tok voice asked from a hidden speaker.

"I've told and told and there isn't . . . I don't know, Lord," she whimpered. "I want to go home. . . . I've told you, I barely saw the foreign devil . . . he only visited us this once that I know of, Lord. . . . I don't remember, it was years ago, oh can I go now I've told you everything, everything. . . ."

Armstrong was watching her through the one-sided mirror in the darkened observation room, Wu beside him. Both men were set-faced and ill-at-ease. Sweat beaded Wu's forehead even though the room was pleasantly air conditioned. A tape recorder turned noiselessly. There were microphones and a bank of electronic equipment behind them.

"I think she's told us everything we need," Armstrong said, sorry for her.

"Yes sir." Wu kept his nervousness out of his voice. This was the first time that he had ever been part of an SI interrogation. He was frightened and excited and his head ached.

"Ask her again where she got the purse."

Wu did as he was ordered. His voice was calm and authoritative.

"But I've told you again and again," the old woman whimpered. "Please can I g—"

"Tell us again and then you can go."

"All right . . . all right . . . I'll tell you again. . . . It belonged to my Mistress who gave it to me on her deathbed, she gave it to me, I swear it and—"

"The last time you said it was given to you the day before she died. Now which is the truth?"

Anxiously Ah Tam plucked at her ratty queue. "I . . . I don't remember, Lord. It was on her . . . it was when she died . . . I don't remember." The old woman's mouth worked and no sound came out and then said in a querulous rush, "I took it and hid it after she died and there were those old photos . . . I've no picture of my Mistress so I took them too and there was one tael of silver too and this paid for part of my journey to Hong Kong during the famine. I took it because none of her rotten sons or daughters or family who hated her and hated me would give me anything so I took it when no one was . . . she gave it to me before she died and I just hid it it's mine, she gave it to me. . . ."

They listened while the old woman went on and on and they let her talk herself out. The wall clock read 1:45. They had been questioning her for half an hour. "That's enough for now, Wu. We'll repeat it in three hours just for safety but I think she's told us everything." Wearily Armstrong picked up a phone, dialed. "Armstrong—you can take her back to her cell now," he said into the phone. "Make sure she's comfortable and well looked after and have the doctor reexamine her." It was normal SI procedure to give prisoners an examination before and after each interrogation. The doctor had said that Ah Tam had the heart and the blood pressure of a twenty-year-old.

In a moment they saw the white, almost hidden door open. A uniformed SI policewoman beckoned Ah Tam kindly. Ah Tam hobbled out. Armstrong dipped the lights, switched the tape recorder to rewind. Wu mopped his brow.

"You did very well, Wu. You learn quickly."

"Thank you, sir."

The high-pitched whine of the tape recorder grew. Armstrong watched it silently, still in shock. The sound ceased and the big man took the reel out of the machine. "We always mark the date, exact time and exact duration of the interrogation and use a code name for the suspect. For safety and secrecy." He looked up a number in a book, marked the tape, then began to make out a form. "We cross-check with this form. We sign it as interrogators and put Ah Tam's code down here—V-11-3. This's top secret and filed in the safe." His eyes became very hard. Wu almost quailed. "I repeat: You'd better believe that a closed mouth catches no flies and that everything in SI, everything that you have been party to today is top secret."

"Yes sir. Yes, you can count on me, sir."

"You'd better also remember that SI's a law unto itself, the governor and the minister in London. Only. Good old English law and fair play and normal police codes do *not* apply to SB or SI—habeas corpus, open trials, and appeal. In an SI case there's no trial, no appeal and it's a deportation order to the PRC or Taiwan, whichever's worse. Understand?"

"Yes sir. I want to be part of SI, sir, so you can believe me. I'm not one to slake my thirst on poison," Wu assured him, sick with hope.

"Good. For the next few days you're confined to this HQ."

Wu's mouth dropped open. "But sir, my . . . yes sir."

Armstrong led the way out and locked the door after him. He gave the key and the form to an SI agent who was on guard at the main desk. "I'll keep the reel for the moment. I've signed the receipt."

"Yes sir."

"You'll take care of Constable Wu? He's our guest for a couple of days. Start getting his particulars—he's been very very very helpful. I'm recommending him for SI."

"Yes sir."

He left them and went to the elevator and got out on his floor, a sick-sweet-sour taste of apprehension in his mouth. SI interrogations were anathema to him. He hated them though they were fast, efficient and always obtained results. He preferred to have an old-fashioned battle of wits, to use patience and not these new, modern psychological tools. "It's all bloody dangerous if you ask me," he muttered, walking along his corridor, the faint musty smell of headquarters in his nostrils, hating Crosse and SI and everything it stood for, hating the knowledge he had unearthed. His door was open. "Oh hi, Brian," he said, closing it, his face grim. Brian Kwok had his feet up on the desk and was idly reading one of the Communist Chinese morning papers, the windows rain-streaked behind him. "What's new?"

"There's quite a big piece on Iran," his friend said, engrossed in what he was reading. "It says 'capitalist CIA overlords in conjunction with the tyrant Shah have put down a people's revolutionary war in Azerbaijan, thousands have been killed' and so on. I don't believe all that but it looks as though the CIA and the Ninety-second Airborne have defused that area and the Yanks have done right for once."

"Lot of bloody good that'll do!"

Brian Kwok looked up. His smile faded. "What's up?"

"I feel rotten." Armstrong hesitated. "I sent for a couple of beers, then we'll have lunch. How about a curry? All right?"

"Fine, but if you're feeling rotten let's skip lunch."

"No, it's not that sort of rotten. I . . . . I just hate doing white interrogations . . . gives me the creeps."

Brian Kwok stared at him. "You did the old *amah* there? What the hell for?"

"It was Crosse's order. He's a bastard!"

Brian Kwok put his paper down. "Yes he is, and I'm sure I'm right about him," he said softly.

"Not now, Brian, over lunch maybe but not now. Christ, I need a drink! Bloody Crosse, and bloody SI! I'm not SI and yet he acts like I'm one of his."

"Oh? But you're coming on the 16/2 this evening. I thought you'd been seconded."

"He didn't mention it. What's on?"

"If he didn't mention it, I'd better not."

"Of course." It was normal SI procedure, for security, to minimize the spread of information so that even highly trustworthy agents working on the same case might not be given all the facts. "I'm bloody not going to be seconded," Armstrong said grimly, knowing that if Crosse ordered it there was nothing he could do to prevent it. "Is the intercept to do with Sevrin?"

"I don't know. I hope so." Brian Kwok studied him then smiled. "Cheer up, Robert, I've some good news for you," he said and Armstrong noticed again how handsome his friend was, strong white teeth, golden skin, firm jaw, dancing eyes with that devil-may-care confidence about him.

"You're a good-looking sod," he said. "What good news? You leaned on friend One Foot at the Para Restaurant and he's given you the first four winners for Saturday?"

"Dreamer! No, it's about those files you snatched yesterday at Bucktooth Lo's and passed over to Anti-Corruption. Remember? From Photographer Ng?"

"Oh? Oh yes."

"It seems our fair-weather American-Chinese guest, Thomas K. K. Lim, who's 'somewhere in Brazil,' is quite a character. His files were golden. Very golden indeed! And in English, so our Anti-Corruption fellows went through them like a dose of salts. You came up with treasure!"

"He's connected with Tsu-yan?" Armstrong asked, his mind diverted immediately.

"Yes. And a lot of other people. Very important people, ve—"

"Banastasio?"

Brian Kwok smiled with his mouth. "Vincenzo Banastasio himself. That ties John Chen, the guns, Tsu-yan, Banastasio and Peter Marlowe's theory nicely."

"Bartlett?"

"Not yet. But Marlowe knows someone who knows too much that we don't know. I think we should investigate him. Will you?"

"Oh yes. What else about the papers?"

"Thomas K. K. Lim's a Catholic, a third-generation American-Chinese who's a magpie. He collects all sorts of inflammatory correspondence, letters, notes, memos, etcetera." Brian Kwok smiled his humorless smile again. "Our Yankee friends are worse than we thought."

"For instance?"

"For instance, a certain well-known, well-connected New England family's involved with certain generals, U.S. and Vietnamese in building several very large, very unnecessary U.S.A.F. bases in Vietnam—very profitably—for them."

"Hallelujah! Names?"

"Names, ranks and serial numbers. If the principals knew friend Thomas had it documented, it would send a shudder of horror down the Hallowed Halls of Fame, the Pentagon and various expensive smoke-filled rooms."

Armstrong grunted. "He's the middle man?"

"Entrepreneur he calls himself. Oh he's on very good terms with lots of notables. American, Italian, Vietnamese, Chinese, both sides of the fence. The papers document the whole fraud. Another scheme's to channel millions of U.S. funds into another phony Vietnam aid program. 8 million to be exact—one is already paid over to them. Friend Lim even discussed how the one million *h'eung yau*'s to be diverted to Switzerland."

"Could we make it stick?"

"Oh yes, if we catch Thomas K. K. Lim and if we wanted to make it stick. I asked Crosse but he just shrugged and said it wasn't our affair, that if Yanks wanted to cheat their government, that's up to them." Brian Kwok smiled but his eyes didn't. "It's powerful info, Robert. If even part became common knowledge it'd create one helluva stinky stink right up to the top."

"Is he going to pass it on to Rosemont? Leak it?"

"I don't know. I don't think so. In one way he's right. It's nothing to do with us. Bloody stupid to put it all down! Stupid! They deserve to get chopped! When you've a minute read the papers, they're juicy."

"Any connection between Lim and those other villains? Bucktooth Lo and the other man? Are they stealing CARE funds?"

"Oh yes, must be, but all their files're in Chinese so it'll take longer to pin them." Brian Kwok added strangely, "Curious that Crosse sniffed that one out, almost as though he knew there'd be a connection." He dropped his voice. "I know I'm right about him."

The silence gathered. Armstrong's mouth felt parched and tasted bad. He pried his eyes off the rain and looked at Brian Kwok.

"What've you got?"

"You know that vice-consul in the U.S. Consulate—the homo, the one who's selling visas?"

"What about him?"

"Last month Crosse had dinner with him. In *his* flat."

Armstrong rubbed his face nervously. "That proves nothing. Listen, tomorrow, tomorrow we get the files. Tomorrow Sind—"

"Perhaps *we* won't get to read them."

"Personally I don't give a shit. That's SI business and I'm CID and that's wh—"

A knock stopped him. The door opened. A Chinese waiter came in with a tray and two tankards of cold beer and beamed toothily. "Afternoon, sah," he said, offering one to Brian Kwok. He gave the other to Armstrong and went out.

"Good luck," Armstrong said, hating himself. He drank deeply then went to his safe to lock the tape away.

Brian Kwok studied him. "You sure you're all right, old chum?"

"Yes, yes of course."

"What did the old woman say?"

"In the beginning she told lots of lies, lots of them. And then the truth. All of it. I'll tell you over lunch, Brian. You know how it is—you catch the lies eventually, if you're patient. I'm fed up with lies." Armstrong finished his beer. "Christ, I needed that."

"Do you want mine too? Here."

"No, no thanks, but it's me for a whiskey and soda before curry and maybe another one. Drink up and let's get the show on the road."

Brian Kwok put his half-empty tankard down. "That's enough for me." He lit a cigarette. "How's the nonsmoking going?"

"Rough." Armstrong watched him inhale deeply. "Anything on Voranski? Or his assassins?"

"They vanished into thin air. We've got their photos so we'll catch them, unless they're over the border."

"Or in Taiwan."

After a pause, Brian Kwok nodded. "Or Macao or North Korea, Vietnam or wherever. The minister's hopping mad with Crosse over Voranski, so's MI-6, so's the CIA. The CIA top echelon in London have been chewing the minister's tail so he's passing it on. We'd better get those buggers before Rosemont or we'll lose all face. Rosemont's under fire too to come up with their heads. I hear he's got every man out looking, thinking it's to do with Sevrin, and the carrier. He's petrified there's going to be an incident involving the nuclear carrier." Brian Kwok added, his voice hardening, "Bloody stupid to offend the PRC by bringing her here. That monster's an open invitation to every agent in Asia."

"If I was Soviet I'd try to infiltrate her. SI's probably trying right now. Crosse'd love to have a plant aboard. Why not?" The big man watched the smoke curling. "If I was Nationalist perhaps I'd plant a few mines and blame the PRC—or vice versa and blame Chiang Kai-shek."

"That's what the CIA'd do to get everyone hopping mad at China."

"Come off it, Brian!"

Brian Kwok took a last sip then got up. "That's enough for me. Come on."

"Just a moment." Armstrong dialed. "This's Armstrong, set up another session at 1700 hours for V-11-3. I'll want . . ." He stopped, seeing his friend's eyes flutter, then glaze and he caught him easily as he fell and let him slump back in the chair. Out of himself, almost watching himself, he put the phone back on its cradle. Now there was nothing for him to do but wait.

I've done my job, he thought.

The door opened. Crosse came in. Behind him were three plainclothed SI agents, all British, all senior agents, all taut-faced and tense. Quickly one of the men put a thick black hood over Brian Kwok's head, picked him up easily and went out, the others following.

Now that it was done Robert Armstrong felt nothing, no remorse or shock or anger. Nothing. His head told him that there was no mistake though his head still told him equally that his friend of almost twenty years could not possibly be a Communist mole. But he was. The proof was irrefutable. The evidence he had found proved conclusively that Brian Kwok was the son of Fang-ling Wu, Ah Tam's old employer, when according to his birth certificate and personal records his mother and father were supposed to have been surnamed Kwok and murdered by Communists in Canton in '43. One of the photographs had showed Brian Kwok standing beside a tiny Chinese lady in front of a pharmacy at a crossroads in a village. The quality was poor but more than good enough to read the characters of the shop sign and to recognize a face, his face. In the background was an ancient car. Behind it stood a European, his face half turned away. Spectacles Wu had identified the store as the pharmacy at the crossroads in Ning-tok, the property of the Tok-ling Wu family. Ah Tam had identified the woman as her mistress.

"And the man? Who's the man standing beside her?"

"Oh that's her son, Lord. I've told you. He's Second Son Chu-toy. Now he lives with the foreign devils across the sea in the north, the north of the Land of the Golden Mountains," the old woman had whimpered from the white room.

"You're lying again."

"Oh no, Lord, he's her son, Chu-toy. He's her Second Son and he was born in Ning-tok and I helped deliver him with my own hands. He was Mother's second born who went away as a child. . . ."

"He went away? He went where?"

"To . . . to the Rain Country, then to the Golden Mountains. Now he has a restaurant and two sons. . . . He's a businessman there and he came to see Father. . . . Father was dying then and he came as a dutiful son should come but then he went away and Mother wept and wept. . . ."

"How often did he visit his parents?"

"Oh, it was only once, Lord, only that once. Now he lives so far away, in such a far place, such a far place but he came as a dutiful son should and then he left. It was just by chance I saw him, Lord. Mother had sent me to visit some relations in the next village but I was lonely and I came back early and saw him. . . . It was just before he left. The young Master left in a foreign devil car. . . ."

"Where did he get the motorcar? It was his?"

"I don't know, Lord. There was no car in Ning-tok. Even the village committee did not possess one, even Father who was the pharmacist in our village. Poor Father who died in such pain. He was a member of the committee. . . . They left us alone, Chairman Mao's people, the Outsiders. . . . Yes they did because though Father was an intellectual and pharmacist he was always a secret Mao supporter though I never knew, Lord, I swear I never knew. Chairman Mao's people left us alone, Lord."

"What was his name, the son of your Mistress? The man in the photo?" he had repeated, trying to shake her.

"Chu-toy Wu, Lord, he was her second born. . . . I remember when he was sent from Ning-tok to . . . to this foul place, this Fragrant Harbor. He was five or six and he was sent to an uncle here and—"

"What was the uncle's name?"

"I don't know, Lord, I was never told, I only remember Mother weeping and weeping when Father sent him away to school. . . . Can I go home please now, I'm tired, please. . . ."

"When you tell us what we want to know. If you tell us the truth."

"Oh I tell you the truth, anything anything. . . ."

"He was sent to school in Hong Kong? Where?"

"I don't know, Lord, my Mistress never said, only to school and then she put him out of her mind and so did I, oh yes, it was better, because he was gone forever, you know always second sons must leave. . . ."

"When did Chu-toy Wu return to Ning-tok?"

"It was some years ago when Father was dying. He only returned that once, it was only once, Lord, don't you remember me saying, I remember saying that. Yes it was the once of the photo. Mother insisted on the photo and wept and begged him to have one taken with her. . . . Surely she felt the hand of death on her now that Father had gone and she was truly alone . . . Oh she wept and wept so Chu-toy let her have her way as a dutiful son should and my Mistress was so pleased. . . ."

"And the barbarian in the photo, who is he?" The man was half turned around, in the background, not easy to recognize if you did not know him, standing beside the car that was parked beside the pharmacy. He was a tall man, European, crumpled clothes and nondescript.

"I don't know, Lord. He was the driver and he drove Chu-toy away but the committee of the village and Chu-toy himself bowed many times to him and it was said he was very important. He was the first foreign devil I had ever seen, Lord. . . ."

"And the people in the other photograph? Who're they?" This photograph was ancient, almost sepia and showed a self-conscious couple in ill-fitting wedding clothes staring bleakly at the camera.

"Oh of course they're Father and Mother, Lord. Don't you remember me saying that? I told you many times. That's Mother and Father. His name was Ting-top Wu and his *tai-tai* my Mistress was Fang-ling. . . ."

"And the cutting?"

"I don't know, Lord, it was just stuck to the photo so I left it there. Mother had stuck it there so I left it. What should I want with foreign devil nonsense or writing. . . ."

Robert Armstrong sighed. The yellowed clipping was from a Chinese newspaper of Hong Kong, dated July 16, 1937, that told of three Chinese youths who had done so well in their term examinations that they had been granted scholarships by the Hong Kong Government to an English public school. Kar-shun Kwok was the first named. Kar-shun was Brian Kwok's formal Chinese name.

"You did very well, Robert," Crosse said, watching him.

"Did I?" he replied through the fog of his misery.

"Yes, very well. You came to me at once with the evidence, you've followed instructions perfectly and now our mole is safely asleep." Crosse lit a cigarette and sat at the desk. "I'm glad you drank the right beer. Did he suspect anything?"

"No. No I don't think so." Armstrong tried to get a hold on himself. "Would you excuse me, sir, please. I feel filthy. I've . . . I've got to get a shower. Sorry."

"Sit down a minute, please. Yes, you must be tired. Very tiring, these sort of things."

Christ, Armstrong wanted to shout in anguish, it's all impossible! Impossible for Brian to be a deep-cover agent but it all fits. Why else would he have a completely different name, different birth certificate? Why else such a carefully constructed cover story—that his parents were killed in Canton during the war, murdered by Communists? Why else would he risk sneaking secretly back to Ning-tok, risking everything so carefully constructed over thirty years unless his own father was really dying? And if those facts are true then others automatically follow: That he must have been in continual contact with the Mainland to know about his father's approaching death, that as a superintendent of H.K. Police he must be totally persona grata with the PRC to be allowed in secretly and allowed out secretly again. And if he was persona grata then he must be one of them, groomed over the years, nurtured over the years. "Christ," he muttered, "he'd've become assistant commissioner easily, perhaps even commissioner . . . !"

"What do you suggest now, Robert?" Crosse asked, his voice soft.

Armstrong tore his mind into the present, his training overcoming his anguish. "Check backwards. We'll find the link. Yes. His father was a tiny Commie cog but a Ning-tok cog nonetheless, so the Hong Kong relation he was sent to would be also. They'd've kept a tight rein on Brian in England, in Canada, here, wherever—so easy to do that, so easy to feed a hatred for *quai lohs*, so easy for a Chinese to hide such a hatred. Aren't they the most patient and secretive people on earth? Yes, you check back and eventually you find the link and find the truth."

"Robert, you're right again. But first you begin his interrogation."

Armstrong felt a chill of horror rush into his stomach. "Yes," he said.

"I'm delighted to tell you that that's your honor."

"No."

"You'll oversee the interrogation. No Chinese in this, just senior British agents. Except Wu, Spectacles Wu. Yes, he'll be a help—just him, he's good that fellow."

"I can't . . . I won't."

Crosse sighed and opened the large manila envelope he had brought with him. "What do you think of this?"

Shakily Armstrong took the photograph. It was an eight-by-ten blowup of a tiny section of the Ning-tok photograph, the European's head that was part of the background beside the car. The man's face was half turned and blurred, the grain from the magnification dense. "I . . . I'd say he saw the camera and turned or was turning to avoid being photographed."

"My thought too. Do you recognize him?"

Armstrong peered at the face, trying to clear his head. "No."

"Voranski? Our dead Soviet friend?"

"Perhaps. No, no I don't think so."

"How about Dunross, Ian Dunross?"

More shaken, Armstrong took it to the light. "Possible but . . . improbable. If . . . if it's Dunross then . . . you think he's the Sevrin plant? Impossible."

"Improbable, not impossible. He's very good friends with Brian." Crosse took the photo back and looked at it. "Whoever he is he's familiar, what you can see of him, but I can't place the man or where I've seen him. Yet. Well, never mind. Brian will remember. Yes." His voice became silky. "Oh, don't worry, Robert, I'll set Brian up for you but you're the one for the coup de grâce. I want to know who this fellow is very quickly, in fact I want to know everything Brian knows very, very quickly."

"No. Get someone els—"

"Oh Robert, don't be so bloody boring! Chu-toy Wu, alias Brian Karshun Kwok, is an enemy mole who's eluded us for years, that's all." Crosse's voice cut into Armstrong. "By the way, you're on the 16/2 tonight at 6:30 and you're also seconded to SI. I've already talked to the commissioner."

"No, and I can't interrog—"

"Oh but my dear fellow you can and you will. You're the only one who can, Brian's far too clever to be caught like an amateur. Of course I'm as astounded he's the mole as you are, as the governor was!"

"Please. I don—"

"He betrayed Fong-fong, another friend of yours, eh? He must have leaked the AMG papers. It must be he who's furnished all our dossiers to the enemy and all the other information. God knows what knowledge he's had access to on the General Staff Course and all the other courses." Crosse puffed his cigarette, his face ordinary. "In SI he has the highest security clearances and I certainly agree he was being groomed for high office—I was even going to make him my number two! So we'd better find out very quickly everything about him. Curious, we were looking for a Soviet mole and it turns out we have a PRC one instead." He stubbed out the cigarette. "I've ordered a Classification One interrogation on him to begin at once."

The color drained out of Armstrong's face and he stared at Crosse, hating him openly. "You're a bastard, a fucking rotten bastard."

Crosse laughed gently. "True."

"Are you a fag too?"

"Perhaps. Perhaps only occasionally and only when it pleases me. Perhaps." Crosse watched him calmly. "Come now, Robert, do you really think I could be blackmailed? Me? Blackmailed? Really, Robert, don't you understand life? I hear homosexuality is quite normal, even in high places."

"Is it?"

"Nowadays, yes, quite normal, almost fashionable, for some. Oh yes, yes it is, my dear fellow, and it's practiced, from time to time, by a most catholic grouping of VIPs everywhere. Even in Moscow." Crosse lit another cigarette. "Of course, one should be discreet, selective and preferably uncommitted, but a penchant for the peculiar could have all sorts of advantages in our profession. Couldn't it?"

"So you justify any sort of evil, any sort of shit, murder, cheating, lying in the name of the bloody SI—is that it?"

"Robert, I justify nothing, I know you're distraught but I think that's enough of that."

"You can't force me into SI. I'll resign."

Crosse laughed scornfully. "But my dear fellow, what about all your debts? What about the 40,000 by Monday?" He got up, his eyes granite. His voice was hardly changed but now there was a vicious edge to it. "We're both over twenty-one, Robert. Break him, and do it very quickly."

45

The closing bell of the Stock Exchange rang but the sound was drowned in the fetid pandemonium of massed brokers desperately trying to complete their final transactions.

For Struan's, the day had been disastrous. Huge amounts of stock had been shoved onto the market to be bought tentatively, then hurled back again as rumors fed on more rumors and more stock was offered. The share price plummeted from 24.70 to 17.50 and there were still 300,000 shares on offer in the sell column. All bank shares were down, the market was reeling. Everyone expected the Ho-Pak to fail tomorrow—only Sir Luis Basilio suspending trading in bank shares at noon had saved the bank from going under then.

"Jesus Christ, what a stinker!" someone said. "Screwed by the sodding bell."

"Look at the tai-pan!" another burst out. "Christ almighty, you'd think it was just another day and not the death knell of the Noble House!"

"He's got balls has our Ian, no doubt about that. Look at that smile on him. Christ, his stock goes from 24.70 to 17.50 in one day when it's never been below 25 since the poor bugger went public and it's as though nothing's happened. Tomorrow Gornt has to get control!"

"I agree—or the bank."

"The Vic? No, they've troubles of their own," another said, joining the excited, sweating group.

"Holy mackerel, you really think Gornt will do it? Gornt tai-pan of the new Noble House?"

"Can't imagine it!" another shouted over the din.

"Better get used to it, old boy. But I agree, you'd never know Ian's world's crashing about his testicles . . ."

"About bloody time!" someone else called out.

"Oh come on, the tai-pan's a good fellow, Gornt's an arrogant bastard."

"They're both bastards!" another said.

"Oh I don't know. But I agree Ian's cold all right. Ian's as cold as charity and that's pretty chilly. . . ."

"But not as cold as poor old Willy, he's dead poor bastard!"

"Willy? Willy who?" someone asked amid the laughter. "Eh?"

"Oh for chrissake, Charlie, it's just a ditty, a poem! Willy rhymes with chilly, that's all. How did you do on the day?"

"I made a pile in commissions."

"I made a pile too."

"Fantastic. I unloaded 100 percent of all my own shares. I'm liquid now, thank God! It'll be tough on some of my clients but easy come easy go and they can afford it!"

"I'm still holding 58,000 Struan's and no takers. . . ."

"*Jesusschriiist!*"

"What's up?"

"The Ho-Pak's finished! They've closed their doors."

"*What!*"

"Every last bloody branch!"

"Christ almighty are you sure?"

"Of course I'm sure and they say the Vic won't open tomorrow either, that the governor'll declare tomorrow a bank holiday! I have it on the highest authority, old boy!"

"Good sweet Christ, *the Vic's closing?*"

"Oh Christ we're all ruined. . . ."

"Listen, I've just talked to Johnjohn. The run's spread to them but he says they'll be all right—not to worry. . . ."

"Thank God!"

"He says there was a riot at Aberdeen half an hour ago when the Ho-Pak branch there failed but Richard Kwang's just put out a press release. He's 'temporarily closed' all their branches except Head Office in Central. There's no need to worry, he's got plenty of money and . . ."

"Lying bastard!"

". . . and anyone with Ho-Pak funds has to go there with their passbook and they'll get paid."

"What about their shares? When they liquidate how much do you think they'll pay? Ten cents on the dollar?"

"God knows! But thousands are going to lose their knickers in this crash!"

"Hey, tai-pan! Are you going to let your stock plummet or are you going to buy?"

"The Noble House's strong as it ever was, old boy," Dunross said easily. "My advice to you is to buy!"

"How long can you wait, tai-pan?"

"We'll weather this slight problem, don't worry." Dunross continued to push through the crowd, heading for the exit, Linc Bartlett and Casey following, questions being fired at him. Most of them he dismissed with a

pleasantry, a few he answered, then Gornt was in front of him and the
two of them were in the middle of a great silence.

"Ah, Quillan, how did you do on the day?" he asked politely.

"Very good, thank you, Ian, very good. My partners and I are 3 or 4
million ahead."

"You have partners?"

"Of course. One doesn't mount an attack on Struan's lightly—of course
one must have very substantial financial backing." Gornt smiled. "Fortunately, Struan's're roundly detested by lots of good people and have been
for a century or more. I'm delighted to tell you I've just acquired another
300,000 shares for sale first thing. That should just about bring your
house atumbling down."

"We're not Humpty-Dumpty. We're the Noble House."

"Until tomorrow. Yes. Or perhaps the next day. Monday at the latest."
Gornt looked back at Bartlett. "Tuesday for dinner is still on?"

"Yes."

Dunross smiled. "Quillan, a man can get burned selling short in such a
volatile market." He turned to Bartlett and Casey and said pleasantly,
"Don't you agree?"

"It sure as hell isn't like our New York exchange," Bartlett replied to a
general laugh. "What's happening here today'd blow our whole economy
to hell. Eh Casey?"

"Yes," Casey replied uneasily, feeling Gornt's scrutiny. "Hello," she
said, glancing at him.

"We're honored to have you here," Gornt said with great charm. "May
I compliment you on your courage last night—both of you."

"I did nothing special," Bartlett said.

"Nor did I," Casey said uncomfortably, very aware she was the only
woman in the room and now the center of so much attention. "If it hadn't
been for Linc and Ian . . . for the tai-pan and you and the others, I'd've
panicked."

"Ah, but you didn't. Your dive was perfection," Gornt said, to cheers.

She said nothing but she was warmed by that thought, not for the first
time. Somehow life had been different since she had taken off her clothes
without thinking. Cavallan had called this morning to ask how she was.
So had others. At the exchange she had felt the looks strongly. There had
been lots of compliments. Many from strangers. She felt that Dunross and
Gornt and Bartlett remembered because she had not failed them. Or herself. Yes, she thought, you gained great face before all the men. And increased the jealousy of all their women. Curious.

"Are you selling short, Mr. Bartlett?" Gornt was saying.

"Not personally," Bartlett told him with a small smile. "Not yet."

"You should," Gornt said agreeably. "There's a great deal of money to
be made in a falling market, as I'm sure you know. A great deal of money
will change hands with control of Struan's." He put his eyes back onto

Casey, excited by her courage and her body and by the thought that she would be coming sailing on Sunday alone. "And you, Ciranoush, are you in the market?" he asked.

Casey heard her name and the way he said it. A thrill took her. Beware, she cautioned herself. This man's dangerous. Yes. And so is Dunross and so is Linc.

Which?

I think I want all three of them, she thought, heat rushing into her.

The day had been exciting and grand from the first moment when Dunross had phoned her so solicitously. Then getting up, feeling no ill effects from the fire or the emetics of Dr. Tooley. Then working away happily all morning on all the cables and telexes and phone calls to the States, tidying business problems of Par-Con's far-flung conglomerate, cementing a merger that had been on their agenda for months, selling off another company very profitably to acquire one that would further enhance Par-Con's stab into Asia—whomever they were in business with. Then, unexpectedly, being invited for lunch by Linc. . . . Dear handsome confident attractive Linc, she thought, remembering the lunch they had had atop the Victoria and Albert in the great, green dining room overlooking the harbor, Linc so attentive, Hong Kong Island and the sea roads obsured by the driving rain. Half a grapefruit, a small salad, Perrier, all perfectly served, just what she wanted. Then coffee.

"How about going to the Stock Exchange, Casey? Say 2:30?" he had said. "Ian invited us."

"I've still got lots to do, Linc, an—"

"But that place is something else and the things those guys get away with's unbelievable. Insider trading's a way of life here and quite legal. Jesus, it's fantastic—wonderful—a great system! What they do here legally every day'd get you twenty years in the States."

"That doesn't make it right, Linc."

"No, but this is Hong Kong and their rules please them and it is their country and they support themselves and their government only creams off 15 percent tax," he had said. "I tell you, Casey, if you want drop dead money it's here for the taking."

"Let's hope! You go, Linc, I've really got a pile of stuff to get through."

"It can wait. Today might be the clincher. We should be in at the kill."

"Gornt's going to win?"

"Sure, unless Ian gets massive financing. I hear the Victoria won't support him. And Orlin won't renew his loan, just as I forecast!"

"Gornt told you?"

"Just before lunch—but everyone knows everything in this place. Never known anything like it."

"Then maybe Ian knows you put up the 2 million to start Gornt off."

"Maybe. It doesn't matter, so long as they don't know Par-Con's on the way to become the new Noble House. How 'bout Tai-pan Bartlett?"

Casey remembered his sudden grin and the warmth flooding out at her
and she felt it now, standing on the floor of the Stock Exchange, watching
him, crowds of men around her, only three important—Quillan, Ian and
Linc—the most vital and exciting of all the men she had ever met. She
smiled back at them equally, then said to Gornt, "No, I'm not in the
market, not personally. I don't like gambling—the cost of my money comes
too high."

Someone muttered, "What a rotten thing to say!"

Gornt paid no attention and kept his eyes on her. "Wise, very wise. Of
course, sometimes there's a sure thing, sometimes you can make a killing."
He looked at Dunross who was watching with his curious smile. "Figuratively, of course."

"Of course. Well, Quillan, see you tomorrow."

"Hey, Mr. Bartlett," someone called out, "have you made a deal with
Struan's or not?"

"Yes," another said, "and what does Raider Bartlett think of a raid
Hong Kong style?"

Another silence fell. Bartlett shrugged. "A raid is a raid wherever," he
said carefully, "and I'd say this one's mounted and launched. But you
never know you've won until you've won and all the votes are counted. I
agree with Mr. Dunross. You can get burned." He grinned again, his eyes
dancing. "I also agree with Mr. Gornt. Sometimes you can make a killing,
figuratively."

There was another burst of laughter. Dunross used it to push through
to the door. Bartlett and Casey followed. At his chauffeured Rolls below,
Dunross said, "Come on, get in—sorry, I've got to hurry, but the car'll take
you home."

"No, that's all right, we'll take a cab. . . ."

"No, get in. In this rain you'll have to wait half an hour."

"The ferry'll do fine, tai-pan," Casey said. "He can drop us there."
They got in and drove off, the traffic snarled.

"What're you going to do about Gornt?" Bartlett asked.

Dunross laughed and Casey and Bartlett tried to gauge the strength of
it. "I'm going to wait," he said. "It's an old Chinese custom: Patience. Everything comes to him who waits. Thanks for keeping mum about our
deal. You handled that rather well."

"You'll announce tomorrow after the market closes, as planned?" Bartlett asked.

"I'd like to leave my options open. I know this market, you don't. Per-
haps tomorrow." Dunross looked at them both clearly. "Perhaps not until
Tuesday when we've actually signed. I presume we still have a deal?
Until Tuesday at midnight?"

"Sure," Casey said.

"Can the announcement time be left to me? I'll tell you beforehand but
I may need the timing to . . . to maneuver."

"Certainly."

"Thank you. Of course, if we're down the pipe then, it's no deal. I understand quite clearly."

"Gornt can get control?" Casey asked. Both of them saw the change in the Scotsman's eyes. The smile was still there but it was only on the surface.

"No, not actually, but of course with enough stock he can force his way immediately onto the board and appoint other directors. Once on the board he will be party to most of our secrets and he'll disrupt and destroy." Dunross glanced back at Casey. "His purpose is to destroy."

"Because of the past?"

"Partially." Dunross smiled, but this time they saw a deep-seated tiredness within it. "The stakes are high, face is involved, huge face, and this's Hong Kong. Here the strong survive and the weak perish but en route the government doesn't steal from you, or protect you. If you don't want to be free and don't like our rules, or lack of them, don't come. You've come for profit, *heya?*" He watched Bartlett. "And profit you will have, one way or another."

"Yes," Bartlett agreed blandly, and Casey wondered how much Dunross knew about the arrangement with Gornt. The thought disquieted her.

"Profit's our motive, yes," she said. "But not to destroy."

"That's wise," he said. "It's better to create than to destroy. Oh, by the way, Jacques asked if you'd both like to dine with him tonight, 8:30-ish. I can't, I've an official do with the governor but I might see you for a drink later."

"Thanks, but I can't tonight," Bartlett said easily, not feeling easy at the sudden thought of Orlanda. "How about you, Casey?"

"No, no thanks. I've a stack to get through, tai-pan, maybe we could take a rain check?" she asked him happily and thought that he was wise to be close-mouthed and Linc Bartlett equally wise to cool it with Struan's for a while. Yes, she told herself, her mind diverted, and it'll be lovely to have dinner with Linc, just the two of us, like lunch. Maybe we can even take in a movie.

Dunross went into his office.

"Oh . . . oh hello, tai-pan," Claudia said. "Mr. and Mrs. Kirk are in the downstairs reception room. Bill Foster's resignation's in your *in* tray."

"Good. Claudia, make sure I see Linbar before he goes." He was watching her carefully and though she was consummate at hiding her feelings, he could sense her fear. He sensed it in the whole building. Everyone pretended otherwise but confidence was tottering. "Without confidence in the general," Sun Tzu had written, "no battle can be won by however many troops and with however many weapons."

Uneasily Dunross rethought his plan and position. He knew he had very few moves, that the only true defense was attack and he could not attack without massive funds. This morning when he had met Lando Mata, he had got only a reluctant perhaps. ". . . I told you I have to consult with Tightfist Tung first. I've left messages but I just can't get hold of him."

"He's in Macao?"

"Yes, yes I think so. He said he was arriving today but I don't know on which ferry. I really don't know, tai-pan. If he's not on the last inbound, I'll go back to Macao and see him at once—if he's available. I'll call you this evening, the moment I've talked to him. By the way, have you reconsidered either of our offers?"

"Yes. I can't sell you control of Struan's. And I can't leave Struan's and run the gambling in Macao."

"With our money you'll smash Gornt, you co—"

"I can't pass over control."

"Perhaps we could combine both offers. We support you against Gornt in return for control of Struan's and you run our gambling syndicate, secretly if you wish. Yes, it could be secret. . . ."

Dunross shifted in his easy chair, certain that Lando Mata and Tightfist were using the trap that he was in to further their own interests. Just like Bartlett and Casey, he thought without anger. Now that's an interesting woman. Beautiful, courageous and loyal—to Bartlett. I wonder if she knows he breakfasted with Orlanda this morning, then visited her flat. I wonder if they know I know about the 2 million from Switzerland. Bartlett's smart, very smart, and making all the correct moves, but he's wide open to attack because he's predictable and his jugular's an Asian girl. Perhaps Orlanda, perhaps not, but certainly a youth-filled Golden Skin. Quillan was clever to bait the trap with her. Yes. Orlanda's a perfect bait, he thought, then put his mind back to Lando Mata and his millions. To get those millions I'd have to break my Holy Oath and that I will not do.

"What calls do I have, Claudia?" he asked, a sudden ice shaft in his stomach. Mata and Tightfist had been his ace, the only one left.

She hesitated, glanced at the list. "Hiro Toda called from Tokyo, person to person. Please return the call when you've a moment. Alastair Struan the same from Edinburgh. . . . David MacStruan from Toronto . . . your father from Ayr . . . old Sir Ross Struan from Nice . . ."

"Uncle Trussler from London," he said, interrupting her, "Uncle Kelly from Dublin . . . Cousin Cooper from Atlanta, cous—"

"From New York," Claudia said.

"From New York. Bad news travels fast," he told her calmly.

"Yes. Then there was . . ." Her eyes filled with tears. "What're we going to do?"

"Absolutely not cry," he said, knowing that a large proportion of her savings was in Struan stock.

"Yes! Oh yes." She sniffed and used a handkerchief, sad for him but thanking the gods she had had the foresight to sell at the top of the market and not buy when the Head of the House of Chen had whispered for all the clan to buy heavily. *"Ayeeyah,* tai-pan, sorry, so sorry, please excuse me . . . yes. But it's very bad, isn't it?"

"Och aye, lassie," he said, aping a broad Scots accent, "but only when you're deaded. Isn't that what the old tai-pan used to say?" The old tai-pan was Sir Ross Struan, Alastair's father, the first tai-pan he could remember. "Go on with the calls."

"Cousin Kern from Houston and Cousin Deeks from Sydney. That's the last of the family."

"That's all of them." Dunross exhaled. Control of the Noble House rested with those families. Each had blocks of shares that had been handed down to them, though by House law he alone voted all the stock—while he was tai-pan. The family holdings of the Dunrosses, descended from Dirk Struan's daughter Winifred, were 10 percent; the Struans from Robb Struan, Dirk's half-brother, 5 percent; the Trusslers and Kellys from Culum and Hag Struan's youngest daughter, each 5 percent; the Coopers, Kerns and Derbys, descended from the American trader, Jeff Cooper of Cooper-Tillman, Dirk's lifetime friend who had married Hag Struan's eldest daughter, each 5 percent; the MacStruans, believed illegitimate from Dirk, 2½ percent; and the Chens 7½ percent. The bulk of the stock, 50 percent, the personal property and legacy of Hag Struan, was left in a perpetual trust, to be voted by the tai-pan "whoever he or she may be, and the profit therefrom shall be divided yearly, 50 percent to the tai-pan, the remainder in proportion to family holdings—but only if the tai-pan so decides," she had written in her firm, bold hand. "If he decides to withhold profit from my shares from the family for any reason he may, then that increment shall go into the tai-pan's private fund for whatever use he deems fit. But let all following tai-pans beware: the Noble House shall pass from safe Hand to safe Hand and the clans from safe Harbor to safe Harbor as *the tai-pan* himself decreed or I shall add my curse, before God, to *his,* on him or her who fails us. . . ."

Dunross felt a chill go through him as he remembered the first time he had read her will—as dominating as the legacy of Dirk Struan. Why are we so possessed by these two? he asked himself again. Why can't we be done with the past, why should we be at the beck and call of ghosts, not very good ghosts at that?

I'm not, he told himself firmly. I'm only trying to measure up to their standards.

He looked back at Claudia, matronly, tough and very together but now scared, scared for the first time. He had known her all his life and she had served old Sir Ross, then his father, then Alastair, and now himself with a fanatical loyalty, as had Phillip Chen.

Ah Phillip, poor Phillip.

"Did Phillip call?" he asked.

"Yes, tai-pan. And Dianne. She called four times."

"Who else?"

"A dozen or more. The more important ones are Johnjohn at the bank, General Jen from Taiwan, Gavallan *père* from Paris, Four Finger Wu, Pug—"

"Four Fingers?" Dunross's hope peaked. "When did he call?"

She referred to her list. "2:56."

I wonder if the old pirate has changed his mind, Dunross thought, his excitement growing.

Yesterday afternoon late he had gone to Aberdeen to see Wu to seek his help but, as with Lando Mata, he had got only vague promises.

"Listen, Old Friend," he had told him in halting Haklo, "I've never sought a favor from you before."

"A long line of your tai-pan ancestors have sought plenty favors and made great profits from my ancestors," the old man had answered, his cunning eyes darting. "Favors? Fornicate all dogs, tai-pan, I have not that amount of money. 20 millions? How could a poor old fisherman like me have that cash?"

"More came out of the Ho-Pak yesterday, old friend."

"*Ayeeyah*, fornicate all those who whisper wrong informations! Perhaps I withdrew my money safely but it all has gone, gone to pay for goods, goods I owed money for."

"I hope not for the White Powder," he had told him grimly. "The White Powder is terrible joss. Rumor has it you are interested in it. I advise against it as a friend. My ancestors, Old Green-Eyed Devil and Hag Struan of the Evil Eye and Dragon's Teeth, they both put a curse on those who deal in the White Powder, not on opium but on all White Powders and those who deal in them," he had said stretching the truth, knowing how superstitious the old man was. "I advise against the Killing Powder. Surely your gold business is more than profitable?"

"I know nothing of White Powder." The old man had forced a smile, showing his gums and a few twisted teeth. "And I don't fear curses, even from them!"

"Good," Dunross had said, knowing it to be a lie. "Meanwhile help me to get credit. 50 million for three days is all I want!"

"I will ask among my friends, tai-pan. Perhaps they can help, perhaps we can help together. But don't expect water from an empty well. At what interest?"

"High interest, if it's tomorrow."

"Not possible, tai-pan."

"Persuade Tightfist, you're an associate and old friend."

"Tightfist is the only fornicating friend of Tightfist," the old man had said sullenly and nothing Dunross could say would change the old man's attitudes.

He reached for the phone. "What other calls were there, Claudia?" he asked as he dialed.

"Johnjohn at the bank, Phillip and Dianne . . . oh I told you about them. . . . Superintendent Crosse, then every major stockholder we have and every managing director of every subsidiary, most of the Turf Club . . . Travkin, your trainer, it's endless. . . ."

"Just a moment, Claudia." Dunross held onto his anxiety and said into the phone, in Haklo, "This is the tai-pan. Is my Old Friend there?"

"Sure, sure, Mr. Dunross," the American voice said politely in English. "Thanks for returning the call. He'll be right with you, sir."

"Mr. Choy, Mr. Paul Choy?"

"Yes sir."

"Your uncle told me all about you. Welcome to Hong Kong."

"I . . . here he is sir."

"Thank you." Dunross concentrated. He had been asking himself why Paul Choy was with Four Fingers now and not busily engaged in worming his way into Gornt's affairs and why Crosse called and why Johnjohn.

"Tai-pan?"

"Yes, Old Friend. You wanted to speak to me?"

"Yes. Can . . . can we meet this evening?"

Dunross wanted to shout, Have you changed your mind? But good manners forbade it and Chinese did not like phones, always preferring to meet face-to-face. "Of course. About eight bells, in the middle watch," he said casually. Near midnight. "As near as I can," he added, remembering he was to meet Brian Kwok at 10:45 P.M.

"Good. My wharf. There will be a sampan waiting."

Dunross replaced the phone, his heart thumping. "First Crosse, Claudia, then bring in the Kirks. Then we'll go through the list. Set up a conference call with my father, Alastair and Sir Ross, make it for five, that's nine their time and ten in Nice. I'll call David and the others in the States this evening. No need to wake them in the middle of their night."

"Yes, tai-pan." Claudia was already dialing. She got Crosse, handed him the phone and left, closing the door after her.

"Yes, Roger?"

"How many times have you been into China?"

The unexpected question startled Dunross for a moment. "That's all a matter of record," he said. "It's easy for you to check."

"Yes, Ian, but could you recall now? Please."

"Four times to Canton, to the fair, every year for the last four years. And once to Peking with a trade commission, last year."

"Did you ever manage to get outside Canton—or Peking?"

"Why?"

"Did you?"

Dunross hesitated. The Noble House had many associations of long standing in China, and many old and trusted friends. Some were now committed Communists. Some were outwardly Communists but inwardly totally Chinese and therefore far-seeing, secretive, cautious and nonpolitical. These men ranged in importance up to one in the Presidium. And all of these men, being Chinese, knew that history repeated itself, that eras could change so quickly and the Emperor of this morning could become the running dog of this afternoon, that dynasty followed dynasty at the whim of the gods, that the first of any dynasty inevitably mounted the Dragon throne with bloodstained hands, that an escape route was always to be sought after—and that certain barbarians were Old Friends and to be trusted.

But he knew most all of the Chinese were a practical people. China needed goods and help. Without goods and help they were defenseless against their historic and only real enemy, Russia.

So many times, because of the special trust in which the Noble House was held, Dunross had been approached officially and unofficially, but always secretly. He had many private potential deals simmering for all kinds of machinery and goods in short supply, including the fleet of jet airliners. Oftentimes he had gone where others could not go. Once he had gone to a meeting in Hangchow, the most beautiful part of China. This was to greet other members of the 49 Club privately, to be wined and dined as honored guests of China. The 49 Club consisted of those companies that had continued to trade with the PRC after 1949, mostly British firms. Britain had recognized Mao Tse-tung's government as the government of China shortly after Chiang Kai-shek abandoned the Mainland and fled to Taiwan. Even so, relations between the two governments had always been strained. But, by definition, relations between *Old Friends* were not, unless an Old Friend betrayed a confidence, or cheated.

"Oh I went on a few side trips," Dunross said airily, not wanting to lie to the chief of SI. "Nothing to write home about. Why?"

"Could you tell me where, please."

"If you're more specific, Roger, certainly," he replied, his voice hardening. "We're traders and not politicians and not spies and the Noble House has a special position in Asia. We've been here quite a few years and it's because of traders the Union Jack flies over . . . used to fly over half the earth. What had you in mind, old chap?"

There was a long pause. "Nothing, nothing in particular. Very well, Ian, I'll wait till we've had the pleasure of reading the papers, then I'll be specific. Thanks, so sorry to trouble you. 'Bye."

Dunross stared at the phone, troubled. What does Crosse want to know? he asked himself. Many of the deals he had made and would be making certainly would not conform to official government policy in London, or, even more, in Washington. His short-term and long-term attitude toward China clearly was opposed to theirs. What they would consider contraband he did not.

Well, as long as I'm tai-pan, he told himself firmly, come hell or typhoon, our links with China will remain our links with China and that's the end of that. Most politicians in London and Washington just won't realize Chinese are Chinese first and Communist second. And Hong Kong's vital to the peace of Asia.

"Mr. and Mrs. Jamie Kirk, sir."

Jamie Kirk was a pedantic little man with a pink face and pink hands and a pleasing Scots accent. His wife was tall, big and American.

"Oh so pleased to m—" Kirk began.

"Yes we are, Mr. Dunross," his wife boomed good-naturedly over him. "Get to the point, Jamie, honey, Mr. Dunross's a very busy man and we've shopping to do. My husband's got a package for you, sir."

"Yes, it's from Alan Medford G—"

"He knows it's from Alan Medford Grant, honey," she said happily, talking over him again. "Give him the package."

"Oh. Oh yes and there's a—"

"A letter from him too," she said. "Mr. Dunross's very busy so give them to him and we can go shopping."

"Oh. Yes, well . . ." Kirk handed Dunross the package. It was about fourteen inches by nine and an inch thick. Brown, nondescript and heavily taped. The envelope was sealed with red sealing wax. Dunross recognized the seal. "Alan said to—"

"To give it to you personally and give you his best wishes," she said with another laugh. She got up. "You're so slow, sweetness. Well, thank you, Mr. Dunross, come along, hon—"

She stopped, startled as Dunross held up an imperious hand and said with polite though absolute authority, "What shopping do you want to do, Mrs. Kirk?"

"Eh? Oh. Oh some clothes, er, I want some clothes made and honey needs some shirts an—"

Dunross held up his hand again and punched a button and Claudia was there. "Take Mrs. Kirk to Sandra Lee at once. She's to take her at once to Lee Foo Tap downstairs and by the Lord God tell him to give Mrs. Kirk the best possible price or I'll have him deported! Mr. Kirk will join her there in a moment!" He took Mrs. Kirk by the arm and before she knew it she was contentedly out of the room, Claudia solicitously listening to what she wanted to buy.

Kirk sighed in the silence. It was a deep, long-suffering sigh. "I wish I could do that," he said gloomily, then beamed. "Och aye, tai-pan, you're everything Alan said you were."

"Oh? I didn't do anything. Your wife wanted to go shopping didn't she?"

"Yes but . . ." After a pause Kirk added, "Alan said that you should, er, you should read the letter while I'm here. I . . . I didn't tell her that. Do you think I should have?"

"No," Dunross said kindly. "Look, Mr. Kirk, I'm sorry to tell you bad news but I'm afraid AMG was killed in a motorcycle accident last Monday."

Kirk's mouth dropped. "What?"

"Sorry to have to tell you but I thought you'd better know."

Kirk stared at the rain streaks, lost in thought. "How terrible," he said at length. "Bloody motorbikes, they're death traps. He was run down?"

"No. He was just found in the road, beside the bike. Sorry."

"Terrible! Poor old Alan. Dear oh dear! I'm glad you didn't mention it in front of Frances, she's, she was fond of him too. I, er, I . . . perhaps you'd better read this letter then . . . Frances wasn't a great friend so I don't . . . poor old Alan!" He stared down at his hands. The nails were bitten and disfigured. "Poor old Alan!"

To give Kirk time, Dunross opened the letter. It read: "My dear Mr. Dunross: This will introduce an old school friend, Jamie Kirk, and his wife Frances. The package he brings, please open in private. I wanted it safely in your hands and Jamie agreed to stop over in Hong Kong. He's to be trusted, as much as one can trust anyone these days. And, please, don't mind about Frances, she's a good sort really, good to my old friend and quite well off from previous husbands which gives Jamie the freedom he requires to sit and to think—a rare, very rare privilege these days. By the way, they're not in my line of work though they know I'm an amateur historian with private means." Dunross would have smiled but for the fact that he was reading a letter from a dead man. The letter concluded, "Jamie's a geologist, a marine geologist, one of the best in the world. Ask him about his work, the last years, preferably not with Frances there—not that she's not party to everything he knows but she does carry on a bit. He has some interesting theories that could perhaps benefit the Noble House and your contingency planning. Kindest regards, AMG."

Dunross looked up. "AMG says you're old school friends?"

"Oh yes. Yes, we were at school together. Charterhouse actually. Then I went on to Cambridge, he to Oxford. Yes. We've, er, kept in contact over the years, haphazardly, of course. Yes. Have you, er, known him long?"

"About three years. I liked him too. Perhaps you don't want to talk now?"

"Oh. Oh no, that's all right. I'm . . . it's a shock of course but well, life must go on. Old Alan . . . he's a funny sort of laddie isn't he, with all his papers and books and pipe and ash and carpet slippers." Kirk sadly steepled his fingers. "I suppose I should say he *was*. It doesn't seem right yet to talk about him in the past tense . . . but I suppose we should. Yes. He always wore carpet slippers. I dinna think I've ever been to his chambers when he wasn't wearing carpet slippers."

"You mean his flat? I've never been there. We always met in my London office though he did come to Ayr once." Dunross searched his memory. "I don't remember him wearing carpet slippers there."

"Ah, yes, he told me about Ayr, Mr. Dunross. Yes, he told me. It was, er, a high point in his life. You're . . . you're very lucky to have such an estate."

"Castle Avisyard's not mine, Mr. Kirk, though it's been in the family for more than a hundred years. Dirk Struan bought it for his wife and family—a country seat so to speak." As always, Dunross felt a sudden glow at the thought of all that loveliness, gentle rolling hills, lakes, moors, forests, glades, six thousand acres or more, good shooting, good hunting and Scotland at its best. "It's tradition that the current tai-pan's always laird of Avisyard—while he's tai-pan. But, of course, all the families, particularly children of the various families, know it well. Summer holidays . . . Christmas at Avisyard's a wonderful tradition. Whole sheep and sides of beef, haggis at New Year, whiskey and huge roaring fires, the pipes sounding. It's a bonnie place. And a working farm, cattle, milk, butter— and not forgetting the Loch Vey distillery! I wish I could spend more time there—my wife just left today to get things ready for the Christmas vacation. Do you know that part of the world?"

"A wee bit. Mostly I know the Highlands. I know the Highlands better. My family came from Inverness."

"Ah, then you must visit us when we're in Ayr, Mr. Kirk. AMG says in his letter you're a geologist, one of the best in the world?"

"Oh. Oh he's too kind—was too kind. My, er, my speciality's marine. Yes. With particular emph—" He stopped abruptly.

"What's the matter?"

"Oh, er, nothing, nothing really, but do you think Frances will be all right?"

"Absolutely. Would you like me to tell her about AMG?"

"No. No I can do that later. No, I . . . I, on second thoughts I think I'm going to pretend he's not dead, Mr. Dunross. You need not have told me, then I won't have to spoil her holiday. Yes. That's best, don't you think?" Kirk brightened a little. "Then we can discover the bad news when we get home."

"Whatever you wish. You were saying? With particular emphasis on?"

"Oh yes . . . petrology, which is, of course, the broad study of rocks including their interpretation and description. Within petrology my field has been narrowed down more recently to sedimentary rocks. I've, er, I've been on a research project for the last few years as a consultant on Paleozoic sedimentaries, porous ones. Yes. The study concentrated on the eastern coastal shelf of Scotland. AMG thought you might like to hear about it."

"Of course." Dunross curbed his impatience. His eyes were looking at the package on his desk. He wanted to open it and call Johnjohn and do a dozen other pressing things. There was so much to do and he did not yet understand the AMG connection between the Nobel House and Kirk. "It sounds very interesting," he said. "What was the study for?"

"Eh?" Kirk stared at him, startled. "Hydrocarbons." At Dunross's blank look he added hastily, "Hydrocarbons are only found in porous sedimentary rocks of the Paleozoic era. Oil, Mr. Dunross, crude oil."

"Oh! You were exploring for oil?"

"Oh no! It was a research project to determine the possibility of hydrocarbons being present offshore. Off Scotland. I'm happy to say I think they'll be there abundantly. Not close in but out in the North Sea." The small man's pink face became pinker and he mopped his brow. "Yes. Yes, I think there'll be quite a number of good fields out there."

Dunross was perplexed, still not seeing the connection. "Well, I know a little about offshore drilling in the Middle East and the Texas Gulf but out in the North Sea? Good God, Mr. Kirk, that sea's the worst in the world, probably the most fickle in the world, almost always in storm with mountainous seas. How could you drill there? How could you make the rigs safe, how would you supply the rigs, how could you possibly get the oil in bulk ashore, even if you found it? And if you got it ashore, my God, the cost'd be prohibitive."

"Oh quite right, Mr. Dunross," Kirk agreed. "Everything you say's quite right, but then it's not my job to be commercial, just to find our elusive, supremely valuable hydrocarbons." He added proudly, "This is the first time we've ever thought they could exist there. Of course, it's still only a theory, my theory—you never know for certain until you drill—but part of my expertise's in seismic interpretation, that's the study of waves resulting from induced explosions, and my approach to the latest findings was a wee bitty unorthodox. . . ."

Dunross listened now with only the surface of his brain, still trying to puzzle out why AMG should consider this important. He allowed Kirk to continue for a while then politely brought him back. "You've convinced me, Mr. Kirk. I congratulate you. How long are you staying in Hong Kong?"

"Oh. Oh just till Monday. Then, er, then we're going to New Guinea."

Dunross concentrated, very concerned. "Where in New Guinea?"

"To a place called Sukanapura, on the north coast, that's in the new Indonesian part. I've been . . ." Kirk smiled. "Sorry, of course you'd know President Sukarno took over Dutch New Guinea in May."

"Stolen might be another way of putting it. If it hadn't been for more ill-advised U.S. pressure, Dutch New Guinea'd still be Dutch and far better off, I think. I don't believe it'd be a good idea at all for you and Mrs. Kirk to go there for a while. It's very dicey, the political situation's very unstable and President Sukarno's hostile. The insurrection in Sarawak is Indonesian-sponsored and supported—he's very antagonistic to the West, to all Malaysia, and pro his Marxists. Besides Sukanapura is a hot, rotten, spooky port with lots of disease on top of all the other troubles."

"Oh you don't have to worry, I have a Scots constitution, and we're invited by the government."

"My point is that, presently, there's very little government influence."

"Ah, but there're some very interesting sedimentaries they want me to look at. You don't have to worry, Mr. Dunross, we're geologists, not political. Everything's arranged—this was the whole purpose of our trip—no need to worry. Well, I should be going."

"There's . . . I'm having a small cocktail party on Saturday from 7:30 to 9:00 P.M.," he said. "Perhaps you and your wife would like to come? Then we can talk further about New Guinea."

"Oh, oh that's awfully kind of you. I, er, we'd love to. Where wo—"

"I'll send a car for you. Now, perhaps you'd like to join Mrs. Kirk—I won't mention AMG if you're sure that's what you want."

"Oh! Oh yes. Poor Alan. For a moment, discussing sedimentaries, I'd forgotten about him. Curious, isn't it, how soon one can forget."

Dunross sent him off with another assistant and closed the door. Carefully he broke the seals of AMG's package. Inside there was an envelope and an inner package. The envelope was addressed: "Ian Dunross, private and confidential." Unlike the other letter, which was neatly handwritten, this was typed: "Dear Mr. Dunross, This comes in haste to you through my old friend Jamie. I've just had some very disquieting news. There is another very serious security leak somewhere in our system, British or American, and it's quite clear our adversaries are stepping up their clandestine attacks. Some of this might even spill over onto me, even to you, hence my anxiety. To you because it could be the existence of our highly classified series of papers has been discovered. Should anything untoward happen to me please call 871-65-65 in Geneva. Ask for Mrs. Riko Gresserhoff. To her, my name is Hans Gresserhoff. Her real name is Riko Anjin. She speaks German, Japanese and English—a little French—and if I'm owed any money please assign it to her. There are certain papers she will give you, some for transmission. Please deliver them personally when convenient. As I said, it's rare to find someone to trust. I trust you. You're the only one on earth who knows about her and her real name. Remember, it is vital that neither this letter nor my previous papers go out of your hands to *anyone*.

"First, to explain about Kirk: Within ten years or so I believe the Arab nations will bury their differences and use the real power they have, not against Israel directly but against the Western world—forcing us into an intolerable position: Do we abandon Israel . . . or do we starve? They use their oil as a weapon of war.

"If they ever manage to work together, a handful of sheiks and feudal kings in Saudi Arabia, Iran, the Persian Gulf States, Iraq, Libya, can, at their whim, cut off Western and Japanese supplies of the one raw material that is indispensable. They have an even more sophisticated opportunity: to raise the price to unprecedented heights and hold our economies to ransom. Oil is the ultimate weapon for Arabia. Unbeatable so long as we're dependent on their oil. Hence my immediate interest in Kirk's theory.

"Nowadays it costs about eight cents American to get one barrel of oil to the surface of an Arabian desert. From the North Sea it would cost seven dollars to bring one barrel ashore, in bulk, to Scotland. If Arabian oil jumped from its present three dollars a barrel on the world market to nine . . . I'm sure you get the point immediately. At once North Sea becomes immensely possible, and a British national treasure.

"Jamie says the fields are to the north and east of Scotland. The port of Aberdeen would be the logical place to bring it ashore. A wise man would start looking at wharfing, real estate, airfields, in Aberdeen. Don't worry about bad weather, helicopters will be the connecting links to the rigs. Expensive yes, but viable. Further, if you will accept my forecast that Labour will win the next election because of the Profumo scandal . . ."

The case had filled the newspapers. Six months before, in March, the Secretary of State for War, John Profumo, had formally denied that he had ever had an affair with a notorious call girl, Christine Keeler, one of several girls who had suddenly sprung to international prominence with their procurer, Stephen Ward—up to that time just a well-known osteopath in London's high society. Unsubstantiated rumors began to circulate that the girl had also been having an affair with one of the Soviet attachés, a well-known KGB agent, Commander Yevgeny Ivanov, who had been recalled to Russia the previous December. In the uproar that followed, Profumo resigned, and Stephen Ward committed suicide.

"It is curious that the affair was revealed to the press at the perfect time for the Soviets," Grant continued. "I have no proof, yet, but it's not just a coincidence in my opinion. Remember it is Soviet doctrine to fragment countries—North Korea and South, East Germany and West, and so on—then to let their indoctrinated underlings do their work for them. So I think the pro-Soviet Socialists will help fragment Britain into England, Scotland, Wales and south and north Ireland (watch Eire and Northern Ireland which is a ready-made arena for Soviet merrymaking).

"Now for my suggested Contingency Plan One for the Noble House: To be circumspect about England and to concentrate on Scotland as a base. *North Sea oil would make Scotland abundantly self-sufficient.* The population is small, hardy and nationalistic. As an entity, Scotland would be practical now, and defensible—with an abundant exportable oil supply. A strong Scotland could perhaps help tip the scales and help a tottering England . . . our poor country, Mr. Dunross! I fear greatly for England.

"Perhaps this is another of my farfetched theories. But reconsider Scotland, Aberdeen, in the light of a new North Sea."

"Ridiculous!" Dunross exploded and he stopped reading for a moment, his mind swept, then cautioned himself, don't go off at half cock! AMG's farfetched sometimes, given to exaggeration, he's a right-wing imperialist who sees fifteen Reds under every bed. But what he says could be possible. If it's possible, then it must be considered. If there were a vast worldwide oil shortage and we were prepared, we could make a fortune, he told himself, his excitement growing. It'd be easy to buy into Aberdeen now, easy to begin a calculated retreat from London without hurting anything—Edinburgh has all the modern amenities of banking, communications, ports, airfields, that we'd need to operate efficiently. Scotland for the Scots, with abundant oil for export? Completely viable, but not separate, somehow within a strong Britain. But if the city of London, Parliament and Threadneedle Street become left-wing choked . . .

The hair on the nape of his neck twisted at the thought of Britain being buried under a shroud of left-wing socialism. What about Robin Grey? Or Julian Broadhurst? he asked himself, chilled. Certainly they'd nationalize everything, they'd grab North Sea oil, if any, and put Hong Kong on the block—they've already said they would.

With an effort he tabled that thought for later, turned the page and read on. "Next, I think I've identified three of your Sevrin moles. The information was expensive—I may need extra money before Christmas—and I am not certain of the accuracy (I'm trying to cross-check at once, realizing the importance to you). The moles are believed to be: Jason Plumm of a company called Asian Properties; Lionel Tuke in the telephone company; and Jacques deVille in Struan's . . ."

"Impossible!" Dunross burst out loud. "AMG's gone mad! Plumm's as impossible as Jacques, totally absolutely impossible. There's no way they co—"

His private phone began ringing. Automatically he picked it up. "Yes?"

"This is the overseas operator calling Mr. Dunross."

"Who's calling him please?" he snapped.

"Will Mr. Dunross accept a collect call from Sydney, Australia, from a Mr. Duncan Dunross?"

The tai-pan's heart missed a beat. "Of course! Hello, Duncan . . . Duncan?"

"Father?"

"Hello, my son, are you all right?"

"Oh yes, sir, absolutely!" he heard his son say and his anxiety fled. "I'm sorry to call you during the working day, Father, but my Monday flight's overbooked an—"

"Dammit, you have a confirmed booking, laddie. I'll get p—"

"No, Father, thank you, that's perfectly all right. Now I'm on an earlier one. I'm on Singapore Airlines Flight 6 which arrives Hong Kong at noon. Don't bother to meet me, I'll get a taxi an—"

"Look for the car, Duncan. Lee Choy will be there. But come to the office before you go home, eh?"

"All right. I've validated my tickets and everything."

Dunross heard the pride in his son's voice and it warmed him. "Good. Well done. By the way, Cousin Linbar will be arriving tomorrow on Qantas at 8:00 P.M. your time. He'll be staying at the house too." Struan's had had a company house in Sydney since 1900 and a permanent office there since the eighties. Hag Struan had gone into partnership with an immensely wealthy wheat farmer named Bill Scragger and their company had flourished until the crash of 1929. "Did you have a good holiday?"

"Oh smashing! Smashing, yes, I want to come back next year. I met a smashing girl, Father."

"Oh?" Half of Dunross wanted to smile, the other half was still locked into the nightmare possibility that Jacques was a traitor, and if traitor and part of Sevrin, was he the one who supplied some of their innermost secrets to Linc Bartlett? No, Jacques couldn't have. He couldn't possibly have known about our bank holdings. Who knows about those? Who wou—

"Father?"

"Yes, Duncan?"

He heard the hesitancy, then his son said in a run, trying to sound manly, "Is it all right for a fellow to have a girl friend a little older than himself?"

Dunross smiled gently and started to dismiss the thought as his son was only just fifteen, but then he remembered Elegant Jade when he himself was not quite fifteen, surely more of a man than Duncan. Not necessarily, he thought honestly. Duncan's tall and growing and just as much a man. And didn't I love her to madness that year and the next year and didn't I almost die the next year when she vanished? "Well," he said as an equal, "it really depends on who the girl is, how old the man is and how old the girl is."

"Oh." There was a long pause. "She's eighteen."

Dunross was greatly relieved. That means she's old enough to know better, he thought. "I'd say that would be perfect," he told Duncan in the same voice, "particularly if the fellow was about sixteen, tall, strong and knew the facts of life."

"Oh. Oh I didn't . . . oh! I wouldn't . . ."

"I wasn't being critical, laddie, just answering your question. A man has to be careful in this world, and girl friends should be chosen carefully. Where did you meet her?"

"She was on the station. Her name's Sheila."

Dunross suppressed a smile. Girls in Australia were referred to as sheilas just as in England they were called birds. "That's a nice name," he said. "Sheila what?"

"Sheila Scragger. She's a niece of old Mr. Tom and she's on a visit from England. She's training to be a nurse at Guy's Hospital. She was ever so super to me and Paldoon's super too. I really can't thank you enough for arranging such a super holiday." Paldoon, the Scragger ranch, or station as it was called in Australia, was the only property they had managed to save from the crash. Paldoon was five hundred miles southwest of Sydney near the Murray River in Australia's rice lands, sixty thousand acres—thirty thousand head of sheep, two thousand acres of wheat and a thousand head of cattle—and the greatest place for a youth to holiday, working all day from dawn to dusk, mustering the sheep or cattle on horseback, galloping twenty miles in any direction and still on your own property.

"Give Tom Scragger my regards and make sure you send him a bottle of whiskey before you leave."

"Oh I sent him a case, is that all right?"

Dunross laughed. "Well laddie, a bottle would have done just as well, but a case is perfect. Call me if there's any change in your flight. You did very well to get it organized yourself, very good. Oh by the way, Mama and Glenna went to London today, with Aunt Kathy, so you'll have to go back to school alone an—"

"Oh jolly good, Father," his son said happily. "After all, I'm a man now and almost at university!"

"Yes, yes you are." A small sweet sadness touched Dunross as he sat in his high chair, AMG's letter in his hand but forgotten. "Are you all right for money?"

"Oh yes. I hardly spent anything on the station except for a beer or two. Father, don't tell Mother about my girl."

"All right. Or Adryon," he said and at once his chest tightened at the thought of Martin Haply together with Adryon and how they went off hand-in-hand. "You should tell Adryon yourself."

"Oh super, I'd forgotten her. How is she?"

"She's in good shape," Dunross said, ordering himself to be adult, wise, and not to worry and it was all quite normal for boys and girls to be boys and girls. Yes, but Christ it's difficult if you're the father. "Well, Duncan, see you Monday! Thanks for calling."

"Oh yes, and Father, Sheila drove me up to Sydney. She . . . she's staying the weekend with friends and going to see me off! Tonight we're going to a movie, *Lawrence of Arabia*, have you seen it?"

"Yes, it's just come to Hong Kong, you'll enjoy that."

"Oh super! Well, good-bye, Father, have to run . . . love you!"

"Love you," he said but the connection was already dead.

How lucky I am with my family, my wife and kids, Dunross thought, and at once added, Please God let nothing happen to them!

With an effort he looked back at the letter. It's impossible for Jason Plumm or Jacques to be Communist spies, he told himself. Nothing they've ever said or done would indicate that. Lionel Tuke? No, not him either. I only know him casually. He's an ugly, unpopular fellow who keeps to himself but he's on the cricket team, a member of the Turf Club and he's been out here since the thirties. Wasn't he even interned at Stanley between '42 and '45? Maybe him, but the other two? Impossible!

I'm sorry AMG's dead. I'd call him right now about Jacques and . . .

First finish the letter, then consider the parts, he ordered himself. Be correct, be efficient. Good God! Duncan and an eighteen-year-old sheila! Thank God it wasn't Tom Scragger's youngest. How old is Priscilla now?

Fourteen, pretty, built much older. Girls seem to mature early Down Under.

He exhaled. I wonder if I should do for Duncan what Chen-chen did for me.

The letter continued, ". . . As I've said, I'm not completely sure but my source is usually impeccable.

"I'm sorry to say the espionage war has hotted up since we uncovered and caught the spies Blake, Vassal—the Admiralty cipher clerk—and Philby, Burgess and Maclean all defected. They've all been seen in Moscow by the way. Expect spying to increase radically in Asia. (We were able to peg First Secretary Skripov of the Soviet Embassy in Canberra, Australia, and order him out of the country in February. This broke his Australian ring which was, I believe, tied to your Sevrin and further involved in Borneo and Indonesia.)

"The free world is abundantly infiltrated now. MI-5 and MI-6 are tainted. Even the CIA. While we've been naive and trusting, our opponents realized early that the future balance would depend on economic power as well as military power, and so they set out to acquire—steal—our industrial secrets.

"Curiously our free-world media fail dismally to point out that all Soviet advances are based originally on one of our stolen inventions or techniques, that without our grain they starve, and without our vast and ever-growing financial assistance and credits to buy our grains and technology they cannot fuel and refuel their whole military-industrial infrastructure which keeps their empire and people enthralled.

"I recommend you use your contacts in China to cememt them to you further. The Soviets increasingly view China as their number one enemy. Equally strangely, they no longer seem to have that paranoiac fear of the U.S. which is, without doubt, now the strongest military and economic power in the world. China, which is economically and militarily weak, except in numbers of available soldiers, really presents no military threat to them. Even so China petrifies them.

"One reason is the five thousand miles of border they share. Another is national guilt over the vast areas of historic Chinese territory Soviet Russia has swallowed over the centuries; another is the knowledge that the Chinese are a patient people with long memories. One day the Chinese will take back their lands. They have always taken back their lands when it was militarily feasible to do so. I've pointed out many times that the cornerstone of Soviet (Imperialist) politics is to isolate and fragment China to keep her weak. Their great bugaboo is a tripartite alliance between China, Japan and the U.S. Your Noble House should work to promote that. (Also a Common Market between the U.S., Mexico and Canada, totally essential, in my opinion, to a stable American continent.) Where else but through Hong Kong—and therefore your hands—will all the inward wealth to China go?

"Last, back to Sevrin: I have taken a major risk and approached our most priceless asset in the inner core of the KGB's ultra-secret Department 5. I have just heard back today that the identity of *Arthur,* Sevrin's leader, is Classification One, beyond even his grasp. The only clue he could give was that the man was English and one of his initials is R. Not much to go on I'm afraid.

"I look forward to seeing you. Remember, my papers must never pass into the hands of anyone else. Regards, AMG."

Dunross committed the Geneva phone number to memory, encoded it in his address book and lit a match. He watched the airmail paper curl and begin to burn.

R. Robert Ralph Richard Robin Rod Roy Rex Rupert Red Rodney and always back to Roger. And Robert. Robert Armstrong or Roger Crosse or—or who?

Holy Christ, Dunross thought, feeling weak.

"Geneva 871-65-65, station to station," he said into his private phone. Tiredness engulfed him. His sleep last night had been disturbed, his dreams dragging him back to war, back to his flaming cockpit, the smell of burning in his nostrils, then waking, chilled, listening to the rain, soon to get up silently, Penn sleeping soundly, the Great House quiet except for old Ah Tat who, as always, had his tea made. Then to the track and chased all day, his enemies closing in and nothing but bad news. Poor old John Chen, he thought, then made the effort to push his weariness away. Perhaps I can kip for an hour between five and six. I'll need all my wits tonight.

The operator made the connections and he heard the number ringing.

"*Ja?*" the gentle voice said.

"*Hier ist* Herr Dunross *im* Hong Kong. Frau Gresserhoff *bitte,*" he said in good German.

"Oh!" There was a long pause. "*Ich bin* Frau Gresserhoff. Tai-pan?"

"*Ah so desu! Ohayo gozaimasu. Anata wa Anjin Riko-san?*" he asked, his Japanese accent excellent. Good morning. Your name is also Riko Anjin?

"*Hai. Hai, dozo. Ah, nihongo wa jotzu desu.*" Yes. Oh you speak Japanese very well.

"*Iye, sukoshi, gomen nasai.*" No, sorry, only a little. As part of his training, he had spent two years in their Tokyo office. "Ah, so sorry," he continued in Japanese, "but I'm calling about Mr. Gresserhoff. Have you heard?"

"Yes." He could hear the sadness. "Yes. I heard on Monday."

"I've just received a letter from him. He said you have some, some things for me?" he asked cautiously.

"Yes, tai-pan. Yes I have."

"Would it be possible for you to bring them here? So sorry, but I cannot come to you."

"Yes. Yes of course," she said hesitantly, her Japanese soft and pleasing. "When should I come?"

"As soon as possible. If you go to our office on Avenue Bern in a couple of hours, say at noon, there will be tickets and money for you. I believe there's a Swissair connection that leaves this afternoon—if that were possible."

Again the hesitation. He waited patiently. AMG's letter writhed in the ashtray as it burned. "Yes," she said. "That would be possible."

"I'll make all the arrangements for you. Would you like someone to travel with you?"

"No, no thank you," she said, her voice so quiet that he had to cup one hand over his ear to hear better. "Please excuse me for causing all this trouble. I can make the arrangements."

"Truly, it's no trouble," he said, pleased that his Japanese was flowing and colloquial. "Please go to my office at noon. . . . By the way, the weather here is warm and wet. Ah, so sorry, please excuse me for asking but is your passport Swiss or Japanese, and under what name would you travel?"

An even longer pause. "I would . . . I think I should . . . It would be Swiss, my travel name should be Riko Gresserhoff."

"Thank you Mrs. Gresserhoff. I look forward to seeing you. *Kiyo-skette,*" he ended. Have a safe journey.

Thoughtfully he put the phone back onto its cradle. The last of AMG's letter twisted and died with a thread of smoke. Carefully he crumbled the ashes into powder.

Now what about Jacques?

46

Jacques deVille plodded up the marble stairs of the Mandarin Hotel to the mezzanine floor, packed with people having late tea.

He took off his raincoat and went through the crowds, feeling very old. He had just talked to his wife, Susanne, in Nice. The specialist from Paris had made another examination of Avril and thought that her internal injuries might not be as bad as first thought.

"He says we have to be patient," Susanne had told him in her gushing Parisienne French. "But Mother of God, how can we be? The poor child's distraught and losing her mind. She keeps saying, 'But I was the driver, it was me, Mumma, me, but for me my Borge would be alive, but for me. . . .' I fear for her, *chéri!*"

"Does she know yet that her . . . about her inside?"

"No, not yet. The doctor says not to tell her until he's sure." Susanne had begun to cry.

In agony he had calmed her as best he could and said he would call her back in an hour. For a while he had considered what he should do, then he had made arrangements and had left his office and come here.

The public phone booth near the newsstand was occupied so he bought an afternoon paper and glanced at the headlines. Twenty killed in resettlement mud slides above Aberdeen . . . Rain to continue . . . Will Saturday's Great Race Day be canceled? . . . JFK warns Soviets not to interfere in Vietnam . . . Atom Test Ban Treaty signed in Moscow by Dean Rusk, Andrei Gromyko and Sir Alec Douglas-Home, rejected by France and China . . . Malayan Communists step up offensive . . . Kennedy's second son, born prematurely, dies . . . Manhunt for the British Great Train Robbers continues . . . Profumo scandal damages Conservative Party . . .

"Excuse me, sir, are you waiting for the phone?" an American woman asked from behind him.

"Oh, oh yes, thank you, sorry! I didn't see that it was empty." He went

into the booth, closed the door, put in the coin and dialed. The ringing
tone began. He felt his anxiety rising.

"Yes?"

"Mr. Lop-sing please," he said, not sure of the voice yet.

"There's no Mr. Lop-*ting* here. Sorry, you have a wrong number."

"I want to leave a message," he said, relieved to recognize Suslev's voice.

"You have a wrong number. Look in your phone book."

When the code was completed correctly, he began, "Sorry to c—"

"What is your number?" interrupted him harshly.

Jacques gave it at once.

"Is it a phone booth?"

"Yes." Immediately the phone clicked off. As he hung up he felt a sudden sweat on his hands. Suslev's number was only to be used in an emergency but this was an emergency. He stared at the phone.

"Excuse me, sir," the American woman called out through the glass
doors. "Can I use the phone? I won't be a moment."

"Oh! Oh I'm—I won't be a second," Jacques said, momentarily flustered.
He saw that three Chinese were waiting impatiently behind her now.
They stared at him balefully. "I'm . . . I'll just be a second." He reclosed
the door, sweat on his back. He waited and waited and waited and then
the phone rang. "Hello?"

"What's the emergency?"

"I . . . I just heard from Nice." Carefully Jacques told Suslev about his
conversation with his wife without mentioning any names. "I'm going
there at once on the evening flight—and I thought I'd better tell you personally so the—"

"No, this evening's too soon. Book tomorrow, on the evening flight."

Jacques felt his world collapse. "But I talked to the tai-pan a few minutes ago and he said it was all right for me to go tonight. I'm booked. I
can be back in three days, she really sounded awful on the phone. Don't
you th—"

"No!" Suslev told him more sharply. "I will call you tonight as arranged. This could all have waited till then. Don't use this number again
unless there's a real emergency!"

Jacques opened his mouth to answer hotly but the phone was already
dead. He had heard the anger. But this is an emergency, he told himself,
enraged, beginning to redial. Susanne needs me there and so does Avril.
And the tai-pan was all for it.

"Good idea, Jacques," Dunross had said at once. "Take all the time you
need. Andrew can cover for you."

And now . . . *Merde,* what do I do? Suslev's not my keeper!
Isn't he?

DeVille stopped dialing, his sweat chilling, and hung up.

"Are you finished, sir?" the American woman called out with her insistent smile. She was in her fifties, her hair fashionably blue. "There's a line waiting."

"Oh . . . oh yes, sorry." He fought the door open.

"You forgot your paper, sir," she said politely.

"Oh, oh thank you." Jacques deVille reached back for it and came out in misery. At once all the Chinese, three men and a woman, surged forward, elbowing him and the American lady out of the way. A heavyset matron got to the door first and slammed it shut behind her, the others crowding to be next.

"Hey . . . it was my turn," the American woman began angrily but they paid no attention to her except to curse her and her antecedents openly and with great vulgarity.

Suslev was standing in the sleazy Kowloon apartment that was one of Arthur's safe houses, his heart still thumping from the suddenness of the call. There was a damp, musky, soiled smell of ancient cooking in the room and he stared down at the phone, furious with Jacques deVille. Stupid motherless turd. Jacques is becoming a liability. Tonight I'll tell Arthur what should be done with him. The sooner the better! Yes, and the sooner you calm down yourself the better, he cautioned himself. Angry people make mistakes. Put away your anger!

With an effort, he did just that and went out onto the dim, paint-peeled landing, locking the door behind him. Another key unlocked Ginny Fu's door next to his.

"You want vodka?" she asked with her saucy smile.

"Yes." He grinned back, pleased to look at her. She was sitting cross-legged on the old sofa and wore only a smile. They had been kissing when his phone had rung the first time. There were two phones in her apartment. Hers and the other one, the secret one in the cupboard that only he used and answered. Arthur had told him it was safe, bootlegged, unlisted and impossible to bug. Even so, Suslev only used the other apartment and its phone for emergencies.

Matyeryebyets, Jacques, he thought, still edgy from the sudden shrilling of his private phone.

"Drink, *tovarich*," Ginny said, offering the glass. "Then drink me, *heya?*"

He grinned back, took the vodka and ran an appreciative hand over her cute little rump. "Ginny, *golubushka*, you're a good girl."

"You bet! I best girl for you." She reached up and fondled his earlobe. "We jig-jig *heya?*"

"Why not?" He drank the fiery liquid sparingly, wanting it to last. Her tiny nimble fingers were undoing his shirt. He stopped her for a moment and kissed her, she welcoming his kiss and returning it equally. "Wait till clothes off, *heya?*" she chuckled.

"Next week I go, eh?" he said, holding her in his bear hug. "How about you coming too, eh? The holiday I've always promised you?"

"Oh? Oh truly?" Her smile was immense. "Wen? Wen? You no tease?"

"You can come with me. We'll stop in Manila, our first stop's Manila, then north and back here in a month."

"Oh a real month . . . oh Gregy!" She hugged him with all her might. "I make best ship's captain girl all China!"

"Yes, yes you will."

"Wen go . . . wen we go?"

"Next week. I'll tell you when."

"Good. Tomorrow I go get passport th—"

"No, no passport, Ginny. They'll never give it to you. Those *viblya-doks*'ll stop you. They won't ever let you come with me . . . oh no, *golubushka*, those dirty police will never let you come with me."

"Then wat I do, *heya*?"

"I'll smuggle you aboard in a chest!" His laugh was rich. "Or perhaps on a magic carpet. Eh?"

She peered up at him, her dark eyes wide and brimming and anxious. "True you take me? True? One month on your ship, *heya*?"

"At least a month. But don't tell anyone. The police watch me all the time and if they know, you won't be able to come with me. Understand?"

"All gods bear witness not tell a weevil, not even my mother," Ginny swore vehemently, then hugged him again with the vastness of her happiness. "Eeeee, I get huge face as captain's lady!" Another hug and then she let her fingers stray and he jerked involuntarily. She laughed and began to undress him again. "I give you best time, best."

She used her fingers and her lips expertly, probing and touching and withdrawing and moving against him, concentrating on her task until he cried out and became one with the gods in the Clouds and the Rain. Her hands and lips stayed on him, not leaving while the last tiny fraction of pleasure remained. Then she ceased and curled against him and listened to the deepness of his breathing, very contented that she had done her job well. She, herself, she had not experienced the Clouds and the Rain though she had pretended to several times, to increase his pleasure. Only twice in all the times that they had pillowed had she reached the zenith and both times she had been very drunk and not really sure if she had or if she had not. It was only with Third Nighttime Sandwich Cook Tok at the Victoria and Albert that she would zenith every time. All gods bless my joss, she thought happily. With one month holiday and the extra money Gregor will give me, and, with joss, one more year with him, we'll have enough money to open our own restaurant and I can have sons and grandsons and become one with the gods. Oh how lucky I am!

She was tired now for she had had to work hard, so she curled more comfortably against him, closed her eyes, liking him, thankful to the gods that they had helped her to overcome her distaste for his size and his white, toadlike skin and his rancid body smell. Thank all gods, she thought happily as she wafted into sleep.

Suslev was not sleeping. He was just drifting, his mind and his body at peace. The day had been good and a little very bad. After meeting with Crosse at the racetrack he had returned to his ship, appalled that there could be a security leak from the *Ivanov*. He had encoded Crosse's information about Operation Dry Run and all the other things and sent it off in the privacy of his cabin. Incoming messages told him that Voranski would not be replaced until the next visit of the *Sovetsky Ivanov*, that the special psychochemical expert, Koronski, was available to arrive from Bangkok at twelve hours' notice, and that he, Suslev, was to assume direction of Sevrin and liaise with Arthur directly. "Do not fail to obtain copies of the AMG files."

He remembered how a chill had gone through him at that "do not fail." So few failures, so many successes, but only the failures remembered. Where was the security leak aboard? Who read the AMG file apart from me? Only Dimitri Metkin, my second-in-command. It could not be him. The leak must be from elsewhere.

How far to trust Crosse?

Not far, but that man's clearly the most priceless asset we have in the capitalistic camp of Asia and must be protected at all costs.

The feel of Ginny against him was pleasing. She was breathing softly, a tiny jerk from time to time, her breast rising and falling. His eyes went through the doorway to the old-fashioned clock that stood in a niche of one of the untidy kitchen shelves among all the half-used bottles and tins and containers. The kitchen was in an alcove off the living room. Here in the only bedroom, the bed was huge and almost filled the room. He had bought it for her when he had begun with her two, almost three years ago. It was a good bed, clean, soft but not too soft, a welcome change from his bunk aboard.

And Ginny, she was welcome too. Pliant, easygoing, no trouble. Her blue-black hair was cut short and straight across her high forehead, the way he liked it—such a contrast to Vertinskaya, his mistress in Vladivostok, her with her sloe, hazel eyes, long wavy dark brown hair and the temper of a wildcat, her mother a true Princess Zergeyev and her father an insignificant half-caste Chinese shopkeeper who had bought the mother at an auction when she was thirteen. She had been on one of the cattle trucks of children fleeing Russia after the holocaust of '17.

Liberation, not holocaust, he told himself happily. Ah, but it's good to bed the daughter of a Princess Zergeyev when you're the grandson of a peasant off Zergeyev lands.

Thinking of the Zergeyevs reminded him of Alexi Travkin. He smiled to himself. Poor Travkin, such a fool! Would they really release the Princess Nestorova, his wife, to Hong Kong at Christmas? I doubt it. Perhaps they will and then poor Travkin will die of shock to see that little old hag of the snows, toothless, wrinkled and arthritic. Better to spare him that agony, he thought compassionately. Travkin's Russian and not a bad man.

Again he looked at the clock. Now it read 6:20. He smiled to himself. Nothing to do for a few hours but sleep and eat and think and plan. Then the oh so careful meeting with the English MP and, late tonight, seeing Arthur again. He chuckled. It amused him very much to know secrets Arthur did not know. But then Arthur holds back secrets too, he thought without anger. Perhaps he already knows about the MPs. He's smart, very smart, and doesn't trust me either.

That's the great law: Never trust another—man, woman or child—if you want to stay alive and safe and out of enemy clutches.

I'm safe because I *know* people, know how to keep a closed mouth and know how to further State policy purely as part of my own life plan.

So many wonderful plans to effect. So many exciting coups to precipitate and be part of. And then there's Sevrin . . .

Again he chuckled and Ginny stirred. "Go to sleep, little princess," he whispered soothingly as to a child. "Go to sleep."

Obediently she did not truly awaken, just brushed her hair out of her eyes and snuggled more comfortably.

Suslev let his eyes close, her body sweet against him. He let his arm rest across her loins. The rain had lessened during the afternoon. Now he noticed it had stopped. He yawned as he went into sleep, knowing the storm had not yet ended its work.

Robert Armstrong drained his beer. "Another," he called out blearily, feigning drunkenness. He was in the Good Luck Girlfriend, a crowded, noisy Wanchai bar on the waterfront, filled with American sailors from the nuclear carrier. Chinese hostesses plied the customers with drink and accepted banter and touch and watered drinks in return at high cost. Occasionally one of them would order a real whiskey and show it to her partner to prove that this was a good bar and they were not being cheated.

Above the bar were rooms but it was not wise for sailors to go to them. Not all of the girls were clean or careful, not from choice just from ignorance. And, late at night, you could be rolled though only the very drunk were robbed. After all, there was no need: sailors were ready to spend everything they had.

"You want jig-jig?" the overpainted child asked him.

Dew neh loh moh on all your ancestors, he wanted to tell her. You should be home in bed with some schoolbooks. But he did not say it. That would do no good. In all probability her parents had gratefully arranged this job for her so that all the family could survive just a little better. "You want drink?" he said instead, hiding that he could speak Cantonese.

"Scottish, Scottish," the child called out imperiously.

"Why not get tea and I'll give you the money anyway," he said sourly.

"Fornicate all gods and the mothers of gods I not a cheater!" Haughtily the child offered the grimy glass the waiter had slapped down. It did contain cheap but real whiskey. She drained it without a grimace. "Waiter! Another Scottish and another beer! You drink, I drink, then we jig-jig."

Armstrong looked at her. "What's your name?"

"Lily. Lily Chop. Twenty-five dollars short time."

"How old are you?"

"Old. How old you?"

"Nineteen."

"Huh, coppers always lie!"

"How'd you know I'm a copper?"

"Boss tell me. Only twenty dollar, *heya?*"

"Who's the boss? Which one's he?"

"She. Behind the bar. She mama-*san.*"

Armstrong peered through the smoke. The woman was lean and scrawny and in her fifties, sweating and working hard, keeping up a running vulgar banter with the sailors as she filled the orders. "How'd she know I was a copper?"

Again Lily shrugged. "Listen, she tell me keep you happy or I out in street. We go upstairs now, *heya?* On house, no twenty dollar." The child got up. He could see her fear now.

"Sit down," he ordered.

She sat, even more afraid. "If I not pleeze she throw m—"

"You please me." Armstrong sighed. It was an old ploy. If you went, you paid, if you didn't go, you paid and the boss always sent a young one. He passed over fifty dollars. "Here. Go and give it to the mama-*san* with my thanks. Tell her I can't jig-jig now because I've got my monthly! Honorable Red's with me."

Lily gawked at him then cackled like an old woman. "Eeeee, fornicate all gods that's a good one!" She went off, hard put to walk on her high heels, her brassy *chong-sam* slit very high, showing her thin, very thin legs and buttocks.

Armstrong finished his beer, paid his bill and got to his feet. At once his table was claimed and he pushed through the sweating, shouting sailors for the door.

"You welcome anytime," the mama-*san* called out as he passed her.

"Sure," he called back without malice.

The rain was just a thin drizzle now and the day growing dark. On the street were many more raucous sailors, all of them American—British sailors had been ordered out of this area for the first few days by their captains. His skin felt wet and hot under his raincoat. In a moment he left Gloucester Road and the waterfront and strolled through the crowds up O'Brien Road, splashing through the puddles, the city smelling good and clean and washed. At the corner he turned into Lochart Road and at length found the alley he sought. It was busy, as usual, with street stalls and shops and scrawny dogs, chickens packed into cages, dried fried ducks and meats hanging from hooks, vegetables and fruits. Just inside the mouth of the alley was a small stall with stools under a canvas overhang to keep off the drizzle. He nodded at the owner, chose a shadowed corner, ordered a bowl of Singapore noodles—fine, lightly fried vermicelli-like noodles, dry, with chili and spices and chopped shrimps and fresh vegetables —and began to wait.

Brian Kwok.

Always back to Brian Kwok.

And always back to the 40,000 in used notes that he had found in his desk drawer, the one he always kept locked.

Concentrate, he told himself, or you'll slip. You'll make a mistake. You can't afford a mistake!

He was weary and felt an overpowering dirtiness that soap and hot water would not cleanse away. With an effort he forced his eyes to seek his prey, his ears to hear the street sounds, and his nose to enjoy the food.

He had just finished the bowl when he saw the American sailor. The man was thin and wore glasses and he towered over the Chinese pedestrians even though he walked with a slight stoop. His arm was around a street girl. She held an umbrella over them and was tugging at him.

"No, not this way, baby," she pleaded. "My room other way . . . unnerstan'?"

"Sure, honey, but first we go this way then we'll go your way. Huh? Come on, darlin'."

Armstrong hunched deeper into the shadows. He watched them approach, wondering if this was the one. The man's accent was Southern and sweet-sounding and he was in his late twenties. As he strolled along the busy street he looked this way and that, seeking his bearings. Then Armstrong saw him spot the tailor's shop on one corner of the alley that was called Pop-ting's Handmade Suits, and, opposite it, a small, open-faced restaurant lit with bare bulbs and with a crudely written sign nailed to a post: WELCOME TO AMERICAN SAILORS. The bold column of Chinese characters over the door read: "A Thousand Years' Health to Mao Tse-tung Restaurant."

"C'mon, honey," the sailor said, brightening. "Let's have a beer here."

"No good place, baby, better come my bar, *heya?* Bett—"

"Goddamnit we're having a beer here." He went into the open shop and sat at one of the plastic tables, bulky in his raincoat. Sullenly she followed. "Beer. Two beers! San Miguel, huh? You savvy huh?"

From where he sat, Armstrong could see them both clearly. One of the tables was filled with four coolies who noisily sucked noodles and soup into their mouths. They glanced at the sailor and the girl briefly. One made an obscene remark and the others laughed. The girl blushed, turning her back to them. The sailor hummed as he looked around carefully, sipping his beer, then stood up. "I gotta use the can." Unerringly he went to the back through the flyblown string curtain, the counterman watching him sourly. Armstrong sighed and relaxed. The trap was sprung.

In a moment the sailor returned. "C'mon," he said, "let's get outta here." He drained his glass, paid, and they went off arm in arm again the way they had come.

"You want more S'pore noodles?" the stall keeper asked Armstrong rudely, his hostile eyes just slits in his high-boned face.

"No thanks. Just another beer."

"No beer."

"Fornicate you and all your line," Armstrong hissed in perfect gutter Cantonese. "Am I a fool from the Golden Mountain? No, I'm a guest in your fornicating restaurant. Get me a fornicating beer or I'll have my men slit your Secret Sack and feed those peanuts you call your treasure to the nearest dog!"

The man said nothing. Sullenly he went to the next street stall and got a San Miguel and brought it back and set it on the counter, opening it. The other diners were still gaping at Armstrong. Abruptly he hawked loudly and spat and put his cold blue eyes on the man nearest him. He saw him shiver and look away. Uneasily the others went back to their bowls too, uncomfortable to be in the presence of a barbarian policeman who had the bad manners to swear so colloquially in their tongue.

Armstrong eased more comfortably on the stool, then let his eyes range the road and the alley, waiting patiently.

He did not have long to wait before he saw the small, squat chunky European coming up the alley, keeping to the side, stopping and peering into the storefront of a cheap shoe shop behind the street stalls that crowded the narrow roadway.

Ah, he's a professional, Armstrong thought, very pleased, knowing the man was using the glass as a mirror to case the restaurant. The man took his time. He wore a shapeless plastic raincoat and hat and appeared nondescript. His body was hidden for a moment as a coolie swayed past him with huge bundles on either end of the bamboo pole on his shoulders. Armstrong noticed his knotted calves, varicose-veined, as he watched the feet of the other man. They moved and he walked out of the alley, covered by the coolie, and did not stop, just continued up the road.

He's very good, the policeman thought admiringly, still having him in sight. This bugger's done this before. Must be KGB to be this smart. Well, it won't be long now, my fine fellow, before you're hooked, he told himself without rancor, as a fisherman would seeing a fat trout teasing the bait.

The man was shop-watching again. Come along, little fish.

The man was acting just like a trout. He made several passes and went away and came back but always very carefully and without attracting attention. At last he went into the open-faced restaurant and sat down and ordered a beer. Armstrong sighed again, happy now.

It seemed to take the man an interminable time before he, too, got up, asked where the toilet was, walked through the few diners and went under the bead curtain. In time he reappeared and went for his table. At once the four coolie diners fell on him from behind, pinioning his arms and holding him helpless, while another strapped a stiff high collar around his neck. Other diners, real customers, and not undercover SI police, gaped, one dropped his chopsticks, a couple fled and the others froze.

Armstrong got up from his stool leisurely and walked over. He saw the tough-looking Chinese behind the counter take off his apron. "Shut up, you bastard," the fellow said in Russian to the man who cursed and struggled impotently. "Evening, Superintendent," he added to Armstrong with a sly grin. His name was Malcolm Sun, he was a senior agent, SI, and ranking Chinese on this 16/2. It was he who had organized the intercept and had paid off the cook who usually worked this shift and had taken his place.

"Evening, Malcolm. You did very well." Armstrong turned his attention to the enemy agent. "What's your name?" he asked pleasantly.

"Who you? Let me go . . . let go!" the man said in heavily accented English.

"All yours, Malcolm," Armstrong said.

At once, Sun said in Russian, "Listen you mother-eater, we know you're off the *Ivanov*, we know you're a courier and you've just picked up a drop from the American off the nuclear carrier. We've already got the bastard in custody and you'd bet—"

"Lies! You've made a mistake," the man blustered in Russian. "I know nothing of any American. Let me go!"

"What's your name?"

"You've made a mistake. Let me go!" A crowd of gaping, gawking onlookers was now surrounding the store.

Malcolm Sun turned to Armstrong. "He's a ripe one, sir. Doesn't understand very good Russian. I'm afraid we'll have to take him in," he said with a twisted smile.

"Sergeant, get the Black Maria."

"Yes sir." Another agent went off quickly as Armstrong went closer. The Russian was gray-haired, a squat man with small, angry eyes. He was held perfectly with no chance of escape and no chance to put a hand into a pocket or into his mouth to destroy evidence, or himself.

Armstrong searched him expertly. No manual or roll of film. "Where did you put it?" he asked.

"I no understand!"

The man's hatred did not bother Armstrong. He bore him no malice, the man was just a target who had been trapped. I wonder who shopped this poor bugger who's frightened to death, rightly, who's now ruined with the KGB and with his own people forever and might as well be a dead man. I wonder why it's our coup and not old Rosemont's and his CIA boys? How is it we're the ones who knew about the drop and not the Yanks? How is it Crosse got to know about this? All Crosse had told him was the where and the how and that the drop was going to be made by a sailor from the carrier and intercepted by someone off the *Ivanov*.

"You're in charge, Robert, and please, don't make a balls up."

"I won't. But please get someone else for Brian K—"

"For the last time, Robert, you're doing the Kwok interrogation and you're seconded to SI until I release you. And if you bitch once more I'll have you out of the force, out of Hong Kong, out of your pension and I hardly need remind you SI's reach is very long. I doubt if you'd work again, unless you go criminal, and then God help you. Is that finally clear?"

"Yes sir."

"Good. Brian will be ready for you at six tomorrow morning."

Armstrong shivered. How impossibly lucky we were to catch him! If Spectacles Wu hadn't come from Ning-tok—if the old *amah* hadn't talked to the Werewolf—if the run on the bank—Christ, so many ifs. But then that's how you catch a fish, a big fish. Pure, bloody, unadulterated luck most times. Jesus Christ, Brian Kwok! You poor bugger!

He shivered again.

"You all right, sir?" Malcolm Sun asked.

"Yes." Armstrong looked back at the Russian. "Where did you put the film, the roll of film?"

The man stared back at him defiantly. "Don't understand!"

Armstrong sighed. "You do, too well." The big black van came through the gawking crowd and stopped. More SIs got out. "Put him in and don't let go of him," Armstrong said to those holding him. The crowd watched and chattered and jeered as the man was frog-marched into the van. Armstrong and Sun got in after him and closed the door.

"Off you go, driver," Armstrong ordered.

"Yes sir." The driver let in his clutch easing through the crowds and joined the snarled traffic heading for Central HQ.

"All right, Malcolm. You can begin."

The Chinese agent took out a razor-sharp knife. The Soviet man blanched.

"What's your name?" Armstrong asked, sitting on a bench opposite him.

Malcolm Sun repeated the question in Russian.

"D . . . Dimitri Metkin," the man muttered, still held viselike by the four men and unable to move a finger or a toe. "Seaman, first class."

"Liar," Armstrong said easily. "Go ahead, Malcolm."

Malcolm Sun put the knife under the man's left eye and the man almost fainted. "That comes later, spy," Sun said in Russian with a chilling smile. Expertly, with a deliberate malevolent viciousness, Sun rapidly sliced the raincoat away. Armstrong searched it very carefully as Sun used the knife deftly to cut away the man's seaman's jersey and the rest of his clothes until he was naked. The knife had not cut or even nicked him once. A careful search and re-search revealed nothing. Nor his shoes, the heels or the soles.

"Unless it's a microdot transfer and we've missed it so far, it must be in him," Armstrong said.

At once the men holding the Russian bent him over and Sun got out the surgical gloves and surgical salve and probed deeply. The man flinched and moaned and tears of pain seeped from his eyes.

"*Dew neh loh moh,*" Sun said happily. His fingers drew out a small tube of cellophane wrapping.

"Don't let go of him!" Armstrong rapped.

When he was sure the man was secure he peered at the cylindrical package. Inside he could see the double-ended circles of a film cartridge. "Looks like a Minolta," he said absently.

Using some tissues he wrapped the cellophane carefully and sat down opposite the man again. "Mr. Metkin, you're charged under the Official Secrets Act for taking part in an espionage act against Her Majesty's Government and her allies. Anything you say will be taken down and used in evidence against you. Now, sir," he continued gently, "you're caught. We're all Special Intelligence and not subject to normal laws, any more than your own KGB is. We don't want to hurt you but we can hold you forever if we want, in solitary if we want. We would like a little cooperation. Just the answers to a few questions. If you refuse we will extract the information we require. We use a lot of your KGB techniques and we can, sometimes, go a little better." He saw a flash of terror behind the man's eyes but something told him this man would be hard to crack.

"What's your real name? Your official KGB name?"

The man stared at him.

"What's your KGB rank?"

The man still stared.

Armstrong sighed. "I can let my Chinese friends have at you, old chum, if you prefer. They really don't like you at all. Your Soviet armies ran all over Malcolm Sun's village in Manchuria and wiped it out and his family. Sorry, but I really must have your official KGB name, your rank on the *Sovetsky Ivanov* and official position."

Another hostile silence.

Armstrong shrugged. "Go ahead, Malcolm."

Sun reached up and jerked the ugly-looking crowbar from its clip and as the four men turned Metkin roughly onto his stomach and spreadeagled him, Sun inserted the tip. The man screamed. "Wait . . . wait . . ." he gasped in guttural English, "wait . . . I'm Dimitri . . ." Another scream. "Nicoli Leonov, major, political commissaaaar . . ."

"That's enough, Malcolm," Armstrong said, astonished by the importance of their catch.

"But sir . . ."

"That's enough," Armstrong said harshly, deliberately protective as Sun was deliberately hostile and angrily slammed the crowbar back into its clips. "Pull him up," he ordered, sorry for the man, the indignity of it. But he had never known the trick to fail to produce a real name and rank, if done at once. It was a trick because they would never probe deeply and the first scream was always from panic and not from pain. Unless the enemy agent broke at once they would always stop and then, at head-quarters, put him through a proper monitored interrogation. Torture wasn't necessary though some zealots used it against orders. This is a dangerous profession, he thought grimly. KGB methods are rougher, and Chinese have a different attitude to life and death, victor and vanquished, pain and pleasure—and the value of a scream.

"Don't take it badly, Major Leonov," he said kindly when the others had pulled him up and sat him back on the bench, still holding him tightly. "We don't want to harm you—or let you harm yourself."

Metkin spat at him and began to curse, tears of terror and rage and frustration running down his face. Armstrong nodded at Malcolm Sun who took out the prepared pad and held it firmly over Metkin's nose and mouth.

The heavy, sick-sweet stench of chloroform filled the stuffy atmosphere. Metkin struggled impotently for a moment, then subsided. Armstrong checked his eyes and his pulse to make sure he was not feigning unconsciousness. "You can let him go now," he told them. "You all did very well. I'll see a commendation goes on all your records. Malcolm, we'd better take good care of him. He might suicide."

"Yes." Sun sat back with the others in the swaying van. It was grinding along in the heavy traffic irritatingly, stopping and starting. Later he said what was in all their minds. "Dimitri Metkin, alias Nicoli Leonov, major, KGB, off the *Ivanov*, and her political commissar. What's a big fish like that doing on a small job like this?"

48

Linc Bartlett chose his tie carefully. He was wearing a pale blue shirt and light tan suit and the tie was tan with a red stripe. A beer was open on the chest of drawers, the can pearled from the cold. All day he had debated with himself whether he should call for Orlanda or not call for her, whether he should tell Casey or not tell Casey.

The day had been fine for him. First, breakfast with Orlanda and then out to Kai Tak to check his airplane and make sure he could use it, for the flight with Dunross to Taipei. Lunch with Casey, then the excitement of the exchange. After the exchange had closed he and Casey had caught the ferry to Kowloon. Canvas storm shades lashed against the rain shut out the view and made the deck claustrophobic and the crossing not pleasant. But it was pleasant with Casey, his awareness of her heightened by the knowledge of Orlanda, and the dilemma.

"Ian's had it, hasn't he, Linc?"

"I'd think so, sure. But he's smart, the battle's not over yet, only the first attack."

"How can he get back? His stock's at bargain prices."

"Compared to last week, sure, but we don't know his earning ratio. This exchange's like a yo-yo—you said so yourself—and dangerous. Ian was right in that."

"I'll bet he knows about the 2 million you put up with Gornt."

"Maybe. It's nothing he wouldn't do if he had the chance. You meeting Seymour and Charlie Forrester?"

"Yes. The Pan Am flight's on time and I've a limo coming. I'll leave soon as we get back. You think they'll want dinner?"

"No. They'll be jet-lagged to hell." He had grinned. "I hope." Both Seymour Steigler III, their attorney, and Charlie Forrester, the head of their foam division, were socially very hard going. "What time's their flight in?"

"4:50. We'll be back around six."

At six they had had a meeting with Seymour Steigler—Forrester was unwell and had gone straight to bed.

Their attorney was a New Yorker, a handsome man with wavy black-gray hair and dark eyes and dark rings under his eyes. "Casey filled me in on the details, Linc," he said. "Looks like we're in great shape."

By prior arrangement, Bartlett and Casey had laid out the whole deal to their attorney, excluding the secret arrangement with Dunross about his ships.

"There're a couple of clauses I'd want in, to protect us, Linc," Steigler said.

"All right. But I don't want the deal renegotiated. We want a wrap by Tuesday, just as we've laid it out."

"What about Rothwell-Gornt? Best I should feel them out, huh? We can kite Struan's."

"No," Casey had said. "You leave Gornt and Dunross alone, Seymour." They had not told Steigler about Bartlett's private deal with Gornt either. "Hong Kong's more complicated than we thought. Best leave it as it is."

"That's right," Bartlett said. "Leave Gornt and Dunross to Casey and me. You just deal with their attorneys."

"What're they like?"

"English. Very proper," Casey said. "I met with John Dawson at noon —he's their senior partner. Dunross was supposed to be there but he sent Jacques deVille instead. He's one of Struan's directors, deals with all their corporate affairs, and some financing. Jacques is very good but Dunross runs everything and decides everything. That's the bottom line."

"How about getting this, er, Dawson on the phone right now? I'll meet with him over breakfast, say here at eight."

Bartlett and Casey had laughed. "No way, Seymour!" she had said. "It'll be a leisurely in by ten and a two-hour lunch. They eat and drink like there's no tomorrow, and everything's the 'old boy' bit."

"Then I'll meet him after lunch when he's mellow and maybe we can teach him a trick or two," Seymour Steigler had said, his eyes hardening. He stifled a yawn. "I've got to call New York before I hit the sack. Hey, I've got all the papers on the GXR merger an—"

"I'll take those, Seymour," Casey said.

"And I bought the 200,000 block of Rothwell-Gornt at 23.50—what're they today?"

"21."

"Jesus, Linc, you're down 300 grand," Casey said, perturbed. "Why not sell and buy back? If and when."

"No. We'll hold the stock." Bartlett was not worried about the Rothwell stock loss for he was well ahead on his share of Gornt's selling-short ploy. "Why don't you quit for the night, Seymour? If you're up we'll have breakfast—the three of us—say about eight?"

"Good idea. Casey, you'll fix me with Dawson?"

"First thing. They'll see you in the morning sometime. The tai-pan . . . Ian Dunross's told them our deal's top priority."

"It should be," Steigler said. "Our down payment gets Dunross off the hook."

"If he survives," Casey said.

"Here today, gone tomorrow so let's enjoy!"

It was one of Steigler's standard sayings and the phrase was still ringing in Bartlett's head. Here today, gone tomorrow . . . like the fire last night. That could've been bad. I could've bashed my head in the way that poor bastard Pennyworth did. You never know when it's your turn, your accident, your bullet or your act of God. From outside or inside. Like Dad! Jesus—bronzed and healthy, hardly sick a day in his life, then the doc says he's got the big C and in three months he's wasted away and stinking and dying in great pain.

Bartlett felt a sudden sweat on his forehead. It had been a bad time then, during his divorce, burying his father, his mother distraught and everything falling apart. Then finalizing the divorce. The settlement had been vicious but he had just managed to retain control of the companies, to pay her off without having to sell out. He was still paying even though she'd remarried—along with an escalating maintenance for his children as well as future settlements—every cent still hurting, not the money itself but the unfairness of California law, the attorney in for a third until death us do part, screwed by my attorney and hers. One day I'll have vengeance on them, Bartlett grimly promised himself again. On them and all the other goddamn parasites.

With an effort he thrust them aside. For today.

Here today, gone tomorrow, so let's enjoy, he repeated as he sipped his beer, tied his tie and looked at himself in the mirror. Without vanity. He liked living within himself and he had made his peace with himself, knowing who he was and what he was about. The war had helped him do that. And surviving the divorce, surviving her, finding out about her and living with it—Casey the only decent thing that whole year.

Casey.

What about Casey?

Our rules are quite clear, always have been. She set them: If I have a date or she has a date, we have dates and no questions and no recriminations.

Then why is it I'm all uptight now that I've decided to see Orlanda without telling Casey?

He glanced at his watch. Almost time to go.

There was a half-hearted knock on the door and instantly it opened and Nighttime Song beamed at him. "Missee," the old man announced and stepped aside. Casey was approaching down the corridor, a sheaf of papers and a notebook in her hand.

"Oh hi, Casey," Bartlett said. "I was just going to phone you."

"Hi, Linc," she called out and then said, "*Doh jeh,*" in Cantonese to the old man as she passed. Her walk was happy as she came into the two-bedroom suite. "Got some stuff for you." She handed him a sheaf of telexes and letters and went to the cocktail bar to pour herself a dry martini. She wore casual, slim-fitting gray pants and flat gray shoes with a gray silk open-necked shirt. Her hair was tied back and a pencil left there was her only decoration. Tonight she was wearing glasses, not her usual contacts. "The first couple deal with the GXR merger. It's all signed, sealed and delivered, and we take possession September 2. There's a board meeting confirmed at 3:00 P.M. in L.A.—that gives us plenty of time to get back. I've ask—"

"Turn down bed, Master?" Nighttime Song interrupted importantly from the door.

Bartlett started to say no, but Casey was already shaking her head. "*Um ho,*" she said pleasantly in Cantonese, pronouncing the words well and with care. "*Cha z'er, doh jeh.*" No thank you, please do it later.

Nighttime Song stared at her blankly. "*Wat?*"

Casey repeated it. The old man snorted, irritated that Golden Pubics had the bad manners to address him in his own language. "Turn down bed, *heya?* Now *heya?*" he asked in bad English.

Casey repeated the Cantonese, again with no reaction, began again then stopped and said wearily in English, "Oh never mind! Not now. You can do it later."

Nighttime Song beamed, having made her lose face. "Yes, Missee." He closed the door with just enough of a slam to make his point.

"Asshole," she muttered. "He had to understand me, I know I said it right, Linc. Why is it they insist on not understanding? I tried it on my maid and all she said was '*wat*' too." She laughed in spite of herself as she aped the coarse guttural, "*Wat you say, heya?*"

Bartlett laughed. "They're just ornery. But where'd you learn Chinese?"

"It's Cantonese. I got a teacher—fitted in an hour this morning—thought I should at least be able to say, Hi, Good morning, Give me the bill please . . . ordinary things. Goddamn but it's complicated. All the tones. In Cantonese there are seven tones—seven ways of saying the same word. You ask for the check, it's *mai dan,* but if you say it just a little wrong, it means fried eggs, they're *mai dan* too, and one'll get you fifty the waiter'll bring you the fried eggs just to put you down." She sipped her martini and added an extra olive. "I needed that. You want another beer?"

Bartlett shook his head. "This's fine." He had read all the telexes.

Casey sat on the sofa and opened her notepad. "Vincenzo Banastasio's secretary phoned and asked me to confirm his suite for Saturday an—"

"I didn't know he was due in Hong Kong. You?"

"I think I remember him saying something about going to Asia the last time we saw him . . . at the track last month—at Del Mar—the time John Chen was there. Terrible about John, isn't it?"

"I hope they get those Werewolves. Bastards to murder him and put that sign on him like that."

"I wrote a condolence note for us to his father and to his wife Dianne—you remember we met her at Ian's and at Aberdeen—Jesus, that seems like a million years ago."

"Yes." Bartlett frowned. "I still don't remember Vincenzo saying anything. He staying here?"

"No, he wants to be Hong Kong side. I confirmed the booking at the Hilton by phone and I'll do it in person tomorrow. He's on JAL's Saturday morning flight from Tokyo." Casey peered at him over her glasses. "You want me to schedule a meeting?"

"How long's he staying?"

"Over the weekend. A few days. You know how vague he is. How about Saturday after the races? We'll be Hong Kong side and it's an easy walk from Happy Valley if we can't get a ride."

Bartlett was going to say, Let's make it Sunday, but then he remembered Taipei on Sunday. "Sure, Saturday after the races." Then he saw her look. "What?"

"I was just wondering what Banastasio's about."

"When he bought 4 percent of our Par-Con stock," he said, "we ran it through Seymour, the SEC and a few others and they're all satisfied his money was clean. He's never been arrested or charged, though there're a lot of rumors. He's never given us any trouble, never wanted in on any board, never turns up for any shareholder meetings, always gives me his proxy, and he came through with the money when we needed it." He stared at her. "So?"

"So nothing, Linc. You know my opinion of him. I agree we can't take the stock back. He bought it free and clear and asked first, and we sure as hell needed his money and put it to great use." She adjusted her glasses and made a note. "I'll fix the meeting and be polite as always. Next: Our company account at the Victoria Bank's operating. I put in 25,000 and here's your checkbook. We've established a revolving fund and First Central's ready to transfer the initial 7 million to the account whenever we say so. There's a confirm telex there. I also opened a personal account for you at the same bank—here's your checkbook with another 25 grand—20 in an HK treasury bill on a daily rollover." She grinned. "That should buy a couple of bowls of chop suey and a good piece of jade though I hear the phonies are hard to tell from the real ones."

"No jade." Bartlett wanted to look at his watch but he did not, just sipped his beer. "Next?"

"Next: Clive Bersky called and asked a favor."

"You told him to blow it out of his muffler?"

She laughed. Clive Bersky was chief executive of their branch of the First Central of New York. He was very meticulous, pedantic and drove

Bartlett crazy with his need for perfect documentation. "He asks that if the Struan deal goes through, we put our funds through the . . ." She referred to her pad. ". . . the Royal Belgium and Far East Bank here."

"Why them?"

"I don't know. I'm checking them out. We've a date for a drink with the local chief exec at eight. The First Central's just bought his bank—it's got branches here, Singapore, Tokyo."

"You deal with him, Casey."

"Sure. I can drink and run. You want to eat afterwards? We could go down to the Escoffier or up to the Seven Dragons or maybe walk up Nathan Road for some Chinese chow. Somewhere close—the weatherman says more rain's expected."

"Thanks but not tonight. I'm going Hong Kong side."

"Oh? Wh—" Casey stopped. "Fine. When are you leaving?"

"About now. No hurry." Bartlett saw the same easy smile on her face as her eyes went down the list but he was sure she had instantly realized where he was going and suddenly he was furious. He kept his voice calm. "What else do you have?"

"Nothing that won't wait," she said in the same nice voice. "I've an early meeting with Captain Jannelli about your Taipei trip—Armstrong's office sent over the documentation temporarily lifting the impounding on the airplane. All you have to do is sign the form agreeing to come back to H.K. I put Tuesday on it. Is that right?"

"Sure. Tuesday's D Day."

She got up. "That's it for tonight, Linc. I'll deal with the banker and the rest of this stuff." She finished her martini and put the glass back on the mirrored cabinet. "Hey that tie, Linc! Your blue one'd go better. See you at breakfast." She blew him her usual kiss and walked off as she usually did and closed the door with her usual, "Sweet dreams, Linc!"

"Why the hell'm I so goddamn mad?" he muttered angrily, out loud. "Casey's done nothing. Son of a bitch!" Unaware, he had crushed his empty beer can. Son of a bitch! Now what? Do I forget it and go or what?

Casey was walking up the corridor toward her own room, seething. I'll bet my life he's going out with that goddamn tramp. I should've drowned her while I had the chance.

Then she noticed that Nighttime Song had opened her door for her and was holding it wide with a smile she read as a smirk.

"Andyoucanblowitoutofyourasstoo!" she snarled at him before she could stop herself, then slammed the door and threw her papers and pad on the bed and was about to cry. "You're not to cry," she ordered herself out loud, tears on the words. "No goddamn man is going to get you down no way. No way!" She stared down at her fingers, which were trembling with the rage that possessed her.

"Oh shit on all men!"

49

7:40 P.M.:

"Excuse me, your Excellency, you're wanted on the phone."

"Thank you, John." Sir Geoffrey Allison turned back to Dunross and the others. "If you'll excuse me a moment, gentlemen?"

They were in Government House, the governor's official residence above Central, the French doors open to the cool of the evening, the air fresh and washed, trees and shrubs dripping nicely, and the governor walked across the crowded anteroom where predinner cocktails and snacks were being served, very pleased with the way the evening had gone so far. Everyone seemed to be having a good time. There was banter and good conversation, some laughter and no friction yet between the Hong Kong tai-pans and the MPs. At his request, Dunross had gone out of his way to soothe Grey and Broadhurst, and even Grey seemed to have mellowed.

The aide closed the door of his study, leaving him alone with the telephone. The study was dark green and pleasing, with blue flock wallpaper, fine Persian carpets from his two-year sojourn in the Teheran embassy, cherished crystal and silver and more showcases with fine Chinese porcelains. "Hello?"

"Sorry to bother you, sir," Crosse said.

"Oh hello, Roger." The governor felt his chest tighten. "No bother," he said.

"Two rather good pieces of information, sir. Somewhat important. I wonder if I might drop by?"

Sir Geoffrey glanced at the porcelain clock on the mantel over the fireplace. "Dinner's served in fifteen minutes, Roger. Where are you now?"

"Just three minutes away from you, sir. I won't delay your dinner. But, if you prefer, I could make it afterwards."

"Come now, I could use some good news. With this whole banking affair and the stock market . . . Use the garden door if you wish. John will meet you."

"Thank you, sir." The phone clicked off. By custom, the head of SI had a key to the iron garden gate which was set into the high surrounding walls.

In exactly three minutes Crosse was crossing the terrace, walking lightly. The ground was very wet. He dried his feet carefully before he came through the French windows. "We've caught a rather big fish, sir, an enemy agent, caught him with his hands in the honey pot," he said softly. "He's a major, KGB, off the *Ivanov,* and her political commissar. We caught him in the middle of an espionage act with an American computer expert off the nuclear carrier."

The governor's face had gone red. "That blasted *Ivanov!* Good God, Roger, a major? Have you any idea of the diplomatic and political storm this will precipitate with the USSR, the U.S. and London?"

"Yes sir. That's why I thought I'd better consult at once."

"What the devil was the fellow doing?"

Crosse gave him the broad facts. He ended, "Both of them are sedated now and very safe."

"What was on the film?"

"It was blank, sir, fogged. Wh—"

"What?"

"Yes. Of course both men denied any espionage was involved. The sailor denied there was a drop, denied everything, said he'd won the $2,000 U.S. we found on him playing poker. Childish to lie once you're caught, childish to make things difficult, we always get the truth eventually. I thought we'd either missed the real film or it was a microdot transfer. We re-searched their clothing and I ordered immediate emetics and stool examinations. Major . . . the KGB agent passed the real negative film an hour ago." Crosse offered the big manila envelope. "These're eight-by-ten prints, sir, frame by frame."

The governor did not open the envelope. "What are they of? In general?"

"One set shows part of the ship's radar guidance system manual." Crosse hesitated. "The other set's a photocopy of a complete manifest of the carrier's arsenal, ammunition, missiles and warheads. Quantities, qualities, their numbers and where stored in the ship."

"Jesus Christ! Including nuclear warheads? No, please don't answer that." Sir Geoffrey stared at Crosse. After a pause he said, "Well, Roger, it's marvelous that the information didn't get into enemy hands. You're to be congratulated. Our American friends will be equally relieved, and they'll owe you a number of very great favors. Good God, in expert hands that knowledge would lay bare the ship's entire strike capability!"

"Yes sir." Crosse smiled thinly.

Sir Geoffrey studied him.

"But what to do about this major of yours?"

"I would send the major to London with a special escort by RAF transport at once. I think they should do the debriefing there even though we're better equipped, more practiced, and more efficient here. My worry is that his superiors will surely know within an hour or so and might attempt to rescue him or to render him useless. They might even use extreme diplomatic pressure to force us to release him to the *Ivanov*. Besides, when the PRC and Nationalists hear we've caught such an official, they might try to acquire him themselves."

"What about the American sailor?"

"It might be politic to turn him over to the CIA at once, with the negative of the film and these—they're the only prints I made. I developed and made them myself for obvious security reasons. I suspect Rosemont would be the best person."

"Ah yes, Rosemont. He's here now."

"Yes sir."

Sir Geoffrey's eyes hardened. "You have copies of all my guest lists, Roger?"

"No sir. Half an hour ago I called the consulate to find out where he was. They told me."

Sir Geoffrey looked back at him under his shaggy eyebrows, disbelieving him, sure that the chief of SI did know whom he invited and when. Never mind, he thought testily, that's his job. And I'll bet a golden guinea to a doughnut that these prints aren't the only copies Roger made, for he knows our Admiralty would love to see them too and it's his duty to provide them. "Could this have any connection with the AMG business?"

"No. No not at all," Crosse said and the governor thought he heard the momentary flutter in Crosse's voice. "I don't think there's any connection."

Sir Geoffrey got out of the tall chair and paced for a moment, his mind sifting possibilities. Roger's right. Chinese Intelligence on both sides of the bamboo fence are bound to find out quickly, as every one of our Chinese police has PRC or Nationalist sympathies. So it's far better to have the spy out of reach. Then no one will be tempted—at least, not here. "I think I should chat with the minister at once."

"Perhaps, under the circumstances, sir, you could *inform* the minister what I've done about the major—sending him to London under es—"

"He's already gone?"

"No sir. But it's well within my authority to expedite that—if you agree."

Thoughtfully Sir Geoffrey glanced again at the clock. At length he said with a small smile, "Very well. It's lunchtime now in London, I'll *inform* him in an hour or so. Is that sufficient time?"

"Oh yes, thank you, sir. Everything's arranged."

"I presumed it was."

"I'll breathe a lot easier when the fellow's en route home, sir. Thank you."

"Yes. And the sailor?"

"Perhaps you could *ask* the minister to approve our handing him over to Rosemont, sir."

There were a dozen questions Sir Geoffrey would like to have asked but he asked none of them. From long experience he knew he was not a good liar, so the less he knew the better. "Very well. Now, what's the second piece of 'good' news. I trust this will be better."

"We've caught the mole, sir."

"Ah! Good. Excellent! Very good. Who?"

"Senior Superintendent Kwok."

"Impossible!"

Crosse kept the pleasure off his face. "I agree, sir. Even so, Superintendent Kwok's a Communist mole and spy for the PRC." Crosse related how Brian Kwok's cover had been penetrated. "I suggest Superintendent Armstrong should get a commendation—also Spectacles Wu. I'm taking him into SI, sir."

Sir Geoffrey was staring out of the window, stunned. "Bless my soul! Young Brian! Why? He would have been an assistant commissioner in a year or two. . . . I suppose there's no mistake?"

"No sir. As I said, the proof is irrefutable. Of course, we don't know the how or the why yet but we soon will."

Sir Geoffrey heard the finality and he saw the thin, hard face and cold eyes and he felt very sorry for Brian Kwok, whom he had liked for many years. "Keep me advised about him. Perhaps we can discover what makes a man like that do such a thing. Good God, such a charming chap and a first-class cricketer too. Yes, keep me advised."

"Certainly, sir." Crosse got up. "Interesting. I could never understand why he was always so anti-American—it was his only flaw. Now it's obvious. I should have spotted that. Sorry sir, and sorry to interrupt your evening."

"You're to be congratulated, Roger. If the Soviet agent's being sent to London perhaps Brian Kwok should go too? The same reasons would apply to him?"

"No sir. No I don't think so. We can deal with Kwok here much quicker and better. We're the ones who need to know what he knows— London wouldn't understand. Kwok's a threat to Hong Kong, not to Britain. He's a PRC asset—the other man's Soviet. The two don't parallel."

Sir Geoffrey sighed heavily, knowing Crosse was right. "I agree. This has really been a quite dreadful day, Roger. First the bank runs, then the stock market . . . the deaths last night, poor Sir Charles Pennyworth and Toxe's wife . . . and this morning the Aberdeen mud-slide deaths . . . the Noble House's tottering . . . it looks as though this storm front's developing into a blasted typhoon which will probably wreck Saturday's racing . . . and now all your news, an American sailor betrays his country and ship and honor for a paltry $2,000?"

Crosse smiled his thin smile again. "Perhaps $2,000 wasn't paltry to him."

We live in terrible times, Sir Geoffrey was going to say, but he knew it was not the times. It was merely that people were people, that greed pride lust avarice jealousy gluttony anger and the bigger lust for power or money ruled people and would rule them forever. Most of them.

"Thank you for coming, Roger. Again, you're to be congratulated. I will so inform the minister. Good night."

He watched Crosse walk off, tall, confident and deadly. When the iron door in the high wall had been bolted behind him by his aide, Sir Geoffrey Allison allowed the real unasked question to surface once more.

Who's the mole in my police?

AMG's paper was quite clear. The traitor's a Soviet asset, not from the PRC. Brian Kwok has been flushed out by chance. Why didn't Roger point out the obvious?

Sir Geoffrey shuddered. If Brian could be a mole anyone could. Anyone.

50

Almost before he took his finger off the bell the door swung open.

"Oh, Linc," Orlanda said breathlessly, her happiness spilling over, "I'd given you up. Please come in!"

"Sorry to be late," Bartlett said, taken aback by her beauty and marvelous warmth. "The traffic's snarled to hell and the ferries jammed and I couldn't get to a phone."

"You're here so you're not late, not at all. I was just afraid that . . ." Then she added in a rush, "I was afraid you wouldn't come back tonight and then I'd've been shattered. There, I've said it and all my defenses are down but I'm so happy to see you I don't care." She stood on tiptoe and kissed him a swift happy kiss, took his arm and shut the door behind them.

Her perfume was delicate and barely there but he felt it as a physical presence. The dress she wore was knee-length white chiffon that sighed as she moved, close at the wrists and neck. It showed but somehow didn't quite show her golden skin. "I'm so happy you're here," she said again and took his umbrella and put it into a rack.

"So am I."

The room was prettier by night, mostly candlelit, the tall glass doors of the terrace open to the air. They were just below the overcast and the city sprawled down the mountain to the sea, the lights misting from time to time as whiskers of the low clouds passed by. Sea level was seven hundred feet below. Kowloon was dim and the harbor dim but he knew the ships were there and he could see the huge carrier at the wharf, her great angled deck floodlit, the needle-nosed jets floodlit, her battle-gray bridge reaching for the sky—the Stars and Stripes hanging damp and listless.

"Hey," he said, leaning on the terrace railing, "what a great night, Orlanda."

"Oh yes, yes it is. Come and sit down."

"I'd rather look at the view, if it's okay."

"Of course, anything you want's fine, anything. That suit's great on you, Linc, and I love your tie." She said it happily, wanting to compliment him even though she did not think the tie matched too well. Never mind, she thought, he's just not color conscious like Quillan, and needs helping. I'll do what Quillan taught me to do, not criticize but go out and buy one I like and give it to him. If he likes it, marvelous, if not never mind, for what does it matter—he's the one who's wearing it. Blue, blue would match Linc's eyes and go better with that shirt. "You dress very well."

"Thanks, so do you." He was remembering what Casey had said about his tie and how furious he had been with her tonight all the way across the ferry, all the time waiting for a cab, and the old woman who had trod on his foot shoving past to usurp his cab but he had foiled her and cursed her back.

It was only now that his rage-temperature had vanished. It was Orlanda's pleasure at seeing me that did it, he told himself. It's years since Casey lit up like a Christmas tree or said anything when I . . . the hell with that. I'm not going to worry about Casey tonight. "The view's fantastic and you're as pretty as a picture!"

She laughed. "So're you and . . . *oh your drink*, sorry . . ." She whirled away for the kitchen, her skirt flying. "I don't know why but you make me feel like a schoolgirl," she called out. In a moment she came back. On the tray was an earthenware pot of pâté and rounds of fresh toast and a bottle of iced beer. "I hope this's right."

It was Anweiser. "How did you know my brand?"

"You told me this morning, don't you remember?" Her warmth flooded over again at his obvious pleasure. "Also that you like drinking it out of the bottle."

He took it and grinned at her. "Is that going to be in the article too?"

"No. No, I've decided not to write about you."

He saw her sudden seriousness. "Why?"

She was pouring herself a glass of white wine. "I decided I could never do you justice in an article so I won't write one. Besides, I don't think you'd like that hanging over you." Her hand went to her heart. "Cross my heart and hope to die, no article, everything private. No article, no journalism, I swear by the Madonna," she added, meaning it.

"Hey, no need to be dramatic!"

She was leaning with her back against the railing, an eighty-foot drop to the concrete below. He saw the sincerity in her face and he believed her completely. He was relieved. The article had been the only flaw, the only danger point for him—that and her being a journalist. He leaned forward and kissed her lightly, deliberately lightly. "Sealed with a kiss. Thanks."

"Yes."

They watched the view for a moment.

"Is the rain over for good?"

"I hope not, Linc. We need a good series of storms to fill the reservoirs. Keeping clean's so hard and we still only get water one day in four." She smiled mischievously as a child would. "Last night during the torrent I stripped and bathed here. It was fantastic. The rain was even heavy enough to wash my hair."

The thought of her naked, here, in the night, touched him. "You'd better be careful," he said. "The railing's not that high. I wouldn't want you to slip."

"Strange, I'm frightened to death of the sea but heights don't bother me a bit. You certainly saved my life."

"C'mon! You would have made it without me."

"Perhaps, but you certainly saved my face. Without you there I would surely have disgraced myself. So thanks for my face."

"And that's more important than life out here, isn't it?"

"Sometimes, yes, yes it is. Why do you say that?"

"I was just thinking about Dunross and Quillan Gornt. Those two're having at each other, mostly over face."

"Yes. You're right, of course." She added thoughtfully, "They're both fine men, in one way, both devils in another."

"How do you mean?"

"They're both ruthless, both very very strong, very hard, adept and . . . and well conversed with life." As she talked she heaped one of the rounds of toast with pâté and offered it to him, her nails long and perfect. "The Chinese have a saying: 'Chan ts'ao, chu ken'—when pulling weeds make sure you get rid of the roots. The roots of those two go deep in Asia, very deep, too deep. It would be hard to get rid of those roots." She sipped her wine and smiled a little smile. "And probably not a good idea, not for Hong Kong. Some more pâté?"

"Please. It's wonderful. You make it?"

"Yes. It's an old English recipe."

"Why wouldn't it be good for Hong Kong?"

"Oh, perhaps because they balance each other. If one destroys the other —oh I don't mean just Quillan or Dunross, I mean the *hongs* themselves, the companies, Struan's and Rothwell-Gornt. If one eats up the other, perhaps the remaining one would be too strong, there would certainly be no competition, then perhaps *the* tai-pan would become too greedy, perhaps he'd decide to dump Hong Kong." She smiled hesitantly. "Sorry . . . I'm talking too much. It's just an idea. Another beer?"

"Sure, in a moment, thanks, but that's an interesting thought." Yes, Bartlett was thinking, and one that hadn't occurred to me—or to Casey. Are those two necessary to each other?

And Casey and I? Are we necessary to each other?

He saw her watching him and he smiled back. "Orlanda, it's no secret

I'm thinking about making a deal with one of them. If you were me, which one would you go with?"

"Neither," she said at once and laughed.

"Why?"

"You're not British, not one of the 'old boys,' not a hereditary member of any of the clubs, and however much your money and power here, it's the Old Boy network that will finally decide what is to be." She took his empty bottle and went and brought another.

"You think I couldn't make a go of it?"

"Oh I didn't mean that, Linc. You asked about Struan's or Rothwell-Gornt, about going into business with one of *them*. If you do, they'll be the winners in the end."

"They're that smart?"

"No. But they're Asian, they belong here. Here the saying is, *T'ien hsia wu ya i pan hei*'—all crows under heaven are black—meaning that all the tai-pans are the same and they'll all stick together to destroy the out-sider."

"So neither Ian nor Quillan would welcome a partner?"

She hesitated. "I think I'm getting out of my depth, Linc. I don't know about business things. It's just that I've never heard of an American who's come here and made it big."

"What about Biltzmann, Superfoods and their takeover of H.K. Gen-eral Stores?"

"Biltzmann's a joke. Everyone hates him and hopes he'll fall on his face, even Pug . . . Pugmire. Quillan's sure he will. No, even Cooper and Tillman didn't make it. They were Yankee traders in the first days, Linc, opium traders—they were even under Dirk Struan's protection. They're even related, the Struans and the Coopers. Hag Struan married her eldest daughter, Emma, to old Jeff Cooper, Old Hook Nose was his nickname when he was in his dotage, the story is that the marriage was payment for his helping her destroy Tyler Brock. Have you heard about them, Linc? The Brocks, Sir Morgan and his father Tyler, and the Hag?"

"Peter Marlowe told us some of the stories."

"If you want to know about the real Hong Kong, you should talk to Auntie Bright Eyes—that's Sarah Chen, Phillip Chen's maiden aunt! She's a great character, Linc, and sharp as a needle. She says she's eighty-eight. I think she's older. Her father was Sir Gordon Chen, Dirk Struan's illegit-imate son by his mistress Kai-Sung, and her mother was the famous beauty Karen Yuan."

"Who's she?"

"Karen Yuan was Robb Struan's granddaughter. Robb was Dirk's half-brother and he had a mistress called Yau Ming Soo with whom he had a daughter Isobel. Isobel married John Yuan, an illegitimate son of Jeff Coo-per. John Yuan became a well-known pirate and opium smuggler, and Isobel died quite notorious as an enormous gambler who had lost two of her husbands' fortunes playing mah-jong. So it was Isobel and John's daughter, Karen, who married Sir Gordon Chen—actually she was his second wife, more like a concubine really, though it was a perfectly legal marriage. Here, even today, if you're Chinese you can legally have as many wives as you like."

"That's convenient!"

"For a man!" Orlanda smiled. "So this tiny branch of the Yuans are Cooper descendents—the T'Chungs and Chens are from Dirk Struan, the Sungs, Tups and Tongs from Aristotle Quance the painter—here in Hong Kong it's the custom for the children to take the name of their mother, usually an insignificant girl who was sold to the pillow by her parents."

"By the parents?"

"Almost always," she told him casually. " 'T'ung t'ien yu ming'—listen to heaven and follow fate. Particularly when you're starving." She shrugged. "There's no shame in that, Linc, no loss of face, not in Asia."

"How come you know so much about the Struans and Coopers and mistresses and so on?"

"This is a small place and we all love secrets but there are no real secrets in Hong Kong. Insiders—true insiders—know almost everything about the others. As I said, our roots go deep here. And don't forget that the Chens, Yuans and Sungs are Eurasian. As I told you, Eurasians marry Eurasians, so we should know who we're from. We're not desired by British or Chinese as wives or husbands, only as mistresses or lovers." She sipped her wine and he was awed by the delicacy of her movements, her grace. "It's custom for Chinese families to have their genealogy written down in the village book, that's the only legality they have—that gives them continuity, they've never had birth certificates." She smiled up at him. "To go back to your question. Both Ian Dunross and Quillan would welcome your money and your inside track into the U.S. market. And with either one you'd make a profit here—if you were content to be a silent partner."

Thoughtfully Bartlett let his eyes stray to the view.

She waited patiently, allowing him his thoughts, staying motionless. I'm very glad Quillan was such a good teacher and such a clever man, she thought. And oh so wise. He was right again.

This morning she had called him in tears on his private line to report what had happened and, "Oh Quillan, I think I've ruined everything. . . ."

"What did you say and what did he say?"

She had told him exactly and he had reassured her. "I don't think you've any need to worry, Orlanda. He'll come back. If not tonight, tomorrow."

"Oh are you sure?" she had said so gratefully.

"Yes. Now dry those tears and listen." Then he had told her what to do and what to wear and above all to be a woman.

Ah how happy I am to be a woman, she thought, and remembered with sadness now the old days when they were happy together, she and Quillan, she nineteen, already his mistress for two years and no longer shy or afraid—of the pillow or him or of herself—how sometimes they would go on his yacht for a midnight cruise, just the two of them and he would lecture her. "You're a woman and Hong Kong *yan* so if you want to have a good life and pretty things, to be cherished and loved and pillowed and safe in this world be female."

"How, my darling?"

"Think only of my satisfaction and pleasure. Give me passion when I need it, quiet when I need it, privacy when I need it, and happiness and discretion all the time. Cook as a gourmet, know great wine, be discreet always, protect my face always and never nag."

"But Quillan, you make it sound all so one-sided."

"Yes. It is, of course it is. In return I do my part with equal passion. But that's what I want from you, nothing less. You wanted to be my mistress. I put it to you before we began and you agreed."

"I know I did and I love being your mistress but . . . but sometimes I'm worried about the future."

"Ah, my pet, you have nothing to worry about. You know our rules were set in advance. We will renew our arrangement yearly, providing *you* want to until you're twenty-four, and then, if you choose to leave me I will give you the flat, money enough for reasonable needs and a handsome dowry for a suitable husband. We agreed and your parents approved. . . ."

Yes they did. Orlanda remembered how her mother and father had enthusiastically approved the liaison—had even suggested it to her when she had just come back from school in America when they told her that Quillan had asked if he might approach her, saying that he had fallen in love with her. "He's a good man," her father had said, "and he's promised to provide well for you, if you agree. It's your choice, Orlanda. We think we would recommend it."

"But Father, I won't be eighteen until next month, and besides I want to go back to the States to live. I'm sure I can get a Green Card to remain there."

"Yes, you can go, child," her mother had said, "but you will be poor. We can give you nothing, no help. What job will you get? Who will support you? This way in a little while you can go with an income, with property here to support you."

"But he's so old. He's . . ."

"A man doesn't wear age like a woman," both had told her. "He's strong and respected and he's been good to us for years. He's promised to cherish you and the financial arrangements are generous, however long you stay with him."

"But I don't love him."

"You talk nonsense in eight directions! Without the protection of the lips the teeth grow cold!" her mother had said angrily. "This opportunity you are being offered is like the hair of the phoenix and the heart of the dragon! What do you have to do in return? Just be a woman and honor and obey a good man for a few years—renewable yearly—and even after that there's no end to the years if you choose and are faithful and clever. Who knows? His wife is an invalid and wasting. If you satisfy him and cherish him enough why wouldn't he marry you?"

"Marry a Eurasian? Quillan Gornt?" she had burst out.

"Why not? You're not just Eurasian, you're Portuguese. He has British sons and daughters already, *heya*? Times are changing, even here in Hong Kong. If you do your best, who knows? Bear him a son, in a year or two, with his permission, and who knows? Gods are gods and if they want they can make thunder from a clear sky. Don't be stupid! Love? What is that word to you?"

Orlanda Ramos was staring down at the city now, not seeing it. How stupid and naive I was then, she thought. Naive and very stupid. But now I know better. Quillan taught me very well.

She glanced up at Linc Bartlett, moving just her eyes, not wanting to disturb him.

Yes, I'm trained very well, she told herself. I'm trained to be the best wife any man could ever have, that Bartlett will ever have. No mistakes this time. Oh no, no mistakes. Quillan will guide me. He will help remove Casey. I will be Mrs. Linc Bartlett. All gods and all devils bear witness; that is what must happen. . . .

Soon he took his eyes off the city, having thought through what she had said. She was watching him, wearing a little smile that he could not read. "What is it?"

"I was thinking how lucky I was to meet you."

"Do you always compliment a man?"

"No, just the ones who please me—and they're as rare as the hair of the phoenix or the heart of a dragon. Pâté?"

"Thanks." He accepted it. "You're not eating?"

"I'm saving for dinner. I have to watch my diet, I'm not like you."

"I work out daily. Tennis when I can, golf. You?"

"I play a little tennis, I'm a good walker but I'm still taking golf lessons." Yes, she thought, I try very hard to be the best at everything I do and I'm the best for you, Linc Bartlett, in the whole wide world. Her tennis was very good and golf quite good because Quillan had insisted she be adept at both—because he enjoyed them. "Are you hungry?"

"Starving."

"You said Chinese food. Is that what you really want?"

He shrugged. "It doesn't matter to me. Whatever you want."

"Are you sure?"

"Positive. Why, what would you like?"

"Come in a moment."

He followed her. She opened the dining room door. The table was set exquisitely for two. Flowers, and a bottle of Verdicchio on ice. "Linc, I haven't cooked for anyone for such a long time," she said in her breathless rush that he found so pleasing. "But I wanted to cook for you. If you'd like it, I have an Italian dinner all set to go. Fresh pasta *aglio e olio*—garlic and oil—veal *piccata*, a green salad, *zabaglione*, espresso, and brandy. How does that sound? It will only take me twenty minutes and you can read the paper while you wait. Then afterwards we can leave everything for when the *amah* comes back and go dancing or drive. What do you say?"

"Italian's my favorite food, Orlanda!" he told her enthusiastically. Then a vagrant memory surfaced, and for a moment he wondered whom he had told about Italian being his favorite. Was it Casey—or was it Orlanda this morning?

51

Brian Kwok jerked out of sleep. One moment he was in a nightmare, the next awake but somehow still in the deep dark pit of sleep, his heart pounding, his mind disordered and no change between sleep and awake. Panic swamped him. Then he realized he was naked and still in the same warm darkness of the cell and remembered who he was and where he was.

They must have drugged me, he thought. His mouth was parched, his head ached, and he lay back on the mattress that was slimy to his touch and tried to collect himself. Vaguely he remembered being in Armstrong's office and before that with Crosse discussing the 16/2 but after that not much, just waking in this darkness, groping for the walls to get his bearings, feeling them close by, biting back the terror of knowing he was betrayed and defenseless in the bowels of Central Police HQ within a box with no windows and a door somewhere. Then, exhaustedly sleeping and waking and angry voices—or did I dream that—and then sleeping again . . . no, eating first, didn't I eat first . . . yes, slop they called dinner and cold tea . . . Come on, think! It's important to think and to remember . . . Yes, I remember, it was bedraggled stew and cold tea then, later, breakfast. Eggs. Was it eggs first or the stew first and . . . yes the lights came on for a moment each time I ate, just enough time to eat . . . no, the lights went off and each time I finished in darkness, I remember finishing in darkness and hating to eat in darkness and then I peed in the pail in darkness, got back onto the mattress and lay down again.

How long have I been here? Must count the days.

Wearily he swung his legs off the cot and stumbled to a wall, his limbs aching to match his head. Got to exercise, he thought, got to help work the drugs out of my system and get my head clear and ready for the interrogation. Must get my mind ready for when they go at me, really begin—when they think I've softened up—then they'll keep me awake until they break me.

No, they won't break me. I'm strong and prepared and I know some of the pitfalls.

Who gave me away?

The effort to solve that was too much for him so he mustered his strength and did a few weak knee bends. Then he heard muffled footsteps approaching. Hastily he groped back for the cot and lay down, pretending sleep, his heart hurting in his chest as he held down his terror.

The footsteps stopped. A sudden bolt clanged back and a trapdoor opened. A shaft of light came into the cell and a half-seen hand put down a metal plate and a metal cup.

"Eat your breakfast and hurry up," the voice said in Cantonese. "You're due for more interrogation shortly."

"Listen, I want . . ." Brian Kwok called out but the trapdoor had already clanged back and he was alone in the darkness with the echo of his own words.

Keep calm, he ordered himself. Calm yourself and think.

Abruptly the cell flooded with light. The light hurt his eyes. When he had adjusted he saw that the light came from fixtures in the ceiling high above, and he remembered seeing them before. The walls were dark, almost black, and seemed to be pressing inward on him. Don't worry about them, he thought. You've seen the dark cells before and though you've never been part of an in-depth interrogation you know the principles and some of the tricks.

A surge of nausea came into his mouth at the thought of the ordeal ahead.

The door was hardly discernible and the trapdoor equally hidden. He could feel eyes though he could see no spyholes. On the plate were two fried eggs and a thick piece of rough bread. The bread was a little toasted. The eggs were cold and greasy and unappetizing. In the cup was cold tea. There were no utensils.

He drank the tea thirstily, trying to make it last, but it was finished before he knew it and the small amount had not quenched his thirst. *Dew neh loh moh* what I wouldn't give for a toothbrush and a bottle of beer an—

The lights went out as suddenly as they had come on. It took him much time to adjust again to the darkness. Be calm, it's just darkness and light, light and darkness. It's just to confuse and disorient. Be calm. Take each day as it comes, each interrogation as it comes.

His terror returned. He knew he was not really prepared, not experienced enough, though he had had some survival training against capture, what to do if the enemy captured you, the PRC Communist enemy. But the PRC's not the enemy. The real enemy are the British and Canadians who've pretended to be friend and teacher, they're the real enemy.

Don't think about that, don't try to convince yourself, just try to convince them.

I have to hold fast. Have to pretend it's a mistake for as long as I can and then, then I tell the story I've woven over the years and confuse them. That's duty.

His thirst was overpowering. And his hunger.

Brian Kwok wanted to hurl the empty cup against the wall and the plate against the wall and shout and call for help but that would be a mistake. He knew he must have great control and keep every particle of strength he could muster to fight back.

Use your head. Use your training. Put theory into practice. Think about the survival course last year in England. Now what do I do?

He remembered that part of the survival theory was that you must eat and drink and sleep whenever you can for you never know when they will cut off food and drink and sleep from you. And to use your eyes and nose and touch and intelligence to keep track of time in the dark and remember that your captors will always make a mistake sometime, and if you can catch the mistake you can relate to time, and if you can relate to time then you can keep in balance and then you can twist them and not divulge that which must not be divulged—exact names and real contacts. Pit your mind against them was the rule. Keep active, force yourself to observe.

Have they made any mistakes? Have these devil barbarian British slipped yet? Only once, he thought excitedly. The eggs! The stupid British and their eggs for breakfast!

Feeling better now and wide awake, he eased off the cot and groped his way to the metal plate and put the cup down gently beside it. The eggs were cold and the grease congealed but he chewed them and finished the bread and felt a little better for the food. Eating with his fingers in darkness was strange and uncomfortable especially with nothing to wipe his fingers on except his own nakedness.

A shudder went through him. He felt abandoned and unclean. His bladder was uncomfortable and he felt his way to the pail that was attached to the wall. The pail stank.

With an index finger he deftly measured the level in the pail. It was partially full. He emptied himself into it and measured the new level. His mind calculated the difference. If they haven't added to it to confuse me, I've peed three or four times. Twice a day? Or four times a day?

He rubbed his soiled finger against his chest and that made him feel dirtier but it was important to use everything and anything to keep balanced and time related. He lay down again. Out of touch with light or dark or day or night was nauseating. A wave of sickness came from his stomach but he dominated it and forced himself to remember the Brian Kwok who they, the enemy, thought was Brian Kar-shun Kwok and not the other man, the almost forgotten man whose parentage was Wu, his generation name Pah and his adult name Chu-toy.

He remembered Ning-tok and his father and mother and being sent to school to Hong Kong on his sixth birthday, wanting to learn and to grow up to become a patriot like his parents and the uncle he had seen flogged to death in his village square for being a patriot. He had learned from his Hong Kong relations that patriot and Communist were the same and not enemies of the State. That the Kuomintang overlords were just as evil as the foreign devils who had forced the unequal treaties on China, and the only true patriot was he who followed the teachings of Mao Tse-tung. Being sworn into the first of many secret Brotherhoods, working to be the best for the cause of China and Mao which was the cause of China, learning from secret teachers, knowing he was part of the new great wave of revolution that would take back control of China from foreign devils and their lackeys, and sweep them into the sea forever.

Winning that scholarship! At twelve!

Oh how proud his secret teachers had been. Then going to barbarian lands, now perfect in their language and safe against their evil thoughts and ways, going to London, the capital of the greatest empire the world has ever seen, knowing it was going to be humbled and laid waste someday, but then in 1937, still in its last flowering.

Two years there. Hating the English school and the English boys . . . Chinkee Chinkee Chinaman sitting on his tail . . . but hiding it and hiding his tears, his new Brotherhood teachers helping him, guiding him, putting questions and answers into context, showing him the wonder of dialectic, of being part of the true real unquestioned revolution. Never questioning, never a need to question.

Then the German war and being evacuated with all the other school boys and girls to safety in Canada, all that wonderful time in Vancouver, British Columbia, on the Pacific shore, all that immensity, mountains and sea and a thriving Chinatown with good Ning-tok cooking—and a new branch of the world Brotherhood and more teachers, always someone wise to talk to, always someone ready to explain and advise . . . not accepted by his schoolmates but still beating them scholastically, in the gym with gloves and at their sports, being a prefect, playing cricket well and tennis well—part of his training. "Excel, Chu-toy, my son, excel and be patient for the glory of the Party, for the glory of Mao Tse-tung who is China," the last words his father had said to him, secret words engraved since he was six—and repeated on his deathbed.

Joining the Royal Canadian Mounted Police had been part of the plan. It was easy to excel in the RCMP, assigned to Chinatown and the wharves and the byways, speaking English and Mandarin and Cantonese —his Ning-tok dialect buried deep—easy to become a fine policeman in that sprawling beautiful city port. Soon he became unique, Vancouver's Chinese expert, trusted, excelling and implacably against the crimes that the triad gangsters of Chinatown fed off of—opium, morphine, heroin, prostitution and the ever-constant illegal gambling.

His work had been commended by his superiors and by Brotherhood leaders alike—they equally against gang rule and drug traffic and crime, assisting him to arrest and uncover, their only secret interest the inner workings of the RCMP, how the RCMP hire and fire and promote and collate and investigate and watch, and who controls what, where and how. Sent from Vancouver to Ottawa for six months, loaned by a grateful chief of police to assist in an undercover investigation of a Chinese drug ring there, making new important Canadian contacts and Brotherhood contacts, learning more and more and breaking the ring and getting promotion. Easy to control crime and get promotion if you work and if you have secret friends by the hundreds, with secret eyes everywhere.

Then the war ending and applying for a transfer for the Hong Kong Police—the final part of the plan.

But not wanting to go, not wanting to leave, loving Canada, and loving her. Jeannette. Jeannette deBois. She was nineteen, French-Canadian from Montreal, speaking French and English, her parents French-Canadians of many generations and them liking him and not disapproving, not against him because he was the *Chinoise*, as they jokingly called him. He was twenty-one then, already known as commandant material with a great career ahead of him, marriage ahead, a year or so ahead . . .

Brian Kwok shifted on the mattress in misery. His skin felt clammy and the dark was pressing down. He closed his leaden eyelids and let his mind roam back to her and that time, that bad time in his life. He remembered how he had argued with the Brotherhood, the leader, saying he could serve better in Canada than in Hong Kong where he would be only one of many. Here in Canada he was unique. In a few years he would be in Vancouver's police hierarchy.

But all his arguments had failed. Sadly he knew that they were right. He knew that if he had stayed, eventually he would have gone over to the other side, would have broken with the Party. There were too many unanswered questions now, thanks to reading RMCQ reports on the Soviets, the KGB, the *gulags*, too many friends, Canadian and Nationalist, now. Hong Kong and China were remote, his past remote. Jeannette was here, loving her and their life, his souped-up car and prestige among his peers, seeing them as equals, no longer barbarians.

The leader had reminded him of his past, that barbarians are only barbarians, that he was needed in Hong Kong where the battle was just beginning, where Mao was still not yet Chairman Mao, not yet victorious, still embattled with Chiang Kai-shek.

Bitterly he had obeyed, hating being forced, knowing he was in their power and obeying because of their power. But then the heady four years till 1949, and Mao's incredible, unbelievable total victory. Then burrowing deep again, using his brilliant skills to fight the crime that was anathema to him and a disgrace to Hong Kong and a blot on the face of China.

Life was very good again now. He was picked for high promotion, the British bound to him, respecting him because he was from a fine English

public school with a fine upper-class English accent and an English sports-
man like the elite of the Empire before him.

And now it's 1963 and I'm thirty-nine and tomorrow . . . no, not tomorrow, on Sunday, on Sunday it's the hill climb and on Saturday there
are the races and Noble Star—will it be Noble Star or Gornt's Pilot Fish
or Richard Kwok's, no Richard *Kwang's* Butterscotch Lass or John Chen's
outsider, Golden Lady? I think I'd put my money on Golden Lady—every
penny I have, yes, all my life's savings and I'm also gambling the Porsche
as well even though that's stupid but I have to. I have to because Crosse
said so and Robert agrees and they both said I've got to put up my life as
well but Jesus Christ now Golden Lady's limping in the paddock but the
gamble's settled and now they're off and running, come on Golden Lady,
come on for the love of Mao, don't mind the storm clouds and the lightning come on, all my savings and my life's riding on your rotten lousy
god-cursed oh Jesus Chairman don't fail me. . . .

He was deep in dreams now, bad dreams, drug-assisted dreams, and
Happy Valley was the Valley of Death. His eyes did not feel the lights
come up gently nor the door swing open.

It was time to begin again.

Armstrong looked down at his friend, pitying him. The lights were carefully dimmed. Beside him was Senior Agent Malcolm Sun, an SI guard
and the SI doctor. Dr. Dorn was a small, dapper, slightly bald specialist
with an animated, birdlike intensity. He took Brian Kwok's pulse and
measured his blood pressure and listened to his heartbeat.

"The client's in fine shape, Superintendent, physically," he said with a
faint smile. "His blood pressure and heartbeat're nicely up but that's to
be expected." He noted his readings on the chart, handed it to Armstrong,
who glanced at his watch, wrote down the time and signed the chart also.

"You can carry on," he said.

The doctor filled the syringe carefully. With great care he gave Brian
Kwok the injection in the rump with a new needle. There was almost no
mark, just a tiny spot of blood that he wiped away. "Dinner time whenever you want," he said with a smile.

Armstrong just nodded. The SI guard had added a measure of urine to
the pail and that was noted on the chart as well. "Very smart of him to
measure the level, didn't think he'd do that," Malcolm Sun commented.
Infrared rays made it easy to monitor a client's most tiny movement from
spyholes set into the ceiling lights. "*Dew neh loh moh,* who'd've imagined
he'd be the mole? Smart, he always was so fornicating smart."

"Let's hope the poor bugger's not too fornicating smart," Armstrong told
him sourly. "The sooner he talks the better. The Old Man won't give up
on him."

The others looked at him. The young SI guard shivered.

Dr. Dorn broke the uneasy silence. "Should we still maintain the two-
hour cycle, sir?"

Armstrong glanced at his friend. The first drug in the beer had been about 1:30 this afternoon. Since then, Brian Kwok had been on a Classification Two—a chemical sleep-wake-sleep-wake schedule. Every two hours. Wake-up injections just before 4:30 P.M., 6:30, 8:30, and this would continue until 6:30 A.M. when the first serious interrogation would begin. Within ten minutes of each injection the client would be artificially pulled out of sleep, his thirst and his hunger increased by the drugs. Food would be wolfed and the cold tea gulped and the drugs therein would quickly take effect. Deep sleep, very deep very quick assisted by another injection. Darkness and harsh light alternated, metallic voices and silence alternated. Then wake-up. Breakfast. And two hours later, dinner, and two hours later breakfast. To an increasingly disoriented mind twelve hours would become six days—more if the client could stand it, twelve days, every hour on the hour. No need for physical torture, just darkness and disorientation, enough to discover that which you wish to discover from the enemy client, or to make your enemy client sign what you want him to sign, soon believing your truth to be his truth.

Anyone.

Anyone after a week of sleep-wake-sleep followed by two or three days of no sleep.

Anyone.

Oh Christ almighty, Armstrong thought, you poor bloody bastard, you'll try to hold out and it won't do you a bit of good. None.

But then most of Armstrong's mind shouted back, but he's not your friend but an enemy agent, just a "client" and enemy who has betrayed you and everything and everyone for years. It was probably him who shopped Fong-fong and his lads who're now in some lousy stinking cell having the same but without doctors and monitoring and care. Still, can you be proud of this type of treatment—can any civilized person?

No. Is it necessary to stuff lousy chemicals into a helpless body?

No . . . yes, yes it is, yes it is sometimes, and killing's necessary sometimes, mad dogs, people—oh yes some people are evil and mad dogs are evil. Yes. You've got to use these modern psychic techniques, developed by Pavlov and other Soviets, developed by Communists under a KGB regime. Ah but do you have to follow them?

Christ I don't know but I do know the KGB're trying to destroy us all and bring us all down to their level an—

Armstrong's eyes focused and he saw them all staring at him. "What?"

"Shall we maintain the two-hour cycle, sir?" the doctor repeated, disquieted.

"Yes. Yes, and at 6:30 we'll begin the first interview."

"Are you doing that yourself?"

"It's on the orders, for chrissake," Armstrong snarled. "Can't you bloody read?"

"Oh sorry," the doctor replied at once. They all knew of Armstrong's friendship for the client and of Crosse's ordering him to do the interrogation. "Would you like a sedative, old chap?" Dr. Dorn asked solicitously.

Armstrong cursed him obscenely and left, angry that he had allowed the doctor to needle him into losing his temper. He went to the top floor, to the officers' mess.

"Barman!"

"Coming up, sir!"

His usual tankard of beer came quickly but tonight the smooth dark liquid he loved, malt heavy and bitter, did not quench his thirst or cleanse his mouth. A thousand times he had worried what he would do if he was caught by *them* and put naked into such a cell, knowing most techniques and practices and being on guard. Better than poor bloody Brian, he thought grimly. Poor bugger knows so little. Yes, but does more knowledge help when you're the client?

His skin felt clammy with fear-sweat as he thought of what was ahead of Brian Kwok.

"Barman!"

"Yes sir, coming up!"

"Evening Robert, can I join you?" Chief Inspector Donald C. C. Smyth asked.

"Oh, hello. Yes . . . sit down," he told the younger man unenthusiastically.

Smyth sat on the bar stool beside him and eased his arm that was in a sling more comfortably. "How's it going?"

"Routine." Armstrong saw Smyth nod and he thought how apt his nickname was. The Snake. Smyth was good-looking, smooth, sinuous like a snake with the same deadly quality of danger there, and the same habit of licking his lips from time to time with the tip of his tongue.

"Christ! It's still impossible to believe it's Brian." Smyth was one of the few in the know about Brian. "Shocking."

"Yes."

"Robert, I've been ordered by the DCID"—Director of Criminal Investigation, Armstrong's ultimate boss—"to take over the Werewolf case from you while you're occupied. And any others you might want me to cover."

"Everything's in the files. Sergeant Major Tang-po's my Number Two . . . he's a good detective, very good in fact." Armstrong quaffed some beer and added cynically, "He's well connected."

Smyth smiled with his mouth. "Good, that's a help."

"Just don't organize my bloody district."

"Perish the thought, old chum. East Aberdeen takes all of my skill. Now, what about the Werewolves? Continue surveillance on Phillip Chen?"

"Yes. And his wife."

"Interesting that before Dianne married that old miser she was Mai-wei

T'Chung, eh? Interesting too that one of her cousins was Hummingbird Sung."

Armstrong stared at him. "You've been doing your homework."

"All part of the service!" Smyth added grimly, "I'd like to get those Werewolves right smartly. We've already had three panic calls in East Aberdeen from people who have had phone calls from the Werewolves demanding *h'eung yau*, 'velly quicklee' or else a kidnapping. I hear it's the same all over the Colony. If three frightened citizens called us, you can bet three hundred haven't had the courage." Smyth sipped his whiskey and soda. "That's not good for business, not good at all. There's only so much fat on the cow. If we don't get the Werewolves quickly the buggers'll have their own mint—a few quick phone calls and money'll be in the mail, the poor bloody victims happy to pay off to escape their attention—and every other bloody villain here with a sense of larceny will have a field day too."

"I agree." Armstrong finished his beer. "You want another?"

"Let me. Barman!"

Armstrong watched his beer being drawn. "You think there's a connection between John Chen and Hummingbird Sung?" He remembered Sung, the wealthy shipping magnate with the oral reputation, kidnapped six years ago, and smiled wryly. "Christ, I haven't thought about him in years."

"Nor me. The cases don't parallel and we put his kidnappers into pokey for twenty years and they'll rot there but you never know. Perhaps there's a connection." Smyth shrugged. "Dianne Chen must have hated John Chen and I'm sure he hated her back, everyone knows that. Same with old Hummingbird." He laughed. "Hummingbird's other nickname, in the trade so to speak, is Nosy-nosy."

Armstrong grunted. He rubbed the tiredness out of his eyes. "Might be worth going to see John's wife, Barbara. I was going to do that tomorrow but . . . well, it might be worthwhile."

"I've already got an appointment. And I'm going out to Sha Tin first thing. Maybe those local buggers missed something in the rain."

"Good idea." Uneasily Armstrong watched the Snake sipping his whiskey. "What's on your mind?" he asked, knowing there was something.

Smyth looked up at him directly. "There're a lot of things I don't understand about this kidnapping. For instance, why was such a huge reward offered by the High Dragons for John's recapture, curiously, dead or alive?"

"Ask them."

"I have. At least, I asked someone who knows one of them." The Snake shrugged. "Nothing. Nothing at all." He hesitated. "We'll have to go back into John's past."

Armstrong felt a shaft of cold that he kept buried. "Good idea."

"Did you know Mary knew him? In the POW camp at Stanley?"

"Yes." Armstrong drank some beer without tasting it.

"She might give us a lead—if John was, say, connected with black market in the camp." His pale blue eyes held Armstrong's pale blue eyes. "Might be worth asking."

"I'll think about that. Yes, I'll think about that." The big man bore the Snake no malice. If he had been the Snake he would have asked too. The Werewolves were very bad news and the first wave of terror had already rushed through Chinese society. How many more people know about Mary and John Chen? he asked himself. Or about the 40,000 that's still burning a hole in my desk, still burning a hole in my soul. "It was a long time ago."

"Yes."

Armstrong lifted his beer. "You've got your 'friends' helping you?"

"Let's just say very substantial rewards and payments are being made—paid gratefully, I hasten to add, by our gambling fraternity." The sardonic smile left Smyth's face. And the banter. "We've got to get those sodding Werewolves very fast or they'll really upset our applecart."

52

9:15 P.M.:

Four Finger Wu was on the tall poop of the motorized junk that was wallowing in the chop at the rendezvous well out to sea, all lights doused. "Listen, Werewolf turd," he hissed irritably at Smallpox Kin who lay quivering on the deck at his feet, mindless with pain, trussed with rope and heavy chain. "I want to know who else is in your fornicating gang and where you got the coin from, the half-coin." There was no answer. "Wake the fornicator up!"

Obligingly Goodweather Poon poured another bucket of seawater over the prostrate youth. When this had no effect, he leaned down with his knife. At once Smallpox Kin screamed and came out of his stupor. "What, what is it, Lord?" he shrieked. "No more . . . what is it, what do you want?"

Four Finger Wu repeated what he had said. The youth shrieked again as Goodweather Poon probed. "I've told you everything . . . everything . . ." Desperately, never believing that there could be so much pain in the universe, beyond caring, he babbled again who were the members of the gang, all their real names and addresses, even about the old *amah* in Aberdeen. ". . . my father gave me the coin . . . I don't know where . . . he gave it to me never saying wh . . . he got it I swearrrrr. . . ." His voice trailed away. Once more he fainted.

Four Fingers spat disgustedly. "The youth of today have no fortitude!"

The night was dark and an ill-tempered wind gusted from time to time under a lowering overcast, the powerful and well-tuned engine purring nicely, making just enough way to lessen the junk's inevitable corkscrewing—the rolling pitch and toss. They were a few miles southwest of Hong Kong, just out of the sea-lanes, PRC waters and the vast mouth of the Pearl River just to port, open sea to starboard. All sails were furled.

He lit a cigarette and coughed. "All gods curse all fornicating triad turds!"

"Shall I wake him again?" Goodweather Poon asked.

"No. No, the fornicator's told the truth as much as he knows." Wu's calloused fingers reached up and nervously touched the half-coin that he wore now around his neck under his ragged sweat shirt, making sure it was still there. A knot of anxiety welled at the thought that the coin might be genuine, might be Phillip Chen's missing treasure. "You did very well, Goodweather Poon. Tonight you'll get a bonus." His eyes went to the southeast, seeking the signal. It was overdue but he was not yet worried. Automatically his nose sniffed the wind and his tongue tasted it, tangy and heavy with salt. His eyes ranged the sky and the sea and the horizon. "More rain soon," he muttered.

Poon lit another cigarette from his butt and ground the butt into the deck with his horny bare foot. "Will it ruin the races on Saturday?"

The old man shrugged. "If the gods will it. I think it will be piss heavy again tomorrow. Unless the wind veers. Unless the wind veers we could have the Devil Winds, the Supreme Winds, and those fornicators could scatter us to the Four Seas. Piss on the Supreme Winds!"

"I'll piss on them if there are no races. My nose tells me it's Banker Kwang's horse."

"Huh! That stinky, mealy-mouth nephew of mine certainly needs a change of joss! The fool's lost his bank!"

Poon hawked and spat for luck. "Thank all gods for Profitable Choy!"

Since Four Fingers and his captains and his people had all successfully extracted all their monies from the Ho-Pak, thanks to information from Paul Choy—and since he himself was still enjoying vast profits from his son's illicit manipulation of Struan stock, Wu had dubbed him Profitable Choy. Because of the profit, he had forgiven his son the transgression. But only in his heart. Being prudent, the old man had showed none of it outwardly except to his friend and confidant, Goodweather Poon.

"Bring him on deck."

"What about this Werewolf fornicator?" Poon's horny toe stabbed Kin. "Young Profitable didn't like him or this matter at all, *heya?*"

"Time he grew up, time he knew how to treat enemies, time he knew real values, not ill-omened, stink-wind, fatuous Golden Mountain values." The old man spat on the deck. "He's forgotten who he is and where his interests lie."

"You said yourself you don't send a rabbit against a dragon. Or a minnow against a shark. You've your investment to consider and don't forget Profitable Choy's returned everything he cost you over fifteen years twenty times over. In the money market he's a High Dragon and only twenty-six. Leave him where he's best, best for you and best for him. *Heya?*"

"Tonight he's best here."

The old seaman scratched his ear. "I don't know about that, Four Fingers. That the gods will decide. Me, I'd have left him ashore." Now Goodweather Poon was watching the southeast. His peripheral vision had caught something. "You see it?"

After a moment Four Fingers shook his head. "There's plenty of time, plenty of time."

"Yes." The old seaman glanced back at the body trussed with chains like a plucked chicken. His face split into a grin. "Eeeee, but when Profitable Choy turned white like a jellyfish at this fornicator's first scream and first blood, I had to break wind to release my laughter to save his face!"

"The young today have no fortitude," Wu repeated, then lit a new cigarette and nodded. "But you're right. After tonight Profitable's going to be left where he belongs to become even more profitable." He glanced down at Smallpox Kin. "Is he dead?"

"Not yet. What a dirty motherless whore to hit Number One Son Noble House Chen with a shovel and then lie about it to us, heya? And to cut off Chen's ear and blame his father and brothers and lie about that too! And then taking the ransom even though they couldn't deliver the goods! Terrible!"

"Disgusting!" The old man guffawed. "Even more terrible to get caught. But then you showed the fornicator the error of his rotten ways, Goodweather Poon."

They both laughed, happy together.

"Shall I cut off his other ear, Four Fingers?"

"Not yet. Soon, yes, very soon."

Again Poon scratched his head. "One thing I don't understand. I don't understand why you told me to put their sign on Number One Son and leave him as they planned to leave him." He frowned at Four Fingers. "When this fornicator's dead that's all the Werewolves dead, heya? So what good is the sign?"

Four Fingers cackled. "All comes clear to he who waits. Patience," he said, very pleased with himself. The sign implied the Werewolves were very much alive. If only he and Poon knew that they were all dead, he could at any time resurrect them, or the threat of them. At his whim. Yes, he thought happily, kill one to terrify ten thousand! The "Werewolves" can easily become a continuous source of extra revenue at very little cost. A few phone calls, a judicious kidnapping or two, perhaps another ear. "Patience, Goodweather Poon. Soon you'll un—" He stopped. Both men had centered their eyes on the same spot in the darkness. A small, dimly lit freighter was just nosing into sight. In a moment two lights flashed at her masthead. At once Wu went to the conn and flashed an answering signal. The freighter flashed the confirm. "Good," Wu said happily, flashing his reconfirm. The deck crew had also seen the lights. One hurried below to fetch the rest of the seamen and the others went to their action stations. Wu's eyes fell on Smallpox Kin. "First him," he said malevolently. "Fetch my son here."

Weakly Paul Choy groped his way on deck. He gulped the fresh air gratefully, the stench from below decks overpowering. He climbed the gangway to the poop. When he saw the red mess on the deck and the partial person on the deck, his stomach revolted and once more he threw up over the side.

Four Finger Wu said, "Give Goodweather Poon a hand."

"What?"

"Are your ears filled with vomit?" the old man shouted. "Give him a hand."

Frightened, Paul Choy reeled over to the old seaman, the helmsman watching interestedly. "What do you . . . you want me to do?"

"Take his legs!"

Paul Choy tried to dominate his nausea. He closed his eyes. His nostrils were filled with the smell of vomit and blood. He reached down, took the legs and part of the heavy chain and staggered, half falling, to the side. Goodweather Poon was carrying most of the weight and he could easily have carried it all and Paul Choy too if need be. Effortlessly he balanced Smallpox Kin on the gunnel.

"Hold him there!" By prearrangement with Four Fingers, the old seaman backed away, leaving Paul Choy on his own, the unconscious, mutilated face and body slumped precariously against him.

"Put him overboard!" Wu ordered.

"But Father . . . please . . . he's . . . he's not de . . . not dead yet. Pl—"

"Put him over the side!"

Beside himself with fear and loathing, Paul Choy tried to pull the body back aboard but the wind squalled and heeled the junk and the last of the Werewolves toppled into the sea and sank without a trace. Helplessly Paul Choy stared at the waves slopping against the teak. He saw that there was blood on his shirt and on his hands. Another wave of nausea racked him, tormenting him.

"Here!" Gruffly Wu handed his son a flask. It contained whiskey, good whiskey. Paul Choy choked a little but his stomach held the whiskey. Wu turned back to the conn, waved the helmsman toward the freighter, the throttle opened to full ahead. Paul Choy almost fell but managed to grab the gunnel and stay on his feet, unprepared for the suddenness of the deep-throated roar and burst of speed. When he had his sea legs he looked at his father. Now the old man was near the tiller, Goodweather Poon nearby, and both were peering into the darkness. He could see the small ship and his stomach reeled, and he hated his father afresh, hated being on board and being involved in what obviously was smuggling—on top of the horror of the Werewolf.

Whatever that poor son of a bitch did, he thought, enraged, it doesn't merit taking the law into your own hands. He should've been handed over to the police to be hanged or imprisoned or whatever.

Wu felt the eyes on him and he glanced back. His face did not change. "Come here," he ordered, his thumbless hand stabbing the gunnel in front of him. "Stand here."

Numbly Paul Choy obeyed. He was much taller than his father and

Goodweather Poon but he was a piece of chaff against either of them.

The junk sped through the darkness on an intercept course, the sea black and the night black with just a little moonlight sifting through the overcast. Soon they were just aft of the vessel and a little to starboard, closing fast. She was small, slow and quite old and she dipped uneasily in the gathering swell. "She's a coastal freighter," Goodweather Poon volunteered, "a Thai trawler we call them. There's dozens of the fornicators in all Asian waters. They're the lice of the seas, Profitable Choy, crewed by scum, captained by scum, and they leak like lobster pots. Most ply the Bangkok, Singapore, Manila, Hong Kong route, and wherever else they've a cargo for. This one's out of Bangkok." He hawked and spat, revolting the young man again. "I wouldn't want to voyage on one of those stinking whores. Th—"

He stopped. There was another brief flashing signal. Wu answered it. Then all on deck saw the splash on her starboard side as something heavy went overboard. At once Four Fingers rang up "all engines stop." The sudden quiet was deafening. Bow lookouts peered into the darkness, the junk wallowing and swerving as she slowed.

Then one of the bow lookouts signaled with a flag. At once Wu gave a little engine and made the correction. Another silent signal and another change of direction and then a sharper, more excited movement of the flag.

Immediately Wu reversed engines. The props bit the sea heavily. Then he killed the thrust, the junk swerving closer to the line of bobbing buoys. The gnarled old man seemed to be part of the ship as Paul Choy watched him with his eyes fixed into the sea ahead. Nimbly Wu maneuvered the ponderous junk into the course of the buoys. In a few moments a seaman with a long, hooked boarding pole leaned out from the main deck and hooked the line. The rough cork buoys were brought aboard deftly, other seamen helping, and the line attached securely to a stanchion. With practiced skill the chief deckhand cut away the buoys and cast them overboard while more seamen made sure that the bales attached to the other end of the line below the surface were safe and secure. Paul Choy could see the bales clearly now. There were two of them, perhaps six foot by three foot by three foot, roped together heavily underwater, their sinking weight keeping the thick line taut. As soon as all was tight and safe, the cargo secure alongside though still five or six feet beneath the surface of the sea, the chief deckhand signaled. At once Four Fingers brought the junk to cruising speed and they sped away on a different tack.

The whole operation had been done in silence, effortlessly and in seconds. In moments the weak riding lights of the Thai trawler had vanished into the darkness and they were alone on the sea once more.

Wu and Goodweather Poon lit cigarettes. "Very good," Goodweather Poon said. Four Fingers did not reply, his ears listening to the pleasing note of the engines. No trouble there, he thought. His senses tested the wind. No trouble there. His eyes ranged the darkness. Nothing there either, he told himself. Then why are you uneasy? Is it Seventh Son?

He glanced at Paul Choy who was at the port side, his back toward him. No. No danger there either.

Paul Choy was watching the bales. They kicked up a small wake. His curiosity peaked and he was feeling a little better, the whiskey warming and the salt smelling good now, that and the excitement of the rendezvous and being away and safe. "Why don't you bring them aboard, Father? You could lose them."

Wu motioned Poon to answer.

"Better to leave the harvest of the sea to the sea, Profitable Choy, until it's quite safe to bring it ashore. *Heya?*"

"My name's Paul, not Profitable." The young man looked back at his father and shivered. "There was no need to murder that fornicator!"

"The captain didn't," Goodweather Poon said with a grin, answering for the old man. "You did, Profitable Choy. You did, you threw him overboard. I saw it clearly. I was within half a pace of you."

"Lies! I tried to pull him back! And anyway he ordered me to. He threatened me."

The old seaman shrugged. "Tell that to a fine, foreign devil judge, Profitable Choy, and that won't be fornicating profitable at all!"

"My name's not Pro—"

"The Captain of the Fleets has called you Profitable so by all the gods Profitable you are forever. *Heya?*" he added, grinning at Four Fingers.

The old man said nothing, just smiled and showed his few broken teeth and that made his grimace even more frightening. His bald head and weathered face nodded his agreement. Then he put his eyes on his son. Paul Choy shivered in spite of his resolve.

"Your secret's safe with me, my son. Never fear. No one aboard this boat saw anything. Did they, Goodweather Poon?"

"No, nothing. By all gods great and small! No one saw anything!"

Paul Choy stared back sullenly. "You can't wrap paper in fire!"

Goodweather Poon guffawed. "On this boat you can!"

"Yes," Wu said, his voice a rasp. "On this boat you can keep a secret forever." He lit another cigarette, hawked and spat. "Don't you want to know what's in those bales?"

"No."

"It's opium. Delivered on shore this night's work will bring a 200,000 profit, just to me, with plenty in bonuses for my crew."

"That profit's not worth the risk, *not to me*. I made you th—" Paul Choy stopped.

Four Finger Wu looked at him. He spat on the deck and passed the conn to Goodweather Poon and went to the great cushioned seats aft that ringed the poop. "Come here, Profitable Choy," he commanded.

Frightened, Paul Choy sat at the point indicated. Now they were more alone.

"Profit is profit," Wu said, very angry. "10,000 is your profit. That's enough to buy an air ticket to Honolulu and back to Hong Kong and have ten days of holiday together." He saw the momentary flash of joy wash across his son's face and he smiled inside.

"I'll never come back," Paul Choy said bravely. "Never."

"Oh yes you will. You will now. You've fished in fornicating dangerous waters."

"I'll never come back. I've a U.S. passport and a—"

"And a Jap whore, *heya?*"

Paul Choy stared at his father, aghast that his father knew, then rage possessed him and he sprang up and bunched his fists. "She's not a whore by all gods! She's great, she's a lady and her folks're th—"

"Quiet!" Wu bit back the expletive carefully. "Very well, she's not a whore, even though to me all women are whores. She's not a whore but an empress. But she's still a fornicating devil from the Eastern Sea, one of those who raped China."

"She's American, she's American like me," Paul Choy flared, his fists clenched tighter, ready to spring. The helmsman and Goodweather Poon readied to interfere without seeming to. A knife slid into Poon's fist. "I'm American, she's American nisei and her father was with the 442 in Italy an—"

"You're Haklo, you're one of the Seaborne Wu, the ship people, and you'll obey me! You will, Profitable Choy, oh yes you will obey! *Heya?*"

Paul Choy stood in front of him shaking with equal fury, trying to keep up his courage, for, in rage, the old man was formidable and he could feel Goodweather Poon and the other men behind his back. "Don't call her names! Don't!"

"You dare bunch your fists at me? Me who's given you life, given you everything? Every chance, even the chance of meeting this . . . this Eastern Sea Empress? *Heya?*"

Paul Choy felt himself spun around as though by a great wind. Goodweather Poon was peering up at him. "This is the Captain of the Fleets. You will respect him!" The seaman's iron hand shoved him back to the seats. "The captain said sit. *Sit!*"

After a moment, Paul Choy said sullenly, "How did you know about her?"

Exasperated, the old man sputtered, "All gods bear witness to this country person I sired, this monkey with the brains and manners of a country person. Do you think I didn't have you watched? Guarded? Do I send a mole among snakes or a civilized whelp among foreign devils unprotected? You're the son of Wu Sang Fang, Head of the Seaborne Wu, and I protect my own against all enemies. You think we don't have enemies enough who would slit your Secret Sack and send me the contents just to spite me? *Heya?*"

"I don't know."

"Well know it very well now, my son!" Four Finger Wu was aware this was a clash to the death and he had to be wise as a father must be when his son finally calls him. He was not afraid. He had done this with many sons and only lost one. But he was grateful to the tai-pan who had given him the information about the girl and about her parentage. That's the key, he thought, the key to this impudent child from a Third Wife whose Golden Gulley was as sweet and as tender as fresh bonefish as long as she lived. Perhaps I'll let him bring the whore here. The poor fool needs a whore whatever he calls her. Lady? Ha! I've heard the Eastern Sea Devils have no pubics! Disgusting! Next month he can bring the strumpet here. If her parents let her come alone that proves she's a whore. If they don't, then that's the end of her. Meanwhile I'll find him a wife. Yes. Who? One of Tightfist's granddaughters? Or Lando Mata's or . . . Ah, wasn't that half-caste's youngest brat trained in the Golden Mountain too, at a school for girls, a famous school for girls? What's the difference to this fool, pure blood or not?

I have many sons, he thought, feeling nothing for him. I gave them life. Their duty is to me and when I'm dead, to the clan. Perhaps a good broad-hipped, hard-footed Haklo boat-girl'd be the right one for him, he thought grimly. Yes, but eeeee, there's no need to cut your Stalk to spite a weakness in your bladder, however rude and ill-mannered the fornicating dumblehead is! "In a month Black Beard will grant you a holiday," he said with finality. "I will see to it. With your 10,000 profit you can take a passage on a flying machine . . . No! Better to bring her here," he added as though it were a fresh thought. "You will bring her here. You should see Manila and Singapore and Bangkok and visit our captains there. Yes, bring her here in a month, your 10,000 will pay for the ticket and pay for everyth—"

"No. I won't. I won't do it. And I don't want drug money! I'll never take drug money and I counsel you to get out of the drug trade immed—"

The whole junk was suddenly floodlit. Everyone was momentarily blinded. The searchlight was to starboard.

"Haul to!" came the order in English over the loud-hailer, then repeated in Haklo, then in Cantonese.

Wu and Goodweather Poon were the first to react and in a split second they were in motion. Wu swung the tiller hard to port away from the Marine Police patrol boat and gunned both the engines to full ahead. Poon had leapt down the gangway to the main deck and now he sliced the cargo line and the wake of bales vanished as the bales sank into the deep.

"Haul to for boarding!" The metallic words ripped through Paul Choy who stood paralyzed with fright. He watched his father reach into a nearby sea locker and bring out some crumpled PRC peaked soldiers' hats and shove one on. "Quick," he ordered, throwing one to him. Petrified, he obeyed and crammed it onto his head. Miraculously all the crew were now wearing the same kind of hat and a few were struggling into equally drab and crumpled army tunics.

His heart stopped. Others were reaching into sea lockers and bringing out PRC army rifles and submachine guns as still others went to the side nearest the police boat and began shouting obscenities. The boat was sleek and battle gray with a deck gun, two searchlights now and her riding lights on. She lay a hundred yards to starboard, her engines growling, keeping pace with them easily. They could see the neat, white-clad sailors and, on the bridge, the peaked British officers' caps.

Four Fingers had a loud-hailer horn now and he went to the side, his hat pulled well down, and he roared, "Go fornicate yourselves, barbarians! Look at our colors!" His hand stabbed toward his masthead. The PRC marine flag fluttered there. Aft on the stern was a fake Canton PRC registration number. "Leave a peaceful patrol alone . . . you're in our waters!"

Poon's face was split into a malevolent grin. A PRC automatic pistol was in his hands and he stood at the gunnel silhouetted in the light, the cap pulled well down to preclude identification by the binoculars he knew were raking the ship. His heart was racing too and there was a sick-sweet-sour bile in his mouth. They were in international waters. Safety and PRC waters were fifteen minutes away. He cocked the gun. Orders were quite clear. No one was boarding tonight.

"Haul to! We're coming aboard!"

They all saw the patrol boat slow and the cutter splash into the sea and many aboard lost their initial confidence. Four Fingers squeezed the throttle forward to get the last fraction of power. He cursed himself for not seeing the police boat or sensing their presence earlier but he knew that they had electronic devices to see in the dark whereas he had to rely on eyes and nose and the sixth sense that so far had kept him and most of his people alive.

It was rare to find a patrol boat so close to Chinese waters. Even so, the boat was there and though his cargo was gone, there were guns aboard and so was Paul Choy. Joss! All gods defecate on that patrol boat! Goodweather Poon was partially right, he told himself. The gods will decide if it was wise or not to bring the youth aboard.

"Go fornicate yourselves! No foreign devil comes aboard a patrol boat of the People's Republic of China!" All the crew cheered enthusiastically, adding their obscenities to the din.

"Haul to!"

The old man paid no attention. The junk was headed toward the Pearl River estuary at maximum speed and he and all aboard prayed that there were no PRC patrols nearby. In the searchlight they could see the cutter with ten armed sailors on an intercept course but it was not fast enough to overtake them.

"For the last time, haul tooooo!"

"For the fornicating last time leave peaceful PRC patrol to their own waters. . . ."

Suddenly the patrol's sirens started *whoopwhoopwhooping* and she seemed to jump forward from the violent thrust of her engines, a high churning wake astern. The searchlight still kept them centered as she charged ahead and cut across the junk's bow and stayed there, her engines growling malevolently, barring the path to safety.

Paul Choy was still staring at the battle gray, sharp-nosed craft with its deck gun manned and machine guns manned, big, with four times the power they had, the gap closing fast with no room to maneuver. They could see the uniformed sailors on her deck and the officers on the bridge, radar aerials sweeping.

"Get your head down," Wu warned Paul Choy who obeyed instantly. Then Wu ran forward to the bow, Goodweather Poon beside him. Both had automatic machine guns.

"Now!"

Carefully he and his friend sprayed the sea toward the patrol boat that was almost on them, taking extreme care that none of the bullets splashed the deck. Instantly the searchlight went out and at once, in the blinding darkness, the helmsman put the junk hard to starboard and prayed that Wu had chosen correctly. The junk slid around the other ship with a few yards leeway as the other craft gunned ahead to get out of the way of the bullets. The helmsman heaved her back on her course and her dash for safety.

"Good," Wu muttered, knowing he had gained another hundred yards. His mind carried the chart of these waters. Now they were in the gray area between Hong Kong and PRC waters, a few hundred yards from real safety. In the darkness all on deck had kept their eyes tightly shut. The moment they felt the searchlight again, they opened their eyes and adjusted more quickly. The attacker was ahead and to port out of machine gun range but still ahead and still in the way. Wu smiled grimly. "Big Nose Lee!" His chief deckhand came promptly, and he handed him the machine gun. "Don't use it till I order it and don't hit one of those fornicators!"

Suddenly the darkness split and the *parrang* of the deck gun deafened them. A split second and a vast spout of water burst from the sea near their bow. Wu was shocked and he shook his fist at the ship. "Fornicate you and all your mothers! Leave us alone or Chairman Mao will sink all Hong Kong!"

He hurried aft. "I'll take the tiller!"

The helmsman was frightened. So was Paul Choy, but at the same time he was curiously excited and vastly impressed with the way his father commanded and the way everyone aboard reacted with discipline instead of as the motley ragtag bunch of pirates he had imagined them to be.

"*Haul to!*"

Again the gap began closing but the patrol boat kept out of machine gun range and the cutter kept out of range aft. Stoically Wu held his course. Another flash then another and *parrang parrannng*. Two shells straddled the junk rocking her.

"Fornicate all mothers," Wu gasped, "all gods keep those gunners accurate!" He knew that the shots were only to frighten. His friend the Snake had given him assurances that all patrols were ordered never to hit or sink a fleeing junk carrying PRC colors in case the colors were real, never to forcibly board unless one of their own seamen was killed or wounded. "Give them a burst," he called out.

Obediently but with great care, the two men on the bow sprayed the waters. The searchlight never wavered, but suddenly it went out.

Wu kept his course firm. Now what? he asked himself desperately. Where's that fornicator going? He searched the darkness, his eyes straining to see the patrol boat and the promontory he knew was nearby. Then he saw the silhouette to port aft. She was bearing down fast in a swirling rush to come up alongside with grappling hooks. Safety was a hundred yards ahead. If he turned from the new danger he would parallel safety and stay in international waters and then the ship would do the same again and shepherd him into open seas until his ammunition was gone or the dawn came and he was lost. He dare not make a real battle for he knew British law had a long arm and the killing of one of their seamen was punished with hanging, and no money or high friends would prevent it. If he held his course the ship could grapple him and he knew how adept and well trained these Cantonese seamen were and how they hated Haklos.

His face split into a grimace. He waited until the patrol boat was fifty yards astern, coming up very fast, the siren whooping deafeningly, then grimly he turned the tiller into her and prayed the captain was awake. For a moment the two ships hung in the balance. Then the patrol boat swung away to avoid the collision, the wash from her props spraying them. Wu wheeled starboard and slammed all throttles forward even though they were already as far forward as they could go. A few more yards were gained.

He saw the patrol boat recover quickly. She roared around in a circle and came back at them on a different tack. They were just within Chinese waters. Without hope Four Fingers left the tiller and picked up another submachine gun and sprayed the darkness, the barking *thwack thwack thwack* and the smell of cordite making his fear more intense. Abruptly the searchlight splashed him, its light vicious. He turned his head, blinded, and blinked, keeping his head and cap well down. When he could see again he pointed the automatic directly at the light and cursed obscenely, frightened that they would grapple him and tow him from safety. The hot barrel shook as he aimed for the light, his finger on the trigger. It would be death if he fired and prison if he didn't. Fear spread through him and throughout his ship.

But the light did not swoop down as he expected. It remained aft and now he saw her bow wave lessening and her wake waves lessening and his heart began to beat again. The patrol boat was letting him go. The Snake had been right!

Shakily he put down the gun. The loud-hailer was nearby. He brought it to his mouth.

"Victory to Chairman Mao!" he bellowed with all his might. "Stay out of our waters, you fornicating foreign devilllls!" The joy-filled words echoed across the waters. His crew jeered, shaking their fists at the light. Even Paul Choy was caught up in the excitement and shouted too as they all realized the patrol boat would not venture into Chinese waters.

The searchlight vanished. When their eyes had adjusted they saw the patrol boat broadside, making hardly any way, her riding lights on now.

"She'll have us on their radar," Paul Choy muttered in English.

"Wat?"

He repeated it in Haklo, using the English word, *radar,* but explaining it as a magic eye. Both Poon and Four Fingers knew about radar in principle though they had never seen one. "What does that matter?" Wu scoffed. "Their magic screens or magic eyes won't help them now. We can lose them easily in the channels near Lan Tao. There's no evidence against us, no contraband aboard, no nothing!"

"What about the guns?"

"We can lose them overboard, or we can lose those mad dogs and keep our guns! Eeeee, Goodweather Poon, when those shells straddled us I thought my anus was jammed shut forever!"

"Yes," Poon agreed happily, "and when we fired into the darkness at the fornicators . . . all gods fornicate! I've always wanted to use those guns!"

Wu laughed too until the tears were running down his face. "Yes, yes, Old Friend." Then he explained to Paul Choy the strategy that the Snake had worked out for them. "Good, *heya?*"

"Who's the Snake?" Paul Choy asked.

Wu hesitated, his small eyes glittering. "An employee, a police employee you might say, Profitable Choy."

"With the cargo gone the night's not profitable at all," Poon said sourly.

"Yes," Wu agreed, equally sourly. He had already promised Venus Poon a diamond ring that he had planned to pay for from tonight's transactions. Now he would have to dip into his savings, which was against all his principles. You pay for whores out of current earnings, never out of savings, so piss on that police boat! he thought. Without the diamond present . . . Eeeee, but her Beauteous Box is everything Richard Kwang claimed, and the wriggle of her rump everything rumor had promised. And tonight . . . tonight after the TV station closes, her Gorgeous Gate is due to open once more!

"Filthy joss, that sharp-nosed bandit finding us tonight," he said, his manhood stirring at the thought of Venus Poon. "All that money gone and our expenses heavy!"

"The cargo's lost?" Paul Choy asked, greatly surprised.

"Of course lost, gone to the bottom," the old man said irritably.

"You haven't got a marker on it, or a beeper?" Paul Choy used the English word. He explained it to them. "I presumed it would have one—or a float that would release itself in a day or two, chemically—so you could recover it or send frogmen to fetch it when it was safe to do so." The two men were gaping at him. "What's the matter?"

"It is easy to find these 'beepers' or to arrange a delayed float for a day or two?" Wu asked.

"Or a week or two weeks if you want, Father."

"Would you write all this down, how to do it? Or you could arrange it?"

"Of course. But why don't you also have a magic eye, like theirs?"

"What do we need with them—and who could work them?" The old man scoffed again. "We have noses and ears and eyes."

"But you got caught tonight."

"Watch your tongue!" Wu said angrily. "That was joss, joss, a joke of the gods. We're safe and that's all that matters!"

"I disagree, Captain," Paul Choy said, without fear now as everything fell into place. "It would be easy to equip this boat with a magic eye—then you can see them as soon or sooner than they can see you. They can't surprise you. So you can thumb your noses at them without fear and never lose a cargo. *Heya?*" He smiled inwardly, seeing them hooked. "Never a mistake, not even a little one. And never danger. And never a lost cargo. And cargo with beepers. You don't even need to be anywhere near the drop. Only a week later, *heya?*"

"That would be perfect," Poon said fervently. "But if the gods are against you, Profitable Choy, even magic eyes won't help. It was close tonight. That whore wasn't supposed to be here."

They all looked at the ship, just lying aft. Waiting. A few hundred yards aft. Wu set the engine to slow ahead. "We don't want to go too deep into PRC waters," he said uneasily. "Those civilized fornicators are not so polite or so law-abiding." A shiver went through him. "We could use a magic eye, Goodweather Poon."

"Why don't you own one of those patrol boats?" Paul Choy said, baiting the hook again. "Or one a little faster. Then you could outrun them."

"One of those? Are you mad?"

"Who would sell us one?" Wu asked impatiently.

"Japanese."

"Fornicate all Eastern Sea Devils," Poon said.

"Perhaps, but they'd build you something like that, radar equipped. They—"

He stopped as the police patrol boat cut in her deep growling engines, and, with her siren *whoopwhoopwhooping,* hurtled off into the night, her wake churning.

"Look at her go," Paul Choy said admiringly in English. "Classy son of a bitch!"

He repeated it in Haklo. "I'll bet she's still got the Thai trawler in her magic eye. They can see everything, every junk, every ship and cove and promontory for miles—even a storm."

Thoughtfully Four Finger Wu gave a new course to the helmsman that kept them just in PRC waters heading north for the islands and reefs around Lan Tao Island where he would be safe to make for the next rendezvous. There they would transfer to another junk with real registrations —PRC and Hong Kong—to slide back into Aberdeen. Aberdeen! His fingers nervously touched the half-coin again. He had forgotten the coin in the excitement. Now his fingers trembled and his anxiety was rekindled as he thought about his meeting with the tai-pan tonight. There was plenty of time. He would not be late. Even so he increased speed.

"Come," he ordered, motioning Poon and Paul Choy to join him on the cushions aft where they would be more private.

"Perhaps we'd be wise to stay with our junks, and not get one of those whores, my son." Wu's finger stabbed the darkness where the patrol boat had been. "The foreign devils would become even madder if I had one of those in my fleet. But this magic eye of yours . . . you could install it and show us how to use it?"

"I could get experts to do that. People from the Eastern Sea—it would be better to use them—not British or German."

Wu looked at his old friend. "Heya?"

"I don't want one of those turds or their magic eyes on my ship. Soon we'd rely on the fornicators and we'd lose our treasures along with our heads," the other man grumbled.

"But to see when others can't?" Wu puffed on his cigarette. "Is there another seller, Profitable Choy?"

"They would be the best. And cheapest, Father."

"Cheapest, heya? How much will this cost?"

"I don't know. 20,000 U.S., perhaps 40—"

The old man exploded. "40,000 U.S.? Am I made of gold? I have to work for my money! Am I Emperor Wu?"

Paul Choy let the old man rave. He was feeling nothing for him anymore, not after all the night's horror and killing and entrapment and cruelty and blackmail, and most of all because of his father's words against his girl. He would respect his father for his seamanship, for his courage and his command. And as Head of the House. Nothing more. And from now on he would treat him like any other man.

When he felt the old man had raved enough, he said, "I can have the first magic eye installed and two men trained at no cost to you, if you want."

Wu and Poon stared at him. Wu was instantly on guard. "How at no cost?"

"I will pay for it for you."

Poon started to guffaw but Wu hissed, "Shut up, fool, and listen. Profitable Choy knows things you don't know!" His eyes were glittering even more. If a magic eye, why not a diamond too? And if a diamond, why not a mink coat and all the necessary plunder that that mealy-mouthed whore will require to sustain her enthusiastic cleft, hands and mouth.

"How will you pay for it, my son?"

"Out of profit."

"Profit on what?"

"I want control, for one month, of your money in the Victoria."

"Impossible!"

"We opened accounts for 22,423,000. Control for one month."

"To do what with?"

"The stock market."

"Ah, gamble? Gamble with my money? My hard-earned cash? Never."

"One month. We split the profit, Father."

"Oh, we split? It is my fornicating money but you want half. Half of what?"

"Perhaps another 20 million." Paul Choy let the sum hang. He saw the avarice on his father's face and knew that though the negotiation would be heated, they would make a deal. It was only a matter of time.

"*Ayeeyah*, that's impossible, out of the question!"

The old man felt an itch below and he scratched the itch. His manhood stirred. Instantly he thought of Venus Poon who had made him stand as he had not stood for years and of their coming bout tonight. "Perhaps I shall just pay for this magic eye," he said, testing the young man's resolve.

Paul Choy took his spirit completely into his own hands. "Yes, yes you can, but then I'm leaving Hong Kong."

Wu's tongue darted spitefully. "You will leave when I tell you to leave."

"But if I can't be profitable and put my expensive training to work, why should I stay? Did you pay all that money for me to be a pimp on one of your Pleasure Boats? A deckhand on a junk that can be raped at will by the nearest foreign devil cutter? No, better I leave! Better I become profitable to someone else so that I can begin to repay your investment in me. I will give Black Beard a month's notice and leave then."

"You will leave when I tell you to leave!" Wu added malevolently. "You have fished in dangerous waters."

"Yes." And so have you, Paul Choy wanted to add, unafraid. If you think you can blackmail me, that I'm on your hook, you're on mine and you've more to lose. Haven't you heard of Queen's evidence, turning Queen's evidence—or plea bargaining? But he kept this future ploy secret, to be used when necessary, and kept his face polite and bland. "All waters are dangerous if the gods decide they're dangerous," he said cryptically.

Wu took a long deep drag of his cigarette, feeling the smoke deep within him. He had noticed the change in this young man before him. He had seen many such changes in many men. In many sons and many daughters. The experience of his long years screamed caution. This whelp's dangerous, very dangerous, he thought. I think Goodweather Poon was right: it was a mistake to bring Profitable Choy aboard tonight. Now he knows too much about us.

Yes. But that's easy to rectify, when I need to, he reminded himself. Any day or any night.

53

"Well, what the devil are you going to do, Paul?" the governor asked Havergill. Johnjohn was with them and they were on the terrace of Government House after dinner, leaning against the low balustrade. "Good God! If the Victoria runs out of money too, this whole Island's ruined, eh?"

Havergill looked around to make sure they were not being overheard, and dropped his voice. "We've been in touch with the Bank of England, sir. By midnight tomorrow night, London time, there'll be an RAF transport at Heathrow stuffed full of five- and ten-pound notes." His usual confidence returned. "As I said, the Victoria is perfectly sound, completely liquid and our assets here and in England substantial enough to cover any eventuality, well almost any eventuality."

"Meanwhile you may not have enough Hong Kong dollars to weather the run?"

"Not if the, er, the problem continues but I'm sure all will be well, sir."

Sir Geoffrey stared at him. "How the devil did we get into this mess?"

"Joss," Johnjohn said wearily. "Unfortunately the mint can't print enough Hong Kong dollar notes for us in time. It'd take weeks to print and to ship the amount we'd need, and it wouldn't be healthy to have all those extra notes in our economy. The British currency's stopgap, sir. We can just announce that the, er, that the mint is working overtime to supply our needs."

"How much do we actually need?" The governor saw Paul Havergill and Johnjohn look at each other and his disquiet increased.

"We don't know, sir," Johnjohn said. "Colony-wide, apart from ourselves, every other bank will also need to pledge its securities—just as we've pledged ours temporarily to the Bank of England—to obtain the cash they need. If every depositor on the Colony wants every dollar back . . ." The sweat was beading the banker's face now. "We've no way of knowing how extended the other banks are, or the amount of their deposits. No one knows."

"Is one RAF transport enough?" Sir Geoffrey tried not to sound sarcastic. "I mean, well, a billion pounds in fives and tens? How in the hell are they going to collect that number of notes?"

Havergill mopped his brow. "We don't know, sir, but they've promised a first shipment will arrive Monday night at the latest."

"Not till then?"

"No sir. It's impossible before then."

"There's nothing else we can do?"

Johnjohn swallowed. "We considered asking you to declare a bank holiday to stem the tide but, er, we concluded—and the Bank of England agreed—if you did that it might blow the top off the Island."

"No need to worry, sir." Havergill tried to sound convincing. "By the end of next week it will all be forgotten."

"I won't forget it, Paul. And I doubt if China will—or our friends the Labour MPs will. They may have a point about some form of bank controls."

Both bankers bridled and Paul Havergill said deprecatingly, "Those two berks don't know their rears from a hole in the wall! Everything's in control."

Sir Geoffrey would have argued that point but he had just seen Rosemont, the CIA deputy director, and Ed Langan, the FBI man, wander out onto the terrace. "Keep me advised. I want a full report at noon. Would you excuse me a moment? Please help yourself to another drink."

He went off to intercept Rosemont and Langan. "How're you two?"

"Great, thank you, sir. Great evening." Both Americans watched Havergill and Johnjohn going back inside. "How're our banker friends?" Rosemont asked.

"Fine, perfectly fine."

"That MP, the Socialist guy, Grey, was sure as hell getting under Havergill's skin!"

"And the tai-pan's," Ed Langan added with a laugh.

"Oh I don't know," the governor said lightly. "A little opposition's a good thing, what? Isn't that democracy at its best?"

"How's the Vic, sir? How's the run?"

"No problems that can't be solved," Sir Geoffrey replied with his easy charm. "No need to worry. Would you give me a moment, Mr. Langan?"

"Certainly, sir." The American smiled. "I was just leaving."

"Not my party, I trust! Just to replenish your drink?"

"Yes sir."

Sir Geoffrey led the way into the garden, Rosemont beside him. The trees were still dripping and the night dark. He kept to a path that was puddled and muddy. "We've a slight problem, Stanley. SI's just caught one of your sailors from the carrier passing secrets to a KGB fellow. Bo—"

Rosemont stopped, aghast. "Off the *Ivanov?*"

"Yes."

"Was it Suslev? Captain Suslev?"

"No. No, it wasn't that name. May I suggest you get on to Roger at once. Both men are in custody, both have been charged under the Official Secrets Act but I've cleared it with the minister in London and he agrees you should take charge of your fellow at once . . . a little less embarrassing, what? He's, er, he's a computer chap I believe."

"Son of a bitch!" Rosemont muttered, then wiped the sudden sweat off his face with his hand. "What did he pass over?"

"I don't know exactly. Roger will be able to fill you in on the details."

"Do we get to interrogate . . . to interview the KGB guy too?"

"Why not discuss that with Roger? The minister's in direct touch with him, too." Sir Geoffrey hesitated. "I, er, I'm sure you'll appreciate . . ."

"Yes, of course, sorry, sir. I'd . . . I'd better get going at once." Rosemont's face was chalky and he went off quickly, collecting Ed Langan with him.

Sir Geoffrey sighed. Bloody spies, bloody banks, bloody moles and bloody Socialist idiots who know nothing about Hong Kong. He glanced at his watch. Time to close the party down.

Johnjohn was walking into the anteroom. Dunross was near the bar. "Ian?"

"Oh hello? One for the road?" Dunross said.

"No, thanks. Can I have a word in private?"

"Of course. It'll have to be quick, I was just leaving. I said I'd drop our friendly MPs at the ferry."

"You're on a pink ticket too?"

Dunross smiled faintly. "Actually, old boy, I have one whenever I want it, whether Penn's here or not."

"Yes. You're lucky, you always did have your life well organized," Johnjohn said gloomily.

"Joss."

"I know." Johnjohn led the way out of the room onto the balcony. "Rotten about John Chen, what?"

"Yes. Phillip's taking it very badly. Where's Havergill?"

"He left a few minutes ago."

"Ah, that's why you mentioned 'pink ticket'! He's on the town?"

"I don't know."

"How about Lily Su of Kowloon?"

Johnjohn stared at him.

"I hear Paul's quite enamored."

"How do you do it, know so much?"

Dunross shrugged. He was feeling tired and uneasy and had been hard put not to lose his temper several times tonight when Grey was in the center of another heated argument with some of the tai-pans.

"By the way, Ian, I tried to get Paul to call a board meeting but it's not in my bailiwick."

"Of course." They were in a smaller anteroom. Good Chinese silk paintings and more fine Persian carpets and silver. Dunross noticed the paint was peeling in the corners of the room and off the fine moldings of the ceiling, and this offended him. This is the British raj and the paint shouldn't be peeling.

The silence hung. Dunross pretended to examine some of the exquisite snuff bottles that were on a shelf.

"Ian . . ." Johnjohn stopped and changed his mind. He began again. "This is off the record. You know Tiptop Toe quite well, don't you?"

Dunross stared at him. Tiptop Toe was their nickname for Tip Tok-toh, a middle-aged man from Hunan, Mao Tse-tung's home province, who had arrived during the exodus in 1950. No one seemed to know anything about him, he bothered no one, had a small office in Princes Building, and lived well. Over the years it was evident that he had very particular contacts within the Bank of China and it came to be presumed that he was an official unofficial contact of the bank. No one knew his position in the hierarchy but rumor had it that he was very high. The Bank of China was the only commercial arm of the PRC outside of China, so all of its appointments and contacts were tightly controlled by the ruling hierarchy in Peking.

"What about Tiptop?" Dunross asked, on guard, liking Tiptop—a charming, quiet-spoken man who enjoyed Cognac and spoke excellent English, though, following a usual pattern, nearly always he used an interpreter. His clothes were well cut, though most times he wore a Maoist jacket, looked a little like Chou En-lai and was just as clever. The last time Dunross had dealt with him was about some civilian aircraft the PRC had wanted. Tip Tok-toh had arranged the letters of credit and financing through various Swiss and foreign banks within twenty-four hours. "Tiptop's canny, Ian," Alastair Struan had said many times. "You have to watch yourself but he's the man to deal with. I'd say he was very high up in the Party in Peking. Very."

Dunross watched Johnjohn, curbing his impatience. The smaller man had picked up one of the snuff bottles. The bottles were tiny, ornate ceramic or jade or glass bottles—many of them beautifully painted *inside*, within the glass: landscapes, dancing girls, flowers, birds, seascapes, even poems in incredibly delicate calligraphy. "How do they do that, Ian? Paint on the inside like that?"

"Oh they use a very fine brush. The stem of the brush's bent ninety degrees. In Mandarin they call it *li myan huai*, 'inside face painting.'" Dunross lifted up an elliptical one that had a landscape on one side, a spray of camellias on the other and tiny calligraphy on the paintings.

"Astonishing! What patience! What's the writing say?"

Dunross peered at the tiny column of characters. "Ah, it's one of Mao's sayings: 'Know yourself, know your enemy; a hundred battles, a hundred victories.' Actually the Chairman took it out of Sun Tzu."

Thoughtfully Johnjohn examined it. The windows beyond him were open. A small breeze twisted the neat curtains. "Would you talk to Tiptop for us?"

"About what?"

"We want to borrow the Bank of China's cash."

Dunross gaped at him. "Eh?"

"Yes, for a week or so. They're full to the gills with Hong Kong dollars and there's no run on them. No Chinese'd dare line up outside the Bank of China. They carry Hong Kong dollars as part of their foreign exchange. We'd pay good interest for the loan and put up whatever collateral they'd need."

"This is a formal request by the Victoria?"

"No. It can't be formal. This's my idea, I haven't even discussed it with Paul—only with you. Would you?"

Dunross's excitement crested. "Do I get my 100 million loan tomorrow by 10:00 A.M.?"

"Sorry, I can't do that."

"But Havergill can."

"He can but he won't."

"So why should I help you?"

"Ian, if the bank doesn't stand as solid as the Peak, the market'll crash, and so will the Noble House."

"If I don't get some financing right smartly I'm in the shit anyway."

"I'll do what I can but will you talk to Tiptop at once? Ask him. I can't approach him . . . no one can officially. You'd be doing the Colony a great service."

"Guarantee my loan and I'll talk to him tonight. An eye for an eye and a loan for a loan."

"If you can deliver his promise of a credit up to half a billion in cash by 2:00 P.M. tomorrow, I'll get you the backing you need."

"How?"

"I don't know!"

"Give that to me in writing by 10:00 A.M. signed by you, Havergill and the majority of the board and I'll go and see him."

"That's not possible."

"Tough. An eye for an eye and a loan for a loan." Dunross got up. "Why should the Bank of China bale out the Victoria?"

"We're Hong Kong," Johnjohn said with great confidence. "*We are*. We're the Victoria Bank of Hong Kong and China! We're old friends of China. Without us there's nothing—the Colony'd fall apart and so would Struan's and therefore so would most of Asia."

"Don't bet on that!"

"Without banking, particularly us, China's in bad shape. We've been partners for years with China."

"Then ask Tiptop yourself."

"I can't." Johnjohn's jaw was jutting. "Did you know the Trade Bank of Moscow has again asked for a license to trade in Hong Kong?"

Dunross gasped. "Once they're in we're all on the merry-go-round."

"We've been offered, privately, substantial Hong Kong dollars immediately."

"The board'll vote against it."

"The point is, my dear chap, if you're no longer on the board, the new board can do what the hell it likes," Johnjohn said simply. "If the 'new' board agrees, the governor and the Colonial Office can easily be persuaded. That'd be a small price to pay—to save our dollar. Once an official Soviet bank's here what other devilment could they get up to, eh?"

"You're worse than bloody Havergill!"

"No old chum, better!" The jesting left the banker's face. "Any major change and we become the Noble House, like it or not. Many of our directors would prefer you gone, at any price. I'm just asking you to do Hong Kong and therefore yourself a favor. Don't forget, Ian, the Victoria won't go under, we'll be hurt but not ruined." He touched a bead of sweat away. "No threats, Ian, but I'm asking for a favor. One day I may be chairman and I won't forget."

"Either way."

"Of course, old chum," Johnjohn said sweetly and went to the sideboard. "How about one for the road now? Brandy?"

Robin Grey was seated in the back of Dunross's Rolls with Hugh Guthrie and Julian Broadhurst, Dunross in the front beside his uniformed chauffeur. The windows were fogged. Idly Grey streaked the mist away, enjoying the deep luxury of the sweet-smelling leather.

Soon I'm going to have one of these, he thought. A Rolls of my very own. With a chauffeur. And soon all these bastards'll be crawling, Ian bloody Dunross included. And Penn! Oh yes, my dear sweet sneering sister's going to see the mighty humbled.

"Is it going to rain again?" Broadhurst was asking.

"Yes," Dunross replied. "They think this storm's developing into a full-scale typhoon—at least that's what the Met Office said. This evening I got a report from *Eastern Cloud,* one of our inbound freighters just off Singapore. She said that the seas were heavy even that far south."

"Will the typhoon hit here, tai-pan?" Guthrie, the Liberal MP asked.

"You never know for certain. They can head for you then veer off at the last minute. Or the reverse."

"I remember reading about Wanda, Typhoon Wanda last year. That was a dilly, wasn't it?"

"The worst I've been in. Over two hundred dead, thousands injured, tens of thousands made homeless." Dunross had his arm across the seat and he was half turned around. "*Tai-fun*, the Supreme Winds, were gusting to 170 mph at the Royal Observatory, 190 at Tate's Cairn. The eye of the storm came over us at high tide so our tides in places were twenty-three feet over normal."

"Christ!"

"Yes. At Sha Tin in the New Territories these gusts blew the tidal surge up the channel and breached the storm shelter and shoved fishing boats half a mile inland onto the main street and drowned most of the village. A thousand known fishing boats vanished, eight freighters aground, millions of dollars in damage, most of our squatters' areas blown into the sea." Dunross shrugged. "Joss! But considering the enormity of the storm, the seaborne damage here was incredibly small." His fingers touched the leather seat. Grey noticed the heavy gold and bloodstone signet ring with the Dunross crest. "A real typhoon shows you how really insignificant you are," Dunross said.

"Pity we don't have typhoons every day in that case," Grey said before he could stop himself. "We could use having the mighty in Whitehall humbled twice a day."

"You really are a bore, Robin," Guthrie said. "Do you have to make a sour remark every time?"

Grey went back to his brooding and shut his ears to their conversation. To hell with all of them, he thought.

Soon the car pulled up outside the Mandarin. Dunross got out. "The car'll take you home to the V and A. See you all Saturday if not before. Night."

The car drove off. It circled the huge hotel then headed for the car ferry which was slightly east of the Golden Ferry Terminal along Connaught Road. At the terminal a haphazard line of cars and trucks waited. Grey got out. "I think I'll stretch my legs, walk back to the Golden Ferry and go across in one of them," he said with forced bonhomie. "I need the exercise. Night."

He walked along the Connaught Road waterfront, quickly, relieved that it had been so easy to get away from them. Bloody fools, he thought, his excitement rising. Well, it won't be long before they all get their come-uppance, Broadhurst particularly.

When he was sure he was clear he stopped under a streetlamp, creating an eddy in the massed stream of pedestrians hurrying both ways, and flagged a taxi. "Here," he said and gave the driver a typed address on a piece of paper.

The driver took it, stared at it and scratched his head sullenly.

"It's in Chinese. It's in Chinese on the back," Grey said helpfully.

The driver paid him no attention, just stared blankly at the English address. Grey reached over and turned the characters toward him. "Here!"

At once the driver insolently turned the paper back and glared at the English again. Then he belched, let in his clutch with a jerk and eased into the honking traffic.

Rude sod, Grey thought, suddenly enraged.

The cab ground its gears continually as it went into the city, doubling back down one-way streets and narrow alleys to get back into Connaught Road.

At length they stopped outside a dingy old apartment building on a dingy street. The pavement was broken and narrow and puddled, the traffic honking irritably at the parked cab. There was no number that Grey could see. He got out and told the driver to wait and walked back a little to what seemed to be a side door. An old man was sitting on a battered chair, smoking and reading a racing paper under a bare bulb.

"Is this 68 Kwan Yik Street in Kennedy Town?" Grey asked politely.

The old man stared at him as though he was a monster from outer space, then let out a stream of querulous Cantonese.

"68 Kwan Yik Street," Grey repeated, slower and louder, "Ken-ned-dy Town?"

Another flood of guttural Cantonese and an insolent wave toward a small door. The old man hawked and spat and went back to his paper with a yawn.

"Sodding bastard," Grey muttered, his temperature soaring. He opened the door. Inside was a tiny, grimy foyer with peeling paint, a sorry row of mailboxes with names on the boxes. With great relief he saw the name he sought.

At the cab he took out his wallet and carefully looked at the amount on the meter twice before he paid the man.

The elevator was tiny, claustrophobic, filthy and it squeaked as it rose. At the fourth floor he got off and pressed the button of number 44. The door opened.

"Mr. Grey, sir, this's an honor! Molly, his nibs's arrived!" Sam Finn beamed at him. He was a big beefy Yorkshireman, florid, with pale blue eyes, an ex-coal miner and shop steward with important friends in the Labour Party and Trades Union Council. His face was deeply lined and pitted, the pores ingrained with specks of coal dust. "By gum, 'tis a pleasure!"

"Thank you, Mr. Finn. I'm glad to meet you too. I've heard a lot about you." Grey took off his raincoat and gratefully accepted a beer.

"Sit thee down."

The apartment was small, spotlessly clean, the furniture inexpensive. It smelt of fried sausages and fried potatoes and fried bread. Molly Finn came out of the kitchen, her hands and arms red from years of scrubbing and washing up. She was short and rotund, from the same mining town as her husband, the same age, sixty-five, and just as strong. "By Harry," she said warmly, "thee could've knocked us'n down with feather when we heard thee'd be a-visiting us'n."

"Our mutual friends wanted to hear firsthand how you were doing."

"Grand. We're doing grand," Finn said. " 'Course it's not like home in Yorkshire and we miss our friends and the Union Hall but we've a bed and a bit of board." There was the sound of a toilet flushing. "We've a friend we thought thee'd like to meet," Finn said and smiled again.

"Oh?"

"Aye," Finn said.

The toilet door opened. The big bearded man stuck out his hand warmly. "Sam's told me a lot about you, Mr. Grey. I'm Captain Gregor Suslev of the Soviet Marine. My ship's the *Ivanov*—we're having a small refit in this capitalist haven."

Grey shook his hand formally. "Pleased to meet you."

"We have some mutual friends, Mr. Grey."

"Oh?"

"Yes, Zdenek Hanzolova of Prague."

"Oh! Oh yes!" Grey smiled. "I met him on a Parliamentary Trade Delegation to Czechoslovakia last year."

"How did you like Prague?"

"Very interesting. Very. I didn't like the repression though . . . or the Soviet presence."

Suslev laughed. "We're invited there, by them. We like to look after our friends. But much goes on I don't approve of either. There, in Europe. Even in Mother Russia."

Sam Finn said, "Sit thee down, please sit thee down."

They sat around the dining room table in the living room that now had a neat white tablecloth with a potted aspidistra on it.

"Of course, you know I'm not a Communist, and never have been one," Grey said. "I don't approve of a police state. I'm totally convinced our British democratic socialism's the way of the future—Parliament, elected officials and all that it stands for—though a lot of Marxist-Leninist ideas are very worthwhile."

"Politics!" Gregor Suslev said deprecatingly. "We should leave politics to politics."

"Mr. Grey's one of our best spokesmen in Parliament, Gregor." Molly Finn turned to Grey. "Gregor's a good lad too, Mr. Grey. He's not one of them nasties." She sipped her tea. "Gregor's a good lad."

"That's right, lass," Finn said.

"Not too good, I hope," Grey said and they all laughed. "What made you take up residence here, Sam?"

"When we retired, Mrs. Finn and me, we wanted to see a bit of the world. We'd put a bit of brass aside and we cashed in a wee coop insurance policy we had, and got a berth on a freighter . . ."

"Oh, my, we did have a good time," Molly Finn broke in. "We went to

so many foreign parts. It were proper lovely. But when we cum here Sam
was a bit poorly, so we got off and were to pick up a freighter when she
cum back."

"That's right, lass," Sam said. "Then I met a right proper nice man and
he offered me a job." He beamed and rubbed the black pits in his face. "I
was to be consultant to some mines he was superintendent for, in some
place called Formosa. We went there once but no need to stay so we cum
back here. That's all there is to it, Mr. Grey. We make a little brass, the
beer's good, so Mrs. Finn and me we thought we'd stay. The kids are all
growed up. . . ." He beamed again, showing his obviously false teeth.
"We're Hong Kongers now."

They chatted pleasantly. Grey would have been totally convinced by
the Finns' cover story if he had not read his very private dossier before he
left London. It was known only to very few that for years Finn had been
a card-carrying member of the BCP, the British Communist Party. On his
retirement he had been sent out to Hong Kong by one of their secret
inner committees, his mission to be a fountain of information about anything to do with the Hong Kong bureaucracy and legislature.

In a few minutes Molly Finn stifled a yawn. "My my, I'm that tired! If
thee will excuse me I think I'll go to bed."

Sam said, "Off thee go, lass."

They talked a little more about inconsequential affairs then he too
yawned. "If thee'll excuse me, I think I'll go too," adding hastily, "Now
don't thee move, chat to thy heart's content. We'll see thee before thee
leaves Hong Kong, Mr. Grey . . . Gregor."

He shook hands with them and closed the bedroom door behind him.
Suslev went over to the television and turned it on with a laugh. "Have
you seen Hong Kong TV? The commercials are very funny."

He adjusted the sound high enough so they could talk yet not be overheard. "One can't be too careful, eh?"

"I bring you fraternal greetings from London," Grey said, his voice as
soft. Since 1947 he had been an inner-core Communist, even more secretly than Finn, his identity only known to half a dozen people in England.

"And I send them back." Suslev jerked his thumb at the closed door.
"How much do they know?"

"Only that I'm left-wing and potential Party material."

"Excellent." Suslev relaxed. Center had been very clever to arrange this
private meeting so neatly. Roger Crosse, who knew nothing of his connection with Grey, had already told him there were no SI tails on the MPs.
"We're quite safe here. Sam's very good. We get copies of his reports too.
And he asks no questions. You British are very close-mouthed and very
efficient, Mr. Grey. I congratulate you."

"Thank you."

"How was your meeting in Peking?"

Grey took out a sheaf of papers. "This's a copy of our private and pub-lic reports to Parliament. Read it before I go—you'll get the full report through channels. Briefly, I think the Chinese are totally hostile and revisionist. Madman Mao and his henchman Chou En-lai are implacable enemies to international communism. China is weak in everything except the will to fight, and they will fight to protect their land to the last. The longer you wait the harder it will be to contain them, but so long as they don't get nuclear weapons and long-range delivery systems they'll never be a threat."

"Yes. What about trade? What did they want?"

"Heavy industries, oil cracking plants, oil rigs, chemical plants, steel mills."

"How are they going to pay?"

"They said they've plenty of foreign exchange. Hong Kong supplies much of it."

"Did they ask for arms?"

"No. Not directly. They're clever and we didn't always talk or meet as a group. They were well briefed about me and Broadhurst and we weren't liked—or trusted. Perhaps they talked privately to Pennyworth or one of the other Tories—though that won't've helped them. You heard he died?"

"Yes."

"Good riddance. He was an enemy." Grey sipped his beer. "The PRC want arms, of that I'm sure. They're a secretive lot and rotten."

"What's Julian Broadhurst like?"

"An intellectual who thinks he's a Socialist. He's the dregs but useful at the moment. Patrician, old school tie," Grey said with a sneer. "Because of that he'll be a power in the next Labour government."

"Labour will get in next time, Mr. Grey?"

"No, I don't think so, even though we're working very hard to help Labour and the Liberals."

Suslev frowned. "Why support Liberals? They're capitalists."

Grey laughed sardonically. "You don't understand our British system, Captain Suslev. We're very lucky, we've a three-party vote with a two-party system. The Liberals split the vote in our favor. We have to encour-age them." Happily he finished his beer and got two more from the refrig-erator. "If it wasn't for the Liberals, Labour would have *never* got in, not never! And never will again."

"I don't understand."

"At the best of times the vote for Labour's only about 45 percent of the population, a little under 45 percent. Tory—Conservatives—are about the same, usually a little more. Most of the other 10-odd percent vote Liberal. If there was no Liberal candidate the majority'd vote with the Conser-vatives. They're all fools," he said smugly. "The British are stupid, com-rade, the Liberal Party's Labour's permanent passport to power—therefore ours. Soon the BCP'll control the TUC, and so Labour completely—

secretly of course." He drank deeply. "The great British unwashed are stupid, the middle class stupid, the upper class stupid—it's almost no challenge anymore. They're all lemmings. Only a very few believe in democratic socialism. Even so," he added with great satisfaction, "we pulled down their rotten Empire and pissed all over them with Operation Lion." Operation Lion was formulated as soon as the Bolsheviks had come to power. Its purpose, the destruction of the British Empire. "In just eighteen years, since 1945, the greatest empire the world has ever seen's become nonexistent."

"Except for Hong Kong."

"Soon that will go too."

"I cannot tell you how important my superiors consider your work," Suslev said with pretended open admiration. "You and all our fraternal British brothers." His orders were to be deferential to this man, to debrief him on his Chinese mission, to pass on instructions as requests. And to flatter him. He had read Grey's dossier and the Finns'. Robin Grey had a Beria-KGB classification 4/22/a: "An important British traitor paying lip service to Marxist-Leninist ideals. He is to be used but never trusted, and, should the British Communist Party ever reach power, is subject to immediate liquidation."

Suslev watched Grey. Neither Grey nor the Finns knew his real position, only that he was a minor member of the Vladivostok Communist Party—which was also on his SI dossier.

"You have some information for me?" Grey asked.

"Yes, *tovarich*, and also, with your permission, a few questions. I was told to ask about your implementation of Directive 72/Prague." This highly secret directive put top priority on infiltrating covert, hard-core experts into positions as shop stewards, in every car-manufacturing plant throughout the U.S. and the West—the motor industry, because of its countless allied industries, being the core of any capitalist society.

"We're full speed ahead," Grey told him enthusiastically. "Wildcat strikes are the way of the future. With wildcats we can get around union hierarchies without disrupting existing unionism. Our unions're fragmented. Deliberately. Fifty men can be a separate union and that union can dominate thousands—and so long as there's never a secret ballot, the few will always rule the many!" He laughed. "We're ahead of schedule, and now we've fraternal brothers in Canada, New Zealand, Rhodesia, Australia—particularly Australia. Within a few years we'll have trained agitators in every key machine-shop union in the English-speaking world. A Brit will lead the workers wherever there's a strike—Sydney, Vancouver, Johannesburg, Wellington. It'll be a Brit!"

"And you're one of the leaders, *tovarich!* How marvelous!" Suslev let him continue, leading him on, disgusted that it was so easy to flatter him. How dreadful traitors are, he told himself. "Soon you'll have the democratic paradise you seek and there'll be peace on earth."

"It won't be long," Grey said fervently. "We've cut the armed services and we'll cut them even more next year. War's over forever. The bomb's done that. It's only the rotten Americans and their arms race who stand in the way but soon we'll force even them to lay down their arms and we'll all be equal."

"Did you know America's secretly arming the Japanese?"

"Eh?" Grey stared at him.

"Oh, didn't you know?" Suslev was well aware of Grey's three and a half years in Japanese POW camps. "Didn't you know the U.S. has a military mission there right now asking them if they'd accept nuclear weapons?"

"They'd never dare."

"But they have, Mr. Grey," Suslev said, the lie coming so easily. "Of course it's all totally secret."

"Can you give me details I could use in Parliament?"

"Well, I'll certainly ask my superiors to furnish that to you if you think it'd be of value."

"Please, as soon as possible. Nuclear bombs . . . Christ!"

"Are your people, your trained experts, in British nuclear plants too?"

"Eh?" Grey concentrated with an effort, heaving his mind off Japan. "Nuclear plants?"

"Yes. Are you getting your Brits?"

"Well, no, there's only one or two plants in the U.K. and they're unimportant. The Yanks're really arming the Japs?"

"Isn't Japan capitalist? Isn't Japan a U.S. protégé? Aren't they building nuclear plants too? If it wasn't for America . . ."

"Those American sods! Thank God you've the bombs too or we'd all have to kowtow!"

"Perhaps you should concentrate some effort on your nuclear plants, eh?" Suslev said smoothly, astounded that Grey could be so gullible.

"Why?"

"There's a new study out, by one of your countrymen. Philby."

"Philby?" Grey remembered how shocked and frightened he had been at Philby's discovery and flight, then how relieved he was that Philby and the others had escaped without giving lists of the inner core of the BCP that they must have had. "How is he?"

"I understand he's very well. He's working in Moscow. Did you know him?"

"No. He was Foreign Office, stratosphere. None of us knew he was one of us."

"He points out in this study that a nuclear plant is self-sustaining, that one plant can generate fuel for itself and for others. Once a nuclear plant is operating, in effect it is almost perpetual, it requires only a few highly skilled, highly educated technicians to operate it, no workers, unlike oil or coal. At the moment all industry in the West's dependent on coal or oil.

He suggests it should be our policy to encourage use of oil, not coal, and completely discourage nuclear power. Eh?"

"Ah, I see his point!" Grey's face hardened. "I shall get myself on the parliamentary committee to study atomic energy."

"Will that be easy?"

"Too easy, comrade! Brits are lazy, they want no problems, they just want to work as little as possible for as much money as possible, to go to the pub and football on Saturdays—and no unpaid work, no tedious committees after hours, no arguments. It's too easy—when we have a plan and they don't."

Suslev sighed, very satisfied, his work almost done. "Another beer? No, let me get it, it's my honor, Mr. Grey. Do you happen to know a writer who's here at the moment, a U.S. citizen, Peter Marlowe?"

Grey's head snapped up. "Marlowe? I know him very well, didn't know he was a U.S. citizen though. Why?"

Suslev kept his interest hidden and shrugged. "I was just asked to ask you, since you are English and he originally was English."

"He's a rotten upper-class sod with the morals of a barrow boy. Hadn't seen him for years, not since '45, until he turned up here. He was in Changi too. I didn't know he was a writer until yesterday, or one of those film people. What's important about him?"

"He's a writer," Suslev said at once. "He makes films. With television, writers can reach millions. Center keeps track of Western writers as a matter of policy. Oh yes, we know about writers in Mother Russia, how important they are. Our writers have always pointed the way for us, Mr. Grey, they've formed our thinking and feeling, Tolstoy, Dostoevski, Chekhov, Bunin . . ." He added with pride, "Writers with us are pathfinders. That's why nowadays we must guide them in their formation and control their work or bury it." He looked at Grey. "You should do the same."

"We support friendly writers, Captain, and damn the other shower whichever way we can, publicly and privately. When I get home, I'll put Marlowe on our formal BCP media shit list. It'll be easy to do him some harm—we've lots of friends in our media."

Suslev lit a cigarette. "Have you read his book?"

"The one about Changi? No, no I haven't. I'd never heard of it until I got here. It probably wasn't published in England. Besides, I don't have much time to read fiction and if he did it, it's got to be upper-class shit and a penny-dreadful and . . . well Changi's Changi and best forgotten." A shudder went through him that he did not notice. "Yes, best forgotten."

But I can't, he wanted to shout. I can't forget and it's still a never-ending nightmare, those days of the camp, year after year, the tens of thousands dying, trying to enforce the law, trying to protect the weak against black market filth feeding off the weak, everyone starving and no hope of ever getting out, my body rotting away and only twenty-one with no women and no laughter and no food and no drink, twenty-one when I was caught in Singapore in 1942 and twenty-four, almost twenty-five when the miracle happened and I survived and got back to England—home gone, parents gone, world gone and my only sister sold out to the enemy, now talking like the enemy, eating like them, living like them, married to one, ashamed of our past, wanting the past dead, me dead, nobody caring and oh Christ, *the change*. Coming back to life after the no-life of Changi, all the nightmares and the no sleeping in the night, terrified of life, unable to talk about it, weeping and not knowing why I was weeping, trying to adjust to what fools called normal. Adjusting at length. But at what cost, oh dear sweet Jesus at what a cost . . .

Stop it!

With an effort Grey pulled himself off the descending spiral of Changi. Enough of Changi! Changi's dead. Let Changi stay dead. It's dead—Changi's got to stay dead. But Ch—

"What?" he said, jerked into the present again.

"I just said, your present government is completely vulnerable now."

"Oh? Why?"

"You remember the Profumo scandal? Your minister of war?"

"Of course. Why?"

"Some months ago, MI-5 began a very secret, very searching investigation into the alleged connection between the now famous call girl, Christine Keeler, and Commander Yevgeny Ivanov, our naval attaché, and other London social figures."

"Is it finished?" Grey asked, suddenly attentive.

"Yes. It documents conversations the woman had with Commander Ivanov. Ivanov had asked her to find out from Profumo when nuclear weapons would be delivered to Germany. It claims," Suslev said, deliberately lying now to excite Grey, "that Profumo had been given security warnings by MI-5 about Ivanov *some months before* the scandal broke—that Commander Ivanov was KGB and also her lover."

"Oh Christ! Will Commander Ivanov substantiate it?"

"Oh no. Absolutely not. That would not be correct—or necessary. But MI-5's report tells the facts accurately," Suslev lied smoothly. "The report's true!"

Grey let out a shout of laughter. "Oh Christ, this'll blow the government off the front bench and bring about a general election!"

"And Labour in!"

"Yes! For five wonderful years! Oh yes and once we're in . . . oh my God!" Grey let out another bellow of laughter. "First he lied about Keeler! And now you say he *knew* about Ivanov all the time! Oh bloody Christ, yes, that'll cause the government to fall! This'll be worth all the years of taking the shit from those middle-class sods. You're sure?" he asked with sudden anxiety. "It's really true?"

"Would I lie to you?" Suslev laughed to himself.

"I'll use it. Oh God will I use it." Grey was beside himself with joy. "You're absolutely sure? But Ivanov. What happened to him?"

"Promotion of course for a brilliantly executed maneuver to discredit an enemy government. If his work helps to bring it down, he'll be decorated. He's presently in Moscow waiting for reassignment. By the way, at your press conference tomorrow, do you plan to mention your brother-in-law?"

Grey was suddenly on guard. "How did you know about him?"

Suslev stared back calmly. "My superiors know everything. I was told to suggest you might consider mentioning your connection at the press conference, Mr. Grey."

"Why?"

"To enhance your position, Mr. Grey. Such a close association with the tai-pan of the Noble House would make your words have much greater impact here. Wouldn't they?"

"But if you know about him," Grey said, his voice hard, "you also know about my sister and me, that we've an agreement not to mention it. It's a family matter."

"Matters to do with the State take preference over family matters, Mr. Grey."

"Who are you?" Grey was suddenly suspicious. "Who are you really?"

"Just a messenger, Mr. Grey, really." Suslev put his great hands on Grey's shoulders and held him warmly. "*Tovarich,* you know how we must use everything in our power to push the cause. I'm sure my superiors were only thinking of your future. A close family connection with such a capitalist family would help you in Parliament. Wouldn't it? When you and your Labour Party get in next year they'll need well-connected men and women, eh? For cabinet rank you need connections, you said so yourself. You'll be the Hong Kong expert, with special connections. You can help us tremendously to contain China, put her back on the right track, and put Hong Kong and all Hong Kong people where they belong—in the sewer. Eh?"

Grey thought about that, his heart thumping. "We could obliterate Hong Kong?"

"Oh yes." Suslev smiled. The smile broadened. "There is no need to worry, you wouldn't have to volunteer anything about the tai-pan or break your word to your sister. I can arrange for you to be asked a question. Eh?"

54

Dunross was waiting for Brian Kwok in the Quance Bar of the Mandarin, sipping a long brandy and Perrier. The bar was men only and almost empty. Brian Kwok had never been late before but he was late now.

Too easy to have an emergency in his job, Dunross thought, unperturbed. I'll give him a couple more minutes.

Tonight Dunross did not mind waiting. He had plenty of time to get to Aberdeen and Four Finger Wu and as Penn was safely en route to England, there was no pressure to get back.

The trip will be good for her, he told himself. London, the theater, and then Castle Avisyard. It will be grand there. Soon autumn and crisp mornings, your breath visible, the grouse season, and then Christmas. It will be grand to be home for Christmas in the snow. I wonder what this Christmas will bring and what I'll think when looking back to this time, this bad time. Too many problems now. The plan working but creaking already, everything bad and not in control, my control. Bartlett, Casey, Gornt, Four Fingers, Mata, Tightfist, Havergill, Johnjohn, Kirk, Crosse, Sinders, AMG, his Riko, all moths around the flame—and now a new one, Tiptop, and Hiro Toda arriving tomorrow instead of Saturday.

This afternoon he had talked at length to his Japanese friend and ship-building partner. Toda had asked about the stock market and about Struan's, not directly English style but obliquely, politely Japanese style. Even so, he had asked. Dunross had heard the gravity under the smooth, American-tinged voice—the product of two years postgraduate school at Harvard.

"Everything's going to be fine, Hiro," Dunross had told him. "It's a temporary attack. We take delivery of the ships as planned."

Will we?

Yes. Some way or another. Linbar goes to Sydney tomorrow to try to resurrect the Woolara deal and renegotiate the charter. A long shot.

Inexorably his mind turned back to Jacques. Is Jacques truly a Communist traitor? And Jason Plumm and Tuke? And R. Is he Roger Crosse or Robert Armstrong? Surely neither of them and surely not Jacques! For God's sake I've known Jacques most of my life—I've known the deVilles for most of my life. It's true Jacques could have given Bartlett some of the information about our inner workings, but not all of it. Not the company part, that's tai-pan knowledge only. That means Alastair, Father, me or old Sir Ross. All unthinkable.

Yes.

But someone's a traitor and it isn't me. And then there's Sevrin.

Dunross looked around. The bar was still almost empty. It was a small, pleasing, comfortable room with dark-green leather chairs and old polished oak tables, the walls lined with Quance paintings. They were all prints. Many of the originals were in the long gallery in the Great House, most of the remainder in the corridors of the Victoria and Blacs banks. A few were privately owned elsewhere. He leaned back in the alcove, at ease, glad to be surrounded by so much of his own past, feeling protected by it. Just above his head was a portrait of a Haklo boat-girl with a fair-haired boy in her arms, his hair in a queue. Quance was supposed to have painted this as a birthday present for Dirk Struan from the girl in the picture, May-may T'Chung, the child in her arms supposed to be their son, Duncan.

His eyes went across the room to the portraits of Dirk and his half-brother Robb beside another painting of the American trader Jeff Cooper, and landscapes of the Peak and the praya in 1841. I wonder what Dirk would say if he could see his creation now. Thriving, building, reclaiming, still the center of the world, the Asian world which is the only world.

"Another, tai-pan?"

"No thanks, Feng," he said to the Chinese barman. "Just a Perrier, please."

A phone was nearby. He dialed.

"Police headquarters," the woman's voice said.

"Superintendent Kwok please."

"Just a moment, sir."

As Dunross waited he tried to decide about Jacques. Impossible, he thought achingly, not without help. Sending him to France to pick up Susanne and Avril isolates him for a week or so. Perhaps I'll talk to Sinders, perhaps they already know. Christ almighty, if AMG hadn't put the R down I'd've gone directly to Crosse. Is it possible that he could be Arthur?

Remember Philby of the Foreign Office, he told himself, revolted that an Englishman of that background and in such a high position of trust could be a traitor. And the other two equally, Burgess and Maclean. And Blake. How far to believe AMG? Poor bugger. How far to trust Jamie Kirk?

"Who's calling Superintendent Kwok please?" a man's voice asked on the phone.

"Mr. Dunross of Struan's."

"Just a moment please." A short wait then a man's voice that he recognized at once. "Evening, tai-pan. Robert Armstrong . . . sorry but Brian's not available. Was it anything important?"

"No. We just had a date for a drink now and he's late."

"Oh, he never mentioned it—he's usually spot on about something like that. When did you make the date?"

"This morning. He called to tell me about John Chen. Anything new on those bastards?"

"No. Sorry. Brian had to go out of town—a quick trip, you know how it is."

"Oh of course. If you talk to him tell him I'll see him Sunday at the hill climb, if not before."

"Do you still intend to go to Taiwan?"

"Yes. With Bartlett. Sunday, back Tuesday. I hear we can use his plane."

"Yes. Please make sure he comes back on Tuesday."

"If not before."

"Nothing I can do for you?"

"No thank you, Robert."

"Tai-pan, we've, we've had another rather disturbing encounter, here in Hong Kong. Not to worry you but take it easy until tomorrow with Sinders, eh?"

"Of course. Brian said the same. And Roger. Thanks, Robert. Night."

Dunross hung up. He had forgotten that he had an SI bodyguard following him. The fellow must be better than the others. I didn't notice him at all. Now what to do about him? He's certainly unwelcome with Four Fingers.

"I'll be back in a moment," he said.

"Yes, tai-pan," the barman said.

Dunross went out and strolled to the men's room, watching without watching. No one followed him. When he had finished he went into the noisy crowded mezzanine, across and down the main staircase to the newsstand in the foyer to buy an evening paper. There were crowds everywhere. Coming back, he zeroed in on a slight, bespectacled Chinese who was watching him over a magazine from a chair in the foyer. Dunross hesitated, went back to the foyer and saw the eyes following him. Satisfied, he went back up the crowded stairs. "Oh hello, Marlowe," he said, almost bumping into him.

"Oh hello, tai-pan."

At once Dunross saw the great weariness in the other man's face. "What's up?" he asked, instantly sensing trouble, stepping out of the way of the crowds.

"Oh nothing . . . nothing at all."

"Something's up." Dunross smiled gently.

Peter Marlowe hesitated. "It's, it's Fleur." He told him about her.

Dunross was greatly concerned. "Old Tooley's a good doctor so that's
one thing." He related to Marlowe how Tooley had filled him, Bartlett
and Casey full of antibiotics. "Are you all right?"

"Yes. Just a touch of the runs. Nothing to worry about for a month or
so." Peter Marlowe told him what Tooley had said about hepatitis. "That
doesn't worry me, it's Fleur and the baby, that's the worry."

"Do you have an *amah?*"

"Oh yes. And the hotel's marvelous, the room boys are all pitching in."

"Have you time for a drink?"

"No, no thanks, I'd better be getting back. The *amah's* not . . . there's
no room for her so she's just baby-sitting. I've got to drop by the nursing
home on the way back, just to check."

"Oh, then another time. Please give your wife my regards. How's the
research going?"

"Fine, thank you."

"How many more of our skeletons have you wheedled out of our Hong
Kong *yan?*"

"Lots. But they're all good." Peter Marlowe smiled faintly. "Dirk
Struan was one helluva man. Everyone says you are too and they all hope
you'll best Gornt, that you'll win again."

Dunross looked at him, liking him. "Do you mind questions about
Changi?" He saw the shadow pass across the rugged used face that was
young-old.

"That depends."

"Robin Grey said you were a black marketeer in the camp. With an
American. A corporal."

There was a long pause and Peter Marlowe's face did not change. "I
was a trader, Mr. Dunross, or actually, an interpreter for my friend who
was a trader. He was an American corporal. He saved my life and the life
of my friends. There were four of us, a major, a group captain, a rubber
planter and me. He saved dozens of others too. His name was King and he
was a king, King of Changi in a way." Again the faint smile. "Trading
was against Japanese law—and camp law."

"You said Japanese, not Jap. That's interesting," Dunross said at once.
"After all those horrors at Changi, you don't detest them?"

After a pause Peter Marlowe shook his head. "I don't detest anyone.
Even Grey. It takes all of my mind and energy to appreciate that I'm
alive. Night!" He turned to go.

"Oh, Marlowe, one last thing," Dunross said quickly, making a decision. "Would you like to go to the races Saturday? My box? There'll be a
few interesting people . . . if you're researching Hong Kong you might as
well do it in style, eh?"

"Thank you. Thank you very much but Donald McBride's invited me. I'd like to stop by for a drink though, if I may. Any luck on the book?"

"Sorry?"

"The book on the history of Struan's, the one you're going to let me read."

"Oh yes, of course. I'm having it retyped," Dunross said. "It seems there's only one copy. If you'll bear with me?"

"Of course. Thanks."

"Give my best to Fleur." Dunross watched him go, glad that Marlowe understood the difference between trading and black marketeering. His eyes fell on the Chinese SI man who still watched him over the magazine. He walked slowly back to the bar as though lost in thought. When he was safe inside he said quickly, "Feng, there's a bloody newsman downstairs I don't want to see."

At once the barman opened the countertop. "It's a pleasure, tai-pan," he said, smiling, not believing the excuse at all. His customers frequently used the servants' exit behind the bar. As women were not allowed inside the bar, it was usual that it was a woman who was to be avoided outside. Now what whore would the tai-pan want to avoid? he asked himself, bemused, watching him leave a generous tip and hurry away through the exit.

Once on the street in the side alley Dunross walked quickly around the corner and got a taxi, hunching down into the back.

"Aberdeen," he ordered and gave directions in Cantonese.

"*Ayeeyah*, like an arrow, tai-pan," the driver said at once, brightening as he recognized him. "May I ask what are the chances for Saturday? Rain or no rain?"

"No rain, by all the gods."

"Eeeee, and the winner of the fifth?"

"The gods haven't whispered it to me, nor the foul High Tigers who bribe jockeys or drug horses to cheat honest people out of an honest gamble. But Noble Star will be trying."

"All the fornicators'll be trying," the driver said sourly, "but who's the one chosen by the gods and by the High Tiger of Happy Valley Racetrack? What about Pilot Fish?"

"The stallion's good."

"Butterscotch Lass? Banker Kwang needs a change of luck."

"Yes. The Lass's good too."

"Will the market go down more, tai-pan?"

"Yes, but buy Noble House at a quarter to three on Friday."

"At what price?"

"Use your head, Venerable Brother. Am I Old Blind Tung?"

* * *

Orlanda and Linc Bartlett were dancing very close in the semi-darkness of the nightclub, feeling the length of each other. The music was soft and sensual, the beat good, the band Filipino, and the great mirrored luxurious room was deftly pool lit, with private alcoves and low deep chaises around low tables and tuxedoed waiters with pencil flashlights like so many fireflies. Many girls in colorful evening dresses sat together chatting or watching the few dancers. From time to time singly or in pairs they would join a man or men at the tables to ply them with laughter and conversation and drinks and, after a quarter of an hour or so, move on, their movements delicately orchestrated by the ever-watchful mama-*san* and her helpers. The mama-*san* here was a lithe attractive Shanghainese woman in her fifties, well dressed and discreet. She spoke six languages and was responsible to the owner for the girls. On her depended the success or failure of the business. The girls obeyed her totally. So did the bouncers and waiters. She was the nucleus, the queen of her domain, and as such, fawned upon.

It was rare for a man to bring a date though it was not resented—providing the tip was generous and the drinks continuous. Dozens of these pleasure places of the night were spread about the Colony, a few private, most open, catering to men—tourists, visitors or Hong Kong *yan*. All were well stocked with dancing partners of all races. You paid them to sit with you, to chat or to laugh or to listen. Prices varied, quality varied with your choice of place, the purpose always the same. Pleasure for the guest. Money for the house.

Linc Bartlett and Orlanda were closer now, swaying more than dancing, her head soft against his chest. One of her hands was gently on his shoulder, the other held by his, cool to his touch. He had one arm almost around her, his hand resting on her waist. She felt his warmth deep in her loins and almost absently, her fingers caressed the nape of his neck and she eased a little closer, drawn by the music. Her feet followed his perfectly, so did her body. In a moment she felt his stirring and then his length.

How do I deal with him tonight? she asked herself dreamily, loving the night and how perfect it had been. Do I or don't I? Oh how I want . . .

Her body seemed to be moving of its own volition, now even closer, her back slightly arched, loins forward. A wave of heat swept her.

Too much heat, she thought. With an effort she pulled herself back.

Bartlett sensed her leaving him. His hand stayed on her waist and he held her against him, feeling nothing but her body under his hand, no undergarment. So rare. Just flesh under the gossamer chiffon . . . and more warmth than flesh. Jesus!

"Let's sit for a moment," she said throatily.

"When the dance ends," he muttered.

"No, no, Linc, my legs feel weak." With an effort she put both hands around his neck and leaned back a little, keeping herself against him but letting him take some of her weight. Her smile was vast. "I may fall. You wouldn't want me to fall, would you?"

"You can't fall," he said, smiling back. "No way."

"Please . . ."

"You wouldn't want me to fall would you?"

She laughed and her laugh thrilled him. Jesus, he thought, slow down, she's got you going.

For a moment they danced, but apart, and that cooled him a little. Then he turned her and followed her close and they sat down at their table, lounging on their sofa, still aware of their closeness. Their legs touched.

"The same, sir?" the dinner-jacketed waiter asked.

"Not for me, Linc," she said, wanting to curse the waiter for his ineptness, their drinks not yet finished.

"Another crème de menthe?" Bartlett said.

"Not for me, truly, thanks. But you have one."

The waiter vanished. Bartlett would have preferred a beer but he didn't want that smell on his breath and, even more, he did not want to spoil the most perfect meal he had ever had. The pasta had been wonderful, the veal tender and juicy with a lemon and wine sauce that was mouth tingling, the salad perfect. Then *zabaglione*, mixed in front of him, eggs and Marsala and magic. And always her radiance, the touch of her perfume.

"This is the best evening I've had in years."

She raised her glass with mock solemnity. "Here's to many more," she said. Yes, here's to many many more but after we're married, or at least engaged. You're too heady, Linc Bartlett, too tuned in to my psyche, too strong. "I'm glad you've enjoyed it. So have I. Oh yes, so have I!" She saw his eyes slide off her as a hostess brushed by, her gown low cut. The girl was lovely, barely twenty, and she joined a group of boisterous Japanese businessmen with many girls at a corner table. At once another girl got up and excused herself and went away. Orlanda watched him watching them, her mind now crystal clear.

"Are they all for hire?" he asked involuntarily.

"For pillowing?"

His heart missed a beat and he glanced back at her, all attention. "Yes, I suppose that's what I meant," he said cautiously.

"The answer's no, and yes." She kept her smile gentle, her voice soft. "That's like most things in Asia, Linc. Nothing's ever really no or yes. It's always maybe. It depends on the availability of a hostess. It depends on the man, the money and the amount she's in debt." Her smile was mischievous. "Perhaps I shall just point you in the right direction but then you'd be up to no good—because you fascinate all pretty ladies, big strong man like you *heya?*"

"Come on, Orlanda!" he said with a laugh as she aped a coolie accent.

"I saw you notice her. I don't blame you, she's lovely," she said, envying the girl her youth but not her life.

"What did you mean about debts?"

"When a girl first comes to work here she has to look pretty. Clothes are expensive, hairdressing expensive, stockings, makeup, everything expensive, so the mama-*san*—that's the woman who looks after the girls—or the nightclub owner will advance the girl enough to buy all the things she needs. Of course in the beginning all the girls are young and frivolous, fresh like a first rose of summer, so they buy and buy and then they have to pay back. Most have nothing when they begin, just themselves—unless they've been a hostess in another club and have a following. Girls change nightclubs, Linc, naturally, once they're out of debt. Sometimes an owner will pay the debts of a girl to acquire her and her followers—many girls are very popular and sought after. For a girl it can be well paying, if you can dance, converse and speak several languages."

"Their debts're heavy then?"

"Perpetual. The longer they stay the harder it is to look pretty so the more the cost. Interest on the debt is 20 percent at the very least. In the first months the girl can earn much to pay back much but never enough." A shadow passed over her face. "Interest builds up, the debt builds up. Not all patrons are patient. So the girl has to seek other forms of financing. Sometimes she has to borrow from loan sharks to pay back the patron. Inevitably she seeks help. Then one night the mama-*san* points out a man. 'He wants to buy you out,' she'll say. An—"

"What does that mean, to buy a girl out?"

"Oh that's just a nightclub custom here. All the girls have to be here promptly, say eight, when the club opens, neat and groomed. They have to stay till 1:00 P.M. or they'll be fined—and fined also if they are absent or if they're late or not neat and not groomed and not pleasant to the customers. If a man wants to take a girl out by himself, for dinner or whatever, and many customers just take the girls for dinner—many even take a couple of girls for dinner, mostly to impress their friends—he buys the girl out of the club, he pays the club a fee, the amount depends on the time left before closing. I don't know how much she gets of the fee, I think it's 30 percent, but what she makes outside is all hers, unless the mama-*san* negotiates for her before she leaves. Then the house gets a fee."

"Always a fee?"

"It's a matter of face, Linc. In this place, which is one of the best, to buy a girl out it would cost you about 80 HK an hour, about $16 U.S."

"That's not much," he said absently.

"Not much to a millionaire, my dear. But for thousands here, 80 HK has to last a family for a week."

Bartlett was watching her, wondering about her, wanting her, so glad that he didn't have to buy her out. Shit, that'd be terrible. Or would it? he asked himself. At least that way it'd be a few bucks, then in the sack and move on again. Is that what I want?

"What?" she asked.

"I was just thinking what a rotten life these girls have."

"Oh not rotten, not rotten at all," she said with the immense innocence he found shattering. "This is probably the best time in their lives, certainly the first time in their lives they've ever worn anything pretty, been flattered and sought after. What other kind of job can they get if you're a girl without a great education? Secretarial if you're lucky, or else in a factory, twelve to fourteen hours a day for 10 HK a day. You should go to one, Linc, see the conditions. I'll take you. Please? You must see how people work, then you'll understand about us here. I'd love to be your guide. Now that you're staying you should know everything, Linc, experience everything. Oh no, they think themselves lucky. At least for a short time in their lives they live well and eat well and laugh a lot."

"No tears?"

"Always tears. But tears is a way of life for a girl."

"Not for you."

She sighed and put her hand on his arm. "I've had my share. But you make me forget all the tears I've ever had." A sudden burst of laughter made them look up. The four Japanese businessmen were hunched down with six girls, their table loaded with drinks and more arriving. "I'm so happy I don't have to . . . have to serve the Japanese," she said simply, "I bless my joss for that. But they are the biggest spenders, Linc, much more than any other tourists. They spend even more than the Shanghainese, so they get the best service even though they're hated and they know they're hated. They don't seem to care that their spending buys them nothing except falsehoods. Perhaps they know it, they're clever, very clever. Certainly they have a different attitude to pillowing and to Ladies of the Night, different from other people." Another burst of laughter. "Chinese call them *lang syin gou fei* in Mandarin, literally 'wolf's heart, dog's lungs,' meaning men without conscience."

He frowned. "That doesn't make sense."

"Oh but it does! You see Chinese cook and eat every part of fish, fowl or animal except for a wolf's heart and a dog's lungs. They're the only two things that you cannot flavor—they always stink whatever you do to them." She looked back at the other table. "To Chinese, Japanese men're *lang syin gou fei*. So is money. Money has no conscience either." She smiled a strange smile and sipped her liqueur. "Nowadays many mama-*sans* or owners will advance money to a girl to help her learn Japanese. To entertain, of course you have to communicate, no?"

Another bevy of girls went past and she saw them look at Bartlett and then at her speculatively and look away again. Orlanda knew they despised her because she was Eurasian and with a *quai loh* customer. They joined another table. The club was filling up.

"Which one do you want?" she asked.

"What?"

She laughed at his shock. "Oh come now, Linc Bartlett, I saw your wandering eye. Is—"

"Stop it, Orlanda!" he said uncomfortably, a sudden edge to his voice. "In this place it's impossible not to notice."

"Of course, that's why I suggested it," she said immediately, forcing her smile steady, her reactions very fast and again she touched him, her hand tender on his knee. "I picked this place for you so you could feast your eyes." She snapped her fingers. Instantly the maître d' was there, kneeling politely beside their low table. "Give me your card," she said imperiously in Shanghainese, almost sick with an apprehension that she hid perfectly. At once the man produced what looked like a playbill. "Leave me your flashlight. I'll call you when I need you."

The man went away. Like a conspirator she moved closer. Now their legs were touching. Linc put his arm around her. She directed the pencil light at the playbill. There were photographs, portraits of twenty or thirty girls. Underneath each were rows of Chinese characters. "Not all these girls will be here tonight, but if you see one you like we'll bring her over."

He stared at her. "Are you serious?"

"Very serious, Linc. You don't have to worry, I'll negotiate for you, if you like her, after you've met her and talked to her."

"I don't want one of these, I want you."

"Yes. Yes I know, my darling, and . . . but for tonight, bear with me, please. Play a little game, let me design your night."

"Jesus, you're something else!"

"And you're the most marvelous man I've ever known and I want to make your night perfect. I can't give you me now, much as I want to, so we'll find a temporary substitute. What do you say?"

Bartlett was still staring at her. He finished his drink and did not taste it. Another appeared out of nowhere. He drank half of it.

Orlanda knew the chance she was taking but felt that either way she would draw him tighter to her. If he accepted he would be beholden to her for an exciting night, a night that Casey or any *quai loh* woman would never in a thousand years have offered to him. If he refused, then he would still be grateful for her generosity. "Linc, this is Asia. Here sex is not Anglo-Saxon mumbo-jumbo and guilt-ridden. It's a pleasure to be sought like great food or great wine. What's the value of one night to a man, a real man, with one of these Pleasure Ladies? A moment of pleasure. A memory. Nothing more. What has that to do with love, real love? Nothing. I'm not for *one* night or for hire. I felt your yang. . . . No please, Linc," she added quickly as she saw him bridle. "About yang and yin things we cannot lie or tell falsehoods, that would destroy us. I felt you and I was filled with joy. Didn't you feel me? You're strong and a man, yang, and I'm a woman, yin, and when the music is soft and . . .

Oh, Linc." She put her hand around his and looked up at him beseechingly. "I beg you, don't be bound by Anglo-American nonsense. This is Asia and I—I want to be everything a woman could be for you."

"Jesus, you really mean it?"

"Of course. By the Madonna, I would like to be everything that you could desire in a woman," she said. "Everything. And I also swear that when I'm old or you no longer desire me I will help arrange *that* part of your life to be joyous, openly, freely. All that I would ask is to be *tai-tai,* to be part of your life." Orlanda kissed him lightly. And then she saw the sudden change in him. She saw the awe and his defenselessness and she knew she had won. Her glee almost swamped her. Oh Quillan, you're a genius, she wanted to shout. I never believed, truly believed, that your suggestion would be so perfect, I never believed that you were so wise, oh thank you thank you.

But her face showed none of this and she waited patiently, motionless.

"What does *tai-tai* mean?" he asked throatily.

Tai-tai meant "supreme of the supreme," wife. By ancient Chinese custom, in the home the wife was supreme, all powerful. "To be part of your life," she said softly, her whole being shouting caution.

Again she waited. Bartlett leaned down and she felt his lips brush hers. But his kiss was different and she knew that from now on their relationship would be on a different plane. Her excitement soared. She broke the spell. "Now," she said as though to a naughty child, "now, Mr. Linc Bartlett, which one do you choose?"

"You."

"And I choose you, but meanwhile we have to decide which one you're going to consider. If these aren't to your liking we'll go to another club." Deliberately she kept her voice matter-of-fact. "Now what about her?" The girl was lovely, the one he had looked at. Orlanda had already decided against her and had chosen the one that she would prefer but, she thought contentedly, very sure of herself, the poor boy's entitled to an opinion. Oh I'm going to be such a perfect wife for you! "Her résumé says she's Lily Tee—all the girls have working names they choose themselves. She's twenty, from Shanghai, speaks Shanghainese and Cantonese and her hobbies are dancing, boating and . . ." Orlanda peered at the tiny characters and he saw the lovely curve of her neck. ". . . and hiking. What about her?"

His eyes went to the picture. "Listen, Orlanda, I haven't been with a whore for years, not since I was in the army. I've never been much on them."

"I understand completely and you're right," she told him patiently, "but these aren't whores, not in the American sense. There's nothing vulgar or secret about them or what I propose. These are Pleasure Ladies who *may* offer you their youth *which has great value,* in exchange for some of your money which has almost none. It's a fair exchange, given and received

with face on both sides. For instance, you should *know* in advance how
much she should receive and you must never give her the money directly,
you must only put it into her handbag. That's important, and it's very important to me that your first encounter be perfect. I've got to protect your
face too, an—"

"Come on, Orlan—"

"But I'm serious, Linc. This choosing, this gift from me to you has
nothing to do with you and me, nothing. What happens with us is joss.
It's just important to me for you to enjoy life, to know what Asia is, really
is, not what Americans think it is. Please?"

Bartlett was floundering now, all his well-tested signposts and guides
shattered and useless against this woman who fascinated and astounded
him.

He was drunk with her warmth and tenderness. All of him believed
her.

Then, suddenly, he remembered and his inner self screamed caution.
His euphoria fled. He had just remembered to whom he had mentioned
how much he loved Italian food. Gornt. Gornt, a couple of days ago. Talking about the best meal he had ever had. Italian food with beer. Gornt.
Jesus are these two in cahoots? Can't be, just can't be! Maybe I told her
about the same meal. Did I?

He searched his mind but could not remember exactly, all of him rocked
but his eyes kept seeing her waiting there, smiling at him, loving him.
Gornt and Orlanda? They can't be in cahoots! No way! Even so, be cautious. You know almost nothing about her, so watch out for chrissake,
you're in a web, her web. Is it a Gornt web too?

Test her, the devil in him shouted. Test her. If she means what she says
then that's something else and she's from outer space and just as rare and
you'll have to decide about her—you'll only have her on her terms.

Test her while you've the chance—you've nothing to lose.

"What?" she asked, sensing a change.

"I was just thinking about what you said, Orlanda. Shall I choose
now?"

55

11:35 P.M.:

Suslev was sitting in the half-dark of their safe house at 32 Sinclair Towers. Because of his meeting with Grey he had changed the rendezvous with Arthur to here.

He sipped his drink in the dark. Beside him on the side table was a bottle of vodka, two glasses and the telephone. His heart thumped heavily as it always did when he was waiting for a clandestine meeting. Will I never get used to them? he asked himself. No. Tonight I'm tired though everything has gone beautifully. Grey's programmed now. That poor fool, driven by hatred and envy and jealousy! Center must further caution the leadership of the BCP about him—the trend's too vulnerable. And Travkin, once a prince, now nothing, and Jacques deVille—that impetuous incompetent—and all the others.

Never mind! Everything goes excellently. Everything's prepared against tomorrow and the arrival of the man Sinders. An involuntary shudder went through Suslev. I wouldn't want to be trapped by them. MI-6 are dangerous, committed and fanatic against us, like the CIA, but much worse. If the CIA and MI-6 plan, code name Anubis, to join Japan, China, England, Canada and America together ever comes to pass, Mother Russia will be ruined forever. Ah my country my country! How I miss Georgia, so beautiful and gentle and verdant.

The songs of his childhood, the folk songs of Georgia, welled up and took him back. He wiped away a small tear at the thought of so much beauty, so far away. Never mind, my leave's due soon. Then I'll be home. And my son will be home on leave at the same time from Washington with his young wife and their infant son, born so wisely in America. No trouble about a passport for him. He'll be our fourth generation to serve. We advance.

The darkness was pressing down on him. At Arthur's request, for further safety he had drawn the curtains and kept the windows closed though there was no possibility they could be seen. The apartment had air conditioning but again for safety he had been asked to leave it off, as well as the lights. It had been wise to leave the Finns' apartment before Grey in case there had been a change of plan and there was an SI tail on him. Crosse had told him there would be none tonight, though tomorrow another man would be assigned to him.

He had caught a taxi and stopped at Golden Ferry for the evening papers, pretending to lurch drunkenly in case he was being observed, then went to Rose Court and Clinker's and down the tunnel and then here. There was an SI man stationed outside Rose Court. The man was still outside and would stay there or not stay there. It made no difference.

The phone jangled. The sound made him jump even though the bell was carefully muted. Three rings, then silence. His heart picked up a beat. Arthur would be here shortly.

He touched the automatic that was secreted behind one of the cushions. Orders from Center. It was one of many orders he disapproved of. Suslev did not like guns, handguns. Guns could make mistakes, poison never. His fingers touched the tiny phial that was buried in his lapel close enough for his mouth to reach it. What would it be like to live *without* instant death so close?

Deliberately he relaxed and concentrated his senses like radar, wanting to sense Arthur's presence before it was actually there. Would Arthur use the front door or the back?

From where he was sitting he could see both doors. His ears searched carefully, mouth slightly open to increase their sensitivity. The whine of the elevator. His eyes went to the front door but the whine ceased floors below. He waited. The back door opened before he sensed anything. His insides fell over as he failed to recognize the dark shape. For a moment he was paralyzed. Then the shape straightened one shoulder and the slight stoop vanished.

"*Kristos!*" Suslev muttered. "You gave me a fright."

"All part of the service, old boy." The soft, clipped words were mixed with the dry, hacking, put-on cough. "Are you alone?"

"Of course!"

The shape moved noiselessly into the living room. Suslev saw the automatic being put away and he relaxed the hold on his but left it ready in hiding. He got up and stretched out his hand warmly. "You're on time for once."

They shook hands. Jason Plumm did not remove his gloves. "I very nearly didn't arrive," he said in his normal voice, the smile on the surface of his face only.

"What's wrong?" the Russian asked, reading the quality of the smile. "And why all the 'pull the curtains and keep the windows closed'?"

"I think this place may be under surveillance."

"Eh?" Suslev's disquiet soared. "Why didn't you mention it before?"

"I said, I *think* it may be. I'm not sure. We've gone to a lot of trouble to make this a safe house and I don't want it blown for any reason." The tall Englishman's voice had a raw edge to it. "Listen, comrade, all hell's broken loose. SI's caught a fellow called Metkin off your ship. He—"

"What?" Suslev stared at him with pretended shock.

"Metkin. He's supposed to be political comm—"

"But that's impossible," Suslev said shakily, his acting consummate, hiding his delight that Metkin had fallen into his trap. "Metkin would never make a pickup himself!"

"Even so, SI have him! Armstrong got him and an American off the carrier. They caught them in the act. Does Metkin know about Sevrin?"

"No, absolutely not."

"You're sure?"

"Yes. Even I didn't know until a few days ago when Center told me to take over from Voranski," Suslev said, the twisted truth coming easily.

"You're sure? Roger almost hit the roof! Metkin's supposed to be your political commissar, and a major, KGB. Is he?"

"Yes, but it's ridic—"

"Why the devil didn't he or you or someone tell us you've an operation going so we could have been prepared in case of a foul-up! I'm head of Sevrin and now you're operating here without liaising or keeping me advised. It was always agreed. Voranski always told us in advance."

"But, comrade," Suslev said placatingly, "I didn't know anything about a pickup. Metkin does what he wants. He's the chief, the senior man on the ship. I'm not party to everything—you know that!" Suslev was suitably apologetic and irritable, keeping up his perpetual cover that he was not the real arbiter of Sevrin. "I can't think what possessed Metkin to have made a pickup himself. Stupid! He must've been mad! Thank God he's a dedicated man and his lapel's poisoned so there's no n—"

"They got him intact."

Suslev gasped, now in real shock. He'd expected Metkin to be long since dead. "You're sure?"

"They got him intact. They got his real name, rank and serial number and right now he's on an RAF transport under heavy guard heading for London."

Suslev's mind blanked out for a moment. He had cunningly set up Metkin to take over from the agent who should have made the pickup. For months now he had found Metkin increasingly critical of him and nosy and therefore dangerous. Three times in the last year he had intercepted private reports to Center, written by his number two, criticizing the easy way he ran his ship and his job, and his liaison with Ginny Fu. Suslev was sure Metkin was preparing a trap for him, maybe even trying to guarantee his retirement to the Crimea—a plum posting—by pulling off some coup, like, for example, whispering to Center that he suspected there was a security leak aboard the *Ivanov* and that it must be Suslev.

Suslev shuddered. Neither Metkin, nor Center nor any of the others would need proof, just suspicion would damn him.

"It's definite Metkin's alive?" he asked, thinking through this new problem.

"Yes. You're absolutely sure he knows nothing about Sevrin?"

"Yes. Yes, I've already told you." Suslev sharpened his voice. "You're the only one who knows all the members of Sevrin, eh? Even Crosse doesn't know them all, does he?"

"No." Plumm went to the refrigerator and took out the bottle of water. Suslev poured himself a vodka, delighted that Sevrin had so many important safety valves within it: Plumm not aware that Roger Crosse was a KGB informer on the side . . . Crosse alone knowing Suslev's own real position in Asia but neither Crosse nor Plumm knowing his longtime connection with deVille . . . none of the other members knowing each other . . . and none of them aware of Banastasio and the guns or of the real extent of the Soviet thrust into the Far East.

Wheels within wheels within wheels and now Metkin, one of the faulty wheels, gone forever. It had been so easy to drop the honey to Metkin that safe acquisition of the carrier's armament manifest would guarantee promotion for the agent involved. "I'm surprised they caught him alive," he said, meaning it.

"Roger told me they had the poor bugger pinioned and a neck collar on him before he could get his teeth into the lapel."

"Did they find any evidence on him?"

"Roger didn't say. He had to work so damned fast. We thought the best thing to do was to whisk Metkin out of Hong Kong as quickly as possible. We were petrified he knew about us, being so senior. It'll be easier to deal with him in London." Plumm's voice was grave.

"Crosse will resolve Metkin."

"Perhaps." Uneasily Plumm drank some more water.

"How did SI get to know about the pickup?" Suslev asked, wanting to find out how much Plumm knew. "There must be a traitor aboard my ship."

"No. Roger said the leak came through an informer MI-6 has aboard the carrier. Even the CIA didn't know."

"*Kristos!* Why the hell did Roger have to be so efficient?"

"It was Armstrong. SI has checks and balances. But so long as Metkin knows nothing there's no harm!"

Suslev felt the Englishman's scrutiny. He kept his face guileless. Plumm was no fool. The man was strong, cunning, ruthless, a secret protégé and selectee of Philby's. "I'm certain Metkin knows nothing that could damage us. Even so, Center should be informed at once. They can deal with it."

"I've already done that. I asked for Priority One help."

"Good," Suslev said. "You've done very well, comrade. You and Crosse.

Acquiring Crosse for the cause was a brilliant coup. I must congratulate you again." Suslev meant the compliment. Roger Crosse was a professional and not an amateur like this man and all the others of Sevrin.

"Perhaps I acquired him, perhaps he acquired me. I'm not sure sometimes," Plumm said thoughtfully. "Or about you, comrade. Voranski I knew. We'd done business over the years but you, you're a new, untried quantity."

"Yes. It must be difficult for you."

"You don't seem too upset about the loss of your superior."

"I'm not. I must confess I'm not. Metkin was mad to put himself in such danger. That was totally against orders. To be frank . . . I think there have been security leaks from the *Ivanov*. Metkin was the only long-term member of the crew, apart from Voranski, who had access ashore. He was considered to be beyond reproach but you never know. Perhaps he made other mistakes, a loose tongue in a bar, eh?"

"Christ protect us from fools and traitors. Where did AMG get his information?"

"We don't know. As soon as we do, that leak will be plugged."

"Are you going to be Voranski's permanent replacement?"

"I don't know. I have not been told."

"I don't like change. Change is dangerous. Who killed him?"

"Ask Crosse. I want to know too." Suslev watched Plumm back. He saw him nod, apparently satisfied. "What about Sinders and the AMG papers?" he asked.

"Roger's covered everything. No need to worry. He's sure we'll get to look at them. You'll have your copy tomorrow." Again Plumm watched him. "What if we're named in the reports?"

"Impossible! Dunross would have told Roger at once—or one of his friends in the police, probably Chop Suey Kwok," Suslev said with a sneer. "If not him, the governor. Automatically it would get back to Roger. You're all safe."

"Perhaps, perhaps not." Plumm went to the window and looked at the brooding sky. "Nothing's ever safe. Take Jacques. He's a risk now. He'll never make tai-pan."

Suslev let himself frown and then, as though it was a sudden idea, he said, "Why not guide him out of Hong Kong? Suggest to Jacques he ask to be posted to . . . say Struan's in Canada. He could use his recent tragedy as an excuse. In Canada he'll be in a backwater and he'll die on the vine there. Eh?"

"Very good idea. Yes, that should be easy. He has a number of good contacts there which might be useful." Plumm nodded. "I'll be a lot happier when we've read those files, and even happier when you find out how the hell AMG discovered us."

"He discovered Sevrin, not you. Listen, comrade, I assure you you're safe to continue your vital work. Please continue to do everything you can to agitate the banking crisis and the stock market crash."

"No need to worry. We all want that to happen."

The phone came to life. Both men stared at it. It only sounded once. One ring. The code, *danger,* leaped into their heads. Aghast Suslev grabbed the hidden gun, remembering his fingerprints were on it as he hurtled through the kitchen for the back door, Plumm close behind him. He ripped open the door, letting Plumm through first onto the exit landing. At that moment there was the pounding of approaching feet and a crash against the front door behind them which held but buckled slightly. Suslev closed the back door silently, easing a bar into place. Another crash. He peered through a crack. Another crash. The front locks shattered. For an instant he saw the silhouettes of four men against the hall light, then he fled. Plumm was already down the stairs, covering him from the next landing, automatic out, and Suslev went down the steps three at a time past him to the next landing, then turned to cover in his turn. Above him the back door buckled nauseatingly. Silently Plumm ran past him and again covered him as they fled downward to the next landing. Then Plumm pulled away some camouflaging crates from the false door exit that branched off the main one. Footsteps noisily raced up toward them from downstairs. Another crash against the back door above. Suslev guarded as Plumm squeezed through the opening into the dark and he followed, pulling the partial door closed after him. Already Plumm had found the flashlight that was waiting in a clip. Footsteps raced closer. Cautiously Plumm led the way downward, both men moving well and silently. The footsteps passed with the sound of muffled voices. Both men stopped momentarily, trying to hear what was being said. But the sound was too indistinct and muted and they could not even tell if it was English or Chinese.

Plumm turned again and led the way downward. They hurried but with great caution, not wanting to make any unnecessary noise. Soon they were near the secret exit. Without hesitation the two men lifted the false floor and went below into the cool wet of the culvert. Once they were there and safe, they stopped for breath, their hearts pounding with the suddenness of it all.

When he could talk, Suslev whispered, "Kuomintang?"

Plumm just shrugged. He wiped the sweat off. A car rumbled overhead. He directed his light to the dripping ceiling. There were many cracks and another avalanche of stones and mud cascaded. The floor was awash with half a foot of water that covered their shoes.

"Best we part, old chap," Plumm said softly and Suslev noticed that though the man was sweating, his voice was icy calm and the light never wavered. "I'll get Roger to deal with whatever shower that was at once. Very bloody boring."

Suslev's heart was slowing. He still found it difficult to speak. "Where do we meet tomorrow?"

"I'll let you know." The Englishman's face was stark. "First Voranski, then Metkin and now this. Too many leaks." He jerked a thumb upward. "That was too close. Maybe your Metkin knew more than you think he did."

"No. I tell you he knew nothing about Sevrin, nothing, or about that apartment or Clinker or any of it. Only Voranski and me, we're the only ones who knew. There's no leak from our side."

"I hope you're right." Plumm added grimly, "We'll find out, Roger'll find out one way or another, one day, and then God help the traitor!"

"Good. I want him too."

After a pause Plumm said, "Call me every half an hour from various phone booths, from 7:30 P.M. tomorrow."

"All right. If for any reason there's a problem I'll be at Ginny's from eleven onwards. One last thing. If we don't get to look at the AMG papers, what's your opinion about Dunross?"

"His memory's incredible."

"Then we isolate him for a chemical interrogation?"

"Why not?"

"Good, *tovarich*. I'll make all the preparations."

"No. We'll snatch him and we'll deliver him. To the *Ivanov*?"

Suslev nodded and told him Metkin's suggestion of blaming the Werewolves, not saying it was Metkin's idea. "Eh?"

Plumm smiled. "Clever! See you tomorrow." He handed Suslev the flashlight, took out a pencil light and turned, going down the culvert, his feet still under water. Suslev watched until the tall man had turned the corner and vanished. He had never followed the culvert below. Plumm had told him not to, that it was dangerous and subject to rockfalls.

He took a deep breath, now over his fright. Another car rumbled heavily overhead. That's probably a truck, he thought absently. More mud and a piece of the concrete fell with a splash, startling him. Suslev waited, then began to pick his way carefully up the slope. Another tiny avalanche. Suddenly Suslev hated the subterranean tube. It made him feel insecure and doom ridden.

56

Dunross was looking at the sad hulk of the burned-out *Floating Dragon* restaurant that lay on her side in twenty feet of Aberdeen water. The other multistoried eating palaces that floated nearby were still blazing with lights, gaudy and noisy, filled to capacity, their new, hastily erected, temporary kitchens on barges beside their mother ships, cauldrons smoking, fires under the cauldrons, and a mass of cooks and helpers like so many bees. Waiters hurried up and down precarious gangways with trays and dishes. Sampans sailed nearby, tourists staring, Hong Kong *yan* gaping, the hulk a great attraction.

Part of the hulk's superstructure jutted out of the water. Salvage crews were already working on her under floodlights, salvaging her, readying to float what remained of her. On her part of the wharf and parking lot temporary roofing and kitchens were set up. Vendors were busily selling photographs of the blaze, souvenirs, foods of a hundred kinds, and a huge floodlit sign in Chinese and English proudly proclaimed that the new, ONLY TOTALLY MODERN AND *FIREPROOF* FLOATING RESTAURANT, THE FLOATING DRAGON would soon be in business, bigger than ever, better than ever . . . meanwhile sample the foods of our famous chefs. It was business as usual except that temporarily the restaurant was on land and not on the sea.

Dunross walked along the wharf toward one of the sea steps. There were clusters of sampans nearby, big and small. Most of these were for hire, each small craft with one sculler, a man, woman or child of any age, each craft with a hooped canvas covering that sheltered half of the boat from sun or rain or prying eyes. Some of the sampans were more elaborate. Those were the nighttime Pleasure Boats. Inside were reclining pillows and low tables, the better craft luxurious with plenty of room for two to eat and drink and then to pillow, the single oarsman discreetly not part of the cabin. You could hire one for an hour or a night and the boat would lazily float the byways. Other sampans would come with all manner of drinks and foods, fresh foods served piping hot, served delicately, and you and your lady could dream the night away in perfect privacy.

You could go alone if you wished. Then, out near one of the vast islands of boats, your sampans would rendezvous with Ladies of the Night and you could choose and barter and then drift. In the harbor you could satisfy any wish, any thirst, any desire—at little cost, the price fair whoever you were—if you could pay and were a man. Opium, cocaine, heroin, whatever you wanted.

Sometimes the food was bad or the singsong girl bad, but this was just joss, a regretted mistake and not deliberate. Sometimes you could lose your wallet but then only a simpleton would come among such prideful poverty to flaunt his wealth.

Dunross smiled, seeing a heavyset tourist nervously ease himself into one of the craft, helped by a *chong-sam*ed girl. You're in good hands, he thought, very glad with the hustle and bustle of business all around him, buying, selling, bartering. Yes, he told himself, Chinese are the real capitalists of the world.

What about Tiptop and Johnjohn's request? What about Lando Mata and Tightfist and Par-Con? And Gornt? And AMG and Riko Anjin and Sinders and . . .

Don't think about them now. Get your wits about you! Four Finger Wu hasn't summoned you to discuss the weather.

He passed the first sea steps and headed along the wharf to the main ones, the light from the streetlamps casting strong shadows. At once all the sampans there began to jostle for position, their owners calling out, beckoning. When he got to the top of the steps the commotion stopped.

"Tai-pan!"

A well-set Pleasure Boat with a Silver Lotus flag aft eased directly through them. The boatman was short, squat with many gold teeth. He wore torn khaki pants and a sweat shirt.

Dunross whistled to himself, recognizing Four Finger Wu's eldest son, the *loh-pan*, the head of Wu's fleet of Pleasure Boats. No wonder the other boats gave him leeway, he thought, impressed that Goldtooth Wu met him personally. Nimbly he went aboard, greeting him. Goldtooth sculled swiftly away.

"Make yourself at home, tai-pan," Goldtooth said easily in perfect English-accented English. He had a B.Sc. from London University and had wanted to remain in England. But Four Fingers had ordered him home. He was a gentle, quiet, kind man whom Dunross liked.

"Thank you."

On the lacquered table were fresh tea and whiskey and glasses, brandy and bottled water. Dunross looked around carefully. The cabin was neat and lit with little lights, clean, soft and expensive. A small radio played good music. This must be Goldtooth's flagship, he thought, amused and very much on guard.

There was no need to ask where Goldtooth was taking him. He poured himself a little brandy, adding soda water. There was no ice. In Asia he never used ice.

"Christ," he muttered suddenly, remembering what Peter Marlowe had said about the possibility of infectious hepatitis. Fifty or sixty people have that hanging over their heads now, if they know it or not. Gornt's one of them too. Yes, but that sod's got the constitution of a meat ax. The bugger hasn't even had a touch of the runs. What to do about him? What's his permanent solution?

It was cool and pleasant in the cabin, half open to the breeze, the sky dark. A huge junk moved past, chugging throatily, and he lay back enjoying the tensions he felt, the anticipation. His heart was steady. He sipped the brandy, drifting, being patient.

The side of the sampan scraped another. His ears focused. Bare feet padded aboard. Two sets of feet, one nimble the other not. "Halloa, tai-pan!" Four Fingers said, grinning toothlessly. He ducked under the canopy and sat down. "How you okay?" he said in dreadful English.

"Fine and you?" Dunross stared at him, trying to hide his astonishment. Four Finger Wu was dressed in a good suit with a clean white shirt and gaudy tie and carried shoes and socks. The last time Dunross had seen him like this was the night of the fire and before that, the only other time years ago, at Shitee T'Chung's immense wedding.

More feet approached. Awkwardly Paul Choy sat down. "Evening, sir. I'm Paul Choy."

"Are you all right?" he asked, sensing great discomfort, and fear.

"Sure, yes, thank you, sir."

Dunross frowned. "Well this's a pleasure," he said, letting it pass. "You're working for your uncle now?" he asked, knowing all about Paul Choy, keeping up the pretense he and Four Fingers had agreed to, and very impressed with the young man. He had heard of his stock market coup through his old friend Soorjani.

"No sir. I'm with Rothwell-Gornt's. I just started a couple of days ago. I'm here to interpret . . . if you need me." Paul Choy turned to his father and explained what had been said.

Four Fingers nodded. "Blandeee?"

"It's fine, thank you." Dunross raised his glass. "Good you see, *heya*," he continued in English, waiting for the old man to begin in Haklo. It was a matter of face and, with the presence of Paul Choy, Dunross's latent caution had increased a thousandfold.

The old seaman chatted inconsequentially for a while, drinking whiskey. Paul Choy was not offered a drink, nor did he take one. He sat in the shadows, listening, frightened, not knowing what to expect. His father had sworn him to perpetual secrecy with hair-raising blood oaths.

Finally Wu gave up waiting the tai-pan out and started in Haklo. "Our families have been Old Friends for many years," he said, speaking slowly and carefully, aware that Dunross's Haklo was not perfect. "Very many years."

"Yes. Seaborne Wu and Struan's like brothers," the tai-pan replied cautiously.

Four Fingers grunted. "The present is like the past and the past the present. *Heya?*"

"Old Blind Tung says past and present same. *Heya?*"

"What does the name Wu Kwok mean to the tai-pan of the Noble House?"

Dunross's stomach twisted. "He your great-grandfather, *heya?* Your illustrious forebear. Son and chief admiral of even more illustrious sea warlord, Wu Fang Choi, whose flag, the Silver Lotus, flew all four seas."

"The very one!" Four Fingers leaned closer and Dunross's caution doubled. "What was the connection between Green-Eyed Devil . . . between the first tai-pan of the Noble House and the illustrious Wu Kwok?"

"They meet at sea. They meet in Pearl River Estuary off Wh—"

"It was near here, off Pok Liu Chau, between Pok Liu Chau and Aplichau." The old man's eyes were slits in his face.

"Then they meet off Hong Kong. The tai-pan went aboard Wu Kwok's flagship. He went alone and . . ." Dunross searched for the word. ". . . and he negotiate a, a bargain with him."

"Was the bargain written onto paper and chopped?"

"No."

"Was the bargain honored?"

"It is fornicating ill-mannered to ask such question from Old Friend when Old Friend opposite knows answer!"

Paul Choy jerked involuntarily at the sudden venom and slashing cut of the words. Neither man paid any attention to him.

"True, true, tai-pan," the old man said, as unafraid as Dunross. "Yes, the bargain was honored, though twisted, part was twisted. Do you know the bargain?"

"No, not all," Dunross said truthfully. "Why?"

"The bargain was that on each of your twenty clippers we put one man to train as a captain—my grandfather was one of these. Next, Green-Eyed Devil agreed to take three of Wu Kwok's boys and send them to his land to train them as foreign devils in the best schools, everything like his own sons would be trained. Next the tai—"

Dunross's eyes widened. "What? Who? Who are these boys? Who did they become?"

Four Finger Wu just smiled crookedly. "Next, Green-Eyed Devil agreed to get for the illustrious Wu Fang Choi a foreign devil clipper ship, armed and rigged and beautiful. Wu Fang Choi paid for her but the tai-pan arranged for her and called her *Lotus Cloud.* But when Culum the Weak delivered her, almost two years later, your fornicating chief admiral,

Stride Orlov, the Hunchback, came out of the east like an assassin in the night and murdered our ship and Wu Kwok with her."

Dunross sipped his brandy, waiting, outwardly at ease, inwardly his brain shocked. Who could those boys be? Was that truly part of the bargain? There's nothing in Dirk's diary or testament about Wu Kwok's sons. Nothing. Who co—

"Heya?"

"I know about *Lotus Cloud*. Yes. And about men, captains. I think it was nineteen and not twenty clippers. But I know nothing about three boys. About *Lotus Cloud*, did my ancestor promise not to fight ship after he had give ship?"

"No. Oh no, tai-pan, no he did not promise that. Green-Eyed Devil was clever, very clever. Wu Kwok's death? Joss. We must all die. Joss. No, Green-Eyed Devil kept his bargain. Culum the Weak kept the bargain too. Will you keep his bargain?" Four Finger Wu opened his fist.

In it was the half-coin.

Dunross took it carefully, his heart grinding. They watched him like snakes, both of them, and he felt the strength of their eyes. His fingers shook imperceptibly. It was like the other half-coins that were still in Dirk's Bible, in the safe in the Great House, two still left, two gone, already redeemed, Wu Kwok's one of them. Fighting to control the trembling of his fingers, he handed the coin back. Wu took it, careless that his hand shook.

"Perhaps real," Dunross said, his voice sounding strange. "Must check. Where get it?"

"It's genuine, of course it's fornicating genuine. You acknowledge it as genuine?"

"No. Where get it?"

Four Fingers lit a cigarette and coughed. He cleared his throat and spat. "How many coins were there at first? How many did the illustrious Mandarin Jin-qua give Green-Eyed Devil?"

"I not sure."

"Four. There were four."

"Ah, one to your illustrious ancestor, Wu Kwok, paid and honored. Why would great Jin-qua give him two? Not possible—so this stolen. From whom?"

The old man flushed and Dunross wondered if he had gone too far.

"Stolen or not," the old man spat, "you grant favor. *Heya?*" Dunross just stared at him. "*Heya?* Or is the face of Green-Eyed Devil no longer the face of the Noble House?"

"Where get it?"

Wu stared at him. He stubbed out the cigarette on the carpet. "Why should Green-Eyed Devil agree to four coins? Why? And why would he swear by his gods that he and all his heirs would honor his word, *heya?*"

"For another favor."

"Ah, tai-pan, yes for a favor. Do you know what favor?"

Dunross stared back at him. "Honorable Jin-qua loaned *the tai-pan*, my great-great-grandfather, forty lacs of silver."

"Forty lac—$4 million. One hundred twenty years ago." The old man sighed. His eyes slitted even more. Paul Choy was breathless, motionless. "Was a paper asked for? A debt paper chopped by your illustrious forebear—on the chop of the Noble House?"

"No."

"Forty lacs of silver. No paper no chop just trust! The bargain was just a bargain between Old Friends, no chop, just trust, *heya?*"

"Yes."

The old man's thumbless hand snaked out palm upward and held the half-coin under Dunross's face. "One coin, grant favor. Whoever asks. I ask."

Dunross sighed. At length he broke the silence. "First I fit half to half. Next make sure metal here same metal there. Then you say favor." He went to pick up the half-coin but the fist snapped closed and withdrew and Four Fingers jerked his good thumb at Paul Choy. "Explain," he said.

"Excuse me, tai-pan," Paul Choy said in English, very uneasily, hating the closeness of the cabin and the devil-borne currents in the cabin, all because of a promise given twelve decades ago by one pirate to another, both murdering cutthroats if half the stories were true, he thought. "My uncle wants me to explain how he wants to do this." He tried to keep his voice level. "Of course he understands you'll have reservations and want to be a thousand percent sure. At the same time he doesn't want to give up possession, just at this time. Until he's sure, one way or the other, he'd pr—"

"You're saying he doesn't trust me?"

Paul Choy flinched at the viciousness of the words. "Oh no, sir," he said quickly and translated what Dunross had said.

"Of course I trust you," Wu said. His smile was crooked. "But do you trust me?"

"Oh yes, Old Friend. I trust very much. Give me coin. If real, I tai-pan of Noble House will grant your ask—if possible."

"Whatever ask, whatever, is granted!" the old man flared.

"*If possible.* Yes. If real coin I grant favor, if not real, I give back the coin. Finish."

"Not finish." Wu waved his hand at Paul Choy. "You finish, quickly!"

"My . . . my uncle suggests the following compromise. You take this." The young man brought out a flat piece of beeswax. Three separate imprints of the half-coin had been pressed into it. "You'll be able to fit the other half to these, sir. The edges're sharp enough for you to be sure, almost sure. This's step one. If you're reasonably satisfied, step two's we go together to a government assayer or the curator of a museum and get him to test both coins in front of us. Then we'll both know at the same time." Paul Choy was dripping with sweat. "That's what my uncle says."

"One side could easily bribe the assayist."

"Sure. But before we see him we mix up the two halves. We'd know ours, you'd know yours—but he wouldn't, huh?"

"He could be got at."

"Sure. But if we . . . if we do this tomorrow and if Wu Sang gives you his word and you give him your word not to try a setup, it'd work." The young man wiped the sweat off his face. "Jesus, it's close in here!"

Dunross thought a moment. Then he turned his cold eyes on Four Fingers. "Yesterday I ask favor, you said no."

"That favor was different, tai-pan," the old man replied at once, his tongue darting like a snake's. "That was not the same as an ancient promise collecting an ancient debt."

"You ask your friends concerning my ask, heya?"

Wu lit another cigarette. His voice sharpened. "Yes. My friends are worried about the Noble House."

"If no Noble House, no noble favor, heya?"

The silence thickened. Dunross saw the cunning old eyes dart at Paul Choy and then back to him again. He knew he was entrapped by the coin. He would have to pay. If it was genuine he would have to pay, whether stolen or not. Stolen from whom, his mind was shouting. Who here would have had one? Dirk Struan never knew who the others had been given to. In his testament he had written that he suspected one went to his mistress May-may but there was no reason for such a gift by Jin-qua. If to May-may, Dunross reasoned, then it would have passed down to Shitee T'Chung, who was presently the head of the T'Chung line, May-may's line. Maybe it was stolen from him.

Who else in Hong Kong?

If the tai-pan or the Hag couldn't answer that one, I can't. There's no family connection back to Jin-qua!

In the heavy silence Dunross watched and waited. Another bead of sweat dropped off Paul Choy's chin as he looked at his father, then back at the table again. Dunross sensed the hate and that interested him. Then he saw Wu sizing up Paul Choy strangely. Instantly his mind leaped forward. "I'm the arbiter of Hong Kong," he said in English. "Support me and within a week huge profits can be made."

"Heya?"

Dunross had been watching Paul Choy. He had seen him look up, startled. "Please translate, Mr. Choy," he said.

Paul Choy obeyed. Dunross sighed, satisfied. Paul Choy had not translated "I'm the arbiter of Hong Kong." Again a silence. He relaxed, more at ease now, sensing both men had taken the bait.

"Tai-pan, my suggestion, about the coin, you agree?" the old man said.

"About my ask, my ask for money support, you agree?"

Wu said angrily, "The two are not interwoven like rain in a fornicating storm. Yes or no on the coin?"

"I agree on the coin. But not tomorrow. Next week. Fifth day."

"Tomorrow."

Paul Choy carefully interjected, "Honored Uncle, perhaps you could ask your friends again tomorrow. Tomorrow morning. Perhaps they could help the tai-pan." His shrewd eyes turned to Dunross. "Tomorrow's Friday," he said in English, "how about Monday at . . . at 4:00 P.M. for the coin?" He repeated it in Haklo.

"Why that time?" Wu asked irritably.

"The foreign devil money market closes at the third hour of the afternoon, Honored Uncle. By that time the Noble House will be noble or not."

"We will always be the Noble House, Mr. Choy," Dunross said politely in English, impressed with the man's skill—and shrewdness to take an oblique hint. "I agree."

"Heya?"

When Paul Choy had finished the old man grunted. "First I will check the Heaven-Earth currents to see if that is an auspicious day. If it is, then I agree." He jerked his thumb at Paul Choy. "Go aboard the other boat."

Paul Choy got up. "Thank you, tai-pan. Good night."

"See you soon, Mr. Choy," Dunross replied, expecting him the next day.

When they were quite alone, the old man said softly, "Thank you, Old Friend. Soon we'll do much closer business."

"Remember, Old Friend, what my forebears say," Dunross said ominously. "Both Green-Eyed Devil and her of Evil Eye and Dragon's Teeth—how they put a great curse and Evil Eye on White Powders and those who profit from White Powders."

The gnarled old seaman in the nice clothes shrugged nervously. "What's that to me? I know nothing of White Powders. Fornicate all White Powders. I know nothing of them."

Then he was gone.

Shakily Dunross poured a long drink. He felt the new motion of the sampan being sculled again. His fingers brought out the waxen imprints. A thousand to one the coin's genuine. Christ almighty, what will that devil ask? Drugs, I'll bet it's something to do with drugs! That about the curse and the Evil Eye was made up—not part of Dirk's bargain at all. Even so, I won't agree to drugs.

But he was ill-at-ease. He could see Dirk Struan's writing in the Bible that he had signed and endorsed, agreeing before God "to grant to whomsoever shall present one of the half-coins, whatsoever he shall ask, if it is in the tai-pan's power to give. . . ."

His ears sensed the alien presence before the sound arrived. Another boat scraped his gently. The pad of feet. He readied, not knowing the danger.

The girl was young, beautiful and joyous. "My name is Snow Jade, tai-pan, I'm eighteen years and Honorable Wu Sang's personal gift for the night!" Lilting Cantonese, neat *chong-sam,* high collar, long stockinged legs and high heels. She smiled, showing her lovely white teeth. "He thought you might be in need of sustenance."

"Is that so?" he muttered, trying to collect himself.

She laughed and sat down. "Oh yes, that's what he said and I'd like your sustenance also—I'm starving, aren't you? Honorable Goldtooth has ordered a morsel or two to whet your appetite: quick fried prawns with peapods, shredded beef in black bean sauce, some deep-fried dumplings Shanghai style, quick fried vegetables spiced with Szechuan cabbage and tangy Ch'iang Pao chicken." She beamed. "I'm dessert!"

FRIDAY

57

12:35 A.M.:

Irritably, Banker Kwang stabbed the doorbell again and again. The door swung open and Venus Poon screeched in Cantonese, "How dare you come here at this time of night without an invitation!" Her chin jutted and she stood with one hand on the door, the other imperiously on her hip, her low-cut evening dress devastating.

"Quiet, you mealy-mouthed whore!" Banker Kwang shouted back at her and shoved past into her apartment. "Who's paying the rent? Who bought all this furniture? Who paid for that dress? Why aren't you ready for bed? Wh—"

"*Quiet!*" Her voice was piercing and easily drowned out his. "You *were* paying the rent, but today's the day when the rent was due and where is it, *heyaheyaheyaheya?*"

"Here!" Banker Kwang ripped the check out of his pocket and waved it under her nose. "Do I forget my fornicating promises—*no!* Do you forget your fornicating promises—*yes!*"

Venus Poon blinked. Her rage disappeared, her face changed, her voice became laden with honey. "Oh did Father remember? Oh I was told you'd forsaken your poor lonely Daughter and gone back to the whores of 1 Blore Street."

"Lies!" Banker Kwang gasped, almost apoplectic even though it was the truth. "Why aren't you dressed for bed? Why are you wear—"

"But I was called by three different people who said you'd been there this afternoon at 4:15. Oh, how terrible people are," she said crooningly, knowing that he was there though he only went to introduce Banker Ching from whom he was trying to borrow funds. "Oh poor Father, how dreadful people are." As she talked placatingly, she moved closer. Suddenly her hand snaked out and she snatched the check before he could withdraw it though her voice continued to be sweet. "Oh thank you, Father, from the bottom of my heart . . . *oh ko!*" Her eyes crossed, her voice hardened and the screech returned. "The check is not signed, you dirty old dogmeat! It's another of your banker tricks! Oh oh oh I think I shall kill myself on your doorstep . . . no, better I shall do it in front of the TV camera, telling all Hong Kong how you . . . Oh oh oh. . . ."

Her *amah* was in the living room now, joining in, wailing and caterwauling, both women swamping him in a swelter of invective, challenges and accusations.

Impotently he cursed them both back but that only made them increase their volume. He stood his ground for a moment, then, vanquished, pulled out a fountain pen with a flourish, grabbed the check and signed it. The noise ceased. Venus Poon took it and examined it carefully. Very very carefully. It vanished into her purse.

"Oh thank you, Honorable Father," she said meekly and abruptly whirled on her *amah*. "How dare you interfere in a discussion between the love of my life and your mistress, you lump of festering dogmeat. It's all your fault for spreading other people's cruel lies about Father's infidelity! Out! Fetch tea and food! Out! Father needs a brandy . . . fetch a brandy, *hurry!*"

The old woman pretended to buckle under the assumed rage and scuttled out in pretended tears. Venus Poon cooed and bustled and her hands were soft on Richard Kwang's neck.

At length, under their magic, he allowed himself to be mollified and helped to drink, groaning aloud all the time at his ill joss and how his subordinates, friends, allies and debtors had maliciously forsaken him, after he alone in the whole Ho-Pak empire had worked his fingers to their tendons, his feet to the flesh, worrying over all of them.

"Oh you poor man," Venus Poon said soothingly, her mind darting while her fingers were tender and deft. She had barely half an hour to reach her rendezvous with Four Finger Wu, and while she knew it would be wise to keep him waiting, she did not want to keep him waiting too long in case his ardor lagged. Their last encounter had excited him so much he had promised her a diamond if the performance was repeated.

"I guarantee it, Lord," she had gasped weakly, her skin clammy with sweat from two hours of concentrated labor, feeling herself afloat with the immensity of his at long last explosion.

Her eyes crossed as she remembered Four Finger Wu's prodigious efforts, his size, conformity and undoubted technique. *Ayeeyah*, she thought, still massaging the neck of her former lover, I will need every tael of energy and every measure of juice the yin can muster to dominate that old reprobate's yowling yang. "How is your neck, my dearest love?" she crooned.

"Better, better," Richard Kwang said reluctantly. His head had cleared and he was well aware that her fingers were as skilled as her mouth and her peerless parts.

He pulled her down onto his knee and confidently slipped his hand into the low-cut black silk evening dress that he had bought for her last week and fondled her breasts. When she did not resist, he slipped one strap off and complimented her on the size, texture, taste and shape of the whole. Her warmth shafted him and he stirred. At once his other hand went for the yin but before he knew it she had neatly squirmed out of his grasp. "Oh no, Father! Honorable Red's visiting me and as much as I wa—"

"Eh?" Banker Kwang said suspiciously. "Honorable Red? Honorable Red's not due till the day after tomorrow!"

"Oh no, he arrived with storm th—"

"Eh? He's due the day after tomorrow. I know. I looked at my calendar and made sure before I came here! Am I a fool? Do I fish for a tiger in a stream? We have a long-standing date tonight, all night. Why else am I supposed to be in Taiwan? You're never early and ne—"

"Oh no it was this morning—the shock of the fire and the greater shock that you had forsaken me, br—"

"Come here, you little baggage,—"

"Oh no, Father, Honorable R—"

Before she could avoid him, his hands darted out and he sat her back on his knees and began to lift her dress but Venus Poon was an old stager in this kind of warfare and champion of a hundred jousts, even though she was only nineteen. She fought him not, just pressed closer, twisted and got one hand on him, caressingly, and whispered throatily, "Oh but Father, it's very bad joss to interfere with Honorable Red and as much as I desire your immensity within, we both know there are other ways for the yin to titillate the vital vortex."

"But first I wan—"

"First? First?" Pleased with herself, she felt him strengthening. "Ah, how strong you are! It's easy to see why all the weevil-mouthed baggages want my old Father, *ayeeyah*, such a strong, violent, marvelous man."

Deftly she revealed the yang. Deftly she dominated it and left him gasping. "Bed, dearest love," he croaked. "First a brandy then a little sleep an—"

"Quite right, but not here oh no!" she said firmly, helping him up.

"Eh? But I'm supposed to be in Tai—"

"Yes, so you'd better go to your club!"

"But I—"

"Oh but you've exhausted your poor Daughter." She feigned weakness as she tidied him and had him up and at the door before he really knew what was happening. There, she kissed him passionately, swore eternal love, promised that she would see him tomorrow and closed the door behind him.

Shakily he stared at the door, his knees gone, his skin clammy, wanting to hammer on it to demand rest in the bed he had paid for. But he didn't. He had no strength and tottered to the elevator.

Going down, he suddenly beamed, delighted with himself. The check he had given her was for one month's rent only. She had forgotten he had agreed the month before to increase the amount by $500 a month. Eeeee, Little Marvelous Mouth, he chortled, the yang outsmarted the yin after all! Oh what a good drubbing I gave you tonight, and oh that Clouds and the Rain! Tonight it was truly the Small Death and the Great Birth and certainly cheap at twice one month's rent even with the increase!

Venus Poon finished brushing her teeth and began to repair her makeup. She spotted her *amah* in the bathroom mirror. "Ah Poo," she called shrilly, "fetch my raincoat, the old black one, and phone for a taxi . . . and hurry or I'll pinch both your cheeks!"

The old woman scurried to obey, delighted that her mistress was out of her foul mood. "I've already phoned for a taxi," she wheezed. "He'll be downstairs, waiting at the side entrance as soon as Mother gets there but you'd better give Father a few minutes in case he suspects something!"

"Huh, that old Turtle Top's good for nothing now! All he has strength for is to fall into the back of his car and be driven to his club!"

Venus Poon put the finishing touches to her lips and smiled at herself in the mirror, admiring herself greatly.

Now for the diamond, she thought excitedly.

"When see again, Paw'll?" Lily Su asked.

"Soon. Next week." Havergill finished dressing and reluctantly picked up his raincoat. The room they were in was small but clean and pleasant, and had a bathroom with hot and cold running water that the hotel management had had installed privately, at great cost, with the clandestine help of some experts in the water board. "I'll call you, as usual."

"Why sad, Paw'll?"

He turned and looked at her. He had not told her that soon he would be leaving Hong Kong. From the bed, she watched him back, her skin shiny and youth-filled. She had been his friend for almost four months now, not his exclusive friend since he did not pay her rent or other expenses. She was a hostess in the Happy Hostess Dance Hall that was his favorite nighttime meeting place, Kowloon side. The owner there, One Eye Pok, was an old and valued client of the bank over many years, and the mama-*san* a clever woman who appreciated his custom. He had had many Happy Hostess friends over the years, most for a few hours, some for a month, very few for longer, and only one bad experience in fifteen years—a girl had tried blackmail. At once he had seen the mama-*san*. The girl had left that very night. Neither she nor her triad pimp was ever seen again.

"Why sad, *heya*?"

Because I'm leaving Hong Kong soon, he wanted to tell her. Because I want an exclusivity I can't have, mustn't have, dare not have—and have never wanted with any before. Dear God in Heaven how I want you.

"Not sad, Lily. Just tired," he said instead, the bank troubles adding to the weight upon him.

"Everything be all good," she said reassuringly. "Call soon, *heya?*"

"Yes. Yes I will." His arrangement with her was simple: a phone call. If he could not reach her directly he would call the mama-*san* and that night he would come to the dance hall, alone or with friends, and he and Lily would dance a few dances for face and drink some drinks and then she would leave. After half an hour he would pay his bill and come here—everything paid for in advance. They did not walk together to this private and exclusive meeting place because she did not wish to be seen on the streets or by neighbors with a foreign devil. It would be disastrous for a girl's reputation to be seen alone with a barbarian. In public. Outside of her place of work. Any girl of beddable age would at once be presumed to be the lowest type of harlot, a foreign devil's harlot and despised as such, sneered at openly, and her value diminished.

Havergill knew this. It did not bother him. In Hong Kong it was a fact of life. "*Doh jeh,*" he said, thank you—loving her, wanting to stay, or to take her with him. "*Doh jeh,*" he just said and left.

Once alone she allowed the yawn that had almost possessed her many times this evening to overwhelm her and she lay back on the bed and stretched luxuriously. The bed was rumpled but a thousand times better than the cot in the room she rented in Tai-ping Shan.

A soft knock. "Honored Lady?"

"Ah Chun?"

"Yes." The door opened and the old woman padded in. She brought clean towels. "How long will you be here?"

Lily Su hesitated. By custom the client in this place of assignation paid for the room for the whole night. Also by custom, if the room was vacated early, the management returned part of the fee to the girl. "All night," she said wanting to enjoy the luxury, not knowing when she would have the opportunity again. Perhaps this client will have lost his bank and everything by next week.

"Joss," she said, then. "Please put on the bath."

Grumbling the old woman did as she was told then went away. Again Lily Su yawned, happily listening to the water gurgling. She was tired too. The day had been exhausting. And tonight her client had talked more than usual as she had rested against him, trying to sleep, not listening, understanding only a word here and there but quite content for him to talk. She knew from long experience that this was a form of release, particularly for an old barbarian. Very odd, she thought, all that work and noise and tears and money to achieve nothing but more pain, more talk and more tears. "Never mind if the yang is weak or if they talk or mumble or mutter their foul-sounding language or weep in your arms. Barbarians do that," her mama-*san* had explained. "Close your ears. And close your nostrils to the foreign devil smell and the old man smell and help this one enjoy a moment of pleasure. He's Hong Kong *yan*, an old friend, also he pays well, promptly, he's getting you quickly out of debt, and it's good face to have such a pillow patron. So be enthusiastic, pretend that he's virile and give value for his money."

Lily Su knew she gave value for money received. Yes, my joss is very good and oh so much better than my poor sister and her patron. Poor Fragrant Flower and Noble House Chen Number One Son. What tragedy! What cruelty!

She shivered. Oh those terrible Werewolves! Terrible to cut off his ear, terrible to murder him and threaten all Hong Kong, terrible for my poor elder sister to be crushed to death by those smelly rotten dogmeat fishermen at Aberdeen. Oh what joss!

It was only this morning that she had seen a newspaper that had printed a copy of John Chen's love letter, recognizing it at once. For weeks they had laughed over it, she and Fragrant Flower, that and the other two letters that Fragrant Flower had left with her for safekeeping. "Such a funny man, with almost no yang at all and almost never even a little upstanding," her elder sister had told her. "He pays me just to lie there for him to kiss, sometimes to dance without clothes, and always promise to tell others how strong he is! Eeeee, he gives me money like water! For eleven weeks I have been his 'own true love'! If this continues for another eleven weeks . . . perhaps an apartment bought and paid for!"

This afternoon, fearfully, she had gone with her father to East Aberdeen Police Station to identify the body. They said nothing about knowing who the patron was. Wisely her father had said to keep that secret. "Noble House Chen will surely prefer that secret. His face is involved too —and the face of the new heir, what's his name, the young one with the foreign devil name. In a day or two I'll phone Noble House Chen and sound him out. We must wait a little. After today's news of what the Werewolves've done to Number One Son, no father'd want to negotiate."

Yes, Father's smart, she thought. It isn't for nothing that his fellow workers call him Nine Carat Chu. Thank all gods I have those other two letters.

After they had identified her sister's body, they had filled out forms with their real names and real family name Chu to claim her money, 4,360 HK in the name of Wisteria Su, 3,000 HK under Fragrant Flower Tak, all money earned outside the Good Luck Dance Hall. But the police sergeant had been inflexible. "Sorry, but now that we know her real name we have to announce it so that all her debtors can claim against her estate." Even a very generous offer of 25 percent of the money for immediate possession could not get through his rough manner. So they had left.

The rotten dogmeat foreign devil slave, she thought disgustedly. Nothing will be left after the dance hall collects their debts. Nothing. *Ayeeyah!*

But never mind, she told herself as she lay down in the bath with glorious contentment. Never mind, the secret of the letters will be worth a fortune to Noble House Chen.

And Noble House Chen has more red notes than a cat has hairs.

Casey was curled up in the window of her bedroom, the lights out except for a small reading lamp over the bed. She was staring gloomily down at the street five stories below. Even this late, almost 1:30 A.M., the street was still snarled with traffic. The sky was low and misty, no moon, making the lights from the huge neon signs and columns of Chinese characters more dazzling, reds and blues and greens that reflected in the puddles and turned ugliness into fairyland. The window was open, the air cool and she could see couples darting between buses and trucks and taxis. Many of the couples were heading for the foyer of the new Royal Netherlands Hotel and a late-night snack at the European coffee shop where she had had a nightcap coffee with Captain Jannelli, their pilot.

Everyone eats so much here, she thought idly. Jesus, and so many people here, so much work to provide, so few jobs, so few at the top, one at the top of each pile, always a man, everyone struggling to get there, to stay there . . . but for what? The new car the new house the new ensemble the new refrigerator the new gimmick or whatever.

Life's one long bill. Never enough of the green stuff to cope with the everyday bills let alone a private yacht or private condo on the shores of Acapulco or the Côte d'Azur, and the means to get there—even tourist.

I hate going tourist. First's worth it, worth it to me. Private jet's better, much better but I won't think about Linc. . . .

She had taken Seymour Steigler to dinner upstairs and they had settled all the business problems, most of them legal problems he kept bringing up.

"We gotta make it watertight. Can't be too cautious with foreigners, Casey," he kept on saying. "They don't play the game according to good old Yankee rules."

As soon as dinner was finished she had feigned a load of work and left him. Her work was all done so she curled up in a chair and began to read, speed-read. *Fortune, Business Week, The Wall Street Journal* and several specialized business magazines. Then she had studied another Cantonese lesson, leaving the book till last. The book was Peter Marlowe's novel, *Changi*. She had found the dog-eared paperback in one of the dozens of street bookstalls in an alley just north of the hotel yesterday morning. It had given her great pleasure bargaining for it. The first asking price was 22 HK. Casey had bargained her down to 7.55 HK, barely $1.50 U.S. Delighted with herself and with her find she had continued window-shopping. Nearby was a modern bookshop, the windows stuffed with picture books on Hong Kong and China. Inside on a rack were three more paperbacks of *Changi*. New, they cost 5.75 HK.

At once Casey had cursed the old woman street seller for cheating her. But then the old hag wasn't cheating you at all, she had reminded herself. She outtraded you. After all, only a moment ago you were chortling because you'd trimmed her profit to nothing and God knows these people need profit.

Casey watched the street and the traffic on Nathan Road below. This morning she had walked up Nathan Road to Boundary Road, a mile and a half or so. It was on her list of things to see. It was a road like any other, snarled, busy, gaudy with street signs, except that everything north of Boundary Road to the border would revert to China in 1997. Everything. In 1898 the British had taken a ninety-nine-year lease on the land that extended from Boundary Road to the Sham Chun River where the new border was to be, along with a number of nearby islands. "Wasn't that stupid, Peter?" she had asked Marlowe, meeting him by chance in the hotel foyer at teatime.

"Now it is," he said thoughtfully. "Then? Well, who knows? It must have been sensible then or they wouldn't have done it."

"Yes, but God, Peter, ninety-nine years is so short. What possessed them to make it so short? Their heads must've been . . . must've been elsewhere!"

"Yes. You'd think so. Now. But in those days when all the British prime minister had to do was belch to send a shock wave around the world? World power makes the difference. In those days the British Lion was still the Lion. What's a small piece of land to the owners of a quarter of the earth?" She remembered how he had smiled. "Even so, in the New Territories there was armed opposition from the locals. Of course it fizzled. The then governor, Sir Henry Blake, took care of it. He didn't war on them, just talked to them. Eventually the village elders agreed to turn the other cheek, providing their laws and customs remained in effect, providing they could be tried under Chinese law if they wished and that Kowloon City remained Chinese."

"The locals here are still tried under Chinese law?"

"Yes, historic law—not PRC law—so you have to have British magistrates skilled in Confucian law. It's really quite different. For instance, Chinese law presumes that all witnesses will naturally lie, that it's their duty to lie and cover up, and it's up to the magistrate to find out the truth. He has to be a sort of legal Charlie Chan. Civilized people don't go in for swearing to tell the truth, all that sort of barbarism—they consider us mad to do that, and I'm not sure they're wrong. They've all kinds of crazy or sensible customs, depending how you look at it. Did you know it's quite legal here, throughout the Colony, to have more than one wife—if you're Chinese."

"Bully for them!"

"Having more than one wife really does have certain advantages."

"Now listen, Peter," she had begun hotly, then realized he was merely teasing her. "You don't need more than one. You've got Fleur. How are you both doing? How's the research? Would she like lunch tomorrow if you're busy?"

"Sorry to say but she's in the hospital."

"Oh God, what's the matter?"

He had told her about this morning and Doc Tooley. "I've just seen her. She's . . . she's not too good."

"Oh I am sorry. Is there anything I can do?"

"No thanks. I don't think so."

"Just ask if there is. Okay?"

"Thanks."

"Linc was right to jump into the water with her, Peter. Honestly."

"Oh of course, Casey. Please don't think for a moment . . . Linc did what I . . . he did it better than I could. You too. And I think you both saved that other girl from lots of trouble. Orlanda, Orlanda Ramos."

"Yes."

"She should thank you forever. Both of you. She was panicked—I've seen too much of it not to know. Smashing-looking bird, isn't she?"

"Yes. How's the research coming?"

"Fine, thanks."

"Sometime I'd like to swap impressions. Hey, by the way, I found your book—I bought it—haven't read it yet but it's on top of the pile."

"Oh!" Casey remembered how he had tried to sound offhand. "Oh. I hope you like it. Well, I've got to be off, it's the kids' teatime too."

"Remember, Peter, if there's anything, just call me. Thanks for tea, and say hi to Fleur. . . ."

Casey stretched, an ache now in her back. She got off her perch and went back to bed. Her room was small and did not have the elegance of their suite—*his* suite now. He had decided to keep the second bedroom. "We can always use it as an office," he had said to her, "or keep it as a spare. Don't worry, Casey, it's all tax deductible and you never know when we might need a spare."

Orlanda? No, she wouldn't need that bed!

Casey, she ordered herself, don't be bitchy, or stupid. Or jealous. You've never been jealous, *so* jealous before. You set the rules. Yes, but I'm glad I moved out. That other night was tough, tough on Linc and tough on me, worse for him. Orlanda will be good for him . . . oh shit on Orlanda.

Her mouth felt dry. She went to the refrigerator and got a bottle of iced Perrier and the nice tang of it made her feel better. I wonder how the earth makes those bubbles, she thought idly, getting onto the bed. Earlier, she had tried to sleep but her mind was jumbled and would not stop working, too much of the new—new foods, new smells, air, mores, threats, people, customs, cultures. Dunross. Gornt. Dunross and Gornt. Dunross and Gornt and Linc. A new Linc. A new you, frightened of a pretty piece of ass . . . yes, ass if you want to be vulgar and that's new for you too. Before you came here you were assured, dynamic, in charge of your world, and now you're not. All over her, not just over her, over that bitch Lady Joanna too with her so upper-class English accent, "Don't you remember, dear, it's our Over Thirty Club Lunch today. I mentioned it at the tai-pan's dinner. . . ."

Goddamn old bitch. Over thirty! I'm not even twenty-seven!

That's right, Casey. But you are all riled up like a mashed cat and it's not just her or Orlanda, it's also Linc and the hundreds of available girls you've already seen and you haven't even looked in the dance halls and bars and houses where they specialize. Didn't Jannelli wind you up too?

"Jesus, Casey," he had said with a great beam, "it's like being back on R and R in my Korean days. It's still only 20 bucks and you're the top banana!"

That evening around ten, Jannelli had called to ask if she'd like to join him and the rest of the crew at the Royal Netherlands for a night snack. Her heart had turned over when the phone rang, thinking it was Linc, and when she had found it wasn't she had pretended that she still had lots to do but had gratefully allowed herself to be persuaded. Once there she had had a double order of scrambled eggs and bacon and toast and coffee that she knew she did not want.

As a protest. A protest against Asia, Hong Kong, Joanna and Orlanda, and oh Jesus I wish I'd never got interested in Asia, never suggested to Linc we should go international.

Why did you?

Because it's the only way for U.S. business to go—the only way—the only way for Par-Con. Export. Multinational but export. And Asia's the biggest, most teeming untapped marketplace on earth and this is the century for Asia. Yes. And the Dunrosses and Gornts've got it made—if they go with us—'cause we've the greatest market in the world to back us, all the cash, technology, growth and expertise to do it.

But why did you go for Hong Kong so hot and heavy?

To get my drop dead money and to fill the time between now and my birthday—the end of the seventh year.

The rate you're going, she told herself, soon you'll have no job, no future, no Linc to say yes or no to. A sigh took her. Earlier, she had gone to the master suite and had left Bartlett a batch of telexes and letters to sign with a "hope you had a good time" note. When she had come back from her night snack she had gone there again and taken back everything she had left him. "It's Orlanda that's really got you going. Don't fool yourself," she said out loud.

Never mind, tomorrow's another day. You can dump Orlanda easy, she told herself grimly, and now, having zeroed in on her enemy she felt better.

Peter Marlowe's dog-eared paperback caught her eye. She picked it up, plumped the pillows more comfortably and began to read. The pages slid by. Abruptly the phone went. She had been so engrossed she jumped and a sudden, vast happiness flooded her. "Hi, Linc, did you have a good time?"

"Casey, it's me, Peter Marlowe. I'm terribly sorry to call so late but I checked and your room boy said your light was still on. . . . I hope I didn't wake you?"

"Oh, oh no Peter." Casey felt sick with disappointment. "What's up?"

"Sorry to call so late but there's a slight emergency, I've got to go to the hospital and I've . . . you said to call. I ho—"

"What is it?" Casey was completely zeroed in now.

"I don't know. They just asked if I'd come at once. The reason I called was about the kids. There'll be a room boy looking in every so often but I wanted to leave a note for them with your number in case they wake up, just in case they wake up, a friendly face to call so to speak. When we all met yesterday in the foyer, they both thought you a smasher. They probably won't wake but just in case. Could they call you? I'm sor—"

"Of course. Even better, why don't I come right over?"

"Oh no, I wouldn't think of it. If you j—"

"I'm not sleepy and you are right next door. It's no problem, Peter, I'm on my way. So you just go ahead to the hospital."

It took her only a minute to dress in pants and blouse and cashmere sweater. Before she even pressed the elevator button, Nighttime Song was there, wide-eyed and inquisitive. She volunteered nothing.

Downstairs, she crossed the foyer and went out onto Nathan Road, across the side road and into the foyer of the Annex. Peter Marlowe was waiting for her. "This's Miss Tcholok," he said hurriedly to the night porter. "She'll be with the kids till I return."

"Yes sir," the Eurasian said, equally wide-eyed. "The boy'll show you up, miss."

"Hope everything's okay, Peter. . . ." She stopped. He was out the swinging doors, trying to hail a cab.

The apartment was small, on the sixth floor, the front door ajar. The floor boy, Nighttime Po, shrugged and went off muttering, cursing barbarians . . . as if he couldn't look after two sleeping children who played hide and seek with him every evening.

Casey closed the door and peeked into the tiny second bedroom. Both children were fast asleep in the bunk, Jane, the little one, in the upper berth and Alexandra sprawled in the lower one. Her heart went out to them. Blond, tousled, angelic, with teddy bears clutched in their arms. Oh how I'd love to have children, she thought. Linc's children.

Would you? All the diapers, always locked in, sleepless nights and no freedom.

I don't know. I think so. Oh yes, for two like these, oh yes.

Casey didn't know whether to tuck them up or not. The air was warm so she decided to do nothing lest she wake them. In the refrigerator she found bottled water and this refreshed her and settled her racing heart. Then she sat in the easy chair. After a moment she took Peter's book out of her handbag and, once more, began to read.

Two hours later he returned. She had not noticed the time pass.

"Oh," she said, seeing his face. "She lost the baby?"

He nodded, dulled. "Sorry to be so long. Would you like a cup of tea?"

"Sure, hey, Peter, let me d—"

"No. No thank you. I know where everything is. I'm sorry to put you to all this trouble."

"It's no trouble. She's all right though? Fleur?"

"They, they think so. It was the stomach cramps that did it, and the touch of enteric. Too soon to tell but there's no real danger there, that's what they said. The, the miscarriage, they said it's always a bit rough, physically and emotionally."

"I am so sorry."

He glanced back at her and she saw the strong, bent, lived-in face. "Not to worry, Casey. Fleur's all right," he said, holding his voice firm. "The, the Japanese believe that nothing's set until after birth, until after thirty days, thirty days for a boy and thirty-one for a girl, nothing's set, there's no soul, no personality, no person . . . up to that time there's no person." He turned back in the tiny kitchen and set the kettle to boil, trying to sound convincing. "It's, it's best to believe that, eh? How could it be anything but . . . but an it. There's no person till then, thirty-odd days after birth, so that doesn't make it so bad. It's still ghastly for the mother but not so bad. Sorry, I'm not making much sense."

"Oh you are. I hope she'll be all right now," Casey said, wanting to touch him, not knowing whether to or not. He looked so dignified in his misery, trying to sound so calm, yet just a little boy to her.

"Chinese and Japanese are really very sensible, Casey. Their . . . their superstitions make life easier. I suppose their infant mortality rate was so awful in olden days that that made some wise father invent that wisdom to save a mother's grief." He sighed. "Or more likely, some wiser mother invented it to succor a broken father. Eh?"

"Probably," she said, out of her depth, watching his hands make the tea. First boiling water into the teapot, the pot rinsed carefully, then the water thrown away. Three spoons of tea and one for the pot, the boiling water brought to the pot. "Sorry we've no tea bags, I can't get used to them though Fleur says they're just as good and cleaner. Sorry, tea's all we've got." He brought the tea tray into the living room and set it on the dining table. "Milk and sugar?" he asked.

"Fine," she said, never having had it that way.

It tasted strange. But strong and life-giving. They drank in silence. He smiled faintly. "Christ, without a cuppa, eh?"

"It's great."

His eyes saw his half-opened book. "Oh!"

"I like what I've read so far, Peter. How true is it?"

Absently he poured himself another cup. "As true as any telling about any happening fifteen years after the event. As best as I can remember the incidents are accurate. The people in the book didn't live, though people like them did and said those sort of things and did those deeds."

"It's unbelievable. Unbelievable that people, youths could survive that. How old were you then?"

"Changi began when I was just eighteen and ended when I was twenty-one—twenty-one and a bit."

"Who're you in the book?"

"Perhaps I'm not there at all."

Casey decided to let that pass. For the time being. Until she had finished. "I'd better go. You must be exhausted."

"No, I'm not. Actually, I'm not tired. I've got some notes to write up—I'll sleep after the kids're off to school. But you, you must be. I can't thank you enough, Casey. I owe you a favor."

She smiled and shook her head. After a pause she said, "Peter, you know so much about this place, who would you go with, Dunross or Gornt?"

"In business, Gornt. For the future, Dunross, if he can weather this storm. From what I hear, though, that's not likely."

"Why Dunross for the future?"

"Face. Gornt hasn't the style to be *the* tai-pan—or the necessary background."

"Is that so important?"

"Totally, here. *If* Par-Con wants a hundred years of growth, Dunross. If you're in just for a killing, a quick in-and-out raid, go with Gornt."

She finished her tea thoughtfully. "What do you know about Orlanda?"

"Lots," he said at once. "But knowing scandal or gossip about a living person isn't the same as knowing legends or gossip about ancient times. Is it?"

She watched him back. "Even for a favor?"

"That's different." His eyes narrowed slightly. "Are you asking for a favor?"

She set her teacup down and shook her head. "No, Peter, not now. I might later but not now." She saw his frown deepen. "What?" she asked.

"I was wondering why Orlanda was a threat to you. Why tonight? Obviously, that leads to Linc. That leads inevitably to: she's out with him now, which explains why you sounded so ghastly when I called."

"Did I?"

"Yes. Oh, of course, I'd noticed Linc looking at her at Aberdeen and you looking at him and her looking at you." He sipped some tea, his face hardening. "That was quite a party. Lots of beginnings at that party, great tensions, big drama. Fascinating, if you can disassociate yourself from it. But you can't, can you?"

"Do you always watch and listen?"

"I try to train myself as an observer. I try to use my ears and eyes and other senses, properly, as they should be used. You're the same. Not much escapes you."

"Maybe, maybe not."

"Orlanda's Hong Kong-trained and Gornt-trained and if you plan a clash with her over Linc you'd better be prepared for a battle royal—if she's decided to try to grab him, which I don't know yet."

"Would Gornt be using her?"

After a pause, he said, "I'd imagine Orlanda's Orlanda's keeper. Aren't most ladies?"

"Most ladies gear their lives to a man, whether they want to or not."

"From what I know about you, you can take care of any opposition."

"What *do* you know about me?"

"Lots." Again the faint, easy, gentle smile. "Amongst them, that you're smart, brave and have great face."

"I'm so tired of face, Peter. In the future . . ." Her smile was equally warm. "From here on in, in my book, a person's going to gain ass—or arse as you call it—or lose it."

He laughed with her. "The way you say it sounds more ladylike."

"I'm no lady."

"Oh but you are." He added more gently, "I saw the way Linc looked at you at Dunross's party too. He loves you. And he'd be a fool to swap you for her."

"Thank you, Peter." She got up and kissed him and left, at peace. When she got out of the elevator on her floor, Nighttime Song was there. He padded ahead of her and opened her door with a flourish. He saw her eyes go to the door at the end of the corridor.

"Master not home," he volunteered grandly. "Not yet come back."

Casey sighed. "You've just lost more ass, old friend."

"Eh?"

She shut the door, feeling pleased with herself. In bed, she began to read again. With the dawn she finished the book. Then she slept.

58

Dunross came around the corner in his Jaguar fast, climbing the winding road easily, then turned into a driveway and stopped an inch from the tall gates. The gates were set into high walls. In a moment a Chinese porter peered through the side door. When he recognized the tai-pan he opened the gates wide and waved him through.

The driveway curled and stopped outside an ornate Chinese mansion. Dunross got out. Another servant greeted him silently. The grounds were well kept and down a slope was a tennis court where four Chinese, two men and two women, were playing mixed doubles. They paid no attention to him and Dunross did not recognize any of them.

"Please follow me, tai-pan," the servant said.

Dunross hid his curiosity as he was shown into an anteroom. This was the first time he or anyone that he knew had ever been invited into Tiptop's home. The interior was clean and busy with the strange, careless but usual Chinese mixture of good lacquer antiques and ugly modern bric-a-brac. Walls were pancled and ornate with a few bad prints hanging on them. He sat down. Another servant brought tea and poured.

Dunross could feel that he was being observed but this too was usual. Most of these old houses had spyholes in the walls and doors—there were many even in the Great House.

When he had got back to the Great House this morning near 4:00 A.M. he had gone straight to his study and opened the safe. There was no doubt, with even a cursory glance, that one of the two remaining coins fitted the imprints that were in Four Finger Wu's beeswax matrix. No doubt at all. His fingers were trembling when he broke the half-coin from its restraining sealing wax in Dirk Struan's Bible and cleaned it. It fitted the indentations perfectly.

"Christ," he had muttered. "Now what?" Then he had put the matrix and the coin back into the safe. His eyes saw the loaded automatic and the empty space where AMG's files had been. Uneasily he had relocked the safe and went to bed. There was a message on his pillow: "Father dear: Will you wake me when you leave? We want to watch the tryouts. Love, Adryon. P.S. Can I invite Martin to the races Saturday please please please? P.P.S. I think he's super. P.P.P.S. You're super too. P.P.P.P.S. You're out late, aren't you? Now it's 3:16!!!!"

He had tiptoed to her room and opened her door but she was fast asleep. When he had left this morning he had had to knock twice to awaken her. "Adryon! It's 6:30."

"Oh! Is it raining?" she said sleepily.

"No. Soon will be. Shall I open the blinds?"

"No, Father dear, thank you . . . doesn't matter, Martin won't . . . won't mind." She had stifled a yawn. Her eyes had closed and, almost instantly, she was deep asleep again.

Amused, he had shaken her lightly but she had not come out of sleep. "Doesn't matter, Father. Martin won't . . ." And now, remembering how lovely she was and what his wife had said about the pill, he decided to make a very serious check on Martin Haply. Just in case.

"Ah, tai-pan, sorry to keep you waiting."

Dunross got up and shook the outstretched hand. "It's good of you to see me, Mr. Tip. Sorry to hear about your cold."

Tip Tok-toh was in his sixties, graying, with a round nice face. He wore a dressing gown and his eyes were red and his nose stuffed, his voice a little hoarse. "It's this rotten climate. Last weekend I went sailing with Shitee T'Chung and I must've caught a chill." His English accent was slightly American, perhaps Canadian. Neither Dunross nor Alastair Struan had ever been able to draw him out about his past, nor had Johnjohn or the other bankers any knowledge of him in banking circles in Nationalist China days, pre-1949. Even Shitee T'Chung and Phillip Chen who entertained him lavishly could not pry anything out of him. The Chinese had nicknamed him the Oyster.

"The weather has been bad," Dunross agreed pleasantly. "Thank God for the rain."

Tiptop motioned to the man beside him. "This is an associate, Mr. L'eung."

The man was nondescript. He wore a drab Maoist jacket and drab trousers. His face was set and cold and guarded. He nodded. Dunross nodded back. "Associate" could cover a multitude of positions, from boss to interpreter, from commissar to guard.

"Would you like coffee?"

"Thank you. Have you tried vitamin C to cure your cold?" Patiently Dunross began the formal chitchat that would precede the real reason for the meeting. Last night while he was waiting for Brian Kwok in the Quance Bar he had thought Johnjohn's proposal was worth a try so he had phoned Phillip Chen then and asked him to request an appointment early today. It would have been just as easy to have called Tiptop direct but that was not correct Chinese protocol. The civilized way was to go through a mutually friendly intermediary. Then, if the request was refused, you would not lose face, nor would the other person, nor would the intermediary.

He was listening to Tiptop with only half his head, making polite conversation, surprised they were still speaking English, because of L'eung. This could only mean the man's English was also perfect, and, possibly, that he did not understand either Cantonese or Shanghainese which Tiptop spoke and Dunross was fluent in. He fenced with Tiptop, waiting for the opening that at length the banker would give him. Then it came.

"This stock market crash on your stock must be very worrying for you, tai-pan."

"Yes, yes it is, but it's not a crash, Mr. Tip, just a readjustment. The market ebbs and flows."

"And Mr. Gornt?"

"Quillan Gornt is Quillan Gornt and always snapping at our heels. All crows under heaven are black." Dunross kept his voice matter-of-fact, wondering how much the man knew.

"And the Ho-Pak mess? That's a readjustment too?"

"No, no that's bad. I'm afraid the Ho-Pak's out of luck."

"Yes, Mr. Dunross, but luck hasn't much to do with it. It's the capitalistic system, that and ineptness by Banker Kwang."

Dunross said nothing. His eyes flicked momentarily to L'eung who sat stiffly, immobile and very attentive. His ears were concentrated and so was his mind, seeking the oblique currents under what was said. "I'm not party to Mr. Kwang's business, Mr. Tip. Unfortunately the run on the Ho-Pak's spilling over to other banks and that's very bad for Hong Kong and also, I think, bad for the People's Republic of China."

"Not bad for the People's Republic of China. How can it be bad for us?"

"China is China, the Middle Kingdom. We of the Noble House have always considered China to be the mother and father of our house. Now our base in Hong Kong's under siege, a siege that's actually meaningless— just a temporary lack of confidence and a week or so of cash. Our banks have all the reserves and all of the wealth and strength they need to perform . . . for old friends, old customers and ourselves."

"Then why don't they print more money if the currency's so strong?"

"It's a matter of time, Mr. Tip. It's not possible for the mint to print enough Hong Kong money." Even more patiently, Dunross answered the questions, knowing now that most were for the benefit of L'eung, which suggested L'eung was senior to Tiptop, a more senior Party member, a nonbanker. "Our interim solution would be to bring in, at once, a few aircraft loads of pounds sterling to cover withdrawals." He saw both men's eyes narrow slightly.

"That would hardly support the Hong Kong dollar."

"Yes, yes our bankers know that. But Blacs, the Victoria and Bank of England decided this would be best in the interim. We just don't have enough Hong Kong cash to satisfy every depositor."

The silence thickened. Dunross waited. Johnjohn had told him he believed the Bank of China did not have substantial reserves of pounds because of the currency restrictions on their movement in and out of Britain but had very substantial amounts of Hong Kong dollars for which there were no export restrictions.

"It would not be at all good for the Hong Kong dollar to be weakened," Tip Tok-toh said. He blew his nose noisily. "Not good for Hong Kong."

"Yes."

Tip Tok-toh's eyes hardened and he leaned forward. "Is it true, tai-pan, that the Orlin Merchant Bank won't renew your revolving fund?"

Dunross's heart picked up a beat. "Yes."

"And true that your fine bank will not cover this loan or advance you enough to stave off the Rothwell-Gornt attack on your stock?"

"Yes." Dunross was very pleased to hear the calm quality of his voice.

"And true that many old friends have refused credit to you?"

"Yes."

"And true that the . . . the person Hiro Toda arrives this afternoon and requires payment for ships ordered from his Japanese shipyards shortly?"

"Yes."

"And true that Mata and Tung and their Great Good Luck Company of Macao have tripled their normal order for gold bullion but will not help you directly?"

"Yes." Dunross's already fine-tuned concentration increased.

"And true that the running-dog Soviet hegemonists have once more, impudently, very very impudently, applied for a banking charter in Hong Kong?"

"I believe so. Johnjohn told me they had. I'm not sure. I would presume he would not tell me a falsehood."

"What did he tell you?"

Dunross repeated it verbatim, ending, "Certainly the application would be opposed by me, the boards of all British banks, all the tai-pans and the governor. Johnjohn also said the hegemonists had the temerity to offer immediate and substantial amounts of HK dollars to assist them in their present trouble."

Tip Tok-toh finished his coffee. "Would you like some more?"

"Thank you." Dunross noted that L'eung poured and he felt he had achieved a great step forward. Last night he had delicately mentioned the Moscow bank to Phillip Chen, knowing that Phillip would know how to pass the information on, which would of course indicate to such an astute man as Tiptop the real reason for the urgent meeting and so give him the necessary time to contact the decision-maker who would assess its importance and ways to acquiesce or not. Dunross could feel a sheen of sweat on his forehead and prayed that neither of the men opposite him noticed it. His anxiety would push the price up—if a deal was to be made.

"Terrible, terrible," Tiptop said thoughtfully. "Terrible times! Old Friends forsaking Old Friends, enemies being welcomed to the hearth . . . terrible. Oh by the way, tai-pan, one of our old friends asks if you could get him a shipment of goods. Thorium oxide I think it was."

With a great effort Dunross kept his face clean. Thorium oxide was a rare earth, the essential ingredient for old-fashioned gas mantles: it made the mantle emit its brilliant white light. Last year he had happened to hear that Hong Kong had recently become the greatest user after the United States. His curiosity had peaked as Struan's were not in what must clearly be a profitable trade. Quickly he had found out that access to the material was relatively easy and that the trade was prodigious, quite secret, with many small importers, all of them very vague about their business. In nature, thorium occurred in various radioactive isotopes. Some of these were easily converted into fissionable uranium 235, and thorium 232 itself was an enormously valuable breeder material for an atomic pile. Of course, these and many other thorium derivatives were restricted strategic materials but he had been astounded to discover the oxide and nitrate, chemically easily convertible, were not.

He could never find out where the thorium oxides actually went. Of course into China. For a long time, he and others had suspected the PRC of having a crash atomic program, though everyone believed it had to be formulative and at least ten years from fruition. The idea of China nuclear armed filled him with mixed feelings. On the one hand, any nuclear proliferation was dangerous; on the other, as a nuclear power China would instantly become a formidable rival to Soviet Russia, even an equal to Soviet Russia, even a threat, certainly unconquerable—particularly if it also had the means to deliver a retaliatory strike.

Dunross saw both men looking at him. The small vein in L'eung's forehead was pulsing though his face was impassive. "That might be possible, Mr. Tip. How much would be needed and when?"

"I believe immediately, as much as can be obtained. As you know, the PRC is attempting to modernize but much of our lighting is still by gas."

"Of course."

"Where would you obtain the oxides or nitrates?"

"Australia would probably be the quickest, though I've no idea at this moment about quality. Outside of the United States," he added delicately, "it's only found in Tasmania, Brazil, India, South Africa, Rhodesia and the Urals . . . big deposits there." Neither man smiled. "I imagine Rhodesia and Tasmania'd be best. Is there anyone Phillip or I should deal with?"

"A Mr. Vee Cee Ng, in Princes Building."

Dunross bit back a whistle as another piece of the puzzle fell into place. Mr. Vee Cee Ng, Photographer Ng, was a great friend of Tsu-yan, the

missing Tsu-yan, his old friend and associate who had mysteriously fled
into China over the Macao border. Tsu-yan had been one of the thorium
importers. Up to now, the connection had been meaningless. "I know Mr.
Ng. By the way, how is my old friend, Tsu-yan?"

L'eung was plainly startled. Bull's-eye, Dunross thought grimly, shocked
that he had never once suspected Tsu-yan of being Communist or having
Communist leanings.

"Tsu-yan?" Tiptop frowned. "I haven't seen him for a week or more.
Why?"

"I heard he was visiting Peking by way of Macao."

"Curious! That's very curious. I wonder why he'd want to do that—an
arch-capitalist? Well, wonders will never cease. If you'd be kind enough to
contact Mr. Ng direct, I'm sure he will give you the details."

"I'll do that this morning. As soon as I get back to the office."

Dunross waited. There would be other concessions before they would
grant what he sought, if it was to be granted. His mind was racing with
the implication of their first request, how to get thorium oxides, whether
to get them, wanting to know how far along the PRC was with its atomic
program, knowing they would never tell him that. L'eung took out a pack
of cigarettes and offered it.

"No thanks," he said.

Both men lit up. Tiptop coughed and blew his nose. "It's curious, tai-
pan," he said, "very curious that you go out of your way to help the Victoria and Blacs and all your capitalist banks while the strong rumor is that
they'll not help you in your need."

"Perhaps they'll see the error of their ways," Dunross said. "Sometimes
it's necessary to forget present advantages for the common good. It would
be bad for the Middle Kingdom for Hong Kong to falter." He noted the
scorn on L'eung's face but it did not bother him. "It's ancient Chinese
doctrine not to forget Old Friends, trusted ones, and as long as I'm tai-pan
of the Noble House and have power, Mr. Tip, I and those like me—Mr.
Johnjohn for one, our governor for another—will give eternal friendship to
the Middle Kingdom and will never permit hegemonists to thrive on our
barren rock."

Tiptop said sharply, "It is *our* barren rock, Mr. Dunross, that is presently administered by the British, is it not?"

"Hong Kong is and always was earth of the Middle Kingdom."

"I will let your definition pass for the moment but everything in Kowloon and the New Territories north of Boundary Road reverts to us in
thirty-five-odd years doesn't it—even if you accept the Unequal Treaties
forced on our forebears which we don't."

"My forebears have always found their Old Friends wise, very wise, and
never men to cut off their Stalks to spite a Jade Gate."

Tiptop laughed. L'eung continued to be set-faced and hostile.

"What do you forecast will happen in 1997, Mr. Dunross?"

"I am not Old Blind Tung, nor a soothsayer, Mr. Tip." Dunross shrugged. "1997 can take care of 1997. Old friends will still need old friends. *Heya?*"

After a pause Tiptop said, "If your bank will not help the Noble House, nor Old Friends, nor Orlin, how will you remain the Noble House?"

"My forebear, Green-Eyed Devil, was asked the same question by the Great and Honorable Jin-qua when he was beset by his enemies, Tyler Brock and his scum, and he just laughed and said, *'Neng che to lao'*—an able man has many burdens. As I'm abler than most I have to sweat more than most."

Tip Tok-toh smiled with him. "And you are sweating, Mr. Dunross?"

"Well, let me put it this way," Dunross told him cheerfully, "I'm trying to avoid the eighty-fourth. As you know, Buddha said that all men have eighty-three burdens. If we succeed in eliminating one we automatically acquire another. The secret of life is to adjust to eighty-three and avoid at all costs acquiring the eighty-fourth."

The older man smiled. "Have you considered selling part of your company, perhaps even 51 percent?"

"No, Mr. Tip. Old Green-Eyed Devil forbade that." The lines around Dunross's eyes crinkled. "He wanted us to sweat."

"Let us hope you don't have to sweat too much. Yes." Tiptop stubbed out his cigarette. "In troubled times it would be good for the Bank of China to have a closer liaison with your banking system. Then these crises would not be so continuous."

Instantly Dunross's mind leaped forward. "I wonder if the Bank of China would consider having a permanent contact stationed within the Vic and an equivalent one in yours?" He saw the fleeting smile and knew he had guessed correctly. "That would ensure close monitoring of any crisis, and assist you should you ever need international assistance."

"Chairman Mao advises self-help and that's what we are doing. But your suggestion might be worthwhile. I will be glad to pass it on."

"I'm sure the bank would be grateful if you would recommend someone to be their contact with the great Bank of China."

"I would be glad to pass that on too. Do you think Blacs or the Victoria would advance the necessary foreign exchange for Mr. Ng's imports?"

"I'm sure they'd be delighted to be of service, the Victoria certainly. After all, the Victoria has had a century and more of association with China. Wasn't it instrumental in making most of your foreign loans, railway loans, aircraft loans?"

"To great profit," Tiptop said dryly. His eyes darted at L'eung who was staring intently at Dunross. "Capitalist profit," he added thinly.

"Quite," Dunross said. "You must excuse us capitalists, Mr. Tip. Perhaps our only defense is that many of us are Old Friends of the Middle Kingdom."

L'eung spoke to Tiptop briefly in a dialect Dunross did not understand. Tiptop answered him affirmatively. Both men looked back at him. "I'm sorry but you must excuse me now, Mr. Dunross, I really must get some medication. Perhaps you'd phone me here after lunch, say around 2:30."

Dunross got up and stretched out his hand, not sure if he had succeeded but very sure he had better do something about the thorium very quickly, certainly before 2:30. "Thank you for seeing me."

"What about our fifth race?" The older man peered up at him, walking with him to the door.

"Noble Star's worth a bet. Each way."

"Ah! Butterscotch Lass?"

"Same."

"And Pilot Fish?"

Dunross laughed. "The stallion's good but not in the same class, unless there's an act of God, or the devil."

They were at the front door now and a servant had opened it wide. Again L'eung spoke in the dialect Dunross did not recognize. Again Tiptop answered affirmatively and led the way outside. At once L'eung walked off down toward the tennis court.

"I'd like you to meet a friend, a new friend, Mr. Dunross," Tiptop said. "He could, perhaps, be doing a lot of business with you in the future. If you wish."

Dunross saw the flinty eyes and his good humor vanished.

The Chinese coming back with L'eung was well formed, fit and in his forties. His hair was blue-black and tousled from his game, his tennis clothes modern, smart and American. On the court behind him, the other three waited and watched. All were fit and well dressed.

"May I introduce Dr. Joseph Yu from California? Mr. Ian Dunross."

"Hi, Mr. Dunross," Joseph Yu said with easy American familiarity. "Mr. Tip's filled me in on you and Struan's—happy to meet you. Mr. Tip thought we should meet before I leave—we're going into China tomorrow, Betty 'n' I, my wife and I." He waved a vague hand toward one of the women on the tennis court. "We're not expecting to come back for some time so I'd like to make a date to meet in Canton in a month or so." He glanced back at Tiptop. "No trouble about Mr. Dunross's visa, anything like that?"

"No, Dr. Yu. Oh no. None at all."

"Great. If I give you a call, Mr. Dunross, or Mr. Tip does, can we arrange something at a couple days' notice?"

"Certainly, if all the paper work's done." Dunross kept the smile on his face, noticing the assured hardness in Yu. "What had you in mind?"

"If you'll excuse us," Tiptop said, "we'll leave you two together." He nodded politely and went back inside with L'eung.

"I'm from the States," Yu continued cheerfully, "American born, Sacramento. I'm third-generation California though I was educated, in part, in

Canton. My Ph.D. is from Stanford, aerospace engineering, my specialty rocketry and rocket fuels. NASA's where I've spent my best years, best since college." Yu was no longer smiling. "The equipment I'll be ordering will be all manner of sophisticated metallurgy and aerospace hardware. Mr. Tip said you'd be our best bet as the importer. The British, then the French and Germans, maybe Japanese will be the manufacturers. You interested?"

Dunross listened with growing concern that he did not bother to hide. "If it's not strategic and not restricted," he said.

"It'll be mostly strategic and mostly restricted. You interested?"

"Why're you telling me all this, Dr. Yu?"

Yu's mouth smiled. "I'm going to reorganize China's space program." His eyes slitted even more as he watched Dunross carefully. "You find that surprising?"

"Yes."

"So do I." Yu glanced at his wife, then back to Dunross. "Mr. Tip says you're to be trusted. He feels you're fair and since you owe him one or two, you'll pass on a message for me." Yu's voice hardened. "I'm telling you so that when you read about my demise or kidnapping or some 'while his mind was disturbed' crap, you'll know it's all lies and as a favor will pass back that message to the CIA and from them up the line. The truth!" He took a deep breath. "I'm leaving of my own free will. We both are. For three generations our folk and my people, who're the best goddamn immigrants there are, have been kicked around in the States by Americans. My old man was in the First World War and I helped make the Big Bang, but the last goddamn straw was two months ago. June 16. Betty 'n' I wanted a house in Beverly Hills. Are you familiar with Beverly Hills in Los Angeles?"

"Yes."

"We were turned down because we were Chinese. The son of a bitch came out and said it. 'I'm not selling to goddamn Chinese.' That wasn't the first time, hell no, but the son of a bitch said it in front of Betty and that was it. That was the big one!" Yu's lips twisted with anger. "Can you imagine the stupidity of that bastard? I'm the best there is in my field and that red-neck horse's ass says 'I'm not selling to Chinese.'" He spun his racket in his hands. "You'll tell them?"

"Do you want me to pass this information on privately or publicly? I will quote you verbatim if you wish."

"Privately to the CIA, but not before next Monday at 6:00 P.M. Okay? Then next month, after our Canton meeting, it's public. Okay, Mr. Dunross?"

"Very well. Can you give me the name of the house seller, the date, any details?"

Yu took out a typed slip of paper.

Dunross glanced at it. "Thank you." There were two names and addresses and phone numbers in Beverly Hills. "Both the same refusal?"

"Yes."

"I'll take care of it for you, Dr. Yu."

"You think that's petty, huh?"

"No, I don't think so at all. I'm just so sorry that it happened and happens everywhere—to all sorts of people. It's greatly saddening." Dunross hesitated. "It happens in China, Japan, here all over the world. Chinese and Japanese, Vietnamese, all manner of people, Dr. Yu, are sometimes equally intolerant and bigoted. Most times very much more so. Aren't we all called *quai loh?*"

"It shouldn't happen Stateside—not Americans to Americans. That's my bitch."

"Do you think once you're inside China, you'll be allowed to go in and out freely?"

"No. But I don't give a damn about that. I'm going freely. I'm not being tempted by money or being blackmailed to go. I'm just going."

"What about NASA? I'm surprised they allowed such nonsense to happen in the first place."

"Oh we had a fine house on offer, but it wasn't where we wanted to live. Betty wanted that goddamn house and we had the money and position to pay for it, but we couldn't get in. It wasn't just that son of a bitch, it was the neighborhood too." Yu wiped a thread of hair out of his eyes. "They didn't want us so I'm going where I am wanted. What about China having a nuclear retaliatory strike force of its own? Like the French, eh? What do you think of that?"

"The idea of anyone having A- or H-bomb tipped rockets fills me with horror."

"They're just the weapons of the day, Mr. Dunross, just the weapons of the day."

"Jesus Christ!" Johnjohn said, aghast.

Havergill was equally shocked. "Dr. Joseph Yu's really top bracket, Ian?"

"Absolutely. I phoned a friend in Washington. Yu's one of two or three in the world—rockets and rocket fuel." It was after lunch. Dunross had just told them what had transpired this morning. "It's also true no one knows he's going over the border, even that he's left Hawaii where he's supposed to be on vacation—he told me he traveled here quite openly."

"Christ," Johnjohn said again. "If China gets experts like him . . ." He twisted the paper knife that was on Havergill's desk. "Ian, have you considered telling Roger Crosse, or Rosemont to prevent that?"

"Of course, but I can't do that. I absolutely can't."

"Of course Ian can't! Have you considered what's at stake?" Havergill jerked an angry thumb at the window. Fourteen floors below he could see an impatient, angry mob of people trying to get into the bank, the police stretched very thin now. "Let's not delude ourselves, the run is on, we're getting down to the bottom of the barrel. We barely have enough cash to last the day, barely enough to pay government employees. Thank God it's Saturday tomorrow! If Ian says there's a chance we could get China's cash, of course he can't risk giving away such a confidence! Ian, did you hear the Ho-Pak's closed its doors?"

"No. I've been chasing around like a blue-arsed fly since I left Tiptop."

"The Ching Prosperity closed too, the Far East and India's tottering, Blacs is eking out its reserves and like us, praying they can last the next half an hour to closing." He shoved the phone across his pristine desk. "Ian, please call Tiptop now, it's just 2:30."

Dunross kept his face stony and his voice level. "There're a couple of things to settle first, Paul. What about the thorium imports?" He had told them he had contacted Photographer Ng who had happily given him an immediate firm order for as much of the rare earth as he could obtain. "Will you provide the foreign exchange?"

"Yes, provided the trade is not restricted."

"I'll need that in writing."

"You'll have it before closing tonight. Please call him now."

"In ten minutes. It's a matter of face. You'll agree to having a permanent Bank of China contact in the building?"

"Yes. I'm sure they'll never let one of our people inside their building, but no matter." Havergill glanced at his watch again, then looked at Johnjohn. "The fellow'd have to be monitored and we might have to change a few procedures for security, eh?"

Johnjohn nodded. "Yes, but that shouldn't cause any problem, Paul. If it was Tiptop himself, that would be perfect. Ian, do you think there's a chance?"

"I don't know. Now, what about the Yu trade?"

Havergill said, "We can't finance any smuggling. You would of necessity be on your own."

"Who said anything about smuggling?"

"Quite. Then let me say we'll have to take a careful look at the Yu trade when and if you are asked to assist them."

"Come on, Paul, you know damn well it's part of the deal—if there's a deal. Why else would they have wanted me to meet him?"

Johnjohn interjected, "Why not table that one, Ian? We'll bend every which way to assist you when the time comes. You told Yu the same thing —that you'd wait and see but no actual commitment, eh?"

"But you agree to help in every way to assist me?"

"Yes, on this and the thorium."

"Then what about my loan?"

Paul Havergill said, "I'm not permitted to grant it, Ian. We've already been through that."

"Then call a board meeting right now."

"I'll consider it. Let's see how things're going, eh?" Paul Havergill pressed a button and spoke into the small speaker. "Stock Exchange, please."

In a moment a voice came over the speaker. Behind the voice they could hear pandemonium. "Yes, Mr. Havergill?"

"Charles, what's the latest?"

"The whole market's off 28 points . . ." Both bankers blanched. The small vein in Dunross's forehead was pulsing. ". . . and it looks like the beginning of a panic. The bank's off 7 points, Struan's is down to 11.50 . . ."

"Christ!" Johnjohn muttered.

". . . Rothwell-Gornt off 7, Hong Kong Power off 5, Asian Land 11 . . . everything's skidding. All bank stocks are tumbling. The Ho-Pak's frozen at 12 and when it gets unfrozen it'll go to a dollar. The Far East and India is only paying out maximum 1,000 a customer."

Havergill's nervousness increased. Far East was one of the biggest in the Colony.

"I hate to be a pessimist but it looks like New York in '29! I th—" The voice was drowned out by a surge of shouting. "Sorry, there's another huge sell offering up on Struan's. 200,000 shares. . . ."

"Christ, where the hell's all the stock coming from?" Johnjohn asked.

"From every Tom, Dick and Harry in Hong Kong," Dunross said coldly. "Including the Victoria."

"We had to protect our investors," Havergill said, then added into the mike, "Thank you, Charles. Call me back at a quarter to three." He clicked the speaker off. "There's your answer, Ian. I cannot in all conscience recommend to the board we bail you out with another unsecured 100 million loan."

"Are you going to call a board meeting right now or not?"

"Your stock's plunging. You've no assets to pledge to support the run on your stock, your bank holdings are already pledged, the stock in your treasury gets more valueless every minute. On Monday or Tuesday, Gornt will buy back in and then he'll control Struan's."

Dunross watched him. "You'll let Gornt take us over? I don't believe you. You'll buy in before he does. Or have you already made a deal to split up Struan's between you?"

"No deal. Not yet. But if you'll resign from Struan's right now, agree in writing to sell us as much of your treasury stock as we want at market price at Monday's closing, agree to appoint a new tai-pan of our board's choosing, we'll announce that we're supporting Struan's totally."

"When would you make the announcement?"

"Monday at 3:10."

"In other words you'll give me nothing."

"You've always said the best thing about Hong Kong was that it was a free marketplace, where the strong survive and the weak perish. Why didn't you persuade Sir Luis to withdraw your stock from trading?"

"He suggested it. I refused."

"Why?"

"Struan's is as strong as ever."

"Wasn't the real reason face—and your foolish pride? Sorry, there's nothing I can do to prevent the inevitable."

"Balls!" Dunross said and Havergill flushed. "You can call a meeting. You can c—"

"No meeting!"

"Ian." Johnjohn tried to soften the open hostility between the two men. "Listen, Paul, how about a compromise: If, through Ian, we get China's cash, you will call a meeting of the board at once, an extraordinary meeting, today. You could do that—there are enough directors in town, and it's fair. Eh?"

Havergill hesitated. "I'll consider it."

"That's not good enough," Dunross said hotly.

"I'll consider it. Kindly call Tipt—"

"When's the meeting? If?"

"Next week."

"No. Today as Johnjohn suggests."

"I said I'll consider it," Havergill said, flaring. "Now please call Tiptop."

"If you'll guarantee to call the board no later than tomorrow at ten!"

Havergill's voice harshened. "I will not be blackmailed as I was the last time. If you don't want to call Tiptop, I will. I can now. If they want to lend us their money, they'll lend it to us whoever the hell calls. You've agreed to the thorium deal, you've agreed to meet Yu next month, we agree to support that deal whoever controls the Noble House. I am not empowered to grant you any further loans. So take it or leave it. I will consider calling a board meeting before Monday's market opens. That's all I promise."

The silence was heavy and electric.

Dunross shrugged. He picked up the phone and dialed.

"*Weyyyyy?*" The woman's voice was arrogant.

"The Honorable Tip Tok-toh please," he said in Cantonese. "This is the tai-pan."

"Ah, the tai-pan. Ah, please wait a moment." Dunross waited. A bead of sweat gathered on the bottom of Johnjohn's chin. "*Weyyyy?* Tai-pan, the doctor's with him, he's very sick. Please call back later!" The phone clicked off before Dunross could say anything. He redialed.

"This's the tai-pan, I wan—"

"This phone is terrible." The *amah* doubled her volume. "He's sick," she shouted. "Call back later."

Dunross called in ten minutes. Now the line was busy. He kept on trying with no luck.

There was a knock and the harassed chief cashier hurried in. "Sorry,
sir, but there's no letup in the queues, we've a quarter of an hour to go. I
suggest we limit withdrawals now, say a thou—"

"No," Havergill said at once.

"But sir, we're almost empty. Don't y—"

"No. The Victoria must keep going. We must. No. Keep honoring
every penny."

The man hesitated, then went out. Havergill mopped his brow. Johnjohn too. Dunross dialed again. Still busy. Just before three he tried a last
time, then dialed the phone company asking them to check the line. "It's
temporarily out of order, sir," the operator said.

Dunross put the phone down. "Twenty to a brass farthing it's deliberately off the hook." His watch read 3:01. "Let's find out about the
market."

Havergill wiped the palms of his hands. Before he could dial, the phone
rang. "Chief cashier, sir. We've . . . we're all right now. Last customer
has been paid. The doors've closed. Blacs just made it too, sir."

"Good. Check the remaining currency in the vault and call me back."

"Thank God it's Friday," Johnjohn said.

Havergill dialed. "Charles? What's the latest?"

"The market finished off 37 points. Our stock's off 8 points."

"Christ," Johnjohn said. The bank had never fallen so much before,
even during the '56 riots.

"Struan's?"

"9.50."

Both bankers looked at Dunross. His face was impassive. He redialed
Tiptop as the stockbroker continued to reel off the closing prices. Again a
busy signal. "I'll call again from the office," he said. "The moment I get
him I'll call you. If no China money, what are you going to do?"

"There are only two solutions. We wait for the pounds, the governor
declaring Monday a bank holiday or as long as we need. Or we accept the
Moscow trade-bank offer."

"Tiptop was bloody clear that'll backfire. That'll throw a monkey
wrench in Hong Kong forever."

"Those are the only solutions."

Dunross got up. "There's only one. By the way, did the governor phone
you?"

"Yes," Havergill said. "He wants us to open the vaults at 6:00 P.M. for
him, you, Roger Crosse and some fellow called Sinders. What's all that
about?"

"Didn't he tell you?"

"No. Just that it was something covered by the Official Secrets Act."

"See you at six." Dunross walked out.

Havergill wiped more sweat off with a handkerchief. "The only good thing about all this is that that arrogant sod's in worse trouble," he muttered angrily. He dialed Tiptop's number. And again. The interoffice phone rang. Johnjohn picked it up for Havergill. "Yes?"

"This is the chief cashier, sir. There's only 716,027 HK in the vault." The man's voice trembled. "We're . . . that's all we've left, sir."

"Thank you." Johnjohn put the phone down and told Havergill. The deputy chairman did not answer, just redialed Tiptop's number. It was still busy. "You'd better open a dialogue with the Soviet contact."

Johnjohn went red. "But that's impossible—"

"*Do it!* Do it now!" Havergill, equally choleric, redialed Tiptop. Still busy.

Dunross went into his office.

"Mr. Toda's here with the usual entourage, tai-pan." Claudia did not hide her distaste or nervousness.

"Show them in please."

"Mr. Alastair called twice—asked that you call him back the moment you come in. And your father."

"I'll call them later."

"Yes sir. Here's the telex for Nelson Trading from Switzerland confirming that they've purchased triple the regular order of gold for the Great Good Luck Company of Macao."

"Good. Send a copy to Lando at once and request the funds."

"This telex is from Orlin Merchant Bank confirming they regret they cannot renew the loan and require payment."

"Telex them, 'Thank you.'"

"I checked with Mrs. Dunross and they arrived safely."

"Good. Get Kathy's specialist's home number so I can call him over the weekend."

Claudia made another note. "Master Duncan called from Sydney to say he had a great evening and he's on the Monday Qantas flight. Here's a list of your other calls."

He glanced at the long list, wondering fleetingly if his son was no longer a virgin, or was not even before the lovely Sheila. Thinking of a lovely sheila reminded him again of the exquisite Snow Jade. Curious her name was Snow Jade—she reminded me so much of Elegant Jade who's somewhere in Taipei in charge of a House of Many Pleasures. Perhaps the time's come to find Elegant Jade and thank her. Once more he remembered old Chen-chen's admonition when he was dying. "Listen, my son," old Chen-chen had whispered, his voice failing, "never try to find her. You will take away her face and take away beauty, both from her and from you. Now she'll be old, her Jade Gate withered and her pleasures will come from good food and good brandy. Children of the Pleasure

World do not age well, nor do their tempers. Leave her to her joss and to her memories. Be kind. Always be kind to those who give you their youth and their yin to succor your yang. Eeeee, how I wish I was as young as you again. . . ."

Dunross sighed. His evening with Snow Jade had been impeccable. And filled with laughter.

"I don't eat dessert," he had replied at once. "I'm on a diet."

"*Oh ko*, not you, tai-pan. I help you lose weight never mind."

"Thank you but no dessert and never in Hong Kong."

"Ah! Four Fingers said you'd say that, tai-pan, and for me not to be shamed." She had beamed and poured him a whiskey. "I'm to say, Have passport can travel."

They had laughed together. "What else did Four Fingers say?"

The tip of her tongue touched her lips. "Only that foreign devils are mighty very peculiar in some things. Like saying no dessert! As if it mattered." She watched him. "I've never been with a barbarian before."

"Oh? Some of us are really quite civilized."

Dunross smiled to himself, remembering how tempted he was, their banter and the great meal, everything good-humored and satisfying. Yes. But that doesn't forgive that old bastard Four Fingers, nor the half-coin, nor the theft of the half-coin, he thought grimly, nor the trap that he thinks he has me in. But all that comes later. First things come first. Concentrate, there's a lot to do before you sleep tonight!

The list Claudia had given him was long, most of the calls urgent, and two hours of work were ahead of him. Tiptop wasn't on the list, nor Lando Mata, Tightfist Tung, Four Fingers or Paul Choy. Casey and Bartlett were there. Travkin, Robert Armstrong. Jacques deVille, Gavallan, Phillip Chen, Dianne Chen, Alan Holdbrook—Struan's in-house stockbroker—Sir Luis, and dozens of others spread throughout the world. "We'll get to them after Hiro Toda, Claudia."

"Yes sir."

"After Toda, I want to see Jacques—then Phillip Chen. Anything on Mrs. Riko Gresserhoff?"

"Her plane's due in at 7:00 P.M. She's booked into the V and A and she'll be met. Flowers are in her room."

"Thank you." Dunross went into his office and stared out of the window. For the time being he had done everything he could for the Noble House and for Hong Kong. Now it was up to joss. And the next problem. The ships. His excitement picked up.

"Hello, tai-pan."

"Hello, Hiro." Dunross shook the outstretched hand warmly.

Hiro Toda, managing director of Toda Shipping Industries was of an age with Dunross, trim, hard, and much shorter, with wise eyes and a ready smile, his accent slightly American from two years of postgraduate

work at UCLA in the late forties. "May I introduce my associates: Mr.
Kazunari, Mr. Ebe, Mr. Kasigi."

The three younger men bowed and Dunross bowed back. They were all
dressed in dark suits, well cut, with white shirts and subdued ties.

"Please sit down." Airily Dunross waved to the chairs around the small
conference table. The door opened and his Japanese interpreter and assistant, Akiko, came in. She brought a tray with green tea, introduced herself, poured the tea delicately, then took her seat near Dunross. Though
his Japanese was easily good enough for a business meeting she was necessary for face.

Partially in Japanese, partially in English, he began the polite conversation about inconsequential matters, that by Japanese custom preceded serious discussion. It was also Japanese custom that business meetings were
shared by many executives, the more senior the executive, usually the
more people who came with him.

Dunross waited patiently. He liked the other man. Hiro Toda was titular head of the great shipping conglomerate that had been founded by his
great-grandfather almost a hundred years before. His forebears were *dai-
myos,* feudal lords, until feudalism and the samurai class was abolished in
1870 and modern Japan began. His authority in Toda Shipping was outwardly all powerful, but as frequently happened in Japan, all real power
was centered in the hands of his seventy-three-year-old father who, ostensibly, was retired.

At length Toda came to the point. "This stock market collapse must be
very worrying, tai-pan."

"A temporary loss of confidence. I'm sure everything will work itself out
over the weekend."

"Ah yes. I hope so too."

"How long are you staying, Hiro?"

"Till Sunday. Yes Sunday. Then on to Singapore and Sydney. I shall
be back for the closing of our business with you next week. I'm glad to tell
you your ships are ahead of schedule." Toda put a sheaf of papers on the
table. "Here's a detailed report."

"Excellent!" Dunross swung to the attack, blessing the gods and AMG
and Kirk. Coming home last night he had suddenly realized the enormity
of the key AMG and Kirk had given him to a plan he had been working
on for almost a year. "Would you like to bring forward your payment
schedule?"

"Ah!" The other man covered his surprise. "Perhaps I could discuss that
with my colleagues later but I'm glad to hear that everything is in control
then, and the takeover bid contained."

"Didn't Sun Tzu say, 'He who exercises no forethought but makes light
of his opponents is sure to be captured by them.' Gornt is certainly snapping at our heels, of course the run on our banks is serious, but the worst is

over. Everything's just fine. Don't you think we should expand the amount of business we're doing together?"

Toda smiled. "Two ships, tai-pan? Giants by present standards. In one year? That's not a minor connection."

"It could perhaps be twenty-two ships," he said, outwardly nonchalant, his whole being concentrated. "I have a proposal for you, in fact for all Japanese shipbuilding industrial complexes. At the moment you just build ships and sell them, either to gai-jin—outsiders—to ourselves for example, or to Japanese shippers. If to Japanese shippers, your operating costs with the high cost of Japanese crews—which by your law you have to carry—are already becoming noncompetitive, like American ships with American crews. Soon you won't be able to compete with the Greeks, with others and with us, because our costs will be so much lower."

Dunross saw them all concentrating on Akiko who was translating almost simultaneously and he thought with glee of another Sun Tzu saying: "In all fighting, the direct method may be used for joining battle but indirect methods will be needed to secure victory." Then he continued, "Second point: Japan has to import everything it needs to support its rising economy and standard of living and its industrial complex, and certainly the 95 percent of all energy it needs to sustain it. Oil's the key to your future. Oil has to come to you seaborne, so do all your bulk raw materials—always carried by bulk cargo ships. *Always* seaborne. You're building the great ships very efficiently, but as shipowners your operating costs and your own internal tax structure are going to drive you out of the marketplace. My proposal for you is simple: You stop trying to own your own uneconomic merchant fleets. You sell your ships abroad on a lease-back basis."

"What?"

Dunross saw them staring at him, astounded. He waited a moment, then continued, "A ship's life is, say fifteen years. You sell your bulk carrier say to us, but as part of the deal lease it back for fifteen years. We supply the captain and crew and operate her. Prior to delivery, you charter the ship to Mitsubishi or another of your own great companies for bulk supplies over fifteen years—coal, iron ore, rice, wheat, oil, whatever you want. This system guarantees Japan a continuous supply of raw material, set up at your whim and controlled by Japanese. Japan Inc. can increase its financing to you, because you yourselves, in effect, are the carriers of your own vital raw materials.

"Your industries can plan ahead. Japan Inc. can afford to assist financially selected buyers of your ships, because the purchase price is easily covered by the fifteen years charter. And since the ships are on long-term charter, our bankers, like Blacs and the Victoria, will also be happy to finance the rest. Everyone gains. You gain most because you ensure a long-term supply line under your control. And I haven't yet mentioned the tax advantages to you, to Toda Industries particularly!"

Dunross got up in a dead silence, the others staring at him, and went to his desk. He brought back some stapled reports. "Here's a tax study done by our people in Japan with specific examples, including methods to depreciate the ship's cost for added profit. Here's a suggested plan for bulk carriers. This one documents various ways Struan's could assist you in charters, should we be one of the foreign shippers chosen. For example, Woolara Mines of Australia are prepared, at our direction, to enter into a contract with Toda Industries to supply 95 percent of their coal output for one hundred years."

Toda gasped. So did the others when Akiko had translated. Woolara Mines was a huge, highly efficient and productive mine.

"We could assist you in Australia which is the treasury of Asia—supplying all the copper, wheat, foodstuffs, fruit, iron ore you need. I'm told privately there are new, immense deposits of high-grade iron ore just discovered in Western Australia within easy access of Perth. There's oil, uranium, thorium, and other precious materials you require. Wool. Rice. With my scheme *you* control your own flow of materials, the foreign shippers get ships and a steady cash flow to finance and order more ships, to lease back, to carry more and more raw materials and more cars, more television sets, more electronic goods, and more goods outward bound to the States—and heavy industry plants and machines to the rest of the world. Last, back to your most vital import of all: oil. Here's a suggested pattern for a new fleet of bulk oil carriers, half a million to a million tons dead weight each."

Toda gasped and abruptly finished the translation himself. Astounded, they all sucked in their breath when he mentioned the half a million to a million tons.

Dunross sat back enjoying the tension. He watched them glance at one another, then at Toda, waiting for him to react.

"I . . . I think we had better study your proposals, tai-pan," Toda said, trying to keep his voice level. "Obviously they are far-reaching. May we get back to you later?"

"Yes. You're coming to the races tomorrow? Lunch'll be 12:45."

"Thank you, yes, if it's not too much trouble," Toda said with sudden nervousness, "but it would be impossible for us to have an answer by that time."

"Of course. You got your invitations and badges?"

"Yes, thank you. I, er, I hope everything turns out well for you. Your proposal certainly sounds far-reaching."

They left. For a moment Dunross allowed himself to enjoy the excitement. I've got them, he thought. Christ, in a year we can have the biggest fleet in Asia, all totally financed, with no risks to financier, builder, operator or supplier, with oil tankers, huge tankers as its nucleus—if we can weather this typhoon.

All I need's some luck. Somehow I've got to stave off the crash till Tuesday when we sign with Par-Con. Par-Con pays for our ships, but what about Orlin and what about Gornt?

"Mr. Jacques's on his way up, tai-pan. Mr. Phillip's in his office and'll come up whenever you're ready. Roger Crosse called, your appointment's at 7:00 P.M. instead of 6:00. He said Mr. Sinders's plane was late. He's informed the governor and everyone connected."

"Thank you, Claudia." He glanced at his list of calls. He dialed the V and A and asked for Bartlett. He was out. "Miss Tcholok please."

"Hello?"

"Hello! Ian Dunross returning your call and Linc Bartlett's call. How're things?"

There was a slight pause. "Interesting. Tai-pan, can I drop by?"

"Of course. How about cocktails at 6:15 at the Mandarin? That'd give me half an hour-odd before my next appointment. Eh?" A twinge of anxiety went through him at the thought of Crosse, Sinders and AMG's admonition about never giving up the files.

"Is it possible for me to come by the office? I could leave now and be there in half to three quarters of an hour? I have something to talk over with you. I'll make it as short as possible."

"All right. I may have to keep you waiting a moment or two but come on over." He put the phone down, frowning. What's up there?

The door opened. Jacques deVille came in. He looked careworn and tired. "You wanted me, tai-pan?"

"Yes, sit down, Jacques. I understood you were going to be on the plane last night."

"We talked, Susanne and I, and she thought it best for Avril if I waited a day or two. . . ."

Dunross listened with fascination as they began to talk, still astounded that Jacques could be a Communist plant. But now he had thought through the possibility. It was easily possible for Jacques, being young, an idealist and in the Maquis during the hated and terrible Nazi occupation of France to have had his idealistic nationalism and anti-Nazi feelings channeled into communism—Christ, wasn't Russia our ally in those days? Wasn't communism fashionable everywhere in those days even in America? Didn't Marx and Lenin seem so sensible then? *Then.* Before we knew the truth about Stalin, about *gulags* and KGB and police state and mass murders and mass conquests and never freedom.

But how could all that Communist nonsense last for someone like Jacques? How could someone like Jacques retain such convictions and keep them buried for so long—if indeed he is the Sevrin plant AMG claimed?

"What did you think of Grey?" Dunross asked.

"A total *cretin,* tai-pan. He's far too left-wing for me. Even Broadhurst's a little too left for my taste. As I'm . . . I'm staying now, can I take over Bartlett and Casey again?"

"No, for the time being I'll deal with them, but you take care of the contract."

"It's being drawn up now. I've already been on to our solicitors. One slight problem. Dawson met with Bartlett's lawyer, Mr. Steigler, this morning. Mr. Steigler wants to renegotiate the payment schedule and put off signing till next weekend."

A wave of fury rushed through Dunross. He tried to keep it off his face. That's got to be the reason for Casey wanting a meeting, he thought. "I'll deal with that," he said, putting the problem aside for the more pressing one: Jacques deVille, who should be innocent until proven guilty.

He looked at him, liking the craggy, chunky man, remembering all the fine times they had had in Avisyard and in France. He, Penelope, Jacques and Susanne, their children along for Christmas or summer holidays, good food and good wine and good laughter and great plans for the future. Jacques certainly the wisest, the most close-mouthed, and until the AMG accusation, possibly the next in line. But now you're not, not until you've proved yourself and I'm certain. Sorry my friend, but you must be tested.

"I'm making some organizational changes," he said. "Linbar went to Sydney today as you know. I'm going to leave him there for a month to try to get the Woolara merger fixed. I don't hope for much. I want you to take over Australia." He saw Jacques's eyes widen momentarily but could not read if it was concern or happiness. "I've pushed the button on our Toda plan and I w—"

"How did he take it?"

"Hook, line and bait."

"*Merde,* but that is great." Dunross saw Jacques beam and read no guile in him. The man had been one of the main planners for the shipping scheme, working out the intricacies of the financing. "What a shame poor John's not alive to know," Jacques said.

"Yes." John Chen had been working closely with Jacques deVille. "Have you seen Phillip?"

"I had dinner with him last night. Poor fellow, he's aged twenty years."

"So have you."

A Gallic shrug. "Life, *mon ami!* But yes, yes I am sad about poor Avril and poor Borge. Please excuse me, I interrupted you."

"I'd like you to take over Australasia—effective today—and be responsible for putting into effect all our Australian and New Zealand plans. Keep this to yourself for the month—I'll tell Andrew only—but get yourself organized and be prepared to leave then."

"Very well." Jacques hesitated.

"What? Susanne never did like Hong Kong—you'll have no problem there, will you?"

"Oh no, tai-pan. Since the accident . . . frankly I was going to ask you if I could move for a while. Susanne's not been happy here and . . . But I was going to ask if I could take over Canada for a year or so."

Dunross was startled at the new thought. "Oh?"

"Yes. I thought that perhaps I could be useful there. My contacts among French-Canadians are good, very good. Perhaps we could shift Struan's Canadian office from Toronto to Montreal or to Ottawa. I could help very much from there. If our Japanese connection goes through, we'll need wood pulp, woods, copper, wheat, coal and a dozen other Canadian raw materials." He smiled wanly, then rushed onward. "We both know how Cousin David's been chomping to get back out here and I thought, if I moved there, he could return. Actually he's better equipped to be here, to deal with Australasia, *non?* He speaks Cantonese, a little Japanese and reads and writes Chinese which I don't. But whatever you say, tai-pan. I'll take Australasia if you wish. It is true I would like a change."

Dunross let his mind range. He had decided to isolate Jacques from Hong Kong while he found out the truth. It would be too easy to tell Crosse or Sinders secretly and ask them to use their sources to investigate, to watch and to probe. But Jacques was a member of the Inner Court. As such he was party to all sorts of skeletons and private informations which would be put to risk. No, Dunross thought, much better to deal with our own. Perhaps it will take longer but I will find out the truth if he is or isn't. One way or another, I'll know about Jacques deVille.

But Canada?

Logically Jacques'd be better there. So would Struan's—I should have thought of that myself—there's never been any reason to question his business loyalty, or acumen. Good old David's certainly been screaming for two years to come back. The switch would be easier. Jacques's right. David's better equipped to do Australasia, and Australia and New Zealand are far more important to us than Canada, far more important—they're vital and the treasure house of all Asia. If Jacques's innocent he can help us in Canada. If he's not, he can harm us less there. "I'll think about that," he said, having already decided to make the change. "Keep this all to yourself and we'll finalize it Sunday."

Jacques got up and stuck out his hand. "Thanks, *mon ami.*"

Dunross shook the hand. But in his heart he wondered whether it was the hand of his friend—or his Judas.

Alone once more, the weight of his burdens swamped him. The phone rang and he dealt with that problem, then another and another—Tiptop's phone still engaged—and he asked for Phillip to come up, and all the time it seemed as though he were sinking into a pit. Then his eyes caught the eye of Dirk Struan on the wall, looking out of the oil painting at him, half-smiling, supremely confident, arrogant, master of clipper ships—the loveliest craft ever built by man. As always, he was comforted.

He got up and stood before *the* tai-pan. "Christ, I don't know what I'd do without you," he said out loud, remembering that Dirk Struan had been beset by far greater burdens and had conquered them. Only to have the tempest, the wrath of nature, kill him at the zenith of his life, just forty-three, undisputed warlord of Hong Kong and Asia.

Is it always "those whom the gods love die young"? he asked himself. Dirk was just my age when the Devil Winds of the Great Typhoon tore our brand-new three-story residence in Happy Valley to pieces and buried him in the rubble. Is that old or young? I don't feel old. Was that the only way for Dirk to die? Violently? In storm? Young? Killed by nature? Or does the expression mean, those whom the gods love die young in heart?

"Never mind," he said to his mentor and friend. "I wish I'd lived to know you. I tell you openly, tai-pan, I hope to God there is a life after death so that in some eon of time, I can thank you personally."

Confident again, he went back to his desk. In his top drawer was Four Finger Wu's matrix. His fingers touched it, caressing it. How do I squeeze out of this one? he asked himself grimly.

There was a knock. Phillip Chen came in. He had aged in the last few days. "Good God, tai-pan, what are we going to do? 9.50!" he said in a rush, a nervous screech in his voice. "I could tear my hair out! *Dew neh loh moh* because of the boom, you remember I bought in at 28.90, every penny of spare cash and a lot more and Dianne bought at 28.80 and sold at 16.80 and demands I make up the difference. *Oh ko* what're we going to do?"

"Pray—and do what we can," Dunross said. "Have you got hold of Tiptop?"

"Eh . . . no, no, tai-pan. I've been trying every few minutes but the phone's still out of order. The phone company says the phone's been left off the hook. I had my cousin in the phone company check it personally. Both lines into his house are off the hook."

"What do you advise?"

"Advise? I don't know, I think we should send a messenger but I didn't want to until I'd consulted with you . . . what with our stock crash and the bank run and poor John and the reporters pestering . . . all my stocks are down, all of them!" The old man went into a paroxysm of Cantonese obscenities and curses on Gornt, his ancestors and all his future generations. "If the Vic goes, what are we going to do, tai-pan?"

"The Vic won't go. The governor will certainly declare Monday a bank holiday if Tiptop fails us." Dunross had already apprised his compradore of his conversations with Tiptop, Yu, Johnjohn and Havergill. "Come on, Phillip, think!" he added with pretended anger, deliberately sharpening his voice to help the old man. "I can't just send a god-cursed messenger there to say 'you've deliberately left your bloody phone off the hook'!"

Phillip Chen sat down, the rare anger pulling him a little together. "Sorry, yes, sorry but everything . . . and John, poor John . . ."

"When's the funeral?"

"Tomorrow, tomorrow at ten, the Christian one, Monday's the Chinese one. I was . . . I was wondering if you'd say a few words, tomorrow."

"Of course, of course I will. Now, what about Tiptop?"

Phillip Chen concentrated, the effort hard for him. At length he said, "Invite him to the races. To your box. He's never been and that would be great face. That's the way. You could say . . . No, sorry, I'm not thinking clearly. Better, much better, tai-pan, I will write. I'll write the note asking him for you. I'll say you wanted to ask personally but unfortunately his phone is out of order—then if he wants to come, or is forbidden by his superiors, his face is saved and so is yours. I could add that 'by the way, the Noble House has already telexed firm orders to Sydney for the thoriums . . .'" Phillip Chen brightened a little. "That will be a very good trade for us, tai-pan, the price offered. . . . I've checked prices and we can supply all their needs easily and get very competitive bids from Tasmania, South Africa and Rhodesia. Ah! Why not send young George Trussler from Singapore to Johannesburg and Salisbury on an exploratory mission for thoriums . . ." Phillip Chen hesitated. ". . . and er, certain other vital aerospace metals and materials. I did some quick checking, tai-pan. I was astounded to discover that, outside Russia, almost 90 percent of all the Free World's supply of vanadium, chrome, platinums, manganese, titanium—all vital and essential in aerospace and rocketry—come from the southern part of Rhodesia and South Africa. Think of that! 90 percent outside Russia. I never realized how vastly important that area is to the Free World, with all the gold, diamonds, uranium, thorium and God knows what other essential raw materials. Perhaps Trussler could also investigate the possibility of opening an office there. He's a sharp young man and due for promotion." Now that his mind was fully occupied, the old man was breathing easier. "Yes. This trade and, er, Mr. Yu's, could be immense for us, tai-pan. I'm sure it can be handled delicately." He looked up at Dunross. "I'd also mention to Tiptop about Trussler, that we were sending an executive, one of the family, in preparation."

"Excellent. Do it immediately." Dunross clicked on the intercom. "Claudia, get George Trussler please." He glanced back at Phillip. "Why would Tiptop cut himself off?"

"To bargain, to increase the pressure on us, to get more concessions."

"Should we keep on calling him?"

"No. After the hand-delivered note, he will call us. He knows we're not fools."

"When will he call?"

"When he has permission, tai-pan. Not before. Sometime before Monday at 10:00 A.M. when the banks are due to open. I suggest you tell that lump of dogmeat Havergill and Johnjohn not to call—they'll muddy already dark waters. You don't use a tadpole to catch a shark."

"Good. Don't worry, Phillip," he said compassionately, "we're going to get out of this mess."

"I don't know, tai-pan. I hope so." Phillip Chen rubbed his red-rimmed eyes tiredly. "Dianne . . . those damned shares! I see no way out of the morass. Th—"

Claudia interrupted on the intercom. "Master Trussler on line two."

"Thank you, Claudia." He stabbed line two. "Hello, George, how's Singapore?"

"Afternoon, sir. Fine, sir, hot and rainy," the breezy, enthusiastic voice said. "This's a pleasant surprise, what can I do for you?"

"I want you to get on the next plane to Johannesburg. Leave at once. Telex me your flight and hotel and call me as soon as you arrive at the hotel in Johannesburg. Got it?"

There was a slight hesitation and slightly less breeziness. "Johannesburg, South Africa, tai-pan?"

"Yes. The next plane out."

"I'm on my way. Anything else?"

"No."

"Right you are, tai-pan. I'm on my way. 'Bye!"

Dunross put the phone down. Power's a marvelous device, he thought with great satisfaction, but being tai-pan's better.

Phillip got up. "I'll deal with that letter at once."

"Just a minute, Phillip. I've another problem that I need your advice on." He opened the desk and brought out the matrix. Apart from himself and previous tai-pans who were still alive, only Phillip Chen in all the world knew the secret of the four coins. "Here. This was giv—"

Dunross stopped, paralyzed, totally unprepared for the effect the matrix had on his compradore. Phillip Chen was staring at it, his eyes almost popped from their sockets, his lips stretched back from his teeth. As though in a dream, everything in slow motion, Phillip Chen reached out and took the matrix, his fingers trembling, and peered at it closely, mouthing soundlessly.

Then Dunross's brain detonated and he realized the half-coin must have belonged to Phillip Chen, that it had been stolen from *him. Of course,* Dunross wanted to shout. Sir Gordon Chen must have been given one of the four coins by Jin-qua! But why? What was the connection between the Chen family and a Co-hong Mandarin that would make Jin-qua give the Eurasian son of Dirk Struan so valuable a gift?

Still in slow motion, he saw the old man raise his head to squint up at him. Again the mouth moved. No sound. Then in a strangled gasp, "Bar . . . Bartlett gave this . . . this to you already?"

"Bartlett?" Dunross echoed incredulously. "What in the name of Christ's Bartlett got to d—" He stopped as another explosion seemed to shatter his head and more pieces of the jigsaw slammed into place. Bartlett's secret knowledge! Knowledge that could only come from one of seven men, all of them unthinkable, Phillip Chen the most unthinkable of all!

Phillip Chen's the traitor! Phillip Chen's working in conjunction with

Bartlett and Casey . . . it's Phillip Chen who's sold us out and passed over our secrets and passed over the coin.

A blinding rage overcame him. It took all of his training to hold the fury bottled. He saw himself get up and stride to the window and stare out of it. He did not know how long he stood there. But when he turned, his mind was purged clean and the vast error in his logic now clear to him.

"Well?" His voice was chilling.

"Tai-pan . . . tai-pan . . ." the old man began brokenly, wringing his hands.

"Tell the truth, compradore. *Now!*" The word frightened Phillip.

"It . . . it was John," he gasped, tears spilling. "It wasn't me I sw—"

"I know that! Hurry up for chrissake!"

Phillip Chen spewed out everything, how he had taken his son's key and opened his son's safety deposit box and discovered the letters to and from Bartlett and the second key and how, at dinner the night of the tai-pan's party, he had suddenly had a premonition about his oh so secret safe buried in the garden and how, after digging it up, he had discovered the worst. He even told the tai-pan about his quarrel with Dianne and how they thought the coin might be on John Chen somehow, and how, when the Werewolf phoned, she suggested calling his cousin, Four Finger Wu, to get his street fighters to follow him, then to follow them. . . .

Dunross gasped but Phillip Chen did not notice it, rambling on in tears, telling how he had lied to the police and had paid over the ransom to the Werewolf youths he would never recognize again and how the street fighters of Four Fingers who were supposed to be guarding him had not intercepted the Werewolves or recaptured John or recaptured his money. "That's the truth, tai-pan, all of it," he whimpered, "there's no more . . . nothing. Nothing until this morning and my poor son's body at Sha Tin with that filthy sign on his chest. . . ."

Helplessly Dunross was trying to collect his wits. He had not known that Four Fingers was Phillip's cousin, nor could he fathom how the old seaman could have got the coin—unless he was the chief Werewolf or in league with them, or in league with John Chen who had masterminded a supposed kidnapping to squeeze money out of the father he hated and then Four Fingers and John Chen had quarreled or . . . or what? "How did John know our secrets, get all those secrets to pass them over to Bartlett—how the House's structured? Eh?"

"I don't know," the old man lied.

"You must have told John—there's only you, Alastair, my father, Sir Ross, Gavallan, deVille or me who know, and of those, only the first four know the structure!"

"I didn't tell him—I swear I didn't."

Dunross's blinding rage began to swell again but once more he held it into place.

Be logical, he told himself. Phillip's more Chinese than European. Deal with him as a Chinese! Where's the link? The missing part of the jigsaw?

While he was trying to work out the problem, his eyes bored into the old man. He waited, knowing that silence too was a vast weapon, in defense or attack. What's the answer? Phillip would never tell John anything that secret, therefore . . .

"Jesus Christ!" he burst out at the sudden thought. "You've been keeping records! Private records! That's how John found out! From your safe! Eh?"

Petrified by the tai-pan's devil rage, Phillip blurted out before he could stop himself, "Yes . . . yes . . . I had to agree . . ." He stopped, fighting for control.

"Had to? Why? Come on goddamnit!"

"Because . . . because my father, before he . . . he passed the House over to me and the coin to me . . . made me swear to keep . . . to record the private dealings of . . . of the Noble House to protect the House of Chen. It was just that, tai-pan, never to use against you or the House, just a protection. . . ."

Dunross stared at him, hating him, hating John Chen for selling Struan's out, hating his mentor Chen-chen for the first time in his life, sick with rage at so many betrayals. Then he remembered one of Chen-chen's admonitions years ago when Dunross was almost weeping with anger at the unfair way his father and Alastair were treating him: "Don't get angry, young Ian, get even. I told Culum the same thing, and the Hag when they were equally young—Culum never listened but the Hag did. That's the civilized way: Don't get angry, get even! "So Bartlett has our structure, our balance sheets. What else's he got?"

Phillip Chen just shivered and stared back blankly.

"Come on for chrissake, Phillip, think! We've all got skeletons, a lot of skeletons! So've you, the Hag, Chen-chen, Shitee T'Chung, Dianne . . . for chrissake, how much more's documented that John could have passed over?" A wave of nausea went through him as he remembered his theory about the connection between Banastasio, Bartlett, Par Con, the Mafia and the guns. Christ, if our secrets get into the wrong hands! "Eh?"

"I don't know, I don't know . . . What, what did Bartlett ask? For the coin?" Then Phillip cried out, "It's mine, it belongs to me!"

He saw the uncontrollable trembling of Phillip's hands and a sudden tinge of gray in his face. There was brandy and whiskey in decanters on the sideboard and Dunross fetched some brandy and gave it to him. Gratefully the old man drank, choking a little. "Than . . . thank you."

"Go home and fetch everything and th—" Dunross stopped and stabbed an intercom button. "Andrew?"

"Yes, tai-pan?" Gavallan said.

"Would you come up a second? I want you to go home with Phillip, he's not feeling too well and there're some papers to bring back."

"On my way."

Dunross's eyes had never left Phillip's.

"Tai-pan, what did, did Bar—"

"Stay away from them on your life! And give Andrew everything—John's letters, Bartlett's letters, everything," he said, his voice chilling.

"Tai-pan . . ."

"Everything." His head ached, he had so much rage in him. He was going to add, I'll decide about you and the House of Chen over the weekend. But he did not say it. "Don't get mad, get even" kept ringing in his ears.

Casey came in. Dunross met her halfway. She carried an umbrella and was again wearing her pale green dress that set off her hair and eyes perfectly. Dunross noticed the shadows behind her eyes. They made her somehow more desirable. "Sorry to keep you waiting." His smile was warm but he enjoyed none of its warmth. He was still appalled over Phillip Chen.

Casey's hand was cool and pleasant. "Thanks for seeing me," she said. "I know you're busy so I'll come to the point."

"First tea. Or would you like a drink?"

"No liquor thanks, but I don't want to put you to any trouble."

"No trouble, I'm going to have tea anyway. 4:40's tea time." As though by magic the door opened and a liveried houseboy brought in a silver tray with tea for two—with thin buttered toast and hot scones in a silver warmer. The man poured and left. The tea was dark brown and strong. "It's Darjeeling, one of our House blends. We've been trading it since 1830," he said sipping it gratefully, as always thanking the unknown genius Englishman who had invented afternoon tea, which, somehow, always seemed to settle the cares of the day and put the world into perspective. "I hope you like it."

"It's great, maybe a mite too strong for me. I had some around 2:00 A.M., and it certainly woke me up."

"Oh? You still on jet lag?"

She shook her head and told him about Peter Marlowe.

"Oh! What bad joss!" He stabbed the intercom. "Claudia, call the Nathan Nursing Home and see how Mrs. Marlowe is. And send some flowers. Thanks."

Casey frowned. "How'd you know she was at the Nathan?"

"Doc Tooley always uses that place in Kowloon." He was watching her closely, astonished that she seemed so friendly when obviously Par-Con was trying to sabotage their deal. If she's been up most of the night, that accounts for the shadows, he thought. Well, shadows or not, watch out, young lady, we shook on the deal. "Another cup?" he asked solicitously.

"No thanks, this's fine."

"I recommend the scones. We eat them like this: a big dollop of Devonshire clotted cream on top, a teaspoon of homemade strawberry jam in the center of the cream and . . . magic! Here!"

Reluctantly she took it. The scone was just bite-sized. It vanished. "Fantastic," she gasped, wiping a touch of the cream off her mouth. "But all those calories! No, really, no more, thanks. I've done nothing but eat since I got here."

"It doesn't show."

"It will." He saw her smile back at him. She was sitting in one of the deep high-backed leather chairs, the tea table between them. Again she crossed her legs and Dunross thought once more that Gavallan had been right about her—that her Achilles' heel was impatience. "May I start now?" she asked.

"You're sure you don't want some more tea?" he asked, deliberately to throw her off balance again.

"No thanks."

"Then tea's over. What's cooking?"

Casey took a deep breath. "It seems that Struan's is way out on a limb and about to go under."

"Please don't concern yourself about that. Struan's really is in very fine shape."

"You may be, tai-pan, but it doesn't look that way to us. Or to outsiders. I've checked. Most everyone seems to think Gornt, and or the Victoria, will make the raid stick. It's almost a general thumbs down. Now our deal's—"

"We have a deal till Tuesday. That's what we agreed," he said, his voice sharpening. "Do I understand you want to renege or change it?"

"No. But in the present state you're in, it'd be crazy and bad business to proceed. So we've two alternatives: It's either Rothwell-Gornt, or we've to help you with some kind of bail-out operation."

"Oh?"

"Yes. I've a plan, a partial plan for how you could maybe extricate yourself and make us all a fortune. Okay? You're the best for us—long-term."

"Thank you," he said, not believing her, all attention, well aware that any concession she offered was going to be prohibitively expensive.

"Try this on for size. Our bankers are the First Central New York—the hated bank here. They want back into Hong Kong so much it hurts, but they'll never get a new charter, right?"

Dunross's interest peaked at this new thought. "So?"

"So recently they bought a small foreign bank with branches in Tokyo, Singapore, Bangkok and Hong Kong: the Royal Belgium and Far East Bank. It's a tiny, nothing bank and they paid 3 million for everything. First Central has asked us to put our funds through the Royal Belgium if our deal goes through. Last night I met with Dave Murtagh who's in charge of Royal Belgium and he was moaning and groaning how bad business was, how they're squeezed out of everything by the Establishment here and though they've got the huge dollar resources of First Central behind them, almost nobody'll open accounts and deposit Hong Kong dollars which they need to make loans. You know about the bank?"

"Yes," he said, not understanding what she was leading to, "but I didn't realize the First Central was behind them. I don't think that's common knowledge. When was it bought out?"

"A couple of months ago. Now, what if the Royal Belgium would advance you Monday 120 percent of the purchase price of the two Toda ships?"

Dunross gaped at her, caught off guard. "Secured by what?"

"The ships."

"Impossible! No bank'd do that!"

"The 100 percent is for Toda, the 20 percent to cover all carrying charges, insurances and the first months of operation."

"With no cash flow, no charterer set?" he asked incredulously.

"Could you charter them in sixty days to give you a cash flow to sustain a reasonable repayment schedule?"

"Easily." Jesus Christ, if I can pay Toda at once I can slam my leaseback scheme into operation with the first two ships, without having to wait. He held onto his hope, wondering what the cost, the real cost would be. "Is this a theory or will they really do it?"

"They might."

"In return for what?"

"In return for Struan's depositing 50 percent of all foreign exchange for a five-year period; a promise you'd keep average cash deposits with them of between 5 and 7 million Hong Kong dollars—one and one half million U.S. dollars worth; that you'd use the bank as your second Hong Kong bank and the First Central as your prime lending American bank outside of Hong Kong for a five-year period. What do you say?"

It took all his training not to bellow with joy. "Is this a firm offer?"

"I think it is, tai-pan. I'm a bit out of my depth—I've never been into ships but 120 percent seemed fantastic and the other terms okay. I didn't know how far I should go negotiating terms but I told him he'd better make it all fair or he'd never get to first base."

An ice shaft went into his guts. "The local man would never have the authority to make such an offer."

"That was Murtagh's next point, but he said we've the weekend and if you'll go for the scheme he'll get on the wire."

Dunross sat back, nonplussed. He put aside three vital questions and said, "Let's hold this for the moment. What's your part in all this?"

"In a minute. There's another wrinkle to his offer. I think he's bananas but Murtagh said he'd try to persuade the brass to put up a revolving $50 million U.S. against the value of the unissued shares you got in your treasury. So you're home free. If."

Dunross felt the sweat break out on his back and on his forehead, well aware what a tremendous gamble that would be, however big the bank. With effort he put his brain to work. With the ships paid for and that revolving fund, he could fight off Gornt and smash his attack. And with Gornt bottled, Orlin'd come back meekly because he'd always been a good customer—and wasn't First Central part of the Orlin Merchant Bank consortium? "What about our deal?"

"That stays as is. You announce at the best time for both of us, for you and for Par-Con as we agreed. If, and it's a big if, if First Central'll go for the gamble, you and we could make a killing, a real killing by buying Struan at 9.50 Monday morning—it has to go back up to 28, maybe to 30, doesn't it? The only part I can't figure is how to deal with the bank runs."

Dunross took out his handkerchief and unashamedly wiped his forehead. Then he got up and poured two brandy and sodas. He gave her one and sat back in his chair again, his mind amok, one moment blank, the next crammed with happiness, instantly to be agitated and hurting with all the hope and fear, the questions, answers, plans and counterplans.

Christallbloodymighty, he thought, trying to calm himself.

The brandy tasted good. The warming bite was very good. He noticed she only sipped hers then set it down and watched him. When his brain had cleared and he was ready, he looked at her. "All this in return for what?"

"You'll have to set the parameters with the Royal Belgium—that's up to you. I don't know accurately enough your net cash flow. Interest charges'll be steep, but worth it to get out from under. You'll have to put up your personal guarantee for every cent."

"Christ!"

"Yes. Plus face." He heard her voice harden. "It'll cost you face to be dealing with the 'yellow bastards.' Wasn't that what Lady Joanna called the First Central people with her big fat sneer and 'But what do you expect, they're . . .' I guess she meant Americans." He saw Casey's eyes flatten and his danger signals came up. "That's some old bitch, that one."

"She's not really," he said. "She's a bit caustic, and rough, but all right usually. She is anti-American, sorry to say, paranoid I suppose. You see, her husband, Sir Richard, was killed at Monte Cassino in Italy by American bombs, their aircraft mistaking British troops for Nazis."

"Oh," Casey said. "Oh I see."

"What does Par-Con want? And what do you and Linc Bartlett want?"

She hesitated, then put Lady Joanna aside for a moment, concentrating again. "Par-Con wants a long-term deal with Struan's—as 'Old Friends.'" He saw the strange smile. "I've discovered what *Old Friend* means, Chinese style, and that's what I want for Par-Con. Old Friend status as and from the moment the Royal Belgium delivers."

"Next?"

"Is that a yes?"

"I'd like to know all the terms before I agree to one."

She sipped the brandy. "Linc wants nothing. He doesn't know about all this."

"I beg your pardon?" Again Dunross was caught off balance.

"Linc doesn't know about the Royal Belgium yet," she said, her voice ordinary. "I brainstormed all this with Dave Murtagh today. I don't know if I'm doing you much of a favor because your . . . because you'll be on the line, you personally. But it could get Struan's off the hook. Then our deal can work."

"Don't you think you should consult with your fearless leader?" Dunross said, trying to work out the implications of this unexpected tack.

"I'm executive director and Struan's is my deal. It costs us nothing but our influence to get you out of your trap and that's what influence's for. I want our deal to go through and I don't want Gornt the winner."

"Why?"

"I told you. You're the best for us long-term."

"And you, Ciranoush? What do you want? In return for using your influence?"

Her eyes seemed to flatten even more and become more hazel, like a lioness's. "Equality. I want to be treated as an equal, not patronized or scoffed at as a woman who's in business on the coat tails of a man. I want equality with the tai-pan of the Noble House. And I want you to help me get my drop dead money—apart from anything to do with Par-Con."

"The second's easy, if you're prepared to gamble. As to the first, I've never patronized or sloughed you o—"

"Gavallan did, and the others."

". . . off, and I never will. As to the others, if they don't treat you as you like, then leave the conference table and leave the battleground. Don't force your presence on them. I can't make you equal. You're not and you never will be. You're a woman and like it or not this's a man's world. Particularly in Hong Kong. And while I'm alive I'm going to continue to treat it as it is and treat a woman as a woman whoever the hell she is."

"Then screw you!"

"When?" He beamed.

Her sudden laugh joined his and the tension fled. "I deserved that," she said. Another laugh. "I really deserved that. Sorry. Guess I lost ass."

"I beg your pardon?"

She explained her version of face. He laughed again. "You didn't. You gained arse."

After a pause she said, "So whatever I do, I can never have equality?"

"Not in business, not on masculine terms, not if you want to be of this world. As I said, like it or not, that's the way it is. And I think you're wrong to try to change it. The Hag was undisputedly more powerful than anyone in Asia. And she got there as a woman, not as a neuter."

Her hand reached out and lifted her brandy and he saw the swell of her breast against the light silk blouse. "How the hell can we treat someone as attractive and smart as you as a non-person? Be fair!"

"I'm not asking for fairness, tai-pan, just equality."

"Be content you're a woman."

"Oh I am. I really am." Her voice became bitter. "I just don't want to be classed as someone whose only real value is on her back." She took a last sip and got up. "So you'll take it from here? With the Royal Belgium? David Murtagh's expecting a call. It's a long shot, but it's worth a try, isn't it? Maybe you could go see him, instead of sending for him—face, huh? He'll need all the support you can give him."

Dunross had not got up. "Please sit down a second, if you've time. There're still a couple of things."

"Of course. I didn't want to take any more of your time."

"First, what's the problem with your Mr. Steigler?"

"What do you mean?"

He told her what Dawson had related.

"Son of a bitch!" she said, obviously irritated. "I told him to get the papers drawn, that's all. I'll take care of him. Lawyers always think they've the right to negotiate, 'to improve the deal' is the way they put it, trying to put you down, I guess. I've lost more deals because of them than you can imagine. Seymour's not as bad as some. Attorneys're the plague of the United States. Linc thinks so too."

"What about Linc?" he asked, remembering the 2 million he had advanced to Gornt to attack their stock. "Is he going to be 100 percent behind this new twist?"

"Yes," she said after a pause. "Yes."

Dunross's mind reached out for the missing piece. "So you'll take care of Steigler and everything stands as before?"

"You'll have to work out title to the ships as we agreed but that shouldn't be a problem."

"No. I can handle that."

"You'll personally guarantee everything?"

"Oh, yes," Dunross said carelessly. "Dirk did all the time. That's the tai-pan's privilege. Listen, Ciranoush, I—"

"Will you call me Casey, tai-pan? Ciranoush is for a different era."

"All right. Casey, whether this works or not, you're an Old Friend and I owe you a thank you for your bravery, your personal bravery at the fire."

"I'm not brave. It must have been glands." She laughed. "Don't forget we've still got the hepatitis over our heads."

"Oh. You thought of that too."

"Yes."

Her eyes were watching him and he could not gauge her. "I'll help you with drop dead money," he said. "How much do you need?"

"2 million, tax free."

"Your tax laws are rigid and tough. Are you prepared to stretch laws?"

She hesitated. "It's the right of every red-blooded American to avoid taxes, but not evade them."

"Got it. So at your bracket you might need 4?"

"My bracket's low, though my capital's high."

"$46,000 at the San Fernando Savings and Loan's not very much," he said, grimly amused to see her blanch. "$8,700 in your checking account at the Los Angeles and California's not too much either."

"You're a bastard."

He smiled. "I merely have friends in high places. Like you." Casually he opened the trap. "Will you and Linc Bartlett have dinner with me tonight?"

"Linc's busy," she said.

"Will you have dinner then? Eight? Let's meet in the lobby of the Mandarin." He had heard the undercurrent and the giveaway and he could almost see her mind waves churning. So Linc's busy! he thought. And what would Linc Bartlett be busy with in that tone of voice? Orlanda Ramos? Has to be, he told himself, delighted he had flushed out the real reason—the real why of her help. Orlanda! Orlanda leading to Linc Bartlett leading to Gornt. Casey's petrified of Orlanda. Is she petrified that Gornt's behind Orlanda's onslaught on Bartlett—or is she just frantic with jealousy and ready to bring Bartlett atumbling down?

59

5:35 P.M.:

Casey joined the packed lines going through the turnstiles at Golden Ferry. People were shoving and pushing and hurrying along the corridor for the next ferry. As the warning bell sounded shrilly, those in front broke into a frantic run. Involuntarily her feet quickened. The noisy, heated crush of humanity carried her along onto the ferry. She found a seat and stared out at the harbor gloomily, wondering if she had pulled off her side of the deal.

"Jesus, Casey," Murtagh had burst out, "head office'll never go for it in a million years!"

"If they don't they'll miss the greatest opportunity of their lives. And so will you. This is your big chance—grab it! If you help Struan's now think how much face everyone gets. When Dunross comes to see you th—"

"If he comes!"

"He'll come. I'll get him to come see you! And when he does, tell him this's all your idea, not mine, and that y—"

"But, Casey, don—"

"No. It's got to be your idea. I'll back you a thousand percent with New York. And when Dunross comes to you, tell him you want Old Friend status too."

"Jesus, Casey, I've got enough troubles without having to explain to those meatheads back home about Old Friend and 'face'!"

"So don't explain that part to them. You pull this off and you'll be the most important American banker in Asia."

Yes, Casey told herself, sick with hope, and I'll have extricated Linc from Gornt's trap. I know I'm right about Gornt.

"The hell you are, Casey!" Bartlett had said angrily this morning, the first time in their life together he had ever flared at her.

"It's obvious, Linc," she had slammed back. "I'm not trying to interfere i—"

"The hell you're not!"

"You brought Orlanda up, I didn't! You're going overboard about—about her great cooking and great dancing and great outfit and great company! All I said was, did you have a nice time?"

"Sure, but you said it with a real crappy harpy jealous tone and I know you meant: I hope you had a lousy time!"

Linc was right, Casey thought in misery. If he wants to be out all night that's up to him. I should have buttoned up like the other times and not made a big deal of it. But this isn't like the other times. He's in danger and won't see it!

"For chrissake, Linc, that woman's after your money and power and that's all! How long have you known her? A couple of days. Where did you meet her? Gornt! She's got to be Gornt's puppet! That guy's as smart as they come! I've done some checking, Linc, her apartment's paid by him, her bills. Sh—"

"She told me all that and all about him and her and that's the past! You can forget Orlanda! Get it? Just don't bad-mouth her anymore. Understand?"

"Par-Con's got a lot riding on whether it's Struan's or Gornt and they'll both use any tactic to undermine you or lay you open to att—"

"And *lay* the operative word? C'mon, Casey, for chrissake! You've never been jealous before—admit you're fit to be tied. She's everything a man could want and you're . . ."

She remembered how he had stopped just before he'd said it. Tears filled her eyes. He's right, goddamnit! I'm not. I'm a goddamn business machine, not feminine like her, not an easy lay and not interested in being a housewife, at least not yet, and I could never do what she's done. Orlanda's soft, pliant, golden, a great cook, he says, feminine, great body great legs great taste, trained and beddable, Jesus, how beddable. And with no thought in her goddamn head but how to catch a rich husband. The Frenchwoman was right: Linc's a patsy for any no-account, harpy, Asian gold digger, and Orlanda's the cream of the Hong Kong crop.

Shit!

But whatever Linc says, I'm still right about her and right about Gornt. Or am I?

Let's face it, I've nothing to go on but a few rumors, and my own intuition. Orlanda's got me on the run, I'm running scared. I made a goddamn mistake letting myself go at Linc. Remember what he said before he left the suite. "From here on in you stay the hell out of my private life!"

Oh God!

There was a fine wind blowing as the ferry skittered across the harbor, engines pounding, sampans and other boats moving nimbly out of the way, the sky brooding and overcast. Oblivious, she dabbed her tears away, took out her mirror and checked that her mascara was not running. A huge freighter sounded its horn, flags fluttering, and moved majestically past, but she did not see it, nor the immensity of the nuclear carrier tied up alongside the Admiralty Wharf, Hong Kong side. "Get hold of yourself," she muttered in misery to her mirror image. "Jesus, you look forty."

The cramped wooden benches were crowded and she shifted uncomfortably, jammed between other passengers, most of whom were Chinese, though here and there were camera-heavy tourists and other Europeans. There was not an inch of free space, all gangways clogged, seats clogged, and already blocks of passengers crowded the ramp exit on both decks. The Chinese beside her were awkwardly reading their newspapers as people would on any subway except that, from time to time, they would hawk noisily to clear their throats. One spat. On the bulkhead right in front of him was a large sign in Chinese and English: NO SPITTING—FINE TWENTY DOLLARS. He hawked again and Casey wanted to take his newspaper and thump him with it. The tai-pan's remark flooded her memory: "We've been trying to change them for a hundred and twenty-odd years, but Chinese don't change easily."

It's not just them, she thought, her head aching. It's everyone and everything in this man's world. The tai-pan's right.

So what am I going to do? About Linc? Change the rules or not?

I have already. I've gone over his head with the bail-out scheme. That's a first. Am I going to tell him about it or not? Dunross won't give me away and Murtagh'll take all the credit, has to, if First Central'll buy it. I'll have to tell Linc sometime.

But whether the bail-out works or not, what about Linc and me?

Her eyes were fixed ahead, unseeing, as she tried to decide.

The ferry was nearing the Kowloon Terminal berth now. Two other ferries leaving for Hong Kong side swirled out of the way for the incomers. Everyone got up and began to jostle for position at the port exit ramp. The ship heeled slightly, unbalanced. Jesus, she thought uneasily, jerked out of her reverie, there must be five hundred of us on each deck. Then she winced as an impatient Chinese matron squeezed past, stomped carelessly on her foot and pushed on through the throng to the head of the line. Casey got up, her foot hurting, wanting to belt the woman with her umbrella.

"They're something else, eh?" the tall American behind her said with grim good humor.

"What? Oh yes, yes . . . something else, some of them." People surrounded her, crowding her, pressing too close. Suddenly she felt claustrophobic and sickened. The man sensed it and used his bulk to force a little room. Those who were pushed aside gave way with ill humor. "Thanks," she said, relieved, the nausea gone. "Yes, thanks."

"I'm Rosemont, Stanley Rosemont. We met at the tai-pan's."

Casey turned, startled. "Oh, sorry, I guess . . . I guess I was a million miles away, I didn't . . . sorry. How's it going?" she asked, not remembering him.

"More of the same, Casey." Rosemont looked down at her. "Not so good with you, huh?" he asked kindly.

"Oh I'm fine. Sure, very fine." She turned away, self-conscious that he'd noticed. Sailors were fore and aft and they tossed out guy lines which were instantly caught and dropped over stanchions. The thick ropes screeched under the tension, setting her teeth on edge. As the ferry eased perfectly into its berth, the drawbridge gate began to lower but before it was down completely the crowd was surging off the boat, Casey carried with it. After a few yards the pressure eased and she walked up the ramp at her own pace, other passengers flooding down the other ramp opposite to board for Hong Kong side. Rosemont caught up with her. "You at the V and A?"

"Yes," she said. "You?"

"Oh no! We've an apartment Hong Kong side—the consulate owns it."

"Have you been here long?"

"Two years. It's interesting, Casey. After a month or so you feel locked in—no place to go, so many people, seeing the same friends day after day. But soon it's great. Soon you get to feel you're at the center of the action, the center of Asia where all the action is today. Sure, Hong Kong's the center of Asia—papers're good, you've great food, good golf, racing, boating and it's easy to go to Taipei, Bangkok or wherever. Hong Kong's okay—course it's nothing like Japan. Japan's something else. That's like out of Oz."

"Is that good or bad?"

"Great—if you're a man. Tough for wives, very tough, and for kids. Your helplessness, your alienness is shoved back at you—you can't even read a street sign. I was there for a two-year tour. I liked it a lot. Athena, my wife, she got to hate it." Rosemont laughed. "She hates Hong Kong and wants to go back to Indochina, to Vietnam or Cambodia. She was a nurse there some years back with the French Army."

Through the fog of her own problems Casey heard an undercurrent and she began to listen. "She's French?"

"American. Her father was ambassador for a tour during the French war."

"You have kids?" she asked.

"Two. Both sons. Athena was married before."

Another undercurrent. "Your sons were from her first marriage?"

"One was. She was married to a Vietnamese. He was killed just before Dien Bien Phu, that was when the French ran the country or were getting run out. Poor guy was killed before young Vien was born. He's like my own son. Yes, both my boys are great. You staying long?"

"Depends on my boss and our deal. Guess you know we're hoping to tie in with Struan's."

"It's the talk of the town—apart from the fire at Aberdeen, the flooding, all the mud slides, the storm, Struan's stock crash, the bank runs and the market falling apart—one thing about Hong Kong: it's never dull. You think he'll make it?"

"The tai-pan? I've just left him. I hope so. He's confident, yes very confident. I like him."

"Yes. I like Bartlett too. You been with him long?"

"Seven years, almost."

They were out of the terminal now, the road just as crowded. On the right was the harbor and they chatted, heading east for the pedestrian underpass that would take them to the V and A. Rosemont pointed at a small shop, the Rice Bowl. "Athena works there from time to time. It's a charity shop, run by Americans. All the profit goes to refugees. Lot of the wives put in a day or two there, keeps them busy. I guess you're busy all the time."

"Only seven days a week."

"I heard Linc say that you were taking off over the weekend for Taipei. Will that be your first visit?"

"Yes—but I'm not going, just Linc and the tai-pan." Casey tried to stop the immediate thought welling but she could not: Is he going to take Orlanda? He's right, it's none of my affair. But Par-Con is. And since Linc's hooked, lined and sinkered by the enemy, the less he knows about the First Central ploy the better.

Pleased that she could come to the decision dispassionately, she continued to talk with Rosemont, answering his questions, not really concentrating, pleased to converse with a friendly soul who was as informative as he was interested. ". . . and Taipei's different, more easygoing, less hardnosed, but a comer," he was saying. "We're popular in Taiwan which's a change. So you're really going to spread? On a big deal like this I guess you've a dozen execs on hand?"

"No. There's just the two of us at the moment, and Forrester—he's head of our foam division—and our attorney." Mentioning him, Casey hardened. Damn him for trying to stymie us. "Linc's got Par-Con organized very well. I handle the day-to-day and he fixes policy."

"You're a public company?"

"Oh sure, but that's okay too. Linc has control and our directors and stockholders don't give us a hassle. Dividends're on the rise, and if the Struan deal goes through they'll skyrocket."

"We could use more U.S. firms in Asia. Trade is what made the Empire great for the British. I wish you luck, Casey. Hey, that reminds me," he added casually, "you remember Ed, Ed Langan, my buddy, who was with me at the tai-pan's party? He knows one of your stockholders. A guy called Bestacio, some name like that."

Casey was startled. "Banastasio? Vincenzo Banastasio?"

"Yes, I think that was it," he told her, lying easily, watching her, and at her look added, "Did I say something?"

"No, it's just a coincidence. Banastasio arrives tomorrow. Tomorrow morning."

"What?"

Casey saw him staring at her and she laughed. "You can tell your friend he's staying at the Hilton."

Rosemont's mind buzzed. "Tomorrow? I'll be goddamned."

Casey said carefully, "He's a good friend of Langan's?"

"No, but he knows him. He says Banastasio's quite a guy. A gambler, isn't he?"

"Yes."

"You don't like him?"

"I've only met him a couple of times. At the races. He's big at Del Mar. I'm not much on gamblers or gambling."

They were weaving through the crowds. People jostled from behind and oncoming hordes jostled from the front. The underpass stank of mildew and bodies. She was very glad to get back into the air once more and looking forward to a shower and an aspirin and a rest before 8:00 P.M. Beyond the buildings ahead was the whole of the eastern harbor. A departing jet barreled into the overcast. Rosemont caught sight of the tall deck derricks of the *Sovetsky Ivanov* tied up alongside. Involuntarily he glanced Hong Kong side and saw how easy it would be for high-powered binoculars to rake the U.S. carrier and almost count her rivets.

"Makes you proud to be an American, doesn't it?" Casey said happily, following his look. "If you're consulate, you'll get to go aboard her?"

"Sure. Guided tour!"

"Lucky you."

"I was there yesterday. The captain had a shindig for locals. I tagged along." Again Rosemont told the lie easily. He had gone aboard late last night and again this morning. His initial interview with the admiral, captain and security chief had been stormy. It was not until he produced photocopies of the secret manifest of the ship's armaments and the guidance systems manual that they had truly believed there had been a vast security leak. Now the traitor was under tight surveillance in the ship's brig, guarded by his own CIA people, twenty-four hours a day. Soon the man would break. Yes, Rosemont thought, and after that, jail for twenty years. If it was up to me I'd drop the bastard in the goddamn harbor. Shit, I've got nothing against the Metkins and the KGB. Those bastards're just doing their job for their side—however wrong they are. But our own Joes?

"Okay, fella, you're caught! First tell us why you did it."

"Money."

Jesus H. Christ! The sailor's dossier had shown that he had come from a small town in the Middle West, his work exemplary with nothing in his past or present to indicate a potential security risk. He was a quiet man, good at computer programming, liked by his compatriots and trusted by his superiors. No left-wing indications, no homosexuality, no problem of blackmail, no nothing. "Then why?" he had asked him.

"This guy came up to me in San Diego and said he'd like to know all about the *Corregidor* and he'd pay."

"But don't you understand about treason? About betraying your country?"

"Hell, all he wanted was a few facts and figures. So what? What's the difference? We can blast the hell outta the goddamn Commies anytime we like. The *Corregidor*'s the greatest carrier afloat! It was a caper and I wanted to see if I could do it and they paid on the dot. . . ."

Jesus, how we going to keep security when there are guys like him with their brains in their asses, Rosemont asked himself wearily.

He walked along, listening to himself chatting with Casey, probing her, trying to decide what sort of a risk she was and Bartlett was, with their tie-in to Banastasio. Soon they joined other people going up the wide steps to the hotel. A smiling pageboy opened the swing doors. The foyer was bustling. "Casey, I'm early for my appointment. Can I buy you a drink?"

Casey hesitated, then smiled, liking him, enjoying chatting. "Sure, thanks. First let me collect my messages, okay?" She went to the desk. There were a sheaf of telexes, and messages from Jannelli, Steigler and Forrester to please call. And a handwritten note from Bartlett. The note contained routine instructions about Par-Con, all of which she agreed to, and asked her to make sure that the airplane was ready to take off on Sunday. The note ended: "Casey, we're going with Rothwell-Gornt. Let's meet for breakfast in the suite, 9:00 A.M. See you then."

She went back to Rosemont. "Can I take a raincheck?"

"Bad news?"

"Oh no, just a load of stuff to deal with."

"Sure, but maybe you'd like dinner next week, you and Linc? I'd like Athena to meet you. She'll give you a call to fix the day, okay?"

"Thanks, I'd like that." Casey left him, her whole being more than ever committed to the course she had decided upon.

Rosemont watched her go, then ordered a Cutty Sark and soda and began to wait, lost in thought. How much money's Banastasio's got in Par-Con and what's he get in return? Jesus H. Christ, Par-Con's hot in defense and space and a lot of secret crap. What's that bum doing here? Thank God I took on Casey today and didn't leave her to one of the guys. He might've missed Banastasio. . . .

Robert Armstrong arrived.

"Jesus, Robert, you look terrible," the American said. "You better get yourself a vacation or a good night's rest or lay off the broads."

"Get stuffed! You ready? We'd better leave."

"You've time for a quick one. The bank date's been changed to seven, there's plenty of time."

"Yes, but I don't want to be late as we're to meet the governor at his office."

"Okay."

Obediently Rosemont finished his drink, signed the bill and they walked back toward the ferry terminal.

"How's Dry Run?" Armstrong asked.

"They're still there with flags flying. Looks like the Azerbaijan revolt fizzled." Rosemont noticed the heaviness on the Englishman. "What's eating you, Robert?"

"Sometimes I don't like being a copper, that's all." Armstrong took out a cigarette and lit it.

"I thought you gave up smoking."

"I did. Listen, Stanley old friend, I'd better warn you: you're in the proverbial creek without a paddle. Crosse's so mad he's fit to be committed."

"So what else's new? A lot of guys think he's a basket case anyway. Jesus, it was Ed Langan who tipped you off about the AMG files in the first place. We're allies for chrissake!"

"True," Armstrong replied sourly, "but that's no license to mount a totally unauthorized raid on a totally clean flat belonging to the totally clean telephone company!"

"Who me?" Rosemont looked pained. "What flat?"

"Sinclair Towers, flat 32. You and your gorillas knocked down the door in the dead of the night. For what, may I ask?"

"How should I know?" Rosemont knew he had to bluff this one through, but he was still furious that whoever was in the apartment had escaped without identification. His rage over the carrier leak, Metkin's not being available for questioning, the whole Sevrin mess and Crosse's perfidy, had prompted him to order the raid. One of his Chinese informants had picked up a rumor that though the apartment was empty most of the time, sometimes it was used by Communist enemy agents—of gender unknown—and there was a meeting tonight. Connochie, one of his best agents, had led the raid and thought he caught a glimpse of two men going out the back but he wasn't sure, and though he searched diligently, they had vanished and he found nothing in the apartment to prove or disprove the rumor, just two half-empty glasses. The glasses were brought back and tested for fingerprints. One was clean, the other well marked. "I've never been to 32 Sinclair Towers, for chrissake!"

"Maybe, but your Keystone Kops were there. Several tenants reported four tall, meaty Caucasians charging up and down the stairs." Armstrong added even more sourly, "All fat-arsed and fat-headed. Have to be yours."

"Not mine. No sir."

"Oh yes they were and that mistake's going to backfire. Crosse's already sent two pretty foul cables to London. The pity of it is you failed to catch anything and we catch hell because of your continual screw-ups!"

Rosemont sighed. "Get off my back. I've got something for you." He told Armstrong of his conversation with Casey about Banastasio. "Of course we knew his connection with Par-Con but I didn't know he was arriving tomorrow. What do you think?"

Armstrong had seen the arrival recorded on Photographer Ng's calendar. "Interesting," he said noncommittally. "I'll tell the Old Man. But you'd better have a good explanation for him about Sinclair Towers and don't mention that I told you." His fatigue was almost overwhelming him. This morning at 6:30 A.M. he had begun the first real probe of Brian Kwok.

It was an orchestrated set piece: while still drugged, Brian Kwok had been taken out of his clean white cell and put naked into a filthy dungeon with dank walls and a stinking thin mattress on the mildewed floor. Then, ten minutes after the wake-up drug had jerked him into parched, aching consciousness, the light had blazed on and Armstrong had ripped the door open and cursed the SI jailer. "For chrissake, what're you doing to Superintendent Kwok? Have you gone mad? How dare you treat him like this!"

"Superintendent Crosse's orders, sir. This client's b—"

"There must be a mistake! I don't give a damn about Crosse!" He had thrown the man out and put his full, kind attention onto his friend. "Here, old chum, do you want a cigarette?"

"Oh Christ. Thank . . . thanks." Brian Kwok's fingers had trembled as he held the cigarette and drew the smoke deep. "Robert, what . . . what the hell's going on?"

"I don't know. I've just heard, that's why I'm here. I was told you'd been on leave for a few days. Crosse's gone mad. He claims you're a Communist spy."

"Me? For God's sake . . . what's the date today?"

"The thirtieth, Friday," he had said at once, expecting the question, adding seven days.

"Who won the fifth race?"

"Butterscotch Lass," he had said, caught off guard, astonished that Brian Kwok was still functioning so well and not at all certain if his own slight hesitation had been read for the lie it was. "Why?"

"Just wondered . . . just . . . Listen, Robert, this's a mistake. You've got to help me. Don't you s—"

On cue Roger Crosse had come in like the wrath of God. "Listen, spy, I want names and addresses of all your contacts right now. Who's your controller?"

Weakly Brian Kwok had stumbled to his feet. "Sir, it's all a mistake. There's no controller and I'm no spy an—"

Crosse had suddenly shoved blowups of the photos in his face. "Then explain how you were photographed in Ning-tok in front of your family pharmacy with your mother Fang-ling Wu. Explain how your real name's

Chu-toy Wu, second son of these parents, Ting-top Wu and Fang-ling Wu . . ."

They had both seen the instant of shock on Brian Kwok's face.

"Lies," he had mumbled, "lies, I'm Brian Kar-shun Kwok and I'm—"

"You're a liar!" Crosse had shouted. "We have witnesses! We have evidence! You are identified by your *gan sun*, Ah Tam!"

Another gasp, covered almost brilliantly, then "I . . . I have no *gan sun* called Ah Tam. I h—"

"You'll spend the rest of your life in this cell unless you tell us everything. I'll see you in a week. You'd better answer everything truthfully or I'll put you in chains! Robert!" Crosse had whirled on him. "You're forbidden to come here without permission!" Then he had stalked out of the cell.

In the silence Armstrong remembered how nauseated he had been, having seen the truth written on his friend's face. He was too well trained an observer to be mistaken. "Christ, Brian," he had said, continuing the game, hating his hypocrisy even so. "What possessed you to do it?"

"Do what?" Brian Kwok had said defiantly. "You can't cheat me—or trick me, Robert . . . It can't be seven days. I'm innocent."

"And the photos?"

"Fake . . . they're fake, dreamed up by Crosse." Brian Kwok had held onto his arm, a desperate light behind his eyes, and whispered hoarsely, "I told you Crosse's the real mole. He's the mole, Robert . . . he's a homo—he's trying to frame me an—"

On cue, the brittle, officious SI jailer jerked the cell door open. "Sorry, sir, but you've got to leave."

"All right, but first give him some water."

"No water's allowed!"

"Goddamn you, get him some water!"

Reluctantly the jailer obeyed. While they were momentarily alone, Armstrong had slipped the cigarettes under the mattress. "Brian, I'll do what I can . . ." Then the jailer was back in the room with a battered cup.

"That's all you can have!" he said angrily. "I want the cup back!"

Thankfully Brian Kwok had gulped it and with it the drug. Armstrong left. The door slammed and the bolts shoved home. Abruptly the lights went out, leaving Brian Kwok in darkness. Ten minutes later Armstrong had gone back in with Dr. Dorn. And Crosse. Brian Kwok was unconscious, deeply drugged again and dreaming fitfully. "Robert, you did very well," Crosse had said softly. "Did you see the client's shock?"

"Yes sir."

"Good. So did I. No mistake about that, or his guilt. Doctor, step up the sleep-wake-up every hour on the hour for the next twenty-four . . ."

"Christ," Armstrong burst out, "don't you th—"

"Every hour on the hour, Doctor, provided he checks out medically—I don't want him harmed, just pliable—for the next twenty-four. Robert, then you interrogate him again. If that doesn't work, we put him into the Red Room."

Dr. Dorn had flinched and Armstrong recalled how his heart had missed a beat. "No," he said.

"For chrissake, the client's guilty, Robert," Crosse snarled, no longer playacting. "Guilty! The client shopped Fong-fong and our lads and has done us God knows what damage. We're under the gun. The orders come from London! Remember Metkin, our great commissar catch from the *Ivanov*? I've just heard the RAF transport's vanished. It refueled in Bombay then vanished somewhere over the Indian Ocean."

60

The governor was in an Olympian rage. He got out of the car and stomped to the side door of the bank where Johnjohn was waiting for him.

"Have you read this?" The governor waved the evening edition of the *Guardian* in the night air. The huge headline read: MPs ACCUSE PRC. "Bloody incompetent fools, what?"

"Yes sir." Johnjohn was equally choleric. He led the way past the uniformed doorman into a large anteroom. "Can't you hang both of them?"

At their afternoon press conference, Grey and Broadhurst had proclaimed publicly everything that he, Johnjohn, Dunross and the other taipans had, at length, patiently condemned as totally against Britain's, Hong Kong's and China's interest. Grey had gone on at length discussing his private and personal opinion that Red China was bent on world conquest and should be treated as the great enemy of world peace. "I've already had one unofficial official scream."

Johnjohn winced. "Oh God, not from Tiptop?"

"Of course from Tiptop. He said, in that calm silky voice of his, 'Your Excellency, when our peers in Peking read how important members of your great English Parliament view the Middle Kingdom, I think they will be really quite angry.' I'd say our chances of getting the temporary use of their money now is nil."

Another wave of anger went over Johnjohn.

"That damned man implied his views were the committee's views, which is totally untrue! Ridiculous to inflame China under any circumstances. Without China's benevolence our position here is totally untenable. Totally! Bloody fool! And we all went out of our way to explain!" The governor took out a handkerchief and blew his nose. "Where are the others?"

"Superintendent Crosse and Mr. Sinders are using my office for a moment. Ian's on his way. What about Ian and Grey, sir, Grey being Ian's brother-in-law? Eh?"

"Extraordinary." Since Grey had mentioned it in response to a question this afternoon he had had a dozen calls about it. "Astonishing that Ian never mentioned it."

"Or Penelope! Very odd. Do you th—" Johnjohn glanced up and stopped. Dunross was walking toward them.

"Evening, sir."

"Hello, Ian. I put the time back to 7:00 P.M. to give me a chance to see Sinders and Stanley Rosemont." The governor held up the paper. "You've seen this?"

"Yes sir. The Chinese evening papers are so incensed, I'm surprised every edition's not on fire and all of Central with them."

"I'd try them for treason," Johnjohn said, his face sour. "What the devil can we do, Ian?"

"Pray! I've already spoken to Gutluie, the Liberal MP, and some of the Tories. One of the *Guardian's* top reporters is interviewing them right now and their opposite opinions will be the morning headlines refuting all this poppycock." Dunross wiped his hands. He could feel the sweat on his back as well. The combination of Grey, Tiptop, Jacques, Phillip Chen, the coin and the AMG files was unnerving him. Christ Jesus, he thought, what next? His meeting with Murtagh of the Royal Belgium had been what Casey had forecast—a long shot but a good one. Coming out of that meeting someone had given him the afternoon papers and the bombshell that such ill-advised remarks was going to create had almost knocked him over. "We'll have to just dismiss the whole thing publicly, and privately work like hell to make sure Grey's bill to bring Hong Kong down to Britain's level never gets to a vote, or is voted down, and Labour never gets elected." He felt his bile rising. "Broadhurst was just as bad if not worse."

"Ian, have you talked to Tiptop?"

"No, Bruce. His line's still busy though I did send a message around." He told them what he had arranged with Phillip Chen. Then the governor related Tiptop's complaint. Dunross was aghast. "When did he call, sir?"

"Just before six."

"He would have had our message by then." Dunross felt his heart thumping. "After this . . . this debacle, I'd lay heavy odds there's no chance for Chinese money."

"I agree."

Dunross was acutely aware they had not mentioned Grey's relationship to him. "Robin Grey's worse than a fool," he said, thinking he might just as well bring it out into the open. "My god-cursed brother-in-law could not have done better for the Soviets if he was a member of the Politburo. Broadhurst as well. Stupid!"

812 JAMES CLAVELL

After a pause the governor said, "As the Chinese say, 'The devil gives you your relations, thank all gods you can choose your friends.'"

"You're so right. Fortunately, the committee's due to leave Sunday. With the races tomorrow and all the . . . all the other problems, perhaps it'll all get lost in the shuffle." Dunross mopped his brow. "It's close in here, isn't it?"

The governor nodded, then added testily, "Is everything ready, John-john?"

"Yes sir. The va—" In the hall the elevator opened and Roger Crosse and Edward Sinders, chief of MI-6, came out.

"Ah, Sinders," the governor said as they both came into the anteroom, "I'd like you to meet Mr. Dunross."

"Pleased to meet you, sir." Sinders shook hands with Dunross. He was a middle-aged, middle height, nondescript man with crumpled clothes. His face was thin and colorless, the stubble of his beard gray. "Please excuse my rumpledness, sir, but I haven't been to the hotel yet."

"Sorry about that," Dunross replied. "This could certainly have waited until tomorrow. Evening, Roger."

"Evening, sir. Evening, Ian," Crosse said crisply. "As we're all here, perhaps we could proceed?"

Obediently Johnjohn began to lead the way but Dunross said, "Just a moment. Sorry, Bruce, could you excuse us a moment?"

"Oh certainly." Johnjohn covered his surprise, wondering what this was all about and who Sinders was, but much too wise to ask. He knew they would tell him if they wanted him to know. The door closed behind him.

Dunross glanced at the governor. "Do you attest, sir, formally, this is Edward Sinders, head of MI-6?"

"I do." The governor handed him an envelope. "I believe you wanted it in writing."

"Thank you, sir." To Sinders, Dunross said, "Sorry, but you understand my reluctance."

"Of course. Good, then that's settled. Shall we go, Mr. Dunross?"

"Who's Mary McFee?"

Sinders was shocked. Crosse and the governor stared at him, perplexed, then at Dunross. "You have friends in high places, Mr. Dunross. May I ask who told you that?"

"Sorry." Dunross kept his gaze on him. Alastair Struan had got the information from some VIP in the Bank of England who had approached someone high up in the government. "All we want to do is to be sure Sinders is who he pretends to be."

"Mary McFee's a friend," Sinders said uneasily.

"Sorry, that's not good enough."

"A girl friend."

"Sorry, neither's that. What's her real name?"

Sinders hesitated, then, his face chalky, he took Dunross by the arm and guided him to the far end of the room. He put his lips very close to Dunross's ear. "Anastasia Kekilova, First Secretary of the Czechoslovak Embassy in London," he whispered, his back to Crosse and the governor.

Dunross nodded, satisfied, but Sinders held onto his arm with surprising strength and whispered even more softly, "You'd better forget that name. If the KGB ever suspect you know they'll get it out of you. Then she's dead, I'm dead and so're you."

Dunross nodded. "Fair enough."

Sinders took a deep breath, then turned and nodded at Crosse. "Now let's have this done with, Roger. Your Excellency?"

Tensely they all followed him. Johnjohn was waiting at the elevator. Three floors below were the vaults. Two plainclothes guards waited in the small hallway in front of the heavy iron gates, one man CID, the other SI. Both saluted. Johnjohn unlocked the gates and let everyone through except the guards, then relocked them. "Just a bank custom."

"Have you ever had a break-in?" Sinders asked.

"No, though the Japanese did force the gates when the keys were, er, lost."

"Were you here then, sir?"

"No. I was lucky." After Hong Kong capitulated, at Christmas 1941, the two British banks, Blacs and the Victoria, became prime Japanese targets and were ordered to be liquidated. All the executives were separated and kept under guard and forced to assist the process. Over the months and years they were all subjected to extreme pressures. They were forced to issue bank notes illegally. And then the Kampeitai, the hated and feared Japanese secret police, had become involved. "The Kampeitai executed several of our fellows and made the lives of the rest miserable," Johnjohn said. "The usual: no food, beatings, privation, shut up in cages. Some died of malnutrition—*starvation's* the real word—and both Blacs and we lost our chief execs." Johnjohn unlocked another grille. Beyond were rows and rows of safe deposit boxes in several interconnecting concrete, reinforced cellars. "Ian?"

Dunross took out his passkey. "It's 16.85.94."

Johnjohn led the way. Very uncomfortable, he inserted his bank key in one lock. Dunross did the same with his. They turned both keys. The lock clicked open. Now all eyes were on the box. Johnjohn took out his key. "I'll . . . I'll be waiting at the gate," he said, glad it was over, and left.

Dunross hesitated. "There are other things in here, private papers. Do you mind?"

Crosse did not move. "Sorry but either Mr. Sinders or myself should ensure we get possession of all the files."

Dunross noticed the sweat on both men. His own back was wet. "Your Excellency, would you mind watching?"

"Not at all."

Reluctantly the two other men retreated. Dunross waited until they were well away, then opened the box. It was large. Sir Geoffrey's eyes widened. The box was empty but for the blue covered files. Without comment he accepted them. There were eight. Dunross slammed the box closed and the lock clicked home.

Crosse came forward, his hand out. "Shall I take them for you, sir?"

"No."

Crosse stopped, startled, and bit back a curse. "But, Exce—"

"The minister set up a procedure—approved by our American friends—which I agreed to," Sir Geoffrey said. "We will all go back to my office. We will all witness the photocopying. Two copies only. One for Mr. Sinders, one for Mr. Rosemont. Ian, I have been directly ordered by the Minister to give Mr. Rosemont copies."

Dunross shrugged, desperately hoping that he still appeared unconcerned. "If that's what the minister wants, that's perfectly all right. When you've photocopied the originals, sir, please burn them." He saw them look at him but he was watching Crosse and he thought he saw an instant of pleasure. "If the files're so special then it's better they shouldn't exist—except in the correct hands, MI-6 and the CIA. Certainly I shouldn't have a copy. If they're not special—then never mind. Most of poor old AMG was too farfetched and now that he's dead I must confess I don't consider the files special so long as they're in your hands. Please burn or shred them, Excellency."

"Very well." The governor turned his pale blue eyes on Roger Crosse. "Yes, Roger?"

"Nothing, sir. Shall we go?"

Dunross said, "I've got to get some corporate papers to check while I'm here. No need to wait for me."

"Very well. Thank you, Ian," Sir Geoffrey said and left with the other two men.

When he was quite alone Dunross went to another bank of boxes in the adjoining vault. He took out his key ring and selected two keys, grimly aware that Johnjohn would have a coronary if he knew he had a duplicate master key. The lock sprang back soundlessly. This box was one of dozens the Noble House possessed under different names. Inside were bundles of U.S. $100 notes, ancient deeds and papers. On top was a loaded automatic. As always, Dunross's psyche was unsettled, hating guns, hating Hag Struan, admiring her. In her "Instructions to Tai-pans," written just before her death in 1917, that was part of her last will and testament and in the tai-pan's safe, she had laid down more rules and one of them was that there should always be substantial amounts of secret cash for the tai-pan's use, on hand, and another that there should be at least four loaded handguns perpetually available in secret places. She wrote: "I abhor guns but I know them to be necessary. On Michaelmas Eve in 1916 when I was infirm and sick, my grandson Kelly O'Gorman, fourth tai-pan (in name only), believing I was on my deathbed, forced me from my bed to the safe in the Great House to fetch the seal-chop of the Noble House—to assign to him absolute power as tai-pan. Instead I took the gun that was secretly in the safe and shot him. He lingered two days then died. I am God-fearing and I abhor guns and some killing, but Kelly became a mad dog and it is the duty of the tai-pan to protect the succession. I regret his death not a jot or tittle. You who read this beware: kith or kin lust for power as others do. Do not be afraid to use *any* method to protect Dirk Struan's legacy . . ."

A bead of sweat trickled down his cheek. He remembered the hair on the nape of his neck rising when he had first read her instructions, the night he had taken over as tai-pan. He'd always believed that Cousin Kelly—eldest son of the Hag's last daughter Rose—had died of cholera in one of the great waves that perpetually washed Asia.

There were other monstrosities she had written about: "In 1894, that most terrible of years, the second of Jin-qua's coins was brought to me. That was the year plague had come to Hong Kong, bubonic plague. Amongst our heathen Chinese, tens of thousands were dying. Our own population was equally savaged and the plague took high and low, Cousin Hannah and three children, two of Chen-chen's children, five grandchildren. Legend foretold that bubonic plague was wind-borne. Others thought it was the curse of God or a flux like malaria, the killing 'bad air' of Happy Valley. Then the miracle! The Japanese research doctors Vitasato and Aoyama we brought to Hong Kong isolated the plague bacillus and proved the pest was flea-borne, and rat-borne, and that correct sanitation and the elimination of rats would cast out the curse forever. The eyesore hillside of Tai-ping Shan that Gordon owns—Gordon Chen, son of my beloved tai-pan—where most of our heathen always lived was a stinking, festering, overcrowded, rat-breeding cauldron for all pestilences, and as much as the authorities cajoled, ordered and insisted, the superstitious inhabitants there disbelieved everything and would do nothing to improve their lot, though the deaths continued and continued. Even Gordon, now a toothless old man, could do nothing—tearing his hair at his loss of rents, saving his energy for the four young women in his household.

"In the stench of late summer when it seemed the Colony was once more doomed, with deaths mounting daily, I had Tai-ping Shan put to the torch by night, the whole monstrous stenching mountainside. That some inhabitants were consumed is on my conscience, but without the cleansing fire the Colony was doomed and hundreds of thousands more doomed. I caused Tai-ping Shan to be fired but thereby I kept troth with Hong Kong. I kept troth with the Legacy. And I kept troth with the second of the half coins.

"On the twentieth of April a man called Chiang Wu-tah presented the half coin to my darling young cousin, Dirk Dunross, third tai-pan, who brought it to me, he not knowing the secret of the coins. I sent for the man Chiang who spoke English. The favor he asked was that the Noble

House should grant immediate sanctuary and succor to a young, Western-educated Chinese revolutionary named Sun Yat-sen; that we should help this Sun Yat-sen with funds; and that we should help him as long as he lived, to the limits of our power in his fight to overthrow the alien Manchu Dynasty of China. Supporting any revolutionary against China's ruling dynasty with whom we had cordial relations and on whom depended much of our trade and revenues was against my principles, and seemingly against the interests of the House. I said no, I would not assist the overthrow of their emperor. But Chiang Wu-tah said, 'This is the favor required from the Noble House.'

"And so it was done.

"At great risk I provided funds and protection. My darling Dirk Dunross spirited Dr. Sun out of Canton to the Colony and from there abroad to America. I wanted Dr. Sun to accompany young Dirk to England—he was leaving on the tide, Master of our steamer *Sunset Cloud*. That was the week I wanted to hand over to him as real tai-pan but he said, 'No, not until I return.' But he was never to return. He and all hands were lost at sea somewhere in the Indian Ocean. Oh how terrible my loss, our loss!

"But death is a part of life and we the living have our duty to be done. I do not yet know to whom I should hand over. It should have been Dirk Dunross, who was named for his grandfather. His sons are too young, none of the Coopers are adequate, or deVilles, Daglish is possible, none of the MacStruans are yet ready. Alastair Struan perhaps but there's a weakness there that comes down from Robb Struan.

"I don't mind admitting to you, future tai-pan, that I am weary unto death. But I am not yet ready to die. Pray God I am given the strength for a few more years. There is not one of my line or my beloved Dirk Struan's line worthy of his mantle. And now there is this Great War to see through, the House to rebuild, our merchant fleet to refurbish—so far German U-boats have sunk thirty of our ships, almost our whole fleet. Yes, and there is the favor of the second coin still to fulfill. This Dr. Sun Yat-sen must and will be supported until he dies and so retain our face in Asia. . . ."

And we did, Dunross thought. The Noble House supported him in all his troubles, even when he tried to join with Soviet Russia, until he died in 1925 and Chiang Kai-shek, his Soviet-trained lieutenant, assumed his mantle and launched China into the future—until his old ally but ancient enemy, Mao Tse-tung, took the future away from him to mount the Dragon Throne in Peking with bloody hands, first of a new dynasty.

Dunross took out a handkerchief and mopped his brow.

The air in the vault was dusty and dry and a little caught in his throat and he coughed. His hands were sweaty too and he could still feel the chill on his back. He rummaged carefully to the bottom of the deep metal box and found his corporate chop that he would need over the weekend in case the Royal Belgium–First Central deal came to pass. I certainly owe Casey more than one favor if the deal is made, he told himself.

His heart was thumping again and he could not resist making sure. With great care he lifted the secret false bottom of the safety deposit box a fraction. In the two-inch space beneath were eight blue-covered files. AMG's real files. Those that moments ago he had passed over to Sinders had been in the sealed package that Kirk and his wife had brought yesterday—those eight counterfeit files and a letter: "Tai-pan: I am terribly worried that both you and I are betrayed and that information contained in previous files may fall into the wrong hands. The enclosed substitute files are safe and very similar. They drop vital names and vital information. You may pass these over if you are forced to do it, but only then. As to the originals, you should destroy them after you have seen Riko. Certain pages contain invisible writing. Riko will give you the key. Please excuse all these diversionary tactics but espionage is not for children; it deals in death, actual and in the future. Our lovely Britain is beset with traitors and evil walks the earth. Bluntly, freedom is under siege as never in history. I beg you to emulate your illustrious ancestor. He fought for freedom to trade, to live and to worship. Sorry, but I don't think he died in a storm. We'll never know the truth but I believe he was murdered, as I will be. Not to worry, my young friend. I've done very well in my life. I've put a lot of nails in the enemy coffin, more than my fair share—I ask you to do the same."

The letter was signed, "With great respect."

Poor bugger, Dunross thought sadly.

Yesterday he had smuggled the counterfeit files into the vault, replacing the originals in the other box. He would have liked to have destroyed the originals then but there was no way to do that safely and anyway he had to wait for his meeting with the Japanese woman. Better and safer to leave them where they are for the moment, he said to himself. Plenty of ti—

Suddenly he felt eyes. His hand sneaked for the automatic. When his fingers had grasped it, he looked around. His stomach seemed to turn over. Crosse was watching him. And Johnjohn. They were at the entrance to the vault.

After a moment Crosse said, "I just wanted to thank you for your cooperation, Ian. Mr. Sinders and I appreciate it."

Relief poured through Dunross. "That's all right. Glad to help." Trying to be casual he relaxed his hold on the automatic and let it slide away. The false bottom fell silently into place. He saw Crosse's scrutiny but shrugged it off. From where the superintendent stood he did not think it possible for him to have seen the real files. Dunross blessed his joss that had prevented him from taking one of the files out to leaf through it. Carelessly he slammed the box shut and his breathing began again. "It really is quite stuffy in here, isn't it?"

"Yes. Again, Ian, thank you." Crosse left.

"How did you open that box?" Johnjohn asked coldly.

"With a key."

"Two keys, Ian. That's against regulations." Johnjohn held out his hand. "May I have our property please."

"Sorry, old chum," Dunross said calmly, "it's not your property."

Johnjohn hesitated. "We always suspected you had a duplicate master key. Paul is right about one thing: you've too much power, you consider this bank yours, our funds yours and the Colony yours."

"We've had a long and happy association with both, and it's only in the last few years when Paul Havergill's had some measure of power that I've had a hard time, me personally, and my House personally. But worse than that, he's old-fashioned and I voted him out for that reason only. You're not, you're modern. You'll be fairer, far-seeing, less emotional and straighter."

Johnjohn shook his head. "I doubt it. If I ever become tai-pan of the bank I'm going to see it's wholly owned by its stockholders and controlled by directors appointed by them."

"It is now. We just own 21 percent of the bank."

"You used to own 21 percent. That stock's pledged against your revolving fund which you can't and probably never will repay. Besides, 21 percent is not control, thank God."

"It very nearly is."

"My whole point." Johnjohn's voice was metallic. "That's dangerous for the bank, very dangerous."

"I don't think so."

"I do. I want 11 percent back."

"No sale, old lad."

"When I'm tai-pan, old lad, I'll get it by hook or by crook."

"We'll see."

"When I'm tai-pan I'm going to make lots of changes. All these locks for example. No master keys, privately owned."

"We'll see." Dunross smiled.

On Kowloon side, Bartlett jumped from the wharf to the pitching boat, helped Orlanda aboard. Automatically she kicked off her high heels to protect the fine teak deck.

"Welcome aboard the *Sea Witch*, Mr. Bartlett. Evening, Orlanda," Gornt said with a smile. He was at the helm and at once he motioned to his deckhand who cast off from the wharf that was near the Kowloon ferry terminal. "I'm delighted you accepted my invitation to dinner, Mr. Bartlett."

"I didn't know I had one until Orlanda told me half an hour ago . . . hey, this's a great boat!"

Gornt jovially put the engines into slow astern. "Until an hour ago I didn't know you two were going to dinner by yourselves. I presumed you'd never seen Hong Kong harbor by night so I thought it'd make a change for you. There were a couple of things I wanted to discuss privately so I asked Orlanda if she'd mind if I invited you aboard."

"I hope it was no trouble to come Kowloon side."

"No trouble, Mr. Bartlett. It's routine to pick up guests here." Gornt smiled a secret smile, thinking about Orlanda and all the other guests he had fetched from this Kowloon wharf over the years. Deftly Gornt backed the motor cruiser away from the Kowloon dock near Golden Ferry where the waves slapped the quay dangerously. He put the engine levers into half ahead and swung the tiller starboard to get out into the roads and set a westerly course.

The boat was seventy feet, trim, elegant, sparkling and she handled like a speedboat. They were on the bridge deck, glass-sided, open to the air aft, awnings overhead tight and crackling in the breeze, the wake churning. Gornt wore rough, casual sea clothes, a light reefer jacket and a jaunty peaked cap sporting the Yacht Club emblem. The clothes and his trimmed black, gray-flecked beard suited him. He swayed easily with the motion of the boat, very much at home.

Bartlett was watching him, at home too in sneakers and casual sweat shirt. Orlanda was beside him and he could feel her though they were not touching. She wore a dark evening pants suit and a shawl against the sea cold and she stood swaying easily, the wind in her hair, tiny without shoes.

He looked aft across the harbor at the ferries, junks, liners and the immense bulk of the battle-gray nuclear carrier, her decks floodlit, her flag fluttering bravely. A jet shrieked into the night sky from Kai Tak and incoming jets approaching Kowloon were stacked up.

He could not see the airport or his own airplane from this angle but he knew where it was parked. This afternoon he had visited it with police permission to check and fetch some papers and provisions.

Orlanda, beside him, touched him casually and he looked at her. She smiled back and he was warmed.

"Great, isn't it?"

Happily she nodded. There was no need to answer. Both knew.

"It is," Gornt said, thinking that Bartlett was talking to him and looked around at him. "It's grand to be afloat at night, master of your own craft. We go west, then almost due south around Hong Kong—about three quarters of an hour." He beckoned his captain who was nearby, a silent lithe Shanghainese wearing neat, starched white ducks.

"*Shey-shey,*" thank you, the man said taking the helm.

Gornt waved to the chairs aft around a table. "Shall we?" He glanced at Orlanda. "You're looking very pretty, Orlanda."

"Thank you," she said.

"You're not too cold?"

"Oh no, Quillan, thank you."

A liveried steward came from below. On his tray were hot and cold canapés. In the ice bucket beside the table was an opened bottle of white wine, four glasses, two cans of American beer and some soft drinks. "What can I offer you, Mr. Bartlett?" Gornt asked. "The wine's Frascati but I hear you prefer iced cold beer out of the can?"

"Tonight Frascati—beer later, if I may?"

"Orlanda?"

"Wine please, Quillan," she said calmly, knowing that he knew she preferred Frascati to any other wine. I'll have to be very wise tonight, she thought, very strong and very wise and very clever. She had agreed to Gornt's suggestion at once for she, too, loved the water at night and the restaurant was a favorite though she would have preferred to have been alone with Linc Bartlett. But it was clearly an . . . No, she thought, correcting herself. It wasn't an order, it was a request. Quillan's on my side. And in this, my side and his side have the same aim in common: Linc. Oh how I enjoy Linc!

When she looked at him she saw he was watching Gornt. Her heart quickened. It was like once when Gornt had taken her to Spain and she had seen a *mano a mano*. Yes, these two men are like matadors tonight. I know Quillan still desires me whatever he says. She smiled back at him, her excitement in place. "Wine would be fine for me."

It was dark on deck, the lighting comfortable and intimate. The steward poured, this wine as always very good, delicate, dry and enticing. Bartlett opened an air carry bag that he had brought with him. "It's an old American custom to bring a gift the first time you go to a home—I guess this is a home." He put the wine bottle on the table.

"Oh that's very kind of . . ." Gornt stopped. Delicately he picked up the bottle and stared at it, then got up and looked at it under the binnacle light. He sat down again. "That's not a gift, Mr. Bartlett, that's bottled magic. I thought my eyes were deceiving me." It was a Château Margaux, one of the great *premier cru* clarets from the Médoc in the province of Bordeaux. "I've never had the '49. That was a dream year for clarets. Thank you. Thank you very much."

"Orlanda said you liked red better than white but I guessed we might have some fish." Casually he put the second bottle beside the first.

Gornt stared at it. It was a Château Haut-Brion. In good years Château Haut-Brion red compared with all the great Médocs, but the white—dry, delicate and little known because it was so scarce—was considered one of the finest of all the great Bordeaux whites. The year was '55.

Gornt sighed. "If you know so much about wines, Mr. Bartlett, why do you drink beer?"

"I like beer with pasta, Mr. Gornt,—and beer before lunch. But wine with food." Bartlett grinned. "Come Tuesday, we'll have beer with the pasta, then Frascati or Verdicchio or the Umbrian Casale with . . . with what?"

"*Piccata?*"

"Great," Bartlett said, not wanting any *piccata* other than Orlanda's. "That's just about my favorite." He kept his attention on Gornt and did not glance at Orlanda but he knew she knew what he meant. I'm glad I tested her.

"Oh did you have a good time?" she had said when she had called for him this morning at the small hotel on Sunning Road. "Oh I do hope so, Linc, darling."

The other girl had been beautiful but there had been no feeling other than lust, the satisfaction of the joining minimal. He had told her.

"Oh then that's my fault. We chose wrong," she had said unhappily. "Tonight we'll have dinner and we'll try somewhere else."

Involuntarily he smiled and looked at her. The sea breeze was making her more beautiful. Then he noticed Gornt watching them. "Are we eating fish tonight?"

"Oh yes. Orlanda, did you tell Mr. Bartlett about Pok Liu Chau?"

"No, Quillan, just that we've been invited for a sail."

"Good. It won't be a banquet but the seafood there's excellent, Mr. Bartlett. You pi—"

"Why don't you call me Linc and let me call you Quillan? The 'mister' bit gives me indigestion."

They all laughed. Gornt said, "Linc, with your permission we'll not open your gift tonight. Chinese food's not for these great wines, they wouldn't complement each other. I'll keep them, if I may, for our dinner Tuesday?"

"Of course."

There was a small silence within the muted thunder of the diesel engines below. Immediately sensing Gornt wanted privacy, Orlanda got up with a smile. "Excuse me a second, I just want to powder my nose."

"Use the forward cabins, the forward gangway, Orlanda," Gornt said, watching her.

"Thank you," she said and walked off, in one way glad, in another hurt. The forward cabins were for guests. She would have automatically gone down this gangway to the main cabin, to the toilet off the master suite—the suite that once was theirs. Never mind. The past is the past and now there's Linc, she thought, going forward.

Bartlett sipped his wine, wondering why Orlanda had seemed to hesitate. He concentrated on Gornt. "How many does this boat sleep?"

"Ten comfortably. There's a regular crew of four—captain-engineer, a deckhand, cook and steward. I'll show you around later if you like." Gornt lit a cigarette. "You don't smoke?"

"No, no thanks."

"We can cruise for a week without refueling. If necessary. We still conclude our deal on Tuesday?"

"That's still D Day."

"Have you changed your mind? About Struan's?"

"Monday'll still decide the battle. Monday at 3:00 P.M. When the market closes, you've got Ian or you haven't and it's a standoff again."

"This time it won't be a standoff. He's ruined."

"It sure as hell looks that way."

"Are you still going to Taipei with him?"

"That's still the plan."

Gornt took a deep drag of his cigarette. His eyes checked the lie of his ship. They were well out into the main channel. Gornt got up and stood beside the captain a moment but the captain had also seen the small unlit junk ahead and he skirted it without danger. "Full ahead," Gornt said and came back. He refilled the glasses, chose one of the deep-fried *dim sum* and looked at the American. "Linc, may I be blunt?"

"Sure."

"Orlanda."

Bartlett's eyes narrowed. "What about her?"

"As you probably know, she and I were very good friends once. Very good. Hong Kong's a very gossipy place and you'll hear all sorts of rumors, but we're still friends though we haven't been together for three years." Gornt looked at him under his shaggy black-gray eyebrows. "I just wanted to say that I wouldn't want her harmed." His teeth glinted with his smile in the gimbaled light over the table. "And she's as fine a person and companion as you could find."

"I agree."

"Sorry, don't want to belabor anything, just wanted to make three points, one man to another. That was the first. The second's that she's as closed-mouthed as any woman I've ever known. The third's that she's nothing to do with business—I'm not using her, she's not a prize, or bait or anything like that."

Bartlett let the silence hang. Then he nodded. "Sure."

"You don't believe me?"

Bartlett laughed. It was a good laugh. "Hell, Quillan, this's Hong Kong! I'm out of my depth in more ways than you can shake a stick at. I don't even know if Pok Liu Chau's the name of the restaurant, a part of Hong Kong or in Red China." He drank the wine, enjoying it. "As to Orlanda, she's great and you've no need to worry. I got the message."

"I hope you don't mind my mentioning it."

Bartlett shook his head. "I'm glad you did." He hesitated, then because the other man was open he decided to get everything into the open. "She told me about the child."

"Good."

"Why the frown?"

"I'm just surprised she'd mention her now. Orlanda must like you very much."

Bartlett felt the power of the eyes watching him and he tried to read if there was envy there. "I hope she does. She said you'd been great to her since you split. And to her folks."

"They're nice people. It's rough in Asia to raise five children, raise them well. It was always our company policy to help families where we could." Gornt sipped his wine. "The first time I saw Orlanda was when she was ten. It was a Saturday at the races in Shanghai. In those days everyone would dress up in their best clothes and stroll the paddocks. It was her first formal coming out. Her father was a manager in our shipping division—a good fellow, Eduardo Ramos, third-generation Macao, his wife pure Shanghainese. But Orlanda . . ." Gornt sighed. "Orlanda was the prettiest girl I'd ever seen. Her dress was white . . . I don't remember seeing her after that until she came back from school. She was almost eighteen then and, well, I fell madly in love with her." Gornt looked up from his glass. "I can't tell you how lucky I felt all those years with her." His eyes hardened. "Did she tell you I broke the man who seduced her?"

"Yes."

"Good. Then you know it all." Gornt added with great dignity, "I just wanted to mention my three points."

Bartlett felt a sudden warmth toward the other man. "I appreciate them." He leaned forward to accept more wine. "Why don't we leave it this way. Come Tuesday all debts and friendships are canceled and we start fresh. *All of us.*"

"Meanwhile, which side are you on?" Gornt asked, the front of his face a smile.

"For the raid, yours, one hundred percent!" Bartlett said at once. "For Par-Con's probe into Asia? I'm in the middle. I wait for the winner. I lean toward you and I hope you're the winner, but I'm waiting."

"The two aren't the same?"

"No. I set the ground rules of the raid way back. I said the raid was a onetime operation, a fool's mate." Bartlett smiled. "Sure, Quillan, I'm a hundred percent with you on the raid—didn't I put up the 2 million with no chop, no paper, just a handshake?"

After a pause, Gornt said, "In Hong Kong, sometimes that's more valuable. I haven't the exact figures but on paper we're between 24 and 30 million HK ahead."

Bartlett raised his glass. "Hallelujah! But meanwhile how about the bank run? How will that affect us?"

Gornt frowned. "I don't think it will. Our market's very volatile but Blacs and the Vic are solid, unbreakable, the government has to support both of them. There's a rumor the governor'll declare Monday a bank holiday and close the banks for as long as needed—it's just a matter of time before cash becomes available to stop the loss of confidence. Meanwhile, a lot will get burned and a lot of banks will go to the wall but that shouldn't affect our plan."

"When do you buy back in?"

"That depends on when you dump Struan's."

"How about noon Monday? That gives you plenty of time before closing for you and your secret nominees to buy after the news leaks and the shares go down some more."

"Excellent. Chinese work on rumors, very much, so the market can swing from boom to bust or vice versa very easily. Noon is fine. You'll do that in Taipei?"

"Yes."

"I'll need a telex confirmation."

"Casey'll give it to you."

"She knows? About the plan?"

"Yes. Now she does. How many shares do you need for control?"

"You should have that information."

"That's the only piece missing."

"When we buy in we'll have enough to give us at least three immediate seats on the board and Ian's through. Once we're on the board Struan's is in our power, and then, very soon, I merge Struan's with Rothwell-Gornt."

"And you're tai-pan of the Noble House."

"Yes." Gornt's eyes glinted. He refilled the glasses. "Health!"

"Health!"

They drank, content with their deal. But in their secret hearts neither trusted the other, not even a little. Both were very glad they had contingency plans—if need be.

Grim-faced, the three men came out of Government House and got into Crosse's car. Crosse drove. Sinders sat in the front, Rosemont in the back and both of them held on tightly to their still unread copies of the AMG files. The night was dark, the sky scudding and the traffic heavier than usual.

Rosemont, sitting in the back, said, "You think the guv'll read the originals before he shreds them?"

"I would," Sinders replied without turning to look at him.

"Sir Geoffrey's much too clever to do that," Crosse said. "He won't shred the originals until your copy's safely in the minister's hands, just in case you don't arrive. Even so he's far too shrewd to read something that could be an embarrassment to Her Majesty's plenipotentiary and therefore Her Majesty's Government."

Again there was a silence.

Then, unable to hold back anymore, Rosemont said coldly, "What about Metkin? Eh? Where was the foul-up, Rog?"

"Bombay. The aircraft had to have been sabotaged there, if it was sabotage."

"For chrissake, Rog, gotta be. Of course someone was tipped. Where was the leak? Your goddamn mole again?" He waited but neither man answered him. "What about the *Ivanov*, Rog? You going to impound her and make a sudden search?"

"The governor checked with London and they thought it unwise to create an incident."

"What the hell do those meatheads know?" Rosemont said angrily. "She's a spy ship, for chrissake! Betcha fifty to a bent hatpin we'd get current code books, a look at the best surveillance gear in the USSR and five or six KGB experts. Huh?"

"Of course you're right, Mr. Rosemont," Sinders said thinly. "But we can't, not without the necessary approval."

"Let me and my guys d—"

"Absolutely not!" Irritably Sinders took out his cigarettes. The pack was empty. Crosse offered his.

"So you're going to let 'em get away with it?"

"I'm going to invite the captain, Captain Suslev, to HQ tomorrow and ask him for an explanation," Sinders said.

"I'd like to be party to that."

"I'll consider it."

"You'll have an official okay before 9:00 A.M."

Sinders snapped, "Sorry, Mr. Rosemont, but if I wish I can override any directives from your brass while I'm here."

"We're allies for chrissake!"

Crosse said sharply, "Then why did you raid 32 Sinclair Towers, uninvited?"

Rosemont sighed and told them.

Thoughtfully Sinders glanced at Crosse, then back at Rosemont. "Who told you that it was an enemy safe house, Mr. Rosemont?"

"We've a wide network of informers here. It was part of a debriefing. I can't tell you who but I'll give you copies of the sets of fingerprints off the glass we got if you want them."

Sinders said, "That would be very useful. Thank you."

"That still doesn't absolve you from a fatuous, unauthorized raid," Crosse said coldly.

"I said I'm sorry, okay?" Rosemont flared and his chin jutted. "We all make mistakes. Like Philby, Burgess and Maclean! London's so goddamn smart, eh? We've a hot tip you've a fourth guy—higher up, equally well placed and laughing at you."

Crosse and Sinders were startled. They glanced at one another. Then Sinders craned around. "Who?"

"If I knew, he'd be jumped. Philby got away with so much of our stuff it cost us millions to regroup and recode."

Sinders said, "Sorry about Philby. Yes, we all feel very bad about him."

"We all make mistakes and the only sin's failure, right? If I'd caught a couple of enemy agents last night you'd be cheering. So I failed. I said I'm sorry, okay? I'll ask next time, okay?"

Crosse said, "You won't but it would save us all a lot of grief if you did."

"What have you heard about a fourth man?" Sinders asked, his face pale, the stubble of his beard making him appear even more soiled than he was.

"Last month we busted another Commie ring, Stateside. Shit, they're like roaches. This cell was four people, two in New York, two in Washington. The guy in New York was Ivan Egorov, another officer in the UN Secretariat." Rosemont added bitterly, "Jesus, why don't our side wake up that the goddamn UN's riddled with plants, and the best Soviet weapon since they stole our goddamn bomb! We caught Ivan Egorov and his wife Alessandra passing industrial espionage secrets, computers. The guys in Washington, both'd taken American names of real people who were dead: a Roman Catholic priest and a woman from Connecticut. The four bastards were tied in with a joker from the Soviet Embassy, an attaché who was their controller. We pounced on him trying to recruit one of our CIA guys to spy for them. Sure. But before we ordered him out of the States, we frightened him enough to blow the cover on the other four. One of them tipped us that Philby wasn't kingpin, that there was a fourth man."

Sinders coughed and lit another cigarette from the stub of the other. "What did he say. Exactly?"

"Only that Philby's cell was four. The fourth's the guy who inducted the others, the controller of the cell and the main link to the Soviets. Rumor was he's up there. VVIP."

"What sort? Political? Foreign Office? Gentry?"

Rosemont shrugged. "Just VVIP."

Sinders stared at him, then went back into his shell. Crosse swung into Sinclair Road, and stopped at his own apartment to let Sinders off, then drove to the consulate that was near Government House. Rosemont got a copy of the fingerprints then guided Crosse to his office. The office was large and well stocked with liquor. "Scotch?"

"Vodka with a dash of Rose's lime juice," Crosse said, eyeing the AMG files that Rosemont had put carelessly on his desk.

"Health." They touched glasses. Rosemont drank his Scotch deeply. "What's on your mind, Rog? You've been like a cat on a hot tin roof all day."

Crosse nodded at the files. "It's them. I want that mole. I want Sevrin smashed."

Rosemont frowned. "Okay," he said after a pause, "let's see what we got."

He picked up the first file, put his feet on the desk and began reading.

It took him barely a couple of minutes to finish, then he passed it over to Crosse who read equally fast. Quickly they went through the files one by one. Crosse closed the last page of the last one and handed it back. He lit a cigarette.

"Too much to comment on now," Rosemont muttered absently.

Crosse caught an undercurrent in the American's voice and wondered if he was being tested. "One thing jumps out," he said, watching Rosemont. "These don't compare in quality with the other one, the one we intercepted."

Rosemont nodded. "I got that too, Rog. How do you figure it?"

"These seem flat. All sorts of questions are unanswered. Sevrin's skirted, so's the mole." Crosse toyed with his vodka then finished it. "I'm disappointed."

Rosemont broke the silence. "So either the one we got was unique and different, written differently, or these're phonies or phonied up?"

"Yes."

Rosemont exhaled. "Which leads back to Ian Dunross. If these're phony, he's still got the real ones."

"Either actually, or in his head."

"What do you mean?"

"He's supposed to have a photographic memory. He could have destroyed the real ones and prepared these, but still remember the others."

"Ah, so he could be debriefed if he . . . if he's cheated us."

Crosse lit another cigarette. "Yes. If the powers-that-be decided it was necessary." He looked up at Rosemont. "Of course, any such debriefing would be highly dangerous and would have to be ordered solely under the Official Secrets Act."

Rosemont's used face became even grimmer. "Should I take the ball and run?"

"No. First we have to be sure. That should be relatively easy." Crosse glanced at the liquor cabinet. "May I?"

"Sure. I'll take another shot of whiskey."

Crosse handed him the refill. "I'll make a deal with you: You really cooperate, completely, you don't do anything without telling me in advance, no secrets, no jumping the gun . . ."

"In return for?"

Crosse smiled his thin smile and took out some photocopies. "How would you like to influence, perhaps even control, certain presidential hopefuls—perhaps even an election?"

"I don't follow you."

Crosse passed over the letters of Thomas K. K. Lim that Armstrong and his team had acquired in the raid on Bucktooth Lo two days before. "It seems that certain very rich, very well-connected U.S. families are in league with certain U.S. generals to build several large but unnecessary airfields in Vietnam, for personal gain. This documents the how, when and who." Crosse told him where and how the papers had been found and added, "Isn't Senator Wilf Tillman, the one that's here now, a presidential hopeful? I imagine he'd make you head of the CIA for these goodies—*if* you wanted to give them to him. These two're even juicier." Crosse put them on the desk. "These document how certain rather well-connected politicians and the same well-connected families have got congressional approval to channel millions into a totally fraudulent aid program in Vietnam. 8 millions have already been paid over."

Rosemont read the letters. His face went chalky. He picked up the phone. "Get me Ed Langan." He waited a moment, then his face went suddenly purple. "I don't give a goddamn!" he rasped. "Get off your goddamn butt and get Ed here right now." He slammed the phone back onto its hook, cursing obscenely, opened his desk, found a bottle of antacid pills and took three. "I'll never make fifty at this rate," he muttered. "Rog, this joker, Thomas K. K. Lim, can we have him?"

"If you can find him, be my guest. He's somewhere in South America." Crosse put down another paper. "This's Anti-Corruption's confidential report. You shouldn't have any trouble tracking him."

Rosemont read it. "Jesus." After a pause he said, "Can we keep this between us? It's liable to blow the roof off a couple of our national monuments."

"Of course. We have a deal? Nothing hidden on either side?"

"Okay." Rosemont went to the safe and unlocked it. "One good turn deserves another." He found the file he was looking for, took out some papers, put the file back and relocked the safe. "Here, these're photocopies. You can have 'em."

The photocopies were headed "Freedom Fighter" dated this month and last month. Crosse went through them quickly and whistled from time to time. They were espionage reports, their quality excellent. All the items dealt with Canton, happenings in and around that vital capital city of Kwantung Province: troop movements, promotions, appointments to the local presidiums and Communist Party, floods, food shortages, the military, numbers and types of East German and Czechoslovak goods available in the stores. "Where'd you get these?" he asked.

"We've a cell operating in Canton. This's one of their reports, we get them monthly. Shall I give you a copy?"

"Yes. Yes thank you. I'll check it out through our sources for accuracy."

"They're accurate, Rog. Of course top secret, yes? I don't want my guys blown like Fong-fong. We'll keep this between you'n me, okay?"

"All right."

The American got up and put out his hand. "And Rog, I'm sorry about the raid."

"Yes."

"Good. As to this joker, Lim, we'll find him." Rosemont stretched wearily then went and poured himself another drink. "Rog?"

"No thanks, I'll be off," Crosse said.

Rosemont stabbed a blunt finger at the letters. "About those, thanks. Yeah, thanks but . . ." He stopped a moment, near tears of rage. "Sometimes I'm so sick to my stomach what our own guys'll do for goddamn dough even if it's a goddamn pile of goddamn gold I'd like to die. You know what I mean?"

"Oh yes!" Crosse kept his voice kind and gentle but he was thinking, How naive you are, Stanley!

In a moment he left and went to police HQ and checked out the fingerprints in his private files, then got back into his car and headed haphazardly toward West Point. When he was sure that he was not being followed, he stopped at the next phone booth and dialed. In a moment the phone was picked up at the other end. No answer, just breathing. At once Crosse coughed Arthur's dry hacking cough and spoke in a perfect imitation of Arthur's voice. "Mr. Lop-sing please."

"There's no Mr. Lop-*ting* here. Sorry, you have a wrong number."

Contentedly Crosse recognized Suslev. "I want to leave a message," he said continuing the code in the same voice that both he and Jason Plumm used on the telephone, both of them finding it very useful to be able to pretend to be Arthur whenever necessary, thus further covering each other and their real identities.

When the code was complete, Suslev said, "And?"

Crosse smiled thinly, glad to be able to dupe Suslev. "I've read the material. So has Our Friend." Our friend was Arthur's code name for himself, Roger Crosse.

"Ah! And?"

"And we both agree it's excellent." Excellent was a code word meaning counterfeit or false information.

A long pause. "So?"

"Can our friend contact you, Saturday at four?" Can Roger Crosse contact you tonight at 10:00 P.M. at safe phones?

"Yes. Thank you for calling." Yes. Message understood.

Crosse replaced the receiver.

He took out another coin and dialed again.

"Hello?"

"Hello, Jason, this's Roger Crosse," he said affably.

"Oh hello, Superintendent, this's a pleasant surprise," Plumm replied. "Is our bridge game still on for tomorrow?" Did you make the intercept of the AMG files?

"Yes," Crosse said, then added casually, "But instead of six could we make it eight?" Yes, but we're safe, no names were mentioned.

There was a great sigh of relief. Then Plumm said, "Shall I tell the others?" Do we meet tonight as arranged?

"No, no need to disturb them tonight, we can do that tomorrow." No. We'll meet tomorrow.

"Fine. Thank you for calling."

Crosse went back down the crowded street. Very pleased with himself, he got into his car and lit a cigarette. I wonder what Suslev—or his bosses —would think if they knew I was the real Arthur, not Jason Plumm. Secrets within secrets within secrets and Jason the only one who knows who Arthur really is!

He chuckled.

The KGB would be furious. They don't like secrets they're not party to. And they'd be even more furious if they knew it was I who inducted Plumm and formed Sevrin, not the other way around.

It had been easy to arrange. When Crosse was in Military Intelligence in Germany at the tail end of the war, information was whispered to him privately that Plumm, a signals expert, was operating a clandestine transmitter for the Soviets. Within a month he had got to know Plumm and had established the truth of this but almost immediately the war had ended. So he had docketed the information for future use—to barter with, or against a time he might want to switch sides. In espionage you never know when you're being set up, or betrayed, or being sold for something or someone more valuable. You always need secrets to barter with, the more important the secrets the safer you are, because you never know when you or an underling or overling will make the mistake that leaves you as naked and as helpless as a spiked butterfly. Like Voranski. Like Metkin. Like Dunross with his phony files. Like Rosemont with his naive idealism. Like Gregor Suslev, his fingerprints from the glass now on record with the CIA and so in a trap of my own choosing.

Crosse laughed aloud. He let in the clutch, easing out into the traffic. Switching sides and playing them all off against each other makes life exciting, he told himself. Yes, secrets really do make life very exciting indeed.

61

9:45 P.M.:

Pok Liu Chau was a small island southwest of Aberdeen, and dinner the best Chinese food Bartlett had ever had. They were on their eighth course, small bowls of rice. Traditionally rice was the last dish at a banquet.

"You're not really supposed to eat any, Linc!" Orlanda laughed. "That sort of dramatizes to your host that you're full to bursting!"

"You can say that again, Orlanda! Quillan, it's been fantastic!"

"Yes, yes it was, Quillan," she echoed. "You chose beautifully."

The restaurant was beside a small wharf near a fishing village—drab and lit with bare bulbs and furnished with oilcloth on the tables and bad chairs and broken tiles on the floor. Behind it was an alley of fish tanks where the daily catch of the island was kept for sale. Under the proprietor's direction they chose from what was swimming in the tanks: prawns, squid, shrimps, lobster, small crabs and fish of all kinds of shapes and sizes.

Gornt had argued with the proprietor over the menu, settling with what fish they could agree on. Both were experts and Gornt a valued customer. Later they had sat down at a table on the patio. It was cool and they drank beer, happy together, the three of them. All knew that at least during dinner there was a truce and no need for guards.

In moments the first dish had arrived—mounds of succulent quick-fried shrimps, sea-sweet and as delicious as any in the world. Then tiny octopus with garlic and ginger and chili and all the condiments of the East. Then some chicken wings deep fried which they ate with sea salt, then the great fish steamed with soy and slivers of fresh green onions and ginger and laid on a platter, the cheek, the delicacy of the fish, given to Bartlett as the honored guest. "Jesus, when I saw this dump, sorry, this place, I figured you were putting me on."

"Ah, my dear fellow," Gornt said, "you have to know the Chinese. They aren't concerned with the surroundings, just the food. They'd be very suspicious of any eating place that wasted money on decoration or tablecloths or candles. They want to see what they eat—hence the harsh light. Chinese are at their best eating. They're like Italians. They love to laugh and eat and drink and belch. . . ."

They all drank beer. "That goes best with Chinese food though Chinese tea's better—it's more digestive and breaks down all the oil."

"Why the smile, Linc?" Orlanda asked. She was sitting between them.

"No reason. It's just that you really know how to eat here. Say, what's this?"

She peered at the dish of fried rice mixed with various kinds of fish. "Squid."

"What?"

The others laughed and Gornt said, "The Chinese say if its back faces heaven it's edible. Shall we go?"

As soon as they were back on board and out to sea, away from the wharf, there was coffee and brandy. Gornt said, "Will you excuse me for a while? I've got some paper work to do. If you're cold, use the forward stateroom." He went below.

Thoughtfully Bartlett sipped his brandy. Orlanda was across from him and they were lounging in the deck chairs on the aft deck. Suddenly he wished that this was his boat and they were alone. Her eyes were on him. Without being asked, she moved closer and put her hand on the back of his neck, kneading the muscles gently and expertly.

"That feels great," he said, wanting her.

"Ah," she replied, very pleased, "I'm very good at massage, Linc. I took lessons from a Japanese. Do you have a regular massage?"

"No."

"You should. It's very important for your body, very important to keep every muscle tuned. You tune your aircraft, don't you? So why not your body? Tomorrow I'll arrange it for you." Her nails dug into his neck mischievously. "She's a woman, but not to be touched, heya!"

"Come on, Orlanda!"

"I was teasing, silly," she told him at once, brightly, taking away the sudden tension easily. "This woman's blind. In olden days in China and even today in Taiwan, blind people are given a monopoly on the art and business of massage, their fingers being their eyes. Oh yes. Of course there are lots of quacks and charlatans who pretend to have knowledge but don't, not really. In Hong Kong you soon know who's real and who isn't. This is a very tiny village." She leaned forward and brushed her lips against his neck. "That's because you're beautiful."

He laughed. "I'm supposed to say that." He put his arm around her, bewitched, and gave her a little hug, very conscious of the captain at the helm ten feet away.

"Would you like to go forward and see the rest of the ship?" she asked.

He stared at her. "You a mind reader too?"

She laughed, her lovely face a mirror of joy. "Isn't it the girl's part to notice if her . . . if her date's happy or sad or wanting to be alone or whatever? I was taught to use my eyes and senses, Linc. Certainly I try to read your mind but if I'm wrong you must tell me so that I can get better. But if I'm correct . . . doesn't that make it grander for you?" And so much easier to ensnare you beyond escape. To control you on a line you can so easily break if you wish, my art being to make the too thin line like a steel mesh.

Oh but that was not easy to learn! Quillan was a cruel teacher, oh so cruel. Much of my education was done in anger, Quillan cursing me, "For chrissake can't you ever learn to use your bloody eyes? It should have been crystal clear when I came here that I was feeling rotten and had a rotten day! Why the hell didn't you get me a drink at once, touch me gently at once and then keep your bloody mouth shut for ten minutes while I recoup—just tender and understanding for ten bloody minutes and then I'd be fine again!"

"But Quillan," she had whimpered through her tears, frightened by his rage, "you came in so angrily you upset me and th—"

"I've told you fifty times not to be upset just because I'm bloody upset! It's your job to take the tension out of me! Use your bloody eyes and ears and sixth sense! All I need's ten minutes and I'm docile again and putty. For chrissake, don't I watch over you all the time? Don't I use my bloody eyes and try to defuse you? Every month at the same time you're always edgy, eh? Don't I take care to be as calm as possible then and keep you calmed? *Eh?*"

"Yes but d—"

"To hell with *but!* By God, now I'm in a worse temper than when I came in! It's your bloody fault because you're stupid, unwomanly, and you of all people should know better!"

Orlanda remembered how he had slammed out of the apartment and she had burst into tears, the birthday dinner she had cooked ruined and the evening wrecked. Later, he had come back, calm now, and had taken her into his arms and held her tenderly as she wept, sorry for the row that she agreed was unnecessary and her fault. "Listen, Orlanda," he had said so gently. "I'm not the only man you'll have to control in this life, not the only one on whom you'll depend—it's a basic fact that women depend on some man, however rotten and evil and difficult. It's so easy for a woman to be in control. Oh so easy if you use your eyes, understand that men are children and, from time to time—most of the time—stupid, petulant and awful. But they supply the money and it's hard to do that, very hard. It's very hard to keep supplying the money day after day whoever you are. *Moh ching moh meng* . . . no money no life. In return the woman's got to supply the harmony—the man can't, not all the time. But the woman can *always* cheer her man if she wants to, can *always* take the poison out of him. *Always.* Just by being calm and loving and tender and under-

JAMES CLAVELL

standing for such a short time. I'll teach you the game of life. You'll have
a Ph.D. in survival, as a woman, but you've got to work . . ."

Oh how I worked, Orlanda thought grimly, remembering all her tears.
But now I know. Now I can do instinctively what I forced myself to
learn. "Come on, let me show you the forward part of the ship." She got
up, conscious of the captain's eyes, and led the way confidently.

As they walked she slipped her arm momentarily in Linc's, then took
the railing of the gangway and went below. The stateroom was big, with
comfortable chaises and sofas and deep chairs fixed to the deck. The cocktail cabinet was well stocked. "The galley's forward in the fo'c'sle with the
crew quarters," she said. "They're cramped but good for Hong Kong." A
small corridor led forward. Four cabins, two with a double bunk, two with
bunks one over the other. Neat and shipshape and inviting. "Aft's Quillan's master stateroom and the master suite. It's luxurious." She smiled
thoughtfully. "He enjoys the best."

"Yes," Bartlett said. He kissed her and she responded, fully responded.
His desire made her limp and liquid and she let herself go into his desire,
matching his passion, certain that he would stop and that she would not
have to stop him.

The game had been planned that way.

She felt his strength. At once her loins pressed closer, moving slightly.
His hands roved her and hers responded. It was glorious in his arms, better than she had ever known with Quillan who was always teacher, always in control, always unsharable. They were on the bunk when Bartlett
backed off. Her body cried out for his, but still she exulted.

"Let's go back on deck," she heard him say, his voice throaty.

Gornt crossed the fine stateroom and went into the master suite and
locked the door behind him. The girl was sweetly asleep in the huge bed
under the light blanket. He stood at the foot of the bed, enjoying the sight
of her before he touched her. She came out of sleep slowly. "*Ayeeyah*, I
slept so well, Honored Sir. Your bed is so inviting," she said in Shanghainese with a smile and a yawn and stretched gloriously as a kitten would
stretch. "Did you eat well?"

"Excellently," he replied in the same language. "Was yours equally
fine?"

"Oh yes, delicious!" she said politely. "Boat Steward Cho brought the
same dishes you had. I particularly liked the octopus with black bean and
garlic sauce." She sat up in the bed and leaned against the silk pillows,
quite naked. "Should I get dressed and come on deck now?"

"No, Little Kitten, not yet." Gornt sat on the bed and reached out and
touched her breasts and felt a little shiver run through her. Her Chinese
hostess name was Beauty of the Snow and he had hired her for the evening from the Happy Hostess Night Club. He had considered bringing

Mona Leung, his present girl friend instead, but she would be far too independent to remain below happily and only come on deck at his whim.

He had chosen Beauty of the Snow very carefully. Her beauty was extraordinary, in face and body and the texture of her skin. She was eighteen, and had been in Hong Kong barely a month. A friend in Taiwan had told him about her rarity and said that she was about to join the Happy Hostess Night Club from the sister club in Taiwan. Two weeks ago he had gone there and made an arrangement that had proved profitable to both of them. Tonight when Orlanda had told him she was dining with Bartlett and he had invited them aboard, at once he had called the Happy Hostess and bought Beauty of the Snow out of the club for the night and hurried her aboard.

"I'm playing a game on a friend tonight," he had told her. "I want you to stay here in this cabin, in this place, until I bring you on deck. It may be an hour or two but you are to stay here, quiet as a mouse, until I fetch you."

"*Ayeeyah,* in this floating palace, I am prepared to stay a week without charge. Just my food and more of the champagne . . . though pillowing would be extra. May I sleep in the bed if I wish?"

"Certainly, but please shower first."

"A shower? Bless all gods! Hot and cold water? That will be paradise—this water shortage is very unhygienic."

Gornt had brought her tonight to taunt Orlanda if he decided he wanted to taunt her. Beauty of the Snow was much younger, prettier, and he knew that the sight of her wearing one of the elegant robes that once Orlanda had worn would send her into a spasm. All through dinner, he had chortled to himself, wondering when he should produce her for maximum effect: to excite Bartlett and to remind Orlanda that she was already old by Hong Kong standards, and that without his active help she would never get Bartlett, not the way she wanted.

Do I want her married to Bartlett? he asked himself, bemused.

No. And yet, if Orlanda were Bartlett's wife he would always be in my power because *she is and ever will be.* So far she hasn't forgotten that. So far she's been obedient and filial. And frightened.

He laughed. Oh revenge will be sweet when I lower the boom on you, my dear. As I will, one day. Oh yes, my dear, I haven't forgotten the snickers of all those smug bastards—Pug, Plumm, Havergill or Ian bloody Dunross—when they heard that you couldn't wait to leap into bed with a stud half my age.

Should I tell you now that you're my *mui jai?*

When Orlanda was thirteen her Shanghainese mother had come to see him. "Times are very hard, Lord, our debts to the company are huge and your patience and kindness overwhelm us."

"Times are bad for everyone," he had told her.

"Unfortunately, since last week, my husband's department no longer exists. At the end of the month he is to leave, after seventeen years of service, and we cannot pay our debts to you."

"Eduardo Ramos is a good man and will easily find a new and better position."

"*Yin ksiao shih ta*," she had said: We lose much because of a small thing.

"Joss," he had said, hoping the trap was sprung and all the seeds he had sown would, at long last, bear fruit.

"Joss," she had agreed. "But there is Orlanda."

"What about Orlanda?"

"Perhaps she could be a *mui jai*." A *mui jai* was a daughter given by a debtor to a creditor forever, in settlement for debts that could not otherwise be paid—to be brought up as the creditor wished, or used or given away as the creditor wished. It was an ancient Chinese custom, and quite legal.

Gornt remembered the glow he had felt. The negotiations had taken several weeks. Gornt agreed to cancel Ramos's debts—the debts that Gornt had so carefully encouraged, agreed to reinstate Ramos, giving the man a modest guaranteed pension and help in setting up in Portugal, and to pay for Orlanda's schooling in America. In return the Ramoses guaranteed to provide Orlanda to him, virgin and suitably enamored, on or before her eighteenth birthday. There would be no refusal. "This, by all the gods, will be a perpetual secret between us. I think, too, it would be equally better to keep it secret from her, Lord, forever. But we know and she will know where her rice bowl lies."

Gornt beamed. The good years were worth all the patience and planning and the little money involved. Everyone gained, he told himself, and there is enjoyment yet to come.

Yes, he thought and concentrated on Beauty of the Snow. "Life is very good," he said, fondling her.

"I am happy you're happy, Honored Sir. I am happy too. Your shower was a gift of the gods. I washed my hair, everything." She smiled. "If you don't want me to play the prank yet on your friends, would you care to pillow?"

"Yes," he said, delighted as always by the forthrightness of a Chinese pillow partner. His father had explained it early: "You give them money, they give you their youth, the Clouds and the Rain and entertain you. In Asia it's a fair and honorable exchange. The more their youth, the more the laughter and gratification, the more you must pay. That's the bargain, but don't expect romance or real tears—that's not part of their commitment. Just temporary entertainment and pillowing. Don't abuse the fairness!"

Happily Gornt took off his clothes and lay beside her. She ran her hands over his chest, the hair dark, muscles sleek, and began. Soon she was making the small noises of passion, encouraging him. And though she had been told by the mama-*san* that this *quai loh* was different and there was no need to pretend, instinctively she was remembering the first rule of being a pillow partner to strangers: "Never let your body become involved with a customer for then you cannot perform with taste or daring. Never forget, when with a *quai loh*, you must always pretend to enjoy him greatly, always pretend to achieve the Clouds and the Rain, otherwise he'll consider that somehow it's an affront to his masculinity. *Quai loh* are uncivilized and will never understand that the yin cannot be bought and that your gift of coupling is for the customer's enjoyment solely."

When Gornt was finished and his heart had slowed, Beauty of the Snow got out of bed and went to the bathroom and showered again, singing happily. In euphoria he rested and put his hands under his head. Soon she came back with a towel. "Thank you," he said and dried himself and she slid in beside him once more.

"Oh I feel so clean and marvelous. Shall we pillow again?"

"Not now, Beauty of the Snow. Now you can rest and I will let my mind wander. You have settled the yang very favorably. I will inform the mama-*san*."

"Thank you," she said politely. "I would like you as my special customer."

He nodded, pleasured by her and her warmth and sensuousness. When would it be best for her to come on deck? he asked himself again, quite confident that Bartlett and Orlanda would be there now and not in bed as a civilized person would be.

A chuckle went through him.

There was a porthole beside the bed and he could see the lights of Kowloon in the distance, Kowloon and the dockyard of Kowloon. The engines throbbed sweetly, and in a moment he got out of the bed and went to the cupboard. In it were some very expensive nightdresses and underthings and multicolored robes and rich lounging housecoats that he had bought for Orlanda. It amused him to keep them for others to wear.

"Make yourself very pretty and put this on." He gave her a yellow silk, floor-length *chong-sam* that had been one of Orlanda's favorites. "Wear nothing underneath."

"Yes, certainly. Oh, how beautiful it is!"

He began to dress. "If my prank works you may keep it, as a bonus," he said.

"Oh! Oh, then everything will be as you wish," she said fervently, her open avarice making him laugh.

"We're going to drop my passengers Hong Kong side first." He pointed out of the porthole. "You see that big freighter, the one tied up at the wharf with the Hammer and Sickle flag?"

"Ah yes, Lord. The ship of ill-omen? I see it now!"

"When we are broadside please come on deck."

"I understand. What should I say?"

"Nothing. Just smile sweetly at the man and the woman, then at me and come below again and wait for me here."

Beauty of the Snow laughed. "Is that all?"

"Yes, just be sweet and beautiful and smile—particularly at the woman."

"Ah! Am I to like her or hate her?" she asked at once.

"Neither," he said, impressed with her shrewdness, ecstatically aware that they would both loathe each other on sight.

In the privacy of his cabin aboard the *Sovetsky Ivanov*, Captain Gregor Suslev finished encoding the urgent message, then sipped some vodka, rechecking the cable. "*Ivanov* to Center. Arthur reports the files may be counterfeit. His friend will supply me with copies tonight. Delighted to report Arthur's friend also intercepted the carrier information. Recommend he be given an immediate bonus. I have had extra copies sent by mail to Bangkok for the pouch, also London and Berlin for safety."

Satisfied, he put the code books back into the safe and locked it, then picked up the phone. "Send me the duty signalman. And the first officer." He unbolted the cabin door then went back and stared out the porthole at the carrier across the harbor, then saw the passing pleasure cruiser. He recognized the *Sea Witch*. Idly he picked up his binoculars and focused. He saw Gornt on the aft deck, a girl and another man with his back toward him sitting around a table. His high-powered lenses raked the ship and his envy soared. That bastard knows how to live, he thought. What a beauty! If only I could have one such as her on the Caspian, berthed at Baku!

Not so much to pray for, he told himself, watching the *Sea Witch* pass, not after so much service, so profitable to the cause. Many commissars do—senior ones.

Again his glasses centered the group. Another girl came up from below, an Asian beauty, and then there was a polite knock on his door.

"Evening, Comrade Captain," the signalman said. He accepted the message and signed for it.

"Send it at once."

"Yes sir."

The first officer arrived. Vassili Boradinov was a tough, good-looking man in his thirties, captain, KGB, graduate of the espionage department of Vladivostok University with a master mariner's ticket. "Yes, Comrade Captain?"

Suslev handed him a decoded cable from the pile on his desk. It read: "First Officer Vassili Boradinov will assume Dimitri Metkin's duties as commissar of the *Ivanov* but Captain Suslev will be in complete command on all levels until alternate arrangements are made."

"Congratulations," he said.

Boradinov beamed. "Yes sir. Thank you. What do you want me to do?"

Suslev held up the key to the safe. "If I fail to contact you or return by midnight tomorrow, open the safe. Instructions are in the package marked 'Emergency One.' They will tell you how to proceed. Next . . ." He handed him a sealed envelope. "This gives two phone numbers where I can be reached. Open it only in an emergency."

"Very well." Sweat beaded the younger man's face.

"No need to worry. You're perfectly capable of taking command."

"I hope that will not be necessary."

Gregor Suslev laughed. "So do I, my young friend. Please sit down." He poured two vodkas. "You deserve the promotion."

"Thank you." Boradinov hesitated. "What happened to Metkin?"

"The first thing is he made a stupid and unnecessary mistake. Next, he was betrayed. Or he betrayed himself. Or the god-cursed SI tailed him and caught him. Or the CIA pegged him. Whatever happened, the poor fool should never have exceeded his authority and put himself into such danger. Stupid to risk himself, to say nothing of our whole security. Stupid!"

The first officer shifted nervously in his chair. "What's our plan?"

"To deny everything. And to do nothing for the moment. We're due to sail on Tuesday at midnight; we keep to that plan."

Boradinov looked out of the porthole at the carrier, his face tight. "Pity. That material could have jumped us forward a quantum."

"What material?" Suslev asked, his eyes narrowing.

"Didn't you know, sir? Before Dimitri left, the poor fellow whispered he'd heard that this time we were to get some incredible information—a copy of the guidance system and a copy of their armament manifest, including atomics—that's why he was going himself. It was too important to trust to an ordinary courier. I must tell you I volunteered to go in his place."

Suslev covered his shock that Metkin had confided in anyone. "Where did he hear that?"

The other man shrugged. "He didn't say. I presume the American sailor told him when Dimitri took the call at the phone box to arrange the drop." He wiped a bead of sweat away. "They'll break him, won't they?"

"Oh yes," Suslev said thinly, wanting his subordinate suitably indoctrinated. "They can break anyone. That's why we have to be prepared." He fingered the slight bulge of the poison capsule in the point of his lapel and Boradinov shuddered. "Better to have it quickly."

"Bastards! They must have been tipped to capture him before he did it. Terrible. They're all animals."

"Did . . . did Dimitri say anything else? Before he left?"

"No, just that he hoped we'd all get a few weeks' leave—he wanted to visit his family in his beloved Crimea."

Satisfied that he was covered, Suslev shrugged. "A great pity. I liked him very much."

"Yes. Such a shame when he was due to retire so soon. He was a good man even though he made such a mistake. What will they do to him?"

Suslev considered showing Boradinov one of the other decoded cables on his desk that said in part: ". . . Advise Arthur that, following his request for a Priority One on the traitor Metkin, an immediate intercept was ordered for Bombay." No need to give away that information, he thought. The less Boradinov knows the better. "He'll just vanish—until we catch a bigger fish of theirs to use as an exchange. The KGB looks after their own," he added piously, not believing it, knowing that the younger man did not believe it either, but the saying of it was obligatory and policy.

They'd have to exchange me, he thought, very satisfied. Yes, and very quickly. I know too many secrets. They're my only protection. If it wasn't for what I know they'd order a Priority One on me as fast as they did on Metkin. So would I if I was them. Would I have bit my lapel as that stupid turd should have done?

A shudder went through him. I don't know.

He sipped his vodka. It tasted very good to him. I don't want to die. This life is too good.

"You're going ashore again, Comrade Captain?"

"Yes." Suslev concentrated. He handed the younger man a note he had typed and signed. "You're in command now. Here's your authority—post it on the bridge."

"Thank you. Tomorr—" Boradinov stopped as the ship's intercom came on and the urgent voice said rapidly: "This's the bridge! There're two police cars converging on the main gangway filled with police . . ." Both Suslev and Boradinov blanched. ". . . about a dozen of them. What should we do? Stop them, repel them, what do we do?"

Suslev jerked the sending switch on. "Do nothing!" He hesitated then switched on the ship's intercom. "All hands: Emergency, Red One . . ." This order meant: "Hostile visitors are coming aboard. Radio and radar rooms: arm destructs on all secret equipment." He switched the sender off and hissed at Boradinov, "Go on deck, down the gangway, greet them, delay for five minutes then *invite* the leaders aboard, only them if you can. *Go on!*"

"Surely they daren't come aboard to sear—"

"Intercept them—*now!*"

Boradinov rushed out. Once alone Suslev armed the secret destruct on his safe. If anyone but him tried to open it now its incendiary napalm would obliterate everything.

He tried to put his panicked mind at ease. Think! Is everything covered against a sudden search? Yes. Yes we've done the Red One drill a dozen times. But God curse Roger Crosse and Arthur! Why the devil didn't we get a warning? Was Arthur caught? Or Roger? *Kristos,* let it not be Roger! What ab—

His eyes caught the pile of coded and decoded cables. Frantically he scooped them into an ashtray, cursing himself for not doing it earlier, not knowing if there was enough time now. He found his lighter. His fingers were trembling. The lighter flamed as the intercom crackled on: "Two men're coming aboard with Boradinov, two men, the rest're staying below."

"All right, but delay them. I'll come on deck." Suslev doused the flame with a curse and stuffed the cables in his pocket. He grabbed a half-empty vodka bottle, and took a deep breath, put a broad beam on his face and went on deck. "Ah, welcome aboard! What's the trouble, eh?" he said, a slight slur now in his voice, keeping up his well-known cover. "One of our sailors has himself in trouble, Superintendent Armstrong?"

"This is Mr. Sun. May we have a word with you?" Armstrong said.

"Of course, of course!" Suslev said with a forced joviality he did not feel. He had never seen the Chinese before. He examined the cold-eyed, sallow, hate-filled face. "Follow me please," he said, then added in Russian to Boradinov who spoke perfect English, "You too," then again to Armstrong with continuing forced good humor, "Who's going to win the fifth race, Superintendent?"

"I wish I knew, sir."

Suslev led the way to the small wardroom that adjoined his cabin. "Sit down, sit down. Can I offer you tea or vodka? Orderly, bring tea and vodka!"

They came quickly. Expansively Suslev poured vodka even though the two policemen refused politely. "*Prosit*," he said and laughed jovially. "Not what's the trouble?"

"It seems that one of your crew is engaged in espionage against Her Majesty's Government," Armstrong said politely.

"Impossible, *tovarich!* Why joke with me, eh?"

"We've caught one. Her Majesty's Government is really quite upset."

"This is a peaceful freighter, trading. You've known us for years. Your Superintendent Crosse has watched us for years. We don't deal in espionage."

"How many of your crew are ashore, sir?"

"Six. Now listen, I don't want any trouble. I've had enough cursed trouble this voyage already with one of my innocent seamen murdered by unkn—"

"Ah yes, the late Major Yuri Bakyan of the KGB. Very unfortunate."

Suslev pretended sullen anger. "His name was Voranski. I know nothing of this major you talk about. I know nothing about that, nothing."

"Of course. Now, sir, when are your sailors back from shore leave?"

"Tomorrow, at dusk."

"Where are they staying?"

Suslev laughed. "They're ashore, on leave. Where else should they be but with a girl or in a bar? With a girl, eh, happily, eh?"

"Not all of them are," Armstrong said coldly. "At least one is very miserable right now."

Suslev watched him, glad that he knew Metkin was gone forever and they could not bluff him. "Come now, Superintendent, I know nothing about any espionage."

Armstrong put the eight-by-ten photos on the table. They showed Metkin going into the restaurant, then under guard, then being hustled into the Black Maria, then a mug shot of him, terror in the face.

"*Kristos!*" Suslev gasped, a consummate actor. "Dimitri? It's impossible! It's another false arrest! I will have my gov—"

"It's already been reported to your government in London. Major Nicoli Leonov admitted espionage."

Now Suslev's shock was real. He had never expected Metkin to break so quickly. "Who? Who did you say?"

Armstrong sighed. "Major Nicoli Leonov of your KGB. That's his real name and rank. He was also political commissar on this ship."

"Yes . . . yes that is true but his . . . his name is Metkin, Dimitri Metkin."

"Oh? You have no objection if we search this ship?" Armstrong began to get up. Suslev was aghast, Boradinov equally.

"Oh yes I object," Suslev stuttered. "Yes, Superintendent, so sorry but I formally object, and I mu—"

"If your ship is not engaged in espionage and is a peaceful freighter why should you object?"

"We have international protections. Unless you have a formal search warrant th—"

Armstrong's hand went into his pocket and Suslev's stomach turned over. He would have to comply with a formal warrant and then he would be ruined because they would find more evidence than even they could ever hope for. That god-cursed son of a whore bitch Metkin must've told them something vital. He wanted to shout in rage, the decoded and coded messages in his pocket suddenly lethal. His face had gone white. Boradinov was paralyzed. Armstrong's hand came out of his pocket with only a pack of cigarettes. Suslev's heart began again though his nausea still almost overwhelmed him. "*Matyeryebyets!*" he muttered.

"Sir?" Armstrong asked innocently. "Is anything the matter?"

"No, no, nothing."

"Would you care for an English cigarette?"

Suslev fought for control, wanting to smash the other man for tricking him. Sweat was on his back and on his face. He took the cigarette shakily. "These things are . . . are terrible, eh? Espionage and searches and threats of searches."

"Yes. Perhaps you'd be kind enough to leave tomorrow, not Tuesday."

"Impossible! Are we being hounded like rats?" Suslev blustered, not knowing how far he dare go. "I will have to inform my government and th—"

"Please do. Please tell them we have intercepted Major Leonov of the KGB, caught him in an espionage act, and that he has been charged under the Official Secrets Act."

Suslev wiped the sweat off his face, trying to stay calm. Only the knowledge that Metkin was probably dead now kept him in one piece. But what else did he tell them, he was shrieking in his head, what else? He looked at Boradinov who was standing beside him, white-faced.

"Who're you?" Armstrong asked sharply, following his glance.

"First Officer Boradinov," the younger man said, his voice strangled.

"Who's the new commissar, Captain Suslev? Who took over from your Mr. Leonov? Who's the senior Party man aboard?"

Boradinov went ashen and Suslev was thankful that some of the pressure was turned off him.

"Well?"

Suslev said, "He is. First Officer Boradinov."

At once Armstrong put his icy eyes on the younger man. "Your full name please?"

"Vassili Boradinov, first officer," the man stuttered.

"Very well, Mr. Boradinov, you're responsible for getting this ship under way by midnight Sunday at the latest. You are formally warned we have reason to believe there might be an attack on you by triads—by Chinese bandits. The rumor is the attack's planned for the early hours of Monday—just after midnight Sunday. It's a very strong rumor. Very. There are lots of Chinese bandits in Hong Kong, and Russians have stolen lots of Chinese land. We are concerned for your safety and health. I suggest it politic . . . eh?"

Boradinov was ashen. "Yes, yes, I understand."

"But my . . . my repairs," Suslev began, "if my repai—"

"Please see they're completed, Captain. If you need extra help or a tow outside Hong Kong waters, just ask. Oh yes, and would you be kind enough to appear at police headquarters at 10:00 A.M. Sunday—sorry about the weekend."

Suslev blanched. "Eh?"

"Here's your formal invitation." Armstrong handed him an official letter. Suslev accepted it, began to read as Armstrong took out a second copy, wrote in Boradinov's name. "Here's yours, Commissar Boradinov." He shoved it into his hand. "I suggest you confine the rest of your crew aboard—with the exception of yourselves of course—and bring your shore party back right smartly. I'm sure you'll have lots to do. Good night!" he added with startling suddenness, got up and went out of the wardroom, closing the door behind him.

There was a stunned silence. Suslev saw Malcolm Sun get up and leisurely head for the door. He got up to follow but stopped as the Chinese whirled on them.

"We'll get you, all of you!" Sun said malevolently.

"For what? We've done nothing," Boradinov gasped. "We've d—"

"Espionage. Spying? You KGB think you're so clever, *matyeryebyets!*"

"You get to hell off my ship," Suslev snarled.

"We'll get you all—I don't mean us police . . ." Abruptly Malcolm Sun switched to fluent Russian. "Get out of our lands, hegemonists! China's on the march! We can lose fifty million soldiers, a hundred and still have double that left. Get out while you've time!"

"We'll blast you off the earth!" Suslev bellowed. "We'll atomize all China. We'll ta—" He stopped. Malcolm Sun was laughing at him.

"Your mother's tit in your atomics! We've our own atomics now! You start we finish. Atomics, fists, ploughshares!" Malcolm Sun's voice dropped. "Get out of China while you've the chance. We're coming out of the East like Genghis Khan, all of us, Mao Tse-tung, Chiang Kai-shek, me, my grandsons, their grandsons, we're coming and we'll clean you off the earth and take back all our lands, *all of them!*"

"Get off my ship!" Suslev felt his chest hurting. Almost blind with rage, he readied to hurl himself at his tormentor, Boradinov as well.

Unafraid, Malcolm Sun came back a pace. *"Yeb tvoyu mat'* Turdhead!" Then in English, "Hit me and I'll arrest you for assault and impound your ship!"

With a great effort the two men stopped. Choked with rage, Suslev stuffed his fists into his pockets. "Please, you will . . . you will leave. Please."

"Dew neh loh moh on you, your mother, your father and the whole of your turd-eating Soviet hegemonists!"

"You—will—leave—now."

Equally enraged, Sun cursed them in Russian and shouted back, "We're coming out of the East like locusts. . . ." Then there was a sudden noisy altercation outside on deck and a slight dull boom. At once he turned and went for the door, the other two rushing after him.

Appalled, Suslev saw that now Armstrong was standing at the doorway of the radio room which was next to his cabin. The door was burst open, the two frightened operators staring at the Englishman, aghast, paralyzed deckhand guards nearby. Already the beginning of smoke was welling from the innards of the radio equipment. Red One ordered the senior radio man to trigger the destruct on the secret scrambling device the instant a hostile opened the door or tried to break the lock.

Armstrong turned to face Suslev. "Ah, Captain, so sorry, I stumbled. So sorry," he said innocently. "I thought this was the loo."

"What?"

"The toilet. I stumbled and the door burst open. So sorry." The police-

man glanced back into the radio room. "Good God! It seems there's a fire.
I'll call the fire brigade at once. Malcolm, get th—"

"No . . . no!" Suslev said, then snarled in Russian to Boradinov and
the deck crew, "Get the fire out!" He jerked a fist out of his pocket and
shoved Boradinov into motion. Unnoticed by him his cuff caught one of
his decoded cables and it fell on to the deck. Smoke was pouring out from
behind one of the complex radio panels. Already one of the deckhands
had a fire extinguisher.

"Dear oh dear! What could have happened? You're sure you don't want
assistance?" Armstrong asked.

"No, no thank you," Suslev said, his face mottled with rage, "thank
you, Superintendent. I'll . . . I'll see you Sunday."

"Good night, sir. Come along, Malcolm." In the growing confusion
Armstrong headed for the gangway but stooped and before Suslev realized
what was happening picked up the piece of paper and was halfway down
the gangway, Malcolm Sun following him.

Appalled, Suslev's hand went to his pocket. Forgetting the fire he
rushed into his cabin to check which cable was missing.

Below on the wharf, uniformed police had long since fanned out, covering both gangways. Armstrong was getting into the back of the car beside
Sinders. The eyes of the chief of MI-6 were dark-rimmed and his suit a
little rumpled but he was icily alert. "Well done, you two! Yes. I imagine
that'll interrupt their communications for a day or so."

"Yes sir." Armstrong began rummaging in his pocket for his lighter, his
heart pounding. Sinders watched Malcolm Sun get into the driver's seat.

"What's the matter?" he asked thoughtfully, seeing his face.

"Nothing, nothing really, sir." Malcolm Sun craned around, the sweat
on his back, his heart hurting and the sick-sweet excitement rage-fear taste
still in his mouth. "When . . . when I was conducting delaying tactics for
the superintendent I . . . they got me going, those two bastards."

"Oh? How?"

"Just . . . they started cursing, so I . . . I just cursed them back." Sun
faced the front, settled himself, not wanting Sinders's penetrating eyes on
his. "Just cursing," he added, trying to sound light.

"Pity one of them didn't hit you."

"Yes, yes I was ready."

Sinders glanced at Armstrong briefly as the big man clicked the lighter
on, lit a cigarette and, under the light of the flame, peered at the paper.
Sinders glanced up at the ship above. Once more Suslev was standing at
the head of the gangway staring down at them. "He looks very angry indeed. Good." The flicker of a smile went over him. "Very good." With Sir
Geoffrey's approval he had ordered the sudden arrival and attempt to disrupt the *Ivanov*'s communications—and complacency—to put pressure on

Arthur and the Sevrin moles, hoping to flush them out. "And our police mole," Sir Geoffrey had added grimly. "It's impossible that Brian Kwok's the spy mentioned in the AMG papers. Eh?"

"I agree," he had said.

Armstrong clicked the lighter off. In the semidarkness of the car he hesitated. "You'd better get the detail organized, Malcolm. No need to waste any more time here. All right, Mr. Sinders?"

"Yes. Yes we can go now."

Obediently Malcolm Sun left. Armstrong was watching Suslev on the deck. "You, er, you read Russian, don't you sir?"

"Yes, yes I do. Why?"

Carefully Armstrong passed over the paper, holding it by the edges. "This fell out of Suslev's pocket."

Equally carefully Sinders took the paper but his eyes never left Armstrong's. "You don't trust senior agent, Sun?" he asked softly.

"Yes. Oh yes. But Chinese are Chinese and it's in Russian. I don't read Russian."

Sinders frowned. After a moment he nodded. Armstrong lit the flame for him. The older man scanned the paper twice and sighed. "It's a weather report, Robert. Sorry. Unless it's in code, it's just a meteorological report." Carefully he folded the paper in its original creases. "The fingerprints might be valuable. Perhaps it's code. Just for safety I'll pass it on to our cipher fellows."

Sinders settled back more comfortably in the car. The paper had read: "Advise Arthur that, following his request for a Priority One on the traitor Metkin, an immediate intercept was ordered for Bombay. Second, the meeting with the American is brought forward to Sunday. Third and final, the AMG files continue to be Priority One. Maximum effort must be made by Sevrin to achieve success. Center."

Now which American! Sinders asked himself patiently, and is it Arthur's meeting or whose? Captain Suslev? Is he as innocent as he appears? Which American? Bartlett, Tcholok, Banastasio or who? Peter Marlowe—Anglo-American-Know-all writer with his curious theories?

Did Bartlett or Tcholok make contact with Center in June in Moscow when they were there, with or without Peter Marlowe, who also happened to be there when a highly secret meeting of foreign agents was taking place?

Or is the American not a visitor at all but someone who lives here in Hong Kong?

Is it Rosemont? Or Langan? Both would be perfect.

So much to wonder about.

Like who's the fourth man? Who's the VVIP above Philby? Where will those threads lead? Into *Burke's Peerage*? Perhaps to some castle, or even a palace?

Who's this mysterious Mrs. Gresserhoff who took Kiernan's second call and then vanished like a smoke ring?

And what about those bloody files? What about bloody AMG and bloody Dunross trying to be so bloody clever. . . .

It was getting toward midnight and Dunross and Casey were sitting happily side-by-side in the glassed-in forward section of one of the Golden Ferries, which swerved confidently toward its berth Kowloon side. It was a good night though the clouds still scudded low. Canvas storm panels still closed in and protected the open part of the decks, but here where they were, the view was good and a fine sea-salt breeze came through one of the open windows.

"It is going to rain again?" she asked, breaking their comfortable silence.

"Oh yes. But I certainly hope the heavy stuff stays away till late tomorrow afternoon."

"You and your races! Are they that important?"

"To all Hong Kong *yan,* oh yes. To me, yes and no."

"I'll put my entire fortune on your Noble Star."

"I wouldn't do that," he said. "You should always hedge a bet."

Casey glanced across at him. "Some bets you don't hedge."

"Some bets you can't hedge," he said, correcting her with a smile. Casually he lifted her arm and linked his with hers and settled his hand back in his lap. The contact pleased both of them. It was their first real touch. All during their stroll from the Mandarin Hotel to the ferry Casey had wanted to take his arm. But she had fought back the impulse and now she pretended not to notice their interlinking though, instinctively, she had moved a fraction closer.

"Casey, you never finished your story of George Toffer—did you fire him?"

"No, no I never did, not as I thought I would. When we'd won control I went to his boardroom. Of course he was fit to be tied but by that time I'd found out he wasn't the hero he claimed to be and a few other things. He just waved one of my letters about the money he owed me in my face and shouted that I'd never get that back, never." She shrugged. "I never did, but I got his company."

"What happened to him?"

"He's still around, still cheating someone. Say, can we stop talking about him, it gives me indigestion."

He laughed. "Perish that thought! Terrific night, isn't it?"

"Yes." They had dined impeccably in the Dragon Room atop the skyscraper hotel. Chateaubriand, a few thread-thin French fries, salad and *crème brûlée.* The wine was Château Lafite.

"Celebration?" she had asked.

"Just a thank you for the First Central New York."

"Oh, Ian! They agreed?"

"Murtagh agreed to try."

It had taken just a few seconds to fix the terms based on the bank's agreeing to the financing that Casey had laid out as possible: 120 percent of the cost of both ships, a 50 million revolving fund. "Everything covered by your personal guarantee?" Murtagh had asked.

"Yes," he had said, committing his future and his family's future.

"We, er, I figure with Struan's great management you'll make a profit so our money's secure and . . . but Mr. Dunross, sir, we gotta keep this secret as hell. Meanwhile, I'll give it the old college try." Murtagh was trying to hide his nervousness.

"Please do, Mr. Murtagh. The very best old college try you can. How about joining me for the races tomorrow? Sorry, I can't invite you to lunch, I'm crammed to the gills and overbooked, but here, here's a pass if you're free to join us from 2:30 on."

"Oh Jesus, tai-pan, you mean it?"

Dunross smiled to himself. In Hong Kong an invitation to a steward's box was like being presented at court, and just as useful.

"Why the smile, tai-pan?" Casey asked, shifting slightly, feeling his warmth.

"Because all's well, at the moment, in the world. At least all the various problems are in their compartments." Going ashore and out of the ferry terminal he explained his theory that the only way to deal with problems was the Asian way: to put them into individual compartments and take them up only when ready for them.

"That's good, if you can do it," she said, walking close beside him but not touching now.

"If you can't you'll go under—ulcers, heart attack, old before your time, your health broken."

"A woman cries, that's her safety valve. She cries and then she feels better. . . ." Casey had wept earlier, before leaving the V and A to meet him. Because of Linc Bartlett. Part rage, part frustration, part longing, and part need—physical need. It was six months since she had had one of her rare, very casual and very short affairs. When the need became too strong she would go away for a few days, skiing or sunning and she would choose whom she would allow into her bed. Then, as quickly, she would forget him.

"But oh, isn't it very bad, Ciran-chek," her mother had once said, "to be so callous?"

"Oh no, Mama darling," she had told her. "It's a fair exchange. I enjoy sex—I mean I enjoy it when I'm in the mood, though I try to keep the mood as infrequent as possible. I love Linc and no one else. But I th—"

"How can you love him and go to bed with someone else?"

"It's, it's not easy, in fact, it's awful. But Mama, I work hard for Linc all hours, weekends and Sundays, I work hard for all of us, for you and Uncle Tashjian and Marian and the kids, I'm the wage earner now that Marian's on her own and I love it, truly I enjoy it, you know I do. But sometimes it all gets too much so I just go away. And that's when I choose a partner. Honestly, Mama, it's just biological, there's no difference that way between us and men, and now that we've the God-blessed pill *we* can choose. It's not like in your day, thank God, my darling . . ."

Casey stepped aside to avoid a phalanx of oncoming pedestrians and bumped Dunross slightly. Automatically she took his arm. He did not withdraw.

Since she had asked him for equality this afternoon and had been turned down . . . No, that's not fair, Casey, she told herself. Ian didn't turn me down, he just gave me the truth from his point of view. From mine? I don't know. I'm not sure. But the one thing I'm not is a fool and so tonight I dressed carefully, a little differently, and put on perfume and made my makeup more definite and tonight I bit my tongue three to thirty times and held back, not giving measure for measure, playing it more conventionally, saying sweetly, "That's interesting!"

And most times it was. He was attentive, entertaining and receptive and I felt marvelous. Ian's certainly one helluva man. Dangerous and oh so tempting.

The wide marble steps up to the V and A were ahead. Discreetly she let go of his arm and felt nearer to him because of her understanding. "Ian, you're a wise man. Do you think it's fair to make love to someone—if you don't love them?"

"Eh?" He was startled out of the pleasantness. Then he said lightly, "*Love* is a Western word, lady. Me, I'm *China*-man!"

"Seriously."

He laughed. "I don't think it's time to be serious."

"But do you have an opinion?"

"Always."

They went up the stairs into the foyer, crowded even this late. At once he felt many eyes and recognition which was why he had not left her on the steps. Every little helps, he thought. I must seem calm and confident. The Noble House is inviolate! I will not and cannot allow myself the luxury of normal fear—it would spill over and wreck others and do untold damage.

"Would you like a nightcap?" she asked. "I'm not sleepy. Maybe Linc'll join us if he's in."

"Good idea. Tea with lemon would be fine." The smiling headwaiter appeared miraculously. And an empty table. "Evening, tai-pan."

"Evening, Nighttime Gup."

"Tea and lemon's fine with me too," she said. A waiter scurried away. "I'll just check my messages."

"Of course." Dunross watched her walk away. Tonight, from the first moment in the Mandarin foyer, he had noticed how much more feminine she had seemed, nothing discernible, just a subtle change. Interesting woman. A sexuality that's waiting to explode. How the devil can I help her to get her drop dead money quickly?

Nighttime Gup was bustling around and he said quietly in Cantonese, "Tai-pan, we certainly hope you can deal with the stock market and Second Great House."

"Thank you." Dunross chatted awhile, exuding confidence, then his eyes strayed back to Casey at the front desk.

Nighttime Gup's shrewd old eyes twinkled. "The gun-runner's not in the hotel, tai-pan."

"Eh?"

"No. He left early with a girl. Around 7:00 P.M., I'd just come on duty," the neat old man said airily. "The gun-runner was dressed very casually. For a sail I imagine. A girl was with him."

Dunross concentrated now. "There are many girls in Hong Kong, Nighttime Gup."

"Not like this one, tai-pan." The old man guffawed carefully. "Once she was the mistress of Black Beard."

"Eeeee, old man, you have sharp eyes and a long memory. Are you sure?"

"Oh very sure!" Nighttime Gup was delighted with the way his news was received. "Yes," he added loftily, "since we hear the Americans may be joining the Noble House if you can extricate yourself from all those other fornicators it might be good for you to know that. Also that Golden Pubics has moved her ro—"

"Who?"

Nighttime Gup explained the reason for the nickname. "Can you imagine, tai-pan?"

Dunross sighed, astounded as always at how fast gossip traveled. "She's changed her room?"

"Oh yes, it's along the corridor, 276, on the same floor. Eeeee, tai-pan, I heard she was weeping in the night, two nights ago, and again this evening before she left. Yes. Third Toiletmaid Fung saw her crying tonight."

"They had a row? She and the gun-runner?"

"Oh no, not a row, no shoutings. But, *oh ko*, if Golden Pubics knows about the Orlanda flower that's cause enough for dragons to belch." Nighttime Gup smiled toothily at Casey as she came back, a sheaf of cables and messages in her hand. Dunross noticed that now there was a shadow in her eyes. No message from Linc Bartlett, he surmised, getting up. Nighttime Gup solicitously pulled a chair away for her, poured her tea, continuing in his gutter Cantonese, "Never mind, tai-pan, Golden Pubics or not it's all the same in the dark, *heya*?" The old man chuckled and left.

Dunross glanced at her papers. "Trouble?"

"Oh no, just more of the same." She looked at him directly, "I've got them all compartmentalized for tomorrow. Tonight's mine. Linc's not back yet." She sipped her tea, enjoying it. "So I can monopolize you."

"I thought I was doing the monopolizing. Isn't—" He stopped as he noticed Robert Armstrong and Sinders come in through the swing doors. The two men stood at the entrance, looking for a table.

"Your police work overtime," Casey said, and, as the men's gaze fell on them, waved back half-heartedly. The two men hesitated, then went to a vacant table at the other end of the room. "I like Armstrong," she said. "Is the other man police?"

"I imagine so. Where did you meet Robert?"

She told him. "Still nothing on the smuggled guns. Where they came from or whatever."

"Rotten business."

"Would you like a brandy?"

"Why not? One for the road, then I must be going. Waiter!" He ordered the drinks. "The car'll be here tomorrow at twelve sharp to pick you up."

"Thank you. Ian, the invitation read, 'Ladies Hats and Gloves.' Do you really mean that?"

"Of course." He frowned. "Ladies have always worn hats and gloves at the races. Why?"

"I'll have to buy a hat. I haven't worn one in years."

"Actually, I like ladies in hats." Dunross glanced around the room. Armstrong and Sinders were watching him covertly. Is it a coincidence they're here? he wondered.

"You feel the eyes too, tai-pan? Everyone here seems to know you."

"It's not me, it's just the Noble House and what I represent."

The brandy came. "Health!" They touched glasses.

"Will you answer my question now?"

"The answer's yes." He swirled the brandy in the glass and inhaled it. "Yes what?"

Abruptly he grinned. "Yes nothing, yes it's not fair but yes it happens all the time and I'm not going to get into one of those lovely self-analyzing 'Have you stopped beating your wife recently?' things, though I do hear that most ladies like being beaten occasionally but with great care, with or without hats!"

She laughed and most of her shadows vanished. "It depends, does it?"

"It depends!" He watched her, his calm, easy smile on his face and he was thinking and she was thinking it depends on who and when and where and timing, circumstance and need, and right now it would be grand.

He reached out with his glass and touched hers. "Health," he said. "And here's to Tuesday."

She smiled back and lifted her glass, her heart quickening. "Yes."

"Everything can wait till then. Can't it?"

"Yes. Yes, I hope so, Ian."

"Well, I'll be on my way."

"I had a lovely time."

"So did I."

"Thanks for inviting me. Tomorr—" She stopped as Nighttime Gup bustled up to them.

"Excuse me, tai-pan, telephone."

"Oh, thank you. I'll be right there." Dunross sighed. "No peace for the wicked! Casey, shall we?"

"Sure, sure, tai-pan." She got up too, her heart beating strongly, a sad sweet ache possessing her. "I'll take care of the check!"

"Thanks, but that's already done. They'll just send it on to the office." Dunross left a tip and guided her toward the elevator, both of them conscious of the eyes following them. For a second he was tempted to go upstairs with her just to set the tongues wagging. But that'd really be tempting the devil and I've enough devils surrounding me already, he thought. "Good night, Casey, see you tomorrow and don't forget cocktails 7:30 to 9:00 P.M. Give my best to Linc!" He waved cheerily and walked for the front desk.

She watched him go, tall, immaculate and confident. The elevator doors closed. If this wasn't Hong Kong you wouldn't escape, not tonight, Ian Dunross. Oh no, tonight we'd make love. Oh yes, yes we would.

Dunross stopped at the front desk and picked up the phone. "Hello, this is Dunross."

"Tai-pan?"

"Oh hello, Lim," he said, recognizing his majordomo's voice. "What's up?"

"Mr. Tip Tok-toh just phoned, sir." Dunross's heart picked up tempo. "He asked me to try to reach you and would you please call him back. He said you could call him any time before two o'clock or after 7:00 A.M."

"Thank you. Anything else?"

"Miss Claudia called at eight and said she's settled your guest . . ." There was a rustle of paper. ". . . Mrs. Gresserhoff at the hotel and that your appointment in your office at 11:00 A.M.'s confirmed."

"Good. Next?"

"Missee called from London—everything fine there—and a Dr. Samson from London."

"Ah!" Kathy's specialist. "Did he leave a number?" Lim gave it to him and he scribbled it down. "Anything else?"

"No, tai-pan."

"Is Number One Daughter back yet?"

"No, tai-pan. Number One Daughter came in about 7:00 P.M. for a few minutes with a young man and then they left."

"Was it Martin Haply?"

"Yes, yes it was."

"Thanks, Lim. I'll call Tiptop then get a ferry home."

He hung up. Wanting more privacy, he went to the phone booth that was near the stationer's. He dialed.

"*Weyyyy?*"

He recognized Tiptop's voice. "Good evening, this's Ian Dunross."

"Ah, tai-pan! Just a minute." There was the sound of a hand being put over the mouthpiece and muffled voices. He waited. "Ah, sorry to keep you waiting. I've had some very disquieting news."

"Oh?"

"Yes. It seems your police once again are like dog's lungs and wolf's heart. They have falsely arrested a very good friend of yours, Superintendent Brian Kwok. He—"

"*Brian Kwok?*" Dunross gasped. "But why?"

"I understand he's been falsely accused of being a spy for the PRC, an—"

"Impossible!"

"I agree. Ridiculous! Chairman Mao has no need of capitalist spies. He should be released at once, at once—and if he wishes to leave Hong Kong he should be permitted to do so and go wherever he wishes to go . . . at once!"

Dunross tried to get his mind working. If Tiptop said the man called Brian Kwok was to be released at once and permitted to leave Hong Kong if he wished, then Brian *was* a PRC spy, one of their spies, and that was impossible impossible impossible. "I . . . I don't know what to say," he said, giving Tiptop the opening he required.

"I must point out Old Friends could hardly be expected to consider assisting Old Friends when their police are so errored. *Heya?*"

"I agree," he heard himself saying with the right amount of concern, his mind shouting, Christ almighty, they want to trade Brian for the money! "I'll . . . I'll talk to the authorities first thing tom—"

"Perhaps you could do something tonight."

"It's too late to call the governor now but . . ." Then Dunross remembered Sinders and Armstrong and his heart leaped. "I'll try. At once. I'm sure there's some mistake, Mr. Tip. Yes. It must be a mistake. In any event I'm sure the governor will be helpful. And the police. Surely such a . . . a mistake could be handled satisfactorily—like the Victoria's request for the temporary use of the illustrious bank's cash?"

There was a long silence. "It's possible that could be done. It's possible. Old Friends should assist Old Friends, and help correct mistakes. Yes, it could be possible."

Dunross heard the unsaid *when* left hanging and automatically continued the negotiation, most of his mind still beset by what he had been told. "Did you happen to get my note, Mr. Tip? I've taken care of everything else. By the way, the Victoria will certainly assist the financing of the thorium." He added delicately, "Also most other further requests—at advantageous terms."

"Ah yes, thank you. Yes, I received your note and your very kind invitation. So sorry that I was unwell. Thank you, tai-pan. How long would your government require the cash loan, if it was possible?"

"I imagine thirty days would be more than enough, perhaps even two weeks. But it's the Victoria, Blacs and the other banks and not the Hong Kong Government. I could tell you that tomorrow. Do we have the privilege of seeing you at the races for lunch?"

"I regret not for lunch but perhaps after lunch, if that's possible."

Dunross smiled grimly. The perfect compromise. "Of course."

"Thank you for calling. By the way, Mr. Yu was most impressed with you, tai-pan."

"Please give him my regards. I look forward to seeing him soon. In Canton."

"I was astonished to read your brother-in-law's comments about the Middle Kingdom."

"Yes. So was I. My wife and her brother have been estranged for years. His views are alien, enemy and totally misguided." Dunross hesitated. "I hope to neutralize him."

"Yes. Yes I agree. Thank you. Good night." The phone went dead.

Dunross hung up. Christ! Brian Kwok! And I'd almost given him the AMG papers. Christ!

Collecting his wits with a great effort, he went back into the foyer. Armstrong and Sinders were still there. "Evening, may I join you a moment?"

"Of course, Mr. Dunross. This is a pleasant surprise. May I offer you a drink?"

"Tea, Chinese tea. Thanks."

Their table was away from others and when it was safe Dunross leaned forward. "Robert, I hear you've arrested Brian Kwok," he said still hoping it wasn't true. The two men stared at him.

"Who told you that?" Armstrong asked.

Dunross recounted his conversation. Both men listened noncommittally though from time to time he saw them glance at one another. "Obviously it's a trade," he told them. "Him for the cash."

Sinders sipped his hot chocolate. "How important's the money?"

"Completely important, urgent and the sooner the better." Dunross mopped his brow. "The cash will completely stop the bank runs, Mr. Sinders. We've got t—" He stopped, aghast.

"What is it?" Sinders asked.

"I—I suddenly remembered what AMG wrote in the intercepted report. That the '. . . police mole may or may not be part of Sevrin.' Is he?"

"Who?"

"For chrissake, don't play with me," Dunross said angrily, "this's serious. You think I'm a bloody fool? There's a Sevrin plant in Struan's. If Brian's part of Sevrin I've a right to know."

"I quite agree," Sinders said calmly though his eyes had become very flinty. "The moment the traitor's uncovered you may rest assured you'll be informed. Have you any idea who it could be yet?"

Dunross shook his head, controlling his anger.

Sinders watched him. "You were saying? 'We've got to . . .' Got to what, Mr. Dunross?"

"We've got to get that cash at once. What's Brian done?"

After a moment Sinders said, "Banks don't open till Monday. So Monday's D Day?"

"I imagine the banks will have to get the money before then—to open and have the money in the tills. What the devil's Brian done?"

Sinders lit a cigarette for himself and for Armstrong. "If this person Brian actually has been arrested I don't think that's really a very discreet question, Mr. Dunross."

"I'd've bet anything," the tai-pan said helplessly, "anything, but Tiptop'd never suggest a trade unless it was true. Never. Brian must be bloody important but Christ, what's the world coming to? Will you handle the trade or will Mr. Crosse—I suppose the governor's approval will be needed."

Thoughtfully the chief of MI-6 blew the tip of his cigarette. "I doubt if there will be a trade, Mr. Dunross."

"Why not? The money's more impor—"

"That's a matter of opinion, Mr. Dunross, if this Brian Kwok actually is under arrest. In any event, Her Majesty's Government could hardly be subject to blackmail. Very poor taste."

"Quite. But Sir Geoffrey will agree at once."

"I doubt it. He impressed me as being much too clever to do that. As to trading, Mr. Dunross, I thought you were going to give us the AMG files."

Dunross felt an ice pick in his stomach. "I did, this evening."

"For chrissake, don't play with me, this's serious! You think I'm a bloody fool?" Sinders said in exactly the same tone that Dunross had used. Abruptly he laughed dryly and continued with the same chilling calm, "You certainly gave us a version of them but unfortunately they just don't compare in quality with the one intercepted." The rumpled man's eyes became even more flinty and curiously menacing though his face did not change. "Mr. Dunross, your subterfuge was deft, commendable but unnecessary. We really do want those files, the originals."

"If those don't satisfy you, why not go through AMG's papers?"

"I did." Sinders smiled without humor. "Well, it's like the old highwayman saying, 'The money or your life.' Possession of those files may be lethal to you. You agree, Robert?"

"Yes sir."

Sinders puffed his cigarette. "So, Mr. Dunross, your Mr. Tiptop wants to trade, eh? Everyone in Hong Kong wants to trade. It's in the air. Eh? But to trade you have to give value for value. I imagine if you want concessions to get concessions from the *enemy* . . . well, all's fair in love and war, they say. Isn't it?"

Dunross kept his face guileless. "So they say. I'll talk to the governor first thing. Let's keep this strictly confidential for the moment until I've talked to him. Night."

They watched him walk through the swing doors and disappear.

"What do you think, Robert? Did Dunross switch the files on us?"

Armstrong sighed. "I don't know. His face said nothing. I was watching closely. Nothing. But he's as sharp as a tack."

"Yes." Sinders pondered a moment. "So the enemy want a trade, eh? I'd say we have possession of this particular client for twenty-four hours at the most. When do you do his next interrogation?"

"6:30 A.M."

"Oh! Well if you've an early start we'd better be going." Sinders called for the check. "I'll consult with Mr. Crosse but I know what he'll say— what in fact London has ordered."

"Sir?"

"They're very concerned because the client's been party to too many secrets, the General Staff Course, the Royal Canadian Mounted Police." Sinders hesitated again. "On second thought, Robert, now irrespective of what Mr. Dunross does our only course is to step up the debriefing. Yes. We'll cancel the 6:30 interrogation, continue with the hourly schedule, providing he's medically fit, and into the Red Room."

Armstrong blanched. "But si . . ."

"I'm sorry," Sinders said, his voice gentle. "I know he's a friend, was a friend, but now your Mr. Tiptop and your Mr. Dunross have taken away our time."

SATURDAY

62

The JAL jet from Tokyo came in low over the sea and touched down perfectly at Kai Tak with a puff of smoke from its wheels. At once its engines went into reverse thrust and it howled toward the airport complex, decelerating.

Passengers, aircrew and visitors were milling in the busy terminal, Customs and Immigration and waiting areas. Outward-bound was easy. Incoming was mostly easy. Except for Japanese nationals. Chinese have long memories. The years of the Japanese war occupation of China and Hong Kong were too near, too strong, too vicious to forget. Or to forgive. So Japanese nationals were checked more thoroughly. Even members of the JAL crew now going through, even the pert, pretty, polite air hostesses, some of whom were hardly alive when that occupation had ended, they too were given back their travel documents with a frigid stare.

Next to them in line was an American. "'Morning," he said handing his passport to the official.

"'Morning." The young Chinese flipped the book open and glanced at the photograph and at the man and leafed through to find the visa. Unnoticed, his foot touched a hidden switch. This alerted Crosse and Sinders who were in a nearby observation office. They went to the one-way mirror and looked at the man waiting at immigration in front of one of the six crowded lines of passengers.

The passport, a year old, said, "Vincenzo Banastasio, male, born New York City, August 16, 1910. Hair gray, eyes brown." Casually the official checked the other visas and stamps: England, Spain, Italy, Holland, Mexico, Venezuela, Japan. He stamped the dull gray book, handed it back noncommittally.

Banastasio walked through to Customs, an expensive crocodile briefcase under his arm, carrying duty-free liquor in a gaudy plastic carrier, camera swinging off his shoulder.

"Good-looking fellow," Sinders said. "He takes care of himself." They saw him disappear into the crowds. Crosse clicked on the portable CB. "Do you have him covered?" he asked into it.

"Yes sir," came the instant answer.

"I'll keep monitoring this frequency. Keep me advised."

"Yes sir."

To Sinders, Crosse said, "We'll have no problem tailing him."

"No. Glad I've seen him. I always like to see an enemy in the flesh."

"Is he? Enemy?"

"Mr. Rosemont thinks so. Don't you?"

"I meant our enemy. I'm sure he's a crook—I meant I'm not sure he's tied into Intelligence."

Sinders sighed. "You've checked the bugs?"

"Yes." Late last night a team of SI experts had secretly put bugs into the bedroom Banastasio had booked at the Hilton. Also the office and private suite of Photographer Ng, Vee Cee Ng.

They waited patiently. On the table the CB hissed and crackled slightly.

After a pause Sinders said absently, "What about our other client?"

"Who? Kwok?"

"Yes. How long do you think it'll take?"

"Not long." Crosse smiled to himself.

"When do you put him into the Red Room?"

"I thought noon might be rather apt. Before if he's ready."

"Armstrong'll do the interrogation?"

"Yes."

"Armstrong's a good man. He handled himself very well at the *Ivanov*."

"Next time would you mind keeping me advised? After all, this is my area."

"Certainly, Roger. It was a sudden decision by London."

"What's the idea? About the Sunday summons."

"The minister is sending special instructions." Sinders frowned. "Brian Kwok's records say he's strong. We don't have too much time. He'll've been well indoctrinated to be hidden so deep, so long."

"Oh yes. But I'm quite confident. Since I had the room built I've experimented on myself three times. The most I've ever stayed was five minutes and each time I was sick as a dog—and that was without any disorientation scheduling. I'm confident we'll have no problem." Crosse stubbed out his cigarette. "It's very effective—an exact pattern of the KGB prototype."

After a moment Sinders said, "Pity these methods have to be used. Very dicey. Disgusting really. I preferred it when . . . well, even then, I suppose our profession was never really clean."

"You mean during the war?"

"Yes. I must say I preferred it then. Then there was no hypocrisy on the part of some of our leaders—or the media. Everyone understood we were at war. But today when our very survival's threatened we—" Sinders stopped, then pointed. "Look, Roger, isn't that Rosemont?" The American was standing with another man by the exit door.

"Yes, yes it is. That's Langan with him. The FBI man," Crosse said. "Last night I agreed to a joint effort with him on Banastasio though I do wish those bloody CIA'd leave us alone to do our job."

"Yes. They really are becoming quite difficult."

Crosse picked up the CB and led the way outside. "Stanley, we've got him well covered. We agreed last night that on this operation we handle this part, you handle the hotel. Right?"

"Sure, sure, Rog. 'Morning, Mr. Sinders." Grim-faced, Rosemont introduced Langan who was equally taut. "We're not interfering, Rog, though that bum is one of our nationals. That's not the reason we're here. I'm just seeing Ed off."

"Oh?"

"Yes," Langan said. He was as tired and gaunt as Rosemont. "It's those photocopies, Rog. Thomas K. K. Lim's papers. I've got to deliver them personally. To the Bureau. I read part to my chief and his pots blew and he began to come apart at the seams."

"I can imagine."

"There's a request on your desk to let us have the originals and th—"

"No chance," Sinders said for Crosse.

Langan shrugged. "There's a request on your desk, Rog. Guess your brass'll send orders from heaven if ours really need them. I'd better get on board. Listen, Rog, we can't thank you enough. We—I owe you one. Those bastards . . . yeah we owe you one." They shook hands and he hurried off onto the tarmac.

"Which piece of information blew the seams, Mr. Rosemont?"

"They're all lethal, Mr. Sinders. It's a coup for us, for us and the Bureau, mostly the Bureau. Ed said his folk went into hysterics. The political implications for Democrats and Republicans are immense. You were right. If Senator Tillman—the presidential hopeful who's in town right now—if he got hold of those papers, there's no telling what he'd do." Rosemont was no longer his usual good-humored self. "My brass telexed our South American contacts to put an all-points on Thomas K. K. Lim so we'll be interviewing him pretty damn soon—you'll get a copy don't worry. Rog, was there anything else?"

"I beg your pardon?"

"With these choice pieces, were there others we could use?"

Crosse smiled without humor. "Of course. How about a blueprint for financing a private revolution in Indonesia?"

"Oh Jesus . . ."

"Yes. How about photostats of arrangements for payments into a French bank account of a very important Vietnamese lady and gentleman —for specific favors granted?"

Rosemont had gone chalky. "What else?"

"Isn't that enough?"

"Is there more?"

"For chrissake, Stanley, of course there's more, you know it, we know it. There'll always be more."

"Can we have them now?"

Sinders said, "What can you do for us?"

Rosemont stared at them. "Over lunch we'll ta—"

The CB crackled into life. "The target's got his bags now and he's walking out of Customs, heading for the taxi rank . . . Now he's . . . Now he's . . . ah, someone's meeting him, a Chinese, good-looking man, expensive clothes, don't recognize him. . . . They're going over to a Rolls, registration HK. . . . ah, that's the hotel limousine. Both men're getting in."

Into the sender Crosse said, "Stay on this frequency." He switched frequencies. Static and muffled traffic and noise.

Rosemont brightened. "You bugged the limo?" Crosse nodded. "Great, Rog. I'd've missed that!"

They listened, then clearly, ". . . good of you to meet me, Vee Cee," Banastasio was saying. "Hell you shouldn't've come all this wa—"

"Oh it's my pleasure," the cultured voice replied. "We can chat in the car, perhaps that'll save you coming to the office and then in Ma—"

"Sure . . . sure," the American voice overrode the other man. "Listen, I got something for you, Vee Cee . . ." Muffled sounds then a sudden high-pitched whine that totally dominated the airwave, completely obliterating the clarity and voices. At once Crosse switched frequencies but the others were operating perfectly.

"Shit, he's using a portable shaver to block us," Rosemont said disgustedly. "That bastard's a pro! Fifty to a blown cent they block all the bugs we got, hundred says when they come back on this channel it'll all be goddamn chitchat. I told you Banastasio was cream."

63

"Tai-pan, Dr. Samson calling from London. He's on line three."

"Oh thank you, Claudia." Dunross punched the button. "Hello, Doctor. You're up late."

"I've just come back from the hospital—sorry not to call before. You were calling about your sister, Mrs. Gavallan?"

"Yes. How is she?"

"Well, sir, we've begun another stringent series of tests. Mentally, I must say she's in very good shape. I'm afraid physically not so good. . . ."

Dunross listened with a sinking heart as the doctor went into detail about multiple sclerosis, how no one really knew much about it, that there was no known cure and that the disease went in descending plateaus— once some deterioration of the nerve structure had taken place it was not possible with present medications to climb back to the previous level. "I've taken the liberty of calling in Professor Klienberg from the clinic at UCLA in Los Angeles for a consultation—he's the world expert on the disease. Please rest assured we will do everything we can for Mrs. Gavallan."

"It doesn't sound as if you can do anything at all."

"Well, it's not quite as bad as that, sir. If Mrs. Gavallan takes care, rests, and is sensible, she can have a normal life for many years."

"How long is many years?" Dunross heard the long hesitation. Oh Kathy, poor Kathy!

"I don't know. Many times this sort of problem's in the hands of God, Mr. Dunross. Patients do not follow the same time patterns. In Mrs. Gavallan's case I could answer you better in six months, perhaps by Christmas. Meanwhile, I have taken her on as a National Health patient so then—"

"No. She should be a private patient, Dr. Samson. Please send all bills to my office."

"Mr. Dunross, there's no difference in the quality of service I give to her. She just has to wait a little while in my waiting room and be in a ward, not a private room at the hospital."

"Please make her a private patient. I would prefer it, so would her husband."

Dunross heard the sigh and hated it. "Very well," the doctor was saying. "I have all your numbers and I'll call you the instant Professor Klienberg has made his examination and the tests are concluded."

Dunross thanked him and replaced the phone. Oh Kathy, poor dear Kathy.

Earlier when he had got up at dawn he had talked to her and to Penelope. Kathy had said how much better she felt and how Samson was most encouraging. Penn had told him later that Kathy was looking very tired. "It doesn't seem very good, Ian. Is there any chance you could come here for a week or two before October 10?"

"Not at the moment, Penn, but you never know."

"I'm going to take Kathy to Avisyard as soon as she gets out of the hospital. Next week at the latest. She'll be better there. The land will make her better, don't worry, Ian."

"Penn, when you get to Avisyard, would you go out to the Shrieking Tree for me?"

"What's the matter?"

He heard the concern in her voice. "Nothing, darling," he told her, thinking about Jacques and Phillip Chen—how can I explain about them? "Nothing particular, just more of the same. I just wanted you to say hello to our real Shrieking Tree."

"Our Jacaranda there's no good?"

"Oh yes, she's fine, but not the same. Perhaps you should bring a cutting back to Hong Kong."

"No. Better we leave it where it is. Then you have to come home, don't you, Ian?"

"Can I make a bet for you this afternoon?"

Again a pause. "Ten dollars on the horse you choose. I'll back your choice. I'll always back your choice. Call me tomorrow. Love you . . . 'bye."

He remembered the first time she had said, I love you, and then, later, when he had asked her to marry him, all the refusals and then eventually, through shattering tears, the real reason: "Oh Christ, Ian, I'm not good enough for you. You're upper class, I'm not. The way I talk now, I acquired. It was because I was evacuated at the beginning of the war to the country—my God I'd only been outside London twice in my whole life till then, just to the seaside. I was evacuated to a wonderful old manor house in Hampshire where all the other girls were from one of your fine upperclass schools, Byculla was its name. There was a mix-up, Ian, my whole school went somewhere else, just me to Byculla, and it was only then that I found I talked different, differently—there, you see I still forget sometimes! Oh God, you've no idea how awful it was to find out so young that . . . that I was common and talked common and that there are such limitless differences in England, the way we talk—the way we talk so important!

"Oh how I worked to imitate the others. They helped me and there was one teacher who was so wonderful to me. I hurled myself into the new life, theirs, and I swore to better myself and never go back, never, never, never, and I won't. But I can't marry you, my darling—let's just stay lovers —I'll never be good enough."

But in time, her time, they had married. Granny Dunross had persuaded her. Penelope had agreed but only after going out to the Shrieking Tree, alone. She had never told him what she had said.

I'm lucky, Dunross thought. She's the best wife a man could have.

Since coming back from the track at dawn he had worked steadily. Half a hundred cables. Dozens of international phone calls. Countless locals. At 9:30 he had called the governor about Tiptop's proposal. "I'll have to consult the minister," Sir Geoffrey had said. "The earliest I could call him would be four this afternoon. This must be kept entirely secret, Ian. Dear oh dear, Brian Kwok must be very important to them!"

"Or perhaps just another convenient concession for the money."

"Ian, I don't think the minister will agree to a trade."

"Why?"

"Her Majesty's Government might consider it a precedent, a bad one. I would."

"The money's vital."

"The money's a temporary problem. Precedents unfortunately last forever. You were at the track?"

"Yes sir."

"How's the form?"

"They all looked in fine fettle. Alexi Travkin says Pilot Fish's our main opposition and the going will be soft. Noble Star's grand though she's never raced in the wet."

"Will it rain?"

"Yes. But perhaps we'll be lucky, sir."

"Let's hope so. Terrible times, Ian. Still, these things are sent to try us, eh? Are you going to John's funeral?"

"Yes sir."

"So am I. Poor fellow . . ."

At the funeral this morning Dunross had said kind words about John Chen for the face of the House of Chen and for all the Chen forebears who had served the Noble House so long and hard.

"Thank you, tai-pan," Phillip Chen had said simply. "Again, I'm sorry."

Later he had said to Phillip Chen privately, "Sorry is sorry but that still doesn't help us extricate ourselves from the trap your son, and you, put us into. Or solve bloody Four Fingers and the third coin."

"I know, I know!" Phillip Chen had said, wringing his hands. "I know, and unless we can get the stock back up we're ruined, we're all ruined! *Oh ko,* after you'd announced the boom I bought and bought and now we're ruined."

Dunross had said sharply, "We've got the weekend, Phillip. Now listen to me, damnit! You will claim every favor you're owed. I want Lando Mata and Tightfist Tung's backing by Sunday midnight. At least 20 million."

"But, tai-pan, don—"

"If I don't get that by Sunday midnight, have your resignation on my desk by 9:00 A.M., you're no longer compradore, your son Kevin's out and all your branch is out forever and I'll choose a new compradore from another branch."

Now he exhaled heavily, hating that Phillip Chen and John Chen—and probably Jacques deVille—had betrayed their trust. He went to the coffee tray and poured himself some coffee. Today it did not taste good to him. The phones had been incessant, most of the calls about the looming collapse of the market, the banking system. Havergill, Johnjohn, Richard Kwang. Nothing from Tightfist or Lando Mata or Murtagh. The only bright spot had been his call to David MacStruan in Toronto: "David, I want you here for a conference on Monday. Can you g—" He had been swamped by the bellow of joy.

"Tai-pan, I'm on my way to the airport. Goo—"

"Hang on, David!" He had explained his plan about transferring Jacques to Canada.

"Och, laddie, if you do that I'm your slave forever!"

"I'm going to need more than slaves, David," he had said carefully.

There was a long pause and the voice on the other end hardened. "Anything you want, tai-pan, you've got. Anything."

Dunross smiled, warmed by the thought of his distant cousin. He let his eyes drift out of the windows. The harbor was misted, the sky low and dark but no rain yet. Good, he thought, so long as it docsn't rain till after the fifth race. After four o'clock it can rain. I want to smash Gornt and Pilot Fish and oh God let First Central come up with my money, or Lando Mata or Tightfist or Par-Con! Your bet's covered, he told himself stoically, every way you can. And Casey? Is she setting me up like Bartlett? And like Gornt? What about . . .

The intercom clicked on. "Tai-pan, your eleven o'clock appointment's here."

"Claudia, come in a second." He took an envelope out of his drawer with the $1,000 in it and gave it to her. "Betting money, as promised."

"Oh thank you, tai-pan." There were care lines in her jolly face and shadows under the smile.

"You're in Phillip's box?"

"Oh yes. Yes, Uncle Phillip invited me. He . . . he seems very upset," she said.

"It's John." Dunross wasn't sure if she knew. She probably does, he thought, or soon will. There're no secrets in Hong Kong. "What do you fancy?"

"Winner's Delight in the first, Buccaneer in the second."

"Two outsiders?" He stared at her. "You've inside info?"

"Oh no, tai-pan." A little of her normal good humor came back. "It's just the form."

"And in the fifth?"

"I'm not betting the fifth, but all my hopes're on Noble Star." Claudia added worriedly, "Is there anything I can do to help, tai-pan? Anything? The stock market and . . . we have to slaughter Gornt somehow."

"I'm rather fond of Gornt—he's such a *fang-pi*." The Canton obscenity was picturesque and she laughed. "Now show in Mrs. Gresserhoff."

"Yes, yes tai-pan," Claudia said. "And thanks for the *h'eung yau!*"

In a moment, Dunross got up to greet his guest. She was the most beautiful woman he had ever seen. "*Ikaga desu ka?*" he asked in shock, his Japanese fluent—How are you?—astounded that she could have been married to Alan Medford Grant whose name, God help us, was also supposed to be Hans Gresserhoff.

"*Genki*, tai-pan. *Domo. Genki desu! Anatawa?*" Fine, tai-pan, thank you. And you?

"*Genki.*" He bowed slightly in return and did not shake hands though he noticed her hands and feet were tiny and her legs long. They chatted for a moment then she switched to English with a smile. "Your Japanese is oh very good, tai-pan. My husband, he did not tell me you were so tall."

"Would you care for coffee?"

"Thank you . . . but oh please let me get it for you too." Before he could stop her she had gone to the coffee tray. He watched her pour delicately. She offered him the first cup with a little bow. "Please." Riko Gresserhoff—Riko Anjin—was barely five feet, perfectly proportioned with short hair and lovely smile and she weighed about ninety pounds. Her blouse and skirt were auburn silk, well cut and French. "Thank you for the expense money Miss Claudia gave me."

"It's nothing. We owe your, your husband's estate about 8,000 pounds. I'll have a cashier's check for you tomorrow."

"Thank you."

"You have me at a disadvantage, Mrs. Gresserhoff. You kn—"

"Please call me Riko, tai-pan."

"Very well, Riko-*san*. You know me but I know nothing about you."

"Yes. My husband said I was to tell you whatever you wanted to know. He told me that, that once I had made sure you were the tai-pan, then I was to give you an envelope I have brought from him to you. May I bring it later?" Again the little interrogative smile. "Please?"

"I'll come back with you now and collect it."

"Oh no, that would be too much trouble. Perhaps I can bring it to you after luncheon. Please."

"How big is it? The envelope?"

Her tiny hands measured the air. "It is an ordinary envelope but not so thick. You could put it easily into your pocket." Again the smile.

"Perhaps you'd like to . . . I tell you what," he said, charmed by her presence. "In a minute or two I'll send you back by car. You can fetch the envelope and come right back." Then he added, knowing it would ruin the seating arrangements but not caring, "Would you join us for lunch at the races?"

"Oh but . . . but I would have to change and . . . oh thank you but no, it would be too much trouble for you. Perhaps I could deliver the letter later, or tomorrow? My husband said I was only to put it into your hands."

"No need to change, Riko-*san*. You look lovely. Oh! Do you have a hat?"

Perplexed she stared at him. "Please?"

"Yes, it's, er, yes, it's our custom that ladies wear hats and gloves to the races. Silly custom but do you? Have a hat?"

"Oh yes. Every lady has a hat. Of course."

A wave of relief went through him. "Good, then that's settled."

"Oh! Then if you say so." She got up. "Shall I go now?"

"No, if you've time, please sit down. How long were you married?"

"Four years. Hans . . ." She hesitated. Then she said firmly, "Hans told me to tell you, but you alone, if ever he was to die and I was to come as I have come, to tell you that our marriage was of convenience."

"What?"

She reddened a little as she continued. "Please excuse me but I was to tell you. It was a convenience to both of us. I obtained a Swiss citizenship and passport and he obtained someone to care for him when he came to Switzerland. I . . . I did not wish to marry but he asked me many times and he . . . and he stressed that it would protect me when he died."

Dunross was startled. "He knew he was going to die?"

"I think so. He said the marriage contract was for five years only but that we should have no children. He took me to an advocate in Zurich who drew up a contract for five years." She opened her purse, her fingers trembling but not her voice, and pulled out an envelope. "Hans told me to give you these. They're copies of the contract, my, my birth and marriage certificate, his will and birth certificate." She took out a tissue and pressed it against her nose. "Please excuse me." Carefully she untied the string around the envelope and took out a letter.

Dunross accepted it. He recognized AMG's handwriting. "Tai-pan: This will confirm my wife, Riko Gresserhoff—Riko Anjin—is who she says she is. I love her with all my heart. She merits and merited far better than

me. If she needs help . . . please please please." It was signed Hans Gresserhoff.

"I do not merit better, tai-pan," she said with a sad, small confident
voice. "My husband was good to me, very good. And I'm sorry he is dead."

Dunross watched her. "Was he ill? Did he know he was going to die
from an illness?"

"I don't know. He never told me. One of his asks before I . . . before I
married him was that I would not question him or question where he
went, why, or when he was to return. I was just to accept him as he was."
A small shiver went through her. "It was very hard living thus."

"Why did you agree to live like that? Why? Surely it wasn't necessary?"

Again Riko hesitated. "I was born in Japan in 1939 and went as an infant with my parents to Berne—my father was a minor official in the Japanese Embassy there. In 1943 he went back to Japan but left us in Geneva.
Our family is—our family comes from Nagasaki. In 1945 my father was
lost and all our family was lost. There was nothing to go back to and my
mother wanted to stay in Switzerland, so we went to live in Zurich with a
good man who died four years ago. He . . . they paid for my education
and kept me and we had a happy family. For many years I knew they
were not married though they pretended and I pretended. When he died
there was no money, or just a little money. Hans Gresserhoff was an ac-
quaintance of this man, my, my stepfather. His name was Simeon Tzerak.
He was a displaced person, tai-pan, a stateless person from Hungary who
had taken up residence in Switzerland. Before the war he was an account-
ant, he said, in Budapest. My mother arranged my marriage to Hans Gresserhoff." Now she looked up from the carpet at him. "It was . . . it was a
good marriage, tai-pan, at least I tried very hard to be whatever my husband wanted and my mother wanted. My *giri*, my duty was to obey my
mother, *neh?*"

"Yes," he said kindly, understanding duty and *giri*, that most Japanese
of words, most important of words that sums up a heritage and a way of
life. "You have performed your *giri* perfectly, I'm sure. What does your
mother say is your *giri* now?"

"My mother is dead, tai-pan. When my stepfather died she did not
wish to live. The moment I was married she went up the mountain and
skied into a crevasse."

"Terrible."

"Oh no, tai-pan, very good. She died as she wished to die, at a time
and place of her choosing. Her man was dead, I was safe, what more was
there for her to do?"

"Nothing," he told her, hearing the softness of her voice, the sincerity,
and the calm. The Japanese word *wa* came to his mind: harmony. That's
what this girl has, he thought. Harmony. Perhaps that's what's so beautiful about her. *Ayeeyah* that I could acquire such *wa!*

One of his phones sounded. "Yes, Claudia?"

"It's Alexi Travkin, tai-pan. Sorry, he said it was important."

"Thank you." To the girl he said, "Excuse me a moment. Yes, Alexi?"

"Sorry to interrupt, tai-pan, but Johnny Moore's sick and he won't be able to ride." Johnny Moore was their chief jockey.

Dunross's voice sharpened. "He seemed all right this morning."

"He's running 103-degree temperature, the doctor said it might be food poisoning."

"You mean he's been tampered with, Alexi?"

"I don't know, tai-pan. I only know he's no good for us today."

Dunross hesitated. He knew he was better than the rest of his jockeys though the extra weight Noble Star would have to carry would load the deck against the horse. Should I or shouldn't I? "Alexi, schedule Tom Wong. We'll decide before the race."

"Yes. Thank you."

Dunross replaced the phone. "Anjin's a curious name," he said. "It means pilot, just pilot, or navigator, doesn't it?"

"The legend in my family is that one of our forebears was an Englishman who became a samurai and advisor to the Shōgun Yoshi Toranaga, oh very many years ago, long long ago. We have many stories but they say first he had a fief in Hemi, near Yokohama, then went with his family to Nagasaki as inspector general of all foreigners." Again the smile and the shrug and the tip of her tongue moistened her lips. "It is just legend, tai-pan. He is supposed to have married a highborn lady called Riko." Her chuckle filled the room. "You know Japanese! A *gai-jin,* a foreigner, marrying a highborn lady—how could that be possible? But anyway, it is a pleasing story and an explanation of a name, *neh?*" She got up and he got up. "I should go now. Yes?"

No, he wanted to say.

The black Daimler pulled up outside the V and A, the Struan arms discreetly on the doors. Casey and Bartlett waited at the top of the stairs, Casey wearing a green dress, self-conscious in a pert green pillbox hat and white gloves, Bartlett broad-shouldered, wearing a blue tie to match his well-cut suit. Both were set-faced.

The chauffeur approached them. "Mr. Bartlett?"

"Yes." They came down the steps to meet him. "You our limo?"

"Yes sir. Excuse me sir, but do you both have your badge tickets, and the invitation card?"

"Yes, here they are," Casey said.

"Ah, good. Sorry but without them . . . My name's Lim. The, er, the custom is for the gentlemen to tie both badges through the hole in their lapels and the ladies usually have a pin."

"Whatever you say," Bartlett said. Casey got in the back and he followed. They sat far apart. Silently they began to fix the small, individually numbered badges.

Blandly Lim closed the door, noticing the frigidity, and chortled inwardly. He closed the electric glass partition window and switched on his intercom mike. "If you want to talk to me, sir, just use the microphone above you." Through his rear mirror he saw Bartlett use the switch momentarily.

"Sure, thank you, Lim."

Once Lim was in the traffic he reached under the dash and touched a hidden switch. At once Bartlett's voice came through the speaker.

". . . going to rain?"

"I don't know, Linc. The radio said it would but everyone's praying." A hesitation, then coldly, "I still think you're wrong."

Lim settled back happily. His trusted older brother Lim Chu, majordomo to the tai-pans of the Noble House, had arranged for another younger brother, an expert radio mechanic, to install this bypass switch so that he could overhear his passengers. It had been done at great cost to protect the tai-pan and older brother Lim had ordered it was never to be used when the tai-pan was in the car. Never never never. It never had been. Yet. Lim felt queasy at the thought of being caught but their wish to know—of course to protect—overcame their anxiety. Oh oh oh, he chortled, Golden Pubics is certainly in a rage!

Casey was seething.

"Let's quit this, Linc, huh?" she said. "Since our breakfast meeting you've been like a bear with a sore ass!"

"And what about you?" Bartlett glared at her. "We're going with Gornt —the way I want it."

"This's my deal, you've said that fifty times, you promised, you've always listened before. Jesus, we're on the same side. I'm only trying to protect you. I know you're wrong."

"You *think* I'm wrong. And it's all because of Orlanda!"

"That's a crock! I went through my reasons fifty times. If Ian gets out of the trap then we're better off to go with him than Gornt."

Bartlett's face was cold. "We've never had a bust before, Casey, but if you want to vote your shares, I'll vote mine and your ass'll be in a vise before you can count to ten!"

Casey's heart was thumping. Ever since their breakfast meeting with Seymour Steigler, the day had been heavy going. Bartlett was adamant that their best course lay with Gornt and nothing she could say would dissuade him. After an hour of trying she had closed the meeting and gone off to deal with a pile of overnight telexes, then, remembering suddenly at the last moment, had rushed out in a panic and bought her hat.

When she had met Bartlett in the foyer with great trepidation, wanting the hat to please him, she had begun to make peace but he had interrupted her. "Forget it," he had said. "So we disagree. So what?"

She had waited and waited but he hadn't even noticed. "What do you think?"

"I told you. Gornt's best for us."

"I meant my hat."

She had seen his blank stare.

"Oh that's what's different! Hey, it's okay."

She had felt like tearing it off and hurling it at him. "It's Parisian," she had said half-heartedly. "It says hats and gloves on the invitation, remember? It's a crock but Ian said that la—"

"What makes you think he can get out of the trap?"

"He's clever. And *the* tai-pan."

"Gornt's got him on the run."

"It looks that way. So let's forget it for now. Maybe we'd better wait outside. The car's coming at noon promptly."

"Just a minute, Casey. What have you got cooking?"

"What do you mean?"

"I know you better than anyone. What do you have on the burner?"

Casey hesitated, unsure of herself, wondering if she should reveal the First Central ploy. But there's no reason to, she reassured herself. If Ian gets the credit and squeezes out, I'll be the first to know. Ian promised. Then Linc can cover his 2 million with Gornt and they can buy back in to cover their selling short and make a huge profit. At the same time Ian, Linc and I get in at the bottom of the market and make our own killing. I'll be the first to know after Murtagh and Ian. Ian promised. Yes, yes he did. But can I trust him?

A wave of nausea went through her. Can you trust anyone in business here, or anywhere? Man or woman?

At dinner last night she had trusted him. Influenced by the wine and food she had told him about her relationship with Linc, and about the bargain they had made.

"That's a bit rough, isn't it? On both of you?"

"Yes, yes and no. We were both over twenty-one, Ian, and I wanted so much more than being just Mrs. Linc Bartlett, a mother-mistress-servant-dishwasher-diaperwasher-slave and a left-at-home. That's the thing that kills off any woman. You're always left. At home. So home becomes a prison in the end, and it drives you mad, being trapped until death do us part! I've seen it too many times."

"Someone has to look after the home and the children. It's the man's job to make the money. It's the wife's j—"

"Yes. Most times. But not for me. *I'm* not prepared to accept that and I don't think it's wrong to want a different sort of life. I'm the wage earner for my family. My sister's husband died so there's my sister and her kids, and my Ma and uncle are getting on. I'm educated and good and better than most in business. The world's changing, everything's changing, Ian."

"I said before, not here thank God!"

Casey remembered how she had readied to return measure for measure, but had bitten back the old Casey and said instead, "Ian, what about the Hag? How did she do it? What was her secret? How did she become more equal than anyone?"

"She kept her hands on the purse strings. Absolutely. Oh she conceded outward position and face to Culum and following tai-pans but she kept the books, she hired and fired through him—she was the strength of that family. When Culum was dying, it was easy to persuade him to make her tai-pan. He gave her the Struan chop, family chop and all the reins and all the secrets. But, wisely, she kept it all very secret and after Culum she only appointed those she could control, and never once gave any one of them the purse strings, or real power, not until she herself was dying."

"But ruling through others, is that enough?"

"Power is power and I don't think it matters so long as you rule. For a woman—after a certain age—power only comes with control of the purse. But you're right about drop dead money. Hong Kong's the only place on earth you can get it to keep it. With money, real money, you can be more equal than anyone. Even Linc Bartlett. I like him, by the way. I like him very much."

"I love him. Our partnership's worked, Ian. I think it's been good for Linc—oh how I hope so. He's our tai-pan and I'm not trying to become one. I just want to succeed as a woman. He's helped me tremendously, of course he has. Without him I'd never have made it. So we're in business together, until my birthday. November 25 this year. That's D Day. That's when we both decide."

"And?"

"I don't know. I honestly don't know. Oh I love Linc, more than ever, but we're not lovers."

Later, coming back on the ferry, she had been sorely tempted to ask him about Orlanda. She had decided not to. "Perhaps I should have," she muttered out loud.

"Eh?"

"Oh!" She came out of her reverie, finding herself in the limo on the car ferry en route to Hong Kong. "Sorry, Linc, I was daydreaming."

She looked at him and saw that he was as handsome as ever, even though now he stared back coldly. You're more attractive to me than either Ian or Quillan, she thought. And yet, right now, I'd prefer to pillow with either of them than with you. Because you're a bastard.

"Do you want to have at it?" he said. "You want to vote your shares against mine?"

Casey stared back at him, enraged. Tell him to go screw, the devil half of her screamed, he needs you more than you need him, you've got the reins of Par-Con, you know where the bodies are buried, you can take apart what you helped to create. But the other half of her urged caution.

She remembered what the tai-pan had said about this man's world, and about power. And about the Hag.

So she dropped her gaze a moment and allowed tears to seep. At once she saw the change in him.

"Jesus, Casey, don't cry, I'm sorry . . ." he was saying and his arms reached out for her. "Jesus, you've never cried before . . . Listen, we've been through the mill a dozen times, hell, fifty times, there's no need to get so uptight. We've got Struan's and Gornt locked into battle. There's no difference in the end. We'll still be the Noble House, but up front, up front Gornt's better, I know I'm right."

Oh no, you're not, she thought contentedly, warm in his embrace.

64

12:32 P.M.:

Brian Kwok was screaming and beyond terror. He knew he was in prison and in hell and it had gone on forever. His whole insane world was an instant of never-ending blinding light, everything blood-colored, the cell walls floor ceiling blood-colored, no doors or windows, and the floor awash with blood, but everything twisted and all upside down for somehow he was lying on the ceiling, his whole being in torment, frantically trying to claw his way down to normality, each time falling back into the mess of his own vomit, then the next instant once more in the blackness, grinding pulsating voices laughing, drowning out his friend, drowning out Robert who pleaded with the devils to stop stop for the love of God stop, then once more the eye-tearing head-exploding bloodlight, seeing the blood waters that would not fall, groping desperately, stretching down for the chairs and table that sat in the blood water but falling back, always falling back, floor meeting ceiling everything wrong upside sideways madness madness the devil's invention . . .

Bloodlight and darkness and laughter and stench and blood again, on and on and on . . .

He knew he had begun raving years ago, begging them to stop, begging them to let him go, swearing he would do anything but let him go, that he was not the one they sought, not due for hell . . . It's a mistake, it's all a mistake, no it's not a mistake I was the enemy who was the enemy what enemy? Oh please let the world turn right side up and let me lie where I should be lying up there, down there, where oh Jesus Christ Robert Christ help, help meeeeee . . .

"All right, Brian. I'm here. I'm putting everything right. I am. I'm putting everything right!" He heard the compassionate words come soaring out of the maelstrom, drowning the laughter. The enveloping blood went away. He felt his friend's hand, cool and gentle, and he clutched it, terrified lest it was another dream within a dream within a dream, oh Christ Robert don't leave me. . . .

Oh Jesus it's impossible! Look there! The ceiling's there where it should be and I'm here, I'm lying on the bed where I should be and the room's dim but soft where it should be, everything's clean, flowers, blinds drawn but flowers and the water properly in the vase and I'm right side up, I'm right side up. "Oh Christ, Robert . . ."

"Hello, chum," Robert Armstrong said gently.

"Oh Jesus Robert thank you thank you, I'm right side up oh thank you thank you . . ."

It was hard to talk and he felt weak, his strength gone, but it was glorious just to be here, out of the nightmare, his friend's face misted but real. And smoking, am I smoking? Oh yes. Yes I think I remember Robert left me a packet of cigarettes though those devils came and found them and took them away last week . . . thank God for smoke . . . When was it, last month, last week, when? I remember yes but Robert came back again and gave me a secret drag last month, was it last month? "Oh that tastes so good, so good and the peace, no nightmare, Robert, not seeing blood up there, the ceiling awash, not lying up there but down here not in hell oh thank you thank you . . ."

"I must go now."

"Oh Christ don't go they may come back no don't go sit and stay please stay. Look, we'll talk, yes, that's it, talk, you wanted to talk . . . don't leave. Please talk . . ."

"All right, old friend, then talk. I won't go while we talk. What do you want to tell me, eh? Certainly I'll stay while you talk. Tell me about Ning-tok and your father. Didn't you go back to see him?"

"Oh yes, I went back to see him once, yes, just before he died, my friends helped me, they helped me it only took a day, my friends helped me . . . that, that was so long ago. . . ."

"Did Ian go with you?"

"Ian? No it . . . was it Ian? I can't remember . . . Ian, the tai-pan? Someone went with me. Was it you, Robert? Ah, with me in Ning-tok? No it wasn't you or Ian it was John Chancellor from Ottawa. He hates the Soviets too, Robert, they're the great enemy. Even in school, and devil Chiang Kai-shek and his assassins Fong-fong and . . . and . . . Oh I'm so tired and so pleased to see you. . . ."

"Tell me about Fong-fong."

"Oh him. He was a bad man, Robert, him and all his spy group they were against us, the PRC, and pro-Chiang, I know; don't worry as soon as I read the . . . What are you asking me, eh? What?"

"It was that rotten Grant, eh?"

"Yes, yes it was and I almost fainted when he knew I was . . . I . . . where was I oh yes but I stopped Fong-fong at once. . . . Oh yes."

"Who did you tell?"

"Tsu-yan. I whispered it to Tsu-yan. He's back in Peking now . . . Oh he was very high up, though he didn't know who I really was, Robert, I was all very hush-hush. . . . Yes then it was in school, my father sent me after old Sh'in was murdered . . . thugs came and flogged him to death in the village square because he was one of us, one of the people, one of Chairman Mao's people, and when I was in Hong Kong I stayed with . . . with Uncle . . . I went to school . . . and he schooled me at night. . . . Can I sleep now?"

"Who was your uncle, Kar-shun, and where did he live?"

"I don't . . . don't remember. . . ."

"Then I must go. Next week I'll come ba—"

"No wait, Robert, wait, it was Wu Tsa-fing, on . . . on Fourth Alley in Aberdeen . . . number 8, lucky 8, fifth floor. There, I can remember! Don't go!"

"Very good, old chum. Very good. Were you at school long in Hong Kong?" Robert Armstrong kept his voice soft and kind and his heart went out to his friend that once was. He was astonished that Brian had broken so easily, so quickly.

The client's mind was open now, ready for him to take apart. He kept his eyes on the shell of the man who lay on the bed, encouraging him to remember so that the others who listened secretly could record all the facts and figures and names and places, the undercover truths and half-truths that were spilling out and would continue to spill out until Brian Kar-shun Kwok was a husk. And he knew that he would continue to probe, to cajole or threaten or become impatient or angry or pretend to want to leave or curse the jailer away who would interrupt, if necessary. With Crosse and Sinders monitoring the in-depth debriefing, he was just a tool like Brian Kwok had been a tool for others who had used his mind and talents for their own purposes. His job was just to be the medium, to keep the client talking, to bring him back when he rambled or became incoherent, to be his sole friend and his sole prop in this unreal universe, the one who brought the truth forth—like John Chancellor of Ottawa, who's he? Where does he fit? I don't know yet.

We'll get everything the client has now, he thought. We'll get all his contacts, his mentors, enemies and friends. Poor old Fong-fong and the lads. We'll never see them again—unless they turn up as agents of the other side. What a rotten filthy business this is, selling out your friends, working with the enemy who, everyone knows, wants you enslaved.

". . . in Vancouver it was wonderful, wonderful, Robert. There was a girl there who . . . Yes and I almost married her but Sensible Tok, Sensible was my 489, he lived . . . he lived on . . . oh yes it was Pedder Street in Chinatown and he owned the Hoho-tok Restaurant . . . yes Sensible Tok said I should honor Chairman Mao before any *quai loh*. . . . Oh how I loved her but he said it was the *quai lohs* who raped China for centuries. . . . You know that's true that's true. . . ."

"Yes that's true," he said, humoring him. "Sensible Tok was your only friend in Canada?"

"Oh no Robert I have dozens. . . ."

Armstrong listened, astounded by the wealth of information about the inner workings of the Canadian Mounted Police, and the extent of Chinese Communist infiltration throughout the Americas and Europe and particularly on the Western seaboard—Vancouver, Seattle, San Francisco, Los Angeles, San Diego—wherever a Chinese restaurant or shop or business existed there was the potential of pressure, of funds and most of all of knowledge. ". . . and the Wo Tuk on Gerrard Street in London's the Center where I . . . when I was . . . Oh my head aches I'm so thirsty. . . ."

Armstrong gave him the water that contained stimulant. When he or Crosse considered the moment correct, the client would be given the thirst-quenching, delicately flavored Chinese tea that was his favorite. This contained the soporific.

Then it was up to Crosse and Sinders what happened, whether it was more of the same, more of the Red Room or the end of the exercise and then, carefully, the gradual bringing back of the client to reality, with great care, so that no permanent damage was done.

It's up to them, he thought. Sinders was right to put on the pressure while we've time. The client knows too much. He's too well trained, and if we'd had to give him back without knowing what he knows, well that would have been irresponsible. We've got to keep ahead.

Armstrong lit two cigarettes and inhaled his own deeply. I'll give up smoking for Christmas. I can't now, not with all this horror. It was Brian Kwok's wailing screams so soon, barely twenty minutes after being put into the room for the second time that had shattered him. He had been watching through spyholes with Crosse and Sinders, watching the insanity of trying to reach the ceiling that was the floor that was the ceiling, astonished that someone so strong, so well trained as Brian Kwok would break so quickly. "It's impossible," he had muttered.

"He may be faking," Sinders said.

"No," Crosse had said. "No. It's real, for him. I know."

"I don't believe he'd break so easily."

"You will, Robert." And then when Brian Kwok had been carried out to be brought to this room, clean and nice and the Red Room had been mopped clean, Roger Crosse had said, "All right, Robert, try it, then you'll see."

"No, no thanks. It's like something out of *The Cabinet of Dr. Caligari*," he had muttered. "No thanks!"

"Please try it, just for a minute. It's an important experience for you. You may be caught by them, the other side, some day. You should be prepared. One minute might save your sanity. Test it, for your own safety."

So he had agreed. They had closed the door. The room was totally scarlet, small but everything tilted, the lines all wrong, angles all wrong, the floor meeting the ceiling in one corner, perspectives all wrong, no angles ordinary. The tilted ceiling far above was a sheer sheet of scarlet glass. Above the glass, water washed down to be recycled and come down again. Attached to this tilted glass ceiling surface were scarlet chairs and a table and pens and paper casually on the table, scarlet cushions on the chairs, making it seem the floor, a false door nearby, almost ajar . . .

Sudden blackness. Then the blinding strobe and the stunning impact of the scarlet. Blackness, scarlet, blackness, scarlet. Involuntarily he groped for the reality of the table and chairs and the floor and door and stumbled and fell, unable to get his bearings, water above, the glass vanished, just insane scarlet water on the floor above. Blackness and now voices pounding and again blood-colored hell. His stomach told him that he was upside down though his mind said it was just a trick and to close your eyes it's a trick it's a trick it's a trick . . .

After an eternity, when at length normal lights came on and the real door opened, he was lying on the real floor, retching. "You bastard," he had snarled at Crosse, barely able to talk. "You said a minute, you lying bastard!" His chest heaved and he fought to his feet, reeling, barely able to stand or to stop vomiting.

"Sorry, but it was only a minute, Robert," Crosse said.

"I don't believe it. . . ."

"Honestly, it was," Sinders said. "I timed it myself. Really! Extraordinary. Most effective."

Again Armstrong felt his chest heave at the thought of the water above and the table and chairs. He put those thoughts away and concentrated on Brian Kwok, feeling that he had let the client ramble enough and it was now time to bring him back. "You were saying? You passed over our dossiers to your friend Bucktooth Lo?"

"Well no, it wasn't . . . I'm tired, Robert, tired . . . what ar—"

"If you're tired I'll leave!" He got up and saw the client blanch. "Next month I'll se—"

"No . . . no . . . please don't go . . . they . . . no, don't go. Pleasssssssse!"

So he sat back, continuing the game, knowing it to be unfair, and that with the client so totally disoriented he could be made to sign anything, say anything at whim. "I'll stay while you talk, old friend. You were saying about Bucktooth Lo—the man in Princes Building? He was the go-between?"

"No . . . not . . . yes in a way . . . Dr. Meng . . . Dr. Meng would pick up any package that I left . . . Meng never knew that I . . . that it was me . . . the arrangements were by phone or by letter . . . he would take them to Lo who was paid . . . Bucktooth Lo was paid to give them to another man, I don't know who . . . I don't know . . ."

"Oh I think you do, Brian, I don't believe you want me to stay."

"Oh Christ I do . . . I swear it . . . Bucktooth . . . Bucktooth would know . . . or perhaps Ng, Vee Cee Ng, Photographer Ng, he's on our side, he's on our side Robert . . . Ask him, he'll know . . . he was with Tsu-yan importing thoriums . . ."

"What're thoriums?"

"Rare earths for . . . for atomics, for our atomics . . . oh yes we'll have our own A-bombs and H-bombs in a few months. . . ." Brian Kwok went into a paroxysm of laughter. "The first in a few weeks . . . our first explosion in just a few weeks now oh of course not perfect but the first and soon an H-bomb, dozens, Robert, soon we'll have ours to defend against those hegemonists who threaten to wipe us out, in a few weeks! Christ, Robert, think of that! Chairman Mao's done it, he has, he's done it . . . yes and then next year H-bombs and then Joe, yes we'll get back our lands, oh yes, with atomics we cancel out theirs . . . we will, Joe's going to help, Joe Yu's going to . . . Oh we'll stop them now, stop them we'll stop them and take our lands back." His hand reached out and he held Robert Armstrong's arm but his grip was weak. "Listen, we're at war already, us and the Soviets, Chung Li told me, he's my emergency . . . em, em contact . . . there's a war, a shooting war going on right now. In the north, divisions, not patrols near the Amur they're they're killing more Chinese and stealing more land but . . . but not for long." He lay back weakly and began to mumble, his mind wandering.

"Atomics? Next year? I don't believe it," Armstrong said, pretending to scoff, his mind blown as he listened to the continued outpouring that was giving chapter and verse and names. Christ, A-bombs in a few months? A few months? The world's been told that's ten years away. China with A-and H-bombs?

Carefully he let Brian Kwok peter out and then he said casually, "Who's Joe? Joe Yu?"

"Who?"

He saw Brian Kwok turn and stare at him, eyes strange, different, boring into him. Instantly he was on guard and he prepared. "Joe Yu," he said even more offhand.

"Who? I don't know any Joe Yu . . . no. . . . What, what . . . what am I doing here? What is this place? What's happening? Yu? Why . . . why should I know him? Who?"

"No reason," Armstrong said, calming him. "Here, here's some tea, you must be very thirsty, old chum."

"Oh yes . . . yes I am . . . where . . . yes . . . Christ what's happ . . . happening?"

Armstrong helped him drink. Then he gave him another cigarette and further calmed him. In a few moments Brian Kwok was again deeply asleep. Armstrong wiped his palms and his forehead, exhausted too.

The door opened. Sinders and Crosse came in.

"Very good, Robert," Sinders said excitedly, "very good indeed!"

"Yes," Crosse said. "I felt he was coming back too. Your timing was perfect."

Armstrong said nothing, feeling soiled.

"My God," Sinders chortled, "this client's gold. The minister will be delighted. Atomics in a few months and a shooting war going on right now! No wonder our Parliamentary Trade Commission made such marvelous progress! Excellent, Robert, just excellent!"

"You believe the client, sir?" Crosse said.

"Absolutely, don't you?"

"I believe he was telling what he knew. Whether it's fact, that's another matter. Joe Yu? Does Joe or Joseph Yu mean anything to you?" The others shook their heads. "John Chancellor?"

"No."

"Chung Li?"

Armstrong said, "There's a Chung Li who's a friend of Br—the client's, a car enthusiast—Shanghainese, big industrialist—could be him."

"Good. But Joe Yu, that triggered something in him. Could be important." Crosse glanced at Sinders. "Proceed?"

"Of course."

65

A roar of excitement went up from fifty thousand throats as the seven entries for the first race, jockeys up, came up the ramp out from under the stands to prance and skitter to the owners' paddock where trainers and owners waited. The owners and their wives were dressed in their very best, many of the wives laden and over-minked, Mai-ling Kwang and Dianne Chen among them, conscious of the envious stares of the multitude craning to see the horses—and them.

Either side of the soggy grass paddock and winner's circle, the packed mass of the crowds went down to the white sparkling rails and the perfectly kept turf of the encircling track. The winning post was opposite and beside it, on the other side of the track, was the huge totalizator that would carry the names of the horses and jockeys and odds, race by race. The totalizator was owned and operated by the Turf Club, as was the course. There were no legal bookmakers here or outside or any legal off-course betting places. This was the only legal form of betting in the Colony.

The sky was dark and forbidding. Earlier there had been a few sprinkles but now the air was clear.

Behind the paddock and winner's circle, on this level, were the jockeys' changing rooms and the offices of the officials—food concessions and the first banks of betting windows. Above them were the stands, four terraced tiers, each cantilevered floor with its own bank of betting windows. The first tier was for nonvoting members, next for voting members, and the two top floors set aside for the private boxes and radio room. Each box had its own private kitchen. Each of the ten annually elected stewards had a box and then there were some permanent ones: first his Excellency the governor, patron of the club; then the commander-in-chief; one each for Blacs and the Victoria. And last, Struan's. Struan's was in the best position, exactly opposite the winning post.

"Why's that, tai-pan?" Casey asked.

"Because Dirk Struan began the Turf Club, set the rules, brought out a famous racing expert, Sir Roger Blore, to be the first secretary of the club. He put up all the money for the first meeting, money for the stands, money to import the first batch of horses from India and helped persuade the first plenipotentiary, Sir William Longstaff, to deed the land to the Turf Club in perpetuity."

"Come now, tai-pan," Donald McBride, the track steward for this meeting, said jovially, "tell it as it happened, eh? You say Dirk 'helped persuade'? Didn't Dirk just 'order' Longstaff to do it?"

Dunross laughed with the others still seated at the table he had hosted, Casey, Hiro Toda and McBride, who had just arrived to visit. There was a bar and three round tables in the box, each seating twelve comfortably. "I prefer my version," he said. "In any event, Casey, the legend is that Dirk was voted this position by popular acclaim when the first stands were built."

"That's not true either, Casey," Willie Tusk called out from the next table. "Didn't old Tyler Brock demand the position as the right of Brock and Sons? Didn't he challenge Dirk to put up the position on a race, man to man, at the first meeting?"

"No, that's just a story."

"Did those two race, tai-pan?" Casey asked.

"They were going to. But the typhoon came too soon, so they say. In any event Culum refused to budge so here we are. This's ours while the course exists."

"And quite right too," McBride said, with his happy smile. "The Noble House deserves the best. Since the very first stewards were elected, Miss Casey, the tai-pan of Struan's has always been a steward. Always. By popular acclaim. Well, I must be off." He glanced at his watch, smiled at Dunross. With great formality he said, "Permission to start the first race, tai-pan?"

Dunross grinned back at him. "Permission granted." McBride hurried off.

Casey stared at Dunross. "They have to ask your permission to begin?"

"It's just a custom." Dunross shrugged. "I suppose it's a good idea for someone to say, 'All right, let's begin,' isn't it? I'm afraid that unlike Sir Geoffrey, the governors of Hong Kong in the past haven't been known for their punctuality. Besides, tradition is not a bad thing at all—gives you a sense of continuity, of belonging—and protection." He finished his coffee. "If you'll excuse me a moment, I must do a few things."

"Have fun!" She watched him go, liking him even more than last night. Just then Peter Marlowe came in and Dunross stopped a moment. "Oh hello, Peter, good to see you. How's Fleur?"

"Getting better, thank you, tai-pan."

"Come on in! Help yourself to a drink—I'll be back in a moment. Put your money on number five, Excellent Day, in the first! See you later."

"Thanks, tai-pan."

Casey beckoned to Peter Marlowe but he did not see her. His eyes had fixed on Grey who was with Julian Broadhurst out on the balcony, haranguing some of the others. She saw his face close and her heart leaped, remembering their hostility, so she called out, "Peter! Hi, come and sit down."

His eyes unglazed. "Oh! Oh hello," he said.

"Come sit down. Fleur's going to be fine."

"She certainly appreciated your going to see her."

"It was a pleasure. Are the kids okay?"

"Oh yes. You?"

"Fantastic. This is the only way to go to a race!" Lunch in the Struan box for the thirty-six guests had been a lavish buffet of hot Chinese foods or, if they preferred, hot steak-and-kidney pie and vegetables, with plates of smoked salmon, hors d'oeuvres and cold cuts, cheeses and pastries of all kinds and as a topper, a meringue sculpture of the Struan Building—all prepared in their own kitchen. Champagne, with the best red and white wines, liqueurs. "I'm gonna have to diet for fifty years."

"Not you. How goes it?"

She felt his probing eyes. "Fine. Why?"

"Nothing." He glanced off at Grey again, then turned his attention to the others.

"May I introduce Peter Marlowe? Hiro Toda of Toda Shipping Industries of Yokohama. Peter's a novelist-screenwriter from Hollywood." Then all at once his book rushed into her mind and Changi and three and a half years as a prisoner of war and she waited for the explosion. There was a hesitation between both men. Toda politely offered his business card and Peter Marlowe gave his in return, equally politely. He hesitated a moment then put out his hand. "How're you?"

The Japanese shook it. "This's an honor, Mr. Marlowe."

"Oh?"

"It's not often one meets a famous author."

"I'm not, no, not at all."

"You're too modest. I liked your book very much. Yes."

"You've read it?" Peter Marlowe stared at him. "Really?" He sat and looked at Toda, who was much shorter than he, lithe and well built, more handsome and well dressed in a blue suit, a camera hanging on his chair, his eyes equally level, the two men of an age. "Where did you find it?"

"In Tokyo. We have many English bookshops. Please excuse me, I read the paperback, not the hardback. There was no hardback on sale. Your novel was very illuminating."

"Oh?" Peter Marlowe took out his cigarettes and offered them. Toda took one.

Casey said, "Smoking's not good for you, you both know that!"

They smiled at her. "We'll give them up for Lent," Peter Marlowe said.

"Sure."

Peter Marlowe looked back at Toda. "You were army?"

"No, Mr. Marlowe. Navy. Destroyers. I was at the Battle of the Coral Sea in '42, then at Midway, sub-lieutenant, later at Guadalcanal. I was sunk twice but lucky. Yes, I was lucky, apparently more lucky than you."

"We're both alive, both in one piece, more or less."

"More or less, Mr. Marlowe. I agree. War is a curious way of life." Toda puffed his cigarette. "Sometime, if it would please you and not hurt, I would like to talk about your Changi, about its lessons and our wars. Please?"

"Sure."

"I'm here for a few days," Toda said. "At the Mandarin, back next week. A lunch, or dinner perhaps?"

"Thank you. I'll call. If not this time perhaps next. One day I'll be in Tokyo."

After a pause the Japanese said, "We need not discuss your Changi, if you wish. I would like to know you better. England and Japan have much in common. Now if you'll excuse me, I think I should place my bet." He bowed politely and walked off. Casey sipped her coffee.

"Was that very hard for you? Being polite?"

"Oh no, Casey. No, it wasn't, not at all. Now we're equal, he and I, any Japanese. The Japanese—and Koreans—I hated were the ones with bayonets and bullets when I had none." She saw him wipe the sweat off, noticing his twisted smile. "'Mahlu, I wasn't ready to meet one here."

"'Mahlu? What's that, Cantonese?"

"Malayan. It means 'ashamed.'" He smiled to himself. It was a contraction of puki mahlu. Mahlu ashamed, puki a Golden Gulley. Malays grant feelings to that part of a woman: hunger, sadness, kindness, rapaciousness, hesitancy, shame, anger—anything and everything.

"No need to be ashamed, Peter," she said, not understanding. "I'm astonished you'd talk to any of them after all that POW horror. Oh I really liked the book. Isn't it marvelous that he'd read it too?"

"Yes. That threw me."

"May I ask you one question?"

"What?"

"You said Changi was genesis. What did you mean?"

He sighed. "Changi changed everyone, changed values permanently. For instance, it gave you a dullness about death—we saw too much of it to have the same sort of meaning to outsiders, to normal people. We're a generation of dinosaurs, we the few who survived. I suppose anyone who goes to war, any war, sees life with different eyes if they end up in one piece."

"What do you see?"

"A lot of bull that's worshipped as the be-all and end-all of existence. So much of 'normal, civilized' life is bull that you can't imagine it. For us ex-Changi-ites—we're lucky, we're cleansed, we know what life is really all

about. What frightens you, doesn't frighten me, what frightens me, you'd
laugh at."

"Like what?"

He grinned at her. "That's enough about me and my karma. I've a hot
tip for th—" He stopped and stared off. "Good sweet Christ who's that?"

Casey laughed. "Riko Gresserhoff. She's Japanese."

"Which one's Mr. Gresserhoff?"

"She's a widow."

"Hallelujah!" They watched her go across the room, out onto the terrace.

"Don't you dare, Peter!"

His voice became Olympian. "I'm a writer! It's a matter of research?"

"Baloney!"

"You're right."

"Peter, they say all first novels are autobiographical. Who were you in
the book?"

"The hero of course."

"The King? The American trader?"

"Oh no. Not him. And that's quite enough of my past. Let's talk about
you. You sure you're all right?" His eyes held hers, willing the truth out of
her.

"What?"

"There was a rumor that you were in tears last night."

"Nonsense."

"Sure?"

She looked back at him, knowing he saw inside of her. "Of course. I'm
fine." A hesitation. "Sometime, sometime I might need a favor."

"Oh?" He frowned. "I'm in McBride's box, two down the hall. It's
quite okay to visit if you want." He glanced off at Riko. His pleasure
faded. Now she was talking to Robin Grey and Julian Broadhurst, the
Labour MPs. "Guess it's not my day," he muttered. "I'll be back later, got
to bet. See you, Casey."

"What's your hot tip?"

"Number seven, Winner's Delight."

Winner's Delight, an outsider, won handily by half a length over the
favorite, Excellent Day. Hugely pleased with herself, Casey joined the
line in front of the winner's pay window clutching her winning tickets,
well aware of the envious stares of others who walked along the corridor
outside the boxes. Agonized bettors were already putting down their
money at other windows for the second race that was the first leg of the
double quinella. To win a quinella they had to forecast the first and second runners in any order. The double quinella put the second race together with the fifth that was today's big race. The double quinella payout
would be huge, the odds against forecasting four horses immense. The
minimum bet was 5 HK. There was no maximum. "Why's that, Linc?"

she had asked just before the race, craning over the balcony watching the horses in the gate, all Hong Kong *yan* with their binoculars focused.

"Look at the tote." The electronic numbers were flashing and changing as money went onto different horses, narrowing the odds, to freeze just before the off. "Look at the total money invested on this race, Casey! It's better than three and a half million Hong Kong. That's almost a dollar for every man woman and child in Hong Kong and it's only the first race. This's gotta be the richest track in the world! These guys are gambling crazy."

A vast roar went up as the starters' gate opened. She had looked at him and smiled. "You okay?"

"Sure. You?"

"Oh yes."

Yes I am, she thought again, waiting her turn to collect her money. I'm a winner! She laughed out loud.

"Oh hello, Casey! Ah, you won too?"

"Oh! Oh hello, Quillan, yes I did." She moved out of her place back to Gornt, the others in the line all strangers to her. "I only had 10 on her but yes I won."

"The amount doesn't matter, it's the winning." Gornt smiled. "I like your hat."

"Thank you." Curious, she thought, both Quillan and Ian had mentioned it immediately. Damn Linc!

"It's very lucky to pick the first winner, first time at the track."

"Oh I didn't. It was a tip. Peter gave it to me. Peter Marlowe."

"Ah yes. Marlowe." She saw his eyes change slightly. "You're still on for tomorrow?"

"Oh. Oh yes. Is it weather permitting?"

"Even if it's raining. Lunch anyway."

"Great. The dock at ten sharp. Which's your box?" She noticed an instant change which he tried to hide.

"I don't have one. I'm not a steward. Yet. I'm a fairly permanent guest at the Blacs box and from time to time I borrow the whole place for a party. It's down the corridor. Would you care to come by? Blacs is an excellent bank an—"

"Ah but not as good as the Vic," Johnjohn called out good-naturedly as he passed. "Don't believe a word he says, Casey. Congratulations! Good joss to get the first. See you both later."

Casey watched him thoughtfully. Then she said, "What about all the bank runs, Quillan? No one seems to care—it's as though they're not happening, the stock market's not crashing, and there's no pending doom."

Gornt laughed, conscious of the ears that were tuned to their conversation. "Today is race day, a rarity, and tomorrow will take care of tomorrow. Joss! The stock market opens 10:00 A.M. Monday and next week will decide a lot of fates. Meanwhile every Chinese who could get his money out, has it in his fist, here today. Casey, it's your turn."

She collected her money. 15 to one. 150 HK. "Hallelujah!" Gornt collected a vast bundle of red notes, 15,000. "Hey, fantastic!"

"Worst race I've ever seen," a sour American voice said. "Hell, it was fantastic they didn't bust the jockey and disallow the win."

"Oh hello, Mr. Biltzmann, Mr. Pugmire." Casey remembered them from the night of the fire. "Bust who?"

Biltzmann stood in the place line. "Stateside there'd be an objection a mile wide. Coming into the straight out of the last bend you could see Excellent Day's jockey pull the bejesus out of her. It was a fix—he wasn't trying."

Those in the know, the very few, smiled to themselves. The whisper in the jockeys' rooms and trainers' rooms had been that Excellent Day wasn't to win but Winner's Delight would.

"Come now, Mr. Biltzmann," Dunross said. Unnoticed, he'd heard the exchange as he was passing and had stopped. "If the jockey wasn't trying, or if there was any tampering, the stewards would be on to it at once."

"Maybe it's okay for amateurs, Ian, and this little track but on any professional track at home, Excellent Day's jockey'd be banned for the rest of his life. I had my glasses on him all the time." Biltzmann sourly collected his place winnings and stomped off.

Dunross said quietly, "Pug, did you see the jockey do anything untoward? I didn't watch the race myself."

"No, no I didn't."

"Anyone?" Those nearby shook their heads.

"Seemed all right to me," someone said. "Nothing out of the ordinary."

"None of the stewards queried anything." Then Dunross noticed the large roll of notes in Gornt's hand. He looked up at him. "Quillan?"

"No. But I must tell you frankly I find that berk's manner appalling. I hardly think he'd be a proper addition to the Turf Club." Just then he saw Robin Grey go past to place a bet and smiled at a sudden thought. "Excuse me, will you?" He nodded politely and walked off. Casey saw Dunross watching the roll of notes that Gornt put into a pocket and was inwardly aghast at the momentary look on his face.

"Could Biltzmann . . . could he've been correct?" she asked nervously.

"Of course." Dunross put his full attention on her. "Fixing happens everywhere. That's really not the point. There's been no objection from any of the stewards or jockeys or trainers." His eyes were slate gray. The small vein in his forehead was pulsating. "That's not the real point at issue." No, he was thinking. It's a matter of bloody manners. Even so, calm yourself. You have to be very cool and very calm and very collected this weekend.

All day he had had nothing but trouble. The only bright moment had been Riko Anjin Gresserhoff. But then AMG's last letter had once more filled him with gloom. It was still in his pocket and it had told him that if by chance he had not destroyed the original files, to heat a dozen specified pages that were spread throughout, the secret information written in invisible ink on these pages to be passed privately to the prime minister or the current head of MI-6, Edward Sinders, personally—and a copy given to Riko Anjin in a sealed envelope.

If I do that then I have to admit the files I gave him were false, he thought, weary of AMG, espionage and his instructions. Goddamnit, Murtagh doesn't arrive till later, Sir Geoffrey can't call London till 4:00 P.M. about Tiptop and Brian Kwok and, Christ Jesus, now some rude bastard calls us all amateurs . . . which we are. I'll bet a hundred to a bent hatpin Quillan knew before the race.

At a sudden thought he said casually, "How did you pick the winner, Casey? With the proverbial pin?"

"Peter gave it to me. Peter Marlowe." Her face changed. "Oh! Do you think he heard it was fixed?"

"If I thought that for a moment, the race would have been set aside. There's nothing I can do now. Biltzmann . . ." Suddenly he gasped as the idea hit him in all its glory.

"What's the matter?"

Dunross took her arm and led her aside. "To get your drop dead money are you prepared to gamble?" he asked softly.

"Sure, sure, Ian, if it's legal. But gamble what?" she asked, her innate caution uppermost.

"Everything you've got in the bank, your house in Laurel Canyon, your stock in Par-Con against 2 to 4 million within thirty days. How about it?"

Her heart was thumping, his obvious excitement sweeping her. "Okay," she said and then wished she hadn't said it, her stomach fluttering. "Jesus!"

"Good. Stay here a second. I'll go and find Bartlett."

"Wait! Is he part of this? What is this, Ian?"

He beamed. "A modest business opportunity. Yes, Bartlett's essential. Does that make you change your mind?"

"No," she told him uneasily, "but I said I wanted to get my . . . my stake outside of Par-Con."

"I haven't forgotten. Wait here." Dunross hurried back into his box, found Bartlett and brought him back, led the way down the bustling corridor to the Struan kitchen, greeting people here and there. The kitchen was small, busy and sparkling. The staff paid no attention to them. A door opened into a tiny private room, carefully soundproofed. Four chairs, a table and phone. "My father had this constructed during his tenure—lots of business is done at the races. Sit down please. Now"—he looked at Bartlett—"I've a business proposal for you, for you and Casey as individuals, outside of our Par-Con deal, nothing to do with the Par-Con–Struan proposal. Are you interested?"

"Sure. This a Hong Kong scam?"

"Do you mind?" Dunross beamed. "It's an honest-to-God Hong Kong business proposal."

"Okay, let's have it."

"Before I lay it out there are ground rules: It's my game, you two're bystanders but you're in for 49 percent of the profits, to be shared equally between you two. Okay?"

"What's the full game plan, Ian?" Bartlett asked cautiously.

"Next: You put up $2 million U.S. by Monday 9:00 A.M. into a Swiss bank of my choosing."

Bartlett's eyes narrowed. "Against what?"

"Against 49 percent of the profit."

"What profit?"

"You put up $2 million for Gornt, no paper, no chop, no nothing except against potential profit."

Bartlett grinned. "How long have you known about that?"

Dunross smiled back. "I told you, there're no secrets here. Are you in?" Dunross saw Bartlett glance at Casey and he held his breath.

"Casey, you know what this's all about?"

"No, Linc." Casey turned to Dunross. "What *is* the scam, Ian?"

"First I want to know if I get the 2 million advance free and clear—*if* you go for this scheme."

"What's the profit potential?" Casey asked.

"$4 to $12 million. Tax free."

Casey blanched. "Tax free?"

"Free of any Hong Kong taxes and we can help you avoid States taxes if you want."

"What's . . . what's the payout period?" Bartlett asked.

"The profit'll be set in thirty days. The payout will take five to six months."

"The $4 to $12 million's the total, or our share only?"

"Your share."

"That's a lot of profit for something completely, twenty-four-carat legal."

There was a great silence. Dunross waited, willing them onward.

"$2 million cash?" Bartlett said. "No security, no nothing?"

"No. But after I've laid it out you can put up or pass."

"What's Gornt to do with this?"

"Absolutely nothing. This venture has nothing to do with Gornt, Rothwell-Gornt, Par-Con, your interest in them or us or the Par-Con deal. This is totally outside, whatever happens—my word on that. And my word before God, that I'll never tell him you've put up this $2 million, that you two are my partners and in for a piece—or, by the way, that I know about the three of you selling me short." He smiled. "That was a very good idea by the way."

"The deal's swung by my $2 million?"

"No. Greased. I haven't $2 million U.S. cash as you know, otherwise you wouldn't be invited in."

"Why us, Ian? You could raise 2 mill from one of your friends here, easy, if it's so good."

"Yes. But I choose to sweeten the lure to you two. By the way, you are held to Tuesday at midnight." Dunross said it flat. Then his voice changed and the others felt the glee. "But with this—this business venture —I can dramatize how much superior we are to Rothwell-Gornt, how much more exciting it'll be being associated with us than him. You're a gambler, so am I. Raider Bartlett they call you and I'm tai-pan of the Noble House. You gambled a paltry $2 million with Gornt, with no chop, why not with me?"

Bartlett glanced at Casey. She gave him neither a yes or a no though he knew the lure had her in spades.

"Since you're setting the rules, Ian, answer me this: I put up the $2 million. Why should we share equally, Casey and I?"

"I remember what you said over dinner about drop dead money. You've got yours, she hasn't. This could be a device to get her hers."

"Why're you so concerned over Casey? You trying to divide and rule?"

"If that's possible then you shouldn't be in a very special partnership and business relationship. She's your right arm, you told me. She's clearly very important to you and to Par-Con so she's entitled to share."

"What does she risk?"

"She'll put up her house, her savings, her Par-Con stock—that's everything she has—alongside yours. She'll sign it all over for a half share. Right?"

Casey nodded, numb. "Sure."

Sharply Bartlett glanced at Casey. "I thought you said you knew nothing about this?"

She looked at him. "Couple of minutes ago, Ian asked if I'd gamble my all to get some drop dead money, big money." She gulped and added, "I said okay and already wish I hadn't."

Bartlett thought a moment. "Casey, blunt: You want in or you want out?"

"In."

"Okay." Then Bartlett beamed. "Okay, tai-pan, now who do we have to kill?"

Nine Carat Chu, who was a sometime gold coolie for the Victoria Bank and also the father of two sons and two daughters—Lily Su who was Havergill's occasional friend and Wisteria who was John Chen's mistress, whose joss was to be trampled to death outside the Ho-Pak at Aberdeen— waited his turn at the betting window.

"Yes, old man?" the impatient teller said.

He pulled out a roll of money. It was all the money he had and all the money he could borrow, leaving only enough for three inhalations of the White Powder that he would need to see him through his night shift tonight. "The double quinella, by all the gods! Eight and five in the second race, seven and one in the fifth."

The teller methodically counted out the crumpled bills. 728 HK. He pressed the buttons of those numbers and checked the first ticket. It was correct: five and eight—second race; seven and one—fifth race. Carefully he counted 145 tickets, each of 5 HK, the minimum bet, and gave them to him with 3 HK change. "Hurry up, by all the gods," the next in line called out. "Are your fingers in your Black Hole?"

"Be patient!" the old man muttered, feeling faint, "this is serious business!" Carefully he checked his tickets. The first, three random ones and the last were correct, and the number of tickets correct, so he gave up his place and pushed his way out of the press into the air. Once in the air he felt a little better, still nauseated but better. He had walked all the way from his night shift of work at the construction site of the new high rise up above Kotewall Road in Mid Levels to save the fare.

Again he checked his tickets. Eight and five in this race and seven and one in the fifth, the big race. Good, he thought, putting them carefully into his pocket. I've done the best I can. Now it is up to the gods.

His chest was hurting him very much so he fought through the crowd to the toilet and there he lit a match and inhaled the smoke from the bubbling White Powder. In time he felt better and went outside again. The second race was already on. Beside himself with anxiety he pushed and shoved his way to the rails, careless of the curses that followed him. The horses were rounding the far bend, galloping toward him into the last straight for the winning post, now past in a thundering blur as he strained his rheumy old eyes to find his numbers.

"Who's leading?" he gasped but no one paid any attention to him, just shouted their own choice on to victory in a growing seething roar that was all possessing, then vanished as the winner won.

"Who won?" Nine Carat Chu gasped, his head exploding.

"Who cares!" someone said with a stream of curses. "It wasn't mine! All gods piss on that jockey forever!"

"I can't read the tote, who won?"

"It was a photo finish, old fool, can't you see! There were three horses bunched together. Fornicate all photo finishes! We must wait."

"But the numbers. . . . what are the numbers?"

"Five and eight and four, Lucky Court, my horse! Come on you son of a whore's left tit! Four and eight for the quinella by all the gods!"

They waited. And waited. The old man thought he would faint so he put his mind on to better things, like his conversation with Noble House Chen this morning. Three times he had called and each time a servant had answered and hung up. It was only when he had said "Werewolf" that Noble House Chen himself had come to the phone.

"Please excuse me for mentioning the terrible slayers of your son," he had said. "It wasn't me, Honored Sir, oh no. I am just the father of your late honorable son's mistress, Wisteria Su, to whom he has written his undying love in the letter that was printed in all the newspapers."

"Eh? Liar! All lies. Do you think I'm a fool to be squeezed by any dog-meat caller? Who are you?"

"My name is Hsi-men Su," he had said, the lie coming easily. "There are two more letters, Honorable Chen. I thought you might wish to have them back even though they're all we have from my poor dead daughter and your poor dead son who I considered like my own son over all the months that he an—"

"More lies! The mealy-mouthed strumpet never had any letters from my son! Our deadly police put forgers in jail, oh yes! Am I a peasant-headed monkey from the Outer Provinces? Beware! Now I suppose you'll produce an infant that you'll claim my son sired? Eh? *Eh?*"

Nine Carat Chu almost dropped the phone. He had discussed and arranged that very ploy with his wife and his sons and Lily. It had been easy to find a relation who would lend a babe in arms for a fee.

"Eh," he spluttered in shock, "am I a liar? Me who fairly, for modest cash, gave his only virgin daughter to be your son's whore and *only love.*" He used the English words carefully, his daughter Lily having coached him for hours so that he could say it properly. "By all the gods we've protected your great name at no charge! When we went to claim my poor daughter's body we did not tell the deadly police who desire, *oh ko,* yes, who desire to find out who the writer was to trap the Werewolves! All gods curse those evil sons of whores! Haven't four Chinese papers already offered rewards for the name of the writer, *heya?* It is only fair I offer the letters to you before collecting the newspapers' reward, *heya?*"

Patiently he had listened to the stream of invective that had begun the negotiation. Several times both sides had pretended they were going to put the phone down, but neither side broke off the bargaining. At length it was left that if a photocopy of one of the other letters was sent to Noble House Chen as proof that it and the others were no forgery, then "it might be, Honorable Su, the other letters—and this one—might be worth a very modest amount of Fragrant Grease."

Nine Carat Chu chortled to himself now. Oh yes, he thought contentedly, Noble House Chen will pay handsomely, particularly when he reads the parts about himself. Oh if those were printed surely it would hold him up to ridicule before all Hong Kong and take his face away forever. Now, how much should I settle f—

A sudden roar surrounded him and he almost fell over. His heart began pounding, his breath short. He held on to the rails and peered at the distant tote. "Who . . . what are the numbers?" he asked, then screeched over the noise and tugged at his neighbors. "The numbers, tell me the numbers!"

"The winner's eight, Buccaneer, the gelding of the Noble House. *Ayeeyah,* can't you see the tai-pan leading him into the winner's circle now? Buccaneer's paying 7 to 1."

"The second? Who was the second horse?"

"Number five, Winsome Lady, 3 to 1 for a place. . . . What's wrong, old man, have you a palsy?"

"No . . . no . . ." Weakly Nine Carat Chu groped away. At length he found a small empty patch of concrete and spread his racing form on the wet concrete and sat down, his head on his knees and arms, his mind sweeping him into the ecstasy of winning the first leg. Oh oh oh! And nothing to do now but wait, and if the time of waiting is too long I will use one more of the White Powders, yes, and that will leave me the last to see me through tonight's work. Now, all gods concentrate! The first leg was won by my own shrewdness. Please concentrate on the fifth! Seven and one! All gods concentrate. . . .

Over by the winner's circle the stewards and owners and officials clustered. Dunross had intercepted his horse and congratulated the jockey. Buccaneer had run a fine race and now as he led the gelding into the winner's circle amid another burst of cheering and congratulations he kept his exuberance deliberately open. He wanted to let the world see his pleasure and confidence, very aware that winning this race was an immense omen, over and above the fact of winning. The omen would be doubled and tripled if he won with Noble Star. Two horses in the double quinella would absolutely set Gornt and his allies back on their heels. And if Murtagh works his magic or if Tiptop keeps his bargain to swap the money for Brian Kwok or if Tightfist or Lando or Four Fingers . . .

"Hey, Mr. Dunross, sir, congratulations!"

Dunross glanced at the crowd on the rails. "Oh hello, Mr. Choy," he said, recognizing Four Finger Wu's Seventh Son and supposed nephew. He went closer and shook hands. "Did you have the winner?"

"Yes sir, sure, I'm with the Noble House all the way! We're on the double quinella, my uncle and me. We just won the first leg five and eight, and we've seven and eight in the fifth. He's got 10,000 riding, me, my whole week's salary!"

"Then let's hope we win, Mr. Choy."

"You can say that again, tai-pan," the young man said with his easy American familiarity.

Dunross smiled and walked over to Travkin. "Are you sure Johnny Moore can't ride Noble Star? I don't want Tom Wong."

"I told you, tai-pan, Johnny's sicker than a drunken cossack."

"I need the win. Noble Star is to win."

Travkin saw Dunross look at Buccaneer speculatively. "No, tai-pan, please don't ride Noble Star. The going's bad, very bad and very dangerous and it'll get worse as they hack up the turf. *Kristos!* I suppose that'll only make you want to ride her more."

"My future could ride on that race—and the face of the Noble House."

"I know." Angrily the gnarled old Russian slapped the switch he carried perpetually against his ancient jodhpurs, shining with use. "And I know you're better than all the other jockeys but that turf's danger—"

"I don't trust anyone in this, Alexi. I can't afford any mistake." Dunross dropped his voice. "Was the first race fixed?"

Travkin stared back levelly. "They weren't doped, tai-pan. Not to my knowledge. The police doctor has put the fear of God into those who might be tempted."

"Good. But was it fixed?"

"It wasn't my race, tai-pan. I'm only interested in my horses and my races. I didn't watch that race."

"That's convenient, Alexi. Seems that none of the other trainers did either."

"Listen, tai-pan. I have a jockey for you. Me. I'll ride Noble Star."

Dunross's eyes narrowed. He glanced at the sky. It was darker than before. There'll be rain soon, he thought and there's much to do before the rain. Me or Alexi? Alexi's legs are good, his hands the best, his experience immense. But he thinks more of the horse than of winning. "I'll consider it," he said. "After the fourth race I'll decide."

"I'll win," the older man said, desperate for the chance to extricate himself from his agreement with Suslev. "I'll win even if I have to kill Noble Star."

"No need to do that, Alexi. I'm rather fond of that horse."

"Tai-pan, listen, perhaps a favor? I've a problem. Can I see you tonight or Sunday, Sunday or Monday late, say at Sinclair Towers?"

"Why there?"

"We made our deal there, I'd like to talk there. But if it's not all right the day after."

"You're going to leave us?"

"Oh no, no it's not that. If you've time. Please."

"All right but it can't be tonight, or Sunday or Monday, I'm going to Taipei. I could see you Tuesday at 10:00 P.M. How's that?"

"Fine, Tuesday's fine yes, thank you."

"I'll be down after the next race."

Alexi watched the tai-pan walk for the elevators. He was near tears, an overwhelming affection for Dunross possessing him.

His eyes went to Suslev who was in the general stands nearby. Trying to appear casual he held up the prearranged number of fingers: one for tonight, two for Sunday, three Monday, four Tuesday. His eyes were very good and he saw Suslev acknowledge the signal. *Matyeryebyets,* he thought. Betrayer of Mother Russia and all us Russians, you and all your KGB brethren! I curse you in the name of God, for me and *all* Russians if the truth be known.

Never mind that! I'm going to ride Noble Star, he told himself grimly, one way or another.

Dunross got into the elevator amid more congratulations and much envy. At the top floor Gavallan and Jacques were waiting for him. "Is everything ready?" he asked.

"Yes," Gavallan replied. "Gornt's there, and the others you wanted. What's cooking?"

"Come along and you'll see. By the way, Andrew, I'm switching Jacques and David MacStruan. Jacques will take over Canada for a year, David—"

Jacques's face lit up. "Oh thank you tai-pan. Yes, thanks very much. I'll make Canada very profitable, I promise."

"What about the changeover?" Gavallan asked. "Do you want Jacques to go there first or will David come here?"

"He arrives Monday. Jacques, you hand over everything to David, then next week you can both go back together for a couple of weeks. You go via France, eh? Pick up Susanne and Avril, she should be well enough by then. There's nothing urgent in Canada at the moment—it's more urgent here."

"Oh yes, *ma foi!* Yes, yes thank you, tai-pan."

Gavallan said thoughtfully, "It'll be good to see old David." He liked David MacStruan very much but he was still wondering why the change, and did this mean that Jacques was out of the running to inherit the tai-pan's mantle and David in and his own position changed, changing or threatened—if there was anything left to inherit after Monday. And what about Kathy?

Joss, he told himself. What is to be will be. Oh goddamn everything!

"You two go on ahead," Dunross said. "I'll get Phillip." He turned into the Chen box. By ancient custom the compradore of the Noble House was automatically a steward. Perhaps for the last year, Dunross thought grimly. If Phillip doesn't deliver help in the form of Four Finger Wu, Lando Mata, Tightfist or something tangible by Sunday at midnight he's blackballed.

"Hello, Phillip," he said, his voice friendly, greeting the other guests in the packed box. "You ready?"

"Oh yes, yes, tai-pan." Phillip Chen was looking older. "Congratulations on the win."

"Yes, tai-pan, a marvelous omen—we're all praying for the fifth!" Dianne Chen called out, trying equally hard to hide her apprehension, Kevin beside her, echoing her.

"Thank you," Dunross said, sure that Phillip Chen had told her about their meeting. She wore a hat with bird of paradise feathers, and too many jewels.

"Champagne, tai-pan?"

"No thanks, later perhaps. Sorry, Dianne, have to borrow Phillip for a moment or two. Won't be long."

Outside in the corridor he stopped a moment. "Any luck, Phillip?"

"I've . . . I've talked to all the . . . all of them. They're meeting tomorrow morning."

"Where? Macao?"

"No, here." Phillip Chen dropped his voice even more. "I'm sorry about . . . about all the mess my son's caused . . . yes, very sorry," he said, meaning it.

"I accept your apology. If it hadn't been for your carelessness and treachery, we'd never have become that vulnerable. Christ Jesus, if Gornt gets our balance sheets for the last few years and our interlocking corporate structures, we're up the creek without a paddle."

"I . . . I had a thought, tai-pan, how to extract our—how to extract the House. After the races, could I . . . a little time, please?"

"You're coming for drinks tonight? With Dianne?"

"Yes, if . . . yes please. May I bring Kevin?"

Dunross smiled fleetingly to himself. The heir apparent, officially and so soon. Karma. "Yes. Come along."

"What's this all about, tai-pan?"

"You'll see. Please say nothing, do nothing, just accept—with great confidence—that you're part of the package, and when I leave follow me, spread the word and good cheer. If we fail, the House of Chen fails first, come hell, high water or typhoon!" He turned into the McBride box. There were more immediate congratulations and many said it was great joss.

"Good God, tai-pan," McBride said, "if Noble Star wins the fifth, wouldn't it be marvelous!"

"Pilot Fish will beat Noble Star," Gornt said confidently. He was at the bar with Jason Plumm getting a drink. "10,000 says he'll finish ahead of your filly."

"Taken," Dunross said at once. There were cheers and hoots of derision from the thirty-odd guests and once more Bartlett and Casey, who had by arrangement with Dunross ostensibly just wandered in a few minutes ago to visit Peter Marlowe, were inwardly staggered at the festive air and Dunross's high-flying confidence.

"How're you doing, Dunstan?" Dunross asked. He paid Casey and Bartlett no attention, concentrating on the big florid man who was more florid than usual, a double brandy in his hand.

"Very well, thank you, Ian. Got the first, and Buccaneer—made a bundle on Buccaneer, but blew my damned quinella. Lucky Court let me down."

The room was the same size as the Struan box but not as well decorated, though equally well filled with many of the Hong Kong elite, some invited here a moment ago by Gavallan and McBride for Dunross. Lando Mata, Holdbrook—Struan's in-house stockbroker—Sir Luis Basilio—head of the stock exchange—Johnjohn, Havergill, Southerby—chairman of Blacs— Richard Kwang, Pugmire, Biltzmann, Sir Dunstan Barre, young Martin Haply of the *China Guardian*. And Gornt. Dunross looked at him. "Did you get the winner of the last race too?"

"No. I didn't fancy any runner. What's all this about, Ian?" Gornt said, and everyone's attention soared. "You want to make an announcement?"

"Yes, as a courtesy I thought you should know, along with other VIPs." Dunross turned to Pugmire. "Pug, the Noble House is formally contesting the American Superfoods takeover of your H.K. General Stores."

There was a vast silence and everyone stared at him. Pugmire had gone white. "What?"

"We're offering $5 a share more than Superfoods, we'll further improve their bid by making it 30 percent cash and 70 percent stock, everything done within thirty days!"

"You've gone mad," Pugmire burst out. Didn't I sound everyone out first, he wanted to shout, including you? Didn't you and everyone approve or at least not disapprove? Isn't that the way it's done here for God's sake— private chats at the Club, here at the races, over a private dinner or wherever? "You can't do that," he muttered.

"I already have," Dunross said.

Gornt said harshly, "All you've done, Ian, is to make an announcement. How are you going to pay? In thirty or three hundred days."

Dunross just looked at him. "The bid's public. We complete in thirty days. Pug, you'll get the official papers by 9:30 A.M. Monday, with a cash down payment to cement the tender."

Momentarily he was drowned out as others began talking, asking questions, everyone immediately concerned how this astonishing development would affect them personally. No one had ever contested a prearranged takeover before. Johnjohn and Havergill were furious that this had been done without consultation, and the other banker, Southerby of Blacs, who was merchant-banking the Superfoods takeover, was equally upset that he had been caught off balance. But all the bankers, even Richard Kwang, were counting possibilities, for if the stock market was normal and Struan's stock at its normal level, the Struan bid could be very good for both sides. Everyone knew that Struan's management could revitalize the rich but stagnant *hong*, and the acquisition would strengthen the Noble House immeasurably, put their end-of-year gross up at least 20 percent and of course increase their dividends. On top of all that, the takeover would keep all the profits in Hong Kong, and not have them trickle away to an outsider. Particularly Biltzmann.

Oh my God, Barre was thinking with vast admiration and not a little envy, for Ian to make the tender here, in public, on a Saturday, with never the breath of a rumor that he was contemplating the unthinkable, with nothing to give you an inkling so that you could have bought in quietly last week at bottom to make a fortune with one phone call, was brilliant. Of course Pug's General Stores shares will soar first thing on Monday. But how in the hell did Ian and Havergill keep it quiet? Christ I could've made a bundle if I'd known, perhaps I still can! The rumors about the Victoria not supporting Struan's is obviously a lot of cobblers. . . .

Wait a minute, Sir Luis Basilio was thinking, didn't we buy a huge block of General Stores last week for a nominee buyer? Good God, has the tai-pan outsmarted all of us? But Madonna, wait a minute, what about the run on his stock, what about the market crashing, what about the cash he'll have to put up to fix the tender, what about . . .

Even Gornt was counting, his mind flooded with fury that he had not thought of the ploy first. He knew the bid was good, perfect in fact, that he could not top it, not at the moment. But then, Ian can't complete. There's no wa—

"Can we go to press on this, tai-pan?" Martin Haply's incisive Canadian voice cut through the excited uproar.

"Certainly, Mr. Haply."

"May I ask a few questions?"

"It depends what they are," Dunross said easily. Looking at the penetrating brown eyes, he was grimly amused. We could use a right rotten young bastard in the family—if he could be trusted with Adryon. "What had you in mind?"

"This's the first time a takeover's ever been contested. May I ask why you're doing it at this time?"

"Struan's have always been innovative. As to timing, we considered it perfect."

"Do you consider this Sat—"

Biltzmann interrupted harshly, "We have a deal. It's set. Dickie?" He whirled on Pugmire. "Eh?"

"It was all set, Mr. Biltzmann," Dunross said crisply. "But we're contesting your tender, just as it's done in the States, according to American rules. I presume you don't mind a contest? Of course we are amateurs here but we enjoy trying to learn from our peers. Until the stockholders' meeting nothing's final, that's the law isn't it?"

"Yes, but . . . but it was set!" The tall gray-haired man turned to Pugmire, hardly able to speak he was so angry. "You said it was all agreed."

"Well, the directors had agreed," Pugmire said uneasily, conscious of everyone listening, particularly Haply, one half of him ecstatic with the vastly improved offer, the other furious that he, too, had had no advance warning so he could have bought in heavily. "But, er, but of course it has to be ratified by the stockholders at the Friday meeting. We had no idea there'd be a . . . Er, Ian, er, Chuck, don't you think this is hardly the place to dis—"

"I agree," the tai-pan said. "But at the moment there's little to discuss. The offer's made. By the way, Pug, your own deal stands, except that it's extended from five to seven years, with a seat on Struan's board for the same period."

Pugmire's mouth dropped open. "That's part of the tender?"

"We'd need your expertise, of course," Dunross said airily, and everyone knew Pugmire was hooked and landed. "The rest of the package as negotiated by you and Superfoods stands. The papers will be on your desk by 9:30. Perhaps you'll put our tender to your stockholders on Friday." He went over to Biltzmann and put out his hand. "Good luck. I presume you'll be coming back with a counteroffer at once."

"Well, er, I have to check with head office, Mr., er, tai-pan." Biltzmann was flushed and angry. "We . . . we put our best foot forward and . . . That's a mighty fine offer you made. Yes. But with the run on your stock, the run on the banks and the market going down, that's going to be kinda hard to close, isn't it?"

"Not at all, Mr. Biltzmann," Dunross said, gambling everything that Bartlett would not renege on the promise of cash, that he would close with Par-Con, extricate himself from Gornt and put his stock back into its rightful place by next weekend. "We can close with no trouble at all."

Biltzmann's voice sharpened. "Dickie, I think you'd better consider our bid carefully. It's good till Tuesday," he said, confident that by Tuesday Struan's would be in a shambles. "Now I'll make me a bet on the next race." He stalked out. Tension in the box went up several decibels.

Everyone began talking but Haply called out, "Tai-pan, may I ask a question?"

Again attention zeroed. "What is it?"

"I understand it's customary in takeovers for there to be a down payment, in cash, a measure of good faith. May I ask how much Struan's is putting up?"

Everyone waited breathlessly, watching Dunross. He held the pause as his eyes raked the faces, enjoying the excitement, knowing everyone wanted him humbled, almost everyone, except . . . except who? Casey for one, even though she's in the know. Bartlett? I don't know, not for certain. Claudia? Oh yes, Claudia was staring at him, white-faced. Donald McBride, Gavallan, even Jacques.

His eyes stopped on Martin Haply. "Perhaps Mr. Pugmire would prefer to have that detail in private," he said, leading them on. "Eh, Pug?"

Gornt interrupted Pugmire and said, as a challenge, "Ian, since you've decided to be unorthodox, why not make it all public? How much you put down measures the value of your tender. Doesn't it?"

"No. Not really," Dunross said. He heard the distant muted roar of the off for the third race and was sure, watching the faces, that no one heard it except him. "Oh, very well," he said, matter-of-fact. "Pug, how about $2 million, U.S., with the papers at 9:30 Monday? In good faith."

A gasp went through the room. Havergill, Johnjohn, Southerby, Gornt, were aghast. Phillip Chen almost fainted. Involuntarily Havergill began, "Ian, don't you think we, er, th—"

Dunross wheeled on him. "Oh, don't you consider it enough, Paul?"

"Oh yes, yes of course, more than enough, but, er . . ." Havergill's words trailed off under Dunross's gaze.

"Oh for a moment . . ." Dunross stopped, pretending to have a sudden thought, "Oh, you needn't worry, Paul, I haven't committed you without your approval of course. I have alternate financing for this deal, external financing," he continued with his easy charm. "As you know, Japanese banks and many others are anxious to expand into Asia. I thought it better —to keep everything secret and prevent the usual leaks—to finance this externally until I was ready to announce. Fortunately the Noble House has friends all over the world! See you all later!"

He turned and left. Phillip Chen followed. Martin Haply started for the phone and then everyone was talking and saying I don't believe it, Christ if Ian's got that sort of external funds . . .

In the hubbub Havergill asked Johnjohn, "Which Japanese bank?"

"I wish I knew. If Ian's got finance for this . . . my God, $2 million U.S.'s twice as much as he needed to offer."

Southerby, who was alongside them, wiped his palms. "If Ian pulls this off it'll be worth $10 million U.S. the first year at least." He smiled sardonically. "Well, Paul, now it looks as though we're both out of this particular pie."

"Yes, yes it does, but I just don't see how Ian could . . . and to keep it so quiet!"

Southerby bent closer. "Meanwhile," he asked softly, "more important, what about Tiptop?"

"Nothing, nothing yet. He hasn't returned my calls, or Johnjohn's." Havergill's eyes fell on Gornt who was now talking privately with Plumm. He turned his back on him. "What will Quillan do now?"

"Buy first thing Monday morning. He has to. Has to now, too dangerous to hold on," Southerby said.

"I agree," Sir Luis Basilio added, joining them. "If Ian can toss that sort of cash around, those who've been selling him short better watch out. Come to think of it, we've been buying General Stores for nominees this last week. Probably Ian, eh? He has to have taken a position, lucky devil!"

"Yes," Johnjohn muttered. "For the life of me I can't figure . . . Good sweet Christ, and now if he wins with Noble Star! With joss like that he could turn his whole mess about, you know what Chinese're like!"

"Yes," Gornt said, butting in, startling them. "But thank God we're not all Chinese. We've yet to see the cash."

"He must have it—must have it," Johnjohn said. "Matter of face."

"Ah, face." Gornt was sardonic. "9:30 A.M., eh? If he'd really been smart he would have said noon, or 3:00 P.M., then we wouldn't know all day and he could've manipulated us all day. As it is now . . ." Gornt shrugged. "I win either way, millions, if not control." He glanced across the noisy box, nodded noncommittally to Bartlett and Casey, then turned away.

Bartlett took Casey's arm and led her on to the balcony. "What do you think?" he asked softly.

"About Gornt?"

"About Dunross."

"Fantastic! He's fantastic. 'Japanese bank'—that was a stunning red herring," she said excitedly. "He's put this whole group into a tailspin, you could see that, and if this group, the whole of Hong Kong. You heard what Southerby said?"

"Sure. It looks like we've all got it made—if he can squeeze out of Gornt's trap."

"Let's hope." Then she noticed his smile. "What?"

"You know what we just did, Casey? We just bought the Noble House for the promise of 2 million bucks."

"How?"

"Ian's gambling I will put up the 2."

"That's no gamble, Linc, that was the deal."

"Sure. But say I don't. His whole pack of cards collapses. If he doesn't get the 2 he's finished. Yesterday I told Gornt I might jerk the rug Monday morning. Say I withdraw Ian's 2 before the market opens. Ian's down the tube."

She stared at him, appalled. "You wouldn't?"

"We came here to raid and become the Noble House. Look what Ian did to Biltzmann, what they all did to him. That poor bastard didn't know what hit him. Pugmire made a deal but reneged to take Ian's better offer. Right?"

"That's different." She looked at him searchingly. "You're going to renege after making a deal?"

Bartlett smiled a strange smile, looked down at the packed crowds and at the tote. "Maybe. Maybe that depends on who does what to whom over the weekend. Gornt or Dunross, it's all the same."

"I don't agree."

"Sure, Casey, I know," he said calmly. "But it's my $2 million and my game."

"Yes, and your word and your face! You shook on the deal."

"Casey, these guys here would eat us for breakfast if they got the chance. You think Dunross wouldn't sell us out if he had to choose between him and us?"

After a pause she said, "You're saying a deal's never a deal, no matter what?"

"You want $4 million tax free?"

"You know the answer to that."

"Say you're in for 49 percent of the new Par-Con–Gornt company, free and clear. It's got to be worth that."

"More," she said, afraid of this line of talk and for the first time in her life suddenly not sure of Bartlett.

"You want that 49 percent?"

"In return for what, Linc?"

"In return for getting in back of Gornt–Par-Con 100 percent."

Her stomach felt weak and she looked at him searchingly, trying to read his mind. Normally she could, but not since Orlanda. "Are you offering that?"

He shook his head, his smile the same, his voice the same. "No. Not yet."

She shivered, afraid she would take the deal if it were really offered. "I'm glad, Raider. I guess, yes, I'm glad."

"The point's straight and simple, Casey: Dunross and Gornt play the game to win but for different stakes. Why this box would mean more to both of them than $2 or $4 million. We came here, you and I, to profit and to win."

They both glanced at the sky as a few raindrops spattered. But it was from the roof overhang and not a new shower. She began to say something, stopped.

"What, Casey?"

"Nothing."

"I'm going to circulate, see what the reaction is. See you back in our box."

"What about the fifth?" she asked.

"Wait for the odds. I'll be back before the start."

"Have fun!" She followed him with her eyes, out of the door, then turned and leaned on the balcony to hide from him and everyone. She had almost blurted out, Are you going to pull the rug and renege?

Jesus, before Orlanda—before Hong Kong—I'd never have needed to ask that question. Linc would never go back on a deal before. But now, now I'm not sure.

Again she shivered. What about my tears? I've never pulled that one before, and what about Murtagh? Should I tell Linc about Murtagh now —or later—because he must be told, certainly before 9:30 Monday. Oh God, I wish we'd never come here.

The patter of rain splashed the stadium and someone said, "Christ, I hope it doesn't get any worse!" The track was already scarred and muddy and very slippery. Outside the main entrance the road was slicked, puddled, traffic heavy and many late-coming people still hurried through the turnstiles.

Roger Crosse, Sinders and Robert Armstrong got out of the police car and went through the barriers and the checkpoints to the members' elevator, their blue lapel badges fluttering. Crosse had been a voting member for five years, Armstrong for one. Crosse was also a steward this year. Every year the commissioner of police suggested to the stewards that the police should have their own box and each year the stewards agreed enthusiastically and nothing happened.

In the members' stand Armstrong lit a cigarette. His face was lined, his eyes tired. The huge, crowded room went half the length of the stands. They went to the bar and ordered drinks, greeting other members. "Who's that?" Sinders asked.

Armstrong followed his glance. "That's a little of our local color, Mr. Sinders." His voice was sardonic. "Her name's Venus Poon and she's our top TV starlet."

Venus Poon was wearing a full-length mink and surrounded by an admiring group of Chinese. "The fellow on her left's Charles Wang—he's a film producer, multimillionaire, cinemas, dance halls, nightclubs, bars, girls and a couple of banks in Thailand. The small old man who looks like a bamboo and's just as tough is Four Finger Wu, one of our local pirates—smuggling's his life's work and he's very good."

"Yes," Crosse said. "We almost caught him a couple of days ago. We think he's into heroin now—of course gold."

"Who's the nervous one in the gray suit? The fellow on the outside?"

"That's Richard Kwang of the Ho-Pak disaster," Armstrong said. "The banker. He's her current, or was her current—what's the word—*patron?*"

"Interesting." Sinders concentrated on Venus Poon. Her dress was low-cut and saucy. "Yes, very. And who's that? Over there—the one with the European."

"Where? Oh. That's Orlanda Ramos, Portuguese which usually means Eurasian here. Once she was Quillan Gornt's mistress. Now, now I don't know. The man's Linc Bartlett, the 'gun-runner.' "

"Ah! She's unattached?"

"Perhaps."

"She looks expensive." Sinders sipped his drink and sighed. "Delectable, but expensive."

"I'd say very," Crosse told him distastefully. Orlanda Ramos was with several middle-aged women, all couturier dressed, around Bartlett. "Rather overdone for my taste."

Sinders glanced at him, surprised. "I haven't seen so many smashers in years—or so many jewels. Have you ever had a raid here?"

Crosse's eyes soared. "In the Turf Club? Good God, surely no one'd dare."

Armstrong smiled his hard smile. "Every copper who does duty here, from the high to the low, spends most of the time trying to work out the perfect heist. The final day's take must be 15 million at least. It's baffled us all. Security's too tight, too clever—Mr. Crosse set it up."

"Ah!"

Crosse smiled. "Would you like a snack, Edward? Perhaps a sandwich?"

"Good idea. Thank you."

"Robert?"

"No thank you, sir. If you don't mind I'll study the form and see you later." Armstrong was achingly aware that after the seventh race, they were due to return to HQ where Brian Kwok was scheduled for another session.

"Robert's a serious punter, Edward. Robert, do me a favor, show Mr. Sinders the ropes, where to bet, and order him a sandwich. I'd better see if the governor's free for a moment—I'll be back in a few minutes."

"Glad to," Armstrong said, hating the idea, the envelope with 40,000 *h'eung yau* dollars that he had taken from his desk on an impulse now a never-ending fire in his pocket. Christ, do I or don't I? he asked himself over and over, grimly trying to decide and all the while trying to push away the horror of his friend Brian and the next session—no, no longer his friend but a committed, highly trained foreign asset and enormously valuable catch that they had by a miracle uncovered.

"Robert," Crosse said, keeping his voice deliberately kind, "you've done a very good job today. Very good."

"Yes," Sinders agreed. "I'll see the minister's aware of your help, and of course the CP."

Crosse went for the elevator. Wherever he went nervous Chinese eyes followed him. On the top floor he bypassed the governor's box and went into Plumm's.

"Hello, Roger!" Plumm greeted him affably. "Drink?"

"Coffee would be fine. How're things?"

"Lost my shirt so far, though a number of us have the first leg of the quinella. You?"

"I've just arrived."

"Oh, then you missed the drama!" Plumm told Crosse about Dunross's takeover bid. "Ian's thrown a monkey wrench into Pug."

"Or given him a great offer," someone volunteered.

"True, true."

Plumm's box was as packed as all the others. Lots of chatter and laughter, drinks and good food. "Tea'll be up in half an hour. I'm just going along to the stewards' committee room, Roger. Would you like to stroll with me?"

The committee room was at the end of the corridor, through guarded swing doors. It was small with a table and twelve chairs, a phone, good windows over the track and a tiny balcony. And empty. At once Plumm's easygoing facade vanished. "I talked to Suslev."

"Oh?"

"He's furious about the raid on the *Ivanov* last night."

"I can imagine. That was ordered by London. I wasn't even told till this morning. Bloody Sinders!"

Plumm became even grimmer. "They couldn't be on to you, could they?"

"Oh no. It's routine. Just Special Branch, MI-6 and Sinders flexing their wings. They're a secretive lot and quite right, nothing to do with SI. Go on."

"He said if you came that he'd be by a phone booth." Plumm handed him a slip of paper. "Here's the number. He'll be there exactly at the off of the next three races. Please call him—he said it was urgent. What the hell was the raid for?"

"Just to frighten all the KGB aboard, to frighten them enough to flush out Sevrin. Pressure. Same as the order for Suslev and the new commissar to appear at HQ on Sunday. It was just to frighten."

"Suslev's frightened all right." A sardonic smile flickered over Plumm's handsome face. "His sphincter's out of joint for ten years at least. They'll all have some explaining to do. When Armstrong 'happened' to bust open the radio room, Red One operated and they dutifully and unnecessarily wrecked all their scramble and decoding equipment, along with their classified radar scanners."

Crosse shrugged. "The *Ivanov*'s leaving and they've got plenty to replace them with. It wasn't Suslev's fault, or ours. We can send a report telling Center what happened. If we want."

Plumm's eyes narrowed. "If?"

"Rosemont and his CIA thugs picked up a glass in their raid on Sinclair Towers. Suslev's prints are all over it."

Plumm went white. "Christ! Now he's on file?"

"Has to be. He's in our files as you know, not as KGB, and I think I've the only copies of his fingerprints existing. I removed them from his dossier years ago. I'd say it's only a matter of time before the CIA are on to him, so the sooner he leaves Hong Kong the better."

"You think we should tell Center?" Plumm asked uneasily. "They'll throw their book at him for being so careless."

"We can decide over the weekend. We knew Voranski over a number of years, knew he was to be trusted. But this man?" Crosse left the word hanging, keeping up the pretense that his contact with Suslev was recent, the same as Plumm's. "After all, isn't he only a minor KGB officer, a jumped-up courier. He's not even Voranski's official replacement and we've ourselves to think of."

"True!" Plumm hardened. "Maybe he's a real berk. I know I wasn't followed to Sinclair Towers. And as to the decoded cable—God stone the crows!"

"What?"

"The decoded cable—the one he dropped and Armstrong picked off the *Ivanov's* deck. We've got to decide about that."

Crosse turned away to hide his shock and fought for control, appalled that neither Armstrong nor Sinders had mentioned any cable. He pretended to stifle a yawn to cover. "Sorry, I was up most of the night," he said, making a major effort to keep his voice matter-of-fact. "Did he tell you what was in it?"

"Of course. I insisted."

Crosse saw Plumm watching him. "Exactly what did he tell you was in it?"

"Oh? You mean he might be lying?" Plumm's anxiety showed. "It went something like: 'Inform Arthur that following his request for a Priority One on the traitor Metkin an immediate intercept was ordered for Bombay. Second, the meeting with the American is brought forward to Sunday. Third and final: The AMG files continue to be Priority One. Maximum effort must be made by Sevrin to achieve success. Center.'" Plumm licked his lips. "Is it correct?"

"Yes," Crosse said, gambling, almost wet with relief. He began weighing odds on Armstrong and Sinders. Now why, deliberately, why didn't they tell me that?

"Terrible, eh?" Plumm said.

"Yes, but not serious."

"I don't agree," Plumm said irritably. "It absolutely ties the KGB to Sevrin, absolutely confirms Arthur's existence and Sevrin's existence."

"Yes, but the AMG files have already done that. Calm down, Jason, we're quite safe."

"Are we? There've been too many leaks for my liking. Far too many. Perhaps we should close down for a time."

"We are closed down. It's only those bloody AMG files that are causing us any grief."

"Yes. At least that bugger Grant wasn't completely accurate."

"You mean about Banastasio?"

"Yes. I still wonder where the hell he fits in."

"Yes." In AMG's intercepted file Banastasio had been named erroneously as Sevrin's American connection. It was only after the file that Crosse had learned from Rosemont who Banastasio actually was.

"The fellow who met him was Vee Cee Ng," Crosse said.

Plumm's eyebrows soared. "Photographer Ng? How does he connect?"

"I don't know. Shipping, ships, smuggling. He's into all kinds of shady deals." Crosse shrugged.

"Could that writer fellow's theory work? What's his name? Marlowe. Could the KGB be doing an op in our territory without telling us?"

"Possible. Or it could be an utterly different department, perhaps GRU, instigated in America by the KGB or GRU there. Or just a coincidence." Crosse was back in control now, the fright of the cable wearing off. He was thinking much clearer. "What's Suslev want that's so urgent?"

"Our cooperation. Koronski arrives by the afternoon plane."

Crosse whistled. "Center?"

"Yes. There was a message this morning. Now that the *Ivanov*'s equipment is wrecked I'm the go-between."

"Good. What's his cover name?"

"Hans Meikker, West German. He's to stay at the Seven Dragons." Plumm's anxiety increased. "Listen, Suslev said Center's ordered us to prepare to snatch Ian an—"

"They've gone mad!" Crosse exploded.

"I agree but Suslev says it's the only way to find out quickly if the files are counterfeit or not, and if so, where they're hidden. He claims Koronski can do it. In a chemical debriefing, well, Ian's memory can be . . . can be emptied."

"That's madness," Crosse said. "We're not even sure if the files are counterfeit. That's a complete supposition for God's sake!"

"Suslev says Center told him we can blame it on the Werewolves— those buggers snatched John Chen so why wouldn't they go after the big money, the tai-pan?"

"No. Too dangerous."

Plumm wiped his hands. "To snatch Ian now'd put the tai-pans and Hong Kong into a furor. It could be a perfect time, Roger."

"Why?"

"The Noble House would be in total disarray and with all the bank runs and the stock market disaster, Hong Kong'd be down the sewer and that'd send all China into shock. We'd jump the Cause forward ten years and immeasurably assist international communism and the workers of the world. Christ, Roger, aren't you sick of just sitting and being a messenger? Now we can fulfill Sevrin with hardly any risk. Then we close everything down for a time."

Crosse lit a cigarette. He had heard the tension in Plumm's voice. "I'll think about it," he said at length. "Leave it for the moment. I'll call you tonight. Did Suslev say who the American in the cable was?"

"No. He just said it wasn't anything to do with us."

Crosse's voice hardened. "Everything here's to do with us."

"I agree." Plumm watched him. "It could also be a code word, a code for anyone."

"Possible."

"I have a wild one for you. Banastasio."

"Why him?" Crosse asked, having jumped to the same conclusion.

"I don't know why, but I'll bet that whole scam, if it is a scam, has to be KGB inspired, or assisted. It's classic Sun Tzu: using the enemy's strength against himself—both enemies, the U.S. and China. A strong unified Vietnam's guaranteed militantly anti-Chinese. Eh?"

"Possible. Yes, it all fits," Crosse agreed. Except one thing, he thought: Vee Cee Ng. Until Brian Kwok had blurted out, "Vee Cee's one of us," he had had no inkling that the man was anything other than a swinging photographer and trader-shipping capitalist. "If Banastasio's the American, we'll know." He finished his cigarette. "Was there anything else?"

"No. Roger, consider Dunross. Please. The Werewolves make it possible."

"It's considered."

"This weekend would be perfect, Roger."

"I know."

Orlanda was watching the horses through her high-powered binoculars as they broke out of the starting gate for the fourth race. She stood in a corner of the members' balcony, Bartlett happily beside her, everyone watching the horses except him. He was watching her, the curve of her breasts under the silk, the angle of her cheekbones and the intensity of her excitement. "Come on, Crossfire," she muttered, "come on! He's lying fifth, Linc, oh come on, you beauty, come on . . ."

He chuckled, Orlanda oblivious. They had arranged to meet here between the third and fourth race. "Are you a voting member?" he had asked her last night.

"Oh no, my darling, I'm just going with friends. Old friends of my family. Another drink?"

"No, no thanks—I'd better go."

They had kissed and again he had felt her overpowering welcome. It had kept him unsettled and on edge all the way back across the harbor home and most of the night. Much as he tried, he found the wanting of her difficult to contain and to keep in perspective.

You're hooked, old buddy, he told himself, watching her, the tip of her tongue touching her lips, her eyes concentrating, everything forgotten but her $50 on the nose of the big gray, the favorite.

"Come on . . . come . . . oh he's moving up, Linc . . . oh he's second. . . ."

Bartlett looked at the pack galloping now into the last stretch: Crossfire, the big gray well placed to Western Scot, a brown gelding who was slightly in the lead, the going very slow—one horse had fallen in the third race. Now a contender made his dash, Winwell Stag, a gelding belonging to Havergill that Peter Marlowe had tipped to win, and he was coming up strong on the outside with Crossfire and Western Scot neck and neck just ahead, all whips out now in the gathering roar.

"Oh come on come on come on Crossfire . . . oh he's won, he's won!"

Bartlett laughed in the pandemonium as Orlanda's glee burst out and she hugged him. "Oh Linc, how wonderful!"

In a moment there was another roar as the winning numbers were flashed up on the tote board, confirming their order. Now everyone waited for the final odds. Another great cheer. Crossfire paid 5 to 2.

"That's not much," he said.

"Oh but it is it is it is!" Orlanda had never looked prettier to him, her hat cute, much better than Casey's—he'd noticed it at once and complimented her on it. She moved forward and leaned on the railing and looked down at the winner's circle. "There's the owner, Vee Cee Ng, he's one of our Shanghainese trader-shipping millionaires. My father knew him quite well." She gave him the glasses.

Bartlett focused. The man leading the garlanded horse into the winner's circle was expensively dressed, a beaming, well-set Chinese in his fifties. Then Bartlett recognized Havergill leading in his Winwell Stag, second, defeated by a nose. In the paddock he saw Gornt, Plumm, Pugmire and many of the stewards. Dunross was near the rails talking to a smaller man. The governor was walking from group to group with his wife and aide. Bartlett watched them, envying them a little, the owners standing there with their caps and raincoats and shooting sticks and expensive women and girl friends, greeting one another, all members of the inner club, the powerhouse of Hong Kong, there and in the boxes above. All very British, he thought, all very clever. Will I fit in better than Biltzmann? Sure. Unless they want me out as much as they wanted him out. I'll be a voting member easy. Ian said as much. Would Orlanda fit there? Of course. As wife or girl friend, it's all the same.

"Who's that?" he asked. "The man talking to Ian?"

"Oh that's Alexi Travkin, he's the tai-pan's trainer. . . ." She stopped as Robert Armstrong came up to them.

"Afternoon, Mr. Bartlett," he said politely. "Did you back the winner too?"

"No, no I lost this one. May I introduce Miss Ramos, Orlanda Ramos, Superintendent Robert Armstrong, CID."

"Hello." She smiled back at Armstrong, and he saw her immediate caution. Why are they all frightened of us, the innocent as well as the guilty? he asked himself, when all we do is try to enforce *their* laws, try to protect them from villains and the ungodly. It's because everyone breaks some law, even a little one, every day, most days, because a lot of laws are stupid—like our betting laws here. So everyone's guilty, even you, pretty lady with the oh so sensual walk and oh so promising smile. For Bartlett. What crime have you committed today, to snare this poor innocent? Sardonically he smiled to himself. Not so innocent in most things. But against someone trained by Quillan Gornt? A beautiful, hungry Eurasian girl with no place to go but down? *Ayeeyah!* But oh how I'd like to swap places! Yes, you with your guns, money, birds like Casey and this one and meetings with the offal of the world like Banastasio, oh yes—I'd give ten years of my life, more, because today I swear to God I loathe what I have to do, what only I can do for good old England.

"Did you back the favorite too?" she was asking.

"No, no unfortunately."

"This's her second winner," Bartlett said proudly.

"Ah, if you're on a winning streak, who do you fancy in the fifth?"

"I've been trying to decide, Superintendent. I've no tips—it's wide open. What's yours?"

"Winning Billy's tipped, I hear. I can't make up my mind either. Well, good luck." Armstrong left them, heading for the betting windows. He had put 500 on the third-placed horse, covering his other bets. He always chose a main bet and then hedged it with others, hoping to come out ahead. Most times he did. This afternoon he was a little behind, but he still hadn't touched the 40,000.

In the corridor he hesitated. The Snake, Chief Inspector Donald C. C. Smyth, was turning away from one of the crowded winning windows, a roll of money in his hand. "Hello, Robert. How're you doing?"

"So-so. You're in the big time again?"

"I try." The Snake bent closer. "How is everything?"

"Proceeding." Once more Armstrong felt nauseated at the thought of more of the Red Room, then sitting there, letting Brian Kwok's mind spill out his most secret secrets, working against the clock that was ticking away —all of them aware that the governor was asking London for permission to trade.

"You're not looking so good, Robert."

"I don't feel so good. Who's going to win the fifth?"

"I leaned on your friend Clubfoot at the Para. The word is Pilot Fish. He did tip Buccaneer in the first, though with this going anything could happen."

"Yes. Anything on the Werewolves?"

"Nothing. It's a dead end. I'm having the whole area combed but with this rain it's almost hopeless. I did interview Dianne Chen this morning— and John Chen's wife Barbara. They gave me sweet talk. I'd lay a fiver to a bent hatpin they know more than they're telling. I had a brief talk with Phillip Chen but he was equally uncooperative. Poor bugger's pretty shook." The Snake looked up at him. "By chance did Mary have any clue about John?"

Armstrong looked back at him. "I haven't had a chance to ask her. Tonight—if they give me any peace."

"They won't." Smyth's face crinkled with a twisted smile. "Put your 40 on Pilot Fish."

"What 40?"

"A dickie bird twittered that a certain golden nest egg has flown your coop—to mix metaphors." The smaller man shrugged. "Don't worry, Rob-

ert, have a flutter. There's plenty more where that came from. Good luck."
He went away. Armstrong stared after him, hating him.

The bugger's right though, he thought, his chest hurting. There's
plenty more but once you take the first, what about the second and
though you give nothing, admit nothing, guarantee nothing, there will
come a time. As sure as God made little apples there's always a return payment.

Mary. She needs that holiday, needs it so much and there's the stockbroker's bill and all the other bills and oh Christ, with this market gone
crazy I'm almost wiped out. God curse money—or the lack of it.

40 on a winning quinella'd solve everything. Or do I put it all on Pilot
Fish? All or half or none. If it's all, there's plenty of time to place bets at
other windows.

His feet took him to one of the betting lines. Many recognized him and
those who did, feeling their instant internal fear, wished the police had
their own box and own windows and did not mix with honest citizens.
Four Finger Wu was one of these. Hastily he put 50,000 on a quinella of
Pilot Fish and Butterscotch Lass and fled back to the members' room,
gratefully to sip his brandy and soda. Dirty dogmeat police to frighten
honest citizens, he thought, waiting for Venus Poon to return. Eeeee, he
chortled, her Golden Gully's worth every carat of the diamond I promised
her last night. Two Clouds and Rain before dawn and a promise of another bout on Sunday when the yang recovers his ju—

A sudden roar from outside diverted his mind. At once he shoved his
way through the crowds packing the balcony. The names of the fifth race-
horses and their jockeys were coming up on the board, one by one. Pilot
Fish, number one, got a full-bellied cheer; then Street Vendor, an outsider, two; Golden Lady, three and a ripple of excitement went through
her many backers. When Noble Star, seven, flashed up there was a great
roar and when the last, number eight, the favorite, Butterscotch Lass,
there was an even greater roar.

Down by the rail Dunross and Travkin were grimly inspecting the turf.
It was torn and slippery. The nearer the rail, the worse it was. Above, the
sky was blacker and lowering. A sprinkle started and a nervous groan
slipped from fifty thousand throats.

"It's rotten, tai-pan," Travkin said, "the going's rotten."

"It's the same for everyone." Dunross let his mind reestimate the odds a
last time. If I ride and win, the omen will be immense. If I ride and lose,
the omen will be very bad. To be beaten by Pilot Fish would be even
worse. I could be hurt easily. I can't afford . . . the Noble House can't
afford to be headless today, tomorrow or Monday. If Travkin rides and
loses or finishes behind Pilot Fish that would be bad but not as bad. That
would be joss.

But I won't get hurt. I'll win. I want this race more than anything in the world. I won't fail. I'm not sure about Alexi. I can win—if the gods are with me. Yes but how much are you prepared to gamble on the gods?

"Eeee, young Ian," Old Chen-chen had told him many times, "beware of expecting help from the gods, however much you petition them with gold or promises. Gods are gods and gods go out to lunch and sleep and get bored and turn their eyes away. Gods are the same as people: good and bad, lazy and strong, sweet and sour, stupid and wise! Why else are they gods, *heya?*"

Dunross could feel his heart thumping and could smell the warm, acrid, sweet-sour horse sweat, could sense the mind-blinding, spirit-curdling motioning, hands gripping the whip, bunched in the corner, now into the far straight, now into the last corner, the aching, grand sweet terror of speed, wielding the whip, jamming your heels in, outstretched now, carefully bumping Pilot Fish into the rails, putting him off his stride, and now into the straight, ripping into the straight, Pilot Fish behind, winning post ahead . . . come on come on . . . winning. . . .

"We have to decide, tai-pan. It's time."

Dunross came back slowly, bile in his mouth. "Yes. You ride," he said, putting the House before himself.

And now that he had said it he put the rest aside and clapped Travkin warmly on the shoulders. "Win, Alexi, win by God."

The older man, gnarled and leathery, peered up at him. He nodded once, then walked off to change. As he went he noticed Suslev in the stands watching him through binoculars. A tremor went through him. Suslev had promised that this Christmas Nestorova would come to Hong Kong, she would be allowed to join him in Hong Kong—and stay in Hong Kong—at Christmas. If he cooperated. If he cooperated and did what was asked.

Do you believe that? No. No, not at all, those *matyeryehyets* are liars and betrayers but maybe this time . . . Christ Jesus why should I be ordered to meet Dunross at Sinclair Towers by night, late at night? Why? Christ Jesus, what should I do? Don't think, old man. You're old and soon you'll be dead but your first duty is to win. If you win, the tai-pan will do your bidding. If you lose? If you win or lose, how can you live with the shame of betraying the man who befriended you and trusts you?

He went into the jockeys' room.

Behind him Dunross had turned to glance at the tote. The odds had shortened, the total amount at risk already two and a half million. Butterscotch Lass was 3 to 1, Noble Star 7 to 1, still no jockey listed, Pilot Fish 5 to 1, Golden Lady 7 to 1. Early yet, he thought, and so much time left to gamble. Travkin will shorten the odds. A cold shaft took him. I wonder if there's a deal going on right now, a deal among the trainers and jockeys? Christ, we all better be watching this one very carefully indeed.

"Ah Ian!"

"Oh hello, sir." Dunross smiled at Sir Geoffrey who came up to him then looked at Havergill who was with the governor. "Pity about Winwell Stag, Paul, I thought he ran a grand race."

"Joss," Havergill said politely. "Who's riding Noble Star?"

"Travkin."

The governor's face lit up. "Ah, very good choice. Yes, he'll make a good race of it. For a moment, Ian, I was afraid you might be tempted."

"I was. Still am, sir." Dunross smiled faintly. "If Alexi gets hit by a bus between now and then, I'm riding her."

"Well, for the sake of all of us and the Noble House, let's hope that doesn't happen. We can't afford to have you hurt. The going looks terrible." Another swirl of rain came and passed by. "We've been very lucky so far. No bad accidents. If the rain starts in earnest, it might be worthwhile considering abandoning."

"We've already discussed it, sir. We're running a little late. The race'll be delayed ten minutes. So long as the weather holds for this race most people will be satisfied."

Sir Geoffrey watched him. "Oh by the way, Ian, I tried the minister a few minutes ago but I'm afraid he was already in meetings. I left word and he'll call back the moment he can. It seems the ramifications of this damned Profumo scandal are once more tearing at the very roots of the Conservative government. The press are screaming, quite rightly, in case there have been breaches of security. Until the Commission of Enquiry comes out next month, settling once and for all security aspects and rumors that others in the government are implicated or not, there'll be no peace."

"Yes," Havergill said. "But surely the worst's over, sir. As to the report, certainly it won't be adverse."

"Adverse or not, this scandal will wreck the Conservatives," Dunross said soberly, remembering AMG's forecast in the last report.

"Good God, I hope not." Havergill was aghast. "Those two twits, Grey and Broadhurst, in power amongst all the other Socialist shower? If their press conference was any indication, we might as well all go home."

"We are home, and it all comes home to roost. Eventually," Sir Geoffrey said sadly. "Anyway, Ian made the correct decision, not to ride." He glanced at Havergill and his gaze sharpened. "As I said, Paul, it's important to make correct decisions. It would be a very poor show if the Ho-Pak's depositors were wiped out, perhaps just because of poor judgment by Richard Kwang and the lack of a benevolent decision by those who could avoid such a disaster if they wished—perhaps to great profit. Eh?"

"Yes sir."

Sir Geoffrey nodded and left them.

Dunross said, "What was that about?"

"The governor thinks we should rescue the Ho-Pak," Havergill said offhandedly.

"Why don't you?"

"Let's talk about the General Stores takeover."

"First let's finish the Ho-Pak. The governor's right, it would benefit all of us, Hong Kong—and the bank."

"You'd be in favor?"

"Yes, of course."

"You'll approve, you and your block will approve making the takeover?"

"I don't have a block but certainly I'll support a reasonable takeover."

Paul Havergill smiled thinly. "I was thinking of 20 cents on the dollar on Richard's holdings."

Dunross whistled. "That's not much."

"By Monday night he'll have zero. He'll probably settle for that—his holdings would give the bank control. We could easily stand surety for 100 percent of his depositors."

"He's got that amount of securities?"

"No, but with the normalization of the market and our judicious management, over a year or two it's true the acquisition of the Ho-Pak could greatly benefit us. Oh yes. And there's a desperate need to restore confidence. Such a takeover would help immeasurably."

"This afternoon would be a perfect announcement time."

"I agree. Anything on Tiptop?"

Dunross studied him. "Why the sudden change around, Paul? And why discuss it with me?"

"There's no change around. I've considered the Ho-Pak very carefully. The acquisition would be good bank policy." Havergill watched him. "We'll give him face and offer him a seat on our board."

"So the rumors about the Big Bank are true?"

"Not to my knowledge," the banker said coldly. "As to why discuss it with you? Because you're a director of the bank, presently the most important one, with substantial influence on the board. That's a sensible thing to do, isn't it?"

"Yes, but."

Havergill's eyes became colder. "The interests of the bank have nothing to do with my distaste for you, or your methods. But you were right about Superfoods. You made a good offer at a perfect time and sent a wave of confidence soaring through everyone here. It's bound to spread over all Hong Kong. It was brilliant timing and now if we follow it up and announce we've assumed all the Ho-Pak responsibilities to its depositors, that's another immense vote of confidence. All we need to do is get back confidence. If Tiptop comes to our assistance with his cash, Monday is boom day for Hong Kong. So first thing on Monday morning, Ian, we buy Struan's heavily. By Monday evening we'll assume control. However I'll make you a deal right now: we'll put up the 2 million for General Foods in return for half your bank stock."

"No thanks."

"We'll have it all by next weekend. We'll guarantee that 2 million in any event to cover the takeover and guarantee the overall offer you made to Pug—if you fail to avoid your own takeover."

"I won't."

"Of course. But you don't mind if I mention it to him and to that nosy little cretin Haply?"

"You're a bastard, aren't you?"

Havergill's thin lips twisted with his smile. "This is business—I want your block of bank stock. Your forebears bought it for nothing, practically stole it from the Brocks after smashing them. I want to do the same. And I want control of the Noble House. Of course. Like a great number of others. Probably even your American friend Bartlett if the truth were known. Where's the 2 million coming from?"

"It's manna from heaven."

"We'll find out sooner or later. We're your bankers and you owe us rather a lot of money! Will Tiptop bail us out?"

"I can't be sure but I talked to him last night. He was encouraging. He agreed to come here after lunch but he hasn't arrived yet. That's ominous."

"Yes." Havergill brushed some drizzle off his nose. "We've had a very positive response from the Trade Bank of Moscow."

"Even you're not that fat-headed!"

"It's a last resort, Ian. A serious last resort."

"You'll call an immediate board meeting to discuss the Ho-Pak takeover?"

"Good lord, no." Havergill was sardonic. "You think I'm that much of a fool? If we did that you could table the other directors about an extension of your loan. No, Ian, I propose to ask them individually, like you. With your agreement I have a majority already, the others of course fall into line. I do have your agreement?"

"At 20 cents on the dollar and full payout of investors, yes."

"I might need leeway to go to 30 cents. Agreed?"

"Yes."

"Your word?"

"Oh yes, you have my word."

"Thank you."

"But you'll call a board meeting before Monday's opening?"

"I agreed to consider it. Only. I've considered it and the answer now is *no*. Hong Kong's a freebooting society where the weak fail and the strong keep the fruits of their labors." Havergill smiled and he glanced at the tote. The odds had shortened. 2 to 1 on Butterscotch Lass, well known for liking the wet. Pilot Fish now 3 to 1. While they watched, Travkin's name flashed up alongside Noble Star and a huge roar accompanied it. "I think the governor was wrong, Ian. You should have ridden. Then I'd've put my modest bet on you. Yes. You'd have gone out in a blaze of glory. Yes, you would have won. I'm not sure about Travkin. Good afternoon."

He raised his hat and headed for Richard Kwang who stood with his wife and trainer to one side. "Ah Richard! Can I have a word wi—" He was drowned by a huge roar from the crowd as the first of the eight runners for the fifth race began to trickle out from under the stands. Pilot Fish led the pack, the slight drizzle making his black coat shimmer.

"Yes, Paul?" Richard Kwang asked, following him into an empty space.

"I wanted to talk to you but didn't want to interrupt you with the governor and the tai-pan. Now," he said with forced joviality, "I've a plan. Let's lump all the Ho-Pak's securities together and if you'll lend me 50 mill—"

"No thank you, Richard," Havergill said crisply. "But we do have a proposal that's good till five o'clock today. We'll bail out the Ho-Pak and guarantee all your depositors. In return we'll buy your personal holdings at par an—"

"Par? That's a fiftieth of their value!" Richard Kwang screeched. "That's a fiftieth of their worth—"

"Actually it's 5 cents on the dollar which is about all their value. Is it a deal?"

"No of course not. *Dew neh loh moh,* am I a dogmeat madman?" Richard Kwang's heart was almost bursting. A moment ago he had thought, impossibly, that Havergill was granting him a reprieve from the disaster that by now he was convinced was absolute, however much he pretended otherwise, however much it was not his fault but the work of rumormongers and malicious fools who had led him into inept banking deals. But now he was in the vise. *Oh ko!* Now he would be squeezed and whatever he did he could not escape the tai-pans. Oh oh oh! Disaster on disaster and now that ungrateful strumpet Venus Poon making me lose face in front of Uncle Four Fingers, Charlie Wang and even Photographer Ng and that even after I delivered to her personally the new mink coat that she trails in the mud so carelessly.

"New?" she had flared this morning. "You claim this miserable secondhand coat is new?"

"Of course!" he had shouted. "Do you think I am a monkey? Of course it's new. It cost 50,000 cash *oh ko!*" The 50,000 was an exaggeration but the cash wasn't and they both were well aware that it would be uncivilized not to exaggerate. The coat had cost him 14,000, through an intermediary, after much bargaining from a *quai loh* who had fallen on hard times and another 2,000 to the furrier who had overnight shortened and altered it enough to fit and not to be recognized, with a guarantee that the furrier would swear by all the gods that he had sold it under price at 42 even though it was actually worth 63,500.

"Paul," Richard Kwang said importantly. "The Ho-Pak's in better shape th—"

"Kindly shut up and listen," Havergill said overriding him. "The time has come to make a serious decision—for you, not us. You can go under on

Monday with nothing. . . . I understand trading's opening on your stock first thing."

"But Sir Luis assured me th—"

"I heard it was open for trading, so by Monday night you'll have no bank, no stock, no horses, no dollymoney to pay for mink coats for Venus P—"

"Eh?" Richard Kwang blanched, aware his wife was standing not twenty paces away, lugubriously watching them. "What mink coat?"

Havergill sighed. "All right, if you're not interested." He turned away but the banker caught him by the arm.

"5 cents is ridiculous. 80 is nearer what I can get on the open mar—"

"Perhaps I can go to 7."

"7?" The banker began cursing, more to give himself time to think than anything. "I'll agree to a merger. A seat on the bank's board for ten years at a salary of f—"

"For five years, provided you give me your notarized resignation, un-dated, in advance, that you always vote exactly as *I* wish and at a salary equal to other directors."

"No resignation in adv—"

"Then so sorry no deal."

"I agree to that clause," Richard Kwang said grandly. "Now as to money. I th—"

"No. As to money, so sorry, Richard, I don't want to enter into a pro-tracted negotiation. The governor, the tai-pan and I agree we should res-cue the Ho-Pak. It is decided. I will see you retain face. We guarantee to keep the takeover price secret and are quite prepared to call it a merger—oh by the way, I want to make the announcement at 5:00 P.M., just after the seventh race. *Or not at all.*" Havergill's face was grim, but inside he was filled with glee. If it hadn't been for Dunross's announcement and the way it was being received he would have never considered doing the same. That bugger's quite right! It is time to be innovative and who better than us? It'll stop Southerby in his tracks and make us equal to Blacs at long last. With Struan's in our pocket next week, by next year . . .

"57 cents and that's a steal," Kwang said.

"I'll go to 10 cents."

Richard Kwang wheedled and twisted and almost wept and inside he was ecstatic with the chance of the bail-out. *Dew neh loh moh,* he wanted to shout, a few minutes ago I wouldn't be able to pay for Butterscotch Lass's feed next week let alone the diamond ring and now I'm worth at least $3½ million U.S. and with judicious manipulation much more. "30 by all the gods!"

"11."

"I'll have to commit suicide," he wailed. "My wife will commit suicide, my children will . . ."

"Your pardon, Lord," his Chinese trainer said in Cantonese, coming up to him. "The race's put back ten minutes. Are there any instructions you wa—"

"Can't you see I'm busy, toad-belly! Go away!" Richard Kwang hissed in Cantonese with more obscenities, then said to Havergill, a final abject plea, "30, Mr. Havergill, and you'll have saved a poor man and his fam—"

"18 and that's final!"

"25 and it's a deal."

"My dear fellow, so sorry but I must place a bet. 18. Yes or no?"

Richard Kwang kept up a pathetic patter but he was estimating his chances. He had seen the flash of irritation on his opponent's face. Dirty lump of dogmeat! Is now the time to close? Between now and five o'clock this leper dung could change his mind. If the tai-pan's got all this new financing perhaps I could . . . No, no chance. 18's three times as good as the opening bid! It's clear you are a clever fellow and a good negotiator, he chortled to himself. Has the time come to close?

He thought of Venus Poon, how she had abused his expensive gift and deliberately brushed her exquisite breasts against Four Fingers's arm, and tears of rage welled from his eyes.

"Oh oh oh," he said in an abject whisper, delighted that his stratagem to produce real tears had worked so well. "20, by all the gods, and I'm your slave forever."

"Good," Havergill said, very contentedly. "Come to my box at quarter to five. I'll have a provisional letter of agreement ready for signature—and your undated resignation. At five we'll announce the merger, and Richard, until that time not a whisper! If the news leaks, the deal is off."

"Of course."

Havergill nodded and left and Richard Kwang walked back to his wife. "What's going on?"

"Quiet!" he hissed. "I've agreed to a merger with the Victoria."

"At what price for our holdings?"

He lowered his voice even more. "20 cents on the, er, official book value."

Glee lit her eyes. "*Ayeeyah!*" she said and quickly dropped her gaze for safety. "You did very well."

"Of course. And a directorship for five years an—"

"Eeee, our face will be huge!"

"Yes. Now listen, we've got until five today to make some private deals on Ho-Pak stock. We must buy in today—at fire-sale prices before every dogmeat gambler steals our rightful profits from us. We can't do it ourselves or others'll instantly suspect. Who can we use?"

She thought for a moment. Again her eyes gleamed. "Profitable Choy. Give him 7 percent of anything he makes for us."

"I'll offer 5 to begin with, perhaps I can settle for 6½ percent! Excellent! And I'll also use Smiler Ching, he's a pauper now. He lost everything. Between the two of them . . . I'll meet you back at the box." Importantly he turned away and went to his trainer and carefully kicked him in the shin. "Oh so sorry," he said for the benefit of those nearby who might have seen him, then hissed, "Don't interrupt me when I'm busy, you cheating lump of dogmeat turd! And if you cheat me like you cheated Big Belly Tok I'll—"

"But I told you about that, Lord," the man said sourly. "He knew about it too! Wasn't it his idea? Didn't you both make a fortune?"

"*Oh ko,* if my horse doesn't win this race I'll ask my Uncle Four Fingers to send his street fighters and mash your Heavenly Orbs!"

A sprinkle of rain swept the paddock and they all looked anxiously at the sky. In the stands and on the balconies above, everyone was equally anxious. The shower turned into a slight drizzle and on the members' balcony Orlanda quivered, tense with excitement.

"Oh Linc, I'm going to bet now."

"You're sure?" he asked with a laugh for she had been agonizing over her decision all afternoon, first Pilot Fish then Noble Star, then a hot tip, the outsider Winning Billy, and back to Butterscotch Lass again. The odds were even on Butterscotch Lass, 3 to 1 on both Pilot Fish and Noble Star—the moment Travkin was announced the money started pouring on—6 to 1 on Golden Lady, the rest hardly in the running. The total amount so far at risk was a staggering 4,700,000 HK. "How much are you going to bet?"

She shut her eyes and said in a rush, "All my winnings and an extra . . . an extra 100! Won't be a moment, Linc!"

"Good luck. I'll see you after the race."

"Oh yes, sorry, in the excitement I forgot. Have fun!" She gave him a glorious smile and rushed off before he could ask her what she was betting. He had already bet. This race was a quinella, as well as the second leg of the double quinella. 10,000 HK on any combination of Pilot Fish and Butterscotch Lass. That should do it, he thought, his own excitement growing.

He left the balcony and weaved through the tables heading for the elevators that would take him back upstairs. Many people watched him, some greeted him, most envious of the little badges fluttering in his lapel.

"Hi, Linc!"

"Oh hello," he said to Biltzmann who had intercepted him. "How's it going?"

"You heard about the foulup? Of course, you were there!" Biltzmann said. "Say, Linc, you got a moment?"

"Sure." Bartlett followed him down the corridor, conscious of the curious gazes of passersby.

"Listen," Biltzmann said when they reached a quiet corner, "you'd better watch yourself with these limey bastards. We sure as hell had a deal with General Stores."

"You going to rebid?" Bartlett asked.

"That's up to head office, but me, hell, me I'd let this whole goddamn Island drown."

Bartlett did not reply, aware of glances in their direction.

"Say, Linc!" Biltzmann dropped his voice and bent closer with a twisted grin. "You got something special going with that girl?"

"What are you talking about?"

"The broad. The Eurasian. Orlanda, the one you were talking to."

Bartlett felt the blood rush into his face but Biltzmann continued, "Mind if I put my two cents in?" He winked. "Make a date. Ask her for a date?"

"It's . . . it's a free country," Bartlett said, suddenly hating him.

"Thanks. She's got a great ass." Biltzmann beamed and came even closer. "How much does she charge?"

Bartlett gasped, totally unprepared. "She's not a hooker, for chrissake!"

"Didn't you know? Hey it's all over town. But Dickie said she was lousy in bed. That a fact?" Biltzmann misread the look on Bartlett's face. "Oh, you haven't got there yet? Hell, Linc, all you gotta do's flash a little of the green st—"

"Listen you son of a bitch," Bartlett hissed, almost blind with rage, "she's no hooker and if you talk to her or go near her I'll stick my fist down your throat. Got it?"

"Listen, take it easy," the other man gasped. "I didn'—"

"You get the message?"

"Sure sure, no need to . . ." Biltzmann backed off. "Take it easy. I asked, didn't I? Dickie . . ." He stopped, frightened, as Bartlett came closer. "For chrissake it's not my fault—take it easy, huh?"

"Shut up!" Bartlett contained his rage with an effort, knowing this was not the time or the place to smash Biltzmann. He glanced around but Orlanda had already disappeared. "Get lost, you son of a bitch," he grated, "and don't go near her or else!"

"Sure, sure take it easy, okay?" Biltzmann backed off another pace, then turned and fled thankfully. Bartlett hesitated, then went into the men's room and splashed a little water on his face to calm himself. The tap water, specially connected for the races, was brackish and seemed unclean. In a moment he found his elevator and walked to Dunross's box. It was tea time. The guests were being served little sandwiches, cakes, cheese and great pots of Indian tea with milk and sugar but he did not notice any of it, numb.

Donald McBride, bustling past, stopped briefly on his way back to his own box. "Ah, Mr. Bartlett, I must tell you how happy we all are that you and Casey are going to be in business here. Pity about Biltzmann but all's fair in business. Your Casey's such a charming person. Sorry, got to dash."

He hurried off. Bartlett hesitated in the doorway.

"Hey, Linc," Casey called out joyously from the balcony. "You want tea?" As they met halfway her smile faded. "What's the matter?"

"Nothing, nothing, Casey." Bartlett forced a smile. "They at the starting gate?"

"Not yet but any moment now. You sure you're okay?"

"Of course. What did you bet on?"

"Noble Star, what else? Peter's tipping Doc Tooley's outsider, Winning Billy, for a place so I put 50 on him. You don't look well, Linc. Not your stomach, is it?"

He shook his head, warmed by her concern. "No. I'm fine. You okay?"

"Sure. I've been having a wonderful time. Peter's in great form and Old Tooley's a gas." Casey hesitated. "I'm glad it's not your stomach. Doc Tooley says we should be safe from those lousy Aberdeen bugs, since we haven't gotten the trots yet. Of course we won't know for sure for twenty days."

"Jesus," Bartlett muttered, trying to force his mind off what Biltzmann had said. "I'd almost forgotten about Aberdeen and the fire and that whole mess. The fire seems a million years ago."

"To me too. Where did the time go?"

Gavallan was nearby. "It's Hong Kong," he said absently.

"How do you mean?"

"It's a Hong Kong characteristic. If you live here there's never enough time, whatever your work. Always too much to do. People are always arriving, leaving, friends, business people. There's always a crisis—flood, fire, mud slide, boom, scandal, business opportunity, funeral, banquet or cocktail party for visiting VIPs—or some disaster." Gavallan shook off his anxieties. "This's a small place and you soon get to know most people in your own circle. Then we're the crossroads of Asia and even if you're not in Struan's you're always on the move, planning, making money, risking money to make more, or you're off to Taiwan, Bangkok, Singapore, Sydney, Tokyo, London or wherever. It's the magic of Asia. Look what happened to you both since you got here: poor John Chen was kidnapped and murdered, guns were found on your aircraft, then there was the fire, the stock market mess, the run on our stock, Gornt after us and we after him. And now the banks may close on Monday or if Ian's right, Monday will be boom time. And we're in business together. . . ." He smiled wearily. "What do you think of our tender?"

Casey held back her immediate comment and watched Bartlett.

"Great," Bartlett said, thinking about Orlanda. "You think Ian will be able to turn things around?"

"If anyone can, he can." Gavallan sighed heavily. "Well, let's hope, that's all we can do. Have you put your money on the winner yet?"

Bartlett smiled and Casey felt easier. "Who you backing, Andrew?"

"Noble Star and Winning Billy for the quinella. See you later." He left them.

"Curious what he was saying about Hong Kong. He's right. It makes the U.S. seem a million miles away."

"Yes, but it isn't, not truly."

"You want to stay here, Casey?"

She looked at him, wondering what was under the question, what he was really asking her. "That's up to you, Linc."

He nodded slowly. "Think I'll get me some tea."

"Hey, I'll do that for you," she said, then she saw Murtagh standing nervously at the doorway and her heart missed a beat. "You haven't met our banker, Linc. Let me bring him over."

She went through the throng. "Hi, Dave."

"Hi, Casey, have you seen the tai-pan?"

"He's busy till after the race. Is it yes or no?" she whispered urgently, keeping her back to Bartlett.

"It's a maybe." Nervously Murtagh wiped his brow and took off his wet raincoat, his eyes red rimmed. "Couldn't get a goddamn cab for an hour! Jesus!"

"Maybe what?"

"Maybe maybe. I gave them the plan and they told me to haul ass back home because I'd clearly gone mad. Then, after they calmed down, they said they'd get back to me. Those knuckleheads called me at 4:00 A.M., asked me to repeat the whole scheme then S.J. himself came on." His eyes rolled. "S.J. said I was full of sh— I was loco and hung up on me."

"But you said 'maybe.' What happened next?"

"I called them back and I've been on the phone five hours in the last ten trying to explain my brilliance to them since your harebrained scheme blew my mind." Murtagh suddenly grinned. "Hey, I'll tell you one thing, Casey. Now S.J. sure as hell knows who Dave Murtagh III is!"

She laughed. "Listen, don't mention it to anyone here. Anyone. Except the tai-pan, okay?"

He looked at her, pained. "You think I'm about to tell everybody my ass's chewed to hamburger?"

There was a burst of cheering and someone in the balcony called out, "They're approaching the gate!"

"Quick," Casey said, "go put your bundle on the quinella. One and seven. Quick while you've time."

"Which are they?"

"Never mind. You've no time." She gave him a little shove and he rushed off. She collected herself, picked up a cup of tea and joined Bartlett and all the others crowding the balcony.

"Here's your tea, Linc."

"Thanks. What did you tell him to bet?"

"One and seven."

"I did one and eight."

Another huge roar distracted them. The horses were cantering past and beginning to mill around the gate. They saw Pilot Fish skeetering and weaving, his jockey well up, knees tight, holding on firmly, guiding him to his post position. But the stallion wasn't ready yet and tossed his mane and neighed. At once the mare and the two fillies, Golden Lady and Noble Star, shivered, nostrils flaring and whinnied back. Pilot Fish brayed stridently, reared and pawed the air and everyone gasped. His jockey, Bluey White, cursed softly, dug his steel-strong hands into his mane, hanging on. "C'mon, sport," he called out with a curse, gentling him. "Let the sheilas have a look at your dingledangle!"

Travkin on Noble Star was nearby. The filly had got the stallion's scent and it had unsettled her. Before Travkin could prevent it she twisted and backed and shoved her rump carelessly into Pilot Fish who swerved, startled, to bump the outsider Winning Billy, a bay gelding moving up to his gate. The gelding skeetered, shook his head angrily and whirled away for a few paces, almost trampling Lochinvar, another brown gelding.

"Get that bugger under control, Alexi, for chrissake!"

"Just stay out of my way, *ublyudok*," Travkin muttered, his knees conscious of the untoward tremors racing through Noble Star. He sat very high, part of his mount, stirrups short, and he wondered, cursing, if Pilot Fish's trainer had smeared some of the stallion's musk onto his chest and flanks to agitate the mare and fillies. It's an old trick, he thought, very old.

"Come on!" the starter called out, his voice stentorian. "Gentlemen, get your mounts into their stalls!"

Several were already there, Butterscotch Lass, the brown mare still heavily the favorite, was pawing the ground, nostrils flared, excitement of the coming race and the nearness of the stallion sending shiver after shiver through her. She had stall eight from the rails, Pilot Fish now entering the stall in post position one. Winning Billy had stall three between Street Vendor and Golden Lady, and the smell of them and the stallion's brazen challenge tore the gelding's mind. Before the gate could close behind him he backed out and, once free, fought the bit and reins, shaking his head violently from side to side, twirling like a dancer on the slippery turf, almost colliding with Noble Star who swerved deftly out of the way.

"Alexi, come along!" the starter called out. "Hurry it up!"

"Yes, certainly," Travkin called back but he was not hurried. He knew Noble Star and he walked the trembling, big brown filly well away from the stallion, letting her prance, the wind under her tail. "Gently, my darling," he crooned in Russian, wanting to delay, wanting to keep the others off balance, now the only one not in the gate. A flash of lightning lit the eastern sky but he paid it no attention, or the ominous roll of thunder. The drizzle became stronger.

His whole being was concentrated. Just after the weigh-in, one of the other jockeys had sidled up to him. "Mr. Travkin," he had said softly, "you're not to win."

"Oh? Who says?"

The jockey shrugged.

"Who's the winner?"

Again the jockey shrugged.

"If the trainers and jockeys have a fix then let them know I'm not part of it. I never have been, not in Hong Kong."

"You'n the tai-pan won with Buccaneer, that should satisfy you."

"It satisfies me but in this race I'm a trier."

"Fair enough, sport. I'll tell them."

"Who's them?"

The jockey had gone away, the crowded changing room noisy and sweat-filled. Travkin was well aware who the ring was, some of them, who fixed races now and then, but he had never been a participant. He knew it was not because he was more honest than the others. Or less dishonest. It was only that his needs were few, a sure thing did not excite him and the touch of money did not please him.

The starter was becoming impatient. "Come along, Alexi! Hurry it up!"

Obediently he jabbed the spurs and walked Noble Star forward into her stall. The gate clanged behind her. A moment's hush. Now the racers were under starter's orders.

66

4:00 P.M.:

In their stalls, jockeys dug their fingers into the horses' manes, all of them nervous, those in the know ready to crowd Noble Star. Then the doors flew open and in a mad instant the eight runners were galloping, packed together along a short part of the straight, now past the winning post, now racing into the first bend. The riders were all crouched high up, side by side, almost touching, some touching, the horses getting their pace, hurtling through the first part of the bend that would take them a quarter of the course into the far straight. Already Pilot Fish was half a length ahead on the rails, Butterscotch Lass in fine position not flat out yet, Winning Billy alongside, back a little from Noble Star on the outside, crowding the others for a better place in the pack, all jockeys knowing that all binoculars were trained on them so any pulling or interference better be clever and cautious. They had all been warned that millions would be won or lost and it would cost each one of them their future to foul up.

They pounded through the turn, mud splattering those behind, the going bad. As they came out of the turn into the straight still together, shoving for position, they lengthened their strides, the sweat-smell and the speed exciting horses and riders alike. Winning Billy took the bit and closed up alongside Butterscotch Lass, now half a length behind Pilot Fish, going well, the rest bunched, all waiting to make their run. Now Butterscotch Lass felt the spurs and she leapt forward and passed Pilot Fish, fell back a little and passed him again, Pilot Fish still hugging the rails carefully.

Travkin was holding the filly well, lying back in the pack, still outside, then he gave her the spurs and she increased speed and he cut closer to the leaders, herding the others, almost bumping Lochinvar. The rain increased. The sting of it was in his eyes, his knees and legs tight and already hurting. There was not a length between them as they galloped out of the stretch into the corner. Going into the far turn they were all packed close to take advantage of the corner when a whip came from nowhere and lashed across Travkin's wrists. The suddenness and pain unlocked his grip an instant and almost unbalanced him. A split second later he was in control again. Where the blow came from he did not know, or care, for they were well into the corner, the going dreadful. Abruptly, the gray outsider Kingplay on the rails just behind Pilot Fish slipped and stumbled, his jockey felt the earth twist and they went down smashing into the rails, pulling two horses with them. Everyone in the stadium was on their feet.

"Christ who's down . . ."

"Is it . . . it's Noble Star . . ."

"No, no it isn't . . . Winning Bill—"

"No he's lying third . . ."

"Come on for Christ's sweet sake . . ."

In the uproar in the stewards' room Dunross, whose binoculars were rock steady, called out, "It was Kingplay who fell . . . Kingplay, Street Vendor and Golden Lady . . . Golden Lady's on her feet but Christ the jockey's hurt . . . Kingplay won't get up . . . he's hurt . . ."

"What's the order, what's the order?"

"Butterscotch Lass by a nose, then Pilot Fish on the rails, Winning Billy, Noble Star, nothing to choose amongst them. Now they're going into the last turn, the Lass's ahead by a neck, the others hacking at her . . ." Dunross watched the horses, his heart almost stopped, excitement possessing him. "Come on, Alexi . . ." His shout added to those of others, Casey as excited, but Bartlett watching, uninvolved, his mind below.

Gornt in the Blacs box had his glasses focused as steadily as the tai-pan, his excitement as controlled. "Come on," he muttered, watching Bluey White give Pilot Fish the whip in the turn, Noble Star well placed on the outside, Winning Billy alongside the Lass who was a neck in front, the angle of the turn making it difficult to see.

Again Travkin felt the lash on his hands but he dismissed it and eased a little closer in the bend, the remaining five horses inches apart, Butterscotch Lass crowding the rails.

Bluey White on Pilot Fish knew it would soon be time to make his dash. Ten yards, five, four three two *now!* They were coming out of the turn and he gave Pilot Fish the whip. The stallion shot forward, inches from the rails, flat out now as Butterscotch Lass got the spurs and whip an instant later, for all the jockeys knew it was now or never.

Travkin, stretched out parallel to Noble Star's neck, leaned forward and let out a cossack scream near Noble Star's ear and the filly took the primeval call and lengthened her stride, nostrils flared, foam on her mouth. Now the five runners were pounding the stretch, Noble Star on the outside, Winning Billy inching ahead of the Lass, all their withers sweatfoamed, now the Lass, now Pilot Fish ahead, and now the dappled gelding Lochinvar made his bid to conquer and he took the lead from Pilot Fish, taking the post position, all whips out and spurs in and only the winning post ahead.

One hundred yards to go.

In the stands and on the balconies and in the boxes, there was but one voice. Even the governor was pounding the balcony rail—"Come on come on Butterscotch Lasssss!"—and down by the winning post Nine Carat Chu was almost crushed against the rails by the press of the crowd craning forward.

Ninety yards, eighty . . . mud scattering, all runners flat out, all caught by the excitement and the crescendoing roar.

"The Lass's pulling away . . ."

"No, look at Pilot F—"

"Christ it's Lochinvarrrrr . . ."

"Winning Billy . . ."

"Come on come on come on . . ."

Travkin saw the winning post bearing down on them. There was another flash of lightning. Out of the corner of his eyes he saw Lochinvar ahead by a neck, then the Lass, now Winning Billy, now Pilot Fish easing forward taking the lead, now Winning Billy, Lochinvar crowding him.

Then Bluey White saw the opening he'd been promised and he gave the stallion the final whip. Like an arrow he darted for the opening and swung up alongside Butterscotch Lass, then passed her. He was ahead by a neck. He saw the Lass's jockey, not in the know, give the mare the whip, shouting her onward. Travkin screamed exultantly and Noble Star put out her final effort. The five horses came down the final yards neck and neck, now Pilot Fish ahead, now Winning Billy, Noble Star closing, just a neck behind, just a nose, just a nostril, the crowd a single, mindless raving lunatic, all the runners bunched, Noble Star on the outside, Winning Billy inching away, the Lass closing, Pilot Fish closing, now ahead by a nose.

Forty . . . thirty . . . twenty . . . fifteen . . .

Noble Star was ahead by a nostril, then Pilot Fish, then the Lass then Noble Star . . . Winning Billy . . . and now they were past the winning post not one of them sure who had won—only Travkin sure he had lost. Abruptly he sawed the bit a vicious two inches and held it left in an iron hand, the movement imperceptible but enough to throw her off her stride and she shied. With a shriek she barreled down into the mud and threw her rider at the rails, the Lass almost falling but holding, the other three safe. Travkin felt himself sailing, then there was an impossible chest tearing, head-splitting blackness.

The crowd gasped, the race momentarily forgotten. Another blinding flash of lightning, pandemonium swooped over them, the downpour increased, mixing nicely with the thunder above.

"Pilot Fish by a nose . . ."

"Balls, it was Noble Star by a hair . . ."

"You're wrong, old boy, it was Pilot Fish . . ."

"*Dew neh loh moh* . . ."

"Christ what a race . . "

"Oh Christ! Look! There's the stewards' objection flag . . ."

"Where? Oh my God! Who fouled . . ."

"I didn't see anything, did you . . ."

"No. Difficult in this rain, even with glasses . . ."

"Christ, now what? Those bloody stewards, if they take victory from my winner by Christ . . ."

Dunross had rushed for the elevator the moment he saw Noble Star fall and throw Travkin. He had not seen the cause. Travkin was too clever.

Others were excitedly crowding the corridors waiting for the elevator, everyone talking, no one listening. "We won by a nostril . . ."

"What's the objection for chrissake? Noble St—"

"What's the objection, tai-pan?"

"That's up to the stewards to announce." In the uproar Dunross stabbed the button again.

Gornt hurried up as the doors opened, everyone packing in, Dunross wanting to bellow with rage at the slowness. "It was Pilot Fish by a nose, Ian," Gornt shouted above the uproar, his face flushed.

"What a race!" someone shouted. "Anyone know what the objection is?"

"Do you, Ian?" Gornt asked.

"Yes," he replied.

"It's against my Pilot Fish?"

"You know the procedure. First the stewards investigate, then they make an announcement." He saw Gornt's flat brown eyes and he knew his enemy was suddenly blind with rage that he wasn't a steward. And you won't become one, you bastard, Dunross thought, enraged. I'll blackball you till I'm dead.

"Is it against Pilot Fish, tai-pan?" someone shouted.

"Good God," he called back. "You know the procedure."

The elevator stopped at every level. More owners and friends crammed in. More shouts about what a great race but what the hell's the objection? At last they reached ground level. Dunross rushed out onto the track where a group of ma-foo and officials surrounded Travkin who lay there crumpled and inert. Noble Star had fought to her feet, unhurt, and was now on the far side galloping riderless around the course, stable hands scattered and waiting to intercept her. Up the track on the last bend, the vet was kneeling beside the agonized roan gelding, Kingplay, his back leg broken, the bone jutting through. The sound of the shot did not penetrate the roars and counter roars of the impatient onlookers, their eyes fixed on the tote, waiting for the stewards' judgment.

Dunross knelt beside Travkin, one of the ma-foo holding an umbrella over the unconscious man. "How is he, Doctor?"

"He didn't slam into the rails, missed them by a miracle. He's not dead, at least not yet, tai-pan," Dr. Meng, the police pathologist, said nervously, used to dead bodies, not live patients. "I can't tell, not until he comes around. There's no apparent hemorrhaging externally. His neck . . . and his back seem all right . . . I can't tell yet . . ."

Two St. John's ambulance men hurried up with a stretcher. "Where should we take him, sir?"

Dunross looked around. "Sammy," he said to one of his stableboys, "go and fetch Doc Tooley. He should be in our box." To the ambulance men he said, "Keep Mr. Travkin in the ambulance till Doc Tooley gets here. What about the other three jockeys?"

"Two are just shook up, sir. One, Captain Pettikin, has a broken leg but he's already in a splint."

Very carefully the men put Travkin on the stretcher. McBride joined them, then Gornt and others. "How is he, Ian?"

"We don't know. Yet. He seems all right." Gently Dunross lifted one of Travkin's hands, examining it. He had thought he had seen a blow in the far turn and Travkin falter. A heavy red weal disfigured the back of his right hand. And the other one. "What could have caused this, Dr. Meng?"

"Oh!" More confidently the little man said, "The reins perhaps. Perhaps a whip, could be a blow . . . perhaps in falling."

Gornt said nothing, just watched, inwardly seething that Bluey White could have been so inept when everything had been so neatly set up beforehand with a word here, a promise there. Half the bloody stadium must have seen him, he thought.

Dunross examined Travkin's ashen face. No marks other than inevitable bruising. A little blood seeped out of the nose.

"It's already coagulating. That's a good sign," Dr. Meng volunteered.

The governor hurried up. "How is he?"

Dunross repeated what the doctor had said.

"Damned bad luck, Noble Star shying like that."

"Yes."

"What's the stewards' objection, Ian?"

"We're just going to discuss that, sir. Would you care to join us?"

"Oh, no, no thank you. I'll just wait and be patient. I wanted to make sure Travkin was all right." The governor felt the rain running down his back. He looked up at the sky. "Blasted weather—looks like it's here to stay. Are you going to continue the meet?"

"I'm going to recommend we cancel, or postpone."

"Good idea."

"Yes," McBride said. "I agree. We can't afford another accident."

"When you have a moment, Ian," Sir Geoffrey said, "I'll be in my box."

Dunross's attention focused. "Did you talk to the minister, sir?" he asked, trying to sound matter-of-fact.

"Yes." Sir Geoffrey was equally casual. "Yes, he called on the private line."

Abruptly the tai-pan was conscious of Gornt and the others. "I'll walk you back, sir." To McBride he said, "I'll follow you at once," then turned away and the two of them walked for the elevator.

Once alone Sir Geoffrey muttered, "Hardly the place for a private conversation, what?"

"We could exmaine the course, sir." Dunross led the way to the rail, praying. "The turf's terrible, isn't it?" he said, pointing.

"Very." Sir Geoffrey also kept his back to the eyes. "The minister was very perturbed. He left the decision about Brian to me, providing Mr. Sinders and Mr. Crosse first agree to the release, pro—"

"Surely they'll agree with you, sir?" Uneasily Dunross recalled his conversation with them last night.

"I can only advise. I will advise them it is necessary providing you assure me it is. You personally."

"Of course," Dunross said slowly. "But surely Havergill, Southerby or the other bankers would carry more weight."

"In banking matters, Ian, yes. But I think I require your personal assurance and cooperation also."

"Sir?"

"This matter will have to be handled very delicately, by you, not by them. Then there's the problem of those files. The AMG files."

"What about them, sir?"

"That's for you to answer. Mr. Sinders told me of his conversation with you last night." Sir Geoffrey lit his pipe, his hands cupping the flame, protecting it from the rain. After the tai-pan's call to him this morning he had at once sent for Crosse and Sinders to discuss the matter of the exchange prior to asking the minister. Sinders had reiterated his concern that the files might have been doctored. He said he might agree to release Kwok if he was sure of those files. Crosse had suggested trading Kwok for Fongfong and the others.

Now Sir Geoffrey looked at Dunross searchingly. "Well, Ian?"

"Tiptop's due, or was due this afternoon. May I assume that I can say yes to his proposal?"

"Yes, providing you first get Mr. Sinders's agreement. And Mr. Crosse's."

"Can't you give that to me, sir?"

"No. The minister was quite clear. If you want to ask them now, they are in the members' stands."

"They know the result of your call?"

"Yes. Sorry but the minister made it very clear." Sir Geoffrey was gentle. "It seems the reputation for fairness and honesty of the present tai-pan of the Noble House is known even in those hallowed places. Both the minister and I bank on it." A burst of cheering distracted them. Noble

Star had broken through the cordon of *ma-foo* trying to recapture her, and galloped past them, officials and stableboys scattering. "Perhaps you'd better deal with the race objection first. I'll be in my box. Join me for tea or a cocktail if you wish."

Dunross thanked him then hurried for the stewards' room, his mind in turmoil.

"Ah, Ian," Shitee T'Chung, the nominal chairman called out anxiously as he came in, all the stewards now present. "We really have to decide quickly."

"That's hard without Travkin's evidence," Dunross said. "How many of you saw Bluey White slash at him?"

Only McBride put up his hand.

"That's only two of us out of twelve." Dunross saw Crosse watching him. "I'm certain. And there was a weal across both his hands. Dr. Meng said it could have been made by a whip or the reins in falling. Pug, what's your opinion?"

Pugmire broke an uncomfortable silence. "I saw nothing malicious, personally. I was watching like hell because I was on Noble Star, 1,000 on the nose. Whether there was a blow or not it didn't seem to make much difference. I didn't see her falter, or any of the pack, other than Kingplay. Noble Star was well in the running till the post and everyone had their whips out." He tossed over one of the copies of the photo finish.

Dunross picked it up. The photo was as he had seen it: Pilot Fish by a nose from Noble Star, by a nostril from Butterscotch Lass, by a nose from Winning Billy.

"They've all got their whips out," Pugmire continued, "and they had in the turn, quite rightly. It could easily have been accidental—if there was a blow."

"Shitee?"

"I must confess, old boy, I was watching my Street Vendor and cursing Kingplay. I thought your filly'd pipped Pilot Fish. We, er, we've polled the other trainers and there's, er, no formal complaint. I agree with Pug."

"Roger?"

"I saw nothing untoward."

"Jason?"

To his surprise Plumm shook his head and disagreed and Dunross wondered again about AMG and his astonishing accusation of Plumm and Sevrin. "We all know Bluey White's cunning," Plumm was saying. "We've had to warn him before. If the tai-pan and Donald say they saw it I vote we debar him and disqualify Pilot Fish when it comes to a vote."

Dunross polled the other stewards, the rest wavering.

"Let's call in the jockeys, White last."

They did. All the jockeys muttered permutations of the same thing: they were too busy with their own mounts to notice anything.

Now the stewards looked at Dunross, waiting. He stared back, well

aware that if he said, I vote we unanimously debar Bluey White for interference and disqualify Pilot Fish, all in favor say aye! that they would concede and vote as he wished.

I saw him do it, he told himself, so did Donald, and others, and it shook
Alexi for that necessary split second. Even so, in all honesty I don't think
that cost Noble Star the race. I blew the race myself. Alexi was the wrong
choice for this race. He should have shoved Pilot Fish into the rails on the
second corner when he had the chance, or put his whip across Bluey
White's face, not his hands as I'd have done, oh yes, without hesitation.
And there are other considerations.

"There's no doubt in my mind there was interference," he said. "But
whether by accident or design I doubt if even Alexi will know. I agree it
didn't cost Noble Star the race so I suggest we just caution Bluey and let
the result stand."

"Excellent." Shitee T'Chung exhaled and beamed and they all relaxed,
none of them, least of all Pugmire, wanting a confrontation with the tai-
pan. "Anyone against? Good! Let's release the photo finish to the papers
and make the announcement over the loudspeakers. Will you do that, tai-
pan?"

"Certainly. But what about the rest of the program? Look at the rain."
It was pelting down now. "Listen, I've an idea." He told it to them.

A whoop of excitement and they all laughed. "Very good, oh very
good!"

"Grand!" Dunstan Barre exploded.

"That'll give the buggers something to think about!" Pugmire said.

"Great idea, tai-pan!" McBride beamed. "Oh very good."

"I'll go to the control center—perhaps you'd get Bluey back and give
him what for, scare him, eh?"

Pugmire said, "A word, Ian?"

"Can we make it later?"

"Of course. Roger, can I have a word?"

"Of course. I'll be down in the members' stand with Sinders."

"Oh, not in your box?"

"No, I let the commissioner have it for a private party."

"Ian?"

"Yes, Jason?"

"Do you think they'll hold the hill climb tomorrow?"

"If this keeps up, no. That whole area'll be a quagmire. Why?"

"Nothing. I was planning a cocktail party early Sunday evening to celebrate your Superfoods coup!"

Shitee T'Chung chortled. "Jolly good idea! Congratulations, Ian! Did
you see Biltzmann's face?"

"Ian, would you be free? I won't invite Biltzmann," Plumm added to
much laughter. "It'll be at our company flat in Sinclair Towers."

934 JAMES CLAVELL

"Sorry, I'm going to Taipei early afternoon, sorry, at least that's my present plan. Th—"

Pugmire interrupted with sudden concern, "You won't be here Monday? What about our papers, and everything?"

"No problem, Pug. 9:30 we close." To Plumm Dunross said, "Jason if I cancel or postpone Taipei, I'll accept."

"Good. 7:30 to 9:30 casual."

Dunross walked off, his frown deepening, surprised that Plumm was so friendly. Ordinarily he was the opposition on all the boards they shared, siding with Gornt and Havergill against him, particularly on the Victoria's board.

Outside the stewards' room there were milling clusters of anxious reporters, owners, trainers and bystanders. Dunross brushed aside the barrage of questions all the way to the control room. It was on the top floor.

"Hello, sir," the announcer said, everyone tense in the small glass booth that had the best view of the course. "Marvelous race, pity about . . . Do you have the decision? It's Bluey, isn't it, we all saw the whip. . . ."

"May I use the mike?"

"Oh of course." The man hastily moved and Dunross sat in his place. He clicked on the switch. "This is Ian Dunross, the stewards have asked me to make two announcements. . . ."

The silence was vast as his words echoed and re-echoed over the stadium. The fifty thousand held their breaths, careless of the rain, in the stands and on every soaring level. "First, the result of the fifth race." Dead silence but for the sound of the rain. Dunross took a deep breath. "Pilot Fish by a nose from Noble Star by a whisker from Butterscotch Lass. . . ." but the last was drowned by the cheers and counter cheers, happiness and disgust, and everyone throughout the stadium was shouting, arguing, cheering, cursing and, down in the paddock, Gornt was astonished, having been convinced that his jockey had been seen as he had seen him, had been caught and carpeted and the result would be set aside. In the pandemonium the winning numbers flashed on to the tote: one, seven, eight.

Dunross waited a moment and breezily repeated the result in Cantonese, the crowd more docile, their pent-up anxieties allayed, for the stewards' decision was final. "Second, the stewards have decided, due to the weather and bad conditions, to cancel the rest of the meet . . ." A vast groan went over the crowd. ". . . actually to postpone until next Saturday for another special meet." A sudden great roar and excitement picked up. "We will have a meet of eight races and the fifth will be the same as today, with the same runners, Pilot Fish, Butterscotch Lass, Winning Billy, Street Vendor, Golden Lady, Lochinvar and Noble Star. A special return challenge with double stakes, 30,000 added. . . ."

Cheers and more cheers, applause and roars and someone in the booth said, "Christ what a great idea, tai-pan! Noble Star'll take that black bastard!"

"Oh no he won't! Butterscotch . . ."

"Great idea, tai-pan."

Into the mike Dunross said, "The stewards appreciate your continued support." He repeated it in Cantonese, adding, "There will be a further special announcement in a few minutes. Thank you!" in both languages.

Another huge cheer and those in the rain scurried for cover or for the winning windows, everyone chattering, groaning, cursing the gods or blessing them, choking the exits, long lines of men, women and children seeking the long way home, a wonderful new happiness possessing them. Only those who possessed the winning double quinella numbers, eight and five in the second, one and seven in the fifth, stood paralyzed, staring at the tote, waiting for the winning odds to be declared.

"Another announcement, tai-pan?" the announcer asked anxiously.

"Yes," Dunross said. "Around five." Havergill had told him that the deal with Richard Kwang had been struck and had asked him to go to the Victoria box as soon as possible. He reached the exit door and went down the steps three at a time to the next level, very pleased with himself. Giving the race to Pilot Fish's got to throw Gornt, he thought. Gornt knew and I knew it was a carve-up and that Alexi was set up whatever he did—which is the major reason I didn't ride. They'd've tried it on me and I would have killed someone. But next Saturday . . . ah, next Saturday I'll ride and Bluey White won't dare, nor will the other trainers, next Saturday'll be fair game and they'll be on notice by God. His excitement picked up a beat. Then ahead in the crowded corridor he saw Murtagh waiting for him.

"Oh tai-pan, can I se—"

"Of course." Dunross led him through the kitchen into his private room.

"That was a great race. I won a bundle," the young man said excitedly, "and great about Saturday."

"Good." Then Dunross noticed the sweat on the man's forehead. Oh Christ, he thought. "Are we in business, Mr. Murtagh?"

"Please call me Dave, the brass said, er, they said maybe. They've scheduled a board meeting for tomorrow, 9:00 A.M. their time. Our time that's . . ."

"10:00 P.M. this evening. Yes. Excellent, Mr. Murtagh, then call me on this number." Dunross wrote it down. "Please don't lose it and don't give it to anyone else."

"Oh, of course, tai-pan, I'll call the very moment . . . How late can I call?"

"The moment you put the phone down to them. Keep calling till you get me." Dunross got up. "Sorry but there's rather a lot to do."

"Oh sure, sure!" Murtagh added uneasily, "Say, tai-pan, I just heard about the 2 million down on the General Stores tender. 2 million from us by 9:30 Monday's gotta be kinda pushing it."

"I rather expected it would be—for your group. Fortunately, Mr. Murtagh, I never planned on that modest amount of cash being your money. I know First Central is inclined to be like the mills of God—they grind slowly—unless they wish to remove themselves from the arena," he added, remembering many friends who had been hurt by their precipitous withdrawal years back. "Not to worry, my *new* external source of credit's more th—"

"What?" Murtagh blanched.

"My new external source of finance reacts at once to any sudden business opportunities, Mr. Murtagh. This took them just eight minutes. They seem to have more confidence than your principals."

"Hell, tai-pan, please call me Dave, it's not lack of confidence but, well, they've no idea of Asia. I've got to convince them the General Stores takeover's got to double your gross in three years."

"In one," Dunross interrupted firmly, enjoying himself. "So sorry your group won't share in our huge profits from that minor section of our immense expansion plans. Do have some tea in the box, sorry, I just have to make a phone call." He took Murtagh's elbow and firmly led him out of the door, shutting it after him.

In the kitchen Murtagh was staring at the closed door, the happy clatter of plates and Cantonese obscenities from the twenty cooks and helpers a vast din. "Jesus," he muttered in near panic, "eight minutes? Shit, are the goddamn Swiss horning in on our client?" He tottered away.

Inside the room Dunross was on his private phone, listening to the ringing tone. "*Weyyyyy?*"

"Mr. Tip please," he said carefully in Cantonese. "This is Mr. Dunross calling."

He heard the phone put down with a clatter and the *amah* shriek, "It's the phone! For you, Father!"

"Who is it?"

"A foreign devil."

Dunross smiled.

"Hello?"

"Ian Dunross, Mr. Tip. I was just concerned that your illness wasn't worse."

"Ah, ah, yes, so sorry I could not arrive. Yes. I, I had some pressing business, you understand? Yes. Very pressing. Oh by the way, that was bad joss about Noble Star. I just heard on the wireless that Pilot Fish won by a nose after an objection. What was the objection?"

Patiently Dunross explained and answered questions about his General Stores takeover bid, delighted that that news had already reached him. If Tiptop, then all newspapers. Good, he thought, waiting Tiptop out but Tiptop outsmarted him. "Well, thank you for calling, tai-pan."

At once Dunross said, "It was my pleasure, oh by the way, confidentially, I understand it may well be possible that the police have discovered one of their underlings has made a mistake."

"Ah. I presume the mistake will be corrected immediately?"

"I would presume very soon, if the person concerned wishes to resign and take advantage of permission to travel abroad."

"How soon might very soon be, tai-pan?"

Dunross was picking his words carefully, deliberately vague though formal now. "There are certain formalities, but it is possible that it could be quickly achieved. Unfortunately VIPs have to be consulted elsewhere. I'm sure you understand."

"Certainly. But the mighty dragon is no match for the native serpent, heya? I understand there is one of your VVIPs already in Hong Kong. A Mr. Sinders?"

Dunross blinked at the extent of Tiptop's knowledge. "I have certain approvals already," he said, disquieted.

"I would have thought very few approvals were necessary. True gold fears no fire."

"Yes. Is there somewhere I could call you this evening—to report progress?"

"This number will find me. Please call me at 9:00 P.M." Tiptop's voice became even drier. "I understand it might well be possible that your last suggestion about banking might be serviced. Of course any bank would need proper documentation to secure an immediate half billion Hong Kong dollars in cash, but I hear that the Victoria's chop, the governor's chop and yours would be all that's required to secure the loan for thirty days. This . . . minor amount of cash is ready, for a limited time, whenever the correct procedures are entered into. Until that time this matter is confidential, very strictly confidential."

"Of course."

"Thank you for calling."

Dunross put the phone down and wiped his palms. "For a limited time" was branded on his mind. He knew, and he knew Tiptop knew he understood that the two "procedures" were absolutely interlinked but not necessarily. Christ Jesus I love Asia, he thought happily as he rushed off.

The corridors were filled, many people already crowding the elevators to go home. He peered into his box, caught Gavallan's eye. "Andrew, go down to the members' stand and get hold of Roger Crosse—he's there with a fellow called Sinders. Ask them if they've a moment to join me in my box! Hurry!"

Gavallan took off. Dunross hurried along the corridor past the betting windows.

"Tai-pan!" Casey called out. "Sorry about Noble Star! Did y—"

"Be back in a minute, Casey. Sorry, can't stop!" Dunross called back on the run. He noticed Gornt at the winning window but it did not take away his happiness. First things first, he thought. "How do you want the 10,000? Our bet?"

"Cash will do very nicely, thank you," Gornt said.

"I'll send it around later."

"Monday will do just as well."

"Later tonight. Monday I'll be busy." Dunross walked off with a polite nod.

In the packed Victoria box the uproar was the same as everywhere. Drinks, laughter, excitement and some cursing about Pilot Fish but already wagers were being placed on next Saturday's race. As Dunross came in there were more cheers, condolences and another volley of questions. He fielded them all casually and one from Martin Haply who was jammed beside the door with Adryon.

"Oh, Father, what rotten luck about Noble Star. I lost my shirt and my month's allowance!"

Dunross grinned. "Young ladies shouldn't bet! Hello, Haply!"

"Can I ask ab—"

"Later. Adryon darling, don't forget cocktails. You're hostess."

"Oh yes, we'll be there. Father, can you advance me my next mon—"

"Certainly," Dunross said to her astonishment, gave her a hug and pushed his way over to Havergill, Richard Kwang nearby.

"Hello, Ian," Havergill said. "Bad luck, but clearly Pilot Fish had the edge."

"Yes, yes he did. Hello, Richard." Dunross gave him the copy of the photo finish. "Damned bad luck for both of us." Others crowded to see it.

"Good God, by a whisker . . ."

"I thought Noble Star . . ."

Taking advantage of the diversion Dunross bent closer to Havergill. "Is everything signed?"

"Yes. 20 cents on the dollar. He agreed to and signed the provisional papers. Formal papers by the end of the week. Of course the rotter tried to wheedle but it's all signed."

"Marvelous. You did a terrific deal."

Havergill nodded. "Yes. Yes, I know."

Richard Kwang turned around. "Ah, tai-pan." He dropped his voice and whispered, "Has Paul told you about the merger?"

"Of course. May I offer congratulations."

"Congratulations?" Southerby echoed, coming up to them. "Damned bad luck if you ask me! I had my bundle on Butterscotch Lass!"

The tempo of the room picked up as the governor came in. Havergill went to meet him, Dunross following. "Ah, Paul, Ian. Damned bad luck but an excellent decision! Both of them." His face hardened nicely. "Next Saturday will certainly be a needle match."

"Yes sir."

"Paul, you wanted to make a formal announcement?"

"Yes sir." Havergill raised his voice. "May I have your attention please . . ." No one took any notice until Dunross took a spoon and banged it against a teapot. Gradually there was silence. "Your Excellency, ladies and gentlemen, I have the honor to announce, on behalf of the directors of the Victoria Bank of Hong Kong and China, that an immediate merger has been arranged with the great Ho-Pak Bank of Hong Kong . . ." Martin Haply dropped his glass. ". . . and that the Victoria totally guarantees 100 percent of all Ho-Pak depositors and . . ."

The rest was drowned out with a great cheer. Guests in the nearby boxes craned over the balconies to see what was happening. The news was shouted across as others came in from the corridors and soon there were more cheers.

Havergill was besieged with questions and he held up his hand, delighted with the effect of his announcement. In the silence Sir Geoffrey said quickly, "I must say, on behalf of Her Majesty's Government, that this is marvelous news, Paul, good for Hong Kong, good for the bank, good for you, Richard, and the Ho-Pak!"

"Oh yes, Sir Geoffrey," Richard Kwang said, jovial and loud, sure that now he was a giant step nearer his knighthood. "I decided—of course with our directors—I decided it would be good for the Victoria to have a major foothold in the Chinese community an—"

Hastily Havergill interrupted and overrode him. "Richard, perhaps I'd better finish the formal announcement and leave the details to our press conference." He glanced at Martin Haply. "We have scheduled a formal press conference for Monday at noon but all details of the, er, merger have been agreed. Isn't that so, Richard?"

Richard Kwang began to make another variation but quickly changed his mind, seeing both Dunross's and Havergill's look. "Er, yes, yes," he said but could not resist adding, "I'm delighted to be partners with the Victoria."

Haply called out quickly, "Excuse me, Mr. Havergill, may I ask a question?"

"Of course," Havergill said affably, well aware of what he would be asked. This bastard Haply has to go, he thought, one way or another.

"May I ask, Mr. Havergill, how you propose to pay out all the Ho-Pak customers and yours, Blacs and all the other banks when there's a run on all of them and not enough cash in the till?"

"Rumors, rumors, Mr. Haply," Havergill replied airily and added to laughter, "Remember: A swarm of mosquitoes can create a noise like thunder! Hong Kong's economy has never been stronger. As to the so-called run on the Ho-Pak, that's over. The Victoria guarantees the Ho-Pak's depositors, guarantees the Struan-General Stores takeover and guarantees to be in business for the next hundred and twenty years."

"But Mr. Havergill, would you ans—"

"Not to worry, Mr. Haply. Let's leave the details of our . . . our benevolent umbrella for the Ho-Pak till our press conference on Monday." At once he turned to the governor. "If you'll excuse me, sir, I'll make it public." There were more cheers as he started through the crush toward the door.

Someone began singing, "For he's a jolly good fellow . . ." Everyone joined in. The noise became deafening. Dunross said to Richard Kwang in Cantonese, quoting an old expression, " 'When it is enough, stop.' Heya?"

"Ah, ah yes. Yes, tai-pan. Yes indeed." The banker smiled a sickly smile, understanding the threat, reminding himself of his good fortune, that Venus Poon would certainly kowtow now that he was an important director on the board of the Victoria. His smile broadened. "You're right, tai-pan. 'Inside the red doors there is much waste of meat and wine!' My expertise will greatly benefit our bank, heya?" He went off importantly.

"My God, what a day!" Johnjohn muttered.

"Yes, yes, marvelous! Johnjohn, old fellow," McBride said, "you must be very proud of Paul."

"Yes, of course." Johnjohn was watching Havergill leave.

"Are you feeling all right?"

"Oh yes, I was just working late." Johnjohn had been up most of the night estimating how they could safely effect the takeover, safely for the bank and for the Ho-Pak depositors. He had been the architect and this morning he had spent more wearisome hours trying to convince Havergill that now was the time to be innovative. "We can do it, Paul, and create such a resurgence of confid—"

"And a very dangerous precedent! I don't think your idea's as important as you imagine!"

It was only when Havergill had seen the enormous and immediate gain in confidence after Dunross's dramatic announcement that he had reconsidered. Never mind, Johnjohn thought wearily, we're all gainers. The bank, Hong Kong, the Ho-Pak. Certainly we'll do very well for their investors, stockholders and backers, far better than Richard! When I'm tai-pan I'll use the Ho-Pak as a pattern for future bail-outs. With our new management the Ho-Pak will be a marvelous asset. Like any one of a dozen enterprises. Even like Struan's!

Johnjohn's tiredness vanished. His smile broadened. Oh hurry up, Monday—when the market opens!

In the Struan box Peter Marlowe was gloomily leaning on the rail, watching the crowds below. Rain cascaded off the jutting overhang protecting the boxes. The three cantilever balconies of the members and non-voting members were not so protected. Bedraggled horses were being led down the ramps, bedraggled grooms joining the bedraggled thousands streaming away.

"What's up, Peter?" Casey asked.

"Oh nothing."

"Not Fleur, no problem there I hope?"

"No."

"Was it Grey? I saw you both having at it."

"No, no it wasn't Grey, though he's a pain, ill-mannered and stridently anti-everything of value." Marlowe smiled curiously. "We were just discussing the weather."

"Sure. You were looking depressed as hell just then. You lost the fifth?"

"Yes, but it wasn't that. I'm ahead, well ahead on the day." The tall man hesitated then motioned at the boxes and all around. "It's just that I was thinking that there're fifty thousand-odd Chinese here and another three or four million out there, and each one's got a vast heritage, marvelous secrets, and fantastic stories to tell, to say nothing of the twenty-odd thousand Europeans, high and low, the tai-pans, the pirates, freebooters, accountants, shopkeepers, government people here—why did they choose Hong Kong too? And I know that however much I try, however much I read or listen or ask, I'll never really know very much about Hong Kong Chinese or about Hong Kong. Never. I'll only ever scratch the surface."

She laughed. "It's the same everywhere."

"Oh no, no it isn't. This's the potpourri of Asia. Take that guy—the one in the third box over—the rotund Chinese. He's a millionaire many times over. His wife's a kleptomaniac so whenever she goes out he has his people follow her secretly and every time she steals something, his fellows pay for it. All the stores know her and him and it's all very civilized—where else in the world would you do that? His father was a coolie and his father a highwayman and *his* a Mandarin and *his* a peasant. One of the men near him's another multimillionaire, opium and illegal stuff into China, and his wife's . . . ah well, that's another story."

"What story?"

He laughed. "Some wives have stories just as fascinating as their husbands, sometimes more so. One of the wives you met today, she's a nympho an—"

"Oh come on, Peter! It's like Fleur says, you're making it all up."

"Perhaps. Oh yes, but some Chinese ladies are just as . . . just as predatory as any ladies on earth, on the quiet."

"Chauvinist! You're sure?"

"Rumor has it . . ." They laughed together. "Actually they're so much smarter than we are, the Chinese. I'm told the few Chinese married ladies here who have a wandering eye usually prefer a European for a lover, for safety—Chinese adore gossip, love scandal, and it'd be rare to find a Chinese swinger who'd be able to keep such a secret or protect a lady's honor. Rightly, the lady would be afraid. To be caught would be very bad, very bad indeed. Chinese law's quite strict." He took out a cigarette. "Maybe that makes it all the more exciting."

"To have a lover?"

He watched her, pondering what she would say if he told her her nickname—whispered gleefully to him by four separate Chinese friends. "Oh yes, ladies here get around, some of them. Look over there, in that box— the fellow holding forth wearing a blazer. He wears a green hat—that's a Chinese expression meaning he's a cuckold, that his wife's got a lover, actually in her case it was a Chinese friend of his."

"Green hat?"

"Yes. Chinese are marvelous! They have such a terrific sense of humor. That fellow took out an ad in one of the Chinese papers some months ago that said, 'I know I wear a green hat but the wife of the man who gave it to me had two of his sons by other men!' "

Casey stared at him. "You mean he signed his name to it?"

"Oh yes. It was a pun on one of his names, but everyone of importance knew who it was."

"Was it true?"

Peter Marlowe shrugged. "It doesn't matter. The other fellow's nose was neatly out of joint and his wife got hell."

"That's not fair, not fair at all."

"In her case it was."

"What did she do?"

"Had two sons by anoth—"

"Oh come on, Mr. Storyteller!"

"Hey look, there's Doc Tooley!"

She searched the course below, then saw him. "He doesn't look happy at all."

"I hope Travkin's all right. I heard Tooley went to examine him."

"That was some spill."

"Yes. Terrible."

Both had been subjected to Tooley's searching questions about their health, knowing the specter of typhus, perhaps cholera, and certainly hepatitis still hung over them.

"Joss!" Peter Marlowe had said firmly.

"Joss!" she had echoed, trying not to be worried about Linc. It's worse for a man, she thought, remembering what Tooley had said: Hepatitis can mess up your liver—and your life, forever, if you're a man.

After a moment she said, "People here do seem to be more exciting, Peter. Is that because of Asia?"

"Probably. The mores are so different. And here in Hong Kong we collect the cream. I think Asia's the center of the world and Hong Kong the nucleus." Peter Marlowe waved to someone in another box who waved at Casey. "There's another admirer of yours."

"Lando? He is a fascinating man."

Casey had spent time with him between races.

"You must come to Macao, Miss Tcholok. Perhaps we could have dinner tomorrow. Would 7:30 be convenient?" Mata had said with his marvelous old world charm and Casey had got the message very quickly.

During lunch Dunross had warned her a little about him. "He's a good fellow, Casey," the tai-pan had said delicately. "But here, for a *quai loh* stranger, particularly someone as beautiful as you, on a first trip to Asia, well it's sometimes better to remember that being over eighteen isn't always enough."

"Got you, tai-pan," she had told him with a laugh. But this afternoon she had allowed herself to be mesmerized by Mata, in the safety of the tai-pan's box. Alone, her defenses would be up as she knew they would be tomorrow evening: "It depends, Lando," she had said, "dinner would be fine. It depends what time I get back from the boat trip—I don't know if it's weather permitting or not."

"With whom are you going? The tai-pan?"

"Just friends."

"Ah. Well, if not Sunday, my dear, perhaps we could make it Monday. There are a number of business opportunities for you, here or in Macao, for you and Mr. Bartlett if you wish, and Par-Con. May I call you at seven tomorrow to see if you are free?"

I can deal with him, one way or another, she reassured herself, the thought warming her, though I'll watch the wine and maybe even the water in case the old Mickey Finn.

"Peter, the men here, the ones on the make—are they into Mickey Finns?"

His eyes narrowed. "You mean Mata?"

"No, just generally."

"I doubt if a Chinese or Eurasian would give one to a *quai loh* if that's what you're asking." A frown creased him. "I'd say you'd have to be fairly circumspect though, with them and with Europeans. Of course, to be blunt, you'd be high on their list. You have what it takes to send most of them into an orgiastic faint."

"Thanks much!" She leaned on the balcony, enjoying the compliment. I wish Linc were here. Be patient. "Who's that?" she asked. "The old man leering at the young girl? Down on the first balcony. Look, he's got his hand on her butt!"

"Ah, that's one of our local pirates—Four Finger Wu. The girl's Venus Poon, a local TV star. The youth talking to them is his nephew. Actually the rumor is that he's a son. The fellow's got a Harvard business degree and a U.S. passport and he's as smart as a whip. Old Four Fingers is another multimillionaire, rumored to be a smuggler, gold and anything, with one official wife, three concs of various ages and now he's after Venus Poon. She was Richard Kwang's current. Was. But perhaps now with the Victoria takeover she'll dump Four Fingers and go back to him. Four Fingers lives on a rotten old Aberdeen junk and hoards his enormous wealth. Ah, look there! The wrinkled old man and woman the tai-pan's talking to."

She followed his glance to the next box but one.

"That's Shitee T'Chung's box," he said. "Shitee's a direct descendent of May-may and Dirk through their son Duncan. Did the tai-pan ever show you Dirk's portraits?"

"Yes." A small shiver touched her as she remembered the Hag's knife jammed through the portrait of her father, Tyler Brock. She considered telling him about it but decided not to. "There's a great likeness," she said.

"There certainly is! Wish I could see the Long Gallery. Anyway, that old couple he's talking to live in a tenement, a two-room, sixth-floor walk-up over in Glessing's Point. They own a huge block of Struan stock. Every year before each annual board meeting, the tai-pan, whoever he is, has to go cap in hand to ask for the right to vote the stock. It's always granted, that was part of the original agreement, but he still has to go personally."

"Why's that?"

"Face. And because of the Hag." A flicker of a smile. "She was a great lady, Casey. Oh how I would like to have met her! During the Boxer revolt in 1899–1900, when China was in another of her conflagrations, the Noble House had all its possessions in Peking, Tiensin, Foochow and Canton wiped out by the Boxer terrorists who were more or less sponsored and certainly encouraged by Tz'u Hsi, the old dowager empress. They called themselves the Righteous Harmonious Fists and their battle cry was 'Protect the Ch'ing and kill all foreign devils!' Let's face it, the European powers and Japan had pretty much partitioned China. Anyway, the Boxers fell on all foreign business houses, settlements, the unprotected areas, and obliterated them. The Noble House was in terrible straits. At that time the nominal tai-pan was again old Sir Lochlin Struan—he was Robb Struan's last son, born with a withered arm. He was tai-pan after Culum. The Hag had appointed him when he was eighteen, just after Culum died—then again after Dirk Dunross—and she'd kept him tied to her apron strings till he died in 1915 at the age of seventy-two."

"Where do you get all this information, Peter?"

"I make it up," he said grandly. "In any event, the Hag needed a lot of money fast. Gornt's grandfather had bought up a lot of Struan's paper and he had lowered the boom. There was no normal source of finance, nowhere she could borrow, for all Asia—all the *hongs*—were equally in turmoil. But that fellow's father, the father of the one the tai-pan's talking to, was the King of the Beggars in Hong Kong. Begging used to be a huge business here. Anyway, this man came to see her, so the story goes. 'I come to buy a fifth part of the Noble House,' this man said with great dignity, 'is it for sale? I offer 200,000 taels of silver,' which was exactly the amount she needed to redeem her paper. For face they haggled and he settled for a tenth, 10 percent—an incredibly fair deal—both knowing that he could have had 30 or 40 percent for the same amount because by that time the Hag was desperate. He required no contract other than her chop and her promise that once a year she, or the tai-pan, would come to him or his descendents wherever he or they lived, to ask for the vote of the stock. 'So long as the tai-pan asks—the voting power is given.'

"'But why, Honorable King of the Beggars? Why save me from my enemies?' she asked.

"'Because your grandfather, old Green-Eyed Devil, once saved my grandfather's face and helped him become the first King of the Beggars of Hong Kong.'"

Casey sighed. "Do you believe that, Peter?"

"Oh yes." He looked out at Happy Valley. "Once this was all a malarial swamp. Dirk cleaned that up too." He puffed his cigarette. "One day I'll write about Hong Kong."

"If you continue to smoke you'll never write anything."

"Point well taken. Okay, I'll stop. Now. For today. Because you're pretty." He stubbed the cigarette out. Another smile, different. "Eeeee, but I could tell some stories about lots of the people you met today. I won't, that's not fair, not right. I can never tell the real stories, though I know lots!" She laughed with him, letting her eyes wander from the strange old couple down to the other stands. Involuntarily she gasped. Sitting in the lee of the members' balcony she saw Orlanda. Linc was with her. He was very close. Both were very happy together, that was easy to see, even from this distance.

"What's th—" Peter Marlowe began, then he saw them too. "Oh! Not to worry."

After a pause she took her eyes away. "Peter, that favor. May I ask for that favor, now?"

"What do you want as a favor?"

"I want to know about Orlanda."

"To destroy her?"

"For protection. Protection for Linc against her."

"Perhaps he doesn't want to be protected, Casey."

"I swear I'll never use it unless I honest to God feel it's necessary."

The tall man sighed. "Sorry," he said with great compassion, "but nothing I could tell you about her would give you or Linc protection. Nothing to destroy her or make her lose face. Even if I could I wouldn't, Casey. That really wouldn't be cricket. Would it?"

"No, but I'm still asking." She stared back at him, forcing the issue. "You said a favor. I came when you needed a hand. I need a hand now. Please."

He watched her a long time. "What do you know about her?"

She told him what she had learned—about Gornt supporting Orlanda, Macao, about the child.

"Then you know everything I know, except perhaps that you should be sorry for her."

"Why?"

"Because she's Eurasian, alone, Gornt her only support and that's as precarious as anything in the world. She's living on a knife edge. She's young, beautiful and deserves a future. Here there's none for her."

"Except Linc?"

"Except Linc or someone like him." Peter Marlowe's eyes were slate color. "Perhaps that wouldn't be so bad from his point of view."

"Because she's Asian and I'm not?"

Again the curious smile. "Because she's a woman and so are you but you hold all the cards, and the only real thing you have to decide is if you really want that war."

"Level with me, Peter, please. I'm asking. What's your advice? I'm running scared—there, I'll admit it to you. Please?"

"All right, but this isn't the favor I owe you," he said. "Rumor has it you and Linc are not lovers though you obviously love him. Rumor has it you've been together for six or seven years in close proximity but with no . . . no formal contact. He's a terrific fellow, you're a terrific lady and you'd make a great couple. The key word is *couple*, Casey. Maybe you want money and power and Par-Con more than you do him. That's your problem. I don't think you can have both."

"Why not?"

"It seems to me you choose Par-Con and power and riches and no Bartlett, other than as a friend—or you become Mrs. Linc Bartlett and behave and *love* and be the kind of woman there's no doubt in hell Orlanda would be. Either way you have to be a hundred percent—you and Linc are both too strong and probably have tested each other too many times to be fooled. He's been divorced once, so he's on guard. You're over the age of a Juliet blindness so you're equally on guard."

"Are you a psychiatrist too?"

He laughed. "No, nor a father-confessor, though I like to know about people and like to listen but not to lecture and never to give advice—that's the most thankless task in the world."

"So there's no compromise?"

"I don't think so, but then I'm not you. You have your own karma. Irrespective of Orlanda—if it's not her it'll be another woman, better or worse, prettier though maybe not, because win, lose or draw, Orlanda's quality and has what it takes to make a man content, happy, alive as a *man*. Sorry, I don't mean to be chauvinistic, but since you asked, I'd advise you to make up your mind quickly."

Gavallan hurried into Shitee T'Chung's box and joined the tai-pan. "Afternoon," he said politely to the old couple. "Sorry, tai-pan, Crosse and the other fellow you wanted had already left."

"Blast!" Dunross thought a second, then excused himself and walked out with Gavallan. "You're coming to the cocktail party?"

"Yes, if you want me there—afraid I'm not very good company."

"Let's go in here a second." Dunross led the way into his private room. Tea was laid out and a bottle of Dom Pérignon in an ice bucket.

"Celebration?" Gavallan asked.

"Yes. Three things: the General Stores takeover, the Ho-Pak rescue and the dawn of the new era."

"Oh?"

"Yes." Dunross began to open the bottle. "For instance you: I want you to leave for London Monday evening with the children." Gavallan's eyes widened but he said nothing. "I want you to check on Kathy, see her specialist, then take her and the kids to Castle Avisyard. I want you to take over Avisyard for six months, perhaps a year or two. Six months certain—take over the whole of the east wing." Gavallan gasped. "You're going to head up a new division, very secret, secret from Alastair, my father, every member of the family including David. Secret from everyone except me."

"What division?" Gavallan's excitement and happiness showed.

"There's a fellow I want you to get close to tonight, Andrew. Jamie Kirk. His wife's a bit of a bore but invite them to Avisyard. I want you to slide into Scotland, particularly Aberdeen. I want you to buy property, but very quietly: factory areas, wharfage, potential airfields, heliports near the docks. Are there docks there?"

"Christ, tai-pan, I don't know. I've never been there."

"Nor have I."

"Eh?"

Dunross laughed at the look on Gavallan's face. "Not to worry. Your initial budget is a million pounds sterling."

"Christ, where the hell's a million coming fr—"

"Never mind!" Dunross twisted the cork and held it, deadening the explosion neatly. He poured the pale, oh so dry wine. "You've a million sterling to commit in the next six months. A further 5 million sterling over the next two years."

Gavallan was gaping at him openly.

"In that time I want the Noble House, oh so quietly, to become the power in Aberdeen, with the best land, best influence on the town councils. I want you laird of Aberdeen—and as far east as Inverness and south to Dundee. In two years. All right?"

"Yes but . . ." Gavallan stopped helplessly. All his life he had wanted to quit Asia. Kathy and the children too, but it had never been possible or even considered. Now Dunross had given him Utopia and he could not take it all in. "But why?"

"Talk to Kirk, beguile his wife, and remember, laddie, a closed mouth." Dunross gave him a glass and took one for himself. "Here's to Scotland, the new era and our new fief." Then he added in his most secret heart, And here's to the North Sea! All gods bear witness: The Noble House is implementing Contingency Plan One.

67

The stands were empty now but for the cleaners, most of the boxes dark. Rain cascaded from the sky, a solid sheet of water. It was near twilight. Traffic was snarled all around the racecourse. The thousands plodded homeward, sodden but light of heart. Next Saturday was another race day and another fifth race and oh oh oh, another challenge and this time the tai-pan will surely ride Noble Star and perhaps Black Beard will ride Pilot Fish and those two devil *quai loh* will kill themselves for our amusement.

A Rolls going out of the members' entrance splashed some of the pedestrians and they shouted a barrage of obscenities but none of the Chinese really minded. One day I'll have one of those, everyone thought. All I need's just a little fornicating joss. Just a little joss next Saturday and I'll have enough to buy some land or an apartment to rent out, to barter against a piece of a high rise, to mortgage against an acre of Central. Eeee, how I'll enjoy riding in my Rolls with a lucky number plate like that one! Did you see who it was? Taximan Tok who seven years ago drove a *bo-pi*, an illegal taxi, and found 10,000 HK on his backseat one day and hid it for five years till the statute of limitations had passed, then invested it in the stock market in the boom of three years ago to immense profit then took the profit and bought apartments. Eeee, the boom! Remember what Old Blind Tung wrote in his column about the coming boom! But what about the stock market crash and all the bank runs?

Ayeeyah, that's all over! Didn't you hear the astounding news? Great Bank is taking over the Ho-Pak and standing good for all Banker Kwang's debts. Did you hear about the Noble House buying General Stores? Both such good pieces of news announced on race day. That's never happened before! It's odd! Very odd! You don't think . . . Fornicate all gods! Is it all a foul ploy of those dirty foreign devils to manipulate the market to steal our rightful profits? Oh oh oh, I agree! Yes, it must be a foul plot! It's too much fornicating coincidence! Oh those cunning awful barbarians! Thank all gods I realized it so I can prepare! Now what should I do . . .

As they all headed for home their minds were consumed with growing excitement. Most were poorer than when they came to the track, but a few were much richer. Spectacles Wu, the police constable from the East Aberdeen Police station, was one of those. Crosse had allowed him to go to the races though he had to be back by 6:15 P.M. when the client was due to be interviewed again, Spectacles Wu there as interpreter for the Ning-tok dialect. The young man shivered and his Secret Sack chilled at the thought of how quickly the great Brian Kwok had babbled his innermost secrets.

Ayeeyah, he thought, filled with superstitious dread. These pink barbarians are truly devils who can twist us civilized people as they wish and send us mad. But if I become SI that'll protect me and give me some of their secrets, and with those secrets and other foreign devil secrets I will become an ancestor!

He began to beam. His joss had changed ever since he had caught that old *amah.* Today the gods had favored him greatly. He had forecast one quinella, the daily double and three place horses, each time reinvesting all his winnings and now he was 5,753 HK richer. His plan for the money was already settled. He would finance Fifth Uncle to buy a used plastic molding machine to begin a plastic flower factory in return for 51 percent, another 1,000 would pay for the construction of two dwellings in the resettlement to be rented and the last 1,000 would be for next Saturday!

A Mercedes sounded its horn deafeningly, making him jump. Spectacles Wu recognized one of the men in the back: the man Rosemont, the CIA barbarian with limitless funds to spend. So naive, they are, the Americans, he thought. Last year when his relations had poured over the border in the exodus, he had sent them all down to the consulate on a roster basis, every month a different name and different story, to join the constant and ever-growing band of rice Christians or, to be more exact, rice non-Communists. It was easy to get free meals and handouts from the U.S. Consulate. All you had to do was to pretend to be frightened and say, nervously, that you had just come over the border, that you were staunchly against Chairman Mao and that in your village the Communists did such and such a terrible thing. The Americans would be happy to hear about PRC troop movements, real or imagined. Oh how quickly they would write it all down and ask for more. Any information, any stupid piece of information you could pick up if you could read a newspaper was to them—if whispered with rolling eyes—very valuable.

Three months ago Spectacles Wu had had a brainstorm. Now, with four members of his clan, one of whom was originally a journalist on a Communist newspaper in Canton, Spectacles Wu had offered—but through trusted intermediaries so he and his relations could not be traced —to supply Rosemont with a monthly undercover report, an intelligence pamphlet, code name "Freedom Fighter," on conditions across the Bamboo Curtain in and around Canton. To prove the espionage quality Spectacles

Wu had offered to supply the first two editions free—to catch a mighty tiger it is good business to sacrifice a stolen lamb. If these were considered acceptable to the CIA, the fee would be 1,000 HK each for the next three, and if these were equally valuable, then a new contract would be negotiated for a year of reports.

The first two had been so highly praised that an immediate deal was struck for five reports at 2,000 HK each. Next week they were to get their first fee. Oh how they had congratulated themselves. The content of the reports was culled from thirty Canton newspapers that came down on the daily Canton train that also brought pigs and poultry and foods of all kinds and could be purchased without effort in Wanchai paper shops. All they had had to do was to read them meticulously and copy the articles, after removing the Communist dialectic: articles about crops, building, economics, Party appointments, births, deaths, sentences, extortions and local color—anything they considered of interest. Spectacles Wu translated the stories the others picked.

He felt a huge wave of pleasure. Freedom Fighter had enormous potential. Their costs were almost nil. "But sometimes we must be careful to make a few mistakes," Spectacles Wu had told them, "and occasionally we must miss a month—'we regret our agent in Canton was assassinated for giving away State secrets . . .'" Oh yes. And soon, when I'm a full member of SI and a trained espionage agent, I'll know better how to present the press information to the CIA. Perhaps we'll expand and experiment with a report from Peking, another from Shanghai. We can get day-old Peking and Shanghai papers equally with no trouble and very little investment. Thank all gods for American curiosity!

A taxi honked as it splashed past. He stopped a moment to allow it to pass, then shoved through, careless of the cursing, honking and noise alongside the tall fence that skirted the stadium. He glanced at his watch. He had plenty of time. Headquarters was not far away.

The rain became heavier but he did not feel it, the warmth of winnings in his pocket lightening his footsteps. He squared his shoulders. Be strong, be wise, he ordered himself. Tonight I must be alert. Perhaps they will ask my opinion. I know the Communist Superintendent Brian Kwok is a liar here and there and exaggerating. And as to atomics, what's so important about that? Of course the Middle Kingdom has its own atomics. Any fool knows what's been going on for years in Sinkiang near the shores of Lake Bos-teng-hu. And of course, soon we'll have our own rockets and satellites. Of course! Are we not civilized? Did we not invent gunpowder and rockets but discard them millennia ago as barbaric?

Throughout the stadium on the other side of the fence, women cleaners raked up the sodden leavings of the thousands, patiently sifting the rubbish carefully for a lost coin or ring, fountain pen or bottles that were worth a single copper cash. Crouched beside a pile of garbage cans in the lee of the rain was a man.

"Come on, old fellow, you can't sleep there," a woman cleaner said, not unkindly, shaking him. "It's time to go home!" The old man's eyes fluttered open for an instant, he began to get up but stopped, gave out a great sigh and subsided like a rag doll.

"*Ayeeyah*," One Tooth Yang muttered. She had seen enough of death throughout her seventy years to recognize its finality. "Hey, Younger Sister," she called out politely to her friend and second member of her team. "Come over here! This old man's dead."

Her friend was sixty-four, bent and lined but equally strong and also Shanghainese. She came out of the rain and peered down. "He looks like a beggar."

"Yes. We'd better tell the foreman." One Tooth Yang knelt and carefully went through his ragged pockets. There were 3 HK in change, nothing else. "That's not much," she said. "Never mind." She divided the coins equally. Over the years they had always divided what they found.

"What's that in his left hand?" the other woman asked. One Tooth bent the clawlike hand open. "Just some tickets." She peered at them, then held them close to her eyes and flicked through them. "It's the double quinella . . ." she began, then suddenly cackled, "Eeee, the poor fool got the first leg and lost the second . . . he chose Butterscotch Lass!" Both women laughed hysterically at the mischief of the gods.

"That must have sent the poor old ancient into the seizure—it would me! *Ayeeyah*, to be so close and yet so far, Elder Sister."

"Joss." One Tooth Yang cackled again and tossed the tickets into a garbage can. "Gods are gods and men are men but eee, I can imagine the old fellow dying. I would have too!" The two old women laughed again, the bad joss hurting them and the older one rubbed her chest to ease the pain. "*Ayeeyah*, I must get a physic. Go and tell the foreman about him. Younger Sister, eeee, but I'm tired tonight. Such bad joss, he was close to being a millionaire but now? Joss! Go tell the foreman. I'm tired tonight," she said again, leaning on her rake, her voice wavering.

The other woman went off marveling at the gods and how quickly they can give or take away—if they exist at all, she thought in passing. Ah joss!

Wearily One Tooth Yang continued her work, her head aching, but the moment she was sure she was alone and unobserved she darted for the garbage can and frantically retrieved the tickets, her heart pounding like never in her whole life. Frantically she checked that her eyes had not deceived her and the numbers were correct. But there was no mistake. Each ticket was a winning ticket. Equally frantically she stuffed them in her pocket then made absolutely sure she had not left one carelessly in the rubbish. Quickly she piled more rubbish on top and lifted this can and dumped it into another, all the time her mind shrieking, Tomorrow I can redeem the tickets, I have three days to redeem them! Oh bless all gods,

I'm rich I'm rich I'm rich! There must be a hundred or two hundred tickets and each a 5 HK ticket, each ticket pays 265 HK . . . if there's a hundred tickets that's 26,500 HK, if two hundred tickets 53,000 HK. . . .

Feeling faint, she squatted beside the corpse, leaning against the wall, not noticing it. She knew she dare not count the tickets now, there was no time. Every second was vital. She had to prepare. "Be cautious, old fool," she muttered aloud, then once more almost went into panic. Stop talking aloud! Be careful, you old fool, or Younger Sister will suspect . . . Oh oh oh is she now telling the foreman what she suspects? Oh what shall I do? The joss is mine, I found the old man . . . *ayeeyah*, what shall I do? Perhaps they'll search me. If they see me in this state they're bound to suspect. . . .

Her head was pounding terribly and a wave of nausea went through her. Nearby were some toilets. She groped to her feet and hobbled over to them. Behind her, other cleaners were sifting and tidying up. Tomorrow they would all come again for there would still be plenty to do. Her own shift was due back at nine in the morning. In the empty toilet room she took out the tickets, her fingers trembling, wrapped them in a piece of rag and found a loose brick in the wall and put them behind the brick.

Once safely outside she began to breathe. When the foreman came back with the other old woman he peered down at the man, went through his pockets with great care and found a twist of silver paper they had missed. Within it was a pinch of White Powder. "It will bring 2 HK," he said, knowing it was worth 6.04 HK. "We will split it, 70 for me and 30 for you two." For face, One Tooth argued and they settled that he would try to get 3.10 HK for it, and would split it 60 to him and 40 to them. Satisfied, he went away.

When they were alone again the younger woman began to sift the garbage.

"What're you doing?" One Tooth asked.

"I just wanted to check those tickets, Elder Sister. Your eyes are not so good."

"Please yourself," One Tooth said with a shrug. "I've picked this lot clean. I'm going over there." Her gnarled finger pointed at an unnoticed new source of virgin rubbish under a row of seats. The other woman hesitated then followed and now One Tooth almost chortled with glee, knowing she was safe. Tomorrow I'll come back complaining of stomach sickness. I can retrieve my fortune and go home. Now what shall I do with my wealth?

First the down payment on two *quai loh* dancing dresses for Third Granddaughter in return for half her earnings in the first year. She'll make a fine whore in the Good Luck Dance Hall. Next, Second Son will stop being a coolie on the construction site up on Kotewall Road. He and Fifth Nephew and Second Grandson will become builders, and within the week we will put a down payment on a plot of land and begin to build a building . . .

"You seem very happy, Elder Sister."

"Oh, yes I am, Younger Sister. My bones ache, the ague is with me as ever, my stomach is upset, but I am alive and that old man is dead. It is a lesson from the gods. All gods bear witness, when I first saw him, the first time, I thought it was my husband who died in our flight from Shanghai fifteen years ago. I thought I was seeing a ghost! My spirit almost left me for that old man was like his twin!"

"*Ayeeyah,* how horrible! How terrible! Ghosts! All gods protect us from ghosts!"

Oh yes, the old woman thought, ghosts're terrible. Now, where was I? Oh yes . . . 1,000 will go on the quinella next Saturday. And out of those winnings I will buy . . . I will buy myself a set of false teeth! Eeeee, how wonderful that will be, she wanted to cry out, almost fainting with suppressed pleasure. All her life, all her life since she was fourteen when a Manchu rifle butt had smashed out her teeth in one of the constant revolutions against the foreign Ch'ing Dynasty, she had been nicknamed One Tooth. Always she had hated her nickname. But now . . . oh gods bear witness! I will buy a set of teeth from my winnings next Saturday—and also I will buy and light two candles in the nearest temple in return for such good joss.

"I feel faint, Younger Sister," she said, really faint with near ecstasy. "Could you get me some water?"

The other woman went off grumbling. One Tooth sat down a moment and allowed herself a huge grin, her tongue feeling her gums. Eeeee, when I win, if I win heavily enough, I will have one gold tooth, right in the center, to remind me. Gold Tooth Yang, that has a nice sound to it, she thought, far too clever to mutter it aloud, even though she was completely alone. Yes, Honorable Gold Tooth Yang, of the Yang Constructions empire . . .

68

Suslev was hunched uncomfortably in the front of the small car belonging to Ernie Clinker and they were grinding up the hill. All the windows were steamed up, the rain even heavier. Mud and stones washing down from the steep hillsides made the road surface dangerous. Already they had passed two minor accidents.

"Cor, stone the crows, perhaps you'd better spend the night, old chum," Clinker said, driving with difficulty.

"No, not tonight," Suslev said irritably. "I already told you I promised Ginny and tonight's my last night." Ever since the raid, Suslev had been in a blinding rage, his rage fed by unaccustomed fear—fear of the summons to police HQ in the morning, fear of catastrophic repercussions from the intercepted decoded cable, fear of Center's probable displeasure over the loss of Voranski, being ordered out of Hong Kong, the destruction of their radio equipment, the Metkin affair and now Koronski's arrival and the possible kidnapping of Dunross. Too many things have gone wrong this trip, he thought, chilled—too long in the game to have any illusions. Even his phone conversation during the fifth race with Crosse had not mollified him.

"Not to worry, it's a routine request to appear, Gregor. Just a few questions about Voranski, Metkin and so on," Crosse had said in a disguised voice.

"*Kristos,* what's the 'and so on'?"

"I don't know, Sinders ordered it, not me."

"You'd better cover me, Roger."

"You're covered. Listen, about this possible kidnapping, it's a very bad idea."

"They want it set up, so help Arthur make the arrangements, eh, please? Unless you can delay my departure, we *will* implement it when it is ordered."

"I recommend against it. This is my bailiwick and I rec—"

"Center approves and we will do it if it is ordered!" Suslev wanted to order Roger Crosse to shut up or else, but he was careful not to offend their best asset in Asia. "Can we meet tonight?"

"No, but I'll call you. How about four? At 10:30?" Four was their present code for 32 Sinclair Towers. 10:30 meant 9:30 P.M.

"Is that wise?"

He had heard that dry confident laugh. "Very wise. Would those fools come again? Of course it is wise. And I guarantee it!"

"All right. Arthur will be there. We should cement the plan."

Clinker swerved to avoid a taxi cutting in and he cursed, then ground the gears, peering through the windshield ahead, getting into motion again. Oh his side Suslev rubbed the condensation away. "God-cursed weather," he said, his mind elsewhere. What about Travkin? Stupid motherless turd to fall off after passing the winning post. I thought he'd won. Decadent fool! No real cossack'd ever get caught like that. So he's out now, him and his crippled old crone princess with the broken bones.

Now how do we entice Dunross to the apartment tomorrow instead of Tuesday as Travkin had signaled. It has to be tonight or tomorrow. At the latest it must be tomorrow night. Arthur must arrange it or Roger. They are the keys to the Dunross plan.

And I must get those files—or Dunross—before I leave. One or the other. They're my only real protection against Center.

Bartlett and Casey got out of the Struan limo at the Hilton, the resplendent, turbaned Sikh doorman holding an unnecessary umbrella—the vast overhang already protecting them from the sheets of water.

"I'll be here, sir, whenever you're ready," Chauffeur Lim said.

"Great. Thanks," Bartlett replied. They went up the steps to the ground floor and took the escalator to the foyer.

"You're very quiet, Casey," he said. All the way from the racetrack they had hardly said a word to each other, both locked into their own thoughts.

"So're you, Linc. I thought you didn't want to talk. You seemed distracted." She smiled tentatively. "Maybe it was all the excitement."

"It was a great day."

"You think the tai-pan's going to pull it off? The General Stores takeover?"

"Monday will tell." Bartlett went to the reception desk. "Mr. Banastasio please?"

The handsome Eurasian assistant manager said, "Just a moment please. Oh yes, he changed his room again. Now it's 832." He handed him a house phone. Bartlett dialed.

"Yeah?"

"Vincenzo? Linc, I'm downstairs."

"Hey, Linc, good to hear your voice. Casey with you?"

"Sure."

"You want to come up?"

"On our way." Bartlett went back to Casey.

"You sure you want me along?"

"He asked for you." Bartlett led the way to the elevator, thinking of Orlanda and their date later, thinking of Biltzmann and Gornt and Taipei tomorrow and whether or not he should ask Dunross if he could take her. Shit, life's complicated suddenly. "It'll only be a few minutes," he said, "then it's cocktails with the tai-pan. The weekend's going to be interesting. And next week."

"You out for dinner tonight?"

"Yes. We should have breakfast though. Seymour needs straightening out and as I'm off for a couple of days we'd better have our signals straight."

They crowded into the elevator. Casey casually avoided being trampled on and ground her heel into her assailant's instep. "Oh so sorry," she said sweetly, then muttered "*Dew neh loh moh*" which Peter Marlowe had taught her this afternoon, just loud enough for the woman to hear. She saw the sudden flush. Hastily the woman shoved her way out at the mezzanine floor and Casey knew she had won a great victory. Amused, she glanced at Bartlett but he was lost in thought, staring into space, and she wondered very much what the real problem was. Orlanda?

On the eighth floor they got out. She followed Bartlett down the corridor. "You know what this's all about, Linc? What Banastasio wants?"

"He said he just wanted to say hi and pass the time of day." Bartlett pressed the button. The door opened.

Banastasio was a good-looking man with iron-gray hair and very dark eyes. He welcomed them cordially. "Hey, Casey, you've lost weight— you're looking great. Drink?" He waved a hand at the bar. It was stocked with everything. Casey fixed herself a martini after opening a can of beer for Bartlett, lost in thought. Peter Marlowe's right. So's the tai-pan. So's Linc. All I have to do is decide. By when? Very soon. Today, tomorrow? By Tuesday dinner for sure. Absolutely one hundred percent for sure and meanwhile maybe I'd better begin a few diversionary raids.

"How's it going?" Banastasio was saying.

"Fine. With you?"

"Great." Banastasio sipped a Coke then reached forward and turned on a small tape recorder. Out of it came a confusing mishmash of voices, the sort of background heard at any busy cocktail party.

"Just a habit, Linc, Casey, when I want to talk private," Banastasio said quietly.

Bartlett stared at him. "You think this place's bugged?"

"Maybe, maybe not. You never know who could be listening, huh?"

Bartlett glanced at Casey then back at Banastasio. "What's on your mind, Vincenzo?"

Banastasio smiled. "How's Par-Con?" the man asked.

"Same as ever—great," Bartlett said. "Our growth rate will be better'n forecast."

"By 7 percent," Casey added, all her senses equally sharpened.

"You going to deal with Struan's or Rothwell-Gornt?"

"We're working on it." Bartlett covered his surprise. "Isn't this new for you, Vincenzo? Asking about deals before they happen?"

"You going to deal with Struan's or Rothwell-Gornt?"

Bartlett watched the cold eyes and the strangely menacing smile. Casey was equally shocked. "When the deal's done I'll tell you. The same time I tell the other stockholders."

The smile did not change. The eyes got colder. "The boys and I'd like to get invol—"

"What boys?"

Banastasio sighed. "We've got a good piece of change in Par-Con, Linc, and now we'd like to figure in some of the up-front decisions. We figure I should have a seat on the board. And on the Finance Committee and the New Acquisitions Committee."

Bartlett and Casey stared at him openly. "That was never part of the stock deal," Bartlett told him. "Up front you said it was just an investment."

"That's right," Casey added, her voice sounding thin to her. "You wrote us you were just an investor an—"

"Times've changed, little lady. Now we want in. Got it?" The man's voice was harsh. "Just one seat, Linc. That much stock in General Motors and I'd have two seats."

"We're not General Motors."

"Sure. Sure, we know. But what we want isn't out of line. We want Par-Con to grow faster. Maybe I ca—"

"It's growing just fine. Don't you think it'd be bet—" Again Banastasio turned his bleak gaze on her. Casey stopped. Bartlett's fists began to clench but he held them still. Carefully.

Banastasio said, "It's settled." The smile came back. "I'm on the board from today, right?"

"Wrong. Directors get elected by the stockholders at the annual general meeting," Bartlett said, his voice raw. "Not before. There's no vacancy."

Banastasio laughed. "Maybe there will be."

"Do you want to say that again?"

Abruptly Banastasio hardened. "Listen, Linc, that's not a threat, just a possibility. I can be good on the board. I've got connections. And I want to put in my two cents' worth here and there."

"About what?"

"Deals. For instance, Par-Con goes with Gornt."

"And if I don't agree?"

"A little nudge from us and Dunross'll be on the street. Gornt's our boy, Linc. We checked and he's better."

Bartlett got up. Casey followed, her knees very weak. Banastasio didn't move. "I'll think about all this," Bartlett said. "As of right now it's a toss-up if we make a deal with either one."

Banastasio's eyes narrowed. "What?"

"I'm not convinced that either's good for us. Right, Casey?"

"Yes, Linc."

"My vote says Gornt. Got it?"

"Go screw." Bartlett turned to go.

"Just a minute!" Banastasio stood up and came closer. "No one wants trouble, not me, not the boys, n—"

"What boys?"

Again the other man sighed. "C'mon, Linc, you're over twenty-one. You've had a good ride. We don't want to make waves, just money."

"We have that in common. We'll buy back your stock and give you a profit of si—"

"No deal. It's not for sale." Another sigh. "We bought in when you needed dough. We paid a fair price and you used our cash to expand. Now we want a piece of the exec action. Got it?"

"I'll put it to the stockholders at the annual gen—"

"Goddamnit, now!"

"Goddamnit no!" Bartlett was ready and very dangerous. "Got it?"

Banastasio looked at Casey, his eyes flat like a reptile's. "That your vote too, Miss Executive Vice-President and Treasurer?"

"Yes," she said, surprised that her voice sounded firm. "No seat on the board, Mr. Banastasio. If it comes to a vote, my stock's against you and totally against Gornt."

"When we get control, you're fired."

"When you get control, I'll already have left." Casey walked toward the door, astonished that her legs worked.

Bartlett stood in front of the other man, on guard. "See you around," he said.

"You'd better change your mind!"

"You'd better stay the hell out of Par-Con." Bartlett turned and followed Casey out of the room.

At the elevator he said, "Jesus!"

"Yes," she muttered as helplessly.

"We'd . . . we'd better talk."

"Sure. I think I need a drink. Jesus, Linc, that man petrified me. I've never been so frightened in my whole life." She shook her head, as though trying to clear it. "That was like a goddamn nightmare."

In the bar on the top floor she ordered a martini and he a beer and when the drinks had been silently consumed, he ordered another round.

All the while their minds had been sifting, pitting facts against theories, changing the theories.

Bartlett shifted in his chair. She looked across at him. "Ready for what I think?" she asked.

"Sure, sure, Casey. Go ahead."

"There's always been a rumor he's Mafia or connected with Mafia and after our little talk I'd say that's a good bet. Mafia jumps us to narcotics and all sorts of evil. Theory: maybe it also jumps us somehow to the guns?"

The tiny lines beside Bartlett's eyes crinkled. "I reached that too. Next?"

"Fact: if Banastasio's scared of being bugged that jumps us to surveillance. That means FBI."

"Or CIA."

"Or CIA. Fact: if he's Mafia and if the CIA or FBI're involved, we're in a game we've no right to be in, with nowhere to go but down. Now, as to what he wan—" Casey stopped. She gasped.

"What?"

"I just . . . I just remembered Rosemont, you remember him from the party, Stanley Rosemont, the tall, good-looking, gray-haired man from the consulate? We met on the ferry yesterday, yesterday afternoon. By chance. Maybe it's a coincidence, maybe not, but now that I think of it he brought up Banastasio, said his friend Ed someone, also at the consulate, knew him slightly—and when I said he was arriving today he was knocked for a loop." She recapped her conversation. "I never thought much about it at the time . . . but the consulate and what he said adds up: CIA."

"Got to be. Sure. And if . . . ." He stopped too. "Come to think of it, Ian brought up Banastasio out of the blue too. Tuesday, in the lobby when you were at the phone, just before we went to the gold vaults."

After a pause she said, "Maybe we're in real deep shit! Fact: we got a murder, kidnapping, guns, Banastasio, Mafia, John Chen. Come to think of it, John Chen and Tsu-yan were very friendly with that bum." Her eyes widened. "Banastasio and John Chen's killing. Does that tie? From what the papers've said, the Werewolves don't sound like Chinese—the ear bit. That's, that's brutal."

Bartlett sipped his beer, lost in thought. "Gornt? What about Gornt? Why did Banastasio go for him and not Struan's?"

"I don't know."

"Try this for size, Casey. Say Banastasio's end play is guns, or narcotics, or both guns and narcotics. Both companies would be good for him. Struan's have ships and a huge complex at the airport that dominates inward and outward cargoes, great for smuggling. Gornt has ships and wharfing too. And Gornt's got All Asia Airways. An in with Asia's major feeder airline would give him—them—what they need. The airline goes to Bangkok, India, Vietnam, Cambodia, Japan—wherever!"

"And connects here with Pan-Am, TWA, JAL and all places east, west, north and south! And if we help Gornt to smash Struan's, the two companies together give them everything."

"So, back to the sixty-four-dollar question: what do we do?" Bartlett asked.

"Couldn't we play a waiting game? The Struan-Gornt contest will be solved next week at the latest."

"For this skirmish, we need information—and the right counterforces. Different guns, big guns, guns we don't have." He sipped his beer, even more thoughtful. "We'd better get some top-level advice. And help. Fast. It's Armstrong and the English cops—or Rosemont and the CIA."

"Or both?"

"Or both."

Dunross got out of the Daimler and hurried into police headquarters. "Evening, sir," the young Australian duty inspector on the desk said. "Sorry you lost the fifth—I heard Bluey White was carpeted for interference. Can't trust a bloody Aussie, eh?"

Dunross smiled. "He won, Inspector. The stewards ruled the race was won fair and square. I've an appointment with Mr. Crosse."

"Yes sir, square but not fair dinkum. Top floor, third on the left. Good luck next Saturday, sir."

Crosse met him on the top floor. "Evening. Come on in. Drink?"

"No thanks. Good of you to see me at once. Evening, Mr. Sinders." They shook hands. Dunross had never been in Crosse's office before. The walls seemed as drab as the man and when the door was shut on the three of them the atmosphere seemed to close in even more.

"Please sit down," Crosse said. "Pity about Noble Star—we were both on her."

"She'll be worth another flutter on Saturday."

"You're going to ride her?"

"Wouldn't you?"

Both men smiled.

"What can we do for you?" Crosse asked.

Dunross put his full attention on Sinders. "I can't give you new files— the impossible I can't do. But I can give you something—I don't know what, yet, but I've just received a package from AMG."

Both men were startled. Sinders said, "Hand-delivered?"

Dunross hesitated. "Hand-delivered. Now, please, no more questions till I've finished."

Sinders lit his pipe and chuckled. "Just like AMG to have a bolt-hole, Roger. He always was clever, damn him. Sorry, please go on."

"The message from AMG said the information was of very special importance and to be passed on to the prime minister personally or the current head of MI-6, Edward Sinders, at my convenience—*and if I consid-ered it politic.*" In the dead silence, Dunross took a deep breath. "Since you understand barter, I'll trade you—you directly, in secret, in the pres-ence of the governor alone—whatever the hell 'it' is. In return Brian Kwok is allowed out and over the border, if he wants to go, so we can deal with Tiptop."

The silence deepened. Sinders puffed his pipe. He glanced at Cross. "Roger?"

Roger Crosse was thinking about *it*—and what information was so spe-cial that it was for Sinders or the P.M. only. "I think you could consider Ian's proposal," he said smoothly. "At leisure."

"No leisure," Dunross said sharply. "The money's urgent, and the release is clearly considered urgent. We can't delay past Monday at 10:00 A.M. when the ban—"

"Perhaps Tiptop and money don't come into the equation at all," Sinders interrupted, his voice deliberately brittle. "It doesn't matter a jot or a tittle to SI or MI-6 if all Hong Kong rots. Have you any idea the sort of value a senior superintendent in SI—especially a man with Brian Kwok's qualifications and experience—could have to the enemy, if in fact Brian Kwok is under arrest as you think and this Tiptop claims? Have you also considered that such an enemy traitor's information to us about his contacts and *them* could be of great importance to the whole realm? Eh?"

"Is that your answer?"

"Did Mrs. Gresserhoff hand-deliver the package?"

"Are you prepared to barter?"

Crosse said irritably, "Who's Gresserhoff?"

"I don't know," Sinders told him. "Other than that she's the vanished recipient of the second phone call from AMG's assistant, Kiernan. We're tracing her with the help of the Swiss police." His mouth smiled at Dunross. "Mrs. Gresserhoff delivered the package to you?"

"No," Dunross said. That's not a real lie, he assured himself. It was Riko Anjin.

"Who did?"

"I'm prepared to tell you that after we have concluded our deal."

"No deal," Crosse said.

Dunross began to get up.

"Just a moment, Roger," Sinders said and Dunross sat back. The MI-6 man tapped the pipe stem against his tobacco-discolored teeth. Dunross kept his face guileless, knowing he was in the hands of experts.

At length Sinders said, "Mr. Dunross, are you prepared to swear for-mally under the perjury conditions of the Official Secrets Act that you do not have possession of the original AMG files?"

"Yes," Dunross said at once, quite prepared to twist the truth now—AMG had always had the originals, he had always been sent the top copy.

If and when it came to a formal moment under oath, that would be another matter entirely. "Next?"

"Monday would be impossible."

Dunross kept his eyes on Sinders. "Impossible because Brian's being interrogated?"

"Any captured enemy asset would immediately be questioned, of course."

"And Brian will be a very hard nut to take apart."

"*If* he's the asset, you'd know that better than us. You've been friends a long time."

"Yes, and I swear to God I still think it's impossible. Never once has Brian been anything other than an upright, staunch British policeman. How is it possible?"

"How were Philby, Klaus Fuchs, Sorge, Rudolf Abel, Blake and all the others possible?"

"How long would you need?"

Sinders shrugged, watching him.

Dunross watched him back. The silence became aching.

"You destroyed the originals?"

"No, and I must tell you I also noticed the difference between all the copies I gave you and the one you intercepted. I'd planned to call AMG to ask him why the difference."

"How often were you in contact with him?"

"Once or twice a year."

"What did you know about him? Who suggested him to you?"

"Mr. Sinders, I'm quite prepared to answer your questions, I realize it's my duty to answer them, but the time's not appropriate tonight be—"

"Perhaps it is, Mr. Dunross. We're in no rush."

"Ah, I agree. But unfortunately I've got guests waiting and my association with AMG has nothing to do with my proposal. My proposal requires a simple yes or no."

"Or a maybe."

Dunross studied him. "Or a maybe."

"I'll consider what you've said."

Dunross smiled to himself, liking the cat-and-mouse of the negotiation, aware he was dealing with masters. Again he let the silence hang until exactly the right moment. "Very well. AMG said *at my discretion*. At the moment I don't know what 'it' is. I realize I'm quite out of my depth and should not be involved in SI or MI-6 matters. It's not of my choosing. You intercepted my private mail. My understanding with AMG was quite clear: I had his assurance in writing that he was allowed to be in my employ and that he would clear everything with the government in advance. I'll give you copies of our correspondence if you wish, through the correct channels, with the correct secrecy provisions. My enthusiasm for my offer diminishes, minute by minute." He hardened his voice. "Perhaps it doesn't matter to SI or MI-6 if all Hong Kong rots but it does to me, so

I'm making the offer a last time." He got up. "The offer's good to 8:30 P.M."

Neither of the other men moved. "Why 8:30, Mr. Dunross? Why not midnight or midday tomorrow?" Sinders asked, unperturbed. He continued to puff his pipe but Dunross noticed that the tempo had been interrupted the moment he laid down the challenge. That's a good sign, he thought.

"I have to call Tiptop then. Thanks for seeing me." Dunross turned for the door.

Crosse, sitting behind the desk, glanced at Sinders. The older man nodded. Obediently Crosse touched the switch. The bolts sneaked back silently. Dunross jerked to a stop, startled, but recovered quickly, opened the door and went out without a comment, closing it after him.

"Cool bugger," Crosse said, admiring him.

"Too cool."

"Not too cool. He's tai-pan of the Noble House."

"And a liar, but a clever one and quite prepared to finesse us. Would he obliterate 'it'?"

"Yes. But I don't know if H hour's 8:30 P.M." Crosse lit a cigarette. "I'm inclined to think it is. They'd put immense pressure on him—they have to presume we'd thrust the client into interrogation. They've had plenty of time to study Soviet techniques and they've got a few twists of their own. They must presume we're fairly efficient too."

"I'm inclined to think he hasn't got any more files and 'it' is genuine. If 'it' comes from AMG it must have special value. What's your counsel?"

"I repeat what I said to the governor: If we have possession of the client until Monday at noon we'll have everything of importance out of him."

"But what about *them*? What can he tell them about us when he recovers?"

"We know most of that now. Concerning Hong Kong, we can certainly cover every security problem from today. It's standard SI policy never to let any one person know master plans an—"

"Except you."

Crosse smiled. "Except me. And you in the UK of course. The client knows a lot, but not everything. We can cover everything here, change codes and so on. Don't forget, most of what he passed on's routine. His real danger's over. He's uncovered, fortunately in time. Sure as God made little apples, he'd've been the first Chinese commissioner, and probably head of SI en route. That would have been catastrophic. We can't recover the private dossiers, Fong-fong and others, or the riot and counterinsurrection plans. A riot is a riot and there are only so many contingency plans. As to Sevrin, he knows no more than we knew before we caught him. Perhaps the 'it' could provide keys, possibly keys to questions we should put to him."

"That occurred to me instantly too. As I said, Mr. Dunross is too bloody cool." Sinders lit another match, smoked the match a moment, then tamped the used-up tobacco. "You believe him?"

"About the files, I don't know. I certainly believe he has an 'it' and that AMG came back from the dead. Sorry I never met him. Yes. The 'it' could easily be more important than this client—after Monday at noon. He's mostly a husk now."

Since they had returned, the interrogation of Brian Kwok had continued, most of it rambling and incoherent but details here and there of value. More about atomics and names and addresses of contacts in Hong Kong and Canton, security risks here and patterns of information about the Royal Mounted Police, along with an immensely interesting reiteration of vast Soviet infiltration into Canada.

"Why Canada, Brian?" Armstrong had asked.

"Northern border, Robert . . . the weakest fence in the world, there isn't any. Such great riches in Canada . . . ah I wish . . . there was this girl I almost married, they said my duty . . . if Soviets can disrupt Canadians . . . they're so gullible, and wonderful up there. . . . Can I have a cigarette . . . oh thanks . . . Can I have a drink my . . . So we have counterespionage cells everywhere to disrupt Soviet cells and find out . . . then there's Mexico . . . The Soviets are making a big push there too . . . Yes they have plants everywhere . . . did you know Philby . . ."

An hour had been enough.

"Curious he should break so quickly," Sinders said.

Crosse was shocked. "I guarantee that he's not controlled, not lying, that he's telling absolutely everything he believes, what has happened and will continue to do so un—"

"Yes of course," Sinders said somewhat testily. "I meant curious that a man of his quality should crumble so soon. I'd say he'd been wavering for years, that his dedication was now nonexistent or very small and he was probably ready to come over to us but somehow couldn't extract himself. Pity. He could have been very valuable to us." The older man sighed and lit another match. "After a time it always happens to their deep-cover moles in our societies. There's always some kindness, or girl or man friend or freedom or happiness that turns their whole world upside down, poor buggers. That's why we'll win, in the end. Even in Russia the tables'll be turned and the KGB'll get their comeuppance—from Russians—that's why the pressure now. No Soviet on earth can survive without dictatorship, secret police, injustice and terror." He tapped out his pipe into the ashtray. The dottle was wet at the base. "Don't you agree, Roger?"

Crosse nodded and stared back at the intense, pale blue eyes, wondering what was behind them. "You'll phone the minister for instructions?"

"No. I can take the responsibility for this one. We'll decide at 8:30." Sinders glanced at his watch. "Let's get back to Robert. It's almost time to begin again. Good fellow that, very good. Did you hear that he was a big winner?"

69

"Ian? Sorry to interrupt," Bartlett said.

"Oh hello!" Dunross turned back from the other guests he was chatting with. Bartlett was alone. "You two aren't leaving, I hope—this'll go on till at least 9:30."

"Casey's staying awhile. I've a date."

Dunross grinned. "I hope she's suitably pretty."

"She is, but that comes later. First a business meeting. Do you have a minute?"

"Certainly, of course. Excuse me a moment," Dunross said to the others and led the way out of the crowded anteroom to one of the terraces. The rain had lessened in strength but continued implacably. "The General Stores takeover's almost certain at our figure, without any overbid from Superfoods. We really will make the proverbial bundle—if I can stop Gornt."

"Yes. Monday will tell."

Dunross looked at him keenly. "I'm very confident."

Bartlett smiled, tiredness and concern behind the smile. "I noticed. But I wanted to ask, are we still on for Taipei tomorrow?"

"I was going to suggest we should postpone it till next week, next weekend? Tomorrow and Monday are rather important for both of us. Is that all right?"

Bartlett nodded, hiding his relief. "Fine with me." And that solves my problem about Orlanda, he thought. "Well then, I think I'll be off."

"Take the car. Just send Lim back when you're through with him. You're going to the hill climb if it's on? That's at 10:00 A.M. till about noon."

"Where is it?"

"New Territories. I'll send the car for you, weather permitting. Casey too if she wants."

"Thanks."

"Don't worry about Casey tonight—I'll see she gets back safely. Is she free afterwards?"

"I think so."

"Good, then I'll ask her to join us—a few of us are going for a Chinese supper." Dunross studied him. "No problem?"

"No. Nothing that can't be handled." Bartlett grinned and walked away, girding himself for the next onslaught—Armstrong. He had cornered Rosemont a few moments ago and told him about the meeting with Banastasio.

"Best leave it with us, Linc," Rosemont had said. "As far as you're concerned we're informed officially. The consulate. I'll pass it on to whomever. Leave it all lie—tell Casey, okay? If Banastasio calls either of you, stall him, call us and we'll work out a scam. Here's my card—it's good twenty-four hours a day."

Bartlett was outside the front door now and he joined the others waiting impatiently for their cars.

"Oh hi, Linc," Murtagh said, hurriedly getting out of a cab, almost knocking him over. "Sorry! Party still going on?"

"Sure it is, Dave. What's the rush?"

"Got to see the tai-pan!" Murtagh dropped his voice, his excitement showing. "There's a chance that head office'll go for it, if Ian'll concede a little! Casey still here?"

"Sure," Bartlett said at once and all his senses focused, everything else forgotten. "What concessions?" he asked warily.

"Double the foreign exchange period and he's to deal direct with First Central, giving us first option on all future loans for five years."

"That's not much," Bartlett said, hiding his perplexity. "What's the whole deal now?"

"Can't stop, Linc, gotta get the tai-pan's okay. They're waiting, but it's just as Casey and me laid it out. Hell, if we pull this off the tai-pan'll owe us favors till hell freezes!" Murtagh rushed off.

Bartlett stared after him blankly. His feet began to take him back into the house but he stopped and returned to his place in the line. There's plenty of time, he told himself. No need to ask her yet. Think it out.

Casey had told him about the Royal Belgium's connection with First Central, and Murtagh had elaborated this afternoon, adding how hard it was to get an in here with the Establishment but that was all. Bartlett had noted the Texan's nervousness and Casey's nervousness. At the time he'd put it down to the races.

But now? he asked himself suspiciously. Casey and Murtagh and the tai-pan! "First Central'll go for the deal if" and "the tai-pan'll owe us favors till hell freezes. . . ." and "just as Casey and me laid it out." She's the go-between? Casey'd run rings around that joker and she's no messenger. Hell, Casey has to lead him by the nose. He's no match for her. So probably she put him up to—to what? What does the tai-pan need most?

Credit, fast, in millions by Monday.

Jesus, First Central's going to back him! That's got to be it. If. If he makes concessions, and he's got to make some to get out from under . . .

"You want the car, sir?"

"Oh. Yes, Lim, sure. Police headquarters in Wanchai. Thanks." He got into the back, his mind buzzing.

So Casey's got a private game going. It must've been in the works a day or so but she hasn't told me. Why? If I'm right and the scam succeeds, Ian's got the wherewithal to fight off Gornt, even cream him. She's gone out of her way to help him against Gornt. Without my okay. Why? And in return for what?

Drop dead money! Is the 50–50 a payoff—my 2 mill but she shares 50–50?

Sure. That's one possibility—one that I know about now. What're the others? Jesus! Casey independent, maybe going with the enemy? They're still both enemy, Ian and Gornt.

His excitement increased.

What to do?

The money at risk with Gornt is covered every which way. The 2 mill with Struan's is covered too, and stays. I'd never planned to jerk it—that was just testing Casey. The Struan deal's good either way. The Gornt deal's good, either way. So my plan's still good—I can still jump either way, though the timing's critical.

But now there's Orlanda.

If it's Orlanda, it's the States or somewhere else but not here. It's quite clear she'd never be welcome in Happy Valley's winner's circle. Or in the cliques and clubs. She'd never be freely invited into the great houses, except maybe by Ian. And Gornt, but that'd be to taunt, to jerk the reins, to remind her of the past—like last night when that other girl came on deck. I saw Orlanda's face. Oh she covered, better than anyone could have covered except maybe Casey. She hated that the other girl had been below, in the master suite that was once hers.

Maybe Gornt didn't do that deliberately? Maybe the girl came up on her own. She went back below almost at once. Maybe she wasn't supposed to come up at all. Maybe.

Shit! There's too much going on I can't figure: like the General Stores and the Ho-Pak rescue—too much agreed by a couple of guys on a Saturday—a couple of whiskeys here and a phone call there. It's all dynamite if you're in the club but Jesus watch out if you're not. Here you've got to be British or Chinese to belong.

I'm just as much an outsider as Orlanda.

Still, I could be happy here, for a time. And I could even handle it here with Orlanda, for a short time, on visits. I could handle the Pacific Rim and having Par-Con as a Noble House but for it to be accepted as *the*

Noble House by British and Chinese, it'll still have to be Struan–Par-Con with our name in small letters, or Rothwell-Gornt–Par-Con the same.

Casey?

With Casey, Par-Con could be a Noble House, easily. But is Casey still to be trusted? Why didn't she tell me? Is she sucked in by Hong Kong and beginning to play her own game for Number One?

You'd better choose, old buddy, while you're still tai-pan.

"Yes, Phillip?"

They were in the study under the portrait of Dirk Struan, and Dunross had chosen the place deliberately. Phillip Chen sat opposite him. Very formal, very correct and very weary. "How is Alexi?"

"Still unconscious. Doc Tooley says he'll be all right if he comes out of it in a couple of hours."

"Tiptop?"

"I'm to call him at 9:00 P.M."

"Still no approval of his offer from . . . from the authorities?"

Dunross's eyes narrowed. "You know the arrangement he suggested?"

"Oh yes, tai-pan. I . . . I was asked. I still find it hard to believe . . . Brian Kwok? God help us, but yes . . . my opinion was asked before the suggestion was put to you."

"Why the devil didn't you tell me?" Dunross snapped.

"Rightly you no longer consider me compradore of the Noble House and favor me with your trust."

"You consider yourself trustworthy?"

"Yes. I've proved it in the past many times, so did my father—and his. Even so, if I were you and sitting where you are sitting, I would not be having this meeting, I would not have you in my house and I would already have decided the ways and means of your destruction."

"Perhaps I have."

"Not you." Phillip Chen pointed at the portrait. "He would have, but not you, Ian Struan Dunross."

"Don't bet on it."

"I do."

Dunross said nothing, just waited.

"First the coin: Wait until the favor is asked. I will endeavor to find out what it is in advance. If it is too much th—"

"It will be too much."

"What will he ask for?"

"Something to do with narcotics. There's a strong rumor Four Fingers, Smuggler Yuen and White Powder Lee are in partnership, smuggling heroin."

"It's under consideration. They're not actually partners yet," Phillip Chen said.

"Again, why didn't you tell me? It's your duty as compradore to keep me informed, not to write down intimate details of our secrets and then lose them to enemies."

"Again, I ask forgiveness. But now is the time to talk."

"Because you're finished?"

"Because I might be finished—if once more I cannot prove my worth." The old man looked at Dunross bleakly, seeing the face of many tai-pans in the face of the man opposite him, not liking the face or that of the man above the fireplace whose eyes bored into him—the foreign devil pirate who had forsaken his great-grandfather because of mixed blood, half of which was his own.

Ayeeyah, he thought, curbing his anger. These barbarians and their intolerance! Five generations of tai-pans we've served and now this one threatens to change Dirk's legacy for one mistake?

"About the ask: even if it's connected with heroin or narcotics, it will concern some future performance or action. Agree to it, tai-pan, and I promise I will deal with Four Fingers long before the ask has to be granted."

"How?"

"This is China. I will deal with it in Chinese fashion. I swear it by the blood of my ancestors." Phillip Chen pointed at the portrait. "I will continue to protect the Noble House as I have sworn to do."

"What other trickeries did you have in your safe? I've been through all the documents and balance sheets you gave Andrew. With that information in the wrong hands we're naked."

"Yes, but only in front of Bartlett and Par-Con, providing he keeps them to himself and doesn't pass them over to Gornt or another enemy here. Tai-pan, Bartlett doesn't strike me as a malicious person. Perhaps we can deal with him to get what he has back and ask him to agree to keep the information secret."

"To do that you have to barter with a secret he doesn't want let out. Do you have one?"

"Not yet. As partners to us he should protect us."

"Yes. But he's already dealing with Gornt and advanced $2 million U.S. to cover Gornt selling us short."

Phillip Chen whitened. "Eeeee, I didn't know that." He thought a moment. "So Bartlett will withdraw from us on Monday and go over to the enemy?"

"I don't know. At the moment I think he's fence-sitting. I would if I was him."

Phillip Chen shifted in his chair. "He's very fond of Orlanda, tai-pan."

"Yes, she could be a key. Gornt's got to have arranged that, or pushed her toward Bartlett."

"Are you going to tell him?"

"No, not unless there's a reason. He's over twenty-one." Dunross hardened even more. "What do you propose?"

"Are you agreeing to the new concessions First Central wants?"

"So you know about that too?"

"You must have wanted everyone to know that you're seeking support from them, tai-pan. Why else invite Murtagh to your box at the races, why else invite him here? It was easy to put two and two together, even if one hasn't copies of his telexes y—"

"Have you?"

"Some of them." Phillip Chen took out a handkerchief and wiped his hands. "Will you concede?"

"No. I told him I'd think about it—he's waiting downstairs for my answer but it's got to be no. I can't guarantee to give them first option on all future loans. I can't because the Victoria has so much power here and so much of our paper and they'd squeeze us to death. In any event I can't replace them with an American bank that's already proved to be politically unreliable. They're fine as a backup and fantastic if they'll get us out of this mess but I'm not sure about them long-term. They have to prove themselves."

"They must be ready to compromise too. After all, giving us 2 million to cement the General Stores takeover's a great vote of confidence, *heya?*"

Dunross let that pass. "What had you in mind?"

"May I suggest you counter by making a specific offer: all Canadian, U.S., Australian and South American loans for five years—that covers our expansion in those territories—plus the immediate loan for two giant oil tankers to be purchased through Toda, on the lease-back scheme, and, for an associate, firm orders for a further seven."

"Christ Jesus, who's got that type of operation?" Dunross exploded.

"Vee Cee Ng."

"Photographer Ng? Impossible."

"Within twenty years Vee Cee will have a fleet bigger than Onassis."

"Impossible."

"Very probably, tai-pan."

"How do you know?"

"I've been asked to help finance and arrange a huge extension to his fleet. If we put the first seven tankers into our package with the promise of more, and I can, *I can*, that should satisfy First Central." Phillip Chen wiped the perspiration off his forehead. "*Heya?*"

"Christ, that'd satisfy the Chase Manhattan and the Bank of America jointly! Vee Cee?" Then Dunross's boggled mind jerked into top efficiency. "Ah! Vee Cee plus thoriums plus Old Friends plus all sorts of delicate hardware plus oil plus Old Friends. Eh?"

Phillip smiled tentatively. "All crows under heaven are black."

"Yes." After a pause, he said, "First Central might go for it. But what about Bartlett?"

"With First Central you don't need Par-Con. First Central will be happy to help us get an alternate backer or partner in the States. It'd take a little time, but with Jacques in Canada, David MacStruan here, Andrew in Scotland . . . Tai-pan, I don't know what's in your mind about Andrew and this man Kirk but the theories he's been sporting strike me as farfetched, very farfetched."

"You were saying about Bartlett?"

"I suggest we pray that First Central takes the bait, that Tiptop gives us the money, that I can cover First Central with a syndicate of Mata, Tightfist and Four Fingers. Then you, David MacStruan and I can easily find an alternate to Par-Con. I suggest we open an immediate office in New York. Put David in charge for three months with . . . perhaps Kevin as his assistant." Phillip Chen let that set a moment in the air and rushed on. "Within three months we should know if young Kevin has any value—I think you'll be very impressed, tai-pan, in fact I guarantee it. In three months we'll know what young George Trussler feels about Rhodesia and South Africa. When he has that office set up we could send him to New York. Or we could perhaps tempt your other cousin, the Virginian, Mason Kern, out of Cooper-Tillman and put him in charge of our New York office. After six months Kevin should go to Salisbury and Johannesburg—I have a great feeling that the thorium and precious metal trade will go from strength to strength."

"Meanwhile, we still have our immediate problems. Bartlett, Gornt and the run on our stock?"

"To ensure Bartlett's silence we have to split him totally from Gornt and make him an ally, a complete ally."

"How do you do that, Phillip?"

"Leave that with me. There are . . . there are possibilities."

Dunross kept his eyes on Phillip Chen but the old man did not look up from the desk. What possibilities? Orlanda? Has to be. "All right," he said. "Next?"

"About the market. With the Bank of China supporting us, the bank runs are over. With the General Stores takeover and massive financial backing, the run on our stock has to cease. Everyone will rush to buy and the boom will be on. Now," Phillip Chen said, "I know you didn't want to before, but say we can get Sir Luis to withdraw our stock from trading till Monday at noon we ca—"

"What?"

"Yes. Say no one can trade Struan's officially until noon, say we set the price where it was on Wednesday last—28.80. Gornt is trapped. He has to buy at whatever price he can to cover. If no one offers enough stock below that figure all his profits go out of the window, he might even be mauled."

Dunross felt weak. The idea of jerking the stock now had not occurred to him. "Christ, but Sir Luis'd never go for it."

Phillip Chen was very pale, beads of sweat on his forehead. "If the stock exchange committee agreed that it was necessary 'to stabilize the market' . . . and if the great broking firms of Joseph Stern and Arjan Soorjani also agree not to offer any stock, any bulk stock below 28.80, what can Gornt do?" He wiped his forehead shakily. "That's my plan."

"Why should Sir Luis cooperate?"

"I think . . . I think he will, and Stern and Soorjani owe us many favors." The old man's fingers were twitching nervously. "Between Sir Luis, Stern, Soorjani, you and me, we control most of the major blocks of stock Gornt sold short."

"Stern is Gornt's broker."

"True, but he's Hong Kong *yan* and he needs goodwill more than one client." Phillip Chen shifted more into the light. Dunross noticed the pallor and was greatly concerned. He got up and went to the liquor cabinet and fetched two brandy and sodas. "Here."

"Thank you." Phillip Chen drank his quickly. "Thank God for brandy."

"You think we can line them all up by Monday's opening? By the way, I've canceled my trip to Taipei."

"Good, yes that's wise. Will you be going to Jason Plumm's cocktail party now?"

"Yes. Yes, I said I would."

"Good, we can talk more then. About Sir Luis. There's a good chance, tai-pan. Even if the stock isn't withdrawn, the price has to skyrocket, it must—if we get the support we need."

That's obvious to anyone, Dunross thought sourly. If. He glanced at his watch. It was 8:35. Sinders was to call by 8:30. He had given him half an hour leeway before his call to Tiptop. His stomach seemed to fall apart but he dominated it. Christ, I can't call him, he thought irritably. "What?" he asked, not having heard Phillip Chen.

"The deadline you gave me to have my resignation on your desk—Sunday midnight if Mata and Tightfist or—may I ask that it be extended a week?"

Dunross picked up Phillip Chen's glass to replenish it, liking the Asian subtlety of the request, to extend it to a time when it would have no value, for, in a week's time, the crisis would be long resolved. The way the request was put saved face on both sides. Yes, but he has to make a major effort. Can his health stand it? That's my only real consideration. As he poured the brandy he thought about Phillip Chen, Kevin Chen, Claudia Chen and old Chen-chen and what he would do without them. I need cooperation and service and no more betrayal or treachery. "I'll consider that, Phillip. Let's discuss it just after Prayers on Monday." Then he added carefully, "Perhaps extensions would be justified."

Gratefully Phillip Chen accepted the brandy and took a big swallow, his color better. He had heard the deft plural and was greatly relieved. All I have to do is deliver. That's all. He got up to go. "Thank y—"

The phone jangled irritatingly and he almost jumped. So did Dunross. "Hello? Oh, hello, Mr. Sinders." Dunross could hear the beating of his heart over the rain. "What's new?"

"Very little I'm afraid. I've discussed your suggestion with the governor. If 'it' is in my possession by noon tomorrow, I have reason to believe your friend could be delivered to the Lo Wu border terminal by sunset Monday. I cannot guarantee, of course, that he will wish to cross the border into Red China."

Dunross got his voice going. "There's a lot of 'reason to believe' and 'could be' in that, Mr. Sinders."

"That's the best I can do, officially."

"What guarantees do I have?"

"None, I'm afraid, from Mr. Crosse or myself. It would seem there has to be trust on both sides."

Bastards, Dunross thought furiously, they know I'm trapped. "Thank you, I'll consider what you've said. Noon tomorrow? I'm in the hill climb tomorrow if it's on—ten to noon. I'll come to police headquarters as soon as I can afterwards."

"No need to worry, Mr. Dunross. If it's on, I'll be there too. Noon can be a deadline here or there. All right?"

"All right. Good night." Grimly Dunross put the phone down. "It's a maybe, Phillip. Maybe, by Monday sunset."

Phillip Chen sat down, aghast. His pallor increased. "That's too late."

"We'll find out." He picked up the phone and dialed again. "Hello, good evening. Is the governor there, please? Ian Dunross." He sipped his brandy. "Sorry to disturb you, sir, but Mr. Sinders just called. He said, in effect: perhaps. Perhaps by sunset Monday. May I ask, could you guarantee that?"

"No, Ian, no I can't. I don't have jurisdiction over this matter. Sorry. You have to make any arrangements direct. Sinders struck me as a reasonable man though. Didn't you think so?"

"He seemed very unreasonable," Dunross said with a hard smile. "Thanks. Never mind. Sorry to disturb you, sir. Oh, by the way if this can be resolved, Tiptop said your chop would be required, with the bank's and mine. Would you be available tomorrow, if need be?"

"Of course. And Ian, good luck."

Dunross replaced the phone. After a moment, he said, "Would they agree, the money tomorrow for the fellow Monday sunset?"

"I wouldn't," Phillip Chen said helplessly. "Tiptop was clear. 'Whenever the correct procedures are entered into.' The exchange would be simultaneous."

Dunross sat back in the high chair, sipped his brandy and let his mind roam.

At 9:00 P.M. he dialed Tiptop, and chatted inconsequentially until the moment had come. "I hear the police underling will surely be fired for making such a mistake and that the wronged party could be at Lo Wu at noon Tuesday."

There was a great silence. The voice was colder than ever. "I hardly think that's immediate."

"I agree. Perhaps I might be able to persuade them to bring it forward to Monday. Perhaps your friends could be a little patient. I would consider it a very great *favor*." He used the word deliberately and let it hang.

"I will pass your message on. Thank you, tai-pan. Please call me at seven o'clock tomorrow evening. Good night."

"Night."

Phillip Chen broke the silence, very concerned. "That's an expensive word, tai-pan."

"I know. But I have no option," he said, his voice hard. "Certainly there'll be a return favor asked in payment someday." Dunross brushed his hair away from his eyes and added, "Perhaps it'll be with Joseph Yu, who knows? But I had to say it."

"Yes. You're very wise. Wise beyond your years, much wiser than Alastair and your father, not as wise as the Hag." A small shiver went through him. "You were wise to barter the time, and wise not to mention the money, the bank money, very wise. He's much too smart not to know we need that tomorrow—I'd imagine by evening at the latest."

"Somehow we'll get it. That'll take the Victoria pressure off us. Paul's got to call a board meeting soon," Dunross added darkly. "With Richard on the board, well, Richard owes us many favors. The new board will vote to increase our revolving fund, then we won't need Bartlett, First Central or Mata's god-cursed syndicate."

Phillip Chen hesitated, then he blurted out, "I hate to be the bearer of more bad tidings but I've heard that part of Richard Kwang's arrangement with Havergill included his signed, undated resignation from the Victoria board and a promise to vote exactly as Havergill wishes."

Dunross sighed. Everything fell into place. If Richard Kwang voted with the opposition it would neutralize his dominating position. "Now all we have to do is lose one more supporter and Paul and his opposition will squeeze us to death." He looked up at Phillip Chen. "You'd better nobble Richard."

"I . . . I'll try, but he's nobbled already. What about P. B. White? Do you think he'd help?"

"Not against Havergill, or the bank. With Tiptop he might," Dunross said heavily. "He's next—and last—on the list."

70

The six people piled out of the two taxis at the private entrance of the Victoria Bank building on the side street. Casey, Riko Gresserhoff, Gavallan, Peter Marlowe, Dunross and P. B. White, a spare, spritely Englishman of seventy-five. The rain had stopped, though the poorly lit street was heavily puddled.

"Sure you won't join us for a nightcap, Peter?" P. B. White asked.

"No thanks, P.B., I'd better be getting home. Night and thanks for supper, tai-pan!"

He walked off into the night, heading for the ferry terminal that was just across the square. Neither he nor the others noticed the car pull up and stop down the street. In it was Malcolm Sun, senior agent, SI, and Povitz, the CIA man. Sun was driving.

"This the only way in and out?" Povitz asked.

"Yes."

They watched P. B. White press the door button. "Lucky bastards. Those two broads are the best I've ever seen."

"Casey's okay but the other? There are prettier girls in any dance hall. . . ." Sun stopped. A taxi went past.

"Another tail?"

"No, no I don't think so, but if we're watching the tai-pan you can bet others are."

"Yes."

They saw P. B. White press the button again. The door opened and the sleepy Sikh night guard greeted him, "Evening, sahs, memsahs," then went to the elevator, pressed the button and closed the front door.

"The elevator's rather slow. Antiquated, like me. Sorry," P. B. White said.

"How long have you lived here, P.B.?" Casey asked, knowing there was nothing ancient about him, given the dance in his step or the twinkle in his eyes.

"About five years, my dear," he replied taking her arm. "I'm very lucky."

Sure, she thought, and you've got to be very important to the bank and powerful, must be to have one of the only three apartments in the whole vast building. He had told them one of the others belonged to the chief manager who was presently on sick leave. The last one was staffed but kept vacant. "It's for visiting HRHs, the governor of the Bank of England, prime ministers, those sort of luminaries," P. B. White had said grandly during the light spicy Szechuan food. "I'm rather like a janitor, an unpaid caretaker. They let me in to look after the place."

"I'll bet!"

"Oh it's true! Fortunately there's no connection between this part of the building and the bank proper, otherwise I'd have my hand in the till!"

Casey was feeling very happy, replete with good food and good wine and fine, witty conversation and much attention from the four men, particularly Dunross—and very content that she had held her own with Riko —everything in her life seemingly in place again, Linc so much more her Linc once more, even though he was out with the enemy. How to deal with her? she asked herself for the billionth time.

The elevator door opened. They went into it, crowding into the small area. P. B. White pressed the lowest of three buttons. "God lives on the top floor," he chuckled. "When he's in town."

Dunross said, "When's he due back?"

"In three weeks, Ian, but it's just as well he's out of touch with Hong Kong—he'd be back on the next plane. Casey, our chief manager's a marvelous fellow. Unfortunately he's been quite sick for almost a year and now he's retiring in three months. I persuaded him to take some leave and go to Kashmir, to a little place I know on the banks of the Jehlum River, north of Srinagar. The floor of the valley's about six thousand feet and, up there amongst the greatest mountains on earth, it's paradise. They have houseboats on the rivers and lakes and you drift, no phones, no mail, just you and the Infinite, wonderful people, wonderful air, wonderful food, stupendous mountains." His eyes twinkled. "You have to go there very sick, or with someone you love very much."

They laughed. "Is that what you did, P.B.?" Gavallan asked.

"Of course, my dear fellow. It was in 1915, that was the first time I was there. I was twenty-seven, on leave from the Third Bengal Lancers." He sighed, parodying a lovesick youth. "She was Georgian, a princess."

They chuckled with him. "What were you really in Kashmir for?" Dunross asked.

"I'd been seconded for two years from the Indian General Staff. That whole area, the Hindu Kush, Afghanistan and what's now called Pakistan, on the borders of Russia and China's always been dicey, always will be. Then I was sent up to Moscow—that was late in '17." His face tightened a little. "I was there during the *putsch* when the real government of

Kerenski was tossed out by Lenin, Trotsky and their Bolsheviks. . . ." The elevator stopped. They got out. The front door of his apartment was open, his Number One Boy Shu waiting.

"Come on in and make yourself at home," P.B. said jovially. "The ladies' bathroom's on the left, gentlemen on the right, champagne in the anteroom . . . I'll show you all around in a moment. Oh, Ian, you wanted to phone?"

"Yes."

"Come along, you can use my study." He led the way down a corridor lined with fine oils and a rare collection of icons. The apartment was spacious, four bedrooms, three anterooms, a dining room to seat twenty. His study was at the far end. Books lined three walls. Old leather, smell of good cigars, a fireplace. Brandy, whiskey and vodka in cut-glass decanters. And port. Once the door closed his concern deepened.

"How long will you be?" he asked.

"As quick as I can."

"Don't worry, I'll entertain them—if you're not back in time I'll make your excuses. Is there anything else I can do?"

"Lean on Tiptop." Dunross had told him earlier about the possible deal to exchange Brian Kwok, though nothing about the AMG papers and his problems with Sinders.

"Tomorrow I'll call some friends in Peking and some more in Shanghai. Perhaps they would see the value in helping us."

Dunross had been acquainted with P. B. White for many years though, along with everyone else, he knew very little about his real past, his family, whether he had been married and had children, where his money came from or his real involvement with the Victoria. "I'm just a sort of legal advisor though I retired years ago," he would say vaguely and leave it at that. But Dunross knew him as a man of great charm with many equally discreet lady friends. "Casey's quite a woman, P.B.," he said with a grin. "I think you're smitten."

"I think so too. Yes. Ah, if I was only thirty years younger! And as for Riko!" P.B.'s eyebrows soared. "Delectable. Are you certain she's a widow?"

"Pretty sure."

"I would like three of those please, tai-pan." He chuckled and went over to the bookcase and pressed a switch. Part of the bookcase swung open. A staircase led upward. Dunross had used it before to have private talks with the chief manager. As far as he knew he was the only outsider privy to the secret access—another of the many secrets that he could pass on only to his succeeding tai-pan. "The Hag arranged it," Alastair Struan had told him the night he took over. "Along with this." He had handed him the master passkey to the safety deposit boxes in the vaults. "It's bank policy that Ch'ung Lien Loh Locksmiths Ltd. change locks. Only our tai-pans know we own that company."

Dunross smiled back at P.B., praying that he could be so young when he was so old. "Thanks."

"Take your time, Ian." P. B. White handed him a key.

Dunross ran up the stairs softly to the chief manager's landing. He unlocked a door which led to an elevator. The same key unlocked the elevator. There was only one button. He relocked the outside door and pressed the button. The machinery was well oiled and silent. At length it stopped and the inner door slid open. He pushed the outer door. He was in the chief manager's office. Johnjohn got up wearily. "Now what the hell is all this about, Ian?"

Dunross shut the false door that fitted perfectly into the bookcase. "Didn't P.B. tell you?" he asked, his voice mild, none of his tension showing.

"He said you had to get to the vaults tonight to fetch some papers, that I should please let you in and there was no need to bother Havergill. But why the cloak-and-dagger bit? Why not use the front door?"

"Now give over, Bruce. We both know you've got the necessary authority to open the vault for me."

Johnjohn began to say something but changed his mind. The chief manager had said before he left, "Be kind enough to react favorably to whatever P.B. suggests, eh?" P.B. was on first-name terms with the governor, most of the visiting VVIPs and shared the chief manager's direct line to their skeleton staff in the bank offices still operating in Shanghai and Peking.

"All right," he said.

Their footsteps echoed on the vast, dimly lit main floor of the bank. Johnjohn nodded to one of the night watchmen making his rounds, then pressed the button for the elevator to the vaults, stifling a nervous yawn. "Christ, I'm bushed."

"You architected the Ho-Pak takeover, didn't you?"

"Yes, yes I did, but if it hadn't been for your smashing coup with General Stores, I don't think Paul'd . . . well, that certainly helped. Smashing coup, Ian, if you can pull it off."

"It's in the bag."

"What Japanese bank's backing you with the 2 million?"

"Why did you force Richard Kwang's advance resignation?"

"Eh?" Johnjohn stared at him blankly. The elevator arrived. They got into it. "What?"

Dunross explained what Phillip Chen had told him. "That's not exactly cricket. A director of the Victoria being made to sign an undated resignation like a two-cent operation? Eh?"

Johnjohn shook his head slowly. "No, that wasn't part of my plan." His tiredness had vanished. "I can see why you'd be concerned."

"*Pissed off* would be the correct words."

"Paul must have planned just a holding situation till the chief comes back. This whole operation's precedent-setting so you c—"

"If I get Tiptop's money for you, I want that torn up and a free vote guaranteed to Richard Kwang."

After a pause, Johnjohn said, "I'll support you on everything reasonable —till the chief comes back. Then he can decide."

"Fair enough."

"How much is the Royal Belgium–First Central backing you for?"

"I thought you said a Japanese bank?"

"Oh come on, old chum, everyone knows. How much?"

"Enough, enough for everything."

"We still own most of your paper, Ian."

Dunross shrugged. "It makes no difference. We still have a major say in the Victoria."

"If we don't get China's money, First Central won't save you from a crash."

Again Dunross shrugged.

The elevator doors opened. Dim lights in the vaults cast hard shadows. The huge grille in front of them seemed like a cell door to Dunross. Johnjohn unlocked it.

"I'll be about ten minutes," Dunross said, a sheen to his forehead. "I've got to find a particular paper."

"All right. I'll unlock your box for y—" Johnjohn stopped, his face etched in the overhead light. "Oh, I forgot, you've your own master key."

"I'll be as quick as I can. Thanks." Dunross walked into the gloom, turned the corner and went unerringly to the far bank of boxes. Once there he made sure he was not being followed. All his senses were honed now. He put the two keys into their locks. The locks clicked back.

His fingers reached into his pocket and he took out AMG's letter that gave the numbers of the special pages spread throughout the files, then a flashlight, scissors and a butane Dunhill cigarette lighter that Penelope had given him when he still smoked. Quickly he lifted the false bottom of the box away and slid out the files.

I wish to Christ there was some way I could destroy them now and have done with it, he thought. I know everything that's in them, everything important, but I have to be patient and wait. Sometime soon, they— whoever they are, along with SI, the CIA and the PRC—they won't be following me. Then I can safely fetch the files and destroy them.

Following AMG's instructions with great care, he flicked the lighter and waved it back and forth just under the bottom right quadrant of the first special page. In a moment, a meaningless jumble of symbols, letters and numbers began to appear. As the heat brought them forth, the type in this quadrant began to vanish. Soon all the lettering had gone, leaving just the code. With the scissors he cut off this quarter neatly and put that file aside. AMG had written: "The paper cannot be traced to the files, tai-pan, nor I believe, the information read by any but the highest in the land."

A slight noise startled him and he looked off. His heart was thumping in his ears. A rat scurried around a wall of boxes and vanished. He waited but there was no more danger.

In a moment he was calm again. Now the next file. Again ciphers appeared and the lettering vanished.

Dunross worked steadily and efficiently. When the flame began to fade he was prepared. He refilled the lighter and continued. Now the last file. He cut out the quarter carefully and pocketed the eleven pieces of paper, then slid the files back into their hiding place.

Before he relocked the box he took out a deed for camouflage and laid it beside AMG's letter. Another hesitation, then, shielding AMG's letter with his body, he put the flame to it. The paper twisted as it flared and burned.

"What're you doing?"

Dunross jerked around and stared at the silhouette. "Oh, it's you." He began breathing again. "Nothing, Bruce. Actually it's just an ancient love letter that shouldn't have been kept." The flame died and Dunross pounded the ash to dust and scattered the remains.

"Ian, are you in trouble? Bad trouble?" Johnjohn asked gently.

"No, old chum. It's just the Tiptop mess."

"You're sure?"

"Oh yes." Wearily Dunross smiled back and took out a handkerchief to wipe his forehead and hands. "Sorry to put you to all this trouble."

He walked off firmly, Johnjohn following. The gate clanged after them. In a moment the elevator sighed open and sighed closed and now there was silence but for the scurry of the rats and the slight hiss of the air conditioner. A shadow moved. Silently Roger Crosse came from behind a tall bank of boxes and stood in front of the tai-pan's section. Unhurried, he took out a tiny Minox camera, a flashlight and a bunch of skeleton keys. In a moment, Dunross's box was open. His long fingers reached into it, found the false compartment and brought out the files. Very satisfied he put them in a tidy pile, clipped the flashlight into its socket and, with practiced skill, began to photograph the files, page by page. When he came to one of the special pages he peered at it and the missing section. A grim smile flickered over him. Then he continued, making no sound.

SUNDAY

71

6:30 A.M.:

Koronski came out of the foyer of the Nine Dragons Hotel and hailed a taxi, giving the driver directions in passable Cantonese. He lit a cigarette and slouched back in the seat, keeping a professional watch behind him in the unlikely chance that he was being followed. There was no real risk. His papers as Hans Meikker were flawless, his cover as a sporadic foreign journalist for a West German magazine syndicate real, and he visited Hong Kong frequently as a routine. His eyes reassured him, then he turned to watch the multitudes, wondering who was to be chemically debriefed, and where. He was a short, well-fed, nondescript man, his glasses rimless.

Behind him, fifty yards or so, ducking in and out of the traffic was a small, battered Mini. Tom Connochie, the senior CIA agent was in the back, one of his assistants, Roy Wong, driving.

"He's going left."

"Sure. I see him. Relax, Tom, you're making me nervous for chrissake." Roy Wong was third-generation American, a B.A. Lit., and CIA for four years, assigned to Hong Kong. He drove expertly, Connochie watching carefully—crumpled and very tired. He had been up most of the night with Rosemont trying to sort out the flood of top-secret instructions, requests and orders that the intercepted Thomas K. K. Lim's letters had generated. Just after midnight they'd been tipped by one of their hotel informants that Hans Meikker had just checked in for two days from Bangkok. He had been on their list for years as a possible security risk.

"Son of a bitch!" Roy Wong said as a traffic jam blossomed in the narrow, screeching street near the bustling intersections of Mong Kok.

Connochie craned out of the side window. "He's screwed too, Roy. About twenty cars ahead."

In a moment the jam began to ease, then closed in again as an overladen truck stalled. By the time it had cranked up again, their prey had vanished.

"Shit!"

"Cruise. Maybe we'll get lucky and pick him up."

Two blocks ahead, Koronski got out of the taxi and went down a swarming alley, heading for another swarming road and another alley and Ginny Fu's tenement. He went up the soiled stairs to the top floor. He knocked three times on a drab door. Suslev beckoned him in and locked the door behind him. "Welcome," he said quietly in Russian. "Good trip?"

"Yes, Comrade Captain, very good," Koronski replied, also keeping his voice down by habit.

"Come and sit down." Suslev waved at the table that had coffee and two cups. The room was drab with little furniture. Dirty blinds covered the windows.

"Coffee's good," Koronski said politely, thinking it was hideous, nothing to compare with the French-style coffee of exquisite Bangkok, Saigon and Phnom Penh.

"It's the whiskey," Suslev said, his face hard.

"Center said I was to put myself at your disposal, Comrade Captain. What is it you want me to do?"

"A man here has a photographic memory. We need to know what's in it."

"Where is the client to be interrogated? Here?"

Suslev shook his head. "Aboard my ship."

"How much time do we have?"

"All the time you need. We will take him with us to Vladivostok."

"How important is it to get quality information?"

"Very."

"In that case I would prefer to do the investigation in Vladivostok—I can give you special sedatives and instructions that will keep the client docile during the voyage there and begin the softening-up process."

Suslev rethought the problem. He needed Dunross's information before he arrived in Vladivostok. "Can't you come with me on my ship? We leave at midnight, on the tide."

Koronski hesitated. "My orders from Center are to assist you, so long as I do not jeopardize my cover. Going on your ship would certainly do that —the ship's sure to be under surveillance. If I vanish from the hotel, eh?"

Suslev nodded. "I agree." Never mind, he thought. I'm as well trained an interrogator as Koronski though I've never done an in-depth chemical. "How do you conduct a chemical debriefing?"

"It's quite simple. Intravenous injections of a chemical agent we call Pentothal-V6, twice a day for ten days at twelve-hour intervals—once the client has been put into a suitably frightened, disoriented frame of mind, by the usual sleep-wake method, followed by four days of sleeplessness."

"We've a doctor on the ship. Could he make the injections?"

"Oh yes, yes of course. May I suggest I write down the procedure and supply you with, all the necessary chemicals. You will do the investigation?"

"Yes."

"If you follow the procedure you should have no trouble. The only serious thing to remember is that once the Pentothal-V6 is administered the client's mind is like a wet sponge. It requires great tenderness and even greater care to extract just the right amount of water, the information, at just the right tempo or the mind will be permanently damaged and all other information lost forever." Koronski puffed at a cigarette. "It's easy to lose a client."

"It's always easy to lose a client," Suslev said. "How effective is this Pentothal-V6?"

"We've had great success, and some failures, Comrade Captain," Koronski replied with care. "If the client is well prepared and initially healthy I'm sure you will be successful."

Suslev did not answer, just let his mind reexamine the plan presented so enthusiastically by Plumm late last night, and agreed to reluctantly by Crosse. "It's a cinch, Gregor, everything's falling into place. Now that Dunross's not going to Taipei he's coming to my party. I'll give him a doctored drink that'll make him as sick as a dog—it'll be easy to get him to lie down in one of the bedrooms—the same drug'll put him to sleep. Once the others have left—and I'm keeping the party short and sweet, six to eight— I'll put him in a trunk and have the trunk brought to the car through the side entrance. When he's reported missing I'll say I just left him there sleeping and have no idea what time he left. Now, how are we going to get the trunk aboard?"

"That's no trouble," he had said. "Have it delivered to go-down 7 in the Kowloon Dockyard. We're taking on all kinds of bulk supplies and stores, since our departure's been speeded up, and outward bound there's hardly any check." Suslev had added with grim amusement, "There is even a coffin if we need it. Voranski's body is coming from the morgue at 11:00 P.M., a special delivery. Bastards! Why hasn't our friend caught the bastards who murdered him?"

"He's doing what he can. He is, Gregor. I promise you. He'll catch them soon—but more important, this plan *will* work!"

Suslev nodded to himself. Yes, it's workable. And if the tai-pan's intercepted and discovered? I know nothing, Boradinov knows nothing, though he's responsible and I shall just sail away, leaving Boradinov to blame, if necessary. Roger will cover everything. Oh yes, he told himself grimly, this time it's Roger's neck on the British block if I'm not covered. Plumm's right. The Werewolf kidnapping of the tai-pan will help to create complete chaos for a time, certainly for almost no risk—enough time to cover the Metkin disaster and the intercept of the guns.

He had called Banastasio tonight to make sure the Par-Con ploy was in operation and was shocked to hear of Bartlett's response. "But, Mr. Banastasio, you guaranteed you'd be in control. What do you intend to do?"

"Pressure, Mr. Marshall," Banastasio had told him placatingly, using the alias by which Banastasio knew him. "Pressure all the way. I'll do my part, you do yours."

"Good. Then proceed with your meeting in Macao. I guarantee a substitute shipment will be in Saigon within a week."

"But these jokers here have already said they won't deal without a shipment in their hands."

"It'll be delivered direct to our Viet Cong friends in Saigon. Just you make whatever arrangements you want for payment."

"Sure sure, Mr. Marshall. Where you staying in Macao? Where do I get in touch?"

"I'll be at the same hotel," he had told him, having no intention to make contact. In Macao another controller with the same alias would monitor that end of the operation.

He smiled to himself. Just before he had left Vladivostok, Center had ordered him to be the controller of this independent operation, code name King Kong, that had been mounted by one of the Washington KGB cells. All he knew of the plan was that they were sending highly classified advance-arms delivery schedules to the V.C. in Saigon through diplomatic pouch. In exchange and payment for the information, opium would be delivered FOB Hong Kong—the quantity depending on the numbers of arms hijacked. "Whoever thought of this one deserves immediate promotion," he had told Center delightedly, and had chosen the alias Marshall after General Marshall and his plan that they all knew had ruined the immediate and total Soviet takeover of Europe in the late forties. This is revenge, our Marshall Plan in reverse, he thought.

Abruptly he laughed out loud. Koronski waited attentively, far too practiced to ask what had been so amusing. But without thinking he had analyzed the laugh. There was fear in it. Fear was infectious. Frightened people make mistakes. Mistakes ensnare innocents.

Yes, he thought uneasily, this man smells of cowardice. I shall mention this in my next report, but delicately, in case he's important.

He looked up and saw Suslev watching him and queasily wondered if the man had read his thoughts. "Yes, Comrade Captain?"

"How long will the instructions take to write?"

"A few minutes. I can do it now if you wish, but I will have to go back to the hotel for the chemicals."

"How many different chemicals are to be used?"

"Three: one for sleep, one for wake-up and the last, the Pentothal-V6. By the way, it should be kept cool until used."

"Only the last intravenously?"

"Yes."

"Good, then write it all down. Now. You have paper?"

Koronski nodded and pulled out a small notebook from his hip pocket. "Would you prefer Russian, English or shorthand?"

"Russian. There's no need to describe the wake-sleep-wake pattern. I've used that many times. Just the last phase and don't name Pentothal-V6, just call it medicine. Understand?"

"Perfectly."

"Good. When it's written, put it there." He pointed to a small pile of used newspapers on the moth-eaten sofa. "Put it in the second one from the top. I'll collect it later. As to the chemicals there's a men's room on the ground floor of the Nine Dragons Hotel. Tape them to the underside of the lid, the last booth on the right—and please be in your room at nine o'clock tonight in case I need some clarification. Everything clear?"

"Certainly."

Suslev got up. At once Koronski did the same, offered his hand. "Good luck, Comrade Captain."

Suslev nodded politely as to an inferior and walked out. He went to the end of the corridor and through a bent door up a staircase to the roof. He felt better in the air on the roof. The room smell and Koronski's smell had displeased him. The sea beckoned him, the wide clean ocean and salt-kelp smell. It will be good to be at sea again, away from the land. The sea and the ocean and the ship keep you sane.

Like most roofs in Hong Kong this one was packed with a polyglot of makeshift dwellings, the space rented—the only alternative to the crude, packed mud slopes of the squatter settlements that were far in the New Territories or in the hills of Kowloon or Hong Kong. Every inch of space in the city had long since been taken by the vast influx of immigrants. Most squatters' areas were illegal, like all roof dwellings, and as much as the authorities forbade it and deplored it, wisely they ignored these transgressions for where else were these unfortunates to go? There was no sanitation, no water, not even simple hygiene, but it was still better than on the streets. From the rooftops, the method of disposal was just to hurl it below. Hong Kong *yan* always walked in the center of the street and never on the sidewalk, even if there was one.

Suslev ducked under clotheslines, stepped over the flotsam and jetsam of lifetimes, oblivious of the automatic obscenities that followed him, amused by the urchins who ran before him shrieking, "*Quai loh . . . quai loh!*", laughing together, holding out their hands. He was too Hong Kong *yan* to give them any money though he was touched by them, their poverty and good humor, so he just cursed them genially and tousled a few crew-cut heads.

On the far side of the roof the entrance to Ginny Fu's tenement jutted like an ancient funnel. The door was ajar. He went down.

"Halloa, Gregy," Ginny Fu said, breathlessly opening her front door for him. She was dressed as he had ordered in a drab coolie outfit with a big straw conical hat hanging down her back, her face and hands dirtied. "How I look? Like film star, *heya?*"

"Greta Garbo herself," he said with a laugh as she ran into his arms and gave him a great hug.

"You want jig-jig more 'fore go, *heya?*"

"*Nyet.* Plenty of time in the next weeks. Plenty, *heya?*" He set her down. He had pillowed with her at dawn, more to prove his manhood than out of desire. That's the problem, he thought. No desire. She's boring. "Now, you understand plan, *heya?*"

"Oh yes," she said grandly. "I find go-down 7 and join coolies, carry bales to ship. Once on ship I go door opposite stairway, go in and give paper." She pulled it out of her pocket to show that she had it safely. On the paper was written in Russian, "Cabin 3." Boradinov would be expecting her. "In 3 cabin, can use bath, change to clothes you buy and wait." Another big smile. "*Heya?*"

"Excellent." The clothes had cost little and the buying saved any baggage. Much more simple without baggage. Baggage would be noticed. Nothing about her should be noticed.

"Sure no need bring anything, Gregy?" she asked anxiously.

"No, only makeup things, woman things. Everything in pocket, understand?"

"Of course," she said haughtily. "Am I fool?"

"Good. Then off you go."

Once more she embraced him. "Oh thanks holiday, Gregy—I be bestest ever." She left.

The meeting with Koronski had made him hungry. He went to the battered refrigerator and found the chocolates he sought. He munched on one, then lit the gas stove and began to fry some eggs. His anxiety began to return. Don't worry, he ordered himself. The plan will work, you will get possession of the tai-pan and it will be routine at police headquarters.

Put those things aside. Think of Ginny. Perhaps at sea she won't be boring. She'll divert the nights, some of the nights, the tai-pan the days until we dock. By then he'll be empty and she'll vanish into a new life and that danger will be gone forever and I'll go to my *dacha* where the Zergeyev hellcat'll be waiting and we'll fight, she calling me every obscenity until I lose my temper and tear her clothes off, maybe use the whip again and she'll fight back and fight back until I fight into her and explode, explode taking her with me sometimes, *Kristos* how I wish it was every time. Then sleeping, never knowing when she'll kill me in my sleep. But she's been warned. If anything happens to me my men will give her to lepers on the east side of Vladivostok with the rest of her family.

The radio announced the seven o'clock news in English. "Good morning. This is Radio Hong Kong. More heavy rain is expected. The Victoria Bank has confirmed officially that it will assume all depositor debts of the

Ho-Pak and asks depositors to line up peacefully if they require their money on Monday.

"During the night there were numerous land and mud slides throughout the Colony. Worst hit were the squatters' settlement area above Aberdeen, Sau Ming Ping, and Sui Fai Terrace in Wanchai where six major landslips affected buildings in the area. In all, thirty-three persons are known to have lost their lives and many are feared still buried in the slides.

"There are no new developments in the foul murder and kidnapping of Mr. John Chen by the Werewolf gang. Rewards of $100,000 for information leading to their capture have been posted.

"Reports from London confirm that this year's harvest in the USSR has again failed. . . ."

Suslev didn't hear the rest of the broadcast. He knew the report from London was true. Top-secret KGB forecasts had predicted the harvest would once more be below even that necessary for subsistence.

Kristos, why the hell can't we feed ourselves? he wanted to shout, knowing famine, knowing the bloatedness and pains in his own lifetime let alone the ghastly tales his father and mother would tell.

So there's to be famine once more, tightening the belt once more, having to buy wheat from abroad, using up our hard-earned foreign currency, our future in danger, terrible danger, food our Achilles' heel. Never enough. Never enough skill or tractors or fertilizers or wealth, all the real wealth going for arms and armies and airplanes and ships first, far more important to become strong enough to protect ourselves from capitalist swine and revisionist Chinese swine and carry the war to them and smash them before they smash us, but never enough food for us and our buffer lands—the Balkans, Hungary, Czechoslovakia, Poland, East Germany, the Baltic lands. Why is it those bastards could feed themselves most times? Why is it they falsify their harvests and cheat us and lie and steal from us? We protect them and what do they do? Brood and hate us and yet without our armies and the KGB to keep the filthy scum revisionist dissidents in thrall, they'll foment rebellion—like East Germany and Hungary—and turn the stupid masses against us.

But famine causes revolution. Always. Famine will always make the masses rise up against their government. So what can we do? Keep them chained—all of them—until we smash America and Canada and take their wheatlands for ourselves. Then our system will double their harvest.

Don't fool yourself, he thought, agonized. Our agricultural system doesn't work. It never has. One day it will. Meanwhile we cannot feed ourselves. Those motherless turd farmers should . . .

"Stop it," Suslev muttered aloud, "you're not responsible, it's not your problem. Deal with your own problems, have faith in the Party and Marxist-Leninism!"

The eggs were done now and he made toast. Rain spattered the open windows. An hour ago the all-night torrent had ceased, but across the street and above the opposite tenement there were the dark clouds. More rain there, he thought, lots more. It's either god-cursed drought or god-cursed flood in this cesspit! A gust caught one of the sodden, cardboard makeshift lean-tos on the roof and collapsed it. At once stoic repairs began, children barely old enough to walk helping.

With deft hands, liking neatness, he laid himself a place at the table, humming in time with the radio music. Everything's fine, he reassured himself. Dunross will go to the party, Koronski will supply the means, Plumm the client, Roger the protection, and all I have to do is go to police headquarters for an hour or so, then leisurely board my ship. On the midnight tide I kiss my arse to Hong Kong, leaving the Werewolves to bury the dead. . . .

The hackles of his neck rose as he heard the screech of an approaching police siren. He stood, paralyzed. But the siren whined past and went away. Stoically he sat and began to eat. Then the secret phone rang.

72

The small Bell helicopter swung in over the city, just below the overcast, and continued climbing the slopes to ease past the Peak funicular and the multiple high rises that dotted the steepness. Now the chopper was almost in the bottom layer of cloud.

Warily the pilot climbed another hundred feet, slowed and hovered, then saw the misted helipad in the grounds of the Great House near a great jacaranda tree. Immediately he swooped to the landing. Dunross was already waiting there. He ducked low to avoid the swirling blades, got into the left side of the bubble and buckled on his safety belts and headphones. "Morning, Duncan," he said into the mouth mike. "Didn't think you'd make it."

"Nor me," the older man said, and Dunross adjusted the headphone volume to hear better. "Doubt if we'll be able to get back, tai-pan. The overcast's dropping too fast again. Best leave if we're leaving. You have control."

"Here we go."

Gently Dunross's left hand twisted the throttle grip and increased the revs smoothly and eased the lever up, while his right hand moved the control stick right, left, forward, back, inching it in a gentle tiny circle, seeking and feeling for the air cushion that was building nicely—his left hand controlling speed, climbing or descending, his right hand direction, his feet on the rudder pedals keeping the whole unstable aircraft straight, preventing torque. Dunross loved to fly choppers. It was so much more of a challenge than fixed-wing flying. It required so much concentration and skill that he forgot his problems, the flying cleansing him. But he rarely flew alone. The sky was for professionals or for those who flew daily, so he would always have a pilot-instructor along with him, the presence of the other man not detracting from his pleasure.

His hands felt the cushion building and then the craft was an inch airborne. Instantly he corrected the slight slide to the right as a wind gusted.

He checked his instruments, feeling for dangers, eyes outside, ears tuned to the music of the engine. When all was stable, he increased revs as he raised the left lever, eased the stick forward and left an inch, feet compensating, and went into a skidding left turn, gaining altitude and speed to drop away down the mountainside.

Once he was steady he pushed the transmit button on the stick, reporting in to Air Traffic Control at Kai Tak.

"Watch your revs," Mac said.

"Got it. Sorry." Dunross corrected just a fraction too hastily and cursed himself, then got the helicopter trimmed nicely, cruising sweetly, everything in the green, a thousand feet above sea level heading out across the harbor toward Kowloon, the New Territories and the hill-climb area.

"You really going to do the hill climb, tai-pan?"

"Doubt it, Duncan," he said through the mike. "But I wanted our ride anyway. I've been looking forward to it all week." Duncan MacIver ran this small helicopter business from the airport. Most of his business was local, most from government for surveys. The police hired him sometimes, the fire department, Customs. He was a short man, ex-RAF, with a lined face, very wide, sharp eyes that raked constantly.

Once Dunross was settled and trimmed, MacIver leaned forward and put circles of cardboard over the instruments to force Dunross to fly by feel and sound only, to listen to the pitch and tone; slowing meant the engine was working harder so they were climbing—watch for stalling—and faster, that it was diving, losing altitude.

"Tai-pan, look down there." MacIver pointed at the scar on one of the mountainsides just outside Kowloon; it scored a path through one of the vast squatter hovel slums. "There're mud slides all over. Did you hear the seven o'clock news?"

"Yes, yes I did."

"Let me take her a minute." Dunross took his hands and feet off the controls. MacIver went into a lovely diving turn to swoop nearer the settlement to examine the damage. The damage was great. Perhaps two hundred of the hovels were scattered and buried. Others near the slide were now even more precarious than before. Smoke from the fires that came with every slide still hung like a pall.

"Christ! It looks terrible."

"I was up at dawn this morning. The fire department asked me to help them on Hill Three, over above Aberdeen. They had a slide there a couple of days ago, a child almost got buried. Last night there was another slip in the same area. Very dicey. The slip's about two hundred feet by fifty. Two or three hundred hovels gone but only ten dead—bloody lucky!" MacIver circled for a moment, made a note on a pad, then gunned the ship back to altitude and to course. Once she was steady, level and trimmed he said, "She's all yours." Dunross took control.

Sha Tin was coming up on their right-side horizon. When they were close, MacIver took off the cardboard instrument covers. "Good," he said checking the readings. "Spot on."

"Had any interesting jobs recently?"

"Just more of the same. Got a charter for Macao, weather permitting, tomorrow morning."

"Lando Mata?"

"No, some American called Banastasio. Watch your revs! Oh, there's your landfall."

The fishing village at Sha Tin was near tracks that led back into the hills where the hill climb was to be held. The course consisted of a crude dirt road bulldozed out of the mountainside. At the foot of the slopes were a few cars, some on trailers and trailer rigs, but almost no spectators. Normally there would be hundreds, Europeans mostly. It was the only car-racing event in the Colony. British law forbade using any part of the public road system for racing, and this was the reason that the annual amateur Grand Prix race at Macao had been organized under the joint banner of the Sportscar and Rally Club of Hong Kong and the Portuguese Municipal Council. Last year Guillo Rodriguez of the Hong Kong Police had won the sixty-lap race in three hours twenty-six minutes at an average speed of 72 mph, and Dunross, driving a Lotus, and Brian Kwok in a borrowed E-Type Jag had been neck and neck for second place until Dunross blew a tire, flat out, going into Fisherman's Bend and nearly killed himself at the same spot where his engine blew in '59, the year before he became tai-pan.

Dunross was concentrating on his landing now, knowing that they would be watched.

The chopper was lined up, revs correct for descent, wind ahead and to the right, swirling a little as they came closer to the ground. Dunross held her meticulously. At the exact spot, he corrected and stopped, hovering, in total control, then, keeping everything coordinated, eased off the throttle oh so gently, raising the left lever to change the pitch of the blades to cushion the landing. The landing skids touched the earth. Dunross took off the remaining throttle and smoothly lowered the lever to bottom. The landing was as good as he had ever done.

MacIver said nothing, paying him a fine compliment by pretending to take it for granted, and watched while Dunross began the shutdown drill. "Tai-pan, why don't you let me finish it for you," he said. "Those fellows look somewhat anxious."

"Thanks."

Dunross kept his head down and went to the rain-coated group, his feet squelching in the mud. "Morning."

"It's bloody awful, tai-pan," George T'Chung, Shitee T'Chung's eldest son, said. "I tried my bus out and she stuck on the first bend." He pointed at the track. The E-Type was bogged down with one of its fenders bent. "I'll have to get a tractor." A spatter of rain washed them.

"Bloody waste of time," Don Nikklin said sourly. He was a short, bellicose man in his late twenties. "We should have canceled it yesterday."

Quite true, Dunross thought contentedly, but then I wouldn't have had the excuse to fly, and the extreme pleasure of seeing you here, your morning wasted. "The consensus was to try for today. Everyone agreed it was a long shot," Dunross said sweetly. "You were there. So was your father. Eh?"

McBride said hastily, "I formally suggest we postpone."

"Approved." Nikklin went off back to his brand-new four-wheel-drive truck with its souped-up Porsche under a neat tarp.

"Friendly fellow," someone said.

They watched as Nikklin got his rig into motion and swirled away with great skill on the treacherous dirt road, past the chopper, its engine dying and the rotors slowing down.

"Pity he's such a shit," someone else said. "He's an awfully good driver."

"Roll on Macao, eh, tai-pan?" George T'Chung said with a laugh, his voice patrician and English public school.

"Yes," Dunross said, his voice sharpening, looking forward to November, to beating Nikklin again. He had beaten him three out of six tries but he had never won the Grand Prix, his cars never strong enough to sustain his heavy right foot. "This time I'll win, by God."

"Oh no you won't, tai-pan. This's my year! I've a Lotus 22, the works, my old man sprung for the lot. You'll see my tail for all sixty laps!"

"Not on your nelly! My new E-Type'll . . ." Dunross stopped. A police car was skidding and slipping in the quagmire, approaching him. Why's Sinders here so early? he asked himself, his stomach tightening. He had said noon. Involuntarily his hand moved to check that the envelope was safe in his buttoned-down hip pocket. His fingers reassured him.

Last night when he had returned to P. B. White's study he had taken out the eleven pieces of paper and examined them again under the light. The ciphers were meaningless. I'm glad, he had thought. Then he had gone to the photocopier that was beside the leather-topped desk and made two copies of each page. He put each set into a separate envelope and sealed them. One he marked: "P. B. White—please hand this to the tai-pan of Struan's unopened." That one he put into a book that he chose at random from the bookshelves, replacing it with equal care. Following AMG's instructions, he marked the second with a G for Riko Gresserhoff and pocketed it. The originals he sealed in a last envelope and pocketed that too. With a final check that the secret door was back in place, he unlocked the door and went out. In a few minutes he and Gavallan had left with Casey and Riko and though there was plenty of opportunity to give Riko her set privately, he had decided it was better to wait until the originals were delivered.

Should I give Sinders the originals now or at noon? he asked himself, watching the police car. The car stopped. Chief Inspector Donald C. C. Smyth got out. Neither Sinders nor Crosse was with him.

"Morning," Smyth said politely, touching his peaked cap with his swagger stick, his other arm still in a sling. "Excuse me, Mr. Dunross, is the chopper your charter?"

"Yes, yes it is, Chief Inspector," Dunross said. "What's up?"

"I've a small show on down the road and saw you coming in. Wonder if we could borrow MacIver and the bird for an hour—or if you're going back at once, perhaps we could take her on after?"

"Certainly. I'll be off in a second. The hill climb's canceled."

Smyth glanced at the mountain track and the sky and grunted. "I'd say that was wise, sir. Someone would've been hurt, sure as shooting. If it's all right, I'll talk to MacIver?"

"Of course. Nothing serious I hope?"

"No, no, not at all. Interesting though. The rain's uncovered a couple of bodies that'd been buried in the same area where John Chen's body was found."

The others came closer. "The Werewolves?" George T'Chung asked, shocked. "More kidnap victims?"

"We presume so. They were both young. One had his head bashed in and the other poor bugger half his head cut off, looks like with a spade. Both were Chinese."

"Christ!" Young George T'Chung had gone white.

Smyth nodded sourly. "You haven't heard of any rich sons being kidnapped, have you?"

Everyone shook their heads.

"Not surprised," Smyth said. "Stupid for the families of victims to deal with kidnappers and keep quiet about it. Unfortunately the bodies were discovered by locals so it'll be headlines by tonight from here to Peking!"

"You want to fly the bodies back?"

"Oh no, tai-pan. The hurry's to get some CID experts here to search the area before the rain comes again. We need to try to identify the poor buggers. Can you leave at once?"

"Yes, certainly."

"Thanks. Sorry to bother you. Sorry about Noble Star, but my bundle'll be on you on Saturday." Smyth nodded politely and walked off.

George T'Chung was openly upset. "We're all targets for those bastards, the Werewolves. You, me, my old man, anyone! Christ, how can we protect ourselves against them?"

No one answered him.

Then Dunross said with a laugh, "No need to worry, old chap, we're inviolate, we're all inviolate."

73

The phone rang in the semidarkness of the bedroom. Bartlett scrambled out of sleep. "Hello?"

"Good morning, Mr. Bartlett, this is Claudia Chen. The tai-pan asked if you'd need the car today anyway?"

"No, no thanks." Bartlett glanced at his watch. "Jesus," he muttered aloud, astounded he had slept so long. "Er, thanks, thanks, Claudia."

"The Taipei trip's rescheduled for next Friday, Friday back Monday noon. Is that convenient?"

"Yes, er yes, sure."

"Thank you."

Bartlett hung up and lay back a moment, collecting his wits. He stretched luxuriously, glad that there was no rush for anything, enjoying the rare pleasantness of being just a little lazy.

It had been four o'clock this morning when he had hung up a "do not disturb," cut off the phones till 10:00 A.M. and had gone to bed. Last night Orlanda had taken him to Aberdeen where she had hired a Pleasure Boat. They had drifted the channels, the rain making the hooped cabin more cozy, the brazier warming, the food hot and spicy.

"In Shanghai we cook with garlic and chilies and peppers and all manner of spices," she had told him, serving him, her chopsticks a delicate extension of her fingers. "The farther north you go the hotter the food, the less rice is eaten, more breads and noodles. The north's wheat-eating, only the southern part of China's rice-eating, Linc. More?"

He had eaten well and drunk the beer she had brought with her. The night had been happy for him, the time going unnoticed as she regaled him with stories of Asia and Shanghai, her mind deft and darting. Then, afterward, the rain pattering on the canvas, the dishes taken away and they reclining side-by-side on the cushions, fingers entwined, she had said, "Linc, I'm sorry, but I love you."

It had taken him by surprise.

"No need to be sorry," he had said, not ready yet to reply in kind.

"Oh but I am. It complicates things, oh yes, it complicates things very much."

Yes, he thought. It's so easy for a woman to say I love you, so hard for a man, unwise for a man, for then you're stuck. Is that the right word? Again the answer did not present itself.

As he lay now in bed, his head cradled on his arms, he rethought the night. Touching and leaving alone, then hands searching, his and hers, but not finalizing. Not that she prevented him or stopped him. He just held back. Finally.

"You've never done that before," he muttered out loud. "Once you had a girl going, you went all the way," and he wished he had, remembering how heavy the desire had been upon them. "I'm not a one-night stand or Eurasian tramp" had rung in his ears.

In the taxi to her home they had not spoken, just held hands. That's the goddamnedest part, he thought, feeling foolish, childish, just holding hands. If anyone had told me a month ago, a week ago that I'd settle for that, I'd've said he was a meathead and bet big money.

Money. I have more than enough for Orlanda and me. But what about Casey? And Par-Con? First things first. Let's see if Casey tells me about Murtagh and why she's been sitting on that hot potato. Gornt? Gornt or Dunross? Dunross has style and if Banastasio's against him that's one great vote of confidence.

After he had told Armstrong their theory about Banastasio, Armstrong had said, "We'll see what we can come up with, though Mr. Gornt's credentials are as impeccable as any in the Colony. You can rest assured Vincenzo Banastasio will be high up on our shit list, but isn't his real threat in the States?"

"Oh yes. But I told Rosemont an—"

"Ah, good! That was wise. He's a good man. Did you see Ed Langan?"

"No. Is he CIA too?"

"I don't even know, officially, if Rosemont is, Mr. Bartlett. Leave it with me. Did he have any suggestion about the guns?"

"No."

"Well, never mind. I'll pass on your information and liaise with him—he's very good by the way."

A small tremor went through Bartlett. He'll have to be very good to clobber Mafia, if Banastasio really is Mafia.

He reached over and dialed Casey's room number. No answer, so he called down for his messages. The receptionist told him everything was already under his door. "Would you like your cables and telexes sent up?"

"Sure, thanks. Any message from Casey Tcholok?"

"No sir."

"Thanks."

He jumped out of bed and went to the door. Among the phone messages was an envelope. He recognized her writing. The messages were all business calls except one: "Mr. Banastasio called. Please return his call." Bartlett put that aside. He opened Casey's envelope. The note was timed 9:45 A.M. and read: "Hi, Linc! Didn't want to disturb your beauty sleep—back sixish. Have fun!"

Where's she off to? he asked himself absently.

He picked up the phone to call Rosemont but changed his mind and dialed Orlanda. No answer. He redialed the number. The calling tone droned on and on.

"Shit!" He pushed away his discontent.

You've a date for lunch so what's so tough? Sunday brunch here atop the V and A and lots of time, Sunday brunch where "all the best people go for lunch, Linc. Oh it's super, the hot and cold buffet's the talk of Asia. The very best!"

"Jesus, all this food, by next week I'll weigh a ton!"

"Not you, never never never. If you like, we'll go for a long walk or when the rain stops we'll play tennis. Whatever you want we'll do! Oh Linc, I love you so. . . ."

Casey was leaning on the balustrade at the Kowloon wharf among the crowds. She wore khaki pants and a yellow silk shirt that showed her figure without flaunting it, a matching cashmere sweater tied casually around her neck, sneakers, and in her big handbag was a swimsuit—not that I'll need it today, she told herself, the Peak shrouded to Mid Levels with cloud, black-dark sky to the east and a heavy line of rain squall already touching the Island. A small helicopter putt-putted overhead to go out across the harbor on course for Central. She saw it land on one of the buildings. Isn't that the Struan building? Sure, sure it is. Wonder if Ian's in it?

Wonder if the hill climb's back on again? Last night he had said it was off but that some of them might do it anyway.

Then her eyes saw the approaching motor cruiser. It was big, expensive, the lines sleek, a Red Ensign aft, a colorful pennant on the stubby mast. She picked out Gornt at the helm. He was dressed casually, shirt-sleeves rolled up, canvas pants, his black hair ruffled by the sea breeze. He waved and she waved back. There were others on the bridge main deck: Jason Plumm she had met at the races, Sir Dunstan Barre at the tai-pan's—he was wearing a smart blue blazer and white pants, Pugmire was equally nautical.

Gornt put the cumbersome craft alongside skillfully, fenders out, two deckhands with hooked fending poles. She headed along the quay toward the wet slippery steps. Five Chinese girls were already waiting on the landing, gaily dressed in boating clothes, laughing and chattering and waving. As she watched, they jumped awkwardly aboard helped by a deck-

NOBLE HOUSE   999

hand, kicked their high heels off. One went to Barre, another to Pugmire, another to Plumm as old friends would and the other two went cheerfully below.

I'll be goddamned, she thought disgustedly. It's one of those parties. She began to turn to leave but she saw Gornt leaning over the side, watching her. "Hello, Casey, sorry about the rain, come aboard!"

The craft was dipping and twisting in the swell, waves slapping the steps and the hull. "Come aboard, it's quite safe," he called out. Reacting at once to what she interpreted as a taunt, she came down the steps quickly, refused the proffered help of the deckhand, waited for the correct moment and jumped. "You did that as though you've been aboard a yacht before," Gornt said with admiration, coming to meet her. "Welcome aboard the *Sea Witch*."

"I like sailing, Quillan, though I think maybe I'm out of my depth here."

"Oh?" Gornt frowned and she could read no taunt or challenge there. "You mean the girls?"

"Yes."

"They're just guests of my guests." His eyes bored into her. "I understood you wanted to be treated with equality."

"What?"

"I thought you wanted to be treated equally in a masculine world, in business and pleasure? To be accepted, eh?"

"I do," she said coldly.

His warmth did not change. "Are you upset because the others are married and you've met some of their wives?"

"Yes, I suppose I am."

"Isn't that rather unfair?"

"No, I don't think it is," she said uncomfortably.

"*You're* my guest, *my* guest, the others are my guests' guests. If you want equality, perhaps you should be prepared to accept equality."

"This isn't equality."

"I'm certainly putting you in a position of trust. As an equal. I must tell you the others didn't think you as trustworthy as I consider you." The smile hardened. "I told them they could leave or stay. I do what I like on my ship and I stood surety for your discretion and good manners. This is Hong Kong, our customs are different. This isn't a puritan society though we have very serious rules. You're alone. Unmarried. Very attractive and very welcome. As an equal. If you were married to Linc, you would not have been asked, together or by yourself, though he might have been and what he told you when he came back would be his own affair."

"You're saying this is regular Hong Kong custom—the boys out with the girls bit on a Sunday afternoon?"

"No, not at all. I'm saying my guests asked if they could invite some

guests who'd brighten what might otherwise be a dull luncheon for them."
Gornt's eyes were level.

The *Sea Witch* heeled under another wave and Barre and his girl
friend stumbled and almost lost their footing. She dropped her glass of
champagne. Gornt had not moved. Nor did Casey. She didn't even need
to hold on.

"You've done lots of sailing?" he said with admiration.

"I've an eighteen-footer, fiberglass, Olympic class, sloop-rigged, on a
trailer. I sail some weekends."

"Alone?"

"Mostly. Sometimes Linc comes along."

"He's at the hill climb?"

"No. I heard it was canceled."

"He's going to Taipei this afternoon?"

"No. I heard that was canceled too."

Gornt nodded. "Wise. A lot to do tomorrow." His eyes were kindly.
"I'm sorry you're offended. I thought you different from the usual. I'm
sorry the others came now."

Casey heard the strange gentleness. "Yes, I'm sorry too."

"Would you still like to stay? I hope so, though I will expect your
discretion—I did guarantee it."

"I'll stay," she said simply. "Thanks for trusting me."

"Come on the bridge. There's champagne and I think lunch'll please
you."

Having chosen, Casey put away her reservations and decided to enjoy
the day. "Where're we going?"

"Up by Sha Tin. The sea'll be calm there."

"Say, Quillan, this is a wonderful boat."

"I'll show you around in a moment." There was a spatter of rain and
they moved into the lee of the overhanging deck. Gornt glanced at the
clock tower. It was 10:10. He was about to order their castoff when Peter
Marlowe hurried down the steps and came aboard. His eyes widened as
he noticed Casey.

"Sorry I'm late, Mr. Gornt."

"That's all right, Mr. Marlowe. I was going to give you a couple of
minutes—I know how it is with young children. Excuse me a second, I believe you know each other. Oh, Casey's *my* guest—her discretion's guaranteed." He smiled at her. "Isn't it?"

"Of course."

He turned and left them, going to the bridge to take the conn. They
watched a moment, both embarrassed, the sea breeze freshening the rain
that slanted down.

"I didn't expect to see you, Peter," she said.

"I didn't expect to see you either."

She studied him, her hazel eyes level. "Is one of the, the others yours? Give it to me straight."

His smile was curious. "Even if one was I'd say it wasn't any of your business. Discretion and all that. By the way, are you Gornt's girl friend?"

She stared at him. "No. No, of course not!"

"Then why're you here?"

"I don't know. He . . . he just said I was invited as an equal."

"Oh. Oh I see." Peter Marlowe was equally relieved. "He's got a strange sense of humor. Well, I did warn you. To answer your question, at least eight are part of the Marlowe harem!" She laughed with him and he added more seriously, "You don't have to worry about Fleur. She's very wise."

"I wish I was, Peter. This's all rather new to me. Sorry about . . . yes, sorry."

"It's new to me too. I've never been on a Sunday cruise before. Why did y—" His smile vanished. She followed his glance. Robin Grey had come up from below and was pouring himself a glass of champagne, one of the girls holding out her glass too. Casey turned and stared up at Gornt, watching him glance from man to man, then at her.

"Come aloft," Gornt called out. "There's wine, champagne, Bloody Marys or, if you prefer, coffee." He kept his face expressionless but inside he was vastly amused.

74

11:15 A.M.:

"I repeat, Mr. Sinders, I know nothing of any cable, any Arthur, any files, any American and I know no Major Yuri Bakyan—the man was Igor Voranski, seaman first class." Suslev kept a firm hold on his temper. Sinders sat opposite him, behind the desk in the drab interview room at police headquarters. Suslev had expected Roger Crosse to be there, to help. But he had not seen him since he arrived.

Be careful, he cautioned himself, you're on your own. You'll get no help from Roger. Rightly. That spy has to be protected. And as to Boradinov, he's no help either. He glanced at his first officer who sat beside him, stiff, upright in his chair and greatly ill-at-ease.

"And you still insist this spy Dimitri Metkin's name was not Leonov—Nicoli Leonov—also a major in the KGB?"

"It's nonsense, all nonsense. I shall report this whole incident to my government, I sh—"

"Are your repairs completed?"

"Yes, at least they will be by midnight. We bring good money into Hong Kong and pay our bi—"

"Yes and create nothing but curious troubles. Like Major Leonov, like Bakyan?"

"You mean Metkin?" Suslev glared at Boradinov to take off some of the heat. "Did you know any Leonov?"

"No, Comrade Captain," Boradinov stuttered. "We didn't know anything."

"What a lot of cobblers!" Sinders sighed. "Fortunately Leonov told us quite a lot about you and the *Ivanov* before you murdered him. Yes, your Major Leonov was very cooperative." Suddenly his voice became a whiplash. "First Officer Boradinov, please wait outside!"

The younger man was on his feet before he knew it, white-faced. He opened the door. Outside a hostile Chinese SI agent motioned him to a chair, closing the door once more.

Sinders put his pipe aside, took out a package of cigarettes and leisurely lit one. Rain battered the windows. Suslev waited, his heart grinding. He watched his enemy from under his bushy eyebrows, wondering what Roger Crosse had for him that was so urgent. This morning when the secret phone had rung it was Arthur asking if Suslev would meet Roger Crosse around eight o'clock tonight at Sinclair Towers. "What's so urgent? I should be on my ship and mak—"

"I don't know. Roger said it was urgent. There was no time to discuss anything. Did you see Koronski?"

"Yes. Everything's arranged. Can you deliver?"

"Oh yes. Long before midnight."

"Don't fail, Center's counting on you now," he had added, lying. "Tell our friend it's ordered."

"Excellent. We won't fail."

Suslev had heard the excitement. Some of his dread had left him. Now it was returning. He did not like being here, so near to staying permanently. Sinders's reputation was well known in the KGB: dedicated, smart and given to great leaps of insight. "I'm very tired of these questions, Mr. Sinders," he said, astonished that the head of MI-6 had personally come to Hong Kong and could appear to be so unimportant. He stood up, testing him. "I'm leaving."

"Tell me about Sevrin."

"Sevrin? What is Sevrin? I do not have to stay to answer your questions, I do n—"

"I agree, Comrade Captain, normally, but one of your men has been caught spying and our American friends really want possession of you."

"Eh?"

"Oh yes and I'm afraid they're not as patient as we are."

Suslev's dread swooped back. "More threats! Why threaten me?" he flustered. "We are law-abiding. I'm not responsible for troubles! I demand to be allowed to go back to my ship! Now!"

Sinders just looked at him. "All right. Please leave," he said quietly.

"I can go?"

"Yes, yes of course. Good morning."

Astonished, Suslev stared at him a moment, then turned and went for the door.

"Of course we will certainly leak it to your superiors that you gave us Leonov."

Suslev stopped, ashen. "What, what did you say?"

"Leonov told us, among other things, that you encouraged him to make the intercept. Then you leaked the exchange."

"Lies . . . lies," he said, suddenly aghast that perhaps Roger Crosse had been caught as Metkin was caught.

"Didn't you also leak to North Korean agents about Bakyan?"

"No, no I did not," Suslev stuttered, enormously relieved to discover

Sinders was kiting him, probably without any real information. Some of his confidence returned. "That's more nonsense. I know no North Koreans."

"I believe you, but I'm sure the First Directorate won't. Good morning."

"What do you mean?"

"Tell me about the cable."

"I know nothing about it. Your superintendent was mistaken, I did not drop it."

"Oh but you did. What American?"

"I know nothing about an American."

"Tell me about Sevrin."

"I know nothing of this Severin. What is it, who is it?"

"I'm sure you know your superiors in the KGB are impatient with leaks and very untrusting. If you manage to sail, I suggest you, your first officer, your ship and your entire crew do not come back into these waters again—"

"You threaten me again? This will become an international incident. I will inform my government and yours an—"

"Yes, and so will we, officially and privately. Very privately." Sinders's eyes were freezing though his lips wore a smile.

"I . . . I can go now?"

"Yes. For information."

"What?"

"Who is the American, and who is 'Arthur'?"

"I don't know any Arthur. Arthur who?"

"I will wait till midnight. If you sail without telling me, when I return to London I will make sure information gets to the ears of your naval attaché in London that you leaked Leonov whom you call Metkin, and you leaked Bakyan whom you call Voranski in return for SI favors."

"That's lies, all lies, you know it's lies."

"Five hundred people saw you at the racetrack with Superintendent Crosse. That's when you gave him Metkin."

"All lies." Suslev tried to hide his terror.

Sinders chuckled. "We'll see, won't we? Your new naval attaché in London will clutch at any straws to ingratiate himself with his superiors. Eh?"

"I don't understand," Suslev said, understanding very well. He was trapped.

Sinders leaned forward to tap out his pipe. "Listen to me clearly," he said with absolute finality. "I'll swap you your life for the American and Arthur."

"I don't know any Arthur."

"This will be a secret between you and me only. I'll tell no one. I give you my word."

"I know no Arthur."

"You pinpoint him and you're safe. You and I are professionals, we understand barter—and safety—and an occasional private, very secret deal. You're caught, this time, so you have to deliver. If you sail without telling me who Arthur is, as sure as God made little apples and the KGB exists, I will shop you." The eyes bored into him. "Good morning, Comrade Captain."

Suslev got up and left. When he and Boradinov were in the air once more, in the reality of Hong Kong, both began to breathe. Silently Suslev led the way across the street to the nearest bar. He ordered two double vodkas.

Suslev's mind was ripped. *Kristos,* he wanted to shout, I'm dead if I do and dead if I don't. That goddamned cable! If I finger Banastasio and Arthur, I admit I know Sevrin and I'm in their power forever. And if I don't, my life will surely be finished. One way or another it will be dangerous to return home now, and equally dangerous to come back. One way or another now I need those AMG files or Dunross, or both, for protection. One way or an—

"Comrade Cap—"

He whirled on Boradinov and cursed him in Russian. The younger man whitened and stopped, petrified.

"Vodka! Two more," he called. "Please."

The bar girl brought them. "My name Sally, what your, *heya?*"

"Piss off," Boradinov snarled.

"*Dew neh loh moh* on your piss off, *heya?* You Mr. Pissoff? I no like your face Mr. Pissoff so piss off without swearings." She picked up the vodka bottle and prepared to carry the battle forward.

"Apologize to her," Suslev snapped, wanting no trouble, not sure that she wasn't a plant, the bar being so close to police headquarters.

Boradinov was shocked. "What?"

"Apologize to her, you motherless turd!"

"Sorry," Boradinov muttered, his face flushed.

The girl laughed. "Hey, big man, you want jig-jig?"

"No," Suslev said. "Just more vodka."

Crosse got out of the police car and hurried through the light rain into the Struan Building. Behind him the streets were crowded with umbrellas and snarled traffic, the sidewalks massed, people going to and from work, Sunday not a general holiday. On the twentieth floor he got out.

"Good morning, Superintendent Crosse. I'm Sandra Yi, Mr. Dunross's secretary. This way please."

Crosse followed her down the corridor, his eyes noticing her *chong-samed* rump. She opened a door for him. He went in.

"Hello, Edward," he said to Sinders.

"You're early too, as usual." Sinders was sipping a beer. "Old army habit, eh, five minutes early's on time?" Behind him in the lavish board-room was a well-stocked bar. And coffee.

"Would you care for something, sir? Bloody Marys are mixed," Sandra Yi said.

"Thank you, just coffee. Black."

She served him and went out.

"How did it go?" Crosse asked.

"Our visitor? Fine, just fine. I'd say his sphincter's out of whack." Sinders smiled. "I taped the session. You can listen to it after lunch. Ah, yes, lunch. Roger, can you get fish and chips in Hong Kong?"

"Certainly. Fish and chips it is." Crosse stifled a yawn. He had been up most of the night developing and printing the roll of film he had taken in the vault. This morning he had read and reread AMG's real pages with enormous interest, privately agreeing with Dunross that the tai-pan had been perfectly correct to be so circumspect. AMG gave value for money whatever he cost, he thought. There's no doubt these files're worth a fortune.

The gimbaled clock struck the hour nicely. Noon. The door opened and Dunross strode in. " 'Morning. Thanks for coming here."

Politely the other two got up and shook hands.

"More coffee?"

"No thank you, Mr. Dunross."

As Crosse watched closely Dunross took a sealed envelope out of his pocket and offered it to Sinders. The older man took it, weighing it in his hand. Crosse noticed his fingers were trembling slightly. "Of course you've read the contents, Mr. Dunross?"

"Yes, Mr. Sinders."

"And?"

"And nothing. See for yourself."

Sinders opened the envelope. He stared at the first page, then leafed through all eleven sheets. From where Crosse stood he could not see what was on the pieces of paper. Silently Sinders handed him the top one. The letters and numbers and symbols of the code were meaningless. "Looks like they've been cut from something." Crosse looked at Dunross. "Eh?"

"What about Brian?"

"Where did you get them, Ian?" Crosse saw Dunross's eyes change a little.

"I've kept my side of the trade, are you going to keep yours?"

Sinders sat down. "I did not agree to a trade, Mr. Dunross. I only agreed that it was possible that your request might be complied with."

"Then you won't release Brian Kwok?"

"It's possible that he will be where you want him, when you want him."

"It has to be left like that?"

"Sorry."

There was a long silence. The tick of the clock filled the room. Except for the rain. Another squall came and went. Rain had been falling sporadically since this morning. Weather reports forecast that the storm would be over soon and that the reservoirs, for all the rain, were hardly touched.

Dunross said, "Will you give me the odds? Accurately. Please?"

"First three questions: Did you cut these out of something yourself?"

"Yes."

"From what and how?"

"AMG had written instructions. I was to use a cigarette lighter under the bottom right quadrant of some pages he'd sent—it was an innocuous typed report. When I heated the pages the type disappeared and what you see was left. When I'd finished, again following his instructions, I cut out the pertinent pieces and destroyed the remainder. And his letter."

"Have you kept a copy?"

"Of the eleven pieces? Yes."

"I must ask you for them."

"You may have them when you complete the bargain," Dunross said, his voice pleasant. "Now, what are the odds?"

"Please give me the copies."

"I will, when you complete. Monday at sunset."

Sinders's eyes were even colder. "The copies, now, if you please."

"When you complete. That's a decision. Now, odds please."

"50-50," Sinders said, testing him.

"Good. Thank you. I've arranged that on Tuesday morning all eleven pages will be published in the *China Guardian* and two Chinese papers, one Nationalist and one Communist."

"Then you do so at your peril. Her Majesty's Government does not enjoy coercion."

"Have I threatened you? No, not at all. Those letters and figures are a meaningless mumble-jumble, except perhaps—*perhaps* to some code cipher expert. Perhaps. Perhaps this's all a joke from a dead man."

"I can stop it under the Official Secrets Act."

"You can certainly try." Dunross nodded. "But come hell or the Official Secrets Act, if I choose, those pages will be published somewhere on earth this week. That's a decision too. The matter was left to my discretion by AMG. Was there anything else, Mr. Sinders?"

Sinders hesitated. "No. No, thank you, Mr. Dunross."

Equally politely Dunross turned and opened the door. "Sorry, I've got to get back to work. Thank you for coming."

Crosse let Sinders go first and followed him to the elevator. Sandra Yi, at the reception desk, had already pressed the button for them.

"Oh excuse me, sir," she said to Crosse, "do you know when Superintendent Kwok will be back in the Colony?"

Crosse stared at her. "I'm not sure. I could inquire if you like. Why?"

"We were going to have dinner Friday evening and neither his house-keeper nor his office seems to know."

"I'd be glad to inquire."

The phone buzzer on the switchboard went. "Oh, thank you, sir. Hello, Struan's," she said into the phone. "Just a moment." She began to make the connection. Crosse offered a cigarette to Sinders as they waited, watching the elevator numbers approaching. "Your call to Mr. Alastair, tai-pan," Sandra Yi said into the phone. Again the phone buzzer on the switchboard went.

"Hello," Sandra Yi said. "Just a moment, madam, I'll check." She referred to a typed appointment list as the elevator doors opened. Sinders went in and Crosse began to follow.

"It's for 1:00 P.M., Mrs. Gresserhoff."

At once Crosse stopped and bent down as though to tie his shoelace and Sinders, as efficiently and as casually, held the door.

"Oh that's all right, madam, it's easy to mistake a time. The table's booked in the tai-pan's name. The Skyline at the Mandarin at 1:00 P.M."

Crosse got up.

"All right?" Sinders asked.

"Oh yes." The doors closed on them. Both smiled.

"Everything comes to him who waits," Crosse said.

"Yes. We'll have fish and chips for dinner instead."

"No. You can have them for lunch. We shouldn't eat at the Mandarin. I suggest we just peg her secretly ourselves. Meanwhile, I'll assign surveillance to find out where she's staying, eh?"

"Excellent." Sinders's face hardened. "Gresserhoff, eh? Hans Gresserhoff was the cover name of an East German spy we've been trying to catch for years."

"Oh?" Crosse kept his interest off his face.

"Yes. He was partners with another right rotten bastard, a trained assassin. One of his names was Viktor Grunwald, another Simeon Tzerak. Gresserhoff, eh?" Sinders was silent a moment. "Roger, that publishing business, Dunross's threat. That could be very dicey."

"Can you read the code?"

"Good God, no."

"What could it be?"

"Anything. The pages are for me or the P.M. so they're probably names and addresses of contacts." Sinders added gravely, "I daren't trust them to cables, however coded. I think I'd better return to London at once."

"Today?"

"Tomorrow. I should finish this business first and I'd very much like to identify this Mrs. Gresserhoff. Will Dunross do what he said?"

"Absolutely."

Sinders pulled at his eyebrows, his washed-out blue eyes even more colorless than usual. "What about the client?"

"I'd say . . ." The elevator door opened. They got out and walked across the foyer. The uniformed doorman opened the door of Crosse's car for him.

Crosse cut into the snarled traffic, the harbor misted and the rain stopped for a moment. "I'd say one more session, then Armstrong can begin rebuilding. Monday sunset is too fast but . . ." He shrugged. "I wouldn't suggest any more of the Red Room."

"No. I agree, Roger. Thank God the fellow's got a strong constitution."

"Yes."

"I think Armstrong's ready to crack, poor fellow."

"He can conduct one more. Safely."

"I hope so. My God we've been very lucky. Unbelievable!" The session, at 6:00 this morning, had brought forth nothing. But just as they were about to quit, Armstrong's probing produced gold: at long last, the who and the why and the what of Professor Joseph Yu. Of Cal Tech, Princeton, Stanford. Rocket expert par excellence and NASA consultant.

"When's he due in Hong Kong, Brian?" Armstrong had asked, the whole SI team in the control room breathless.

"I . . . I don't . . . let me think, let me think . . . ah, I can't remember . . . ah yes, it, it's in a we . . . at the end of . . . of this month . . . what is this month? I can't rem . . . remember . . . which day it is. He was to arrive . . . and then go on."

"Where from and where to?"

"Oh I don't know, oh no they didn't tell me . . . except . . . except someone said he . . . he was sailing in Guam on holiday from Hawaii and due here ten days . . . I think it's ten days after . . . after Race Day."

And when Crosse had called in Rosemont and told him—though not where the information had come from—the American was speechless and in panic. At once he had ordered the Guam area scoured to prevent the defection.

"I wonder if they'll catch him," Crosse muttered.

"Who?"

"Joseph Yu."

"I jolly well hope so," Sinders said. "Why the devil do these scientists defect? Damnable! The only good point is he'll launch China's rocketry into the stratosphere and send shivers of horror down all Soviet spines. Bloody good if you ask me. If those two fall out it could help us all immensely." He eased more comfortably in the seat of the car, his back aching. "Roger, I can't risk Dunross publishing those ciphers or keeping a copy."

"Yes."

"He's too damned clever for his own boots is your tai-pan. If it leaks that AMG sent us a ciphered message and if Dunross has the memory he's supposed to have, he's a marked man. Eh?"

"Yes."

They reached the Skyline penthouse restaurant in good time. Crosse was instantly recognized and at once a discreet table was empty at the bar. As Sinders ordered a drink and more coffee Crosse phoned for two agents, one British and one Chinese. They arrived very fast.

At a few minutes to one o'clock Dunross walked in and they watched him go to the best table, maître d' in advance, waiters in tow, champagne already in a silver bucket.

"The bugger's got everyone well trained, eh?"

"Wouldn't you?" Crosse said. His eyes ranged the room, then stopped. "There's Rosemont! Is that a coincidence?"

"What do you think?"

"Ah, look over there. In the far corner. That's Vincenzo Banastasio. The Chinese he's with is Vee Cee Ng. Perhaps that's who they're watching."

"Perhaps."

"Rosemont's clever," Crosse said. "Bartlett went to see him too. It could be Banastasio they're watching." Armstrong had reported Bartlett's conversation about Banastasio to them. Surveillance on the man had been increased. "By the way, I heard he's chartered a helicopter for Macao on Monday."

"We should cancel that."

"It's already done. Engine trouble."

"Good. I suppose Bartlett reporting Banastasio rather clears him, what?"

"Perhaps."

"I still think I'd better go Monday. Yes. Interesting, ah, that Dunross's receptionist had a date with the client. Good God, there's a smasher," Sinders said.

The girl was following the maître d'. Both men were taken by surprise when she stopped at the tai-pan's table, smiled, bowed and sat down. "Christ! Mrs. Gresserhoff's Chinese?" Sinders gasped.

Crosse was concentrating on their lips. "No Chinese'd bow like that. She's Japanese."

"How in the hell does she fit?"

"Perhaps there's more than one guest. Per—oh Christ!"

"What?"

"They're not speaking English. Must be Japanese."

"Dunross speaks Jap?"

Crosse looked at him. "Yes, *Japanese*. And German, French, three dialects of Chinese and passable Italian."

Sinders stared back. "You needn't be so disapproving, Roger. I lost a son on *HMS Prince of Wales*, my brother starved to death on the Burma Road, so don't give me any sanctimonious bullshit, though I still think she's a smasher."

"At least that shows a certain amount of tolerance." Crosse turned back to study Dunross and the girl.

"Your war was in Europe, eh?"

"My war, Edward, is never ending." Crosse smiled, liking the sound of that. "World War Two's ancient history. Sorry about your kin but now Japan's not the enemy, they're our allies, the only real ones we've got in Asia."

For half an hour they waited. He could not read their lips at all.

"She must be Gresserhoff," Sinders said.

Crosse nodded. "Then shall we go? No point in waiting. Shall we fish and chip?"

They went out. The British and Chinese SI agents stayed, waiting patiently, unable to overhear what was being said, envying Dunross, as many did in the room—because he was the tai-pan and because of her.

"*Gehen Sie?*" she asked in German. Are you going?

"To Japan, Riko-*san*? Oh yes," he answered in the same language, "the week after next. We take delivery of a new super-cargo ship from Toda Shipping. Did you chat with Hiro Toda yesterday?"

"Yes, yes I had that honor. The Toda family is famous in Japan. Before the Restoration when the samurai class was abolished, my family served the Toda."

"Your family was samurai?"

"Yes, but of low degree. I, I did not mention about my family to him. Those were ancient days. I would not like him to know."

"As you wish," he said, his curiosity piqued. "Hiro Toda's an interesting man," he added, leading her on.

"Toda-*sama* is very wise, very strong, very famous." The waiter brought their salad and when he had left she said, "Struan's are famous in Japan too."

"Not really."

"Oh yes. We remember Prince Yoshi."

"Ah. I didn't know you knew."

In 1854 when Perry forced the Shōgun Yoshimitsu Toranaga to open up Japan to trade, the Hag had sailed north from Hong Kong, her father and enemy, Tyler Brock, in pursuit. Thanks to her, Struan's was the first into Japan, first to buy land for a trading post and the first outsider to trade. Over the years and many voyages, she made Japan a cornerstone of Struan policy.

During the early years she met a young prince, Prince Yoshi, a relation of the Emperor and cousin to the Shōgun—without whose permission nothing happened in Japan. At her suggestion and with her help, this prince went to England on a Struan clipper to learn about the might of the British Empire. When he returned home a few years later, it was in another Struan ship, and that year some of the feudal barons—*daimyo*—hating the incursion of foreigners, revolted against the Shōgun whose family, the Toranaga, had exclusively ruled Japan for two and a half centuries in an unbroken line back to the great general Yoshi Toranaga. The revolt of the *daimyo* succeeded and power was restored to the Emperor but the land was riven. "Without Prince Yoshi, who became one of the Emperor's chief ministers," she said, unconsciously turning to English, "Japan would still be trembling and torn apart in civil war."

"Why so?" he asked, wanting to keep her talking, her lilting accent pleasing him.

"Without his help, the Emperor could not have succeeded, could not have abolished the Shōgunate, abolished feudal law, the *daimyo*, the whole samurai class, and forced them to accept a modern constitution. It was Prince Yoshi who negotiated a peace among the *daimyo*, and then invited English experts to Japan to build our navy, our banks and our civil service, and help us into the modern world." A small shadow went across her face. "My father told me much about those times, tai-pan, not yet a hundred years ago. Transition from samurai rule to democracy was often bloody. But the Emperor had decreed an ending so there was an ending and all the *daimyo* and samurai dragged themselves painfully into a new life." She toyed with her glass, watching the bubbles. "The Toda were Lords of Izu and Sagami where Yokohama is. For centuries they had had shipyards. It was easy for them and their allies, the Kasigi, to come into this modern age. For us . . ." She stopped. "Oh, but you already know this, so sorry."

"Only about Prince Yoshi. What happened to your family?"

"My great-grandfather became a very minor member of Prince Yoshi's staff, as a civil servant. He was sent to Nagasaki where my family have lived since. He found it difficult not to wear the two swords. My grandfather was also a civil servant, like my father, but only very tiny." She looked up and smiled at him. "The wine is too good. It makes my tongue run away."

"No, not at all," he said, then conscious of the eyes watching them, he added in Japanese, "Let us talk Japanese for a while."

"It is my honor, tai-pan-*san*."

Later, over coffee, he said, "Where should I deposit the money owing to you, Riko-*san*?"

"If you could give me a cashier's check or bank draft"—she used the English words for there was no Japanese equivalent—"before I leave that would be perfect."

"On Monday morning I will have it sent to you. There's £10,625, and a further £8,500 payable in January, and the same the following year," he told her, knowing her good manners would not permit to ask outright. He saw the flash of relief and was glad he had decided to give her two extra years of salary—AMG's information about oil alone was more than worth it. "Would eleven o'clock be convenient for the 'sight draft'?" Again Dunross used the English word.

"Whatever pleases you. I do not wish to put you to any trouble."

Dunross noticed how she was speaking slowly and distinctly to help him. "What will be your travel plans?"

"On Monday I think I will go to Japan, then . . . then I don't know. Perhaps back to Switzerland though I have no real reason to return. I have no relations there, the house was a rented house and the garden not mine. My Gresserhoff life ended with his death. Now I think I should be Riko Anjin again. Karma is karma."

"Yes," he told her, "karma is karma." He reached into his pocket and brought out a gift-wrapped package. "This is a present from the Noble House to thank you for taking so much trouble and such a tiring trip on our behalf."

"Oh. Oh thank you, but it was my honor and pleasure." She bowed. "Thank you. May I open it now?"

"Perhaps later. It is just a simple jade pendant but the box also contains a confidential envelope that your husband wanted you to have, for your eyes only and not for the eyes that surround us."

"Ah. I understand. Of course." She bowed again. "So sorry, please excuse my stupidity."

Dunross smiled back at her. "No stupidity, never, only beauty."

Color came into her face and she sipped coffee to cover. "The envelope is sealed, tai-pan-san?"

"Yes, as he instructed. Do you know what's in it?"

"No. Only that . . . only that Mr. Gresserhoff said that you would give me a sealed envelope."

"Did he say why? Or what you were supposed to do with it?"

"One day someone would come to claim it."

"By name?"

"Yes, but my husband told me I was never to divulge the name, not even to you. Never. Everything else I could tell you but not the . . . the name. So sorry, please excuse me."

Dunross frowned. "You're just to give it to him?"

"Or her," she said pleasantly. "Yes, when I am asked, not before. After it has been digested, Mr. Gresserhoff said the person would repay a debt. Thank you for the gift, tai-pan-san. I will cherish it."

The waiter came and poured the last of the champagne for him then went away again. "How do I reach you in the future, Riko-san?"

"I will give you three addresses and phone numbers that will find me, one in Switzerland, two in Japan."

After a pause he said, "Will you be in Japan the week after next?"

Riko looked up at him and his spirit twisted at such beauty. "Yes. If you wish it," she said.

"I wish it."

75

The *Sea Witch* was tied just offshore beside Sha Tin boat harbor where they had moored for lunch. As soon as they had arrived, the cook, Casey and Peter Marlowe had gone ashore with Gornt in command to select the prawns and shrimps and fish that were still swimming in sea tanks, then on to the bustling market for morning-fresh vegetables. Lunch had been quick-fried prawns with crunchy broccoli, then fish rubbed with garlic and pan-fried, served with mixed Chinese greens, again *al dente*.

The lunch had been laughter filled, the Chinese girls entertaining and happy, all of them speaking varying degrees of salty English, Dunstan Barre choleric and outrageously funny, the others joining in, and Casey thought how different the men were. How much more unrestrained and boyish, and she thought that sad. The talk had turned to business, and in the few short hours she had learned more about Hong Kong techniques than through all the reading she had done. More and more it was clear that unless you were on the inside, real power and real riches would escape you.

"Oh, you'll do very well here, Casey, you and Bartlett," Barre had said. "If you play the game according to Hong Kong rules, Hong Kong tax structures and not U.S. rules, right, Quillan?"

"Up to a point. If you go with Dunross and Struan's—if Struan's and Dunross exist as an entity by next Friday—you'll get some milk but none of the cream."

"With you we'll do better?" she had asked.

Barre had laughed. "Very much better, Casey, but it'll still be milk and very little cream!"

"Let's say, Casey, with us the milk'll be homogenized," Gornt had said amiably.

Now the wonderful smell of freshly roasted coffee, freshly ground, was wafting up from the galley. Conversation was general around the table, banter back and forth, mostly for her benefit, about trading in Asia, supply and demand and the Asian attitude to smuggling, the Chinese girls chattering among themselves.

Abruptly, Grey's voice, a biting rasp to it, cut through. "You'd better ask Marlowe about that, Mr. Gornt. He knows everything about smuggling and blackmailing from our Changi days."

"Come on, Grey," Peter Marlowe said in the sudden silence. "Give over!"

"I thought you were proud of it, you and your Yankee blackmailer mate. Weren't you?"

"Let's leave it, Grey," Marlowe said, his face set.

"Whatever you say, old lad." Grey turned to Casey. "Ask him."

Gornt said, "This is hardly the time to rehash old quarrels, Mr. Grey." He kept his voice calm and the enjoyment off his face, outwardly the perfect host.

"Oh, I wasn't, Mr. Gornt. You were talking about smuggling and black marketeering. Marlowe's an expert, that's all."

"Shall we have coffee on deck?" Gornt got up.

"Good idea. A cuppa coffee's ever so good after grub." Grey used the word deliberately, knowing it would offend them, not caring now, suddenly tired of the banter, hating them and what they represented, hating being the odd-man out here, wanting one of the girls, any one. "Marlowe and his Yankee friend used to roast beans in the camp when the rest of us were starving," he said, his face stark. "Used to drive us mad." He looked at Peter Marlowe, his hate open now. "Didn't you?"

After a pause, Peter Marlowe said, "Everyone had coffee some of the time. Everyone roasted coffee beans."

"Not like you two." Grey turned to Casey. "They had coffee every day, him and his Yankee friend. Me, I was provost marshal and I had it once a month if I was lucky." He glanced back. "How did you get coffee and food while the rest of us starved?"

Casey noticed the vein in Peter Marlowe's forehead knotting and she realized, aghast, that no answer was also an answer. "Robin . . ." she began, but Grey overrode her, his voice taunting.

"Why don't you answer, Marlowe?"

In the silence they all looked from Grey to Peter Marlowe, staring at each other, even the girls tense and on guard, feeling the sudden violence in the cabin.

"My dear fellow," Gornt interrupted, deliberately using that slight nuance of accent he knew would goad Grey, "surely those are ancient times and rather unimportant now. It is Sunday afternoon and we're all friends."

"I think 'em *rather* important, Sunday afternoon or not and Marlowe and I aren't friends, never have been! He's a toff, I'm not." Grey aped the long *a* he loathed and broadened his accent. "Yes. But the war changed everything and us workers'll never forget!"

"You consider yourself a worker and me not?" Peter Marlowe asked, his voice grating.

"We're the exploited, you're the exploiters. Like in Changi."

"Get off that old broken record, Grey! Changi was another world, another place and other time an—"

"It was the same as everywhere. There was bosses and the bossed, workers and them that fed off the workers. Like you and the King."

"Stuff and nonsense!"

Casey was near to Grey and she reached out and took his arm. "Let's have coffee, okay?"

"Of course," Grey said. "But first ask him, Casey." Grimly Grey stood his ground, well aware he had, at long last, brought his enemy to bay in front of his peers. "Mr. Gornt, ask him, eh? Any of you . . ."

They all stood there in silence, embarrassed for Peter Marlowe and shocked with the implied accusations—Gornt and Plumm privately amused and fascinated. Then one of the girls turned for the gangway and left quietly, the others following. Casey would have liked to have gone too but she did not.

"Now is not the time, Mr. Grey," she heard Gornt say gently and she was glad he was there to break it up. "Would you kindly leave this matter alone. Please?"

Grey looked at them all, his eyes ending up on his adversary. "You see, Casey, not one's got the guts to ask—they're all his class, so-called upper class and they look after their own."

Barre flushed. "I say, old chap, don't you th—"

Peter Marlowe said, his voice flat, "It's easy to stop this nonsense. You can't equate Changi—or Dachau or Buchenwald with normality. You just can't. There were different rules, different patterns. We were soldiers, war prisoners, teen-agers most of us. Changi was genesis, everything new, upside down, ev—"

"Were you a black marketeer?"

"No. I was an interpreter in Malay for a friend who was a trader and there's a lot of difference between trading and black marketing an—"

"But it was against camp rules, camp law, and that makes it black marketing, right?"

"Trading with the guards was against *enemy* rules, Japanese rules."

"And tell them how the King'd buy some poor bugger's watch or ring or fountain pen for a pittance, the last bloody thing he had in the world, and sell it high and never tell and cheat on the price, cheat, always cheat. Eh?"

Peter Marlowe stared back. "Read my book. In it th—"

"Book?" Again Grey laughed, goading him. "Tell 'em on your honor as a gent, your father's honor and your family's honor you're so bloody proud of—did the King cheat or didn't he? On your honor! Eh?"

Almost paralyzed, Casey saw Peter Marlowe make a fist. "If we weren't guests here," he hissed, "I'd tell them what a shower you really were!"

"You can rot in hell. . . ."

"Now that's enough," Gornt said as a command and Casey began to breathe again. "For the last time, kindly leave this all alone!"

Grey tore his eyes off Marlowe. "I will. Now, can I get a taxi in the village? I think I'd *rather* get home meself by meself if you don't mind."

"Of course," Gornt said, his face suitably grave, delighted that Grey had asked so that he did not have to finesse the suggestion into the open. "But surely," he added, delivering the coup de grâce, "surely you and Marlowe could shake hands like gentlemen and forget about th—"

"Gentlemen? Ta, but no. No, I've had gentlemen like Marlowe forever. Gentlemen? Thank God England's changing and soon'll be in proper hands again—and the very British Oxford accent won't be a permanent passport to gentry and power, not ever again. We'll reform the Lords and if I have my way . . ."

"Let's hope you don't!" Pugmire said.

Gornt said firmly, "Pug! It's coffee and port time!" Affably he took Grey's arm. "If you'll excuse Mr. Grey and myself a moment . . ."

They went on deck. The chatter of the Chinese girls stopped a moment. Secretly very pleased with himself, Gornt led the way to the gangway and went ashore onto the wharf. Everything was turning out far better than he had thought.

"Sorry about that, Mr. Grey," he said. "I had no idea that Marlowe . . . Disgusting! Well, you never know, do you?"

"He's a bastard, always was, always will be—him and his filthy Yank friend. Hate Yanks too! About time we broke up with that shower!"

Gornt found a taxi easily.

"Are you sure, Mr. Grey, you won't change your mind?"

"Ta, but no thanks."

"Sorry about Marlowe. Clearly you were provoked. When are you and your trade commission off?"

"In the morning, early."

"If there's anything I can do for you here, just let me know."

"Ta. When you come home give me a tinkle."

"Thank you. I will, and thanks for coming." He paid the fare in advance and waved politely as the taxi drove off. Grey did not look around.

Gornt smiled. That revolting bastard's going to be a useful ally in the years to come, he chortled as he walked back.

Most of the others were on deck, drinking coffee and liqueurs, Casey and Peter Marlowe to one side.

"What a bloody berk!" Gornt called out to general agreement. "Frightfully sorry about that, Marlowe, the bugger pr—"

"No, it was my fault," Peter Marlowe said, clearly very upset. "Sorry. I feel terrible that he left."

"No need to apologize. I should never have invited him—thanks for being such a gentleman about it, he clearly provoked you."

"Quite right," Pugmire said to more agreement. "If I'd been you I'd've given him one. Whatever happened is in the past."

"Oh yes," Casey said quickly, "what an awful man! If you hadn't stopped it, Quillan, Grey wou—"

"Enough of that berk," Gornt said warmly, wanting the specter laid to rest. "Let's forget him, let's not allow him to spoil a wonderful afternoon." He put his arm around Casey and gave her a hug. "Eh?" He saw the admiration in her eyes and he knew, gleefully, he was getting there fast. "It's too cold for a swim. Shall we just cruise leisurely home?"

"Good idea!" Dunstan Barre said. "I think I'm going to have a siesta."

"Smashing idea!" someone said to laughter. The girls joined in but the laughter was forced. Everyone was still unsettled and Gornt felt it strongly. "First some brandy! Marlowe?"

"No thank you, Mr. Gornt."

Gornt studied him. "Listen to me, Marlowe," he said with real compassion and everyone fell silent. "We've all seen too much of life, too much of Asia, not to know that whatever you did, you did for good and not evil. What you said was right. Changi was special with special problems. Pug was locked up in Stanley Prison—that's on Hong Kong Island, Casey—for three and a half years. I got out of Shanghai barely with my skin, and blood on my hands. Jason was grabbed by the Nazis after Dunkirk and had a couple of dicey years with them, Dunstan operated in China—Dunstan's been in Asia forever and he knows too. Eh?"

"Oh yes," Dunstan Barre said sadly. "Casey, in war to survive you have to stretch things a bit sometimes. As to trading, Marlowe, I agree, most times you have to equate the problem to the time and place. I thank God I was never caught. Don't think I'd've survived, know I wouldn't." He refilled his port from the decanter, embarrassed to be speaking real truths.

"What was Changi really like, Peter?" Casey asked for all of them.

"It's hard to talk about," he said. "It was the nearest to no-life that you could get. We were issued a quarter of a pound of dry rice a day, some vegetables, one egg a week. Sometimes meat was . . . was waved over the soup. It was different, that's all I can say about it. Most of us had never seen a jungle before, let alone Chinese and Japanese and to lose a war . . . I was just eighteen when Changi began."

"Christ, I can't stand Japs, just can't!" Pugmire said and the others nodded.

"But that's not fair, really. They were just playing the game according to their rules," Peter Marlowe said. "That was fair from the Japanese point of view. Look what wonderful soldiers they were, look how they fought and almost never allowed themselves to be captured. We were dishonored according to their standards by surrendering." Peter Marlowe shivered. "I felt dishonored, still feel dishonored."

"That's not right, Marlowe," Gornt said. "There's no dishonor in that. None."

Casey, standing beside Gornt, put her hand on his arm lightly. "Oh yes. He's right, Peter. He really is."

"Yes," Dunstan Barre said. "But Grey, what the devil got Grey all teed off? Eh?"

"Nothing and everything. He became fanatical about enforcing camp rules—which were Japanese rules—stupidly, a lot of us thought. As I said, Changi was different, officers and men were locked up together, no letters from home, no food, two thousand miles of enemy-occupied territory in every direction, malaria, dysentery, and the death rate terrible. He hated this American friend of mine, the King. It was true the King was a cunning businessman and he ate well when others didn't and drank coffee and smoked tailor-made cigarettes. But he kept a lot of us alive with his skill. Even Grey. He even kept Grey alive. Grey's hatred kept him alive, I'm sure. The King fed almost the whole American contingent—there were about thirty of them, officers and men. Oh they worked for it, American style, but even so, without him they would have died. I would have. I know." Peter Marlowe shuddered. "Joss. Karma. Life. I think I'll have that brandy now, Mr. Gornt."

Gornt poured. "Whatever happened to this man, this fellow you call the King? After the war?"

Pugmire interrupted with a laugh, "One of the buggers in our camp who was a trader became a bloody millionaire afterwards. Is it the same with this King?"

"I don't know," Peter Marlowe said.

"You never saw him again, Peter?" Casey asked, surprised. "You didn't see him back in the States?"

"No, no I never did. I tried to find him but never could."

"That's often the rule, Casey," Gornt said casually. "When you leave a regiment all debts and friendships are canceled." He was very content. Everything's perfect, he told himself, thinking of the double bed in his cabin, and smiled at her across the deck. She smiled back.

Riko Anjin Gresserhoff went into the foyer of the V and A. It was crowded with those having early-afternoon tea or late lunches. As she walked to the elevator a tremor went through her, the eyes bothering her—not the usual lusting eyes of European men or the dislike in the eyes of their women—but Chinese and Eurasian eyes. She had never experienced so much general hatred. It was a strange feeling. This was her first time outside of Switzerland, other than school trips to Germany and two journeys to Rome with her mother. Her husband had taken her abroad only once, to Vienna for a week.

I don't like Asia, she thought, suppressing another shudder. But then it's not Asia, it's Hong Kong, surely it's just here, the people here. And surely, there is right on their side to be antagonistic. I wonder if I'll like Japan? Will I be alien, even there?

The elevator came and she went to her suite on the sixth floor, the room boy not opening her door for her. Alone and with the door bolted, she felt better. The red message light on the phone was blinking but she paid it no attention, quickly taking off her shoes, hat, gloves and coat, putting them at once in a vast closet, the clothes already there neat and organized, like her three pairs of shoes. The suite was small but delicate, a living room, bedroom and bath. Flowers from Struan's were on the table and a bowl of fruit from the hotel.

Her fingers slid the gift wrapping away neatly. Inside was a rectangular black plush box and she opened it. Warmth went through her. The pendant was on a thin gold chain, the jade green with flecks of lighter green, carved like a cornucopia. Light shimmered off the polished surface. At once she put it on, studying it in the mirror, admiring the stone as it lay against her breast. She had never been given jade before.

Underneath the black, plush-covered cardboard was the envelope. It was a plain envelope, not Struan's, the seal equally plain, made of ordinary red sealing wax. With great care she slid a paper knife under the seal and studied the pages, one by one, a small frown on her forehead. Just a jumble of numbers and letters and an occasional symbol. A tiny, satisfied smile touched her lips. She found the hotel letter-writing folder and, settling herself comfortably at the desk, began to copy the pages, one by one.

When she had finished she checked them. She put the copies into a hotel envelope and sealed it, the originals in another envelope, a plain one she took out of her bag. Next she found the new stick of red sealing wax, lit a match and daubed the melting wax on both envelopes, sealing them, making sure the seal on the envelope of the originals was a pattern of the one Dunross had made. The phone rang, startling her. She watched it, her heart thumping, until it stopped. Once more at ease, she went back to her labor, ensuring there were no telltale indentations left on the pad that she had used, examining it under the light. As soon as she was satisfied, she stamped the envelope containing the copies, addressed it to: R. Anjin, Box 154, General Post Office, Sydney, Australia. This and the other envelope with the originals she put into her handbag.

Carefully she rechecked that nothing had been missed, then went to a small refrigerator near the stocked bar and took out a bottle of sparkling mineral water and drank some.

Again the phone rang. She watched it, sipping the soda water, her mind checking and rechecking, thinking about her lunch with Dunross, wondering if she had been wise to accept his invitation to cocktails tonight and, later, to dinner with him and his friends. I wonder if there will be friends or if we will be alone. Would I like to be alone with that man?

Her thoughts went back to the small, untidy, slightly balding Hans

Gresserhoff, and the four years of life that she had led with him, weeks alone, sleeping alone, waking alone, walking alone, no real friends, rarely going out, her husband strangely secretive, cautioning her about making friends, wanting her to be alone and always safe and calm and patient. That was the hardest part to bear, she thought. Patience. Patience alone, patience together, asleep or awake. Patience and outwardly calm. When all the time she was like a volcano, desperate to erupt.

That he loved her was beyond doubt. All she felt for him was *giri*, duty. He gave her money and her life was smooth, neither rich nor poor—even, like the country of their choice. His arrivals and departures had no pattern. When he was with her he always wanted her, wanted to be near her. Their pillowing satisfied him but not her, though she pretended, for his pleasure. But then, she told herself, you have had no other man to judge by.

He was a good man and it was as I told the tai-pan. I tried to be a good wife to him, to obey him in everything, to honor my mother's wish, to fulfill my *giri* to her, and to him. And now?

She looked down at her wedding ring and twisted it on her finger. For the first time since she had married she took it off and looked at it closely in the palm of her hand. Small, empty and uninteresting. So many lonely nights, tears in the nights, waiting waiting waiting. Waiting for what? Children forbidden, friends forbidden, travel forbidden. Not forbidden as a Japanese would: *Kin jiru!* But, "Don't you think, my dear," he would say, "don't you think it would be better if you didn't go to Paris while I'm away? We can go the next time I'm here . . ." both of them knowing they would never go.

The time in Vienna had been terrible. It was the first year. They went for a week. "I have to go out tonight," he had told her the first night. "Please stay in the room, eat in the room till I get back." Two days passed and when he came back he was sallow-faced and drawn, frightened, and then at once, in the darkest part of the night, they had got into their hired car and fled back to Switzerland, going the long way, the wrong way, up through the Tyrolian mountains, his eyes constantly on the rear mirrors in case they were being followed, not talking to her until they were safe across the border once more.

"But why, why, Hans?"

"Because nothing! Please. You're not to ask questions, Riko. That was your agreement . . . our agreement. I'm sorry about the holiday. We'll go to Wengen or Biarritz, it will be grand, it will be grand there. Please remember your *giri* and that I love you with all my heart."

Love!

I do not understand that word, she thought, standing there at the window, looking at the harbor, sullen clouds, the light bad. Strange that in Japanese we do not have such a word. Only duty and shades of duty, affection and shades of affection. Not *lieben*. *Ai*? *Ai* really means respect though some use it for *lieben*.

Riko caught herself thinking in German and she smiled. Most times she thought in German though today, with the tai-pan, she had thought in Japanese. It's such a long time since I spoke my own language. What is my own language? Japanese? That's the language my parents and I spoke. German? That's the language of our part of Switzerland. English? That's the language of my husband even though he claimed that German was his first tongue.

Was he English?

She had asked herself that question many times. It was not that his German was not fluent, it was just attitudes. His attitudes were not German, like mine are not Japanese. Or are they?

I don't know. But now, now I can find out.

He had never told her what his work was and she had never asked. After Vienna it had been very easy to predict that it was clandestine and connected somehow to international crime or espionage. Hans was not the type to be in crime.

So from then on she had been even more cautious. Once or twice she had thought that they were under surveillance in Zurich and when they went skiing, but he had dismissed it and told her not to worry about him. "But be prepared in case of accidents. Keep all your valuables and private papers, passport and birth certificate in your traveling bag, *Ri-chan*," he had said, using her nickname. "Just in case, just in case."

With the death of her husband and his instructions almost all carried out, the money and the tai-pan's phone call and summons, everything had become new. Now she could start again. She was twenty-four. The past was past and karma was karma. The tai-pan's money would be more than enough for her needs for years.

On their wedding night, her husband had told her, "If anything happens to me, you will get a call from a man called Kiernan. Cut the phone wires as I will show you and leave Zurich instantly. Leave everything except the clothes you wear and your travel bag. Drive to Geneva. Here is a key. This key will open a safety deposit box in the Swiss Bank of Geneva on Rue Charles. In it there's money and some letters. Follow the instructions exactly, my darling, oh how I love you. Leave everything. Do exactly as I've said. . . ."

And she had. Exactly. It was her *giri*.

She had cut the phone wires with the wire snips as he had shown her, just behind the box that was attached to the wall so that the cut was hardly noticeable. In Geneva in the bank there had been a letter of instructions, $10,000 U.S. in cash in the safety deposit box, a new Swiss passport, stamped, with her photograph but a new name and new birthday and new birth certificate that documented she was born in the city of Berne twenty-three years ago. She had liked the new name he had chosen for her and she remembered how, in the safety of her hotel room overlooking the lovely lake, she had wept for him.

Also in the safety deposit box had been a savings book in her new name for $20,000 U.S. in this same bank, and a key, an address and a deed. The deed was for a small chalet on the lake, private and furnished and paid for, with a caretaker who knew her only by her new name and that she was a widow who had been abroad—the deed registered in her new name though purchased four years before, a few days prior to her marriage.

"Ah, mistress, I am so happy you have come home at long last. Traveling in all those foreign places must be very tiring," the pleasant, though simple old lady had said in greeting. "Oh, for the last year or so, your home has been rented to such a charming, quiet Englishman. He paid promptly every month, here are the accounts. Perhaps he will come back this year, he said, perhaps not. Your agent is on Avenue Firmet. . . ."

Later, wandering around the lovely house, the lake vast and clean in the bowl of mountains, the house clean like the mountains, pictures on the walls, flowers in vases, three bedrooms and a living room and verandas, tiny but perfect for her, the garden cherished, she had gone into the main bedroom. Among a kaleidoscope of small pictures of various shapes and sizes on one of the walls was what seemed to be part of an old letter in a glass-covered frame, the paper already yellowing. She recognized his writing. It was in English. "So many happy hours in your arms, Ri-chan, so many happy days in your company, how do I say that I love you? Forget me, I will never forget you. How do I beg God to grant you ten thousand days for every one of mine, my darling, my darling, my darling."

The huge double bed was almost convex with its thick eiderdown quilt, multicolored, the windows opened to the tender air, late summer perfumes within it, snow dusting the mountaintops. She had wept again, the chalet taking her to itself.

Within a few hours of being there Dunross had called and she had boarded the first jet and now she was here, most of her work completed, never a need to return, the past obliterated—if she wished it. The new passport was genuine as far as she could tell, and the birth certificate. No reason ever to return to Switzerland—except for the chalet. And the picture.

She had left it on the wall undisturbed. And she had resolved, as long as she owned the house, the picture would stay where he had placed it. Always.

76

Orlanda was driving her small car, Bartlett beside her, his hand resting lightly across her shoulders. They had just come over the pass from Aberdeen and now, still in cloud, were heading down the mountainside in Mid Levels toward her home in Rose Court. They were happy together, aware and filled with expectation. After lunch they had crossed to Hong Kong and she had driven to Shek-O on the southeastern tip of the Island to show him where some of the tai-pans had weekend houses. The countryside was rolling and sparsely populated, hills, ravines, the sea always near, sheer cliffs and rocks.

From Shek-O they had slid along the southern road that curled and twisted until they got to Repulse Bay where she had stopped at the wonderful hotel for tea and cakes on the veranda, looking out at the sea, then on again, past Deepwater Cove to Discovery Bay where she stopped again at a lookout. "Look over there, Linc, that's Castle Tok!" Castle Tok was a vast, incongruous house that looked like a Norman castle and was perched on the cliffside high over the water. "During the war the Canadians—Canadian soldiers—were defending this part of the Island against the invading Japanese and they all retreated to Castle Tok for a last stand. When they were overwhelmed and surrendered there were about two hundred and fifty of them left alive. The Japanese herded them all onto the terrace of Castle Tok and drove them by bayonet over the terrace wall to the rocks below."

"Jesus." The drop was a hundred feet or more.

"Everyone. The wounded, the . . . the others, everyone." He had seen her shiver and at once had reached out to touch her.

"Don't, Orlanda, that's such a long time ago."

"It's not, no, not at all. I'm afraid history and the war's still very much with us, Linc. It always will be. Ghosts walk those terraces by night."

"You believe that?"

"Yes. Oh yes."

He remembered looking back at the brooding house, the surf crashing against the rocks below, her perfume surrounding him as she leaned back against him, feeling her heat, glad to be alive and not one of those soldiers. "Your Castle Tok looks like something out of the movies. You ever been inside?"

"No. But they say there are suits of armor and dungeons and it's a copy of a real castle in France. The owner was old Sir Cha-sen Tok, Builder Tok. He was a multimillionaire who made his money in tin. They say that when he was fifty a soothsayer told him to begin building a 'big mansion' or he would die. So he began to build and he built dozens of places, all mansions, three in Hong Kong, one near Sha Tin and many in Malaya. Castle Tok was the last one he built. He was eighty-nine but hale and hearty and like a middle-aged man. But after Castle Tok the story is he said enough, and quit building. Within a month he was dead and the soothsayer's prophecy came true."

"You're making it all up, Orlanda!"

"Oh no, Linc, I wouldn't, not without telling. But what's true and what's false? Who really knows, eh, my darling?"

"I know I'm mad about you."

"Oh Linc, you must know I feel the same."

They had driven on past Aberdeen, warm and together, his hand on her shoulder, her hair brushing his hand. From time to time she would point out houses and places and the hours went by imperceptibly, delightfully for both of them. Now, as they came down from the pass through the clouds and broke out of them, they could see most of the city below. Lights were not on yet, though here and there the huge colored neon signs down by the water's edge were beginning to brighten.

The traffic was heavy and on the steep mountain roads water still ran in the gutters with piles of fresh mud and rocks and vegetation here and there. She drove deftly, without taking chances, and he felt safe with her though driving on the wrong side of the road had been hair-raising on the bends.

"But we're on the correct side," she said. "You drive on the wrong side!"

"The hell we do. It's only the English who drive on the left. You're as American as I am, Orlanda."

"I wish I were, Linc, oh so very much."

"You are. You sound American and you dress American."

"Ah, but I know what I am, my darling."

He let himself just watch her. I've never enjoyed watching anyone so much, he thought. Not Casey, not anyone in my whole life. Then his mind took him again to Biltzmann and he wished he had that man's neck in his hands.

Put him away, old buddy, away with the shit of the world. That's what he is—he and Banastasio. Bartlett felt another twinge go through him. He had had a phone call just before lunch, and an apology that was really an added threat.

"Let's break bread, baby, you'n me? Hell, Linc, it's shitsville with you'n me hollerin'. How about steaks tonight? There's a great steak house off Nathan Road, the San Francisco."

"No thanks. I've got a date," he had said coldly. "Anyway, you made your point yesterday. Let's leave it at that, okay? We'll get together at the annual board meeting, if you attend."

"Hey Linc, this is me, your old buddy. Remember we came through for you when you needed the cash. Didn't we give you cash up front?"

"Cash up front in return for shares which have been the best investment—the best regular investment you ever had. You've doubled your money in five years."

"Sure we have. Now we want a little of the say-so, that's only fair, isn't it?"

"No. Not after yesterday. What about the guns?" he had asked on a sudden hunch.

There was a pause. "What guns?"

"The ones aboard my airplane. The hijacked M14's and grenades."

"It's news to me, baby."

"My name's Linc. Baby. Got it?"

Another pause. The voice grated now. "I got it. About our deal. You gonna change your mind?"

"No. No way."

"Not now, not later?"

"No."

There had been the silence on the other end of the line and then a click and the endless dial tone began. At once he had called Rosemont.

"Don't worry, Linc. Banastasio's a top target of ours and we have lots of help in these parts."

"Anything on the guns?"

"You're in the clear. The Hong Kong brass here've withdrawn the lien on you. You'll hear that officially tomorrow."

"They found something?"

"No. We did. We checked out your hangar in L.A. One of the night watchmen remembered seeing a couple of jokers fiddling around in your landing bay. He thought nothing about it till we asked."

"Jesus. You catch anybody?"

"No. Maybe never will. No sweat. About Banastasio, he'll be off your back soon enough. Don't worry."

Now, thinking about it, Bartlett felt chilled again.

"What's the matter, darling?" Orlanda asked. "What is it?"

"Nothing."

"Tell me."

"I was just thinking that fear's lousy and can destroy you if you don't watch out."

"Oh yes I know, I know so very well." She took her eyes off the road a second and smiled hesitantly and put her hand on his knee. "But you're strong, my darling. You're afraid of nothing."

He laughed. "I wish that were true."

"Oh but it is. I *know*." She slowed to go around a pile of slush, the road steeper here, water swirling in a minor flood in and out of the gutters. The car was hugging the tall retaining wall as she turned down into Kotewall Road and around the corner to Rose Court. When she came alongside he held his breath as she hesitated a moment, then firmly bypassed the foyer and turned into the steep down-path that led to the garage. "It's cocktail time," she said.

"Great," he said, his voice throaty. He did not look at her. When they stopped he got out and went to her side and opened the door. She locked the car and they went to the elevator. Bartlett felt the pulse in his neck throbbing.

Two Chinese caterers carrying trays of canapés got in with them and asked for the Asian Properties flat. "It's on the fifth floor," she said, and after the caterers had got out Bartlett said, "Asian Properties're the landlords here?"

"Yes," she said. "They're also the original builders." She hesitated. "Jason Plumm and Quillan are good friends. Quillan still owns the penthouse though he sublet it when we broke up."

Bartlett put his arm around her. "I'm glad you did."

"So'm I." Her smile was tender and her wide-eyed innocence tore at him. "Now I am."

They reached the eighth floor and he noticed her fingers tremble slightly as she put the key into her lock. "Come in, Linc. Tea, coffee, beer or a cocktail?" She slipped off her shoes and looked up at him. His heart was pounding and his senses reached out to feel whether the apartment was empty. "We're alone," she said simply.

"How do you know what I'm thinking?"

She shrugged a little shrug. "It's only some things."

He put his hands on her waist. "Orlanda . . ."

"I know, my darling."

Her voice was husky and it sent a tremor through him. When he kissed her, her lips welcomed him, her loins soft and unresisting. His hands traced her. He felt her nipples harden and the throb of her heart equal his. Then her hands left his neck and pressed against his chest but this time he held her against him, his kiss more urgent. The pressure of her hands ceased and once more the hands slid around his neck, her loins closer now. They broke from the kiss but held each other.

"I love you, Linc."

"I love you, Orlanda," he replied, and the sudden truth of it consumed him. Again they kissed, her hands tender but strong, his own hands wandering and in their wake, fire. For him and for her. More of her weight rested on his arms as her knees weakened and he lifted her easily and carried her through the open door into the bedroom. The gossamer curtains that hung from the ceiling to form the four-poster moved gently in the cool sweet breeze from the open windows.

The coverlet was soft and down-filled.

"Be kind to me, my darling," she whispered huskily. "Oh how I love you."

From the stern of the *Sea Witch,* Casey waved good-bye to Dunstan Barre, Plumm and Pugmire who stood on the wharf, Hong Kong side, where they had just been dropped, the late afternoon pleasant but still overcast. The boat was heading back across the harbor again—Peter Marlowe and the girls had already been dropped off at Kowloon—Gornt having persuaded her to stay on board for the extra trip. "I've got to come back to Kowloon again," he had told her. "I've an appointment at the Nine Dragons. Keep me company. Please?"

"Why not?" she had agreed happily, in no hurry, still in plenty of time to change for the cocktail party to which Plumm had invited her this afternoon. She had decided to postpone her dinner with Lando Mata for one day next week.

On the way back from Sha Tin this afternoon she had dozed part of the time, wrapped up warm against a stiff breeze, curled up on the wide, comfortable cushions that circled the stern, the other guests scattered, sometimes Gornt there at the conn, tall, strong and captain of the ship, Peter Marlowe alone in a deck chair dozing at the bow. Later they had had tea and cakes, he and Casey and Barre. During tea, Pugmire and Plumm had appeared, tousled and content, their girls in tow.

"Sleep well?" Gornt had asked with a smile.

"Very," Plumm had said.

I'll bet, she had thought, watching him and his girl, liking her—big, dark eyes, svelte, a happy soul called Wei-wei who stayed with him like his shadow.

Earlier, when she and Gornt had been alone on deck, he had told her that none of these were casual friends, all of them special.

"Does everyone here have a mistress?"

"Good lord no. But, well, sorry, but men and women age differently and after a certain age it's difficult. Bluntly, pillowing and love and marriage aren't the same."

"There's no such thing as faithfulness?"

"Of course. Absolutely. For a woman it means one thing, for a man another."

Casey had sighed. "That's terrible. Terrible and so unfair."

"Yes. But only if you wish it to be."

"That's not right! Think of the millions of women who work and slave all their lives, looking after the man, scrubbing and cleaning and nowadays helping to support their children, to be shoved aside just because they're old."

"You can't blame men, that's the way society is."

"And who runs society? Men! Jesus, Quillan, you've got to admit men are responsible!"

"I already agree it's unfair, but it's unfair on men too. What about the millions of men who work themselves to death to *provide*—that jolly word —to provide the money for others to spend, mostly women. Face it, Ciranoush, men have to go on working until they are dead, to support others, and more than frequently at the end of their lives, a hacking, shrewish wife—look at Pug's wife for God's sake! I could point out fifty who are unnecessarily fat, ugly and stink—literally. Then there's the other neat little female trick of the women who use their sex to trap, get pregnant to ensnare, then cry havoc and scream for a highly paid divorce. What about Linc Bartlett, eh? What sort of a wringer did that wonderful wife of his put him through, eh?"

"You know about that?"

"Of course. You ran a tape on me, I ran one on both of you. Are your divorce laws fair? Fifty percent of everything and then the poor bloody American male has to go to court to decide what proportion of his fifty percent he can retain."

"It's true Linc's wife and her attorney almost put him away. But not every wife's like that. But God, we're not chattel and most women need protection. Women throughout the world still get a raw deal."

"I've never known a real woman to get a raw deal," he said. "I mean a woman like you or Orlanda who understands what femininity means." Suddenly he had beamed at her. "Of course, en route she has to give us poor weak bastards what we want to stay healthy."

She had laughed with him, also wanting to change the subject—too difficult to solve now.

"Ah, Quillan, you're one of the bad ones all right."

"Oh?"

"Yes."

He had turned away to search the sky ahead. She watched him and he looked fine to her, standing there, swaying slightly, the wind ruffling the hairs on his strong forearms, his sea cap jaunty. I'm glad he trusts me and considers me a woman, she had thought, lulled by the wine and the food and by his desire. Ever since she had come aboard she had felt it strongly and she had wondered again how she would deal with it when it manifested itself, as it would, inevitably. Would it be yes or no? Or maybe? Or maybe next week?

Will there be a next week?

"What's going to happen tomorrow, Quillan? At the stock market?"

"Tomorrow can take care of tomorrow," he had said, the wind whipping him.

"Seriously?"

"I will win or I will not win." Gornt shrugged. "Either way I'm covered. Tomorrow I buy. With joss I have him by the shorts."

"And then?"

He had laughed. "Have you any doubt? I take him over, lock, stock and box at the races."

"Ah, you really want that, don't you?"

"Oh yes. Oh yes, that represents victory. He and his forebears have kept me and mine out. Of course I want that."

I wonder if I could make a deal with Ian, she had thought absently. Wonder if I could get the tai-pan to allow Quillan a box, his own box, and help make him a steward. Crazy for these two to be like bulls in a china shop—there's more than enough room for both. Ian owes me a favor if Murtagh delivers.

Her heart fluttered and she wondered what had happened with Murtagh and the bank, and if the answer was yes, what Quillan would do.

And where is Linc? Is he with Orlanda, in her arms, dreaming the afternoon away?

She curled up again on the stern and closed her eyes. The salt air and the throb of the engines and the motion through the sea put her to sleep. Her sleep was dreamless, womblike, and in a few minutes she awoke refreshed. Gornt was sitting opposite her now, watching her. They were alone again, the Cantonese captain at the wheel.

"You have a nice sleeping face," he said.

"Thank you." She moved and rested on one elbow. "You're a strange man. Part devil, part prince, compassionate one minute, ruthless the next. That was a wonderful thing you did for Peter."

He just smiled and waited, his eyes strangely and pleasantly challenging.

"Linc's . . . I think Linc's smitten with Orlanda," she said without thinking and saw a shadow go over him.

"Oh?"

"Yes." She waited but he said nothing, just watched her. Pushed by the silence, she added involuntarily, "I think she's smitten with him." Again a long silence. "Quillan, is that part of a plan?"

He laughed softly and she felt his dominance. "Ah, Ciranoush, you're the strange one. I don—"

"Will you call me Casey? Please? Ciranoush is not right."

"But I don't like Casey. May I use Kamalian?"

"Casey."

"What about Ciranoush today, Casey tomorrow, Kamalian for Tuesday dinner? That's when we close the deal. Eh?"

Her guards came up without thinking. "That's up to Linc."

"You're not tai-pan of Par-Con?"

"No. No, I'll never be that."

He laughed. Then he said, "Then let's make it Ciranoush today, Casey tomorrow and the hell with Tuesday?"

"All right!" she said, warmed by him.

"Good. Now as to Orlanda and Linc," he said, his voice gentle. "That's up to them and I never discuss the affairs of others with others, even a lady. Never. That's not playing the game. If you're asking if I've some devious plot, using her against Linc or you and Par-Con, that's ridiculous." Again he smiled. "I've always noticed that ladies manipulate men, not the other way around."

"Dreamer!"

"One question deserves another: Are you and Linc lovers?"

"No. Not in the conventional sense, but yes I love him."

"Ah, then are you going to marry?"

"Perhaps." Again she shifted and she saw his eyes move over her. Her hands pulled the blanket closer around her, her heart beating nicely, very conscious of him as she knew he was conscious of her. "But I don't discuss my affairs with another man," she said with a smile. "That's not playing the game either."

Gornt reached out and touched her lightly. "I agree, Ciranoush."

The *Sea Witch* came out of the breakwater into the harbor waves, Kowloon ahead. She sat up and turned to watch the Island and the Peak, most of it cloud covered. "It's so beautiful."

"The south coast of Hong Kong's grand around Shek-O, Repulse Bay. I've a place at Shek-O. Would you like to see the boat now?"

"Yes, yes I'd like that."

He took her forward first. The cabins were neat, no sign of having been used. Each had shower stalls and a toilet. A small general cabin served them all. "We're rather popular with ladies at the moment because they can shower to their hearts content. The water shortage does have advantages."

"I'll bet," she said, carried along by his joviality.

Aft, separate from the rest of the boat, was the master cabin. Big double bed. Neat, tidy and inviting.

Her heart was sounding loud in her ears now, and when he casually closed the cabin door and put his hand on her waist she did not back off. He came closer. She had never kissed a man with a beard before. Gornt's body was hard against hers and it felt good to her, her breath picking up tempo, his lips firm and cigar tasting. Most of her whispered: Go, let go, and most of her said, No, don't, and all of her felt sensual in his arms, too good.

What about Linc?

The question barreled into her mind like never before and all at once her mind cleared and, carried along by his sensuality, she knew for the first time with absolute clarity that it was Linc she wanted, not Par-Con or power if that had to be the choice. Yes, it's Linc, just Linc, and tonight I'll cancel our deal. Tonight I'll offer to cancel.

"Now's not the time," she whispered, her voice throaty.

"What?"

"No, not now. We can't, sorry." She reached up and kissed him lightly on the lips, talking through the kisses, "Not now, my dear, sorry, but we can't, not now. Tuesday, perhaps Tuesday . . ."

He held her away from him and she saw his dark eyes searching her. She held her gaze as long as she could, then buried her head against his chest and held him tenderly, still enjoying the closeness, sure that she was safe now, and that he was convinced. That was a close one, she thought weakly, her knees feeling strange, all of her pulsating. I was almost gone then and that wouldn't have been good, good for me or Linc or him.

It would have been good for him, she thought strangely.

Her heart was pounding as she rested against him, waiting, recouping, confident in a moment—with warmth and gentleness and the promise of next week—he would say, "Let's go back on deck."

Then all at once she felt his arms tighten around her and before she knew what was happening she was on the bed, his kisses strong and his hands wandering. She began to fight back but he caught her hands expertly and stretched her out with his great strength and lay across her, his loins pinioning her, making her helpless. At leisure he kissed her and his passion and her heat mingled with her fury and fear and want. As much as she struggled, she could not move.

The heat grew. In a moment he shifted his grip. Instantly she swept to the attack, wanting more though now she was preparing to fight seriously. Again his grip on her hands tightened. She felt herself swamped, wanting to be overpowered, not wanting it, his passion strong, loins hard, the bed soft. And then, as abruptly as he had begun, he released her and rolled away with a laugh.

"Let's have a drink!" he said without rancor.

She was gasping for breath. "You bastard!"

"I'm not actually. I'm very legitimate." Gornt propped himself on an elbow, his eyes crinkling. "But you, Ciranoush, you're a liar."

"Go to hell!"

His voice was calm and genially taunting. "I will, soon enough. Far be it for me to ask a lady to prove such a thing."

She threw herself at him, her nails hacking for his face, furious that he was so controlled when she was not. Easily he caught her hands and held her. "Gently gently catchee monkeeee," he said even more genially. "Calm down, Ciranoush. Remember, we're both over twenty-one, I've already seen you almost naked, and if I really wanted to rape you I'm afraid it wouldn't be much of a contest. You could scream bloody murder and my crew wouldn't hear a thing."

"You're a goddamn lou—"

"Stop!" Gornt kept his smile but she stopped, sensing danger. "The tumble was not to frighten, just to amuse," he said gently. "A prank, nothing more. Truly." He released her and she scrambled off the bed, her breathing still heavy.

Angrily she walked over to the mirror and pushed her hair back into place, then saw him in the mirror, still lying casually on the bed watching her, and she whirled, "You're a black-eyed bastard!"

Gornt let out a bellow of laughter, infectious, belly-shaking, and, all at once, seeing the foolishness of it all, she began to laugh too. In a moment they were both aching with laughter, he spread out on the bed and Casey leaning against the sea chest.

On deck, as good friends, they drank some champagne that was already opened in a silver bucket, the silent, obsequious steward serving them, then going away.

At the dock in Kowloon, she kissed him again. "Thanks for a lovely time. Tuesday, if not before!" She went ashore and waved the ship goodbye a long time, then hurried home.

Spectacles Wu was also hurrying home. He was tired and anxious and filled with dread. The way up through the maze of dwellings and hovels in the resettlement area high above Aberdeen was difficult, slippery and dangerous, mud and mess everywhere, and he was breathing hard from the climb. The runoff in the concrete storm drain had overflowed its banks many times in many places, the flood shoving structures aside and spreading more havoc. Smoke hung over many of the wrecked dwellings, some still smoldering from the fires that had spread so quickly when the slides began. He skirted the deep slide where Fifth Niece had almost perished the day before yesterday, a hundred or more hovels wrecked by new slides in the same area.

The candy shop had vanished and the old woman with it. "Where is she?" he asked.

The scavenger shrugged and continued to sift through wreckage, seeking good wood or good cardboard or corrugated iron.

"How is it above?" he asked.

"As below," the man said in halting Cantonese. "Some good, some bad. Joss."

Wu thanked him. He was barefoot, carrying his shoes to protect them and now he left the storm drain and forced his way over some of the debris wreckage to find the path that meandered upward. From where he was he could not see his area though it seemed there were no slides there. Armstrong had allowed him to come home to check when the radio news had again reported bad slides in this part of the resettlement area. "But be back as quickly as you can. Another interrogation's scheduled for seven o'clock."

"Oh yes, I'll be back," he muttered out loud.

The sessions had been very tiring but for him good, with much praise from Armstrong and the chief of SI, his place in SI assured now, transfer and training to begin next week. He had had little sleep, partially because the session hours bore no relationship to day or night, and partially because of his wish to succeed. The client was shifting from English to

Ning-tok dialect to Cantonese and back again and it had been hard to follow all the ramblings. It was only when his fingers had touched the wonderful, rare roll of bills in his pocket, his winnings at the races, that a lightness had taken hold and carried him through the difficult hours. Again he touched them to reassure himself, blessing his joss, as he climbed the narrow pathway, the path at times a rickety bridge over small ravines, climbing steadily. People passed by, going down, and others were following going up, the noise of hammers and rebuilding, reroofing all over the mountainside.

His area was a hundred yards ahead now, around this corner, and he turned it and stopped. His area was no more, just a deep scar in the earth, the piled-up avalanche of mud and debris two hundred feet below. No dwellings where there had been hundreds.

Numbly he climbed, skirting the treacherous slide, and went to the nearest hovel, banging on the door. An old woman opened it suspiciously. "Excuse me, Honored Lady, I'm Wu Cho-tam's son from Ning-tok. . . ."

The woman, One Tooth Yang, stared at him blankly, then started speaking but Wu did not understand her language so he thanked her and went off, remembering that this was one of the areas settled by the Yang, some of the northern foreigners who came from Shanghai.

Closer to the top of the slide he stopped and knocked on another door. "Excuse me, Honored Sir, but what happened? I'm Wu Cho-tam's son from Ning-tok and my family were there." He pointed at the scar.

"It happened in the night, Honorable Wu," the man told him, speaking a Cantonese dialect he could understand. "It was like the sound of the old Canton express train and then a rumbling from the earth, then screams then some fires came. It happened the same last year over there. Ah yes, the fires began quickly but the rains doused them. *Dew neh loh moh* but the night was very bad." The neighbor was an old man with no teeth and his mouth split into a grimace. "Bless all gods you weren't sleeping there, *heya?*" He shut the door.

Wu looked back at the scar, then picked his way down the hill. At length he found one of the elders of his area who was also from Ning-tok. "Ah, Spectacles Wu, Policeman Wu! Several of your family are there." His gnarled old finger pointed above. "There, in the house of your cousin, Wu Wam-pak."

"How many were lost, Honorable Sir?"

"Fornicate all mud slides how do I know? Am I keeper of the mountainside? There are dozens missing."

Spectacles Wu thanked him. When he found the hut, Ninth Uncle was there, Grandmother, Sixth Uncle's wife and their four children, Third Uncle's wife and baby. Fifth Uncle had a broken arm, now in a crude splint.

"And the rest of us?" he asked. Seven were missing.

"In the earth," grandmother said. "Here's tea, Spectacles Wu."

"Thank you, Honored Grandmother. And Grandfather?"

"He went to the Void before the slide. He went to the Void in the night, before the slide."

"Joss. And Fifth Niece."

"Gone. Vanished, somewhere."

"Could she still be alive?"

"Perhaps. Sixth Uncle's searching for her now, below, and the others, even though she's a useless mouth. But what about my sons, and their sons, and theirs?"

"Joss," Wu said sadly, not cursing the gods or blessing them. Gods make mistakes. "We will light joss sticks for them that they may be reborn safely, if there is rebirth. Joss." He sat down on a broken crate. "Ninth Uncle, our factory, was the factory damaged?"

"No, thank all gods." The man was numbed. He had lost his wife and three children, somehow scrambling out of the sea of mud that had swallowed them all. "The factory is undamaged."

"Good." All the papers and research materials for Freedom Fighter were there—along with the old typewriter and ancient Gestetner copying machine. "Very good. Now, Fifth Uncle, tomorrow you will buy a plastic-making machine. From now on we'll make our own flowers. Sixth Uncle will help you and we will begin again."

The man spat disgustedly, "How can we pay, eh? How can we start? How can we . . ." He stopped and stared. They all gasped. Spectacles Wu had brought out the roll of bills. "Ayeeyah, Honored Younger Brother, I can see that at long last you have seen the wisdom of joining the Snake!"

"How wise!" the others chorused proudly. "All gods bless Younger Brother!"

The young man said nothing. He knew they would not believe him if he said otherwise, so he let them believe. "Tomorrow begin looking for a good secondhand machine. You can pay only $900," he told the older man, knowing that 1,500 was available if necessary. Then he went outside and arranged with their cousin, the owner of this hut, to lease them a corner until they could rebuild, haggling over the price until it was correct. Satisfied that he had done what he could for the Wu clan, he left them and plodded downhill back to headquarters, his heart weeping, his whole soul wanting to shriek at the gods for their unfairness, or carelessness, for taking so many of them away, taking Fifth Niece who but a day or so ago was given back her life in another slide.

Don't be a fool, he ordered himself. Joss is joss. You have wealth in your pocket, a vast future with SI, Freedom Fighter to manufacture, and the time of dying is up to the gods.

Poor little Fifth Niece. So pretty, so sweet.

"Gods are gods," he muttered wearily, echoing the last words he remembered her ever saying, then put her out of his mind.

77

6:30 P.M.:

Ah Tat hobbled up the wide staircase in the Great House, her old joints creaking, muttering to herself, and went along the Long Gallery, hating the gallery and the faces that seemed ever to be watching her. Too many ghosts here, she thought with superstitious dread, knowing too many of the faces in life, growing up in this house, born in this house eighty-five years ago. Uncivilized to hold their spirits in thrall by hanging their likenesses on the wall. Better to act civilized and cast them into memory where spirits belong.

As always when she saw the Hag's knife stuck through the heart of her father's portrait a shudder went through her. *Dew neh loh moh,* she thought, now there was a wild one, her with the unquenchable demon in her Jade Gate, ever secretly bemoaning the loss of *the tai-pan,* her husband's father, bemoaning her fate that she had married the weakling son and not the father, never to be bedded by the father, her Jade Gate unquenchable because of that.

Ayeeyah, and all the strangers that climbed these stairs over the years to enter her bed, barbarians of all nations, of all ages, shapes and sizes, to be cast aside like so much chaff once their essence had been taken and used up, the fire never touched.

Ah Tat shuddered again. All gods bear witness! The Jade Gate and the One-Eyed Monk are truly yin and yang, truly everlasting, truly godlike, both insatiable however much one consumes the other. Thank all gods my parents allowed me to take the vow of chastity, to devote my life to bringing up children, never to be split by a Steaming Stalk, never to be the same ever after. Thank all gods all women do not need men to elevate them to be one with the gods. Thank all gods some women wisely prefer women to cuddle and touch and kiss and enjoy. The Hag had had women too, many, when she was old, finding in their youth-filled arms pleasure but never satisfaction, not like me. Curious she would pillow with a civilized girl but not a civilized man who would surely have put out her fire, one way or another, with pillow tools or without. All gods bear witness, how many times did I tell her? Me the only one she would talk to about such things!

Poor fool, her with her twisted dreams of power, twisted dreams of lust, just like the old dowager empress—nightmares of a lifetime that no shaft could allay.

Ah Tat pulled her eyes off the knife and plodded onward. The House will never be whole until someone pulls out the knife and casts it into the sea—curse or no curse.

The old woman did not knock on the bedroom door but went in noiselessly so as not to wake him and stood over the vast double bed and looked down. This was the time she enjoyed the most, when her manchild was still sleeping, alone, and she could see his sleeping face and study it and not have to worry about Chief Wife's spleen and ill-temper over her comings and goings.

Silly woman, she thought gravely, seeing the lines in his face. Why doesn't she do her duty as Chief Wife and provide my son with another wife, young, child bearing, a civilized person, like old Green-Eyed Devil had. Then this house would be bright again. Yes, the house needs more sons—stupid to risk posterity on the shoulders of one son. And stupid to leave this bull alone, stupid to leave this bed empty, stupid to leave him to be tempted by some mealy-mouthed whore to waste his essence in alien pastures. Why doesn't she realize we have the house to protect! Barbarians.

She saw his eyes open and focus and then he stretched luxuriously. "Time to get up, my son," she said, trying to sound harsh and commanding. "You have to bathe and get dressed and make more phone calls, *heya,* and leave your poor old Mother with more chores and more work, *heya?*"

"Yes, Mother," Dunross mumbled through a yawn in Cantonese, then shook himself like a dog, stretched once more and got out of bed and strode naked for the bathroom.

She studied his tall body critically, the crinkled, savage scars of the old burns from his airplane crash covering most of his legs. But the legs were strong, the flanks strong and the yang resolute and healthy. Good, she thought. I'm glad to see all's well. Even so, she was concerned at his perpetual leanness, with no substantial belly that his wealth and position merited. "You're not eating enough, my son!"

"More than enough!"

"There's hot water in the bucket. Don't forget to wash your teeth."

Contentedly she began to remake the bed. "He needed that rest," she muttered, not realizing she was talking aloud. "He's been like a man possessed for the last week, working all hours, fear in his face and over him. Such fear can kill." When she had finished the bed she called out, "Now don't stay out late tonight. You must take care of yourself and if you go with a whore bring her here like a sensible person, *heya?*"

She heard him laugh and she was glad for it. There hasn't been enough laughter from him the last few days, she thought. "A man needs laughter and youthful yin to nourish the yang. Eh what, what did you say?"

"I said, where's Number One Daughter?"

"In, out, always out, out with that new barbarian," she said going to the bathroom door and peering at him as he doused water over himself. "The one with long hair and crumpled clothes who works for the *China Guardian*. I don't approve of him, my son. No, not at all!"

"Where are they 'out,' Ah Tat?"

The old woman shrugged, chomping her gums. "The sooner Number One Daughter's married the better. Better for her to be another man's problem than yours. Or you should give her a good whip to her rump." He laughed again and she wondered why he laughed this time. "He's getting simple in the head," she muttered, then turned away. At the far door, remembering, she called out, "There's small chow for you before you leave."

"Don't worry about food . . ." Dunross stopped, knowing it was a waste of time. He heard her go off mumbling, closing the door after her.

He was standing in the bath and bailed more cold water over himself. Christ, I wish this bloody water shortage'd cease, he thought. I could use a really long hot shower, his mind inexorably zeroing in on Adryon. At once he heard Penelope's admonition, "Do grow up, Ian! It really is her own life, do grow up!"

"I'm trying," he muttered, toweling himself vigorously. Just before he had slept he had called Penelope. She was already at Castle Avisyard, Kathy still in the London clinic for more tests. "She'll be coming up next week. I do so hope everything will be all right."

"I'm in touch with the doctors, Penn." He told her about sending Gavallan to Scotland. "He's always wanted to be there, Kathy too, it'll be better for both of them, eh?"

"Oh, that's marvelous, Ian. That'll be a marvelous tonic."

"They can take over the whole east wing."

"Oh yes. Ian, the weather's wonderful today, wonderful, and the house so lovely. No chance you can come for a few days I suppose?"

"I'm up to my nose in it, Penn! You heard about the market?"

He had heard the momentary silence and he could see her face change and within her head hear her impotent raging against the market and Hong Kong and business, as much as she tried to cast it away.

"Yes. It must be terrible," she had said, still a thread in her voice. "Poor you. Alastair was carrying on a bit last night. It'll be all right, won't it?"

"Oh yes," he said with great confidence, wondering what she would say if he told her that he would have to guarantee personally the Murtagh loan if it came through. Oh Christ let it come through. He gave her all the news, then told her that AMG had sent him a very interesting message that he would tell her about when he saw her, adding that the messenger was a Japanese-Swiss woman. "She's quite a bird!"

"I hope not too much!"

"Oh no! How's Glenna and how're you?"

"Just fine. Have you heard from Duncan?"

"Yes. He arrives tomorrow—I'll get him to phone you the moment he's home. That's about it, Penn, love you!"

"I love you too and wish you were here. Oh, how's Adryon?"

"More of the same. She and that Haply fellow seem to be inseparable!"

"Do remember she's very grown up, darling, and don't worry about her. Just try to grow up yourself."

He finished drying himself and looked at his reflection in the mirror, wondering if he was old for his years or young, not feeling any different from when he was nineteen—at university or at war. After a moment, he said, "You're lucky to be alive, old chum. You're oh so lucky." His sleep had been heavy and he had been dreaming about Tiptop and, just at waking, someone had said in his dream, "What're you going to do?" I don't know, he thought. How far do I trust that bugger Sinders? Not far. But I got under his guard with my threat . . . no, my promise to publish the eleven pieces of paper. And I will, by God!

I'd better call Tiptop before I leave for Plumm's. I'd better . . .

His ears heard the bedroom door swing open again and Ah Tat padded back across the room to stand at the bathroom door. "Ah, my son, I forgot to tell you, there's a barbarian waiting for you downstairs."

"Oh? Who?"

She shrugged. "A barbarian. Not as tall as you. He has a strange name, and he's more ugly than usual with hair of straw!" She searched in her pocket and found the card. "Here."

The card read, Dave Murtagh III, Royal Belgium and Far East Bank. Dunross's stomach twisted. "How long's he been waiting?"

"An hour, perhaps more."

"What? Fornicate all gods. Why didn't you wake me?"

"Eh? Why didn't I wake you?" she asked caustically. "Why? Why do you think? Am I a fool? A foreign devil? Ayeeyah, what is more important, him waiting or your rest? Ayeeyah!" she added disdainfully and stalked off, grumbling, "As if I didn't know what was best for you."

Dunross dressed hurriedly and rushed downstairs. Murtagh was sprawled out in an easy chair. He awoke with a start as the door opened. "Oh, hi!"

"I'm terribly sorry, I was having a kip and didn't know you were here."

"That's all right, tai-pan." Dave Murtagh was haggard. "The old biddy threatened the hell out of me if I so much as murmured but it didn't matter, I dropped off." He stretched wearily, stifling a yawn and shook his head to try to clear it. "Jesus, sorry to come uninvited but it's better than on the phone."

Dunross held his aching disappointment off his face. It must be a turn-down, he thought. "Whiskey?"

"Sure, with soda. Thanks. Jesus I'm tired."

Dunross went to the decanter and poured, and a brandy and soda for himself. "Health," he said, resisting the urge to ask.

They touched glasses.

"Health. And you got your deal!" The young man's face cracked into an enormous grin. "We did it!" he almost shouted. "They screamed and they hollered but an hour ago they agreed. We got everything! 120 percent of the ships and a $50 million U.S. revolving fund, cash's up Wednesday, but you can commit Monday at 10:00 A.M., the offer of the tanker deals was the clincher. Jesus, we did it for chrissake!"

It took all of Dunross's training to hold in his bellow of triumph and keep the joy off his face and say calmly, "Oh, jolly good," and take another sip of his brandy. "What's the matter?" he asked, seeing the shock on the younger man's face.

Murtagh shook his head and slumped down exhaustedly. "You limeys're something else! I'll never understand you. I give you a hundred percent parole with the sweetest deal God ever gave man and all you say is 'Oh jolly good.'"

Dunross laughed. It was a great bellow of laughter and all his happiness spilled out. He pummeled Murtagh's hand and thanked him. "How's that?" he asked, beaming.

"That's better!" He grabbed his briefcase and opened it and pulled out a sheaf of contracts and papers. "These're just as we agreed. I was up all night drafting them. Here's the main loan agreement, this's your personal guarantee, these're for the corporate seal, ten copies of everything."

"I'll initial one set now which you keep, you initial one which I'll keep and then we'll sign formally tomorrow morning. Can you meet me in my office tomorrow morning, say at 7:30? We'll chop all the documents an—"

The young man let out an involuntary moan. "How 'bout 8:00, tai-pan, or 8:30? I just gotta catch up on some sleep."

"7:30. You can sleep all day." Dunross added at a sudden thought, "Tomorrow night your evening's reserved."

"It is?"

"Yes. You best get all the rest you can, your evening will be busy."

"Doing what?"

"You're not married, you're not attached, so an entertaining evening wouldn't be bad. Eh?"

"Gee." Murtagh brightened perceptibly. "It'd be terrific."

"Good. I'll send you to a friend of mine at Aberdeen. Goldtooth Wu."

"Who?"

"An old friend of the family. Perfectly safe. While I think of it, lunch at the races next week?"

"Oh Jesus, thanks. Yesterday Casey gave me a hot tip and I won a bundle. The rumor is you're going to ride Noble Star Saturday. Are you?"

"Perhaps." Dunross kept his eyes on him. "The deal's really through? No chance of a foul-up?"

"Cross my heart and hope to die! Oh here I forgot." He handed him the confirming telex. "It's as we agreed." Murtagh glanced at his watch. "It's 6:00 A.M. New York time now but you're to call S. J. Beverly, our chairman of the board, in an hour—he's expecting your call. Here's his number." The young man beamed. "They made me VP in charge of all Asia."

"Congratulations."

Dunross saw the time. He would have to leave soon or he would be late and he did not want to keep Riko waiting. His heart picked up a beat. "Let's initial now, shall we?"

Murtagh was already sorting the papers. "Just one thing, tai-pan, S.J. said we got to keep this secret."

"That's going to be difficult. Who typed these?"

"My secretary—but she's American, she's as tight as a clam."

Dunross nodded but inside he was unconvinced. The telex operator—didn't Phillip Chen say he had already had copies of some of the telexes? —or cleaners, or phone operators, it would be impossible to gauge who but the news would be common knowledge soon, whatever he or Murtagh did. Now, how to use everything to the best advantage while it's still secret? he was asking himself, hard put not to dance with joy, the fact of the deal unprecedented and almost impossible to believe. He began to initial his set of papers, Murtagh another. He stopped as he heard the front door open and slam. Adryon shrieked, *"Ah Tat!"* and followed up with a flood of *amah* Cantonese ending, ". . . and did you iron my new blouse by all the gods?"

"Blouse? What blouse, Young Miss with the piercing voice and no patience? The red one? The red one belonging to Chief Wife who told y—"

"Oh, it's mine now, Ah Tat! I told you very seriously to iron it."

Murtagh had stopped too, listening to the stream of screeching Cantonese from both of them. "Jesus," he said tiredly. "I'll never get used to the way the servants go on, no matter what you tell 'em!"

Dunross laughed and beckoned him, opening the door softly. Murtagh gasped. Adryon had her hands on her hips and she was going at Ah Tat who gave it back to her, both of them raucous, both talking over the other and neither listening.

"Quiet!" Dunross said. Both stopped. "Thank you. You really do go on a bit, Adryon!" he said mildly.

She beamed. "Oh hello, Father. Do you th—" She stopped, seeing Murtagh. Dunross noticed the instant change. A warning shaft soared through him.

"Oh, Adryon, may I introduce Dave Murtagh, Vice-President for Asia of the Royal Belgium and Far East Bank?" He looked at Murtagh and saw the stunned expression on his face. "This is my daughter, Adryon."

"You, er, speak Chinese, Miss, er, Dunross?"

"Oh yes, yes of course, Cantonese. Of course. You're new in Hong Kong?"

"Oh no, ma'am, no, I've, er, I've been here half a year or more."

Dunross was watching both of them with growing amusement, knowing that for the moment he was totally forgotten. Ah, boy meets girl, girl meets boy and maybe this one'd be the perfect foil to throw into Haply's works. "Would you like to join us for a drink, Adryon?" he asked casually, the moment their conversation lapsed and she prepared to leave.

"Oh. Oh thank you, Father, but I don't want to disturb you."

"We're just finishing. Come along. How're things?"

"Oh fine, fine." Adryon turned back to Ah Tat who still stood there solidly—she too had noticed the instant mutual attraction. "You'll iron my blouse! Please," she said imperiously in Cantonese. "I have to leave in fifteen minutes."

"*Ayeeyah* on your fifteen minutes, Young Empress." Ah Tat huffed, and went back into the kitchen, grumbling.

Adryon focused on Murtagh who blossomed noticeably, his fatigue vanished. "What part of the States are you from?"

"Texas, ma'am, though I've spent time in Los Angeles, New York and New Orleans. You play tennis?"

"Oh, yes, I do."

"We've some good courts at the American Club. You, maybe you'd like a game next week?"

"I'd love that. I've played there before. Are you good?"

"Oh no, ma'am, er, Miss Dunross, just college class."

"College class could mean very good. Why don't you call me Adryon?"

Dunross gave her the glass of sherry he had poured and she thanked him with a smile though still concentrating on Murtagh. You'd better be top of your class, young fellow, he thought, knowing how competitive she was, or you're in for a drubbing. Carefully keeping his amusement private, he went back to the papers. When he finished initialing his set, he watched the two of them critically, his daughter sitting casually on the edge of the sofa, beautiful and so assured, very much a woman, and Murtagh tall and well mannered, a little shy, but holding his own very well.

Could I stand a banker in the family? I'd better check up on him! God help us, an American? Well he's Texan, and that's not the same, is it? I wish Penn were back here.

". . . oh no, Adryon," Murtagh was saying. "I've a company apartment over at West Point. It's a little bitty place but great."

"That makes such a difference, doesn't it? I live here but I'm going to have my own apartment soon." She added pointedly, "Aren't I, Father?"

"Of course." Dunross added at once, "After university! Here's my set, Mr. Murtagh, do you think you could sign yours?"

"Oh yes . . . oh sorry!" Murtagh almost ran over, hurriedly initialed his set with a flourish. "Here you are, sir. You, er, you said 7:30 at your office tomorrow morning, huh?"

Adryon arched an eyebrow. "You'd better be punctual, Dave, the tai-pan's uncomfortably ornery at unpunctuality."

"Rubbish," Dunross said.

"I love you, Father, but that's not rubbish!"

They chatted for a minute then Dunross glanced at his watch, pretending to be concerned. "Damn! I've got to make a phone call then rush." At once Murtagh picked up his briefcase but Dunross added blandly, "Adryon, you said you were leaving in a few minutes. I wonder, would you have time to drop Mr. Murtagh?"

The young man said at once, "Oh, I can get a cab, there's no need to trouble yoursel—"

"Oh it's no trouble," she said happily, "no trouble at all. West Point's on my way."

Dunross said good night and left them. They hardly noticed his going. He went to his study and closed the door and with the closing of the door, shut out everything else but Tiptop. From the fireplace Dirk Struan watched him. Dunross stared back a moment.

"I've plan A, B or C," he said aloud. "They all add up to disaster if Sinders doesn't perform."

The eyes just smiled in their curious way.

"It was easy for you," Dunross muttered. "When someone got in your way you could kill them, even the Hag."

Earlier he had discussed the plans with Phillip Chen. "They're all fraught with danger," his compradore had said, very concerned.

"Which do you advise?"

"The choice must be yours, tai-pan. You will have to make personal guarantees. It's face too, though I'd support you in everything, and you did ask for a *favor* as an Old Friend."

"What about Sir Luis?"

"I've arranged to see him tonight, tai-pan. I hope for cooperation." Phillip Chen had seemed grayer and older than ever. "It's a pity there's nothing we can give Tiptop in case Sinders reneges."

"What about bartering the tanker fleet? Can we lean on Vee Cee? What about thoriums—or Joseph Yu?"

"Tiptop needs something to barter with, not a threat, tai-pan. Did P.B. say he'd help?"

"He promised to phone Tiptop this afternoon—he said he'd also try one of his friends in Peking."

At exactly seven o'clock Dunross dialed. "Mr. Tip, please. Ian Dunross."

JAMES CLAVELL

"Good evening, tai-pan. How are you? I hear you may be riding Noble Star next Saturday?"

"That's possible." They talked about inconsequential matters, then Tiptop said, "And that unfortunate person? At the latest, when is he going to be released?"

Dunross held on to himself, then committed his future. "Sunset tomorrow, at Lo Wu."

"Do you personally guarantee he will be there?"

"I personally guarantee I've done everything in my power to persuade the authorities to release him."

"That's not the same as saying the man will be there. Is it?"

"No. But he'll be there. I'm . . ." Dunross stopped. He was going to say, "almost certain" and then he knew he would surely fail—not daring to guarantee it because a failure to perform would take away his face, his credulity, forever—but he remembered something Phillip Chen had said about Tiptop having something to barter with and all at once he had an opening. "Listen, Mr. Tip," he began, his sudden excitement almost nauseating. "These are foul times. Old Friends need Old Friends like never before. Privately, very privately, I hear that our Special Branch in the last two days discovered there's a major Soviet spy ring here, a deep-cover ring, the code name of the operation Sevrin. The purpose of Sevrin's the destruction of the Middle Kingdom's link with the rest of the world."

"That's nothing new, tai-pan. Hegemonists will always be hegemonists, Tsarist Russia or Soviet Russia, there's no difference. For four hundred years it's been that way. Four hundred years since their first incursions and theft of our lands. But please go on."

"It's my belief Hong Kong and the Middle Kingdom are equal targets. We're your only window on the world. Old Green-Eyed Devil was the first to see that and it's true. Any interruption here and only the hegemonists will gain. Some documentation, part of the Special Branch documentation has come into my hands." With complete accuracy Dunross began to quote verbatim from the stolen head documents in AMG's report, his mind seeming to read from the pages that effortlessly appeared from his memory. He gave Tiptop all the pertinent details of Sevrin, the spies, and about the police mole.

There was a shocked silence. "What's the date on the Sevrin head document, tai-pan?"

"It was approved by an 'L.B.' on March 14, 1950."

A long sigh. Very long. "Lavrenti Beria?"

"I don't know." The more Dunross thought about this new ploy the more excited he became, certain now that this information and proof positive in the right Peking hands would cause a tidal wave in Soviet-Chinese relations.

"Is it possible to see this document?"

"Yes. Yes it would be possible," Dunross said, sweat on his back, thanking his foresight in photocopying the Sevrin sections of AMG's report.

"And the Czechoslovak STB document you referred to?"

"Yes. The part I have."

"When was that dated?"

"April 6, 1959."

"So our so-called allies were always wolf's heart and dog's lungs?"

"I'm afraid so."

"Why is it Europe and those capitalists in America don't understand who the real enemy in the world is? *Heya?*"

"It's difficult to understand," Dunross said, playing a waiting game now.

After a pause, controlled once more, Tiptop said, "I'm sure my friends would like a copy of this, this Sevrin paper, and any supporting documents."

Dunross wiped the sweat off his forehead but kept his voice calm. "As an Old Friend, it's my privilege to assist in any way I can."

Another silence. "A mutual friend called to offer his support to your request for the Bank of China's cash and a few minutes ago I was told that a very important person called from Peking to suggest any help that could be given in your need would be merited." Another silence and Dunross could almost feel Tiptop and the others who were probably listening on the phone weighing, nodding or shaking their heads. "Could you excuse me a moment, tai-pan, there's someone at the door."

"Would you like me to call you back?" he said at once to give them time to consider.

"No, that won't be necessary—if you don't mind waiting a moment."

Dunross heard the phone put down. A radio was playing in the background. Indeterminate sounds that might be muffled voices. His heart was racing. The waiting seemed to go on forever. Then the phone was picked up again.

"Sorry, tai-pan. Please send those copies early—would after your morning meeting be convenient?"

"Yes, yes certainly."

"Please give Mr. David MacStruan my best wishes when he arrives."

Dunross almost dropped the phone but recovered in time. "I'm sure he would wish me to return them. How is Mr. Yu?" he asked, stabbing in the dark, wanting to scream down the phone "What about the money?" But he was heavily engaged in a Chinese negotiation. His caution increased.

Another silence. "Fine," Tiptop said but Dunross had heard a different tone. "Oh, that reminds me," Tiptop was saying, "Mr. Yu phoned from Canton this afternoon. He would like to bring the date of your meeting forward, if that's possible. To two weeks tomorrow, Monday."

Dunross thought a moment. That was the week he would be in Japan with Toda Shipping negotiating his whole buy–lease-back scheme that, now that First Central was backing him, would have an enormous chance of success. "That Monday's difficult. The following one would be better for me. Could I confirm to you by Friday?"

"Yes, certainly. Well, I won't keep you anymore, tai-pan."

Dunross's tension became almost unbearable now that the final stage had been reached. He listened intently to the pleasant, friendly voice.

"Thank you for your information. I presume that that poor fellow will be at Lo Wu border by sunset. Oh, by the way, if the necessary bank papers are brought in person by Mr. Havergill, yourself and the governor at 9:00 A.M. tomorrow, a half a billion dollars of cash can be transferred to the Victoria immediately."

Instantly Dunross saw through the ploy. "Thank you," he said easily, avoiding the trap. "Mr. Havergill and I will be there. Unfortunately I understand the governor has been ordered by the prime minister's office to remain at Government House until noon, for consultations. But I will bring his authority and chop, guaranteeing the loan," he added, for of course, it would be impossible for the governor to go personally, cap in hand, like a common debtor and so create an unacceptable precedent. "I presume that will be satisfactory."

Tiptop's voice was almost a purr. "I'm sure the bank would be prepared to delay until noon to accommodate the governor's duty."

"Before and after noon he will be on the streets with the riot police, Mr. Tip, and the army, directing possible procedures against misguided riots stirred up by hegemonists. He is of course commander-in-chief, Hong Kong."

Tiptop's voice sharpened. "Surely even a commander-in-chief can take a few precious moments for what is obviously such an important matter?"

"It would be his pleasure, I'm sure," Dunross said, unafraid, knowing the art of Asian negotiation, prepared for rage, honey and everything in between. "But the protection of the Middle Kingdom's interest as well as that of the Colony would be uppermost in his mind. I'm sure, regretfully, he would have to refuse until the emergency was over."

There was a hostile silence. "Then what would you suggest?"

Again Dunross sidestepped the trap, leaping to the next level. "Oh, by the way, his aide-de-camp asked me to mention that his Excellency is having a party for a few of our most important Chinese citizens at the races next Saturday and he wondered if you would happen to be in the Colony so he could send you an invitation?" He held on to his hope. Putting it that way gave Tiptop the option of accepting or refusing without loss of face—and, at the same time, protected the face of the governor who would thus avoid sending such a politically important invitation that might be refused. Dunross smiled to himself, since the governor knew nothing yet about this important party he would be giving.

Another silence while Tiptop considered the political implications. "Please thank him for his consideration. I believe I will be here. May I confirm it Tuesday?"

"I will be glad to pass your message on." Dunross considered mentioning Brian Kwok but decided to leave that in limbo. "Will you be at the bank at 9:00 A.M., Mr. Tip?"

"Oh no. It is really nothing to do with me. I'm merely an interested bystander." Another silence. "Your representatives should see the chief manager."

Dunross sighed, all his senses honed. No mention of the governor's physical presence. Have I won? "I wonder if someone could confirm to Radio Hong Kong, in time for tonight's nine o'clock news, that the Bank of China is extending the Colony an immediate credit of one half a billion dollars of cash."

Another silence. "Oh I'm sure that's not necessary, Mr. Dunross." Tiptop said and now, for the first time, there was a chuckle in his voice. "Surely the word of the tai-pan of the Noble House is sufficient for a simple capitalist radio station. Good night."

Dunross put down the phone. His fingers were trembling. There was an ache in his back and his heart was pounding. "Half a billion dollars!" he muttered, his mind blown. "No paper, no chop, no handshake, a few phone calls, a little negotiation and one half a billion dollars *will be* available for transfer by truck at 9:00 A.M.!"

We've won! Murtagh's money and now China's! Yes. But how to use this knowledge to the best advantage? How? he asked himself helplessly. No point in going to Plumm's now. What to do? What to do?

His knees felt weak, his mind was buzzing with plan and counterplan. Then his pent-up excitement erupted in a huge bellow that ricocheted off his study walls, and he jumped up and down and let out another war cry that melted into a laugh. He went into the bathroom to splash water on his face. He ripped off his soaking shirt, not bothering about the buttons and threw it into a trash can. The study door whirled open. Adryon rushed in, white-faced and anxious. "Father!"

"Good God what's up?" Dunross said, aghast.

"What's up with you? I heard you shout like a mad bull. Are you all right?"

"Oh, oh yes I'm, I, er, I just stubbed my toe!" Dunross's happiness exploded again and he caught her up, lifting her easily. "Thank you, my darling, everything's fine! Oh very fine!"

"Oh, thank God," she said and at once added, "Then I can have my own flat starting next month?"

"Ye—" He caught himself just in time. "Oh no you don't, Miss Smarty Pants. Just because I'm happy th—"

"But Father, do—"

"No. Thank you, Adryon, but no. Off you go!"

She glared at him then burst out laughing. "I almost caught you that time!"

"Yes, yes you did! Don't forget Duncan's in tomorrow on the Qantas noon flight."

"I won't, don't worry. I'll meet him. It'll be fun to have Dunc back, haven't had a good game of billiards since he left. Where're you off to now?"

"I was going to Plumm's at Rose Court to celebrate the General Foods takeover but I don't th—"

"Martin thought that was a wonderful coup! If the stock market doesn't crash. I told the silly man you were bound to arrange everything."

All at once Dunross realized that Plumm's party would be the ideal place. Gornt would be there, Phillip Chen and all the others. Gornt! Now I can put that bugger away for all time, he told himself, his heart racing. "Is Murtagh still downstairs?"

"Oh yes. We were just leaving. He's dreamy."

Dunross turned away to hide a smile and grabbed a clean silk shirt. "Could you hang on a second? I've got some rather good news for him."

"All right." She came over to him, big blue eyes. "My own flat for a Christmas present, pretty please?"

"After university, if you qualify, off you go!"

"Christmas. I'll love you forever."

He sighed, remembering how upset and frightened she had been seeing Gornt in the billiards room. Perhaps I can give you a present of his head tomorrow, he thought. "Not this Christmas, next!"

She hurled her arms around his neck. "Oh thank you Daddy darling but this Christmas, please please please."

"No, because yo—"

"Please please please!"

"All right. But don't tell your mother I agreed for God's sake! She'll skin me alive!"

78

The curtains around Orlanda's bed moved gently, touched by the night breeze, the air clean and salt tasting. She was in his arms as they slept, a pervading warmth between them, and then, as her hand moved, Bartlett awoke. For a moment he wondered where he was and who he was, and then everything came back and his heart picked up a beat. Their lovemaking had been wonderful. He remembered how she had responded, cresting again and again, lifting him to heights he had never experienced before. And then the after. She had got out of bed and walked to the kitchen and warmed water and brought back a hot, wet towel and toweled the sweat off him. "I'm so sorry there's no bath or shower, my darling, that's such a shame, but if you're patient I can make everything nice."

A new clean towel and feeling grand, never before knowing the wonder of a real afterward—her gentle ministrations, tender, loving, unself-conscious, the tiny crucifix around her neck her only adornment. He had noticed it glinting in the half-light. Its implications had begun to seep into his brain but somehow all, at once, she was caressing the alien thoughts away with magic hands and touch and lips until, in time, they had both become one with the gods again and, through their generosity, slid into euphoria—and thence into sleep again.

Idly he watched the curtains that fell from the ceiling waver in the air currents, their surrounding embrace making the bed more intimate, the patterns against the light of the window pleasing, everything pleasing. He lay still, not wishing to move to awaken her, not wanting to break the spell, her breath soft against his chest, her sleep face blemishless.

What to do, what to do, what to do?

Nothing, for the moment, he answered himself. The airplane's free, you're free, she's unbelievable and no woman's ever pleased you more. Never. But can it last, could it last—and then there's Casey.

Bartlett sighed. Orlanda moved again in her sleep. He waited but she did not awaken.

His eyes were mesmerized by the patterns, his spirit at rest. It was neither hot nor cold in the room; everything was perfect, her weight imperceptible. What is it about her? he asked himself. What causes the spell, because sure as death and taxes you're under a spell, enchanted. We've pillowed, that's all, I've made no promises and yet . . . You're enchanted, old buddy.

Yes. And it's wonderful.

He closed his eyes and drifted into sleep.

When Orlanda awoke she was careful not to move. She did not want to awaken him, both for his pleasure and for hers. And she wanted time to think. Sometimes she would do that in Gornt's arms but she knew it was not the same, would never be the same. Always she had been afraid of Quillan, on guard, desperately wanting to please, wondering if she had forgotten anything. No, she thought in ecstasy, this pillowing was better than I ever remember it with Quillan, oh so much better. Linc's so clean and no smoke taste, just clean and wonderful and I promise by the Madonna I will make him a perfect wife, I'll be the best that ever was. I will use my mind and hands and lips and body to please and to satisfy and there will be nothing he needs that I will not do. Nothing. Everything that Quillan taught me I will do for Linc, even the things I did not enjoy, I will enjoy now with Linc. My body and soul will be an instrument for his pleasure, and for mine, when he's learned.

She smiled to herself, curled up in his arms. Linc's technique is nothing in comparison with Quillan's but what my darling lacks in skill he more than makes up with strength and vigor. And tenderness. He has magic hands and lips for me. Never never never before was it ever like this.

"Pillowing's just the beginning of sex, Orlanda," Gornt had said. "You can become an enchantress. You can fill a man with such an unquenchable longing that, through you, he will understand all life." But to reach ecstasy you have to seek it and work for it.

Oh I will seek it for Linc. By the Madonna I will put my mind and my heart and my soul to his life. When he's angry I will turn it into calm. Didn't I stop Quillan's anger a thousand times by being gentle? Isn't it wonderful to have so much power, and oh so easy once I had learned, so very easy and perfect and satisfying.

I will read all the best papers and train my mind, and after the Clouds and the Rain I will not speak, just caress, not to arouse but just for pleasure and I'll never say, "Tell me you love me!" but say only, "Linc I love you." And long before the bloom is off my skin I will have sons to excite him and daughters to delight him and then, long before I'm no longer exciting to him, I will very carefully arrange another for his pleasure, a dullard with beautiful breasts and tight rump and I will be suitably amused and benign—and compassionate when he fails, for, by then he will be much older and less virile and my hands will control the money and I will be ever more essential. And when he tires of the first I will find another, and we will live out our lives, yang and yin, the yin ever dominating the yang!

Yes. I will be *tai-tai*.

And one day he will ask to go to Portugal to see my daughter and I will refuse the first time and the second and the third and then we will go—if I have our son in my arms. Then he will see *her* and love *her* too, and that specter will be laid to rest forever.

Orlanda sighed, feeling wonderful, weightless, with his head resting comfortably against her chest. Pillowing without precautions is so much more glorious, she thought. Ecstasy. Oh so wonderful to feel the surge, knowing you're young and fertile and ready, giving yourself totally, deliberately, praying to create a new life—his life and yours joined forever. Oh yes.

Yes but have you been wise? Have you? Say he leaves you? The only other time in your life you deliberately left yourself free was that single month with Quillan. But that was with permission. This time you have none.

Say Linc leaves you. Perhaps he'll be furious and tell you to stop the child!

He won't, she told herself with complete confidence. Linc's not Quillan. There's nothing to worry about. Nothing. Madonna, please help me! All gods help me! Let his seed grow, oh please please please, I beg you with all my heart.

Bartlett stirred and half awoke. "Orlanda?"

"Yes, my darling, I'm here. Oh how wonderful you are!" She cradled him happily, so glad that she had given her *amah* the day and the night away. "Go back to sleep, we've all the time in the world, sleep."

"Yes but . . ."

"Sleep. In a little while I'm going to fetch some Chinese food an—"

"Maybe you'd like t—"

"Sleep, my darling. Everything's arranged."

79

7:30 P.M.:

Three stories below on the other side of the building, facing the mountainside, Four Finger Wu was watching television. He was in Venus Poon's apartment, in front of her set, his shoes off, his tie loose, sprawled in the easy chair. The old *amah* was sitting on a stiff chair beside him and they both guffawed at the antics of Laurel and Hardy.

"Eeeeee, the Fat One's going to catch his fornicating foot in the scaffolding," he chortled, "and the—"

"And the Thin One's going to hit him with the plank! Eeeeee."

They both laughed at the routine they had seen a hundred times in a hundred re-re-reruns of the old black-and-white movies. Then the film ended and Venus Poon reappeared to announce the next program and he sighed. She was looking directly at him from the box and he—along with every other male viewer—was certain that her smile was for him alone, and though he did not understand her English, he understood her very well. His eyes were glued to her breasts that had fascinated him for hours, examining them closely, never seeing or feeling a sign of the surgical interference that all Hong Kong whispered about.

"I attest your tits are blemishless, certainly the biggest and best I've ever touched," he had volunteered importantly, still mounted, the night before last.

"You're just saying that to please your poor impoverished Daughter oh oh oh!"

"Impoverished? Ha! Didn't Banker Kwang give you that miserable fur yesterday and I hear he added an extra 1,000 to his monthly check! And *me*, didn't I supply the winner of the first, third and the runner-up in the fifth? 30,000 those brought you minus 15 percent for my informant—for less effort than it takes me to fart!"

"P'shaw! That 25,800 HK's not worth talking about, I have to buy my own wardrobe, a new costume every day! My public demands it, I have my public to think of."

They had argued back and forth until, feeling the moment of truth approaching, he had asked her to move her buttocks more vigorously. She had obliged with such enthusiasm that he was left a husk. When at length he had miraculously recovered his spirit from the Void he choked out, "*Ayeeyah*, Little Strumpet, if you can do that one more time I'll give you a diamond ring the—no, no, not now by all the gods! Am I a god? Not now, Little Mealy Mouth, no, not now and not tomorrow but the next day. . . ."

And now it was the next day. Elated and filled with anticipation he watched her on television, all smiles and dimples as she said good night and the new program began. Tonight was her early night and in his mind he could almost see her hurry out of the TV station to his waiting Rolls, sure that she would be just as anxious. He had sent Paul Choy with the Rolls to escort her to the station tonight, to talk English with her, to ensure she arrived safely and returned quickly. And then, after their new bout, the Rolls would take them to the barbarian eating palace in the barbarian hotel with its foul barbarian food and foul smells but one of the places where all the tai-pans go, and all important, civilized persons go with their wives—and, when their wives were busy, with their whores—so he could show off his mistress and how rich he was to all Hong Kong, and she could show off the diamond.

"*Ayeeyah*," he chortled out loud.

"Eh, Honored Lord?" the *amah* asked suspiciously. "What's amiss?"

"Nothing, nothing. Please give me some brandy."

"My mistress doesn't like the brandy smell!"

"Huh, old woman, give me brandy. Am I a fool? Am I a barbarian from the Outer Provinces? Of course I have fragrant tea leaves to chew before our bout. Brandy!"

She went off grumbling but he paid her no attention—she was just trying to protect her mistress's interests and that was perfectly correct.

His fingers touched the small box in his pocket. He had purchased the ring this morning, wholesale, from a first cousin who owed him a favor. The stone was worth 48,000 at least though the real cost was barely half that amount, the quality blue-white and excellent, the carats substantial.

Another bout like the last one will be well worth it, he thought ecstatically, though a little uneasily. Oh yes. Eeee, that last time I thought my spirit was truly gone forever into the Void, taken by the gods at the height of all life! Eeee, how lucky I would be to go thence, at that exact moment! Yes, but more wonderful to come back to storm the Jade Gate again and again and once more!

He laughed out loud, daring the gods, very content. Today had been excellent for him. He had met secretly with Smuggler Yuen and White Powder Lee and they had elected him chief of their new Brotherhood, which was only right, he thought. Hadn't he supplied the link to the marketplace through the foreign devil Ban—whatever his name was—because he had lent money to Number One Son Chen who, in return for such favors, had proposed the gun into opium scheme to him but had had the stupidity to be kidnapped and now murdered? Oh yes. And wasn't he meeting with the same foreign devil in Macao next week to arrange finances, payments, to set into motion the whole vast operation? Of course he should be High Tiger, of course he should have the most profit! With their combined expertise—and Profitable Choy's modern techniques—he could revolutionize the smuggling of the opium into Hong Kong, and once here, revolutionize the conversion of the raw narcotic into the immensely profitable White Powders, and finally, the means of export to the markets of the world. Now that Paul Choy was already in the shipping and air freighting department of Second Big Company and two grandsons of Yuen, also American trained, in their customs broking operation—and another four English university-trained relations of White Powder Lee placed within Noble House's Kai Tak go-down operations and All Asia Air's loading and unloading division, imports and exports would be ever safer, easier and ever more profitable.

They had discussed who they would co-opt in the police, particularly Marine.

"None of the barbarians, never one of those fornicators," White Powder Lee had said hotly. "They won't support us, never. Not in drugs. We must use only the Dragons."

"Agreed. All the Dragons have all been approached and all will cooperate. All except Tang-po of Kowloon."

"We must have Kowloon, he's senior and Marine operates from there. Is he holding out for a better deal personally? Or is he against us?"

"I don't know. At the moment." Four Fingers had shrugged. "Tang-po is up to the High Dragon to solve. The High Dragon has agreed, so it is agreed."

Yes, Four Fingers thought, I outsmarted them to make me High Tiger and I outsmarted Profitable Choy on my money. I didn't give the young fornicator control of my fortune to gamble with as he thought I would. Oh no! I'm not that much of a fool! I only let him have 2 million and promised him 17 percent of all profit—let's see what he can do with that. Yes. Let's see what he can do with that!

The old man's heart picked up and he scratched himself. I'll bet the cunning young man'll triple it within the week, he told himself gleefully, not a little awed—the diamond paid for by his son's wits from the first profit on the stock sale, and a year of Venus Poon already allocated from the same source and not a copper cash of his own capital to lay out! Eeeee! And the cunning schemes Profitable comes up with! Like the one to deal with the tai-pan tomorrow when we meet.

Anxiously his fingers reached up and touched the half-coin that was on the heavy thong around his neck under his shirt, a coin like that his illustrious ancestor, Wu Fang Choi, had called upon to claim a clipper ship to rival the finest in Dirk Struan's fleet. But Wu Fang Choi, he thought grimly, had been the fool—he had never demanded safe passage for the ship as part of his favor and so had been outsmarted by the Green-Eyed Devil, the tai-pan.

Yes, by all the gods, it was Wu Fang Choi's own fault he lost. But he didn't lose everything. He hunted down that hunchback called Stride Orlov who ruled the ships of the Noble House for Culum the Weak. His men caught Orlov ashore in Singapore and brought him in chains to Taiwan where his headquarters were. There he tied him to a post, just at high-water mark, and drowned him very slowly.

I won't be foolish like Wu Fang Choi. No. I will make sure my ask from this tai-pan is watertight.

Tomorrow, the tai-pan will agree to open his ships to my cargoes—secretly of course; will agree to open some of the Noble House accounts for me to hide in—secretly of course, though to his great profit; will agree, equally secretly, to finance with me the vast new pharmaceutical plant that, *oh ko*, Profitable Choy says will be the perfect, legitimate undetectable narcotic smoke screen for me and mine forever; and last, the tai-pan will intercede with the half-person, Lando Mata, and choose my name and my suggested syndicate to replace the existing Macao gold and gambling syndicate of Tightfist Tung and the Chin, and he, the tai-pan, he will promise to be part of it.

Four Finger Wu was filled with ecstasy. The tai-pan will have to agree to everything. Everything. And everything is within his fief.

"Here's the brandy."

Four Finger Wu took it from the *amah* and sipped it dreamily, with vast enjoyment. All gods bear witness: For seventy-six years, I, Four Finger Wu, Head of the Seaborne Wu, have lived life to the full and if you gods will take my spirit during the Clouds and the Rain, I will sing your praises in heaven—if there is a heaven—forever more. And if you don't . . .

The old man shrugged to himself and beamed and curled his toes. He yawned and closed his eyes, warm and toasty and very happy. Gods are gods and gods sleep and make mistakes but as sure as the great storms will come this year and next, Little Strumpet will earn her diamond tonight. Now which way should it be, he asked himself, going to sleep.

The taxi stopped at the foyer below. Suslev got out drunkenly and paid the man, then, reeling slightly, stepped over the rainwater swirling in the gutters and went in.

There was a crowd of people chattering and waiting at the elevator and he recognized Casey and Jacques deVille among them. Unsteadily he belched his way down the stairs to the lower level, crossed the garage and banged on Clinker's door.

"Hello, matey," Clinker said.

"*Tovarich!*" Suslev gave him a bear hug.

"Vodka's up! Beer's up. Mabel, say hello to the captain!" The sleepy old bulldog just opened one eye, chomped her gums and farted loudly.

Clinker sighed and shut the door. "Poor old Mabel! Wish to Christ she wouldn't do that, the place gets proper niffy! Here." He handed Suslev a full glass of water with a wink. "It's your favorite, old mate. 120 proof."

Suslev winked back and slurped the water loudly. "Thanks, old shipmate. Another of these'n I'll sail away from this capitalist paradise happily!"

"Another of those," Clinker guffawed, keeping up the pretense, "an' you'll slip out'uv Hong Kong harbor on your knees!" He refilled the glass. "How long you staying tonight?"

"Just had to have some last drinks with you, eh? So long as I leave here by ten I'm fine. Drink up!" he roared with forced bonhomie. "Let's have some music, eh?"

Happily Clinker turned on the tape recorder, loud. The sad Russian ballad filled the room.

Suslev put his lips close to Clinker's ear. "Thanks, Ernie. I'll be back in good time."

"All right." Clinker winked, still believing Suslev's cover that he had an assignation with a married woman in Sinclair Towers. "Who is she, eh?" He had never asked before.

"No names, no pack drill," Suslev whispered with a broad grin. "But her husband's a nob, a capitalist swine and on the legislature!"

Clinker beamed. "Smashing! Give her one for me, eh?"

Suslev went down the trapdoor and found the flashlight. Water dripped from the cracked concrete roof of the tunnel, the cracks bigger than before. Small avalanches of rubble made the floor precarious and slippery. His nervousness increased, not liking the closeness, nor the necessity to go to meet Crosse, wanting to be far away, safe on his ship with a complete alibi when Dunross was drugged and snatched. But Crosse had been adamant.

"Goddamn it, Gregor, you have to be there! I've got to see you in person and I'm certainly not going aboard the *Ivanov*. It's perfectly safe, I guarantee it!"

Guarantee? Suslev thought angrily again. How can one guarantee anything? He took out the snub-nosed automatic with the silencer, checked it and clicked off the safety catch. Then he continued again, picking his way carefully, and climbed the ladder to the false cupboard. Once on the stairs, he stopped and listened, holding his breath, all his concentration seeking danger. Finding none, he began to breathe easier, went up the stairs silently and into the apartment. Light from the high rise just below and from the city came through the windows and illuminated everything well enough for him to see. He checked the apartment thoroughly. When he had finished he went to the refrigerator and opened a bottle of beer. Absently he stared out of the windows. From where he was he could not see his ship but he knew where she would be and that thought gave him another good feeling. I'll be glad to leave, he thought. And sorry. I want to come back—Hong Kong's too good—but can I?

What about Sinders? Dare I trust him?

Suslev's heart hurt in his chest. Without a doubt, his future was in the balance. It would be easy for his own KGB people to prove he had fingered Metkin. Center could get that out of Roger Crosse by a simple phone call—if they hadn't already come to the same conclusion themselves.

May Sinders rot in hell! I know he'll shop me—I would if I was him. Will Roger know the secret deal Sinders put to me? No. Sinders would keep that secret, secret even from Roger. It doesn't matter. Once I've passed *anything* over to the other side I'm in his power forever.

The minutes ticked by. There was the sound of an elevator. At once he went into a defensive position. His finger slid the safety catch off: a key turned in the lock. The door opened and closed quickly.

"Hello, Gregor," Crosse said softly. "I wish you wouldn't point that bloody thing at me."

Suslev put the safety catch on. "What's so important? What about that turd Sinders? What'd he—"

"Calm down and listen." Crosse took out a roll of microfilm, his pale blue eyes unusually excited. "Here's a gift. It's expensive but all the real AMG files're on that film."

"Eh?" Suslev stared at him. "But how?" He listened as Crosse told him about the vault, ending, "and after Dunross left I photographed the files and put them back."

"Is the film developed?"

"Oh yes. I made one print which I read and at once destroyed. That's safer than giving it to you and risk your being stopped and searched—Sinders is on the warpath. What the devil happened between you and him?"

"First tell me about the files, Roger."

"Sorry, but they're the same as the other ones, word for word. No difference."

"What?"

"Yes. Dunross was telling us the truth. The copies he gave us are exact patterns."

Suslev was shocked. "But we were sure, you were sure!"

Crosse shrugged and passed over the film. "Here's your proof."

Suslev swore obscenely.

Crosse watched him and kept his face grave, hiding his amusement. The real files are far too valuable to pass over—yet—he told himself again. Oh yes. Now's not the time. In due course, Gregor old chap, parts will bring a very great price. And all that knowledge will have to be sifted and offered very carefully indeed. And as to the eleven pieces of code—whatever the devil they mean—they should be worth a fortune, in due course. "I'm afraid this time we've drawn a blank, Gregor."

"But what about Dunross?" Suslev was ashen. He looked at his watch. "Perhaps he's already in the crate?" He saw Crosse shrug, the lean face etched in the half-light.

"There's no need to interrupt that plan," Crosse said. "I've considered that whole operation very carefully. I agree with Jason it'll be good to shake up Hong Kong. Dunross's kidnapping will create all sorts of waves. With the bank runs and the stock market crash—yes it would help us very much. I'm rather worried. Sinders is sniffing around too closely and asking me all sorts of wrong questions. Then there's the Metkin affair, Voranski, the AMG papers, you—too many mistakes. Pressure needs to be taken off Sevrin. Dunross'll do that admirably."

"You're sure?" Suslev asked, needing reassurance.

"Yes. Oh yes, Dunross will do very nicely thank you. He's the decoy. I'll need all the help I can get. You're going to shop Arthur. Aren't you?"

Suslev saw the eyes boring into him and his heart almost stopped but he kept his shock off his face. Just. "I'm glad Sinders told you about our meeting. That saves me the trouble. How can I get out of his trap?"

"How're *you* going to avoid it?"

"I don't know, Roger. Will Sinders do what he threatened?"

Crosse snapped, "Come on, for God's sake! Wouldn't you?"

"What can I do?"

"It's your neck or Arthur's. If it's Arthur's, then the next neck could be mine." There was a long, violent pause and Suslev felt the hair on the nape of his neck twist. "So long as it's not mine—and I know what's going on in advance—I don't care."

Suslev looked back at him. "You want a drink?"

"You know I don't drink."

"I meant water—or soda." The big man went to the refrigerator and took out the vodka bottle and drank from the bottle. "I'm glad Sinders told you."

"For chrissake, Gregor, where've your brains gone? Of course he didn't tell me—the fool still thinks it was a secret, private deal, just you and him, of course he does! Good sweet Christ, this's my bailiwick! I maneuvered him into a room that I'd bugged. Am I a simpleton?" The eyes hardened even more and Suslev felt his chest tighten unbearably. "So it's a simple choice, Gregor. It's you or Arthur. If you shop him I'm in danger and so's everyone else. If you don't concede to Sinders you're finished. Of the two choices I'd prefer you dead—and me, Arthur and Sevrin safe."

"The best solution's that I betray Arthur," Suslev said. "But that before they catch him he flees. He can come aboard the *Ivanov*. Eh?"

"Sinders'll be ahead of you and he'll stop you in Hong Kong waters."

"That's possible. Not probable. I'd resist a boarding at sea." Suslev watched him, the bile in his mouth. "It's that or Arthur commits suicide—or is eliminated."

Crosse stared at him. "You must be joking! You want me to send Jason into the Great Hereafter?"

"You said yourself, it's someone's neck. Listen, at the moment we're just examining possibilities. But it's a fact you're not expendable. Arthur is. The others. I am," Suslev said, meaning it. "So whatever happens it mustn't be you—and preferably not me. I never did like the idea of dying." He took another swig of the vodka and felt the lovely, stomach-warming sensation, then turned his eyes back on his ally. "You are an ally, aren't you?"

"Yes. Oh yes. So long as the money keeps up and I enjoy the game."

"If you *believed*, you would live a longer and better life, *tovarich*."

"The only thing that keeps me alive is that I don't. You and your KGB friends can try and take over the world, infiltrate capitalism and any other ism you like, for whatever purpose you admit, or enjoy, and meanwhile, I shall jolly you along."

"What does that mean?"

"It's an old English expression that means to help," Crosse said dryly. "So you're going to shop Arthur?"

"I don't know. Could you lay a false trail to the airport to give us time to escape Hong Kong waters?"

"Yes, but Sinders has already doubled surveillance there."

"What about Macao?"

"I could do that. I don't like it. What about the others of Sevrin?"

"Let them burrow deeper, we close everything down. You take over Sevrin and we activate again once the storm subsides. Could deVille become tai-pan after Dunross?"

"I don't know. I think it'll be Gavallan. Incidentally, two more Were-wolf victims were discovered out at Sha Tin this morning."

Suslev's hope quickened and some of his dread left him. "What happened?"

Crosse told him how they were found. "We're still trying to identify the poor buggers. Gregor, shopping Arthur's dicey, whatever happens. It might spill back to me. Perhaps with the stock market crashing, the banks all messed up and Dunross vanishing, it might be cover enough. It might."

Suslev nodded. His nausea increased. The decision had to be made. "Roger, I'm going to do nothing. I'm just going to leave and take the chance. I'll, I'll make a private report to forestall Sinders and tell Center what happened. Whatever Sinders does, well, that's up to the future. I've got friends in high places too. Perhaps the Hong Kong disaster and having Dunross—I'll do the chemical debrief myself anyway, just in case he's cheating us and is as clever as you say he is . . . what is it?"

"Nothing. What about Koronski?"

"He left this morning after I got all the chemicals. I rescheduled the debrief to be on the *Ivanov*, not ashore. Why?"

"Nothing. Go on."

"Perhaps the Hong Kong debacle'll placate my superiors." Now that Suslev had made the decision he felt a little better. "Send an urgent report to Center through the usual channels to Berlin. Get Arthur to do the same by radio tonight. Make the report very pro-me, eh? Blame the Metkin affair on the CIA here, the carrier leak, Voranski. Eh? Blame the CIA and the Kuomintang."

"Certainly. For a double fee. By the way, Gregor, if I were you I'd clean my prints off that bottle."

"Eh?"

Sardonically Crosse told him about Rosemont filching the glass in the raid and how, months ago, to protect Suslev he had extracted his prints from his dossier.

The Russian was white. "The CIA have my prints on file?"

"Only if they've a better dossier than ours. I doubt that."

"Roger, I expect you to cover my back."

"Don't worry, I'll make the report so lily-white they'll promote you. In return you recommend my bonus's 100,000 dol—"

"That's too much!"

"That's the fee! I'm getting you out of one helluva mess." The mouth smiled, the eyes did not. "It's fortunate we're professionals. Isn't it?"

"I'll—I'll try."

"Good. Wait here. Clinker's phone's bugged. I'll phone from Jason's flat the moment I know about Dunross." Crosse put out his hand. "Good luck, I'll do what I can with Sinders."

"Thanks." Suslev gave him a bear hug. "Good luck to you too, Roger. Don't fail me on Dunross."

"We won't fail."

"And keep up the good work, eh?"

"Tell your friends to keep up the money. Eh?"

"Yes." Suslev closed the door behind Crosse, then wiped the palms of his hands on his trousers and took out the roll of film. Quietly he cursed it and Dunross and Hong Kong and Sinders, the specter of the KGB questioning him about Metkin swamping him. Somehow I've got to avoid that, he told himself, the cold sweat running down his back. Perhaps I should shop Arthur after all. How to do it, and keep Roger in the clear? There must be a way.

Outside on the landing, Roger Crosse got into the elevator and pressed the ground-floor button. Alone now he leaned exhaustedly against the rickety walls and shook his head to try to get the fear out. "Stop it!" he muttered. With an effort he dominated himself and lit a cigarette, noticing his fingers were trembling. If that bugger chemical debriefs Dunross, he told himself, I'm up the creek. And I'll bet fifty dollars to a pile of dung Suslev still hasn't ruled out the possibility of shopping Plumm. And if he does that, Christ my whole pack of cards can come tumbling down about my ears. One mistake, one tiny slip and I'm finished.

The elevator stopped. Some Chinese got in noisily but he did not notice them.

On the ground floor, Rosemont was waiting.

"And?"

"Nothing, Stanley."

"You and your hunches, Rog."

"You never know, Stanley, there might have been something," Crosse said, trying to get his mind working. He had invented the hunch and invited Rosemont along—to wait below—the ruse just to throw off Rosemont's CIA men he knew were still watching the foyer.

"You all right, Rog?"

"Oh yes. Yes, thanks. Why?"

Rosemont shrugged. "You want a coffee or a beer?" They walked out into the night. Rosemont's car was waiting outside.

"No thanks. I'm going there." Crosse pointed to Rose Court, the highrise that loomed over them on the road above. "It's a cocktail party obligation." He felt his fear welling again. What the hell do I do now?

"What's up, Rog?"

"Nothing."

"Rose Court, huh? Maybe I should get me an apartment there. Rosemont of Rose Court."

"Yes." Crosse mustered his strength. "Do you want to come down to the dock to see the *Ivanov* off?"

"Sure, why not? I'm glad you sent that mother packing." Rosemont stifled a yawn. "We broke that computer bastard tonight. Seems he had all sorts of secrets stacked away."

"What?"

"Bits and pieces about the *Corregidor*, her top speed, where her nukes come from, their arming codes, things like that. I'll give you a rundown tonight. You pick me up at midnight, okay?"

"Yes, yes all right." Crosse turned and hurried off. Rosemont frowned after him, then looked up at Rose Court. Lights blazed from all of the twelve floors. Again the American put his eyes back on Crosse, a small figure now in the dark as he turned the corner, climbing the steep curling roadway.

What's with Rog? he asked himself thoughtfully. Something's wrong.

80

Roger Crosse got out of the elevator on the fifth floor, his face taut, and
went through the open door into the Asian Properties apartment. The
large room was crowded and noisy. He stood at the doorway, his eyes
ranging the guests, seeking Plumm or Dunross. At once he noticed that
there was little happiness here, an air of gloom over most of the guests,
and this added to his disquiet. Few wives were present—the few that were
stood uneasily grouped together at the far end. Everywhere conversation
was heated about the coming debacle of the stock market crash and bank
runs.

"Oh, come on for chrissake, it's all very well for the Victoria to announce a multimillion takeover of the Ho-Pak but where's the cash to
keep us all afloat?"

"It was a merger, not a takeover, Dunstan," Richard Kwang began, "the
Ho-Pak's n—"

Barre's face was suddenly choleric. "For chrissake, Richard, we're all
friends here and we all know there's more in it than a bail-out, for God's
sake. Are we children? My point," Barre said, raising his voice louder to
drown Richard Kwang and Johnjohn out, "my point, old boy, is that
merger or not, we the businessmen of Hong Kong, can't stay afloat if all
you bloody banks have stupidly run out of cash. Eh?"

"It's not our fault, for God's sake," Johnjohn rapped. "It's just a temporary loss of confidence."

"Bloody mismanagement if you ask me," Barre replied sourly to general
agreement, then noticed Crosse trying to pass. "Oh, oh hello, Roger!" he
said with a pasty smile.

Roger Crosse saw the immediate caution that was normal whenever he
caught anyone unawares. "Is Ian here?"

"No. No, not yet," Johnjohn said and Crosse exhaled, wet with relief.
"You're sure?"

"Oh yes. Soon as he arrives I'm leaving," Dunstan said sourly. "Bloody banks! If it wasn't—"

Johnjohn interrupted, "What about those bloody Werewolves, Roger?" The discovery of the two bodies had been the lead item of Radio Hong Kong and all Chinese newspapers—there being no afternoon English Sunday papers.

"I know nothing more than you do," Crosse told them. "We're still trying to identify the victims." His eyes zeroed in on Richard Kwang, who quailed. "You don't know of any sons or nephews, missing or kidnapped, do you, Richard?"

"No, no sorry, Roger, no."

"If you'll excuse me, I'd better see our host." Crosse pushed his way through the crush. "Hello, Christian," he said, easing past the tall, thin editor of the *Guardian*. He saw the desolation the man desperately tried to hide. "Sorry about your wife."

"Joss," Christian Toxe said, attempting to sound calm, and stood in his way. "Joss, Roger. She, well, she'd . . . life has to go on, doesn't it?" His forced smile was almost grotesque. "The *Guardian* has to do its work, eh?"

"Yes."

"Can I have a word later?"

"Certainly—off the record, as always?"

"Of course."

He went on, passing Pugmire and Sir Luis deep in conversation about the General Stores–Struan takeover and noticed Casey in the center of a group on the wide balcony overlooking the harbor, deVille among them, Gornt also part of the group, looking benign, which Crosse found strange. "Hello, Jason," he said coming up behind Plumm who was talking with Joseph Stern and Phillip Chen. "Thanks for inviting me."

"Oh. Oh hello, Roger. Glad you could come."

"Evening," he said to the others. "Jason, where's your guest of honor?"

"Ian phoned to say he'd been delayed but was on his way. He'll be here any moment." Plumm's tension was evident. "The, er, the champagne's ready, and my little speech. Everything's ready," he said, watching him. "Come along, Roger, let me get you a drink. It's Perrier, isn't it? I've got some on ice."

Crosse followed him, equally glad for the opportunity to talk privately but just as they reached the kitchen door there was a momentary hush. Dunross was at the door with Riko, Gavallan beside them. All three were beaming.

"Listen, Jason, I—" Crosse stopped. Plumm had already turned back to the bar and if he hadn't been watching very carefully he would never have seen Plumm's left hand deftly break the tiny vial over one of the filled champagne glasses, then palm the shreds back into his pocket, pick up the tray with four glasses on it and head for the door. Fascinated, he watched Plumm come up to Dunross and offer the champagne.

Dunross let Riko take a glass, then Gavallan. Without any apparent prompting Dunross took the doctored glass. Plumm took the last, giving the tray to an embarrassed waiter. "Welcome, Ian, and congratulations on the coup," Plumm said, casually toasting him, not making a big thing of it. Those nearby politely followed suit. Dunross of course did not drink his own toast.

"Now, perhaps you should toast Richard Kwang and Johnjohn and their merger?" Plumm said, his voice sounding strange.

"Why not?" Dunross replied with a laugh and glanced across the room at Johnjohn. "Bruce," he called out, raising his glass, and there was a small hole in the general level of noise. "Here's to the Victoria!" His voice picked up power and cut through neatly. Others glanced over and stopped in midsentence. "Perhaps everyone should share the toast. I've just heard the Bank of China's agreed to lend you and the other banks half a billion in cash in good time for Monday's opening."

There was a sudden vast silence. Those on the balcony came into the room, Gornt to the fore. "What?"

"I've just heard the Bank of China's lending Hong Kong—lending the Vic to lend to other banks—half a billion in cash and as much more as you want. All bank runs're over!" Dunross raised his glass. "To the Victoria!"

As pandemonium broke out and everyone started asking questions, Crosse got his feet into motion and the moment before Dunross could drink, appeared to stumble and collided with him, knocking the glass out of his hand. It shattered as it hit the parquet flooring. "Oh Christ, I'm sorry," he said apologetically.

Plumm stared at him appalled. "For chrissa—"

"Ah, Jason, I'm so sorry," Crosse overrode him, adding more quickly as a waiter hastily retrieved the pieces, "Perhaps you'd get Ian another glass."

"Er, yes, but . . ." Numbly Plumm went to obey but stopped as Riko said, "Oh, here, tai-pan, please to take mine." Then Johnjohn shouted over the uproar, "Quiet, quiet a moment!" and pushed over to Dunross. "Ian," he said in the utter silence, "you're sure? Sure about the cash?"

"Oh yes," Dunross replied leisurely, sipping Riko's drink, enjoying the moment. "Tiptop called me personally. It'll be on the nine o'clock news."

There was a sudden great cheer and more questions and answers and Dunross saw Gornt staring at him from across the room. His smile hardened and he raised his glass, paying no attention to the barrage of questions. "Your health, Quillan!" he called out, mocking him. Quickly conversation died again. Everyone's attention zeroed on them.

Gornt toasted him back, equally mocking. "Your health, Ian. We've really got China's money?"

"Yes, and by the way, I've just arranged a new revolving fund of 50 million U.S. Now the Noble House's the soundest hong in the Colony."

"Secured by what?" Gornt's voice slashed through the abrupt silence.

"The honor of the Noble House!" With a nonchalance he did not feel,

Dunross turned on Johnjohn. "The loan's from the Royal Belgium, a subsidiary of First Central of New York and backed by them." Deliberately he did not look back at Gornt as he repeated, enjoying greatly the sound, "50 million U.S. Oh by the way, Bruce, tomorrow I'm retiring your loans on both my ships. I no longer need the Vic loan—Royal Belgium's given me better terms."

Johnjohn just stared at him.

"You're joking!"

"No. I've just talked to Paul." Momentarily Dunross glanced at Plumm. "Sorry, Jason, that was why I was late. Naturally I had to see him. Bruce, old fellow, Paul's already down at the bank making arrangements for the transfer of China's cash in time for opening—he asked if you'd go there, at once."

"Eh?"

"At once. Sorry."

Johnjohn stared at him blankly, started to talk, stopped, then erupted with a cheer that everyone took up, and rushed out, cheers following him.

"Christ, tai-pan, but did you . . ."

"Tiptop? That means it's real! Don't you think . . ."

"First Central of New York? Aren't they the berks who . . ."

"Christ, I've been selling short . . ."

"Me too! Shit, I'd better buy first thing or . . ."

"Or I'll be wiped out and . . ."

Dunross saw that Sir Luis, Joseph Stern and Phillip Chen had their heads together, Gornt still staring at him, his face frozen. Then he saw Casey smiling at him so happily and he raised his glass and toasted her. She toasted him back. Gornt saw this and he went over to her and those nearby shivered and fell silent. "First Central's Par-Con's bank. Isn't it?"

"Yes, yes it is, Quillan," she said, her voice sounding small but it went through the room and once more all attention surrounded them.

"You and Bartlett, you did this?" Gornt asked, towering over her.

Dunross said quickly, "I arrange our loans."

Gornt paid no attention to him, just watched her. "You and Bartlett. You helped him?"

She looked back at him, her heart thumping. "I've no control over that bank, Quillan."

"Ah but your fingers're in that pie somewhere," Gornt said coldly. "Aren't they?"

"Murtagh asked *me* if I thought Struan's a good risk," she said, her voice controlled. "I told him, yes, that Struan's was an admirable risk."

"Struan's is on the rocks," Gornt said.

Dunross came up to them. "The whole point is, we're not. By the way, Quillan, Sir Luis has agreed to withdraw Struan's from trading until noon."

All eyes went to Sir Luis who stood stoically, Phillip Chen beside him, then went back to Dunross and Gornt again.

"Why?"

"To give the market time to adjust to the boom."

"What boom?"

"The boom we all deserve, the boom Old Blind Tung forecast." A wave of electricity went through everyone, even Casey. "Also to adjust our stock value," Dunross's voice rasped. "We open at 30."

"Impossible," someone gasped, and Gornt snarled, "You can't! You closed at 9.50 by God! Your stock closed at 9.50!"

"So we offer stock at 30 by God!" Dunross snarled back.

Gornt whirled on Sir Luis. "You're going along with this highway robbery?"

"There isn't any, Quillan," Sir Luis said calmly. "I've agreed, with the committee's unanimous approval, that it's the best for all, for the safety of all investors, that there should be a quiescent period—so that everyone could prepare for the boom. Till noon seemed fair."

"Fair eh?" Gornt grated. "You've got lots of stock I've sold short. Now I buy it all back. What price?"

Sir Luis shrugged. "I'll deal at noon tomorrow, on the floor, not away from the market."

"I'll deal with you right now, Quillan," Dunross said harshly. "How many shares've you sold short? 700,000? 8? I'll let you buy back in at 18 if you will sell the controlling interest in All Asia Air at 15."

"All Asia Air's not for sale," Gornt said, enraged, his mind shouting that at 30 he would be wiped out.

"The offer's good till opening tomorrow."

"The pox on you, tomorrow, and your 30!" Gornt whirled on Joseph Stern. "Buy Struan's! Now, in the morning or at noon! You're responsible!"

"At, at what price, Mr. Gornt?"

"Just buy!" Gornt's face closed and he turned on Casey. "Thanks," he said to her and stomped off, slamming the door behind him. Then conversation exploded, and Dunross was surrounded, people pounding him on the back, swamping him with questions. She stayed alone at the doorway of the veranda, shocked by the violence that had been. Absently, in turmoil, she saw Plumm hurry off, Roger Crosse following, but she paid them little attention, just watched Dunross, Riko now beside him.

In the small back bedroom Plumm reached into the drawer of a bureau that was near the big iron-bound sea trunk. The door swung open and he spun around and when he saw it was Roger Crosse his face twisted. "What the shit're you doing? You deliberately f—"

With catlike speed Crosse was across the room and he belted the man open-handed before Plumm knew what was happening. Plumm gasped and blindly readied to leap at Crosse but again Crosse belted him and Plumm stumbled backward against the bed and fell onto it. "What the f—"

"*Shut up and listen!*" Crosse hissed. "Suslev's going to shop you!"

Plumm gaped at him, the weal from the blows scarlet. At once his anger vanished. "What?"

"Suslev's going to shop you to Sinders, and that means all of us." Crosse's eyes narrowed. "You all right now? For chrissake keep your voice down."

"What? Yes . . . yes. I . . . yes."

"Sorry, Jason, it was the only thing to do."

"That's, that's all right. What the hell's going on, Roger?" Plumm scrambled off the bed, rubbing his face, a thin trickle of blood at the corner of his mouth, now totally controlled. Outside was the rise and fall of indistinct conversation.

"We've got to make a plan," Crosse said grimly and recapped his conversation with Suslev. "I think I've got him convinced, but that bugger's slippery and there's no telling what he'll do. Sinders'll shop him, I'm sure of that, if Suslev doesn't finger Arthur—and if Sinders shops him, Suslev won't come back to Hong Kong. They'll keep him and break him. Then wh—"

"But what about Dunross?" Plumm asked helplessly. "Surely Dunross could've got him out of the mess. Now Gregor's bound to talk. Why stop me?"

"I had to. There was no time to tell you. Listen, after I left Suslev I checked with HQ. They told me Tiptop'd helped those bastards squeeze out of the trap with China's money. Earlier I'd heard that Ian'd arranged his loan," Crosse added, lying. "So the runs're over, the stock market's got to boom, Dunross or not. But worse than that, Jason, I got a whisper from an informant in Special Branch that Sinders has tripled security on Kai Tak, the same on the *Ivanov* wharf, and that, right now, they're opening every crate, every bag, searching every piece of equipment, checking every coolie that goes aboard. If they'd intercepted Dunross, and they would—SI's too smart—we'd be trapped."

Plumm's nervousness increased. A tremor went through him. "What, what about . . . Say we give Sinders Gregor?" he burst out. "What if we gi—"

"Keep your voice down! You're not thinking clearly, for God's sake! Gregor knows all of us. Sinders'd shove him on a sleep-wake-sleep regimen and into the Red Room and he'd tell everything! That'd wreck us, wreck Sevrin and put the Soviets back ten years in Asia."

Plumm shivered and wiped his face. "Then what're we going to do?"

"Let Gregor go aboard and out of Hong Kong, and hope to God he convinces his bosses. Even if he leaks your name to Sinders I think we're buried so deep we can squeeze out of that. You're British, not a foreign national. Thank God we've laws to protect us—even under the Official Secrets Act. Don't worry, nothing'll happen without me knowing and if anything happens I'll know at once. There'll always be time enough for Plan Three." Plan Three was an elaborate escape that Plumm had erected against such an eventuality—with false passports, valid air tickets, ready luggage, clothes, disguises and covers, even including passkeys to airplane waiting areas without going through Immigration—that had a ninety-five percent chance of success given an hour's notice.

"Christ!" Plumm looked down at the waiting trunk. "Christ," he said again, then went to the mirror to look at his face. The redness was going. He doused some water on it.

Crosse watched him, wondering if Plumm was convinced. It was the best he could do under the circumstances. He hated improvisation, but in this case he had little option. What a life we lead! Every one expendable except yourself: Suslev, Plumm, Sinders, Kwok, Armstrong, even the governor.

"What?" Plumm asked, looking at him in the mirror.

"I was just thinking we're in a rough business."

"The Cause makes it worthwhile. That's the only part that counts."

Crosse hid his contempt. I really think you've outlived your usefulness, Jason old fellow, he thought, then went over to the phone. There were no extensions on this line and he knew it was not bugged. He dialed.

"Yes?" He recognized Suslev and coughed Arthur's dry cough. "Mr. Lop-sing please," continuing the code in a perfect imitation of Plumm's voice, then said urgently, "There's been a foul-up. The target did not appear. Be careful at the dock. Surveillance is tripled. We cannot deliver the trunk. Good luck." He hung up. The silence gathered.

"That's his death knell, isn't it?" Plumm said sadly.

Crosse hesitated. He smiled thinly. "Better his death than yours. Eh?"

81

In the noise-filled living room at the other end of the hall, Casey finished her drink and set it down. She was feeling unsettled and very strange. Part of her was joyous at Dunross's reprieve and the other part sad that Gornt was now entrapped. It was quite clear to her with the wheeling and dealing now going on around her that Struan's opening price would be very high. Poor Quillan, she thought. If he doesn't cover his position he'll be in shitsville—and let's face it, I put him there. Didn't I?

Sure, but I had to bail out Dunross because, without him, Gornt would have squeezed us dry—and maybe everyone else. And don't forget, I didn't start the raid on Struan's. That was Linc's raid, not mine. Hasn't Linc always said business and pleasure should never mix? Haven't we both always gone along with that?

Linc. Always back to Linc.

Casey had not seen him all day, nor even heard from him. They were supposed to have met for breakfast but there was a "do not disturb" on his door and a "do not disturb" on his phone so she left him and pushed away the thought of Orlanda—was Orlanda there too? And tonight, when she had returned from the day's sailing, there was a message: "Hi, have fun." So she had showered and changed and bottled her impatience and had come here tonight. It had been no fun in the beginning, everyone gloom and doom-filled, then after the news and Gornt slamming out, no fun again. Shortly afterward Dunross had forced his way over and thanked her again but almost at once he had been surrounded by excited men discussing deals and chances. She watched them, feeling very lonely. Perhaps Linc's back at the hotel now, she thought. I wish . . . never mind, but it is time to go home. No one noticed her slip out.

Roger Crosse was standing at the elevator. He held the door for her then pressed the *down* button.

"Thanks. Nice party, wasn't it?" she said.

"Yes, yes it was," he replied absently.

On the ground floor Crosse let her get out first then strode off out the front door and down the hill. What's his hurry? she asked herself, heading for the group that waited for taxis, glad that it was not raining again. She jerked to a stop. Orlanda Ramos, with packages in her arms, was coming into the foyer. Each woman saw the other at the same instant. Orlanda was the first to recover. "Evening, Casey," she said with her best smile. "How pretty you look."

"So do you," Casey replied. Her enemy did. The pale blue skirt and blouse were perfectly matched.

Orlanda poured a stream of impatient Cantonese over the crumpled concierge who was lounging nearby. At once he took her packages, mumbling.

"Sorry, Casey," she said nicely, a thread of nervousness to her voice, "but there's been a small landslide just down the hill and I had to leave my car there. You're, you're visiting here?"

"No, just leaving. You live here?"

"Yes. Yes I do."

Another silence between them, both readying. Then Casey nodded a polite good night and began to leave.

"Perhaps we should talk," Orlanda said and Casey stopped.

"Certainly, Orlanda, whenever you wish."

"Do you have time now?"

"I think so."

"Would you like to walk with me back to my car? I've got to get the rest of my packages. You won't be able to get a taxi here anyway, below will be easy."

"Sure."

The two women went out. The night was cool but Casey was burning and so was Orlanda, each knowing what was coming, each fearful of the other. Their feet picked a way carefully. The street was wet from the water that rushed downward. There was a promise of more rain soon from the heavy nimbus overcast. Ahead, fifty yards away, Casey could see where the embankment had partially given way, sending a mess of earth and rocks and shrubs and rubble across the road. There was no sidewalk. On the other side of the slip, a line of cars was stopped, impatiently maneuvering to turn around. A few pedestrians scrambled over the embankment.

"Have you lived in Rose Court long?" Casey asked.

"A few years. It's very pleasant. I th— Oh! Were you at Jason Plumm's party, the Asian Properties party?"

"Yes." Casey saw the relief on Orlanda's face and it angered her but she contained the anger and stopped and said quietly, "Orlanda, there's nothing really for us to talk about, is there? Let's say good night."

Orlanda looked up at her. "Linc's with me. He's with me in my apartment. At the moment."

"I presumed that."

"That doesn't bother you?"

"It bothers me very much. But that's up to Linc. We're not married, as you know, not even engaged, as you know—you have your way, I have mine, so th—"

"What do you mean by that?" Orlanda asked.

"I mean that I've known Linc for seven years, you haven't known him for seven days."

"That doesn't matter," Orlanda said defiantly. "I love him and he loves me."

"That's y—" Casey was almost shoved aside by some Chinese who barreled past, chattering noisily. Others were approaching up the incline. Then some of the party guests walked around them, heading down the slope. One of the women was Lady Joanna, and she eyed them curiously but went on.

When they were alone again, Casey said, "That's yet to be proved. Good night, Orlanda," she said, wanting to scream at her, You make your money on your back, I work for mine, and all the love you protest is spelled *money*. Men are such jerks.

"Curiously I don't blame Linc," she muttered out loud seeing the firm jaw, the flashing determined eyes, the perfect, voluptuous yet trim body. "Good night."

She walked on. Now my plan has to change, she was thinking, all her being concentrated. Tonight I was going to love Linc properly, but now everything has to change. If he's in her bed he's under her spell. Jesus, I'm glad I found that out. God, if I'd offered he would have had to say no and then. . . . Now I can. . . . what should I do?

Shit on the Orlandas of the world! It's so easy for them. They have a game plan from day one. But the rest of us?

What do I do? Stick to November 25 and gamble Orlanda will bore the hell out of him by that time?

Not that lady. That one's dynamite and she knows Linc's her passport to eternity.

Her heart picked up a beat. I'm a match for her, she told herself confidently. Maybe not in bed or in the kitchen, but I can learn.

She stepped up and over a boulder, cursing the mud that fouled her shoes, and jumped down the other side of the earth barrier. Dunross's Rolls and his chauffeur were at the head of the line.

"Excuse, Missee, is the tai-pan still there?"

"Yes, yes he is."

"Ah, thank you." The driver locked the car and hurried over the roadblock back up the hill. Casey turned and watched him. Her eyes centered on Orlanda who was approaching and she looked at her, wanting to shove her into the mud. The thought amused her and she stood there, letting her enemy approach, letting her wonder what she would do. She saw the eyes harden and there was no fear on Orlanda's face, just a very confident half-smile. Orlanda passed her fearlessly, and a tremor of apprehension went through Casey that she managed to dominate. Maybe you're just as afraid of me and my power as I am of yours, she thought, her eyes now on Rose Court, a brilliant tower of light, wondering which light surrounded Linc or which darkened window. . . .

When Orlanda had first seen Casey, she had immediately jumped to the conclusion that Casey had been to her apartment and confronted Bartlett—that's what I would have done, she told herself. And, even though she knew now where Casey had been, fear again swept through her at the sight of her rival. Has she power over him through Par-Con? she asked herself, trembling. Can she control Linc through stocks or shares? If Linc's first wife nearly destroyed him financially and Casey saved him as many times as he said, she's bound to have him tied up. I would if I were she, of course I would.

Involuntarily Orlanda glanced back. Casey was still watching Rose Court. Beyond her, Dunross and others—Riko, Toxe, Phillip and Dianne Chen among them—came out of the foyer and started down the hill. She dismissed them and everything except the question of how to deal with Linc when she returned. Should she tell him about meeting Casey or not? Numbly she took the remainder of her packages from her car. I know one thing, she told herself over and over again. Linc's mine, and Casey or no Casey I'll marry him, whatever the cost.

Casey had seen Dunross come out of the foyer and she watched him, enjoying the sight of him, tall, debonair, ten years younger than when she first saw him, and it pleased her very much that she had helped him. Then, just as she turned away, she heard him call out, "Casey! Casey! Hang on a moment!" She glanced back. "How about joining us for dinner?" he called out to her.

She shook her head, not in the mood, and called out, "Thanks but I've a date! See you tomorr—"

At that moment the earth fell away.

82

The landslide had begun further up the mountain on the other side of Po Shan Road, and it swept across the road, smashing into a two-story garage, its mass and velocity so vast that the garage building rotated and toppled off the garden terrace, slid down for a short distance, then fell over. The slide gathered momentum and rushed past a darkened high rise, crossed Conduit Road and smashed into Richard Kwang's two-story house, obliterating it. Then, together with these buildings, the slip, now nine hundred feet long and two hundred feet wide—fifty thousand tons of earth and rock—continued on its downward path across Kotewall Road and struck Rose Court.

The landslide had taken seven seconds.

When Rose Court was struck, it appeared to shudder, and then the building came away from its foundations and moved forward in the direction of the harbor, toppled over and broke up near the middle like a man kneeling then falling.

As it fell, the upper stories struck and ripped off a corner of the upper stories of Sinclair Towers below, then crumpled and disintegrated into rubble. Part of the slide and the demolished building continued on and fell into a construction site farther down the mountain, then stopped. The lights went out as the building collapsed in a cloud of dust. And now over all Mid Levels there was a stunned, vast silence.

Then the screams began. . . .

In the tunnel under Sinclair Road, Suslev was choking, half-buried in rubble. Part of the tunnel roof was torn off, water gushing in now from fractured mains and drains, the tunnel filling rapidly. He scrambled and fought up into the open, his confused mind helpless, not knowing what was happening, what had happened, only that somehow he must have been captured and drugged and now he was in a wake-sleep nightmare from the Red Room. He looked around, panic-stricken. All buildings were dark, power gone, a monstrous pile of shrieking, shifting wreckage surrounding him. Then his glands overpowered him and he fled pell-mell down Sinclair Road. . . .

Far above on Kotewall Road, those on the other side of the barrage were safe though paralyzed with shock. The few still on their feet, Casey among them, could not believe what they had witnessed. The vast slide had torn away all of the roadway as far as they could see. Most of the mountainside that a moment ago was terraced was now an undulating, ugly mud-earth-rock slope—roads vanished, buildings gone, and Dunross and his party carried away somewhere down the slope.

Casey tried to scream but she had no voice. Then, "Oh Jesus Christ! Linc!" tore from her mouth and her feet moved and before she knew what was happening she was scrambling, falling, groping her way toward the wreckage. The darkness was awful now, the screams awful, voices beginning, shouts for help from everywhere, the unbelievable twisted pile of debris still moving here and there, bits still falling and being crushed. All at once the night was lit by power lines exploding, sending cascades of fireballs into the air among the wreckage.

Frantically she rushed to where the foyer once had been. Extended below, far below, the darkness obscuring almost everything, was the twisted mass of rubble, concrete blocks, girders, shoes, toys, pots pans sofas chairs beds radios TVs clothes limbs books, three cars that had been parked outside, and more screams. Then in the light of the exploding power lines she saw the mashed wreckage that was once the elevator down the slope, broken arms and legs jutting from its carcass.

"Linc!" she shrieked at the top of her voice, again and again, not knowing she was crying, the tears streaming down her face. But there was no answer. Desperately she clambered and half fell and groped her way into and over the dangerous rubble. Around her, men and women were shouting, screaming. Then she heard a faint wail of terror nearby and part of the rubble moved. She was on her knees now, stockings torn, dress torn, knees bruised and she pulled away some bricks and found a small cavity, and there was a Chinese child of three or four, beyond terror, coughing, almost choking, trapped under a vast, groaning pile of debris in the rubble dust.

"Oh Jesus you poor darling." Casey looked around frantically but there was no one to help. Part of the rubble shifted, screaming and groaning, a big chunk of concrete with its imbedded, reinforcing iron almost hanging loose. Careless of her safety, Casey fought the debris away, fingers bleeding. Again the wreckage twisted over her as some of it slid farther down the slope. Desperately she clawed a crawlspace and grabbed the child's arm, helping her to squeeze out, then caught her in her arms and darted back to safety as this part of the wreckage collapsed and she stood alone, the trembling child safe and unhurt in her arms, clutching her tightly. . . .

When the avalanche toppled the high rise and tore up most of the roadway and parapet, Dunross and the others on its edge were hurtled down the steep slope, head over heels, brush and vegetation breaking part of their fall. The tai-pan picked himself up in the semidarkness, felt himself blankly, dazed, astonished to find he could stand and was unhurt. From near him came whimpers of agony. The slope was steep and everywhere muddy and sodden as he groped up to Dianne Chen. She was semiconscious, groaning, one leg twisted brutally underneath her. Part of her shinbone jutted through the skin but as far as he could see, no arteries were severed and there was no dangerous bleeding. As carefully as he could he straightened her and her limb, but she let out a howl of pain and fainted. He felt someone nearby and glanced up. Riko was standing there, her dress ripped, her shoes gone, her hair akimbo, a small trickle of blood from her nose.

"Christ, you all right?"

"Yes . . . yes," she said shakily. "It's . . . was it an earthquake?"

At that moment there was another crackling explosion of power cables short-circuiting, and momentarily fireballs lit up the area. "Oh my God!" he gasped. "It's like London in the blitz." Then he caught sight of Phillip Chen in an inert heap around a sapling, sprawled headfirst down the slope. "Stay here with Dianne," he ordered and scrambled down the slope. Hanging onto his dread, he turned Phillip over. His compradore was still breathing. Dunross shook with relief. He settled him as best he could and looked around in the gloom. Others were picking themselves up. Nearby, Christian Toxe was shaking his head, trying to clear it.

"Bloody sodding Christ," he was muttering over and over. "There must be a couple of hundred people living there." He reeled to his feet then slipped in the mud and cursed again. "I've . . . I've got to get to a phone. Give me, give me a hand will you?" Toxe swore as he slipped again. "It's my ankle, the bloody thing's twisted a bit."

Dunross helped him stand and then, with Riko on Toxe's other side, they climbed awkwardly back to the remains of the roadway. People were still standing paralyzed, others clambering over the first slide to see if they could help, a few of the tenants frantic and moaning. One mother was being held back, her husband already running falling clambering toward the wreckage, their three children and *amah* somewhere there.

The moment they were on level ground, Toxe hobbled off down Kotewall Road and Dunross rushed for his car to fetch his flashlight and emergency medical pack.

Lim was nowhere to be seen. Then Dunross remembered his chauffeur had been with them when the avalanche hit. As he found the keys to unlock the trunk he searched his memory. Who was with us? Toxe, Riko, Jacques—no, Jacques had left—Phillip and Dianne Chen, Barre . . . no we left Barre at the party. Jesus Christ! The party! I'd forgotten the party! Who was still there? Richard Kwang and his wife, Plumm, Johnjohn, no he'd gone earlier, Roger Crosse, no wait a minute, didn't he leave?

Dunross jerked open the trunk and found two flashlights and the medical kit, a length of rope. He ran back to Riko, his back hurting him now. "Will you go back and look after Dianne and Phillip till I can get help?" His voice was deliberately firm. "Here." He gave her a flashlight, some bandages and a bottle of aspirin. "Off you go. Dianne's broken her leg. I don't know about Phillip. Do what you can and stay with them till an ambulance comes or I come back. All right?"

"Yes, yes, all right." Her eyes flickered with fear as she looked above. "Will there . . . is there any danger from another slide?"

"No. You'll be quite safe. Go quickly!" His will took away her fear and she started down the slope with the flashlight, picking her way carefully. It was only then he noticed that she was barefoot. Then he remembered Dianne had been barefoot too and Phillip. He stretched to ease his back. His clothes were ripped, but he paid them no attention and rushed for the barrier. In the distance he heard police sirens. His relief became almost nauseating as he broke into a run.

Then he noticed Orlanda at the head of the line of cars. She was staring fixedly at where Rose Court had been, her mouth moving, tiny spasms trembling her face and body, and he remembered the night of the fire when she had been equally petrified and near snapping. Quickly he went to her and shook her hard, hoping to jerk her out of the panic breakdown that he had witnessed so many times during the war. "Orlanda!"

She came out of her almost trance. "Oh . . . oh . . . what, what . . ."

Greatly relieved, he saw her eyes were normal now and the agony normal, the spilling tears normal. "You're all right. Nothing to worry about. Get hold now, you're all right, Orlanda!" he said, his voice kind though very firm, and leaned her against the hood of a car and left her.

Her eyes focused. "Oh my God! Linc!" Then she shrieked after him through her tears, "Linc . . . Linc's there!"

He jerked to a stop, turned back. "Where? Where was he?"

"He's . . . in my, my apartment. It's on the eighth floor . . . it's on the eighth floor!"

Dunross ran off again, his flashlight the only moving speck of light on the morass.

Here and there people were groping blindly, ankle-deep in the soaking earth, their hands cupped around matches, heading for the ruins. As he came nearer the catastrophe, his heart twisted. He could smell gas. Every second the smell became stronger.

"Put out the matches, for chrissake!" he roared. *"You'll blow us all to helllll!"*

Then he saw Casey . . .

The police car following the fire truck roared up the hill, sirens howling, the traffic heavy here and no one getting out of the way. Inside the car Armstrong was monitoring the radio calls: "All police units and fire trucks converge on Kotewall Road. Emergency, emergency emergency! There's a new landslip in the vicinity of Po Shan and Sinclair Road! Callers say Rose Court and two other twelve-story buildings've collapsed."

"Bloody ridiculous!" Armstrong muttered, then, "Watch out for chrissake!" he shouted at the driver who had cut across the road to the wrong side, narrowly missing a truck. "Turn right here, then cut up Castle into Robinson and into Sinclair that way," he ordered. He had been going home from another rebuild session with Brian Kwok, his head aching and exhausted, when he had heard the emergency call. Remembering that Crosse lived on Sinclair Road and that he'd said he would be going to Jason Plumm's party after he'd followed a lead with Rosemont, he had decided to check it out. Christ, he thought grimly, if he's been clobbered who'll take over SI? And do we still let Brian go or hold him or what?

A new voice came on, firm, unhurried, the static on the radio heavy. "This is Deputy Fire Chief Soames. Emergency One!" Armstrong and the driver gasped. "I'm at the junction of Sinclair, Robinson and Kotewall Road where I have set up a command post. Emergency One repeat One! Inform the commissioner and the governor at once, this is a disaster of very great proportions. Inform all hospitals on the Island to be on standby. Order every ambulance and all paramedics to the area. We will require immediate and heavy army assistance. All power is out so we require generators, cables and lights. . . ."

"Jesus Christ," Armstrong muttered. Then sharply, "Get the lead out for chrissake, and hurry it up!"

The police car increased speed. . . .

"Oh, Ian," Casey said beyond tears, the petrified child still in her arms. "Linc's somewhere down there."

"Yes, yes I know," he said above the insane bedlam of screams and cries for help that came through the ominous grinding of the wreckage as it still settled. People wandered around blindly, not knowing where to look, where to start, how to help. "You all right?"

"Oh yes but . . . but Linc. I don—" She stopped. Just ahead, down the slope near the remains of the elevator, a vast pile of twisted beams and shattered fragments of concrete subsided deafeningly, starting a chain reaction all down the slope and as he focused his flashlight on it they saw a loosened mass of debris smash against the elevator, claw it loose and send it reeling, leaving bodies in its wake.

"Oh Jesus," she whimpered. The child clutched her in panic.

"Go back to the car, you'll be saf—" At that moment a man crazed with anxiety rushed up to them, peered at the child in her arms, then grabbed her, clutching her to him, mumbling his thanks to God and to her. "Where, where did you find her?"

Casey pointed numbly.

The man peered at the spot blankly then went off into the night, weeping openly with relief.

"Stay here, Casey," Dunross said urgently, sirens approaching from every direction. "I'll take a quick look."

"Do be careful. Jesus, do you smell gas?"

"Yes, lots of it." Using the flashlight he began to thread his way over and under and through the wreckage, slipping and sliding. It was treacherous, the whole mass uneasy and creaking. The first crumpled body was a Chinese woman he did not know. Ten yards below was a European man, his head mashed and almost obliterated. Quickly he scoured the way ahead with his light but could not see Bartlett among the other dead. Farther below were two broken bodies, both Chinese. Swallowing his nausea, he worked his way under a dangerous overhang toward the European, then, holding the flashlight carefully, reached into the dead man's pockets. The driver's license said: Richard Pugmire.

"Christ!" Dunross muttered. The smell of gas was heavy. His stomach turned over as, far below, more power lines gushed sparks. We'll all go to kingdom come if those bloody sparks reach up here, he thought. Carefully he eased out of the debris and stood at his full height, breathing easier now. A last look at Pugmire's body and he started down the slope again. A few steps later he heard a faint moan. It took a little time to find the source but he centered on it and climbed down, his heart beating heavily. With great care he squirmed into the depths under a monstrous overhang of beams and rubble. His fingers took hold. Using all his strength he tilted the broken concrete and shoved it aside. A man's head was below. "Help," Clinker said weakly. "God love you, mate. . . ."

"Hang on a second." Dunross could see the man was wedged down by a huge rafter but the rafter was also keeping the debris above from crushing him. With the flashlight he searched until he found a broken piece of pipe. With this as a lever he tried to raise the rafter. A pyramid of rubble shifted ominously. "Can you move?" he gasped.

"It's . . . it's me legs, I hurt proper bad, but I can try." Clinker reached out and gripped an imbedded piece of iron. "Ready when you are."

"What's your name?"

"Clinker, Ernie Clinker. Wot's yorn?"

"Dunross. Ian Dunross."

"Oh!" Clinker moved his head painfully and peered upward, his face and head bleeding, hair matted and lips raw. "Thanks, tai-pan," he said. "Ready, ready when you are."

Dunross put his weight and strength onto his makeshift lever. The beam raised an inch. Clinker squirmed but could not dislodge himself. "Bit more, mate," he gasped, in great pain. Again Dunross bore down. He felt the sinews of his arms and legs cry out under the strain. The beam came up a fraction. A trickle of rubble cascaded into the cavity. Higher still. "Now!" he said urgently. "I can't hold it. . . ."

The old man's grip on the iron tightened and he dragged himself out inch by inch. More rubble moved as he shifted his grip. Now he was half-way out. Once his trunk was free, Dunross let the rafter settle back, oh so gently, and when it was completely at rest he grabbed the old man and wrenched him free. It was then that he saw the trail of blood, the left foot missing. "Don't move, old fellow," he said compassionately as Clinker lay panting, half unconscious, trying to stop the whimpers of pain. Dunross tore open a bandage, tying a rough tourniquet just under the knee.

Then he stood up in the small space and looked at the vicious overhang above him, trying to decide what to do next. Next I get the poor bugger out, he thought, loathing the closeness. Then he heard the rumble and shriek of shifting debris. The earth lurched and he ducked, his arms protecting his head. A new avalanche began. . . .

83

9:13 P.M.:

It was just sixteen minutes since Rose Court was struck, but all over the vast area of destruction people were moving. Some had fought themselves out of the rubble. Others were rescuers and down below, near the command post set up at the junction, police cars, four fire trucks and rescue units were there, their mobile lights washing the slope, firemen and police frantically working their way through the wreckage. A small fire flickered and it was quickly doused, everyone aware of the gas danger. An ambulance with wounded or dying had already been dispatched, more were converging.

It was chaotic in the darkness, all streetlighting failed, the rain beginning again. The senior divisional fire officer had arrived a moment ago and had sent for gas company engineers and organized other experts to inspect the foundations of the other high rises and buildings nearby in case they should be evacuated—the whole three tiers of Kotewall, Conduit and Po Shan Roads suspect. "Christ," he muttered, appalled, "this's going to take weeks to dig out and clean up." But he stood in the open, an outward picture of calm. Another patrol car whined to a halt. "Oh hello, Robert," he said as Armstrong joined him. "Yes," he said, seeing his shock, "Christ knows how many're buried th—"

"Look out!" someone shouted and everyone ran for cover as a huge lump of reinforced concrete came crashing down from the mutilated top stories of Sinclair Towers. One of the police cars turned its light upward. Now they could see the shreds of rooms open to the skies. A tiny figure was teetering on the brink. "Get someone up there and see what the hell's going on!"

A fireman took to his heels. . . .

In the darkness at the roadblock up on Kotewall Road, onlookers from nearby buildings had been collecting, everyone petrified that there would be another slide, tenants frantic, not knowing whether to evacuate or not. Orlanda was still leaning numbly against the car, the rain on her face mixing with her tears. Another group of police reinforcements poured over the barrier onto the morass and fanned out with heavy-duty flashlights searching the terrain. One heard a call for help from below and directed his light into the brush, then changed direction quickly as he saw Riko waving and shouting, two figures inert beside her.

Down Kotewall Road at the fork, Gornt's car skidded to a halt. Brushing aside orders from the harassed policeman there, he pressed the keys into his hand and rushed off up the hill. When he got near to the barrier and saw the extent of the disaster he was stunned. Only moments ago he had been there, drinking and flirting with Casey, everything settled, Orlanda settled, then his whole victory upside down and raging at Dunross, but some miracle had sent him away in time and now perhaps all the others were dead and buried and gone forever. Christ! Dunross Orlanda Casey Jason Bar—

"Keep out of the way!" the policeman shouted. More ambulance bearers hurried past, firemen with axes following, up and over the mess of mud and boulders and trees toward the ruins. "Sorry, but you can't stay there, sir."

Gornt moved aside, breathing heavily from his run. "Did anyone get out?"

"Oh yes, of course, I'm sure th—"

"Have you seen Dunross, Ian Dunross?"

"Who?"

"The tai-pan, Dunross?"

"No, no sorry I haven't." The policeman turned away to intercept and calm some disheveled parents.

Gornt's eyes went back to the disaster, still appalled by its immensity.

"Jesus," an American voice muttered.

Gornt turned. Paul Choy and Venus Poon were crammed in a new group who were straggling up. Everyone stared, dumbfounded, into the darkness. "Jesus!"

"What're you doing here, Paul?"

"Oh hello, Mr. Gornt! My . . . my uncle's in there," Paul Choy said, hardly able to talk. "Jesus Christ, lookit!"

"Four Fingers?"

"Yes. He . . ."

Venus Poon overrode him grandly. "Mr. Wu's waiting for me to discuss a movie contract. He's going to be a film producer."

Gornt dismissed the patent fabrication as his mind raced. If he could save Four Fingers, perhaps the old man would help extricate him from the looming stock market debacle. "What floor was he on?"

"The fifth," Venus Poon said.

"Paul, cut around to Sinclair Road and work your way up this side of the slope. I'll work down to meet you! Off you go!"

The young man raced off before Venus Poon could stop him. The policeman was still distracted. Without hesitation Gornt darted for the barrier. He knew Plumm's fifth-floor apartment well—Four Fingers should be nearby. In the darkness he did not notice Orlanda on the other side of the road.

Once over the barrier he moved as fast as he could, his feet sinking into the earth. From time to time he stumbled. "*Heya*, Honored Sir!" he called out in Cantonese to a nearby stretcher bearer. "Do you have a spare flashlight?"

"Yes, yes, here you are!" the man said. "But beware, the path is treacherous. There are many ghosts here."

Gornt thanked him and hurried off, making better time. Nearing where the foyer would have been he stopped. Up the mountainside as far as he could see was the ugly sloping gash of the slide, a hundred yards wide. On the edges of all three tiers were other buildings and high rises, one under construction, and the thought of being caught in one of those nauseated him. All of Conduit Road had gone, trees torn up, parapets gone. When he looked below he shuddered. "It's impossible," he muttered, remembering the size and strength of the high rise and the joy of Rose Court over the years. Then he saw the lights skeetering over the top of Sinclair Towers, the building that he had always hated—had hated Dunross even more for financing and owning—for destroying his wonderful view. When he noticed the upper corner missing, a flash of pleasure went through him, but it quickly turned to bile as he remembered his own penthouse apartment that had been on the twelfth floor of Rose Court, and all the good times he had had with Orlanda, there and on the eighth floor, now rubble and death filled. "Christ," he said out loud, blessing his joss. Then he went onward. . . .

Casey was sitting on a pile of rubble, waiting and in misery. Rescuers were all over the slope working in semidarkness, picking their way over the dangerous surfaces, alternatively calling and listening for calls from those who were trapped. Here and there a few were digging desperately, moving rubble away as another unfortunate was found.

Nervously she got up and peered down the slope, seeking Dunross. He had quickly disappeared from her line of sight into the wreckage, but from time to time she had caught a glint from his flashlight. Now for some minutes she had seen nothing. Her anxiety increased, the minutes hanging, and whenever the wreck settled more fear had whipped her. Linc, Linc's somewhere there, was pounding on her brain. I've got to do something, I can't just sit, better to sit and wait and pray and wait, wait for Ian to come back. He'll find him . . .

In a sudden fright she leapt to her feet. A great section halfway down the slope had broken free, scattering rescuers who ran for their lives. In a moment the chain reaction ceased and it was quiet again but her heart kept up its pounding. There was no moving glint of Dunross's light to reassure her. "Oh Jesus let him be all right!"

"Casey? Casey, is that you?" Gornt came out of the darkness and scrambled up to her.

"Oh Quillan," she began pathetically and he held her in his arms, his strength giving her strength. "Please help Lin—"

"I came as soon as I heard," he told her quickly, overriding her. "It was on the wireless. Christ, I was petrified you were . . . I never expected . . . Hold on, Casey!"

"I'm . . . I'm all right. Linc's in . . . he's in there somewhere, Quillan."

"What? But how? Did he an—"

"He was in Or . . . Orlanda's apartment and Ia—"

"Perhaps you're wrong, Casey. Lis—"

"No. Orlanda told me."

"Eh? She got out too?" Gornt gasped. "Orlanda got out?"

"Yes. She was with me, near me, back there, I saw it all happen, Quillan, I saw the whole terrible avalanche and the whole building collapse and then I ran here, Ian came to help and Linc's d—"

"Dunross? He got out too?" he asked, bile in his mouth.

"Oh yes. Yes, he's down there now. Some of the building shifted and the elevator, the elevator was full of bodies. He's down there somewhere, looking . . . looking in case . . ." Her voice died away.

She saw Gornt shift his attention to the slope. "Who else got out?"

"Jacques, the Chens, that newspaperman, I don't know . . ." She could not see his face so she could not read him. "You're sorry that . . . that Ian's alive?"

"No. On the contrary. Where did he go?"

"Down there." She took his flashlight and directed it. "There, where that outcrop is. He, I haven't seen him for a while but just there. You see the remains of the elevator? Near there." Now she could see his face better, dark eyes, the bearded chiseled face, but it told her nothing.

"Stay here," he said. "You're safe here." He took the flashlight and moved into the wreckage, soon to be swallowed by it.

The rain was heavier now, warm like the night was warm, and Gornt spat the bile out of his mouth, glad that his enemy was alive, hating that he was alive, but wanting him alive more.

It was very slippery as he worked his way down. A slab teetered and gave way. He stumbled, barked his shin and cursed, then moved onward, his flashlight seeking safety where he knew there was none. So Ian bloody tai-pan Dunross got out before it collapsed, he was thinking. That bugger's got a charmed life! Christ! But don't forget, the gods were on your side too. Don't forget th—

He stopped. Faint calls for help from somewhere near. Intently he listened again but he could not identify the direction. He called out, "Where are you, where are you?" listening again. Nothing. Hesitating, he reexamined the way ahead. This whole god-cursed mess can slide down a hundred feet or more at the drop of a hat, he thought. "Where are you?" Still nothing, so cautiously he went on, the gas smell heavy.

When he got nearer to the remains of the elevator he looked at the bodies, not recognizing any of them, went on and eased around a corner, ducking under an overhang. Suddenly a flashlight blinded him.

"What the hell're you doing here, Quillan?" Dunross asked.

"Looking for you," Gornt said grimly, putting the light on him. "Casey told me you were playing hide and seek."

Dunross was resting on some rubble, catching his breath, his arms ripped and bloody, clothes in tatters. When this part of the wreckage had shifted, the way in had shrieked closed. As he had darted for safety the flashlight had been knocked out of his hand and when the avalanche subsided he was trapped with Clinker. It had taken him all his will not to panic in the darkness. Patiently he worked the area, his fingers groping, seeking the flashlight. Inch by inch. And when he was almost ready to give up, his fingers locked on it. In the light once more, fear had left him. The light had pointed a new way out. He stared back at Gornt, then smiled with the skin of his face. "Sorry I'm not dead?"

Gornt shrugged and smiled the same rotten smile. "Yes. Joss. But it'll happen soon enough." The overhang creaked and shifted slightly and his light swung upward. Both men held their breath. It settled back with a sigh. "Sooner if we don't get to hell out of here."

Dunross got up, grunted as a stab of pain went up his back.

"You're not hurt, I hope?" Gornt asked.

Dunross laughed and felt better, the fright of entombment wearing off. "No. Give me a hand will you?"

"What?"

Dunross pointed into the wreckage with his light. Now Gornt could see the old man. "I got trapped down there trying to get him out." At once Gornt moved to help, squatting down, moving what rubble they could to increase the crawlspace.

"His name's Clinker. His legs're a mess and he's lost a foot."

"Christ! Here, let me do that." Gornt got a better grip on the slab, shifted it away, then jumped down into the cavity. In a moment he turned back and peered up at Dunross. "Sorry, the bugger's dead."

"Oh Christ! You're sure?"

Gornt lifted the old man like a doll and they put him into the open.

"Poor bugger."

"Joss. Did he say where he was in the building? What floor? Was anyone with him?"

"He muttered something about caretaker, and being underneath the building, and something about, I think he said Mabel."

Gornt put the flash all around. "Did you hear anything or anyone?"

"No."

"Let's get him out of here," Gornt said with finality.

They picked him up. When they were in the open and relatively safe they stopped to get their breath. Some stretcher bearers were nearby. Dunross beckoned them. "We will take him away, Honored Lord," one said. They bundled the body onto a stretcher and hurried off.

"Quillan, before we get back to Casey. She sai—"

"About Bartlett? Yes, she told me he was in Orlanda's place." Gornt watched him. "Her flat was on the eighth floor."

Dunross looked down the slope. There were more lights than before. "Where would that have ended up?"

"He's got to be dead. The *eighth* floor?"

"Yes. But whereabouts?"

Gornt searched the hillside. "I can't see from here. I might recognize something, but I doubt it. It'd be, it'd be down there, almost at Sinclair Road."

"He could be alive, in a pocket. Let's go and look."

Gornt's face twisted with a curious smile. "You need him and his deal, don't you?"

"No, no not now."

"Bullshit." Gornt clambered onto an outcrop. "Casey!" he shouted, cupping his hands around his mouth. "We're going below! Go back to the barrier and wait there!"

They heard her call back faintly, "Okay, be careful!" Then Gornt said sourly, "All right, Gunga Din, if we're going to play hero, we'd better do it right. I lead." He moved off.

Equally sourly, but needing him, Dunross followed, his anger gathering. The two men worked their way out. Once clear, they scrambled down the slope. From time to time they would see a body or a part of a body but no one they recognized. They passed a few frantic survivors or relatives of those missing, pathetically digging or trying to dig with their hands, a broken piece of wood—anything they could find.

Down at the bottom of the slope Gornt stopped, his flashlight examining the wreckage carefully.

"Anything?" Dunross asked.

"No." Gornt caught sight of some bedraggled curtains that might have been Orlanda's but it had been almost two years since he was in her apartment. His light hesitated.

"What is it?"

"Nothing." Gornt began climbing, seeking clues to her apartment or to the Asian Properties apartment on the fifth floor. "That could be part of

Plumm's furniture," he said. The sofa was torn in half, the springs akimbo.

"Help! Help in the name of all gods!" The faint Cantonese cry came from somewhere in the middle of this section. At once Gornt scrambled toward the sound, thinking he recognized Four Fingers, Dunross close behind, up and over and under. In the center of a mass of debris was an old Chinese man, bedraggled, covered with rubble dust. He was sitting in the wreckage, looking around perplexed, seemingly unhurt. When Gornt and Dunross came up to him he grimaced at them, squinting in their light.

At once they recognized him and now he recognized them. It was Smiler Ching, the banker. "What happened, Honored Sirs?" he asked, his Cantonese heavy-accented, his teeth protruding.

Gornt told him briefly and the man gasped. "By all the gods, that's impossible! Am I alive? Truly alive?"

"Yes. What floor were you on, Smiler Ching?"

"The twelfth—I was in my living room. I was watching television." Smiler Ching searched his memory and his lips opened into another grimace. "I'd just seen Little Mealy Mouth, Venus Poon, and then . . . then there was a thunderous noise from the direction of Conduit Road. The next thing I remember is waking up here, just a few minutes ago, waking up here."

"Who was in the flat with you?"

"My *amah*. First Wife is out playing mah-jong!" The small old man got up cautiously, felt all his limbs and let out a cackle. "*Ayeeyah*, by all the gods, it's a fornicating miracle, tai-pan and second tai-pan! Obviously the gods favor me, obviously I shall recover my bank and become rich again and a steward at the Turf Club! *Ayeeyah!* What joss!" Again he tested his feet and legs then clambered off, heading for safety.

"If this mess was part of the twelfth floor, the eighth should be back there," Dunross said, his light pointing.

Gornt nodded, his face taut.

"If that old bastard can survive, so could Bartlett."

"Perhaps. Let's look."

84

11:05 P.M.:

An army truck swirled up in the heavy rain, spattering mud, and stopped near the command posts. Irish guardsmen in fatigues and raincoats, some with fire axes, jumped down. An officer was waiting for them. "Go up there, Sergeant! Work alongside R.S.M. O'Connor!" He was a young man and he pointed with a swagger stick to the right of the slide, his uniform raincoat, boots and trousers mud filthy. "No smoking, there's still a bloody gas leak, and get the lead out!"

"Where's Alpha Company, sir?"

"Up at Po Shan. Delta's halfway. We've an aid station on Kotewall. I'm monitoring Channel 4. Off you go!"

The men stared at the devastation. "Glory be to God," someone muttered. They charged off, following their sergeant. The officer went back to his command post and picked up the field telephone. "Delta Company, this is Command. Give me a report."

"We've recovered four bodies, sir, and two injured up here. We're halfway across the slope now. One's a Chinese woman called Kwang, multiple fractures but all right, and her husband, he's just shook up a bit."

"What part of the building were they in?"

"Fifth floor. We think the heavy-duty girders protected them. Both casualties're on their way to our aid station at Kotewall. We can hear someone buried deep but, glory be, sir, we can't get at him—the firemen can't use their oxy-acetylene cutters. The gas's too heavy. Nothing else in our area, sir."

"Keep it up." The officer turned around and snapped at an orderly, "Go and chase up those gas board fellows and see what the hell's holding them up! Tell 'em to get their fingers out!"

"Yes sir."

He switched channels. "Kotewall Aid Station, this is Command. What's the score?"

"Fourteen bodies so far, Captain, and nineteen injured, some very bad.

We're getting their names as quick as we can. Sir Dunstan Barre, we dug him out, he just has a broken wrist."

"Keep up the good work! The police've set up a missing persons station on Channel 16. Get them all the names, dead, injured, everyone, quick as you can. We've some pretty anxious people down here."

"Yes sir. The rumor's we're going to evacuate the whole area."

"The governor, commissioner and the fire chief're deciding that right now." The officer rubbed his face tiredly, then rushed out to intercept another incoming truck with Gurkhas from the Engineers Corps, passing the governor, commissioner and senior fire officer who stood at the central command post under the foyer overhang of Sinclair Towers. A white-haired engineer-surveyor from the Public Works Department got out of a car and hurried over to them.

"Evening, sir," he said anxiously. "We've been all through all the buildings now, from Po Shan down to here. I recommend we evacuate nineteen buildings."

"Good God," Sir Geoffrey exploded. "You mean the whole bloody mountainside's going to collapse?"

"No sir. But if this rain keeps up another slip could start. This whole area's got a history of them." He pointed into the darkness. "In '41 and '50 it was along Bonham, '59 was the major disaster on Robertson, Lytton Road, the list's endless, sir. I recommend evacuation."

"Which buildings?"

The man handed the governor a list then waved into the dark at the three levels. "I'm afraid it'll affect more than two thousand people."

Everyone gasped. All eyes went to the governor. He read the list, glanced up at the hillside. The slide dominated everything, the mass of the mountain looming above. Then he said, "Very well, do it. But for God's sake tell your fellows to make it an orderly withdrawal, we don't want a panic."

"Yes sir." The man hurried away.

"Can't we get more men and equipment, Donald?"

"Sorry, not at the moment, sir," the police commissioner replied. He was a strong-faced man in his fifties. "We're spread rather thinly, I'm afraid. There's the massive slip over in Kowloon, another at Kwun Tong—eighty squatters huts've been swamped, we've already forty-four dead in that one so far, twenty children."

Sir Geoffrey stared out at the hillside. "Christ!" he muttered. "With Dunross getting us Tiptop's cooperation I thought our troubles were over, at least for tonight."

The fire chief shook his head, his face drawn. "I'm afraid they're just beginning, sir. Our estimates suggest there may be a hundred or more still buried in that mess." He added heavily, "It'll take us weeks to sift through that lot, if ever."

"Yes." Again the governor hesitated, then he said firmly, "I'm going to go up to Kotewall. I'll monitor Channel 5." He went to his car. His aide opened the door but Sir Geoffrey stopped. Roger Crosse and Sinders were coming back from the great gash across Sinclair Road where the roof of the tunnel culvert had been ripped off. "Any luck?"

"No sir. We managed to get into the culvert but it's collapsed fifty yards in. We could never get into Rose Court that way," Crosse said.

When Rose Court had collapsed and had torn the side from the top four stories of Sinclair Towers, Crosse had been near his own apartment block, seventy yards away. Once he had recovered his wits, his first thought had been for Plumm, the second Suslev. Suslev was closer. By the time he had got to the darkened Sinclair Towers foyer, terrified tenants were already pouring out. Shoving them aside he had pushed and cursed his way up the stairs to the top floor, lighting his way with a pencil flashlight. Apartment 32 had almost vanished, the adjoining back staircase carried away for three stories. As Crosse gaped down into the darkness, it was obvious that if Suslev had been caught here, or caught with Clinker, he was dead—the only possible escape place was the tunnel-culvert.

Back on the ground floor once more, he had gone around the back and slipped into the secret tunnel entrance. The water was a boiling torrent below. Quickly he had hurried to the roadway where the roof of the tunnel had been carried away. The gash was overflowing. More than a little satisfied, for he was certain now that Suslev was dead, he had gone to the nearest phone, called in the alarm, then asked for Sinders.

"Yes? Oh hello, Roger."

He had told Sinders where he was and what had happened, adding, "Suslev was with Clinker. My people know he hasn't come out, so he's buried. Both of them must be buried. No chance they could be alive."

"Damn!" A long pause. "I'll come right away."

Crosse had gone outside again and begun to organize the evacuation of Sinclair Towers and rescue attempts. Three families had been lost when the corner top stories went. By the time uniformed police and fire chiefs had arrived, the dead count was seven including two children and four others dying. When the governor and Sinders had arrived, they had gone back to the open part of the tunnel to see if they could obtain access.

"There's no way we can get in from there, Sir Geoffrey. The whole culvert's collapsed, I'd say gone forever, sir." Crosse was suitably grave, though inwardly delighted with the divine solution that had presented itself.

Sinders was very sour. "Great pity! Yes, very bad luck indeed. We've lost a valuable asset."

"Do you really think he'd've told you who this devil Arthur is?" Sir Geoffrey asked.

"Oh yes." Sinders was very confident. "Don't you agree, Roger?"

"Yes." Crosse was hard put not to smile. "Yes, I'm sure of it."

Sir Geoffrey sighed. "There'll be the devil to pay on a diplomatic level when he doesn't return to the *Ivanov*."

"Not our fault, sir," Sinders said. "That's an act of God."

"I agree, but you know how xenophobic the Soviets are. I'll bet any money they'll believe we have him locked up and under investigation. We'd better find him or his body rather quickly."

"Yes sir." Sinders turned his collar higher against the rain. "What about the departure of the *Ivanov*?"

"What do you suggest?"

"Roger?"

"I suggest we call them at once, sir, tell Boradinov what's happened and that we'll postpone their departure if they wish. I'll send a car for him and whoever he wants to bring to help in the search."

"Good. I'll be up at Kotewall for a while."

They watched Sir Geoffrey go, then went to the lee of the building. Sinders stared at the organized confusion. "No chance he'd still be alive, is there?"

"None."

A harassed policeman hurried up. "Here's the latest list, sir, dead and rescued." The young man gave Crosse the paper and added quickly, "Radio Hong Kong's got Venus Poon coming on any moment, sir. She's up at Kotewall."

"All right, thank you." Rapidly Crosse scanned the list. "Christ!"

"They found Suslev?"

"No. Just a lot of old acquaintances're dead." He handed him the list. "I'll take care of Boradinov then I'm going back to the Clinker area."

Sinders nodded, looked at the paper. Twenty-eight rescued, seventeen dead, the names meaningless to him. Among the dead was Jason Plumm. . . .

At the wharf in Kowloon where the *Ivanov* was tied up, coolies were trudging up and down the gangplanks, laden with last-minute cargo and equipment. Because of the emergency, police surveillance had been cut to a minimum and now there were only two police on each gangway. Suslev, disguised under a huge coolie hat and wearing a coolie smock and trousers, barefoot like the others, went past them unnoticed and up on deck. When Boradinov saw him, he hastily guided the way to Suslev's cabin. Once the cabin door was shut, he burst out, "*Kristos*, Comrade Captain, I'd almost given you up for lost. We're due to le—"

"Shut up and listen." Suslev was panting, still very shaken. He tipped the vodka bottle and gulped the spirit, choking a little. "Is our radio equipment repaired?"

"Yes some of it, yes it is, except the top-security scrambler."

"Good." Shakily he related what had happened. "I don't know how I got out, but the next thing I remember was I was halfway down the hill. I found a taxi and made my way here." He took another swallow, the liquor helping him, the wonder of his escape from death and from Sinders enveloping him. "Listen, as far as everyone else is concerned, I'm still there, at Rose Court! I'm dead or missing presumed dead," he said, the plan leaping into his head.

Boradinov stared at him. "But Com—"

"Get on to police headquarters and say that I've not returned—ask if you can delay departure. If they say no, good, we leave. If they say yes we can stay, we'll stay for a token day, then regretfully leave. Understand?"

"Yes, Comrade Captain, but why?"

"Later. Meanwhile make sure *everyone* else aboard thinks I'm missing. Understand?"

"Yes."

"No one is to come into this cabin until we're safe in international waters. The girl's aboard?"

"Yes, in the other cabin as you ordered."

"Good." Suslev considered her. He could put her back ashore, as he was "missing" and would stay missing. Or keep with his plan. "We stay with that plan. Safer. When the police report I'm missing—I had my usual SI followers so they'll know I'm with Clinker—just tell her our departure's delayed, to stay in the cabin 'until I arrive.' Off you go."

Suslev locked the door, his relief almost overpowering, and switched on the radio. Now he could vanish. Sinders could never betray a dead man. Now he could easily persuade Center to allow him to pass over his duties in Asia to another and assume a different identity and get a different assignment. He could say that the various European security leaks documented in the AMG papers made it necessary for someone new to begin with Crosse and Plumm—if either of them is still alive, he thought. Better they're both dead. No, not Roger. Roger's too valuable.

Happier and more confident than he had been in years he went into the bathroom, found a razor and shaving brush, humming a Beatles tune along with the radio. Perhaps I should request a posting to Canada. Isn't Canada one of our most vital and important posts—on a par with Mexico in importance?

He beamed at himself in the mirror. New places to go to, new assignments to achieve, with a new name and promotion, where a few hours ago there was only disaster ahead. Perhaps I'll take Vertinskaya with me to Ottawa.

He began shaving. When Boradinov returned with police permission to delay their departure, he hardly recognized Gregor Suslev without his mustache and beard.

85

Bartlett was twenty feet down under a cat's cradle of girders that kept the wreckage from crushing him. When the avalanche had hit almost three hours ago he had been standing in the kitchen doorway sipping an ice-cold beer, staring out at the city. He was bathed, dressed and feeling wonderful, waiting for Orlanda to return. Then he was falling, the whole world wrong, unearthly, the floor coming up, the stars below, the city above. There had been a blinding, monstrous, soundless explosion and all air had rushed out of him and he had fallen into the upward pit forever.

Coming back to consciousness was a long process for him. It was dark within his tomb and he hurt everywhere. He could not grasp what had happened or where he was. When he truly awoke, he stared around trying to see where he was, his hands touching things he could not understand. The closed darkness nauseated him and he reeled in panic to his feet, smashing his head against a jutting chunk of concrete that was once part of the outside wall and fell back stunned, his fall protected by the debris of an easy chair. In a little while his mind cleared, but his head ached, arms ached, body ached. The phosphorescent figures on his watch attracted his attention. He peered at them. The time was 11:41.

I remember . . . what do I remember?

"Come on for chrissake," he muttered, "get with it! Get yourself together. Where the hell was I?" His eyes traced the darkness with growing horror. Vague shapes of girders, broken concrete and the remains of a room. He could see little and recognized nothing. Light from somewhere glistened off a shiny surface. It was a wrecked oven. All at once his memory flooded back.

"I was standing in the kitchen," he gasped out loud. "That's it, and Orlanda had just left, about an hour, no less'n that, half an hour. That'd make it around nine when . . . when whatever happened happened. Was it an earthquake? What?"

Carefully he felt his limbs and face, a stab of pain from his right shoulder every time he moved. "Shit," he muttered, knowing it was dislocated. His face and nose were burning and bruised. It was hard to breathe. Everything else seemed to be working, though every joint felt as though he had been racked and his head ached terribly. "You're okay, you can breathe, you can see, you can . . ."

He stopped, then groped around and found a small piece of rubble, carefully raised his hand, then dropped it. He heard the sound the rubble made and his heart picked up. "And you can hear. Now, what the hell happened? Jesus, it's like that time on Iwo Jima."

He lay back to conserve his strength. "That's the thing to do," the old top sergeant had told them, "you lay back and use your goddamn loaf if you're caught in an excavation or buried by a bomb. First make sure you can breathe safe. Then burrow a hole, do anything, but breathe any way you can, that's first, then test your limbs and hearing, you'll sure as hell know you can see but then lay back and get your goddamn head together and *don't panic*. Panic'll kill you. I've dug out guys after four days'n they've been like a pig in shit. So long's you can breathe and see and hear, you can live a week easy. Shit, four days's a piece of cake. But other guys we got to within'n hour'd drowned themselves in mud or crap or their own fear vomit or beaten their goddamn heads unconscious against a goddamn piece of iron when we was within a few feet of the knuckleheads an' if they'd just been lying there like I told you, nice'n easy, quiet like, they'd've heard us and they could've shouted. Shit! Any you bastards panic when you're buried you'd better believe you're dead men. Sure. Me I been buried fifty times. No panic!"

"No panic. No sir," Bartlett said aloud and felt better, blessing that man. Once during the bad time on Iwo Jima, the hangar he had been building was bombed and blown up and he had been buried. When he had dug the earth out of his eyes and mouth and ears, panic had taken him and he had hurled himself at the tomb and then he had remembered, *Don't panic*, and forced himself to stop. He had discovered himself shivering like a cowed dog under the threat of a lash but he had dominated the terror. Once over the terror and whole, he had looked around carefully. The bombing had been during the day so he could see well enough and noticed the beginning of a way out. But he had waited, cautiously, remembering instructions. Very soon he heard voices. He called out, conserving his voice.

"That's another goddamn obvious thing, conserve your voice, huh? You don't shout yourself hoarse the first time you hear help near. Be patient. Shit, some guys I know shouted themselves so goddamn hoarse they was goddamn dumb when we was within easy distance and we lost 'em. Get it through your goddamn heads, we gotta have help to find you. Don't panic! If you can't shout, tap, use anything, make a noise somehow, but give us a sign and we'll get you out, so long's you can breathe—a week's easy, no sweat. You bastards should go on a diet anyways . . ."

Now Bartlett was using all his faculties. He could hear the wreckage shifting. Water was dripping nearby but no sounds of humans. Then, faintly, a police siren which died away. Reassured that help was on the way, he waited. His heart was controlled. He lay back and blessed that old top sergeant. His name was Spurgeon, Spurgeon Roach, and he was black.

It must've been an earthquake, he thought. Has the whole building collapsed or was it just our floor and the next above? Maybe an airplane crashed into . . . Hell, no, I'd've heard the incoming noise. Impossible for a building to collapse, not with building regs, but hey, this's Hong Kong and we heard some contractors don't always obey regulations, cheat a little, don't use first-grade steel or concrete. Jesus if I get, no, *when* I get out . . .

That was another inviolate rule of the old man. "Never forget, so long's you can breathe, you will get out, *you will. . . .*"

Sure. When I get out I'm going to find old Spurgeon and thank him properly and I'm going to sue the ass out of someone. Casey's sure to . . . ah Casey, I'm sure as hell glad she's not in this shit, nor Orlanda. They're both . . . Jesus, could Orlanda have been caught wh—

The wreckage began to settle again. He waited, his heart pounding. Now he could see just a little better. Above him was a twisted mass of steel beams, and pipes half imbedded in broken jagged concrete, pots and pans and broken furniture. The floor he was lying on was equally broken. His tomb was small, barely enough space to stand. Reaching up above with his good arm he could not touch the makeshift ceiling. On his knees now he reached again, then stood, feeling his way, the tiny space claustrophobic. "Don't panic," he said out loud. Groping and bumping into outcrops he circumnavigated the space he was in. "About six feet by five feet," he said out loud, the sound of his voice encouraging. "Don't be afraid to talk out loud," Spurgeon Roach had said.

Again the light glinting off the oven attracted him. If I'm near that, I'm still in the kitchen. Now where was the oven in relation to anything else? He sat down and tried to reconstruct the apartment in his mind. The oven had been set into a wall opposite the big cutting table, opposite the window, near the door, and the big refrigerator was beside the door and across the w—

Shit, if I'm in the kitchen there's food and beer and I can last out the week easy! Jesus, if I could only get some light. Was there a flash? Matches? Matches and a candle? Hey, wait a minute, sure, there was a flash on the wall near the refrigerator! She said they were always blowing fuses and sometimes the power failed and . . . and sure, there were matches in the kitchen drawer, lots of them, when she lit the gas. Gas.

Bartlett stopped and sniffed the air. His nose was bruised and stuffed and he tried to clear it. Again he sniffed. No smell of gas. Good, good he thought, reassured. Getting his bearings from the oven he groped around, inch by inch. He found nothing. After another half an hour his fingers touched some cans of food, then some beer. Soon he had four cans. They were still chilled. Opening one, he felt oh so much better, sipping it, conserving it—knowing that he might have to wait days, finding it eerie down there in the dark, the building creaking, not knowing exactly where he was, rubble falling from time to time, sirens from time to time, water dripping, strange chilling sounds everywhere. Abruptly a nearby tie-beam shrieked, tormented by the thousands of tons above. It settled an inch. Bartlett held his breath. Movement stopped. He sipped his beer again.

Now do I wait or try to get out? he asked himself uneasily. Remember how old Spurgeon'd always duck that one. "It depends, man. It depends," he'd always say.

More creaking above. Panic began to well but he shoved it back. "Let's recap," he said aloud to reassure himself. "I got provisions now for two, three days easy. I'm in good shape an' I can last three, four days easy but you, you bastard," he said to the wreckage above, "what're you going to do?"

The tomb did not answer him.

Another spine-chilling screech. Then a faint voice, far overhead and to the right. He lay back and cupped his hands around his mouth. "Helllp!" he shouted carefully and listened. The voices were still there. "Helllp!"

He waited but now there was a vast emptiness. He waited. Nothing. His disappointment began to engulf him. "Stop it and wait!" The minutes dragged heavily. There was more water dripping, much more than before. Must be raining again, he thought. Jesus! I'll bet there was a landslide. Sure, don't you remember the cracks in the roads? Goddamn son of a bitching landslide! Wonder who all else got caught? Jesus what a goddamn mess!

He tore off a strip of his shirt and tied a knot in it. Now he could tell, the days. One knot for each day. His watch had read 10:16 when his head had first cleared, now it was 11:58.

Again all his attention zeroed. Faint voices, but nearer now. Chinese voices.

"Helllp!"

The voices stopped. Then, "Where you arrrr, *heya?*" came back faintly.

"Down here! Can you hear meeeeee?"

Silence, then more faintly, "Where youuuuarrrrre?"

Bartlett cursed and picked up the empty beer can and began to bang it against a girder. Again he stopped and listened. Nothing.

He sat back. "Maybe they've gone for help." His fingers reached out and touched another can of beer. He dominated his overpowering urge to break it open. "Don't panic and be patient. Help's near. The best I can do's wait an—" At that moment the whole earth twisted and rose up under the strain with an ear-dulling cacophony of noise, the protective girders above grinding out of safety, rubble avalanching down. Protecting his head with his arms, he cowered back, covering himself as best he could.

The shrieking movement seemed to go on for an eternity. Then it ceased. More or less. His heart was thumping heavily now, his chest tight and dust bile in his mouth. He spat it out and sought a beer can. They had vanished. And all the other cans. He cursed, then, cautiously, raised his head and almost banged it against the shifted ceiling of the tomb. Now he could touch the ceiling and the walls without moving. Easily.

Then he heard the hissing sound. His stomach twisted. His hand reached out and he felt the slight draft. Now he could smell the gas. "You'd better get the hell out of here, old buddy," he muttered, aghast.

Getting his bearings as best he could, he eased out of the space. Now that he was on the move, in action, he felt better.

The dark was oppressive and it was very hard to make progress upward. There was no straight line. Sometimes he had to make a diversion and go down again, left then right, up a little, down again under the remains of a bathtub, over a body or part of a body, moans and one time voices far away. "Whereareyouuuu?" he shouted and waited then crawled on, inch by inch, being patient, not panicking. After a while he came into a space where he could stand. But he did not stand, just lay there for a moment, panting, exhausted. There was more light here. When his breathing had slowed he looked at his watch. He gathered his strength and continued but again his upward path was blocked. Another way but still blocked. He slid under a broken pier and, once through, began to squirm onward. Another impasse. With difficulty he retreated and tried another way. And another, never enough space to stand, his bearings lost now, not knowing if he was going deeper into the wreckage. Then he stopped to rest and lay in the wet of his tomb, his chest pounding, head pounding, fingers bleeding, shins bleeding, elbows bleeding.

"No sweat, old buddy," he said out loud. "You rest, then you start again . . ."

MONDAY

86

Gurkha soldiers with flashlights were patiently picking their way over this part of the dangerous, sloping, broken surface calling out, "Anyone there?" then listening. Beyond and all around, up and down the slope, soldiers, police, firemen and distraught people were doing the same.

It was very dark, the arcs set up below not touching this area halfway up the wreckage.

"Anyone there?" a soldier called, listened again, then moved on a few feet. Over to the left of the line one of them stumbled and fell into a crevice. This soldier was very tired but he laughed to himself and lay there a moment, then called down into the earth, "Anyone there?" He began to get up then froze, listening. Once more he lay down and shouted into the wreckage, "Can you hear me?" and listened intently.

"Yesss! . . ." came back faintly, very faintly.

Excitedly the soldier scrambled up. "Sergeant! Sergeant Sah!"

Fifty yards away, on the edge of the wreckage, Gornt was with the young lieutenant who had been directing rescue operations in this section. They were listening to a news broadcast on a small transistor: ". . . slips all over the Colony. And now here is another report direct from Kotewall Road." There was a short silence then the well-known voice came on and the young man smiled to himself. "Good evening. This is Venus Poon reporting live on the single worst disaster to hit the Colony." There was a wonderful throb to her voice, and, remembering the brave, harrowing way she had described the Aberdeen fire disaster that she also had been involved in, his excitement quickened. "Rose Court on Kotewall Road is no more. The great twelve-story tower of light that all Hong Kong could see as a landmark has vanished into an awesome pyre of rubble. My home is no more. Tonight, the finger of the Almighty struck down the tower and those who lived there, amongst them my devoted *gan sun* who raised me from birth. . . ."

"Sir," the sergeant called out from the middle of the slip, "there's one over here!"

At once the officer and Gornt began hurrying toward him. "Is it a man or woman?"

"Man, sah! I think he said his name was Barter or something like that. . . ."

Up at the Kotewall Road barrier Venus Poon was enjoying herself, the center of all attention in the lights of mobile radio and television teams. She continued to read the script that had been thrust into her hand, changing it here and there, dropping her voice a little, raising it, letting the tears flow—though not enough to spoil her makeup—describing the holocaust so that all her listeners felt they were there with her on the slope, felt chills of horror, and thanked their joss that death had passed them by this time, and that they and theirs were safe.

"The rain is still falling," she whispered into the microphone. "Where Rose Court tore away part of the upper stories of Sinclair Towers, seven dead already counted, four children, three Chinese, one English, more still buried. . . ." The tears were seeping out of her eyes now. She stopped and those watching caught their breath too.

In the beginning she had almost torn her hair out at the thought of her apartment gone and all her clothes and all her jewelry and her new mink. But then she had remembered that all her real jewelry was safely in the jewelers being reset—a present of her old suitor, Banker Kwang—and her mink was being altered at the tailor's. And as to her clothes, pshaw, Four Fingers will be happy to replace them!

Four Fingers! Oh oh I hope that old goat got out and will be saved like Smiler Ching, she had prayed fervently. Eeeee, what a miracle! If one, why not another? And surely no building falling can kill old Ah Poo. She'll survive! Of course she will! And Banker Kwang saved! Didn't I weep with happiness that he was saved? Oh lucky lucky day! And now Profitable Choy, such a smart, good-looking interesting fellow. Now if he had money, real money, he would be the one for me. No more of these old bags of fart with their putty yangs for delectable yin, the most delectable . . .

The producer could not wait anymore. He leaped for the mike and said urgently, "We will continue the report as soon as Miss Ven—"

Instantly she came out of her reverie. "No, no," she said bravely, "the show must go on!" Dramatically she wiped her tears away and continued reading and improvising, "Down the slope members of our glorious Gurkha and Irish Guards, heroically risking their lives, are digging out our Brothers and Sisters. . . ."

"My God," an Englishman muttered. "What courage! She deserves a medal, don't you think so, old boy?" He turned to his neighbor and was embarrassed to see the man was Chinese. "Oh, oh sorry."

Paul Choy hardly heard him, his attention on the stretchers that were coming back from the wreckage, the bearers slipping and sliding under the arc lamps that had been erected a few minutes ago. He had just come back from the aid station that was set up at the fork of Kotewall Road under a makeshift overhang where frantic relations like himself were trying to identify the dead or injured or report the names of those who were missing and believed still buried. All evening he had been going back and forth in case Four Fingers had been found somewhere else and was coming in from another direction. Half an hour ago one of the firemen had broken through a mass of wreckage to reach into the area of the collapsed fifth floor. That was when Richard and Mai-ling Kwang had been pulled out, then Jason Plumm with half his head missing, then others, more dead than living.

Paul Choy counted the stretchers. Four of them. Three had blankets covering the bodies, two very small. He shuddered, thinking how fleeting life was, wondering again what would now happen at the stock exchange tomorrow. Would they keep it closed as a mark of respect? Jesus, if they keep it closed all Monday, Struan's is sure to be at 30 by Tuesday opening —gotta be! His stomach churned and he felt faint. Friday, just before closing, he had gambled five times every penny that Four Fingers had reluctantly loaned him, buying on margin. Five times 2 million HK. He had bought Struan's, Blacs, Victoria Bank and the Ho-Pak, gambling that somehow this weekened the tai-pan would turn disaster into victory, that the rumors of China being approached for cash were true, and Blacs or the Victoria had a scam going. Ever since the meeting with Gornt at Aberdeen when he had put his theory of a bail-out by Blacs or the Victoria of the Ho-Pak to Gornt and had seen a flicker behind those cunning eyes, he had wondered if he had sniffed out a scam of the Big Boys. Oh sure, they're Big Boys all right. They've got Hong Kong by the shorts, Jesus, have they got an inside track! And Jesus, oh Jesus when at the races Richard Kwang asked him to buy Ho-Pak and, almost at once, Havergill had announced his takeover, he had gone to the men's room and vomited. 10 million in Ho-Pak, Blacs, Victoria and Struan's, bought at the bottom of the market. And then, tonight, when the nine o'clock news announced that China was advancing half a billion cash so all bank runs were finished, he knew he was a multimillionaire, a multi-multimillionaire.

The young man could not hold his stomach together and rushed off to the bushes by the side of the road and retched till he thought he would die.

The English bystander turned his back on him and said quietly to a friend, "These Chinese fellows really don't have much of a stiff upper lip, do they, old boy?"

Paul Choy wiped his mouth, feeling terrible, the thought of all his maybe money, so near now, too much for him.

The stretchers were passing. Numbly he followed them to the aid station. In the background under the makeshift overhang, Dr. Meng was doing emergency surgery. Paul Choy watched Dr. Tooley turn back the blankets. A European woman. Her eyes were open and staring. Dr. Tooley sighed and closed them. The next was an English boy of ten. Dead too. Then a Chinese child. The last stretcher was a Chinese man, bleeding and in pain. Quickly the doctor gave him a morphia injection.

Paul Choy turned aside and was sick again. When he came back Dr. Tooley said kindly, "Nothing you can do here, Mr. Choy. Here, this'll settle your stomach." He gave him two aspirins and some water. "Why don't you wait in one of the cars? We'll tell you the instant we hear anything about your uncle."

"Yes, thanks."

More stretchers were arriving. An ambulance pulled up. Stretcher bearers got the tagged injured aboard and the ambulance took off into the drizzle. Outside, away from the stench of blood and death, the young man felt better.

"Hello, Paul, how're things going?"

"Oh. Oh hello, tai-pan. Fine, thanks." He had encountered the tai-pan earlier and told him about Four Fingers. Dunross had been shocked and very concerned.

"Nothing yet, Paul?"

"No sir."

Dunross hesitated. "No news is good news perhaps. If Smiler Ching could survive, let's hope for the best, eh?"

"Yes sir." Paul Choy had watched Dunross hurry off up the road toward the barrier, his mind rehashing all the permutations he had worked out. With the tai-pan's fantastic takeover of General Stores—that was so smart, oh so smart—and now sliding out of Gornt's trap, his stock's gotta go to 30. And with Ho-Pak pegged at 12.50, the moment that's back on the board it's gotta go back to 20. Now, figure it, 17.5 percent of 10 million times 50 is—

"Mr. Choy! Mr. Choy!"

It was Dr. Tooley beckoning him from the aid station. His heart stopped. He ran back as fast as he could.

"I'm not sure but follow me, please."

There was no mistake. It was Four Finger Wu. He was dead, seemingly unharmed. On his face was a wonderful calmness and a strange, seraphic smile.

Tears spilled down Paul Choy's cheeks. He squatted beside the stretcher, his grief possessing him. Compassionately Dr. Tooley left him and hurried over to the other stretchers, someone screaming now, another distraught mother clutching the broken body of a child in her arms.

Paul Choy stared at the face, a good face in death, hardly seeing it.

Now what? he asked himself, wiping away his tears, not really feeling he had lost a father but rather the head of the family, which in Chinese families is worse than losing your own father. Jesus, now what? I'm not the eldest son so I don't have to make the arrangements. But even so, what do I do now?

Sobbing distracted him. It was an old man sobbing over an old woman, lying on a nearby stretcher. So much death here, too much, Paul Choy thought. Yes. But the dead must bury the dead, the living must go on. I'm no longer bound to him. And I'm American.

He lifted the blanket as though to cover Four Finger Wu's face and deftly slipped off the thong necklace with its half-coin and pocketed it. Again making sure no one was watching, he went through the pockets. Money in a billfold, a bunch of keys, the personal pocket chop. And the diamond ring in its little box.

He got up and went to Dr. Tooley. "Excuse me, Doc. Would you, would you please leave the old man there? I'll be back with a car. The family, we'd . . . Is that okay?"

"Of course. Inform the police before you take him away, their Missing Persons is set up at the roadblock. I'll sign the death certificate tomorrow. Sorry there's no ti—" Again the kind man was distracted and he went over to Dr. Meng. "Here, let me help. It's like Korea, eh?"

Paul Choy walked down the hill, careless of the drizzle, his heart light, stomach settled, future settled. The coin's mine now, he told himself, certain that Four Fingers would have told no one else, keeping to his usual pattern of secrecy, only trusting those he had to.

Now that I've possession of his personal chop I can chop whatever I like, do whatever I like, but I'm not going to do that. That's cheating. Why should I cheat when I'm ahead? I'm smarter than any of his other sons. They know it, I know it and that's not being crazy. I am better. It's only fair I keep the coin and all the profits on the 2 mill. I'll set the family up, modernize everything, equip the ships, anything they want. But with my profit I'm going to start my own empire. Sure. But first I'm going to Hawaii. . . .

At the head of the line of cars near the first slip Dunross stopped beside his car and opened the door to the backseat. Casey jerked out of a reverie and the color drained out of her face. "Linc?"

"No, nothing yet. Quillan's fairly sure he's pinpointed the area. Gurkhas are combing that part right now. I'm going back to relieve him." Dunross tried to sound confident. "The experts say there's a very good chance he'll be okay. Not to worry. You all right?"

"Yes. Yes thanks."

When he had returned from their first search, he had sent Lim for coffee, sandwiches and a bottle of brandy, knowing the night would be very long. He had wanted Casey to leave with Riko but she had refused. So Riko had gone back to her hotel in the other car with Lim.

"You want a brandy, Ian?" Casey said.

"Thanks." He watched her pour for him, noticing her fingers were steady. The brandy tasted good. "I'll take Quillan a sandwich. Why not put a good slug of brandy into the coffee, eh? I'll take that."

"Sure," she said, glad for something to do. "Have any others been rescued?"

"Donald McBride—he's all right, just shaken. Both he and his wife."

"Oh good. Any, any bodies?"

"None that I know of," he said, deciding not to tell her about Plumm or his old friend Southerby, chairman of Blacs. At that moment Adryon and Martin Haply hurtled up and Adryon threw her arms around him, sobbing with relief. "Oh, Father we just heard, oh, Father, I was petrified."

"There, there," he said, gentling her. "I'm fine. Good God, Adryon, no bloody landslip will ever touch the tai-pan of the Noble Ho—"

"Oh don't say that," she begged him with a shiver of superstitious dread. "Don't ever say that! This's China, gods listen, don't say that!"

"All right, my love!" Dunross hugged her and smiled at Martin Haply who was also wet with relief. "Everything all right?"

"Oh yes sir, we were over in Kowloon, I was covering the other slide when we heard the news." The youth was so relieved. "Goddamn I'm pleased to see you, tai-pan. We . . . afraid we bashed up the car a little getting up here."

"Never mind." Dunross held Adryon away from him. "All right, pet?"

Again she hugged him. "Oh yes." Then she saw Casey. "Oh. Oh hello, Casey I was, er, so—"

"Oh don't be silly. Come on out of the rain. Both of you."

Adryon obeyed. Martin Haply hesitated then said to Dunross, "If you don't mind, sir, I'll just look around."

"Christian got out," Dunross said quickly. "He ph—"

"Yes sir. I called the office. Thanks. Won't be long, honey," he said to Adryon and went off toward the barrier. Dunross watched him go, young, tough and very assured, then caught sight of Gornt hurrying down the hill. Gornt stopped, well away from the car and beckoned him anxiously.

Dunross glanced at Casey, his heart thumping uneasily. From where she was she could not see Gornt. "I'll be back soon as I can."

"Take care!"

Dunross came up to Gornt. The older man was filthy, clothes torn, beard matted and his face set.

"We've pegged him," Gornt said. "Bartlett."

"He's dead?"

"No. We've found him but we can't get at him." Gornt motioned at the thermos. "Is that tea?"

"Coffee with brandy."

Gornt took it, drank gratefully. "Casey's still in the car?"

"Yes. How deep is he?"

"We don't know. Deep. Perhaps it's best not to say anything about him to her, not yet."

Dunross hesitated.

"Better to leave it," the other man said again. "It looks dicey."

"All right." Dunross was weary of all the death and suffering. "All right."

Rain made the night more filthy and the morass even more dangerous. Ahead, past the slide area, Kotewall Road ran almost straight for seventy yards, climbing steeply, then curled up and away around the mountainside. Already tenants were streaming out of buildings, evacuating.

"There's no mistake about Tiptop and the money?" Gornt said, picking his way carefully with the flashlight.

"None. The bank runs're over."

"Good. What did you have to barter?"

Dunross did not answer him, just shrugged. "We'll open at 30."

"That remains to be seen." Gornt added sardonically, "Even at 30 I'm safe."

"Oh?"

"I'll be about $2 million U.S. down. That's what Bartlett advanced."

Dunross felt a glow. That'll teach Bartlett to try a heist on me, he thought. "I knew about that. It was a good idea—but at 30 you'll be down about $4 million, Quillan, his 2 and 2 of yours. But I'll settle for All Asia Air."

"Never." Gornt stopped and faced him. "Never. My airline's still not for sale."

"Please yourself. The deal's on offer until the market opens."

"The pox on your deals."

They plodded onward on the top of the slope, now nearing the foyer area. They passed a stretcher returning. The injured woman was no one either of them knew. If Dunross were on one of those, Gornt thought grimly, it'd solve all my problems neatly . . .

87

The Gurkha sergeant had his flashlight directed downward. Around him were other soldiers, the young lieutenant, firemen hurrying up with one of the fire chiefs.

"Where is he?" Fire Chief Harry Hooks asked.

"There, somewhere down there. His name's Bartlett, Linc Bartlett." Hooks saw the light seep down a few feet then stop, blocked by the maze. He lay down on the ground. Close to the ground the gas smell was heavier. "Down there, Mr. Bartlett! Can you hear me?" he shouted into the wreckage.

They all listened intently. "Yes," came back faintly.

"Are you hurt?"

"No!"

"Can you see our light?"

"No!"

Hooks cursed, then shouted, "Stay where you are for the moment!"

"All right, but the gas is heavy!"

He got up. The officer said, "A Mr. Gornt was here and he's gone to get more help."

"Good. Everyone spread out, see if you can find a passage down to him, or where we can get closer." They did as he ordered. In a moment one of the Gurkhas let out a shout. "Over here!"

It was a small space between ugly broken slabs of concrete, broken timbers and joists and some steel H-beams, perhaps enough for a man to crawl down into. Hooks hesitated then took off his heavy equipment. "No," the officer said. "We'd better try." He looked at his men. "Eh?"

At once they grinned and all moved for the hole. "No," the officer ordered. "Sangri, you're the smallest."

"Thank you, sah," the little man said with a great beam, his teeth white in his dark face. They all watched him squirm underground headfirst like an eel.

Twenty-odd feet below, Bartlett was craning around in the darkness. He was in a small crawlspace, his way up blocked by a big slab of flooring, the smell of gas strong. Then his eyes caught a flicker of light ahead off to one side and he got a quick look at his surroundings. He could hear nothing except the drip of water and the creaking wreckage. With great care he squirmed off toward where he had seen the light. A small avalanche began as he shoved some boards aside. Soon it stopped. Above was another small space. He wormed his way up and along this space and reached a dead end. Another way, dead end. Above he felt some loosened boards in the crumpled flooring. He lay on his back and fought the boards away, coughing and choking in the dust. Abruptly light doused him. Not much, very little, but when his eyes adjusted it was enough for him to see a few yards. His elation vanished as he realized the extent of the tomb. In every direction he was blocked.

"Hello above!"

Faintly, "We hear youuuuu!"

"I'm in the light now!"

After a moment, "Which light?"

"How the hell do I know for chrissake?" Bartlett said. *Don't panic, think and wait,* he almost heard Spurgeon say. Holding on, he waited, then the light he was in moved a little. "That one!" he shouted.

Instantly the light stopped.

"We have you positioned! Stay where you are!"

Bartlett looked around, quartering the area very carefully. A second time with still the same result: there was no way out.

None.

"They'll have to dig me out," he muttered, his fear gathering . . .

Sangri, the young Gurkha, was down about ten feet under the surface but well away to the right from Bartlett. He could go no farther. His way was blocked. He squirmed around and got a purchase on a jagged concrete slab and moved it slightly. At once this part of the wreckage began to shift. He froze, let the slab rest again. But there was no other way to go, so, gritting his teeth and praying that everything would not collapse on him and whoever was below, he pulled the slab aside. The wreckage held. Panting, he put his flash into the cavity, then his head, peering around.

Another dead end. Impossible to go farther. Reluctantly, he pulled back. "Sergeant," he shouted in Nepalese, "I can go no farther."

"Are you sure?"

"Oh yes sah, very sure!"

"Come back!"

Before he left he shouted down into the darkness, "Hello down there!"

"I hear you!" Bartlett called back.

"We're not far away! We'll get you out, sah! Don't worry!"

"Okay!"

With great difficulty Sangri began to back out, retracing his way painfully. A small avalanche pelted him with rubble. Grimly he continued climbing.

Dunross and Gornt clambered over the wreckage to join the clusters of men who were in a chain, removing rubble and beams where they could.

"Evening, tai-pan, Mr. Gornt. We've pegged him but we're not close." Hooks pointed at the man who was holding the flash steady. "That's his direction."

"How far down is he?"

"By the sound of his voice about twenty feet."

"Christ!"

"Aye, Christ it is. The poor bugger's in a pickle. Look't those!" Heavy steel H-beams were blocking the way down. "We daren't use cutters, too much gas."

"There must be another way? From the side?" Dunross asked.

"We're looking. Best we can do's get more men and clear what we can away." Hooks glanced off at an encouraging shout. They all hurried toward the excited soldiers. Below a mess of torn-up flooring that the men had taken away was a rough passageway that seemed to lead downward, twisting out of sight. They saw one of the small men jump into the cavity, then vanish. Others watched, shouting encouragement. The way was easy for six feet, very hard for the next ten feet, twisting and turning, then he was blocked. "Hello down there, sah, can you see my light?"

"Yes!" Bartlett's voice was louder. There was almost no need to shout.

"I'm going to move the light around, sah. Please if it gets near, please give me right or left, up or down, sah."

"Okay." Bartlett could see a tiny part of light up and to his right through a mass of the beams, girders and joists and broken rooms. Directly above him was an impenetrable mess of flooring and girders. Once he lost the light beam but soon picked it up again. "Right a bit," he called, his voice already a little hoarse. Obediently the light moved. "Down! Stop there! Now up a fraction." It seemed to take an age but the light centered on him. "That's it!"

The soldier held the flash steadily, made a cradle for it with rubble, then took his hand away. "All right, sah?" he shouted.

"Yesss! You're on the money!"

"I'm going back for more help."

"All right."

The soldier retreated. In ten minutes he had guided Hooks back. The fire chief gauged the path of the beam and meticulously examined the obstacle course ahead. "Stone the crows, it'll take a month of Sundays," he muttered. Then, containing his dread, he took out his compass and measured the angle carefully.

"Don't you worry, mate," he called down. "We'll get you out nice and easy. Can you get closer to the light?"

"No. I don't think so."

"Just stay where you are and rest. Are you hurt?"

"No, no but I can smell gas."

"Don't worry, lad, we're not far away." Hooks clambered out of the passage. On the surface again, he measured the line on the compass and then paced out over the tilted surface. "He's below this spot, tai-pan, Mr. Gornt, within five feet or so, about twenty feet down." They were two thirds of the way down the slope, closer to Sinclair Road than to Kotewall. There was no way in from the sides that they could see, mud and earth of the slide heavier to the right than to the left.

"The only thing we can do's dig," he said with finality. "We can't get a crane here, so it's elbow grease. We'll try here first." Hooks indicated an area that seemed promising, ten feet away, close to the hole the soldiers had discovered.

"Why there?"

"Safer, tai-pan, in case we start the whole mess a-shifting. Come on, mates, lend a hand. But take care!"

So they began to dig and to carry away everything removable. It was very hard work. All surfaces were wet and treacherous, the wreckage itself unbalanced. Beams, joists, flooring, planks, concrete, plaster, pots, radios, TV sets, bureaus, clothes, all in an untidy impossible jumble. Work stopped as they uncovered another body.

"Get a medic up here!" Hooks shouted.

"She's alive?"

"In a manner of speaking." The woman was old, her once white smock and black trousers tattered and mud-colored, her long hair tied in a ratty queue. It was Ah Poo.

"Someone's *gan sun*," Dunross said.

Gornt was staring incredulously at the place she had been found, a tiny hole within an ugly, almost solid, jagged mess of broken and reinforced concrete. "How the hell do people survive?"

Hooks's face split with his grin, his broken teeth brown and tobacco stained. "Joss, Mr. Gornt. There's always hope so long as a body can breathe. Joss." Then he bellowed below. "Send a stretcher up here, Charlie! On the double!"

It came quickly. The stretcher bearers carried her away. Work continued. The pit deepened. An hour later, four or five feet lower they were blocked by tons of steel beams. "We'll have to detour," Hooks said. Patiently they began again. A few feet later again blocked. "Detour over there."

"Can't we saw through this mess?"

"Oh yes, tai-pan, but one spark and we're all bloody angels. Come on, lads. Here. Let's try here."

Men rushed to obey . . .

88

4:10 A.M.:

Bartlett could hear them loudly now. From time to time dust and dirt would cascade, sodden rubble in its wake, as timbers and beams and mess above were removed. His rescuers seemed to be about ten yards away as far as he could judge, still five or six feet above him, the trickle of light making the waiting easier. His own escape was blocked all around. Earlier he had considered going back, down under this flooring, then down again to try to find another route and seek better safety that way.

"Better wait, Mr. Bartlett!" Hooks had shouted to him. "We knows where you be!"

So he had stayed. He was rain soaked, lying on some boards, not too uncomfortably and well protected by heavy beams. Most of his line of sight was blocked a few feet away. Above was more twisted flooring. There was just enough room to lie down or, with care, to sit up. The smell of gas was strong but he had no headache yet and felt he was safe enough, the air good enough to last forever. He was tired, very tired. Even so, he forced himself to stay awake. From his vantage point he knew it would take them the rest of the night, perhaps part of the day, to work a shaft to him. That did not worry him at all. They were there. And he had made contact. An hour ago he had heard Dunross nearby. "Linc? Linc, it's Ian!"

"What the hell're you doing here?" he had called back happily.

"Looking for you. Don't worry, we're not far away."

"Sure. Say, Ian," he had begun, his anxiety almost overwhelming, "Orlanda, Orlanda Ramos, you know her? I was wai—"

"Yes. Yes I saw her just after the slip hit the building. She's fine. She's waiting up at Kotewall. She's fine. How about you?"

"Hell, no sweat," he had said, almost light-headed now, knowing she was safe. And when Dunross had told him about his own miraculous escape and that Casey had seen the whole catastrophe happen, he was appalled at the thought of how close the others had all been to disaster. "Jesus! A couple of minutes either way and you'd all've been clobbered."

"Joss!"

They had chatted for a while then Dunross had moved out of the way so the rescue could continue.

Thinking about Orlanda now, another tremor shook him and again he thanked God that she was safe and Casey was safe. Orlanda'd never make it underground, he thought. Casey maybe, but not Orlanda. Never. But that's no loss of face either.

He eased himself more comfortably, his soaking clothes making his skin crawl, the shouts and noises of the approaching rescue comforting. To pass the time, he continued his reverie about the two women. I've never known a body like Orlanda's or a woman like her. It's almost as though I've known her for years, not a couple of days. That's a fact. She's exciting, unknown, female, wonderfully dangerous. Casey's no danger. She'd make a great wife, a great partner but she's not female like Orlanda is. Sure Orlanda likes pretty clothes, expensive presents, and if what people here say is true she'll spend money like there's no tomorrow. But isn't that what most of it's for? My ex's taken care of, so're the kids. Shouldn't I have some fun? And be able to protect her from the Biltzmanns of the world?

Sure. But I still don't know what it is about her—or Hong Kong—that's got to me. It's the best place I've ever been and I feel more at home here than back home. "Maybe, Linc, you've been here in a previous lifetime," Orlanda had said.

"You believe in reincarnation?"

"Oh yes."

Wouldn't that be wonderful, he thought in his reverie, not noticing the gas or that now the gas was touching him a little. To have more than one lifetime would be the best luck in all the world an—

"Linc!"

"Hey! Hi, Ian, what's cooking?" Bartlett's happiness picked up. Dunross's voice was quite close. Very close.

"Nothing. We're just going to take a short break. It's heavy going. We've got to detour again but we're only a few yards away. Thought I'd chat. As far as we can judge we're about five feet above you, coming in from the west. Can you see us yet?"

"No. There's a floor above me, all busted up, and beams, but I'm okay. I can last out easy. Hey, you know something?"

"What?"

"Tonight's the first time you called me Linc."

"Oh? I hadn't noticed."

Bullshit, Bartlett thought and grinned to himself. "What y—" A sudden chill took both men as the wreckage began groaning, twisting here and there. In a moment the noise ceased, most of it. Bartlett began to breathe easier. "What you going to do tomorrow?"

"What about?"

"The stock market. How are you going to beat Gornt?" He listened with growing awe as Dunross told him about the Bank of China's money, Plumm's party and his challenge to Gornt, backed by his new 50 million revolving fund.

"Fantastic! Who's supporting you, Ian?"

"Father Christmas!"

Bartlett laughed. "So Murtagh came through, huh?" He heard the silence and smiled again.

"Casey told you?"

"No. No, I had that figured. I told you Casey's as smart as a whip. So you're home free. Congratulations," he said with a grin, meaning it. "I thought I had you, Ian." Bartlett laughed. "You really think your stock'll open at 30?"

"I'm hoping."

"If you're hoping, that means you and your pals have fixed it. But Gornt's smart. You won't get him."

"Oh yes I will."

"No you won't! How about our deal?"

"Par-Con? That stands of course. I thought that was all arranged?"

Bartlett heard the dry innocence. "Quillan must be fit to be tied."

"He is! He's just above. He's helping too."

Bartlett was surprised. "Why?"

There was a pause. "Quillan's a first-class, twenty-four-carat berk but . . . I don't know. Maybe he likes you!"

"Screw you too!" Bartlett was equally good-natured. "What're you going to do about Quillan?"

"I've made him a proposal." Dunross told it to him.

Bartlett grunted. "So my 2 mill's down the sewer?"

"Of course. That 2 million is. But your share of the General Stores takeover'll bring you 5, perhaps more, our Struan–Par-Con deal much more."

"You really figure 5?"

"Yes. You 5, Casey 5."

"Great! I always wanted her to get her drop dead money." I wonder what she'll do now? he asked himself. "She's always wanted to be independent and now she is. Great! What?" he asked, missing what Dunross had said.

"I just said, would you like to talk to her? It's dicey but safe enough."

"No," Bartlett said firmly. "Just say hi, I can say it better when I'm out."

"Casey's said she's not moving till you are." There was a slight pause. "Orlanda too. How about her? You want to say hello or anything?"

"No thanks. Plenty of time later. Tell them both to go home."

"They won't. I'm afraid you're rather popular."

Bartlett laughed and sat up and bumped his head. A pain snaked down his back and he grunted, then moved more comfortably, his head almost touching the roof.

Dunross was cramped in a small space not far away at the bottom of the twisting passage, hating the closeness, his claustrophobia nauseating, a chill cold sweat soaking him because of it. He could see no sign of Bartlett but he had noted his voice sounded strong and confident. Hooks had asked him to keep Bartlett talking while they rested, in case the gas was enveloping him. "You never know, tai-pan, gas can sneak up on you. We need him alert. We'll be needing his help soon now."

The tai-pan squirmed around uneasily, sensing danger. Someone was climbing down, rubble cascading with him. It was Hooks. He stopped a few feet above.

"All right, tai-pan. Best come out now, we'll get some of my lads back in."

"Right away. Linc! Stay awake. We're starting again."

"Okay, no sweat. Say, Ian, would you consider being a best man?"

"Certainly," he said at once, his brain shouting, Which one? "It'd be an honor."

"Thanks," he heard Bartlett say and as much as he wanted to know, he knew he could never ask. He was sure Bartlett would volunteer the who. But all Bartlett said was, "Thanks. Yes, thanks very much." He smiled, surprised. Linc's learning, he told himself. It'll be good to have him as a partner—and a voting member of the Turf Club. Casey too— "We'll have you out in a jiffy!"

Just as he was leaving he heard: "Wouldn't it be great if they could be friends? Guess that's too much to hope for?"

Dunross was not sure if it had been meant for him. "What?" he called out.

"Nothing," Bartlett replied. "Say, Ian, we've got lots to do this week! Hey, I'm glad you won over Gornt!" Yes, he told himself happily. It'll be good maneuvering with you, watching you carefully, building *our* Noble House.

About eight yards away, a few feet up, Dunross turned awkwardly and began to climb back.

Sixteen feet above him, Gornt and the others were waiting beside the greatly widened mouth of the pit. Dawn was lightening the east, a patch of sky now among the enveloping clouds. All over the slope tired men were still digging, searching, calling and listening. Wearily Hooks clambered out of the deepening pit. At that moment there was a tremendous noise from up near Po Shan Road. All heads jerked around. Then far above and to the left they saw part of the slope moving. The noise increased, then a wall of water and mud surged from behind the curve of the hillside up Kotewall Road and, gathering speed, rushed at them. Men began to flee as the sludge crest swept down to where the foyer had been and poured over the slope and wreckage, inundating it, the enormous mass of the sludge pressing the crest forward and down. Gornt saw it coming and hung on to an H-beam, the others hanging on as best they could. The foul, stinking murk swept up to them and passed, Gornt buried to his knees but his grip firm against the suction. The wave surged onward leaving inches of slush over everything, Hooks and the others pulling themselves out, everything else momentarily forgotten.

Gornt had not forgotten.

From where he was he could see down into the pit. He saw Dunross's hands and head appear out of the sludge. The hands grabbed a hold. More sludge was sweeping downward into the pit, finding a level, filling it. Dunross's grip slipped and he was sucked under but he fought out again and hung on precariously.

Gornt watched. And waited. And did not move. The mud poured down. The level rose more.

Dunross felt himself falling, the suction very great. He was choking in the slime, but his fingers held, he forced his toes into a crevice and began to climb. Somehow he tore himself out of the suction and now he was safe, hugging the side, half out of the mud, his chest heaving, heart pounding, retching. Still half in shock, his knees trembling, he wiped the mud from his eyes and mouth and stared around blankly. Then he saw Gornt ten feet above, watching him, resting easily against an outcrop . . .

For an instant his whole being concentrated, seeing the sardonic twisted smile, the hate open and disappointment vast, and he knew that if he had been above and Gornt trapped as he had been trapped, he would have watched and waited too.

Would I?

I'd've watched and waited equally and never never a helping hand. Not for Gornt. And then, at long last, Dirk Struan's curse would be ended, be laid to rest, and those who follow me never bedeviled again.

Then the instant was over. His head cleared. He remembered Bartlett and he stared downward in horror. Where the crawlspace had been was now only a slimy pool.

"Oh Christ! Helllp!" he cried out. Then there was sudden pandemonium and others were in the pit, Hooks and firemen and soldiers, and they hurled themselves impotently at the slime with shovels and with hands.

Dunross pulled himself out. Shakily he stood on the edge. In anguish. Gornt had already gone. In a little while all attempts ceased. The puddle remained.

TUESDAY

89

Dunross stood at the bay window of his penthouse atop the Struan Building, watching the harbor. The sunset was wonderful, visibility unlimited, the sky clear except for a few tinged cumulus westward over Mainland China, reddish there, darkness touching the eastern horizon. Below, the harbor was busy as usual, ordinary as usual, Kowloon glowing in the falling sun.

Claudia knocked and opened the door. Casey came in. Her face was stark, her tawny hair like the sunset. Her grief made her ethereal.

"Hello, Casey."

"Hello, Ian."

There was no need to say any more. Everything about Bartlett had been said already. It had taken until late last night to get his body out. Casey had waited on the slope for him. Then she had gone back to the hotel. This morning she had called and now she was here.

"Drink? Tea? Coffee? There's wine. I made martinis."

"A martini. Thanks, Ian," she said, her voice flat, the hurt in it tearing him. "Yes, I'd like that."

She sat on the sofa. He poured and put in an olive. "Everything can wait, Casey," he said compassionately. "There's no hurry."

"Yes, yes I know. But we agreed. Thanks." She accepted the chilled glass and raised it. "Joss."

"Joss."

She sipped the ice-cold liquor, all her movements studied, almost apart from herself, then opened her briefcase and put a manila envelope on his desk. "This contains all the John Chen papers about Struan's and everything he offered or told us. These're all the copies I have here. The ones in the States I'll shred." Casey hesitated. "You're sure to have made changes by now but, well, it's all there."

"Thanks. Did Linc give anything to Gornt?"

"No, I don't think so." Again the hesitation. "For safety I'd consider part of the information leaked."

"Yes."

"Next, our Par-Con–Struan deal." The sheaf of documents she gave him was quite thick. "All six copies are signed and sealed with the corporate seal. I've the executive power to sign." She hesitated. "We had a deal, Linc and I. I willed him voting power of all my stock for ten years, he did the same for me. So I'm head of Par-Con."

Dunross's eyes widened slightly. "For ten years?"

"Yes," she said without emotion, feeling nothing, wanting nothing except to weep and to die.

Later I can be weak, she thought. Now I must be strong and wise. "For ten years. Linc . . . Linc had voting control. I'll send you a formal verification when it's official."

Dunross nodded. From the lacquer desk he brought back an equivalent set of papers. "These are the same. I've chopped them formally. This"—he put an envelope onto the pile—"this's our private agreement giving Par-Con title to my ships as collateral."

"Thanks. But with your revolving fund that's not necessary."

"Even so, it was part of our agreement." Dunross watched her, admiring her courage. There had been no tears at the new beginning on the slope, just a numbed nod and, "I'll wait. I'll wait until . . . I'll wait." Orlanda had broken at once. He had sent her to a hotel and, later, a doctor to succor her. "It was part of our deal."

"All right. Thanks. But it's not necessary."

"Next: Here is the letter of agreement on our deal on General Stores. I'll get you the formal documents within ten days. I'll nee—"

"But Linc never put up the 2 million."

"Oh but he did. He did it by cable Saturday night. My Swiss bank confirmed the transaction yesterday and the money was duly passed over to the board of General Stores. They accepted so that deal's accomplished now."

"Even though Pug's dead?"

"Yes. His widow agreed to the board's recommendation. It's a very good deal by the way. Far better than the Superfoods tender."

"I don't want that, any part of that."

"When I was down in the pit, chatting with Linc, he said how happy he was that the General Stores deal was going through. His exact words were, 'Great! 5 mill? I always wanted her to get her drop dead money. She always wanted to be independent, and now, she is. Great!'"

"But at what a cost," she told him, her misery welling. "Linc always warned me that drop dead money costs more than you're prepared to pay. It has. I don't want it."

"Money is money. You're not thinking clearly. It was his to give and he gave it to you. Freely."

"You gave it to me."

"You're wrong, he did. I just helped you as you helped me." He sipped his drink. "I'll need to know where to send his profits. You'll remember there were no voting rights included. Who's his trustee?"

"It's a bank. First Central. I'm his executor, along with a man from the bank." She hesitated. "I guess his mother's his heir. She's the only one named in his will—Linc, Linc was open about that, to me. His ex-wife and their kids are well taken care of and specifically excluded from his will. There's just the voting control to me and the rest goes, the rest to his ma."

"Then she'll be very rich."

"That won't help her." Casey was trying very hard to keep her voice level and the tears away. "I talked to her last night and she broke up, poor lady. She's . . . she's in her sixties, nice woman, Linc's her only son." A tear seeped in spite of her resolve. "She, she asked me to bring him back. His will says he's to be cremated."

"Look, Casey," Dunross said quickly, "perhaps I could make the arr—"

"No. Oh no, thanks, Ian. Everything's done. I've done it. I wanted to do it. The airplane's cleared and all the paper work done."

"When do you leave?"

"At ten tonight."

"Oh." Dunross was surprised. "I'll be there to see you off."

"No, no thanks. The car's fine but there's no ne—"

"I insist."

"No. Please?" She looked at him, begging him.

After a moment he said, "What's your plan?"

"Nothing very much. I'm going to . . . I'm going to make sure all his wishes are taken care of, papers, his will, and wind up his affairs. Then I'll reorganize Par-Con—I'll try to reorganize it as he'd want, and then, then I don't know. All that'll take me thirty days. Maybe I'll be back in thirty days to begin, maybe I'll send Forrester or someone else. I don't know. I'll let you know in thirty days. Everything's covered till then. You've got my numbers. Please call me anytime if there's a problem." She started to get up but he stopped her.

"Before you go there's something I should tell you. I didn't last night because the time wasn't right. Perhaps now is, I'm not sure, but just before I left Linc he asked me if I'd consider being a best man." He saw Casey go white and rushed on. "I told him it would be an honor."

"He said me? He wanted to marry me?" she asked incredulously.

"We'd been talking about you. Doesn't that follow?"

"He never mentioned Orlanda?"

"Not at that time. No. Earlier on he'd been very concerned about her because he was in her flat and didn't know what had happened to her." Dunross watched her. "When I told him she was safe he was very relieved, naturally. When I told him you'd almost been caught in the landslide he almost had a heart attack. Then, just as I was leaving I heard him say softly, 'Guess it'd be too much to hope for those two to be friends.' I wasn't sure if I was meant to hear that—while we were digging he'd been talking to himself a lot." He finished his drink. "I'm sure he meant you, Casey."

She shook her head. "It's a good try, Ian. I'll bet it was Orlanda."

"I think you're wrong."

Again a silence. "Maybe. Friends?" She looked at him. "Are you going to be friends with Quillan?"

"No. Never. But that's not the same. Orlanda's a nice person. Truly."

"I'm sure." Casey stared at her drink, sipped but did not taste it. "What about Quillan? What happened today? I'm afraid I didn't hear. What did you do about him? I saw you closed at 30.01 but I . . . I really didn't notice much else."

Dunross felt a sudden glow. Because of the Kotewall catastrophe the governor had ordered the stock market to remain closed all Monday. And the banks, as a sign of mourning. By ten this morning, the Bank of China's cash was on hand in every branch of every bank, throughout the Colony. The bank runs fizzled. By three o'clock many customers were lined up returning to deposit their cash once more.

Just before the market opened at ten o'clock this morning Gornt had called him.

"I accept," he had said.

"You don't want to bargain?"

"I want no quarter from you, just as you expect none from me. The papers are on their way." The phone had gone dead.

"What about Quillan?" she asked again.

"We made a deal. We opened at 28 but I let him buy back in at 18."

She gaped at him. Without thinking she made the quick calculation. "That'd cost him just about 2 million. But that's Linc's 2 million. So Quillan's off the hook!"

"I told Linc the deal and that it'd cost him the 2 million and he laughed. I did point out that with General Stores and the Par-Con deal, his capital loss of 2 is set off against a capital gain of 20 or more." Dunross watched her, gauging her. "I think it's fair that the 2 was forfeit."

"You're not telling me you let Gornt off the hook for nothing?"

"No. I've got my airline back. The control of All Asia Air."

"Ah." Casey shivered remembering the story of that Christmas night when Gornt and his father went unexpectedly to the Great House. Her sadness was brimming. "Do me a favor?"

"Of course. Providing it's not for Quillan."

She had been going to ask Dunross to let Gornt in as a steward, to let him have a box. But now she did not. She knew it would have been a waste of time.

"What favor?"

"Nothing. Nothing now. I'll be off, Ian." Weary, so weary, she got up.

Her knees were trembling. All of her was aching monstrously. She held out her hand. He took it and kissed it with the same grace-filled gesture she remembered from the night of the party, the first night in the Long Gallery when, frightened, she had seen the knife buried in the heart of the portrait. All at once her agony crested and she wanted to scream out her hatred of Hong Kong and the people of Hong Kong who had some-how caused the death of her Linc. But she did not.

Later, she ordered herself, holding on to the limit of her strength. Don't break. Don't let go. Be self-contained. You have to, now. Linc's gone for-ever.

"See you soon, Casey."

" 'Bye, Ian," she said and left.

He stared at the closed door a long time, then sighed and pressed a buzzer.

In a moment Claudia came in. "Evening, tai-pan," she said with her enormous warmth. "There're a few calls that should be dealt with—most important, Master Duncan wants to borrow 1,000 HK."

"What the devil for?"

"It seems he wants to buy a diamond ring for a 'lady.' I tried to pry her name out of him but he wouldn't tell."

Oh God, the sheila, Dunross thought as the memory rushed back of what his son had said about his "girl." Sheila Scragger, the nurse from England, on holiday with Duncan at the Australian station called Pal-doon. "Well, he's not going to buy much for 1,000. Tell him he has to ask me. No, wait!" He thought a moment. "Give him 1,000 out of petty cash —offer it to him at 3 percent interest per month against his written guaran-tee that you can stop it from his pocket money at the rate of 100 a month. If he falls for that it'll teach him a fine lesson. If he doesn't I'll give him the 1,000, but not till next Easter."

She nodded, then added sadly, "Poor Miss Casey. She's dying inside."

"Yes."

"Here are your calls, tai-pan. Master Linbar called from Sydney, please call him back when you have a moment. He thinks he's got Woolara back in line."

Dunross stared at her. "I'll be damned!"

"Mr. Alastair called with congratulations, and your father, and most members of the family. Please call Master Trussler in Jo'burg, it's about thoriums." She sniffed. "Mrs. Gresserhoff called to say good-bye."

"When's she off?" Dunross asked noncommittally, knowing the flight.

"Tomorrow, JAL's early flight. Isn't it awful about Travkin? Oh I'm so sad about him."

"Yes." Travkin had died in the night. Dunross had visited him at the Matilda Hospital several times but his trainer had never recovered con-sciousness since the Saturday accident. "Have we tracked down any next of kin?"

"No. He had no special girl friend or, or anyone. Master Jacques has made the burial arrangements."

"Good. Yes. That's the least we can do for him."

"Are you going to ride Saturday?"

"I don't know." Dunross hesitated. "Remind me to talk to the stewards about making the fifth the Travkin Stakes—a way of thanking him."

"Yes. Oh, that would be wonderful. I did so like him, yes that would be wonderful."

Dunross glanced at his watch. "Is my next appointment downstairs yet?"

"Yes."

"Good," the tai-pan said, his face closing.

He went down to the next floor, to his office. "Afternoon, Mr. Choy, what can I do for you?" He had already sent condolences about Four Finger Wu.

When the door was shut, Paul Choy wiped his hands without noticing it. "I've come about step one, sir. Sorry we had to put it off from yesterday, but, er, the wax impressions—they fitted one of your two remaining half-coins?"

"First I would ask who has the other half, now that Four Fingers is an ancestor."

"The family Wu, sir."

"Who in the family Wu?" Dunross asked harshly, deliberately rough. "The coin was given to an individual who would pass it on to an individual. *Who?*"

"Me. Sir." Paul Choy stared back at the tai-pan, unafraid, even though his heart was beating faster than it had ever beaten—even more than when he was on the junk a lifetime ago—the young Werewolf's blood on his hands, the half-dead, mutilated body leaning against him, and his father shouting at him to throw the man overboard.

"You'll have to prove Four Fingers gave it to you."

"Sorry, tai-pan, I don't have to prove anything," Paul Choy replied confidently. "I just have to present the coin and ask the favor. In secret. Everything secret, that's the deal. If it's the real coin your honor and the face of the Noble House is at stake and the fa—"

"I know what I have at stake." Dunross made his voice grate. "*Do you?*"

"Sir?"

"This is China. Lots of curious things happen in China. You think I'm a fool to be bamboozled by an ancient legend?"

The young man shook his head, his throat tight. "No. You're absolutely no fool, tai-pan. But if I present the coin, you *will* grant the favor."

"What's your favor?"

"First I guess I'd like to know if you're . . . if you're satisfied it's *one* of the four. I'm satisfied."

"Are you now?"

"Yes sir."

"You know this coin was stolen from Phillip Chen?"

Paul Choy stared at him, then recovered quickly. "This coin's from Four Finger Wu. I know of no theft. It came from my father, that's all I know. It was my father's."

"You should give it back to Phillip Chen."

"Did you ever see it, this particular one, in his possession, sir?"

Dunross had already talked to Phillip Chen about the coin. "Is there no way to prove it's yours, Phillip?" he had asked him.

"None, tai-pan. None," the old man had said, wringing his hands.

Dunross kept his eyes boring into the youth. "It's Phillip Chen's."

Paul Choy shifted uneasily. "There were four coins, tai-pan. Mr. Chen's coin must be one of the others. This one belongs, belonged to my father. You remember what he said at Aberdeen?"

Dunross stared at him silently, trying to shake him, dealing with him Western style. Paul Choy wavered but held his gaze steady. Interesting, Dunross thought. You're a tough little bastard and good. Now, are you an emissary of Goldtooth Wu, the eldest son, or a thief and here on your own account? He left the silence hanging, using it to undermine his opponent while he rethought his position. The moment Paul Choy had called yesterday to ask for an appointment he had known the reason. But how to handle it? Four Fingers barely dead and now I've a new enemy, he thought, strong, well trained with lots of balls. Even so, he's got weak links like anyone. Like you have. Gornt's one of them. Riko could be another. Ah, Riko! What is it about her that moves you so much?

Forget that! How do you recover the half-coin before the favor?

"I presume you have your half with you. Let's go to the assayist right now." He got up, testing Paul Choy.

"No sir, sorry but no." Paul Choy felt his heart about to burst, the thong around his neck suddenly a noose, the half-coin burning into his flesh. "Sorry, but I don't think that's a good idea."

"I think it's a very good idea," Dunross continued brusquely, pressuring him. "We'll go and fetch it. Come along!"

"No. No thanks, tai-pan." Paul Choy said it with a polite firmness Dunross recognized. "Could we please do it next week? Say a week Friday? There's no hurry now."

"I won't be in Hong Kong on Friday."

"Yes sir. You'll be in Japan. Could you put aside an hour during your stay there? Anytime to suit you. To go visit an assayist?"

Dunross's eyes narrowed. "You seem to know a lot, Mr. Choy."

"It's easy to find out anything here, sir. Japan would be better for both of us. Less chance of a, a foul-up and in Japan we're both equal."

"You're suggesting you won't be here?"

"No, no, tai-pan. But as you said, this is China, strange things happen in China. Four Fingers and his group're well connected too. The coin's a one shot—person to person—and should be handled that way. That's the way I figure it."

Paul Choy was sweating now, thanking God that part of the "favor" was that everything was to be secret. Ever since he had brought back the body of Four Fingers he had been maneuvering for power in the family. At length he had achieved exactly what he wanted, the very special position—in Mafia terms—of *consigliere*, chief advisor to Goldtooth Wu, the eldest son, now titular head of the Seaborne Wu. That's what we are, he thought, his fear rising again. We're Chinese mafioso. Isn't there blood on me too? I was aboard with the opium. What does Goldtooth know that I don't?

"You can trust me implicitly, Goldtooth," he had said to his brother, fighting for his future.

"I'm afraid I have little choice. I'm in uncharted waters. I need all the help I can get. Your expertise will be very valuable," Goldtooth had said in his clipped English when they were in the final stages of negotiation.

"I figure we can work together."

"Let's be blunt, Brother. We're both university trained, the rest aren't. We need each other and the Seaborne Wu must be modernized. I can't do it. I need serious help—my years running his Pleasure Boats hardly fit me for command. I kept asking but, well, you know our father. Good God, I couldn't even change a girl's hourly rate without getting his approval. His four fingers were on every ship, in every transaction in the fleet."

"Sure, but now if his captains'll go along with change, in a year you'll have the best-run Chinese operation in Asia."

"That's exactly what I want. Exactly."

"What about opium?"

"The Seaborne Wu have always carried that cargo."

"What about guns?"

"What guns?"

"I heard whispers Four Fingers was going into gun-running."

"I know nothing about guns."

"Let's get rid of the opium-heroin racket. Let's stay to hell out of narcotics. Isn't it true he was joining up with those two jokers, Smuggler Yuen and White Powder Lee?"

"Rumors. I'll consider what you suggest. But let me say I'm captain of the fleets and head of the Seaborne Wu now. My decision is final. We'll consult. You'll be *consigliere* with all that means, but if I make a decision it's final. For instance, I heard about the coup, the stock market coup, that you pulled off without his permission. It was brilliant, yes, but there's to be no more of that—I must be consulted and must know in advance."

"Agreed. But from here on in, I'm also in business on my own account.

I've resigned from Gornt's. Next, any private dealings I began with Four Fingers are mine to continue."

"What are they?"

"Friday he advanced me 2 million to play the market. My deal was 17.5 percent of the profits. I want all the profits."

"50 percent."

"90. As of right now, there's nothing to keep me in Hong Kong. Even at 50 percent, if I sell the present holdings—and only I know what they are by the way—I'm worth around 3 million U.S."

They had haggled and settled at 70 percent, Goldtooth's 30 percent to be deposited in a Swiss bank, a numbered account.

"I figure the market'll be on the come for two more days, then I off-load. My decision, okay?"

"Yes. *Profitable* suits you, Younger Brother, better than Paul. I'd like to stay with Profitable. What else were you doing with Four Fingers?"

"There was one last scam. He swore me to secrecy, forever. Forever, with blood oaths. I have to honor his wish."

Reluctantly Goldtooth Wu had agreed and now, waiting for the tai-pan to answer him about Japan, the young man's confidence was brimming. I'm rich. I've all Goldtooth's power if I need it, and I've a U.S. passport and I'm going to Hawaii. In Japan there's a chance I can outsmart Dunross—no, not outsmart him, he's far too good for that, but maybe there I can get a safe, fair shake to prove, once and for all, *my* coin's real.

"Would Japan suit you, tai-pan?" he repeated.

"I hear you made a killing on the market?"

The youth beamed, not expecting the nonsequitur. "Yes sir. I'm about 5.5 million U.S. ahead."

Dunross whistled. "That's not bad for a couple of weeks work, Profitable Choy. At 15 percent tax," he added innocently.

The youth winced and fell into the trap. "Hell, I'm a U.S. citizen, so subject to U.S. taxes every which way." He hesitated. "I've a couple of ideas that'd . . . say, tai-pan, we might make a deal that'd be good for you and good for me."

Dunross saw Paul Choy's eyes flatten and his caution increase.

"My Old Man trusted you," the youth said. "You and he were Old Friends. Maybe I could inherit that—be worth that, one day."

"Return the coin freely and I'll grant all sorts of favors."

"First things first, tai-pan. First we find out if my coin's real. Japan, okay?"

"No. Here, or not at all!" Dunross snapped, deciding to gamble.

Paul Choy's eyes slitted even more. Abruptly he decided too and reached under his shirt and took out the coin and laid it on the desk. "I ask a favor in Jin-qua's name from the tai-pan of the Noble House."

In the silence Dunross stared at the coin. "Well?"

"First, I want Old Friend status, equal to Four Fingers with all that

that implies. Second: I want to be appointed a director of Struan's for a four-year period at a salary equal to other directors—for face I'll buy a block of shares at market bringing my holdings to 100,000 shares." He felt a bead of sweat drop off his chin in the silence. "Next: I want to joint venture, 50-50 partners, a pharmaceutical plant with Struan's, capitalized at 6 million U.S.—I put up half within 30 days."

Dunross stared at him, perplexed. "To do what?"

"The market for pharmaceuticals throughout Asia is vast. We could make a bundle, given your expertise in manufacturing, mine in marketing. Agreed?"

"Is that all? All the favor?"

"Three more things. Th—"

"Only three?" Dunross asked witheringly.

"Three. First, next year I'm going to start another stock exchange. I'll—"

"You'll what?" Dunross gaped at him, thrown.

Profitable Choy grinned and wiped the sweat off his face. "Sure. A stock exchange for Chinese, run by Chinese."

Dunross laughed suddenly, "You've got balls, Profitable Choy. Oh yes. Incidentally, that's not a bad idea at all. What about it, the new exchange?"

"Just your benevolent Old Friend assistance to get started, to stop the big guys from blocking me."

"For 50 percent."

"For very favorable inside terms. Very favorable, guaranteed. Next," the youth held on to his hope, "I want you to introduce me to Lando Mata and tell him you're backing me as part of my father's group to bid for the gambling and gold syndicate monopoly. All right?"

"You said three things. What's last?"

"In three years a stewardship of the Turf Club. In that time I'll guarantee to donate a million U.S. to any charity or charities you name, I'll back all worthy causes and swear by God I'll make it as easy for you as I can." The young man wiped the sweat off. "I'm finished."

Dunross hesitated. "If the coin's real I'll agree to everything except the part about Lando Mata."

"No. That's part of the deal."

"I don't agree."

"I've asked for nothing illegal, nothing you can't gr—"

"Lando Mata's out!"

The young man sighed. He took the coin off the desk, stared at it. "If that's out, then the whole deal's off and I'll put Four Finger Wu's ask in place. It's still the same coin," he said, readying to play his last card.

"And?"

"And that'll make you party to narcotics, guns and everything you detest *but will have to honor*. Sorry, tai-pan, but I'm bucking to be an ancestor." He tossed the coin back on the table. "You choose."

Dunross was suddenly perturbed. The favor was cleverly couched. Nothing illegal, nothing extravagant. Paul Choy had done very well against him. Too well. Four Fingers was a known quantity. But this one, this devil's spawn? I can't risk narcotics—he knows that.

To give himself time Dunross reached into his pocket and found the little silk pouch and put his coin on the table. He moved his half into the other. The fit was perfect.

Without knowing it both men exhaled, staring at the now-joined coin that would lock them immutably together. Dunross knew it was a waste of time but he would go to the assayist anyway. For a moment he held the two halves in his hand. What to do about this cocky young bugger, he asked himself. Ah, now there's a good thought! Phillip Chen should be given the problem!

"All right, Profitable Choy," he said putting him very high on his private Suspected Persons list. "I'll agree to grant your favor—if your half's real—except I'll ask Lando, I can't tell him anything. All right?"

"Thank you, tai-pan, you won't regret it." Wet with relief Profitable Choy took out a list of names. "Here's all the expert assayists in Hong Kong. You like to choose one? I, er, I checked and they're all open to seven o'clock."

Dunross smiled faintly. "You're very sure of yourself, Profitable Choy."

"Just try to keep ahead of the game, sir."

Casey came out of the Struan Building and went to the waiting Rolls. At once Lim opened the door for her. She sank back into the deep cushions feeling nothing, knowing nothing except that her anguish was consuming her and any moment she would break, not even noticing Lim ease the car into the heavy traffic to head for the vehicular ferry.

Tears were very near. So much time before we leave, she thought. Everything packed and sent to the airplane. I'm checked out, all bills paid, but so much time still left.

For a moment she considered just stopping the car and walking off but that would have been worse, no privacy, no protection and she felt so terrible. Yet I've got to get out, be by myself. I've got to. Oh Jesus, Linc poor Linc. "Lim," she said on an impulse, "go to the Peak."

"Missee?"

"Just drive to the top of the Peak, to the lookout. Please?" she said, desperately trying to keep her voice ordinary. "I've, I haven't been there. I want to see it before I go. Please."

"Yes, Missee."

Casey leaned back and closed her eyes against the tears that poured out silently.

90

It was almost sunset.

Up at Lo Wu, the central border village between the Colony and China, the usual crowds of Chinese were crossing the bridge in both directions. The bridge was barely fifty yards long and spanned a trickling muddy stream and yet those fifty yards, for some, were a million miles. At both ends were guard posts and immigration checkpoints and customs, and in the middle, a small removable barrier. Two Hong Kong police stood there and two PRC soldiers. Two train tracks went across the bridge.

In the old days trains came from Canton to Hong Kong and back again, nonstop, but now passenger trains stopped on either side and passengers crossed on foot. And the trains themselves went back the way they came. Freight trains from China went through without problem. Most days.

Each day hundreds of locals crossed the border as they would cross any road. Their fields or work was on both sides of the border and had been so for generations. These border people were a hardy, suspicious lot, hating change, hating interference, hating uniforms, hating police particularly and foreigners of every kind. A foreigner to them, as to most Chinese, was anyone not of their village. To them there was no border, could never be a border.

The Lo Wu bridge was one of the most sensitive single spots in all China—it and the other two crossing points. Of these, one was at Mau Kam Toh where cattle and vegetables came daily over a rickety bridge across this same stream that marked most of the border. The last, at the very eastern tip of the border, was at the fishing village of Tau Kok. Here the border was not marked but, by common consent, was said to run down the middle of the single village street.

These were China's only contact points with the West. Everything was meticulously controlled and monitored—by both sides. The tension and manner of the guards was a barometer.

Today the guards on the PRC side of Lo Wu had been jittery. Because of that, the Hong Kong side was nervous too, not knowing what to expect —perhaps a sudden closure, perhaps a sudden invasion like last year, the Colony existing at the whim of China. "And that's a fact of life," Chief Inspector Smyth muttered. Today he had been assigned here for special duty and he was standing uneasily near the police station that was discreetly set back a hundred yards from the real border so as not to offend or create waves. Christ, he thought, waves? One fart in London could start millions of refugees marching here—if the powers across the border decided that that tiny piece of wind was an affront to the dignity of China.

"Come on, for chrissake," he said impatiently, his khaki shirt sticking to his back, his eyes on the road back to Hong Kong. The road was puddled. It curled away. Then, in the distance, he saw the police car approaching. Greatly relieved, he went to meet it. Armstrong got out. Then Brian Kwok. Smyth saluted Robert Armstrong with his swagger stick to cover his shock. Brian Kwok was in civilian clothes. There was a curious, vacant, petrified look in his eyes. "Hello, Robert," Smyth said.

"Hello. Sorry to be late," Armstrong said.

"It's only a couple of minutes. Actually I was told sunset." Smyth squinted westward. The sun was not yet down. He turned his attention back to Brian Kwok. It was hard to keep the contempt out of his face.

The tall, handsome Chinese took out a pack of cigarettes. His fingers trembled as he offered it to Smyth.

"No thanks," Smyth said coldly. Armstrong took one. "I thought you'd given up smoking?"

"I did. I started again."

Brian Kwok laughed nervously. "Afraid it's me. Robert's been trying to keep . . . to keep Crosse and his angels off my back."

Neither man laughed.

"Is anyone coming? Anyone else?" Smyth asked.

"I don't think so. Not officially." Armstrong looked around. There were the usual gaping bystanders but they appeared haphazard. "They're here though. Somewhere." Both men felt the hackles on their necks rising. "You can get on with it."

Smyth took out a formal document. "Wu Chu-toy, alias Brian Kar-shun Kwok, you are formally charged with espionage against Her Majesty's Government on behalf of a foreign power. Under the authority of the Deportation Order of Hong Kong you are formally ordered out of the Crown Colony. If you return you are formally warned you do so at your peril and are liable for arraignment and imprisonment at Her Majesty's pleasure." Grimly Smyth handed him the paper.

Brian Kwok took it. It seemed to take him time to see and to hear, his senses dulled. "Now . . . now what happens?"

Smyth said, "You walk over that bloody bridge and go back to your pals."

"Eh? You think I'm a fool? You think I believe you're, you're letting me go?" Brian Kwok spun on Armstrong. "Robert, I keep telling you they're playing with me, with you, they'll never let me go free! You know that!"

"You're free, Brian."

"No . . . no, I know what's happening. The moment I, the moment I'm almost there they'll pull me back, the torture of hope, that's it, isn't it?" There was a shrillness creeping into his voice, a fleck of foam at the corner of his lips. "Of course! The torture of hope."

"For chrissake, I've told you you're free! You're free to go," Armstrong said, his voice hard, wanting to end it. "Go for chrissake! Don't ask me why they're letting you go but they are. Go!"

Filled with disbelief, Brian Kwok wiped his mouth, started to speak, stopped. "You're . . . it's a . . . it's a lie, has to be!"

"*Go!*"

"All right, I'll . . ." Brian Kwok went off a pace then stopped. They had not moved. "You're, you really mean it?"

"Yes."

Shakily Brian Kwok put out his hand to Smyth. Smyth looked at it, then into his face. "If it was up to me I'd have you shot."

A flash of hatred went over Kwok's face. "What about you and graft? What about you selling police pro—"

"Don't let's get into that! *H'eung yau*'s part of China!" Smyth snarled and Armstrong nodded uneasily, remembering the first 40,000 gambled on Saturday.

"A little feathering's an old Chinese custom," Smyth continued, shaking with rage. "Treason isn't. Fong-fong was one of my lads before he went to SI. Go get stuffed and get the hell across the bridge or I'll whip you across it!"

Brian Kwok began to speak, stopped. Bleakly he offered his hand to Armstrong. Armstrong shook it without friendship. "That's just for old times' sake, for the Brian I used to know. I don't approve of traitors either."

"I, I know I was drugged but thanks." Brian Kwok backed away, still suspecting a trick, then turned. Every few seconds he looked back, petrified that they were coming after him. When his halting feet reached the bridge he broke into a frantic run. Tension skyrocketed. Police at the barrier did not stop him. Neither did the soldiers. Both sides, forewarned, pretended not to notice him. The crowds streaming across either side of the tracks, bicycles, pedestrians, carts, mostly laden, paid him no attention at all. At the other side of the barrier, Brian Kwok skidded to a stop and turned back.

"We'll win, we'll, we'll win you know," he called back to them, his chest heaving. "We will!" Then still suspecting a trick, he hunched down and fled into China. Near the train they saw a nondescript group of people intercept him but now it was too far away to see clearly. Tension on the bridge subsided. The sun began to set.

In the small observation tower atop the police station, Roger Crosse watched with high-powered binoculars. He was well concealed. Beside him was an SI operator with a telescopic camera, equally concealed. His face closed. One of the men meeting Brian Kwok was Tsu-yan, the missing millionaire.

The sun was almost under the western seas. Casey was at the Peak lookout, all Hong Kong spread below, lights on in the gloaming, part of the city and Kowloon blood-colored, part already dark with deep shadows and blazing highlights. The sun vanished and night, true night, began.

But she saw none of the beauty of it. Her face was wet with the tears that still coursed. She was leaning on the railing at a far corner, oblivious. The other sightseers and people waiting at the nearby bus stops left her alone—too interested in their own affairs.

"By all the gods I made a fortune today. . . ."

"I bought in first thing and doubled my fornicating money. . . ."

"*Ayeeyah* so did I, and I spent most of the day negotiating a loan from Best Bank against my portfolio. . . ."

"Thank all gods the Middle Kingdom bailed out those stupid foreign devils . . ."

"I bought Noble House at 20. . . ."

"Did you hear they dug out two more bodies at Kotewall and now the count's sixty-seven dead. . . ."

"Joss! Isn't it wonderful about the market! Old Blind Tung's prediction came true again. . . ."

"Did you hear about my sister, Third Toiletmaid Fung from Great Hotel? She and her syndicate bought at the darkest time and now she's a millionaire. . . ."

Casey heard nothing, saw nothing, misery overwhelming her. People came and went, a few lovers. The only Europeans were tourists with their cameras. Casey hid from them as best she could.

"Say, can I help?" one of them said.

"No, no thank you," she replied, her voice flat, not looking at him, helpless to stop the tears.

I have to stop, she thought. I have to stop. I have to begin again. I have to begin again and be strong and live, for me and for Linc. I've got to guard him and his, I've got to be strong, be strong.

But how?

"I won't let go," she told herself aloud. I won't. I have to think.

I have to think about what the tai-pan said. Not about marriage, oh Linc, not about that. I have to think about Orlanda.

"Is it too much to hope they'd be friends?" Did he really say that?

What to do about her?

Bury her. She took Linc away from me. Yes. But that was within my rules, the rules I set down. Ian's right. She's not like Quillan and it was Linc—he fell for her, he went out with her. She's not like Quillan Gornt.

Quillan. What about him? He had come to the hotel this afternoon, again offering her whatever help she needed. She had thanked him and refused. "I'm okay, Quillan. I have to work this out myself. No, please don't see me off. Please. I'll be back in thirty days, maybe. Then I'll be more sensible."

"You're signing with Struan's?"

"Yes. Yes, that's what I want to do. Sorry."

"No need to be sorry. You've been warned. But that doesn't preclude dinner the first night you're back. Yes?"

"Yes."

Oh Quillan, what to do about you?

Nothing for thirty days. Linc must have the next thirty days. Totally. I have to protect him against the vultures.

Seymour Steigler for one. This morning he had come to her suite. "Hey Casey, I'll get the coffin arranged and—"

"It's done, everything's done."

"That a fact? Great. Listen, I'm all packed. Jannelli can take my bags and I'll be at the airplane in good time so we c—"

"No. I'm taking Linc home alone."

"But hell, Casey, we've got a lot to talk about. There's his will, there's the Par-Con deal, we got time now to figure it good. We can delay and maybe get us a few extra points. We—"

"It can all wait. I'll see you back in L.A. Take off a couple of days, Seymour. Be back next Monday."

"Monday? For chrissake there's a million things to do! Linc's affairs'll take a year to untangle. We gotta get counsel fast. Sure, the best in town. I'll do that first thing, the best. Don't forget there's his widow and his kids. She'll sue on their behalf, of course she'll sue—and then there's you! For chrissake you're entitled to a fat share. We'll sue too, haven't you been like a wife to him for seven ye—"

"Seymour, you're fired! Get your ass out of here an—"

"What the hell's with you? I'm only thinking of your legal rights an—"

"Don't you hear, Seymore? You're fired!"

"You can't fire me. I've got rights. I got a contract!"

"You're a son of a bitch. You'll get top dollar to settle your contract but if you take after me or Linc or Linc's affairs I'll see to it you get nothing. Nothing. Now get the hell out of here!"

Casey wiped away her tears, remembering her exploding rage. Well he is a son of a bitch. I was never sure before but I am now. I'm glad I fired him. I'll bet any money he'll come sniffing around like a hyena. Sure. I'll bet he'll go see the ex-Mrs. Bartlett if he hasn't already called her and work her into a frenzy, to represent her brood to attack Par-Con and Linc. Sure, I'll bet any money I'll see him in court, one way or another.

Well, God help me, I swear he won't beat me. I'll protect Linc whatever.

Forget that bastard, Casey. Forget the battles you're going to fight, concentrate on the now. What about Orlanda? Linc, Linc liked her—loved her maybe. Did he? I don't know for sure. And never will, not now.

Orlanda.

Should I go see her?

91

Orlanda was sitting in the dark of her room at the Mandarin Hotel staring out at the night. Her grief was spent.

Joss about Linc, she told herself for the ten thousandth time. Joss. Now everything's as before. Everything has to start again. The gods laughed at me again. Perhaps there'll be another chance—of course there'll be another chance. There are other men . . . Oh God! Don't worry, everything will be as it was. Quillan said not to worry, my allowance would contin—

The phone jangled, startling her. "Hello?"

"Orlanda? It's Casey." Orlanda sat bolt upright, astonished. "I'm leaving tonight but I wanted to see you before I go. Is that possible? I'm downstairs."

Her enemy calling her? Why? To gloat? But they'd both lost. "Yes, Casey," she said hesitantly. "Would you like to come up? It's more private here. 363."

"Sure. 363."

Orlanda switched on a light and hurried to the bathroom to check her face. She saw sadness and recent tears—but no age. Not yet. But age is coming, she thought, a shiver of apprehension taking her. A comb to her hair and a little makeup on her eyes. Nothing else needed. Not yet.

Stop it! Age is inevitable. Be Asian! Be aware.

She slipped on her shoes. The waiting seemed long. Her heart was grinding. The bell rang. The door opened. Each saw the desolation of the other.

"Come in, Casey."

"Thanks."

The room was small. Casey noticed two small cases standing neatly beside the bed. "You leaving too?" Her voice sounded far away to her.

"Yes. Yes I'm moving in with friends of my parents. The hotel's a, it's a bit expensive. My friends said I could stay with them until I can find another apartment. Please sit down."

"But you're covered by insurance?"

Orlanda blinked. "Insurance? No, no I don't think so. I never . . . no, I don't think so."

Casey sighed. "So you've lost everything?"

"Joss." Orlanda half-shrugged. "It doesn't matter. I have a little money in the bank and . . . I'm fine." She saw the misery in Casey's face, and her compassion reached out. "Casey," she said quickly, "about Linc. I wasn't trying to trap him, not for anything bad. Oh yes, I loved him and yes, I'd've done anything to marry him, but that's only fair, and honestly I believe I'd've been a wonderful wife for him, I'd've tried so very hard to be the best, honestly. I did love him and . . ." Again Orlanda shrugged her tiny shrug. "You know. Sorry."

"Yes, yes I know. No need to be sorry."

"The first time I met you at Aberdeen, the night of the fire," Orlanda said, rushing on, "I thought how foolish Linc was, perhaps you were for not . . ." She sighed. "Perhaps it's as you said, Casey, there's nothing to talk about. Now most of all." The tears began again. And her tears, the reality of them, brought tears from Casey.

For a moment they sat there, the two women. Then Casey found a tissue, dried her eyes, feeling awful, nothing resolved, wanting now to finish quickly what she had begun. She took out an envelope. "Here's a check. It's for $10,000 U.S. I th—"

Orlanda gasped. "I don't want your money! I don't want anything fr—"

"It's not from me. It's Linc's. Listen a moment." Casey told her what Dunross had said about Bartlett. All of it. The repeating of it tearing her anew. "That's what Linc said. I think it was you he wanted to marry. Maybe I'm wrong. I don't know. Even so, he'd want you to have some drop . . . some protection."

Orlanda felt her heart about to burst at the irony of it all. "Linc said 'best man'? Truly?"

"Yes."

"And to be friends? He wanted us to be friends?"

"Yes," Casey told her, not knowing if she was doing the right thing, what Linc would have wanted. But sitting here now, seeing the tender youthful beauty, the wide eyes, exquisite skin that needed no makeup, perfect figure, again she could not blame her or blame Linc. It was my fault, not his and not hers. And I know Linc wouldn't have left her destitute. So I can't. For him. He wanted us to be friends. Maybe we can be. "Why don't we try?" she said. "Listen, Hong Kong's no place for you. Why not try some other place?"

"I can't. I'm locked in here, Casey. I've no training. I'm nothing. My B.S. means nothing." The tears began again. "I'm just . . . I'd go mad punching a clock."

On a sudden impulse Casey said, "Why not try the States? Maybe I could help you find a job."

"What?"

"Yes. Perhaps in fashion—I don't know what exactly but I'll try."

Orlanda was staring at her incredulously. "You'd help me, really help me?"

"Yes." Casey put the envelope and her card on the table and got up, her whole body aching. "I'll try."

Orlanda went to her and put her arms around her. "Oh thank you, Casey, thank you."

Casey hugged her back, their tears mixing.

The night was dark now with little light from the small moon that came through the high clouds from time to time. Roger Crosse walked silently up to the half-hidden gate in the tall walls that surrounded Government House and used his key. He locked the gate behind him, walked quickly along the path, keeping to the shadows. Near the house he detoured and went to the east side, down some steps to a basement door and took out another key.

This door swung open, equally quietly. The armed sentry, a Gurkha, held his rifle ready. "Password, sir!"

Crosse gave it. The sentry saluted and stepped aside. At the far end of the corridor Crosse knocked. The door was opened by the governor's aide. "Evening, Superintendent."

"I hope I haven't kept you waiting?"

"No, not at all." This man led the way through communicating cellars to a thick iron door set into a concrete box that was crudely constructed in the middle of the big main cellar, wine racks nearby. He took out the single key and unlocked it. The door was very heavy. Crosse went inside alone and closed the door after him. Once inside, the door barred, he relaxed. Now he was totally safe from prying eyes and prying ears. This was the Holy of Holies, a conference room for very private conversations, the concrete room and communications center laboriously built by trusted SI officers, British only, to ensure against enemy listening devices being inserted into the walls—the whole structure tested weekly by Special Branch experts—in case some were somehow infiltrated.

In one corner was the complicated, highly sophisticated transmitter that fed signals into the unbreachable code scrambler, thence to the complex of antenna atop Government House, thence to the stratosphere, and thence to Whitehall.

Crosse switched it on. There was a comforting hum. "The minister, please. This is Asian One." It gave him great pleasure to use his inner code name.

"Yes, Asian One?"

"Tsu-yan was one of the persons meeting the spy, Brian Kwok."

"Ah! So we can strike him off the list."

"Both of them, sir. They're isolated now. On Saturday, the defector Joseph Yu was seen crossing the border."

"Damn! You'd better have a team assigned to monitor him. Do we have fellows at their atomic center at Siankiang?"

"No sir. However there's a rumor Dunross is going to meet Mr. Yu in Canton in a month."

"Ah, what about Dunross?"

"He's loyal—but he'll never work for us."

"What about Sinders?"

"He performed well. I do not consider him a security risk."

"Good. What about the *Ivanov?*"

"She sailed at noon. We haven't found Suslev's body—it'll take weeks to sift and dig out that wreckage. I'm afraid we may never find him in one piece. With Plumm gone too we'll have to rethink Sevrin."

"It's too good a ploy not to have in existence, Roger."

"Yes, sir. The other side will think so too. When Suslev's replacement arrives I'll see what they have in mind, then we can formulate a plan."

"Good. What about deVille?"

"He is to be transferred to Toronto. Please inform the RCMP. Next, about the nuclear carrier: Her complement is 5,500 officers and men, 83,350 tons, eight reactors, top speed sixty-two knots, forty-two F-4 Phantom II's each with nuclear capability, two Hawks Mark V. Curiously her only defense against an attack is one bank of SAMs on her starboard side . . ."

Crosse continued to give his report, very pleased with himself, loving his work, loving being on both sides, on three, he reminded himself. Yes, triple agent, with money to spare, both sides not trusting him completely yet needing him, praying he was on their side—not *theirs.*

Sometimes I almost wonder myself, he thought with a smile.

In the terminal building at Kai Tak, Armstrong was leaning heavily against the information counter, watching the door, feeling rotten. Crowds were milling as usual. To his surprise, he saw Peter Marlowe come in with Fleur Marlowe and their two children, dolls and small suitcases in their hands. Fleur was pale and drawn. Marlowe too. He was laden with suitcases.

"Hello, Peter," Armstrong said.

"Hello, Robert. You're working late."

"No, I've, er, I've just seen Mary off. She's off on a vacation to England for a month. Evening, Mrs. Marlowe. I was sorry to hear."

"Oh, thank you, Superintendent. I'm qu—"

"We're going to Binkok," the four-year-old interrupted gravely. "That's in Minland."

"Oh come along, silly," her sister said. "It's Bunkok in Mainland.

That's China," she added importantly to Armstrong. "We're on vacation too. Mummy's been sick."

Peter Marlowe smiled tiredly, his face creased. "Bangkok for a week, Robert. A holiday for Fleur. Old Doc Tooley said it was important for her to get a rest." He stopped as the two children began to squabble. "Quiet, you two! Darling," he said to his wife, "you check us in. I'll catch you up."

"Of course. Come along. Oh do behave, both of you!" She walked off, the two children skittering ahead.

"Won't be much of a holiday for her, I'm afraid," Peter Marlowe said. Then he dropped his voice. "One of my friends told me to pass on that the meeting in Macao of the narcotics villains is this Thursday."

"Do you know where?"

"No. But White Powder Lee's supposed to be one of them. And an American. Banastasio. That's the rumor."

"Thanks. And?"

"That's all."

"Thanks, Peter. Have a good trip. Listen, there's a fellow in the Bangkok police you should look up. Inspector Samanthajal—tell him I said so."

"Thanks. Rotten about Linc Bartlett and the others, wasn't it? Christ, I was invited to that party too."

"Joss."

"Yes. But that doesn't help him or them, does it? Poor buggers! See you next week."

Armstrong watched the tall man walk away, then went back to the information counter and leaned against it, continuing to wait, sick at heart.

His mind inexorably turned to Mary. Last night they had had a grinding row, mostly over John Chen, but more because of his last few days, Brian and the Red Room and borrowing the money, betting it all on Pilot Fish, waiting in agony, then winning and putting all the $40,000 back in his desk drawer—never a need to touch another penny—paying off his debts and buying her a ticket home but another row tonight and her saying, "You forgot our anniversary! That's not much to remember is it? Oh I hate this bloody place and bloody Werewolves and bloody everything. Don't expect me back!"

Dully he lit a cigarette, loathing the taste yet liking it. The air was humid again, sour. Then he saw Casey come in. He stubbed out his cigarette and went to intercept her, the heaviness in her walk saddening him. "Evening," he said, feeling very tired.

"Oh, oh hello, Superintendent. How, how're things?"

"Fine. I'll see you through."

"Oh that's kind of you."

"I was damned sorry to hear about Mr. Bartlett."

"Yes. Yes, thank you."

They walked on. He knew better than to talk. What was there to say?

Pity, he thought, liking her, admiring her courage, proved at the fire, proved on the slope, proved now, keeping her voice firm when all of her is torn up.

There were no customs outwardbound. The Immigration officer stamped her passport and handed it back with untoward politeness. "Please have a safe journey and return soon." The death of Bartlett had been headlines, among the sixty-seven.

Along corridors to the VIP lounge. Armstrong opened the door for her. To his surprise and her astonishment Dunross was there. The glass door to Gate 16 and the tarmac was open, *Yankee 2* just beyond.

"Oh. Oh hello, Ian," she said. "But I didn't want you to s—"

"Had to, Casey. Sorry. I've a little unfinished business with you and I had to meet a plane. My cousin's coming back from Taiwan—he went to fix the factory sites pending your approval." Dunross glanced at Armstrong. "Evening, Robert. How're things?"

"Same, same as usual." Armstrong put out his hand to Casey and smiled wearily. "I'll leave you now. Have a safe trip. Everything's cleared as soon as you're aboard."

"Thank you, Superintendent. I wish . . . thank you."

Armstrong nodded to Dunross and began to leave.

"Robert, did that consignment get delivered to Lo Wu?"

He pretended to think. "Yes, yes I believe it did." He saw the relief.

"Thanks. Can you hang on a moment? I'd like to hear about it."

"Certainly," Armstrong replied. "I'll be outside."

When they were alone Dunross handed her a thin envelope. "This is a cashier's check for $750,000 U.S. I bought Struan's for you at 9.50 and sold at 28."

"What?"

"Well I, er, I bought in for us first thing—at 9.50 as I promised I would. Your part of the deal was three quarters of a million. Struan's made millions. I made millions, so did Phillip and Dianne, I let them in early too."

She could not take it in. "Sorry, I don't understand."

He smiled and repeated what he had said, then added, "There's also another check—for a quarter of a million dollars U.S. against your share of the General Stores takeover."

She gasped. "I don't believe you."

A smile went over him fleetingly. "Yes. In thirty days another three quarters of a million will be on call. In sixty days we could advance another half million if need be."

Behind her, in the cockpit of *Yankee 2*, Jannelli fired the first jet engine. It shrieked into life.

"Is that enough to tide you over?" he asked.

Her mouth worked but no sound came out, then, "A quarter million?"

"Yes. Actually it comes to a million—these two checks. By the way, don't forget you're tai-pan of Par-Con now. That's Linc's real gift to you.

Tai-pan. The money's unimportant." He grinned at her and gave her a brusque hug. "Good luck, Casey. See you in thirty days. Eh?" The second engine shrieked into life.

"A million U.S.?"

"Yes. I'll get Dawson to send you some tax advice. As your profit is Hong Kong money I'm sure there are legitimate ways to avoid—not evade —taxes." Another engine howled awake.

She was staring at him, speechless. The door of the VIP lounge opened and a tall man came in breezily. "Hello, Ian! They told me I could find you here."

"Hello, David. Casey, this is David MacStruan, my cousin."

Blankly Casey looked at him, half-smiled, but did not really notice him. "Hello. But, Ian, you mean that—you mean what you said?"

"Of course." The last engine exploded into life. "You'd better go aboard! See you next month."

"What? Oh. Oh, but I, yes, see you!" Dazed, she put the envelope in her bag, turned around and left.

They watched her go up the gangway. "So that's the famous Casey," David MacStruan said thoughtfully. He was as tall as Dunross but a few years younger, redheaded, with curious slanting, almost Asian eyes, though green, his face very used, most of the three smaller fingers of his left hand missing where the shrouds of his parachute had mashed them.

"Yes. Yes, that's Kamalian Ciranoush Tcholok."

"Smasher!"

"More than that. Think of her as the Hag."

MacStruan whistled. "Is she that good?"

"She could be, with the right training."

Aboard the airplane Svensen closed the cabin door, locked it. "You want anything, Casey?" he asked kindly, very concerned for her.

"No," she said helplessly. "Just leave me, Sven. I'll, I'll call if I need anything. Okay?"

"Sure." He closed the door.

Now she was alone. Numbly she buckled on her seat belt and looked out of the porthole. Through her tears she saw Dunross and the other man whose name she did not remember wave. She waved back but they did not see her.

Clouds went over the moon. The engines picked up tempo, the airplane taxied away, lined up and shrieked into the black sky, climbing steeply. Casey noticed none of it, Dunross's words still pounding in her brain, over and over, taking her apart and putting her back together again.

Tai-pan. That's Linc's real gift to you, he had said. Tai-pan, the money's unimportant.

Yes, yes that's true but . . .

But . . .

What was it Linc said that time, that first day at the stock market? Wasn't it: "If Gornt wins, we win. If Dunross wins, we win. Either way we become the Noble House—which's why we're here."

The darkness lifted off her. Her mind cleared. The tears stopped.

That's what he wanted, truly wanted, she thought, her excitement growing. He wanted us to be the Noble House. Sure. Maybe that's what I can do for him in return, make that his epitaph—*the Noble House*.

"Oh Linc," she said joyously. "It's worth a try. Isn't it?"

The jetliner barreled into the high clouds, continuing its faultless departure. The night was warm and very dark, the moon crescent, the wind kind.

Below was the Island.

Dunross came out on to the Peak Road fast, heading for home, the traffic light and the engine sounding sweet. On a sudden impulse he changed direction and pulled up at the Peak lookout and stood at the rail, alone.

Hong Kong was a sea of lights. Over in Kowloon another jet took off from the floodlit runway. A few stars came through the high clouds.

"Christ, it's so good to be alive," he said.